# Thermals Of Time

## The Complete Trilogy

### Marcus Lynn Dean

## The Last Ditch Press

The three books that comprise this **THERMALS OF TIME** trilogy are works of fiction. Names, characters, places, incidents, and institutions are the products of the author's imagination or are used fictitiously. Any resemblance to institutions, places, events, or persons, living or dead, is entirely coincidental.

*THE SCREAM OF AN EAGLE*
Copyright © 2019 by Marcus Lynn Dean

*THE FLIGHT TO BLUE RIVER*
Copyright © 2020 by Marcus Lynn Dean

*APOCALYPTIC WINDS*
Copyright © 2021 by Marcus Lynn Dean

Published by: The Last Ditch Press - Grand Junction, Colorado
www.lastditchpress.com

ISBN: 978-1-7376178-4-6 eBook
ISBN: 978-1-7376178-0-8 Paperback

# Contents

# THE SCREAM OF AN EAGLE

## Thermals Of Time - Book One

**For Karen**
**The love of my life**

# PART ONE

S OMEWHERE HIGH OVERHEAD, THE chilling sound of an eagle's scream pierces the quiet stillness of the Colorado morning. The Eagle; of all creatures, the one most loved by the Great Spirit. The eagle teaches the story of life. The man remembers first hearing the legend of the eagle when he was very young. From the veranda where he sits, he can't see the eagle. It is shielded from view by the overhang of the roof. From his vantage point, he sees only a couple of turkey buzzards circling just above the horizon to the northeast. He watches as the buzzards glide down toward the earth. A thought occurs to the man – *the story of life always ends in death.*

# Chapter 1

T HERE WAS, OF COURSE, nothing that the Federal Reserve could do to stop the collapse at that point. Just as there was nothing that the IMF or the rest of the world's central banks could do. They had already done way too much. The "quantitative easing" and debt burdens that had prevented the world's economies from going over the cliff in 2008 had served mainly to astronomically increase the height of that cliff. The climb to the top of that economic peak was decades in the making. The fall, once the economy went over the edge, was a precipitous drop; wiping out those decades of economic gains in just a few short weeks. Fortunately for the world's bankers and elites, having long ago seen what was coming, plans were already in place to take advantage of the crisis.

Robert Mendez sat in the same chair at the same large desk in the same office that he had occupied for the last seven years. The office was on the top floor of a major bank building in downtown Denver. The sign on his office door read Robert James Mendez – Senior VP. He had been promoted to Senior Vice President in charge of the investment division seven years ago, nearly to the day. Under Robert's investment guidance the bank's value, and the shareholders net worth, as well as his own, had grown astronomically. Now, all but the wealthiest and most powerful of those shareholders, and all of the common people who had deposits in the bank were pretty much losing everything.

The three large computer displays on Robert's desk looked almost the same as they had for his entire tenure here. There were, however, some striking differences. The series of ticker tapes still scrolled continuously across the screen on the left, but instead of a series of stock and market listings and numbers, each ticker continuously displayed the same message; **MARKETS CLOSED.** All of the world's financial markets had been forced to close. The world's economic systems were totally frozen.

The central screen showed the same email inbox that it always had. The only difference was the incredible number of unread email messages sitting in wait.

The third screen, the one on the right, was the one that had captured Robert's attention.

The third screen was the one with his favorite newsfeed. He had the volume muted but sat spellbound by the images on the screen. They were mostly a series of views from cities all over the United States, as well as most of the rest of the world. Views of riots in the streets, the rioters anger focused on governments and banks all over the world. Banks that had been locked down, the flow of money shut down completely, as governments and central bankers tried to figure out what to do now. As bank depositors rioted to get their money out of the banks, Robert sat there and knew that the money the depositors thought they had securely stashed away was an illusion. The money had always been, in reality, just an illusion. The world's governments and central banks, the Federal Reserve of the United States and the IMF had, over time, created the world's largest Ponzi scheme; and now, that Ponzi scheme was unraveling and there was nothing anyone could do to stop it. Robert, along with the rest of the world, was now just a witness to the greatest economic disaster of all time. A disaster that would, in later years, come to be known simply as "The Catastrophe".

He decided that it might be best to just go home. Not that there was any chance of rioters being able to breach the bank's security, but there was nothing he could do at this point to change a thing. *No, nothing to be done now,* he thought. It would be a few days before he would need to be back at his desk. It would take a little time for the Federal Reserve and the International Monetary Fund to implement their long-planned policies. If the rabble was protesting now, wait until they saw what came next. Oh, they'd be able to get some of their money out of the banks, but there would be a catch. Most people would be demanding cash, and cash they would get, in strictly limited quantities, of course. But they'd get something else along with the cash they withdrew, they'd get a brand-new tax; a tax on cash.

Most people hadn't given much thought to the tiny magnetic strip that had been placed in bills over the past few decades. They had no idea how that little strip would be used to, once again, force them to "bail out" the "big banks". Robert Mendez knew. Relatively simple really, charge interest on deposits, and let them take the cash out to avoid that interest. Then, when they spend that cash, that tiny little magnetic strip in the bills electronically takes a percentage of the transaction. A truly amazing construct – a tax on cash. A tax that, just like previous bailouts, goes back to where wealth truly belongs, in the hands of the elite few who rule the world's economies and, by extension, the world's governments. Robert may not have been in the very upper echelon of that elite group yet, but he had his plans. He knew his stock in the bank would have to become forfeit, and that it would have to appear that upper bank management had lost a great deal of wealth. He also knew that appearances of loss can be very deceiving.

He took one more look at the three screens on his desk before shutting them down. The elevator that was just across the hall from his office door took him directly to the second level of underground parking. He threw his briefcase into the back seat of the Cadillac SUV, slowly drove up the ramp that came out in the alley behind the bank, and headed home to Castle Pines.

# Chapter 2

S UMMERTIME AT LAST! HE had been anticipating spending some time out at his Grandpa's ranch since school started ten months ago. At twelve years old, it wasn't that he didn't have friends and playmates, but they just couldn't compete with the Blue River Ranch on the western slope near Kremmling. He wouldn't admit it to anyone, but he was especially looking forward to spending time with Anna.

"James, you have to promise me that you will do whatever Grandpa asks. I still don't feel very good about sending you out there by yourself." James smiled at the worried look on his mother's face.

"I'll be fine, Mom. Maybe you and Dad can drive out and pick me up, so I don't have to ride the train back."

Noni Mendez smiled at her son. It had been five years since the Catastrophe, and the world seemed to be getting somewhat back to normal. Public transportation was probably as safe as it had ever been, and she knew that somewhere in the crowd of people getting on the train, there would be at least one member of the Mendez security team. Someone whose sole purpose in being on the train was to keep Robert Mendez' heir safe. It had been Robert's idea to let James experience travel with the masses. Noni wasn't really worried about her son's safety. What really bothered her, more than letting James go to Kremmling by himself, was a longing to go with him. A longing to return to her childhood home.

"I know you'll be fine, James," she tried to hide her longing from her son. "It's your Grandpa I'm worried about. He's not getting any younger, you know. You just make sure you help him every way you can."

Grandpa Chuck didn't seem old at all to James. In a lot of ways, Grandpa Chuck seemed to be in better shape than his dad. Of course, it was probably easier to stay in shape as a rancher than it was sitting behind a desk on the top floor of an office in Denver, even if the office had its own private gym.

"Grandpa's not old, he can probably still ride circles around most anybody else on the ranch."

*He's probably right,* she thought. *Dad probably can still ride circles around most anybody.* She grabbed James by both shoulders, amazed once again that her little boy was nearly as tall as she was. And his shoulders seemed so broad and strong.

"I know you're right James, I just worry about him more since your Grandma died. Wish he didn't have to be all alone on that great big ranch."

James put his arms around his mother and hugged her.

"You know, Mom, he's not really alone. He has the whole Duran family living just down the lane in the old house. You just wish we could live there too, instead of here."

Noni hugged her only son. *He knows me too well,* she thought, as tears formed in her dark brown eyes. *I told myself I wouldn't cry.*

···········

The train ride from Denver to the small town of Kremmling, Colorado was long and slow. At times it seemed like he could have made better time walking. It was one of the combo trains that had been put together in the years after the Catastrophe. With most people no longer able to afford the costs of personal transportation, the quickest solution to transport problems was to add some passenger cars to freight trains to better facilitate mass transit. This particular train had both; one of the old Amtrak cars, and one of the new people mover cars that had been designed to carry more people on shorter trips. It also had ninety-eight freight cars, at least twenty of which were empty coal cars, and thirty loaded fuel cars; as well as the usual thirty or forty blue tanker cars that carried water to the parched west. The whole thing was pulled and pushed over the mountains by three diesel-powered locomotives in the front and two in the rear. All along the way, there were signs of the construction projects that were running power lines along the tracks. Power lines that would, someday, enable the replacement of the diesel locomotives with electrics.

James was lucky enough to get one of the window seats in the new people mover car, where he could watch the scenery slowly passing by. At the moment, the scenery was at a standstill as the train sat on one of the sidings, waiting for another train coming from the west to pass. The only things making much progress were the water in the river and the trucks and a few cars on the old highway across the canyon from the parked train. James had seen this canyon from the other side a few times in his young life, as he and his mother had traveled along highway 40 back and forth from Denver to Kremmling. Most times when they traveled by car, they used I-70 through the old tunnels instead of driving over Berthoud Pass. As he thought about those trips, he realized that he could only recall his father accompanying them once. That was when his grandmother had died. He was very young at the time. The trips by car were always much faster than this trip by train, even though, to James, it always seemed to take forever. James remembered seeing trains on this side of the canyon from Highway 40 on the other side of the river, but this was the first time he had ever seen old Highway 40 from this vantage point.

"Still seems odd to see so little traffic on the old highway," the older man seated next to James said. "Of course, you're probably too young to remember what it was like before; before the Catastrophe that is."

James had been mostly trying to ignore the man, but the man was one of those people who can't help but talk to people, whether they're being ignored or not. James actually could remember when, what everyone now called the Catastrophe, had happened, but he didn't have many memories of the way things were before. He had only been seven years old when his dad came home from the bank, locked the big iron gates at the entrance to their driveway and told him not to dare leave the premises.

"When I was your age," the man continued, "that highway was filled with vehicles of all kinds. It was bumper to bumper traffic, especially on weekends. Now look at it, a few of the autonomous freight haulers and even fewer cars. Only rich folk can afford to travel by car anymore. Normal people can't even afford fuel for their old clunkers, let alone the price of a new EV.

James couldn't help but notice the contempt in the man's voice, especially when he spoke of "rich folk." He hadn't given too much thought to it before, but he knew that his family was included in the "rich folk" that the man spoke of. After all, the Mendez family always traveled by car. Robert Mendez had just recently made his yearly purchase of a brand-new Cadillac. It was totally electric, but what impressed James the most was the seating arrangement. It had two seats in front and two seats in the rear facing each other with a sort of console table in the middle. The two doors, one on each side between the seats, were nearly all glass, offering all four passengers fantastic views of whatever scenery was passing by. No one actually drove the car; the computer that was built into the center console "drove" the car. James wished he was in that car now, speeding along that old highway on the other side of the river.

"How long do we have to sit here?" James asked the man who had spoken to him.

"Not much longer now." The man replied, just as the east-bound train started flashing by the window on the other side of the train. "Where you headed, anyway?"

James felt a little bit uneasy about telling the stranger much, so he just said, "Kremmling," and turned back to the window.

"Kremmling, huh, that's my next stop as well. Bud Johnson," the man said, thrusting his hand out to shake.

James could see the extended hand from the corner of his eye, so he turned toward the man and shook hands. "James Mendez," he said, "I'm going to visit my grandpa." He didn't really know what else to say, so that was it.

"Business trip for me," Bud Johnson was a salesman. That was obvious even to a twelve-year-old boy. "I'm with Pro Foods, meeting with some of the ranchers out there."

James, like most people, had never heard of Pro Foods, but he did catch the part about meeting with ranchers. "My Grandpa's a rancher," he said. "His name's Chuck Pierson."

"What a coincidence, your Grandpa's one of the ranchers I want to meet with. Pro Foods wants to buy all your Grandpa's cattle. We're going to revolutionize the way America eats."

··········

The big old 2019 Ford dually truck was the only vehicle James had ever known his Grandpa to drive. As they dodged the potholes in Highway 9, James wondered why Grandpa Chuck didn't get one of the new autonomous vehicles, maybe even electric instead of diesel.

"Grandpa how come you still drive this same old truck?" he asked. He didn't think his grandpa was poor. He wasn't like so many of the people back on the eastern slope who couldn't afford to own or drive a personal vehicle at all.

"Well James, I bought this truck new back in 2018 when we had a president who was making America great again. At the time, I really believed we were on the road to great things. Guess it's just a reminder of better times. Besides, being a rancher, I get enough fuel subsidy to help pay for the high cost of diesel. Besides that, I don't much like electric vehicles. Suppose I'm just old fashioned."

It was about a twenty-mile drive south on Highway 9 from Kremmling to the confluence of Spider Creek and the Blue River, where the Blue River Ranch was located. On that drive, Chuck and James only met one other vehicle. James noticed that it was also an old beat up looking ranch truck, and Chuck waved at the driver as they met.

"Wonder why John's headed to town?" He muttered, as much to himself as to James. The ranchers who lived sparsely scattered out through this part of the country didn't make the trip to Kremmling very often. Chuck, himself, tried to limit the trip to about once a month. *Probably just needs to stock up,* he thought to himself. *Hope he can find what he needs, shortages are definitely getting to be more common than they used to be.*

"Have you got a horse ready for me to ride?" James' question interrupted his grandpa's thoughts. "Does Anna know I'm coming?" He was getting more excited as they got closer to the ranch.

"Whoa, I thought you came out here to see me, not Anna". Chuck teased. "As for a horse, I have a surprise for you this year. I'm going to let you pick your own out of the herd. If you can catch it and ride it, I'll give it to you for your birthday."

James blushed slightly at the tease about Anna and then frowned. "Dad won't let me have a horse, Grandpa. You know that," he said.

Chuck smiled. "Guess it'll just have to be our little secret. Your horse can live here on the ranch and it'll be yours whenever you're here. Your dad doesn't even need to know." Then the thought occurred to the old rancher that it might be fun if Robert Mendez did know about the horse, just to piss him off.

·····•·····

James was watching anxiously as they drove up the lane to the Blue River Ranch headquarters, but there was no sign of anyone, let alone Anna. Chuck pulled the big Ford truck into the metal shop building near the big house.

"Where is everyone?" James asked.

"The Durans are all helping get the herd up to the high country. Had to trail them up this year, diesel's too expensive to haul 'em. All but Shelly, that is. I bet she's in the house getting dinner ready. You looking for Anna?" Chuck teased, knowing that was the case.

"Ralph and Cody and Anna all got to help move the herd?" James asked, careful to put Ralph and Cody, Anna's younger brothers, ahead of her. "Wish I'd got here sooner, so I could help, too." Trailing the herd seemed like a great adventure to James.

"They've been out for three days. Should be home this evening. It's a long ride up to Elk Park and back. Think you're up to three full days in the saddle?"

"Sure – I love riding." James was as certain as he sounded, the inexperience and optimism of youth blinding him to the rigors of three long days on horseback.

It was almost dusk when James heard the sound of hooves on the graveled lane behind the big house. He'd been sitting on the front porch; Grandpa Chuck was inside. He jumped up and ran to the corner of the house to meet them. Anna was in the lead riding Pintada, her black and white paint, followed by her brothers, Ralph and Cody. The two boys were riding side by side, and Clyde Duran, the longtime ranch foreman, was bringing up the rear. Clyde was leading three pack horses in a line behind him. The pack saddles were all but empty. They'd been used to haul supplies for the two cowboys that would spend the summer with the herd up in the high country. Someone, normally Clyde, would be making that trek with fresh supplies every couple of weeks for the rest of the summer. It would only be a two-day ride, now that the herd was already up there, and James had the thought that maybe he could go next time.

In spite of the dust and grime of the trail, Anna was a beautiful young girl. She had dark skin, long black hair, and eyes that were an even deeper brown than James'. Her face lit up in a radiant smile when she saw James come around the corner of the house. She reined up and dismounted when she got to James. She felt like hugging him, but she knew that would never do. Especially not in front of her dad and her brothers.

"Hi James," was all she could manage to say, as she stood there holding the end of the reins in both hands in front of her. Even that brought a little blush to her face. The blush deepened a little more as she realized she was covered with trail dust and must look a mess.

James couldn't help but think that she looked just like an Indian princess, even though she was dressed head to toe in western cowgirl clothes. From the western style straw hat on her head to the chaps on her legs and the boots on her feet, she was covered with dust from the trail. Anna had definitely changed since he last saw her two years ago. Her face had begun to lose some of the roundness of childhood, and the high cheekbones of her Native American heritage were more pronounced, but what James really noticed were her breasts. She hadn't had breasts when he had last seen her. Now, the youthful mounds were all too obvious underneath her dusty denim shirt. It was his turn to be embarrassed, as he realized he had been staring at her breasts. He looked up into her dark brown eyes.

"Hi Anna," it was as if neither one of them knew what to say.

Fortunately, Ralph and Cody came to the rescue greeting James and asking when he'd arrived, and what he had been up to. Then Clyde Duran pulled up the Buckskin he was riding. Clyde was not as big a man as James' grandfather; he was about six feet tall and probably weighed around a hundred eighty, but he had an imposing presence about him that had a way of making James feel slightly uneasy.

"Yo James," his deep voice didn't help with James' feeling of unease. "Good to see you again."

"Good to see you too, sir – I mean Clyde," James stammered, remembering that Clyde didn't like being called sir.

Clyde swung down off his horse with a groan and stuck his big right hand out to James to shake. "How's your mother?" he asked James as they shook hands.

"She's fine," he answered. He couldn't help but notice that Clyde hadn't asked about his family, or his mom and dad; only about his mother.

"Good to hear," Clyde said to James. Then, to the group, "let's get these horses put away. Come on James, you can help."

Walking side by side with Anna, as she led Pintada to the barn, made the long train trip all worth it. *I get to spend a whole month here*, James thought. At that moment, to his twelve-year-old mind, a month might just as well have been an eternity.

···•··•····

James, Anna, Ralph, and Cody had been playing in the willows that lined the banks of Spider Creek. The willows were so thick that you had to follow the trails and openings made by animals, mostly cows, to get through them. The trails meandered and worked their way through the willows from opening to opening in such a crooked winding manner that the effect was that of a maze, with trails crisscrossing each other and going every which way. The kids, mainly the Duran siblings, since James was only there occasionally, had made various play forts and hideouts from cut willows and scraps of wood, tin, and whatever else they could find. They spent hours on end playing in the willows. It was their own private playground.

James had been at the ranch for three full days now, and he and Anna were both getting tired of the younger boys always being around. James was finding more and more that he wanted to be alone with Anna, instead of having Ralph and Cody tagging along everywhere they went. He seemed to have two main desires. One was to catch and claim one of the horses in the south pasture, the other was to spend time with Anna – alone, just the two of them. So far, he had been unable to satisfy either desire, and he had less than a month before he would have to go back to Castle Pines.

"Let's play hide and seek," James said.

Ralph and Cody were all for it. Without knowing what James had in mind, Anna thought it was too childish. Wondering why James was so intent on playing such a childish game, she finally relented, and after a few rounds of rock, paper, scissors, it was decided that Cody was first to be "it". He stood in one of the play forts, covered his eyes with his hands and began to count out loud to one hundred. Ralph immediately started sneaking down one of the trails toward the creek, moving as quietly as he could to prevent Cody from hearing which direction he had gone. James looked at Anna, put a finger to his lips for silence, and signaled her to follow him in the opposite direction, up a trail that led quickly out of the willows to the back of the log barn. Now Anna's curiosity was definitely piqued. *What is he up to?* she wondered, following behind as quietly as she could.

The log barn was one of the oldest buildings on the ranch. Constructed of logs cut from the surrounding countryside, it had been built so well more than a hundred years ago that it was not only still standing, it was structurally as sound as any of the newer ranch buildings. It was the original horse barn on the BR, with seven stalls and a tack room at ground level and a hayloft above. The hayloft was huge. It was probably twice as tall as the ground floor, with a large set of double doors on the front matching the sliding main entrance doors directly below. The log barn had been designed and built in the days when hay was stacked loose, not baled; the huge volume of space in the loft a requirement of stacking loose hay. There was a large semi-circular corral attached to the back of the log barn. It was actually not round but was constructed of two dozen twelve-foot sections arranged in a semi-circular shape with the back wall of the log barn forming the straight side of the corral. Each section was about eight feet tall, made of spruce and lodgepole pine rails stacked between two large cedar posts. There was another large single cedar post set in the center of the corral. The post in the center was worn totally smooth by the countless ropes that had been wrapped around it over the years, as a multitude of horses had been trained to ride.

"Where are we going?" Anna whispered, even though they were far enough away that they could no longer hear Cody counting.

"I'll show you," James said, as he quietly opened the gate leading into the round corral.

Closing the gate behind them as quietly as he had opened it, he led Anna through the open barn door. Just inside this back door to the barn, there was a ladder made of old rough cut two by fours nailed to the wall. The top edge of most of the boards was rounded and worn smooth by a hundred years of use. A few of the boards had been replaced by newer smooth cut two by fours. James could easily feel the difference between the old boards and the new ones. The top edges of the newer boards were still square and not nearly as smooth as the old ones. He quickly climbed the ladder which led up into the loft above. Anna followed close behind. The hayloft was familiar, both of them having been there many times before. It was mostly empty this time of year, the hay that had filled the cavernous space the previous fall had mostly been fed to the stock over the course of the long winter.

Sunlight shining through the open doors at the west end of the loft illuminated what was left of last year's hay crop. Just a few dozen bales still stacked in the southeast corner. These were the small rectangular hay bales of old. The Blue River ranch had never made the switch to the giant thousand-pound bales that had become so popular in the later years of the twentieth century. Chuck Pierson was somewhat of an enigma that way. He had embraced much of the new technology that had been developed over the course of his life but stubbornly refused to change many of the older ways of doing things.

James walked over and sat down on one of the hay bales, Anna followed and sat down on the bale next to him. James looked at her questioning gaze.

"Anna, do you have a boyfriend?" he asked, the question in a matter of fact way, much as if he'd asked her if she had a pet dog.

Anna wasn't sure how to respond. At eleven years old, with her body changing in ways she was constantly struggling to get used to, she had begun to occasionally find herself thinking about boys in ways she never had before. Whenever the thoughts of boy's bodies and the differences between men and women came to mind, she inevitably thought of James. She could feel herself blush.

"Do you want to be my boyfriend, James?"

By way of answer, James reached over and took her hand.

"Okay, you can be my girlfriend," he said. It wasn't his intention, but it sounded almost begrudging, as if he had resigned himself to the fact that he was going to have to put up with having a girlfriend. "It has to be our secret, though."

Anna smiled, James' touch, just holding hands, sent feelings through her young body that were totally new.

"Okay," she said. "It can be our secret, but James, if we are going to be boyfriend and girlfriend, we should kiss."

They leaned toward each other, not really knowing how to kiss in an adult manner. Turning their faces first one way, and then the other to avoid each other's noses, with closed mouths, their lips came together. James had kissed girls before, usually on a dare, or having lost a bet, but this was like nothing he had ever experienced. It was as if an electric current passed from Anna's lips through his, sending a tingling through his body and shutting out thought. He couldn't have said how long their lips touched. It could have been a split second, or it could have been an eternity.

"Allie allie outs in free, allie allie outs in free!" Cody's yells broke through the spell and the magic of the moment.

"Hurry," James said, breaking away from Anna. "Let's get back before they know where we are. This can be our secret place."

*What secret?* Anna thought as she followed James back down the ladder. *Everyone knows about the hayloft.*

·····•·•····

James woke, startled that the sun was already streaming in the window. He had been dreaming, it took him a minute to realize where he was. In the dream, he'd been on a horse. He was riding bareback without a bridle or even a hackamore for control. The horse was taking him somewhere, his destiny totally under the control of the horse that seemed to be flying through clouds instead of running over the earth. They seemed to be trying to catch someone or some thing that was hidden beyond the cloudy mists. James had awakened just as he was about to glimpse whatever it was that was out there, ahead of them in the clouds.

His room at home, in Castle Pines, was on the west side of the house, but here in the room that was his at the Blue River Ranch, the window faced due east, and the morning sun shone through in all its glory. The smell of frying bacon focused his attention on the hunger that his growing body always awoke to. As he pulled on his jeans and boots, he thought about Anna. Yesterday he got a girlfriend, today he was going to catch himself a horse.

"Grandpa, do you ever eat anything besides bacon and eggs for breakfast?" James asked as he slid the last piece of bacon around on his plate.

"Well, I guess I am kind of a creature of habit," Chuck replied. "Sometimes I have steak and eggs, instead of bacon and eggs. You want me to fix steak and eggs tomorrow?"

"Do you have any cereal?" James asked, hopefully. "Or maybe some donuts or sweet rolls. We'll probably have steaks or burgers again for dinner."

"Well, maybe I can pick something up. I have to go to Kremmling again. The Department of Agriculture says I need to meet with that feller you told me about meeting on the train. You want to ride along?"

James felt instant disappointment. "Not really," he said. "I was hoping we could catch my horse today."

Chuck didn't miss the disappointment in his grandson's voice. "Tell you what, James, how 'bout you go over to the south pasture while I'm gone, and study the horses to see which one you want. Then, tomorrow, I'll help you catch the one you pick. I'd stay away from the big black, though, I'm not too sure about that one." Even as he said it, Chuck had an inward chuckle, thinking that now James wouldn't be able to resist picking Midnight, the big black three-year-old. The one that Chuck had already picked out to be James' horse.

"How can I get across the river?" James asked. The south pasture was on the other side of Spider Creek, and though the river wasn't very deep, there weren't enough stable rocks poking above the water to get across by stepping or leaping from rock to rock. James didn't relish the idea of wading across. "Can I use one of the old ATVs?" There were five old ATVs in the metal shop. They were covered with tarps that were in turn covered with dust.

"I doubt you could even get one started," Chuck answered, "we haven't used those old ATVs for years. The cost of gas got so high that we just went back to using horses. Maybe you could get Anna to saddle up her paint and take you across."

The brightening of James' demeanor at the thought of riding double with Anna wasn't lost on the old cowboy. *Ahh, to be a kid again*, he thought.

·····•·•····

The south pasture wasn't a hay meadow but was about twenty acres of rolling hills that had been cleared of sagebrush and most trees over a century ago. Native dryland grasses had been planted over the years to help keep down the cheatgrass that always wanted to take over any cleared area. Even with the constant fight to eradicate it, there were patches of cheatgrass scattered here and there. Patches of sagebrush had also re-emerged in places between the pinon and juniper trees that dotted the pasture. The entire pasture was surrounded by a five-foot-high, four rail fence that had been very carefully maintained for a full century. It was impossible not to notice the varying ages of the lodgepole and spruce rails that the fence was made of. Some of the rails and a few of the cedar posts had obviously been recently replaced, and then there were others that appeared to be as old as the BR itself.

It wasn't hard to talk Anna into taking him across the river. He had been a little bit embarrassed about having to ride behind a girl, but the thrill of sitting directly behind Anna and being able to put his arms around her middle to hold on as they crossed the river easily outweighed any embarrassment he might have felt. Once again, they had faced the dilemma of how they were going to get away from Ralph and Cody, but that dilemma had been solved by Clyde asking the boys to help him repair some breaks in the barbed wire fence around the big meadow to the north.

At the entrance to the south pasture, somewhat reluctantly, James slid off of Pintada. He planned on opening the gate to let Anna ride through. He was surprised when she also dismounted.

"I can open the gate for you", he said.

"No need," Anna replied. "We can just climb over. We have to leave Pintada here."

"Why?" James asked. He had thought they would just ride up to the horses in the south pasture to get a good close look at all of them.

Anna scowled a little. She was hesitant and a little embarrassed as to how she should answer. "Grullo is in there, and Pintada's in heat." She blushed as she said it, and wondered at James' lack of knowledge of the natural world in general, and the mating habits of horses, in particular. *Such a city boy*, she thought.

She tied her horse to one of the fence rails next to the gate that led into the pasture. Not bothering to open the gate, they both just climbed over. They couldn't see any of the horses from here, they must have been in one of the bottoms behind the hill that was immediately in front of them. They made the short climb to the top of the hill and looked down to the east end of the pasture. Spider Creek swung to the south at that corner of the pasture, and a portion of the fence had been built out into the creek creating a natural watering hole for the horses. The herd was spread out near the river contentedly eating the grass that was plentiful in the bottom. There were eight horses that were visible from their vantage point. Most of the horses were bays or sorrels. There was one buckskin colored horse and one pure black one. That had to be the horse Chuck had warned James about. There was also one big silvery gray grazing somewhat apart from the rest of the herd, as though he was a sentinel.

*That has to be Grullo,* James thought. "Is that all of them," he asked.

"I'm not sure, but I think so. Is your grandpa really going to give you one of those horses?" she asked, at least a hint of skepticism in her voice.

"Whichever one I want." It was almost a brag. "All I have to do is pick one out and catch it. Grandpa did say I should probably stay away from the black one, though."

Anna furrowed her eyebrows. "Why did he want you to stay away from Midnight," she asked. "He's my favorite."

"I don't know. Maybe he doesn't trust him." Even as he said it, he began having doubts. Maybe the black one, Midnight, is Grandpa's favorite, too. Maybe he wants to keep him for himself. That didn't make sense either. Chuck seemed perfectly happy with the big bay horse called Red that he always rode.

Most of the horses were about a hundred yards away, down the hill below where James and Anna sat watching them. Partially concealed by a juniper tree, and downwind from the herd, none of the horses had shown any sign of noticing them yet. The big silver-gray called Grullo was closest to them and seemed totally outstanding to James.

"Maybe I'll catch Grullo," he said quietly.

Once again, Anna was incredulous; amazed at James' innocence and ignorance. "You can't choose Grullo! He's the stallion."

She must have said it louder than she intended. Grullo lifted his head and turned toward them, his full attention, eyes, ears, and nose focused on the top of the hill where they sat. Both Anna and James froze instinctively. Grullo studied the two for a few seconds before his attention was pulled away from the hill by a scent in the air coming from the herd below him. Sticking his nose in the air and turning his head toward the rest of the horses, he took off at a trot, headed directly for the buckskin mare standing a little apart from the rest of the herd. As Grullo approached the mare, his penis started extending below his abdomen, getting longer and longer. The mare, with an air of indifference, seemed to be ignoring his approach. Right up to the point where Grullo stuck his nose up under her tail, that is. She jumped a little then, turning her rear away from Grullo. He, in turn, stuck his nose straight up into the air with his teeth bared in what appeared to be a huge smile. As he did so, his penis, which had been dangling mostly straight down rose toward his belly in anticipation. He moved toward the rear of the mare. She started to turn away again with a little kick half-heartedly aimed his way. Not taking no for an answer, Grullo nipped the base of her neck and moved to mount her. Now the mare acquiesced, as James and Anna watched spellbound.

James had never personally witnessed animals breeding before, and though Anna had seen it many times, she hadn't intimately watched with a boy by her side, and she hadn't been well on her way to womanhood. Though neither yet knew what eroticism was, it was a weirdly erotic experience for both of them. Both were flushed and just sat there in silence, afraid to do or say anything.

Anna, fully aware of the strange feelings stirring in her lower belly, was the first to speak. "Have you ever thought about us doing that?" she asked.

James had thought about it alright, but he had no idea if he could actually do it. He didn't know what to say. Finally, he decided it best to just change the subject to something he was more equipped to deal with. "Why do you think Grandpa told me to stay away from Midnight?" he asked.

Anna, both relieved and a little disappointed at the change of subject, thought about it and had the answer. "He thought telling you to stay away from Midnight would make you want to own him."

James realized immediately that she was right. "Okay, that settles it, I'm going to catch Midnight." He thought about for a bit, and then said, "How can I do that?"

"Come on, I'll help you. We need to get some oats," Anna said, as she stood up. She took James hand as they walked back down the hill toward Pintada.

Something happened on that hill that neither James nor Anna could ever explain. An innocence between them had been lost forever.

# Chapter 3

T HE ONE CONFERENCE ROOM at the Kremmling Hotel was already getting crowded when Chuck arrived. Tables had been arranged in a semi-circle with a small stage and dais in the front of the room. Chuck spotted John Crowley sitting at a table near the center of the room with an empty chair next to him.

"Hey John, is this spot taken?" Chuck asked, tapping John on the shoulder.

"Hi, neighbor. No, Martha didn't want to attend. She didn't know if she could stand to sit through a sales presentation, especially one sponsored by the USDA. Sit down. Do you happen to know any more about this than I do?"

"Guess not. I must've got the same notice as everyone else. Looks like every cattle rancher in the area's here. Have to wonder what the Department of Ag is up to; basically, ordering us to a meeting with something called Pro Foods. Probably can't be a good thing; not with the feds involved."

"Kind of what I've been thinking," John said, fidgeting with his water glass. "Do you know anything about Pro Foods?"

"Not really. Other than they apparently want to buy all the cattle we can produce."

A man stepped forward from the other side of the room and strode to a position behind the dais. He was a fairly short man, but the boots he was wearing made him a little taller. The boots, bolo tie, and the western jacket seemed out of place on the man; and the Stetson hat was about as fitting to this man's head as the deer antlers on a jackalope.

"Good morning," his voice boomed out of the speakers, as he removed the Stetson and placed it on the dais. The light reflected off the top of his bald head when he bent down to adjust the volume on the PA system. "For those of you that I have yet to meet, my name is Bud Johnson, and, as you probably already know, I represent Pro Foods."

With the small talk around the room ended, and everyone's attention on Bud Johnson, he went on; "you're probably wondering what is Pro Foods? And what the hell does the USDA have to do with it?" With that, he touched another button on the dais and the screen above and behind him sprang to life. Listed down the left side of the screen were the names of most of the major food producers in the U.S.; General Mills, Tyson Foods, Kellogg's, Dole, etc. On the right side there were four letters in bold type; USDA. Each of the food company names had a line running from it to a point centered on the USDA.

"Pro Foods is a private-public partnership whose mission is to alleviate hunger in this country." Bud Johnson went on to explain to those gathered that the cuts to social security and other social programs that were forced on the Federal Government by the economic collapse known as the *Catastrophe*, had left many Americans with "food insecurities"; and how the USDA had partnered with all of "these fine companies" to make sure that all Americans at least had food to eat.

There was, of course, not a single person in the room that was unaware of the starvation going on across the country. Many of the ranchers in the room had insecurities themselves. Unlike Chuck, most of the ranchers here, as elsewhere in the country, had been deeply in debt when the Catastrophe hit; and the austerity measures imposed by the good ole Federal Government had left a lot of them in dire straits financially. Most of everything they produced went to prop up the banks and the economic elite that controlled their debt. If not for their ability to grow a lot of their own food, they would have been as bad off as so many of the people living in squalor in the cities.

Chuck Pierson was far better off than most. Unlike most of the other ranchers in the room, Chuck not only owned all of the land that the BR sat on, he owned the mineral rights for the gas and oil that lay beneath the land. Most of the mineral rights in this part of Colorado had been sold for lump-sum payments back in the 1950s and '60s. Back then, the speculators were offering thousands of dollars for mineral deeds and the ranchers were going broke. It seemed stupid not to take the cash; especially before fracking when it seemed that the oil and gas below their land would just stay below their land forever. Charles Pierson senior, Charlie to everyone who knew him, Chuck's father, hadn't seen it that way. He'd refused to sell any part of his mineral rights and he'd managed to hold onto the BR through decades of hard times. When the fracking boom took off in the 1990s, the Blue River Ranch was one of the first places drilled. Charles senior had lived long enough to see the royalties start coming in, and those royalties had grown to become Chuck's main source of income. The BR was indeed a cattle ranch, and Chuck loved ranching, but up until recent times, the BR had been as much about oil and gas as it was about cattle. The income from oil and gas had just about dried up, though. Especially the crude oil income, which was by far the most lucrative. It wasn't that the wells had gone dry, there was still plenty of oil down there; it was the demand for oil that was drying up. The world was shifting away from oil just like the world had shifted away from coal. Chuck had mixed feelings about the shift from fossil fuels to green energy. Climate change could no longer be denied, not with all the weather-related disasters increasing at an exponential pace, but keeping the BR financially viable by raising cattle was definitely not easy.

"We, at the USDA, working with the private sector, have developed Allpro," Bud Johnson continued his spiel, as a new image flashed on the screen above him. The image on the screen appeared to be some kind of meatloaf on a platter with basic nutrition information spelled out below the picture. From the nutrition info, it appeared that three servings of this Allpro would provide nearly a hundred percent of a person's daily nutrition needs. "Since the government can no longer afford to provide monetary food assistance to those in need, we will provide the food instead. Instead of monetary assistance to buy whatever food people choose to eat, those in need will receive vouchers to purchase Allpro. Once the program is fully implemented, no one in this country will ever need to go hungry again."

"Doesn't appear to have missed too many meals, himself, does he," John half-whispered to Chuck.

"And this is where you come in," Bud continued, gesturing to the entire room. "Allpro is a complete food product that contains all of the carbohydrates, fats, and proteins that a person needs to survive; along with vitamins and minerals. It is made from a combination of fruits, vegetables, and meats. It will be produced by the fine companies listed earlier in plants scattered around the country. Here's the interesting thing; nearly any kind of meat can be used. We plan to use a combination of chicken, pork, turkey, and beef; but there's one problem. Beef is simply too expensive. Protein from plants, pork, and especially poultry, is much more economical."

That brought a grumbling murmur to the room. It had been years since anyone had made any money off of their cattle. Even before the Catastrophe, the independent ranchers weren't making money by selling beef. The only ones making any money off of cattle were the very companies who were now, it seemed to many in the room, taking over the USDA.

"Wait a minute," a loud voice spoke up from somewhere behind Chuck and John. "I thought you said you wanted to buy our cattle."

Chuck turned to see that the speaker was Neil Smith. Neil owned a small spread up in the northwest corner of Grand County. *He probably doesn't have more than a hundred head to sell*, Chuck thought. And then the thought struck him that he had reduced the size of his own herd to the point where he wouldn't be able to sell a whole lot more than that, either. This definitely wasn't the good old days when the BR ran a herd that numbered in the thousands. In the years since the Catastrophe, the number of people who could afford to eat beef had gone steadily down, and those who could still afford a good steak had mostly stopped eating beef altogether to help fight climate change. As the demand for beef declined, so did the price that ranchers were paid at market. Chuck had reduced the size of the herd on the BR to around two hundred head, less than ten percent of what had been the norm back in the day. If not for the fact that he loved ranching, and the responsibility he felt to provide a place for Clyde Duran and his family to live and work, he might have sold his entire herd. The royalties on gas and oil were still enough to support one man.

"Pro Foods does want to buy your cattle," Bud answered. "Right now, we need all the cattle we can get, but I need to warn you that isn't going to be the case forever. The long-range plan is to phase out cattle altogether. They're too expensive. Short term, we're phasing out feedlots. They're too hard on the environment and besides, if beef is only a source of protein, it isn't going to matter if it's tender or not. We do want to buy your cattle, that's a fact. But the government, I mean Pro Foods, can't pay market price."

At that, the murmur in the room turned into a roar. Some of the ranchers were standing and yelling at Bud Johnson. Others were still seated, but everyone was angry. "What do you mean market price," someone shouted. "What market?" Another voice yelled out, "First you cut our subsidies and now you want to steal our cattle!" That comment referenced the fact that the latest farm bill had reduced the subsidies that the federal government provided to the agricultural community. Those government subsidies were the only thing that kept many of these ranchers in business.

Bud Johnson stood stoically behind the dais, allowing the questions and verbal abuse to wash over him and slowly subside. Chuck realized it was the reaction that Bud had expected. This obviously wasn't the first group he'd been sent to coerce into accepting Pro Food's plan.

As the roar from the crowd slowly died down, Bud Johnson resumed speaking. "Here's the deal, and this is the true bottom line; the SNAP program is going away. It is not going to be simply reduced further, it is going to be eliminated entirely. Now, I know that demand for your beef cattle has diminished over the past few years, and prices have gone down. But you have to realize that what demand there is, has been propped up by the government giving people the means to buy beef if they so desire. The SNAP program will end in about three months. It will be replaced by a new program, Allpro For All, AFA for short, that will allow the federal government to continue providing nutrition to those Americans in need."

The ranchers had grown quiet as Bud was speaking. Most were looking at him now with a mixture of disgust and dejection; first-hand witnesses to the ongoing breakdown of the U.S. Federal Government.

"Unlike food stamp programs of the past, AFA vouchers can only be used to purchase Allpro, nothing else. Production and distribution facilities for Allpro are ramping up as I speak so there will be plenty available as soon as the program takes effect. We need your beef production to start shipping to the processing plants as soon as possible and we'll be paying you seventy-five percent of current market prices for every pound you ship."

Anger, once again, ran through the crowd. "Are you crazy, you son of a bitch," it was Neil Smith again. "I wouldn't sell to you if you were the last buyer on earth."

"Who the hell do you think you are?" Chuck didn't recognize that voice, but the general din in the room was drowning it out, anyway.

Once again, Bud Johnson simply stood his place waiting for the eruption to end. As the room slowly quieted down, a sad look came over him. "It isn't me," he said solemnly into the microphone. "You have to understand that it isn't me. I understand your anger. I'm angry, too. I can't stand the fact that a few fat cats in Washington have bankrupted our country and driven common people to the point of starvation. But I believe this is the only way to prevent those common people from actually starving. There are no other options. And, as much as I have no other options, neither do you. The USDA is prepared to end all agricultural subsidies to any farmer or rancher who refuses to join the program."

Chuck sat silently in his seat, his emotions perfectly masked. He felt anger, along with everyone else in the room; but he had a deeper sense of sadness than he did of anger. He realized the sadness came from a lifetime of watching the decline of America. It wasn't just the *fat cats* in Washington, as Bud Johnson had put it. It was the system that had put them there. It was the system that produced the ever-widening gap between the haves and the have nots. For a time, it had seemed like the Catastrophe had somewhat leveled the playing field, but Chuck knew that was not really the case. The haves still had, and now, five years after the Catastrophe, they were still rigging the system. He actually felt sorry for Bud Johnson standing there taking the verbal abuse. Bud actually believed that he was on a mission to save people from starving. Chuck wondered if Bud had even considered what was in it for the food companies that had gone along with this plan. *Gone along with it, hell,* he thought; *they're the ones that put the whole thing together.* He stood up and took a look around at the rest of the ranchers who were mostly also standing and yelling; demanding more from Bud Johnson and the Federal Government than they were ever going to get. Without saying a word, Chuck Pierson turned and walked slowly, deliberately out the door. He suddenly wanted nothing more than to be home, alone, on the Blue River Ranch.

..........

After luring Midnight with a bucket of oats and getting him in a halter, James and Anna had led him back to the log barn and put him in one of the stalls. They had then climbed to the loft, broken one of the bales of hay and dropped about half of it through the hole in the floor into the stall's manger.

"Thanks, Anna." James had said, as he had put his hands on her shoulders and kissed her for the second time. Their kiss this time was somehow not as magical as their first, but definitely more natural. Their heads seemed to both know which way to turn and their lips lingered together longer. Then they heard the distinct sound of Chuck's big diesel pickup coming up the lane.

Chuck had parked his truck in the metal shop where he always did and headed straight to the house. James ran after him but didn't catch up until Chuck was already in the house sitting at his big desk.

"You caught Midnight!" Chuck exclaimed, with mock surprise. "All by yourself?"

"Anna helped me." James was reluctant to tell his Grandpa that Anna had actually done most of the catching. "But now that I've caught him, can Midnight really be mine?"

"Well...I guess a deal's a deal. Can you ride him?"

"I haven't ridden him yet, but I'm sure I can. He seems as gentle as Pintada. Can we go for a ride now?" James asked, even though he could see that Chuck seemed to be concentrating on the screen in front of him.

For a moment it seemed that Chuck hadn't even heard the question, but then he turned and smiled at his only grandson. The smile was warm, but there was a kind of sadness in his eyes.

"I can't go for a ride right now James, it's getting late and I have some work that I have to do in here."

"Maybe me and Anna can go for a ride. It won't be dinner time for a while."

"I really think you'd better wait to throw a saddle on Midnight until I can help. Tell you what, if you can find something else to do this evening, I promise we can go for a good long ride first thing tomorrow morning."

James disappointment was evident, but he could see that Chuck had already made up his mind. "Okay," he said, "but remember, you promised to go in the morning. Come on Anna, let's go take care of our horses," he said as he turned and saw Anna standing behind him.

"Hey, if you two see Clyde out there, tell him I need to see him," Chuck called after them, as they headed out the door. Then, muttering "never mind" to himself, he grabbed his comphone and told it to call Clyde.

Clyde found Chuck still sitting at his desk, still studying the screen in front of him. "Grab a chair," was the only thing Chuck said to Clyde, as he stared at the screen. He had been researching everything he could find about Pro Foods, and what he found was troubling, to say the least. It brought a combination of feelings of anger and helplessness. He felt helpless to change what he saw as the downward spiral of the country that he loved, and the more helpless he felt, the angrier he became. At some point in his life, the United States had been stricken with a disease, like a cancer. He couldn't say when the cancer had started growing, and he couldn't say specifically what the cancer was. Was it greed for money? Or, for power? Was it a lack of morals or religion? Maybe too much religion or, more precisely, greed for religious power. Whatever the cancer was that had started growing long ago, it wasn't Pro Foods; but Pro Foods was definitely proof that the cancer had metastasized. The Catastrophe had surely been evidence of the cancer's spread throughout the economy. Pro Foods was proof positive that the cancer had now spread throughout the Federal Government as well.

Since the Catastrophe, every social program under the sun had been slashed or privatized, or both. The privatization of Social Security and subsequent slashing of benefits had been especially hard on Chuck's generation. It had meant starvation and homelessness for way too many elderly Americans. And what had really galled Chuck about it more than anything else, was the knowledge that it had helped enrich his son in law, Robert James Mendez – investment banking guru. And now, Chuck had found, among all of the other information about Pro Foods a list of the board of directors. One name stood out on that list and Chuck just kept staring at it, his mind in turmoil. One name; Robert James Mendez.

"What's up, meeting in town didn't go well?" Clyde's question brought Chuck's attention back to the present.

"No, the meeting didn't go well at all. Stealing cash through taxes wasn't enough. Now, they want our cattle, too."

Clyde looked at the screen that Chuck had been staring at. The heading at the top said, Pro-Foods Corporate Structure. There was a sub-heading below that, Corporate Ownership. Instead of listing the owners, however, there was a statement to the effect that Pro Foods was a private corporation that was jointly owned by the USDA and private interests. Since it was a private, not public, corporation, those private interests were left undisclosed. There was, however, a listing of the Board of Directors, noting how these prominent benefactors were giving their time and efforts to further the cause of ending hunger in America once and for all. Clyde, of course, noticed the inclusion of James' father on that list.

A quick cynical smile played across Clyde's face. "So, not quite as altruistic as they're made out to be, eh?"

"Altruistic my ass!" That scum-bag son-in-law of mine doesn't do anything unless there's money it for him. "Ending hunger - Bullshit!"

*Good thing James isn't here*, Clyde thought. It was, of course, no secret that Chuck Pierson had no use for Noni's husband Robert. He wondered again, as he had many times over the past fifteen years, why Noni had married Robert Mendez. His thoughts started to turn toward fond memories of his youth, growing up with Noni here on the ranch. Those thoughts were interrupted by Chuck.

"We're going to lose our agricultural fuel subsidies, Clyde. Worse than that, I'm afraid we're going to lose the market for our cattle." Chuck went on to explain the details of the meeting in town. How Pro Foods was going to monopolize food production and how they were trying to set themselves up as the only market for beef, pork, turkey and chickens. How they were going to supply a single food item called Allpro.

"Nicely named," Clyde said. "Kind of like that old dog food, Alpo. Probably tastes about the same, too."

Chuck had to smile at that. "Yeah, I'm sure it isn't going to taste anything like a good old rib-eye, is it?"

Clyde thought about it for a second or two and, as usual, saw things differently than Chuck, or most people for that matter. "That's why we won't lose our market," he said. "You think Robert Mendez is going to eat dog food? Sure, there're millions of people who won't have a choice, but there are more than a few rich people that won't be giving up beef steaks anytime soon."

He's right, Chuck thought; as long as there's a one percent or a one-tenth of one percent, there will be a market. Even if the feds outlaw it, there'll be a black market. The rich are going to get what they want one way or another. And, we can get by without the fuel subsidies. We'll just have to cut our fuel use even more than we already have.

The two men discussed the situation some more and decided that they would have to cut the size of the herd down to about a hundred head. That would allow them to lay off the two hands that were up in the high country with the cattle. Chuck and the Duran family could manage the rest of the herd by themselves. Anna, Ralph, and Cody were all old enough to help, and maybe they could get James to help out, at least in the summer. *That'd be a good slap in Robert Mendez' face,* Chuck thought.

"Thinking about it that way," Clyde said, "maybe after Pro Foods locks down the regular markets, beef on the outside of those markets might be worth a whole lot more."

That's when it dawned on Chuck that Clyde was right about steak being worth a whole lot more once the market was locked up, but it wouldn't be ranchers raking in the profit. It would be the Pro Foods investors. They had rigged the system, rigged the government to monopolize the foods produced by independent farmers and ranchers so they could rake in even more money than they already did. There would still be steak and chicken and anything else available to those who could afford it. And there would be Allpro available for those who couldn't. Pro Foods would be the only market that ranchers could sell their beef cattle to, and they would set the price however low they liked, but you could bet your bottom dollar that all of that beef wasn't going into Allpro. There would be a hidden branch or subsidiary, or maybe more than one, that would get the best cuts of beef and the best parts of the chickens and hogs. Those would be sold at a huge profit, and they wouldn't be labeled *Pro Foods*. No, Allpro, that wonder food for the masses, that salvation for the starving - Allpro wouldn't contain the steaks and chops and chicken breasts. Allpro would get the beaks and feet, the hooves and hides, and whatever other parts they could turn into protein meal.

"You're right, Clyde. They will lock down the markets, but they're not going to allow any other market to compete with 'em, either. There'll still be steaks available for Robert Mendez and friends, but they'll be the ones selling those, too. They just won't say Pro Foods on the label."

Clyde could see that Chuck was absolutely right. Pro Foods wasn't a power play to monopolize a part of the food market. Pro Foods was a power play to monopolize all of the food market. "Guess we don't have any choice but to sign up," he said. "At least if we sign up, we'll get to keep our fuel subsidies."

*There is that,* Chuck thought. As much as he hated being any part of it, they only had two choices. Sign on to the Pro Foods market, or stop raising cattle altogether. *If we stop altogether,* he thought, *they'll probably just confiscate the ranch. If they can steal our cattle, they can just as easily steal our land. All they'd have to do is say it was for the "greater good".* Once again, he had a thought that he'd had many times over the course of his life – *we need a revolution. That's what this country really needs; a revolution. Hell, it's not just this country, the whole goddamned world needs a revolution.*

Chuck slid a finger across the screen in front of them and a Pro Foods contract appeared on the screen. "I guess that's settled then. As much as I hate to, I'll sign this damn contract. Guess it's better than shutting down or losing the ranch."

·····•··•·····

It was still early in the morning; James was already in the log barn putting the saddle and bridle on Midnight, something he had done many times over the past several weeks. He had come to think of the horse as a friend more than a possession. He and Anna had ridden nearly every day since the capture of Midnight. *Where is she*, he thought; this is our last day. Tomorrow, Grandpa Chuck would take him to Kremmling and put him on the train, they only had one more day to spend together.

The past few weeks had been quite an emotional roller coaster for James. From the highs of time spent with Anna, to the lows of overheard arguments between his dad and his grandfather. He wasn't very anxious to get home to Castle Pines. He was afraid his father would never let him come back to the ranch. But at the same time, he didn't understand why his grandfather seemed to dislike his father so much. To James, his father was very successful and had always provided James and his mother with everything they could ask for; and yet, this very success was what Chuck seemed to dislike. It was something that was totally beyond his understanding. Grandpa Chuck certainly wasn't poor or deprived, and yet he seemed to have a general dislike for the truly wealthy, just as that salesman on the train, Bud Johnson, had seemed to disdain the wealthy.

James remembered how, when he was younger, he and his Mom had spent a lot of time here at the BR. There had been so many visits that he couldn't remember them all, but his father rarely accompanied them. From summer vacations to holidays, those were mostly all happy memories for James. As he thought about it, James realized that the last time his father had driven them out to Kremmling was when his grandmother died. That was three years ago. Grandma Nancy had died of some kind of cancer at a young age. His mind didn't exactly frame it that way, but James couldn't help but wonder now whether Grandpa Chuck somehow blamed his Grandma's death on the wealthy. His Mom didn't, of that he was sure. This was the first year that she hadn't driven him out to the ranch for his summer vacation, let alone, not even driving out to pick him up. He was sure that she wanted to see Grandpa, and that she loved spending time here at her childhood home, and yet, Grandpa would be putting him on the train tomorrow. He wondered what it meant that his Mom wouldn't be driving out to pick him up.

"Hi, James." The sound of Anna's voice startled him as he was tightening the cinch. He hadn't even heard her come into the barn.

"Morning Anna." His face brightened into a big smile as he spoke. "Where should we go today?"

Anna just said, "I don't know," as she grabbed the bridle and headed to Pintada's stall. James looked after her, the smile fading from his eyes as he realized she was not in a very good mood at all. Come to think of it, he wasn't really in a very good mood himself. *Guess it's just that this is my last day,* he thought.

As it turned out, they mostly just rode about somewhat aimlessly. They rode up to the ranch cemetery, which sat on a hill just to the west of the old homestead. It was a pretty morning view from there, with the sun just a little way up the sky and the headquarters of the BR spread out below them. They lingered there for a little, looking at the headstones marking the graves of both of their ancestors. Each having grandparents and great grandparents buried in the same cemetery seemed to be another link joining them together.

From the cemetery, they rode on up to the big mesa to the west. Riding side by side up the steep two track road that wound its way through the scrub oak, they emerged onto the large gently sloping expanse of cleared pasture. A good part of the big mesa was irrigated hay meadow. The part that wasn't irrigated was mostly sagebrush, with a few pinon and juniper trees scattered here and there.

The knee-high grasses in the irrigated meadow waved in the breeze, like gently lapping waves on a large lake. As they emerged from the scrub oak, which grew all around the mesa's flanks, they startled three buck deer that had been eating the bounty at the edge of the meadow. If you didn't know it already, you could tell the season of the year by simply seeing the bucks grazing peacefully together in the grass hay that was ready for harvest. Having the bucks together, not yet in rut, said that it wasn't yet fall; and seeing that the hay was ready to mow said that summer was almost over. *Just like my vacation is almost over*, James thought.

From the big mesa, they forded Spider Creek, which was a really small stream this late in the summer. Very little snow had fallen in the mountains during the previous winter; the ongoing drought in this part of the country was extreme, to say the least. Even though the BR had the most senior water

MARCUS LYNN DEAN

rights of any ranch around, they hadn't been able to irrigate as much as Grandpa Chuck would have liked.

After crossing the creek, James and Anna followed a series of game and cattle trails winding their way back down through the scrub oak to the southeast. Emerging from a particularly thick stand of brush, they found themselves at the gate to the south pasture where they had caught Midnight just a few weeks ago. Just a few weeks that seemed like forever, on the one hand, and like the blink of an eye on the other. Without saying a word, Anna swung down out of the saddle, and with practiced ease, held the reins of Pintada while opening the gate.

"Isn't Grullo still in there?" James asked as Anna led Pintada through the gate.

"Yes," Anna answered. "But Pintada isn't in heat now."

She wondered if James would ever be observant enough, when it came to a mare, to know when one was in heat. *Probably not,* she thought. *He didn't grow up around horses like I did.*

James rode through the gate, and Anna closed it behind them. She didn't get back on Pintada, though; just started walking, leading the paint. James decided that maybe he should dismount as well, wondering about the strange mood that seemed to have come over Anna. *Actually, Anna had been acting strangely all day,* he thought. Then he thought about his own feelings, this final day before he had to go home to Castle Pines. It wasn't that he didn't want to go home, he just wished that Anna could somehow go with him. It was a totally irrational thought, but he knew he liked being with Anna more than any of his friends back home. Knowing that he now missed his Dad, and especially, his Mom didn't diminish the fact that he knew he would miss Anna a lot.

They led their horses in silence, walking side by side, and found themselves on top of the hill where they had sat just a few weeks before; young voyeurs watching horses in the intimate act of breeding.

Anna didn't say anything, she just took the lunch she had brought from her saddlebag and removed the bridle from Pintada so she could also eat without the bit in her mouth. James followed suit, also in silence. They let the horses go about the business of grazing freely, it wasn't like they could get too far away, and sat together in very nearly the same spot they had sat before.

This time none of the other horses were visible from where they sat. They must have been behind the hill to the south. The two of them sat side by side on the grass, eating their lunch in awkward silence. Anna finally broke the silence.

"I don't want you to go." It was a simple statement, spoken in her soft matter of fact way. "I'm afraid you won't come back."

James swallowed the apple he'd been chewing. "I'll be back, I always get to come back." He wished he was as sure as he sounded. He put his arm around Anna. She leaned against him. They sat in silence, watching a bald eagle as it rode the thermals and slowly floated down to land on one of the large cottonwood trees that grew along the river. For some reason, the eagle gave James a sense of unease, a foreboding feeling that he couldn't quite put his finger on. Truth be known, he too, was afraid he wouldn't be coming back.

# PART TWO

A Chinese man dressed in modern business attire sits behind a desk in a large starkly furnished office in Zhongnanhai in Beijing. There is a knock on the door, and then, before the man even answers the knock, another man dressed in a Chinese military uniform steps briskly through the door. He stops, standing at attention in front of the desk. He speaks just a few words in Mandarin, salutes, pivots and walks back out the door, closing it quietly behind him.

The man sitting at the desk reaches down and plucks an antique telephone receiver off of its cradle. Holding the antique to his ear with one hand, he pushes a series of numbers on the phone's keypad with the other. After a few moments of silence, someone obviously picks up on the other end of the antiquated landline. The Chinese man speaks one sentence into the phone. Incongruously, it is spoken in perfect Farsi. Just one short sentence; *"It is done."* Without saying another word, the man slowly lowers the phone back into its cradle.

# Chapter 4

S NOW WAS FALLING OUTSIDE the window of his room on the fourth floor of the dorm. It was early January, James was a high school sophomore at Colorado One on the north side of Boulder. This was his second year at the new Colorado boarding school which specialized in a highly tailored STEM curriculum. "Unequalled Excellence In Education" was the school's motto. The unequal part was certainly accurate. The school only admitted the most economically elite students. It was said, in a new take on an old saying, that if you had to ask what the cost of tuition was, you couldn't afford it. Classes would resume tomorrow, James was just settling in after being dropped off by Don. Robert hadn't been able to accompany James to Boulder because of a "crucial" meeting he had to attend at his office, and his mother had come down with the flu or something over the holidays.

*Just as well,* he thought. Sometimes it seemed like he enjoyed Don's company more than the company of his parents, anyway. Don was a friendly companion, as much as he was a bodyguard. Next month James would be fifteen, then he could get an Autonomous Vehicle operator's license and "drive" himself wherever he wanted to go. Where he'd wanted to go for Christmas was out to the Blue River Ranch. Once again, that had not been allowed. James had not been allowed to go visit his Grandpa for over two years now. Grandpa Chuck and the Blue River Ranch were hardly ever even mentioned in the presence of his father. James knew that his mother still kept in touch with Grandpa Chuck, but that part of her life was a taboo subject around Robert Mendez. Likewise, James always kept in touch with Anna, but the less his mom and dad knew about it, the better.

Feeling the comphone in his pocket vibrate, James pulled it out and folded it open. Anna was on screen, looking as great as always. James had to wonder if she made herself up before calling, or just looked that good all the time. He touched the screen to allow his image to be seen and smiled brightly into the camera.

"Hi Anna, I was just thinking about you." Truth be known, James thought about Anna most of the time.

"Hi James, are you back at school yet?" She knew he was; otherwise, he would've answered with a text instead of voice video.

By way of answer, James, who was standing with his back to the window, raised the com up above his head letting Anna see the view. "How are you?" he asked, bringing the com back down to face level. "Did you have a good Christmas?"

"I didn't get what I wanted for Christmas," she pouted. "I thought you were going to come see me."

The smile in her eyes belied her pouting lips and James had to laugh. "You know I wanted to," he teased.

Anna's pout turned into a radiant smile. "When is your Dad going to let you come back? I might get another boyfriend if you make me wait too long."

"Maybe this summer; I'll be fifteen. Maybe I'll just come out there whether my Dad wants me to or not." James tried to sound more confident than he was.

Anna started to reply and then vanished. The screen simply went blank. James looked at the status bar; no signal. *That's odd*, he thought. "Hey Assie, what's wrong with my com?" He'd considered naming his digital assistant simply Ass but had decided to lengthen it to Assie after his Mom protested him walking around the house saying *Hey Ass* all the time. There was no reply from his digital assistant. He walked over to the desk and looked down at the DA speaker. The green power light was glowing steady, meaning it definitely had power. What the heck is going on, he thought, as he reached down and pushed the power button. When in doubt, reboot. It was something he'd learned at a very early age. The power light flashed red, then yellow, and finally achieved a steady green glow, as the DA speaker powered up. The green light came on, but there was no familiar greeting from Assie, only silence.

Knowing that the artificial intelligence used by Assie wasn't in the little round speaker on the desk, but rather in massive servers located who knew where, James didn't bother asking Assie to turn on the comscreen on the wall above his desk. Instead, he reached up and manually pushed the comscreen's power button. Like the DA, the comscreen powered up just fine, but instead of his usual home screen, there were just two words in bold red caps in the middle of the screen; **NO CONNECTION.**

James stared at the screen for a few moments. It seemed almost incomprehensible. *How could there be no connection?* The internet linked everything. It had been totally secure since the government made it that way in the wake of foreign interference in the elections of 2016 and 2018, and especially after all of the social media problems of 2020. He turned away from the screen and looked out his window again. The view from his fourth-floor window was to the east. Across the grounds of Colorado One, he could see the tall security fence that ran completely around the school's grounds. Just on the other side of the fence, Highway 36 ran its north-south route between Boulder and Lyons. Highway 36, which usually had quite a bit of traffic moving in both directions now looked more like a parking lot than a highway. There were a few vehicles still moving, mostly along the shoulders and even down in the borrow ditches, but the main traffic lanes were entirely jammed by cars and trucks that were all stopped haphazardly; looking for all the world like everyone had simultaneously shut down their vehicles in the middle of the highway.

As he looked at the chaos on Highway 36, James realized that the only vehicles that were still moving were older cars and trucks that were actually driven by a human driver and not dependent on artificial intelligence and GPS guidance. He could see more and more of the older vehicles trying to work their way out of the stalled traffic and onto the shoulders and down into the borrow ditches, but none of the newer autonomous vehicles were moving at all.

It was getting to be late afternoon, and most of the Colorado One students were settling into their dorms for the new trimester, just as James was doing. There were a few who were just arriving, and a few more were in some of the vehicles that were stalled all over the highway. As James headed to the stairs, he wasn't about to try the elevators, he passed by a window at the end of the hallway with a view of the main entry gates to the school. The gates were made of wrought iron and were opened and closed by the security guards that manned the four guard stations; two guard stations on each side of the ten-foot security fence that surrounded the school. Both the entrance and exit gates were standing open. There was a Mercedes EV blocking the entrance gate and one of the new Jaguars blocking the exit. All eight members of the security guard regiment were milling about the two stalled vehicles with their assault rifles slung over their shoulders. It was obviously not an attack on the school, and there was nothing threatening in sight; other than the eight armed guards at the security gates, that is.

James wasn't the only student who had ventured down to the lobby common area to try to find out what was going on. The dorm building was actually like two separate four-story apartment buildings with a common area between them on the ground floor that housed the lobby, cafeteria, and a large student lounge. The north wing housed the boy's dorms and the south wing housed the girl's. The lobby, cafeteria, and student lounge were shared in the large single-story common area. Boys were not allowed in the girl's wing, and girls were not allowed in the boy's, which made life a little bit tricky for the LGBT students. They were generally placed according to their self-identified gender. James thought they probably should have built a third wing so they could have male, female, and other or undecided.

As James stepped out of the stairwell into the lobby, there were a lot more people than the few dating couples who were usually milling around. There were almost as many students in the common area lounge as there were in the cafeteria on pizza days. Most, if not all, were wearing questioning expressions and talking among themselves. It was obvious that they had no more idea of what was going on than James did. As he looked around, he saw a girl that he hadn't seen before standing by herself off to the side of the main entrance doors. She was standing a little behind the schefflera plant in its large pot, which partially shielded her from his view and provided her some separation from the rest of the students. She was holding something to her ear with one hand. James couldn't tell what it was. He worked his way through the gathering crowd to get closer. As he approached her, he could see that whatever it was she was holding to her ear looked like nothing more than a small black plastic box.

"Hi," James said as he approached the girl. As she looked up at him, he was somewhat taken aback at the extremely concerned look on her face. He also couldn't help but notice in that first instant of eye contact how attractive she was. Her hair was that strawberry blonde color that isn't quite blonde and not quite red. She had a very fair, almost pale, complexion, and her eyes were the clearest blue.

"Oh, hello," she said, never lowering the plastic box from her ear. A smile never even flashed across her face, the ultra-concerned look seeming as permanent as the black plastic box that was stuck to her ear.

"I'm James," he said, trying to get more of a conversation started than just *hello*. "What are you listening to?"

The girl slowly lowered her hand holding what James could now tell was some kind of antique radio thing. As she pulled it away from her ear, he could hear a voice coming out of it. He couldn't make out all of the words, which was obviously why the girl had been holding it up to her ear. He thought he made out the words, *emergency alert*, but he couldn't be sure.

"It's the emergency alert system." The way she said it, she might as well have added, *you idiot*, but she didn't. She also didn't smile, and James was about to just walk away when she added, "I'm Madison Miller," and stuck out her free right hand.

James took her hand lightly to shake but was surprised by her grip. She squeezed his hand firmly and shook much more like a guy than a girl. "So, what's up," he asked, as she released his hand.

"War, I guess; though no one seems to be sure."

That definitely shook James. *War* was not a thought that had even entered his mind. A thousand questions seemed to come to him all at once.

"War? With who?" he asked. It didn't really seem at all possible. Oh sure, the U.S. military still maintained bases all over the world, but the war in Afghanistan had ended years ago. War with North Korea had seemed imminent at one time until it became obvious that it was a war no one could ever win.

"Not sure," she said, returning the radio to her ear. "The only thing that's certain right now is that someone has taken out the internet and most, if not all, of our satellite communications."

# Chapter 5

T HE FALLING SNOW OUTSIDE his window reminded James of the scene two and a half years ago when the war had brought the world to a standstill. This was the same window of the same dorm room that he had occupied every school year since he was a freshman here at Colorado One. Now a senior, he would be graduating and leaving Colorado One behind in just two more months. He could see a few vehicles moving up and down Highway 36, but there wasn't nearly as much traffic as there used to be on a Friday afternoon. Another very notable difference was the number of people who were walking along the shoulders of the highway. Some carried packs, and more than a few were pushing or pulling carts or wagons. *More and more every day,* he thought. *The poor who can't afford any other transportation; worse yet, the homeless, who really have nowhere to go.*

The snow seemed to be ending. *Not even enough to cover the ground. Another winter ending like last winter,* he thought. *Another winter with practically no snowpack.* The ongoing drought was really taking a toll now. Even with trainloads of water being freighted in from the Great Lakes, there wouldn't be enough for everyone to get through another summer. He had the thought that many of those down below who were headed north along Highway 36 sensed the same thing and were trying to get someplace where water was plentiful. *Where are they going,* he thought, *Wyoming, Montana, maybe Canada? A long way to push or pull a wagon or a cart.*

It was mid-March and the daytime high temperatures had already been reaching into the eighties here in Boulder. The cold front that had brought this meager snow would be gone by tomorrow, along with any trace of what little moisture it had brought with it. As he watched the poor headed up the highway, James felt the familiar pangs of guilt. What made him so different than them? How was it that he had a brand-new Jeep parked in the seniors parking lot – underclassmen were not allowed vehicles – and so many others had nothing but the clothes on their backs and whatever they could carry with them?

He thought about the Jeep that had been given to him by his father as a birthday present less than a month ago. It was a pure autonomous vehicle; 4-wheel direct electric drive, lightly armored with bullet-proof glass. It would protect him from the random shots that were sometimes fired at the wealthy, as well as keeping him secure from any random crowd he happened to encounter. The Jeep gave him a sense of freedom that he had never had before. He could go wherever he wanted to go, whenever he wanted to go there. *But what happens if the net goes down again? Won't happen,* he thought.

The Great Mid-East war, as it was now being called, had lasted only a few months, but it had changed the world more than anything had since World War II. The culmination of centuries of religious conflict between Sunni and Shia, between Christian and Muslim, and decades of conflict between Iran and Saudi Arabia, and

Israelis and Palestinians; the war had brought all of these conflicts to an end. At least, for now. The war had also brought a final end to the age of the American Empire. The entire Middle East was mostly in ruins now; the few people who were left were simply surviving, they didn't have time or energy left over for conflict. What the war had failed to take away, was left to the destruction of climate change. Destruction that was more and more pronounced with every passing year.

It had, of course, been China that had taken down much of the infrastructure of the United States, and just as certainly, the U.S.A. had returned the favor. It may have been known as the Great Mid-East war, but it had been as much of a world war as any of the wars of the twentieth century. A few countries had been able to stay out of the conflict. Most notably, those in Central and South America, and a few in central and southern Africa. Even though they had managed to avoid taking part in the conflict, the war brought profound changes to these countries as well. With the previous world order turned upside down and inside out, these countries now had to depend on themselves and their neighbors. There was no longer a World Bank or an International Monetary Fund. Unburdened by the demands of the previously powerful nations of the world, most of these countries would have been thriving, if not for the disasters of climate change.

Although it didn't seem like it to most of its citizens, the United States had actually come through the conflict in better shape than many other countries. Through a lot of behind the scenes diplomatic efforts and threats of nuclear annihilation, the U.S.A, Russia, and China had managed to keep most of the destruction of the war contained to the Middle-East. Much of its influence over the rest of the world was long gone, but at least the U.S.A. was still an intact sovereign nation. And, to the surprise of many, much of the technology that had helped to temporarily make the U.S.A. the world's only super-power continued to function.

The Defense Department had long been aware of the vulnerabilities of the internet and the satellites that everyone depended on. To compensate for those vulnerabilities, top secret dark projects had been in the works since before the end of the twentieth century. There were redundant satellites to replace those that were taken out by the Chinese; some already in orbit and some ready to launch and activate on a moment's notice. As for the internet, that was also ready to be replaced. The infrastructure was already in place on that fateful day, two and a half years ago, when the world wide web went dark. Unlike the rest of the world that struggled to get the web back up and functioning, the U.S. simply activated its replacement. Something the government called Amerinet. Amerinet worked much like the old internet, except that it was most definitely not world-wide. In fact, in the United States, it was no longer possible to even access the wider internet, except by going through special servers that were operated by the new Cyber Security Administration.

James felt the familiar vibration of the com in his pocket. "Diggy, big screen," he said, without even taking the com out of his pocket. He had renamed his digital assistant Diggy. Assy was just too juvenile, now that he considered himself grown up. He turned away from the window to the big screen above his desk and was surprised to see Madison on screen. He'd been expecting a call from Anna.

"Hi Maddi, you're looking great today!" As he said that, he smiled broadly at the screen. Maddi did look great, but then she always did. James had started dating Madison immediately after their meeting on the day the net went dark. It had been an interesting tightrope walk, keeping up a long-distance romance with Anna, while at the same time actively pursuing Maddi.

"Hi, James," Maddi wasn't smiling. Rather, she had kind of a sad look on her face, and her bright blue eyes didn't seem to sparkle like they usually did. He could tell from the background that she wasn't in her dorm room either.

"Maddi, is something wrong?" He felt a little foolish that he hadn't noticed her demeanor right off the bat.

"Can you come down to the lounge?" It seemed almost like a plea.

"Sure. You want me to come down now?" He was supposed to meet her in the lounge in about an hour for a date.

"Please," she said, "I can't wait another hour."

As he walked down the corridor to the stairwell, James hardly ever used the elevators, he thought about Maddi and their relationship. He had a real sense of foreboding. She had said that she couldn't wait another hour. James had been anxiously looking forward to the evening as well. But he was pretty sure that another night of sneaking Maddi into his room and into his bed wasn't what she had in mind. It was definitely what he had in mind; what he had been looking forward to since the last time, which had been almost two weeks ago.

James and Maddi's relationship had developed slowly at first. He had only seen her a couple of times that first year after the net went down. It had been so chaotic then, with the transition from the internet to Amerinet occupying so much of everyone's time and energy. All classes had been canceled at first, and it was thought that everyone would have to go home. It didn't take long for everyone to realize, however, that no one was going to go anywhere soon. Not with so many autonomous vehicles parked all over the streets and highways, unable to function without the connectivity that they depended on. A national state of emergency had been declared along with the declaration of war, and the military had been given the task of getting the nations' infrastructure back up. Interestingly, the military's communications infrastructure never even seemed to go down. Apparently, the military was much more prepared than most of the experts had thought they were. Most American troops had been brought home from all over the world to tackle the infrastructure problems in the United States. Unlike previous wars, troops weren't really needed. As a matter of fact, they were mostly evacuated. The Great Mid-east war had mostly been about the emptying of American, Russian, and Chinese stockpiles of trillions of dollars' worth of bombs, missiles, and even a few nukes. It wasn't so much a war that had been fought, as it was a region of the world that had been blown up. The war had directly claimed the lives of tens of millions of people, but active military personnel made up a very small fraction of all those killed. Most of those killed and injured were civilians. Millions more had been killed indirectly and were still dying all over the world, as a result of the failures of infrastructure and disruptions of fuels, food, and water.

James was remembering the first time he had sneaked Maddi into his room, as he walked down the first flight of stairs. It had been the previous fall shortly after the start of their senior year. Getting her up to his room without getting caught had all been a matter of a simple disguise. The school had a nice co-ed fitness center and gym located a short walk from the dorm. On that day back in October, James and Maddi had separately gone to the fitness center and then met up there. When Maddi went into the fitness center, she was wearing shorts and a light blue windbreaker with her long hair blowing in the wind. She had been carrying a gym bag that was the schools green and gold colors. Within fifteen minutes of Maddi going into the fitness center – James had arrived before her – James, and what appeared to be another boy emerged. They were both wearing black hooded sweatshirts and sunglasses. James was not wearing the hood up on his sweatshirt, but the other boy had his head totally covered. The two walked briskly to the dorm and just as briskly up the stairs, which were seldom used, as most preferred the elevators. It was only when they were safely inside James' room that Maddi took off her sunglasses at the same time as James pushed the hood off her head and kissed her. It wasn't long before, with a lot of awkward inexperience, they were removing the rest of each other's clothes. Before that day, James had always dreamed of Anna being the first. He still had feelings of guilt about having sex with Maddi instead of saving himself for Anna.

He was just about to the bottom of the last flight of stairs when he felt the com vibrate in his pocket again. *Shit,* he thought. He had forgotten about the expected call From Anna. He stopped at the bottom of the stairs to take the call, hesitated, then decided he would just have to call Anna back.

The lounge was mostly empty. There were a couple of guys that James vaguely recognized playing virtual chess at one of the gaming tables; the holographic pieces seeming to float in the air just above the board. Over in the corner by one of the big picture windows, there was a couple who were obviously engaged in a romantic conversation sitting in one of the love seats that were scattered here and there among the overstuffed chairs that were the main furniture.

Looking around, James spotted Madison over in the other corner of the lounge. She was sitting in one of the big overstuffed chairs, half turned to where she could look out the window at the falling snow. As she turned at his approach, he could see that she was crying.

"What's wrong?" he asked, taking a seat in the chair next to hers. The chairs were arranged so they were seated at about a forty-five-degree angle toward each other, with both having a view out the window while carrying on a face to face conversation at the same time.

There were tears in Maddi's blue eyes, as she looked straight into his and said, "I have to stop seeing you, James."

"Why?" The one-word question betrayed his emotions to the extent that it was like a million questions all at once. Why now? What happened? What did I do? Why me? He could feel the tightening in his throat and feel the sting of tears starting to form in his own eyes.

The tears in Maddi's eyes were drying, a steely resolve replacing the sadness on her features. "I have a boyfriend back home." It was a statement of fact spoken flatly, without emotion. "I'm going home next week, and I don't want to see you anymore."

The statement was like a slap in the face. "What do you mean you're going home next week, graduation isn't until May?"

"I have all of my credits and they're letting me graduate early. I'm going back home to start classes at Stanford. Justin is already enrolled...I'm sorry James."

The finality of the way she said, I'm sorry James, drained most of his sadness away, as it was replaced by jealousy. No, not jealousy really; it was more simple anger. The strange thing was, he wasn't really angry at Madison, he was angry at himself. Angry that he had let himself fall for Maddi when the feelings he had for Anna were stronger than anything he had ever felt for the blue-eyed, strawberry blonde from California.

He stood up, the tears in his eyes mostly stopped and the tightness in his throat relaxing. "Fine," he said. "Just so you know, I have a girlfriend, too." He turned and walked away. It was the last time James ever saw or heard from Madison Miller.

..........

On his way back up to his room, James wasn't thinking about Madison, he was thinking about Anna. He was trying to decide if he should tell Anna about Maddi. Maybe that would clear his conscience, but he didn't really have anything to feel guilty about. He had never lied to Anna, except maybe by omission; and they had never talked about not dating other people. For all he knew, Anna had been dating someone else, too. That thought stopped him in his tracks. As he resumed walking, he wondered...for all he knew, Anna might be having sex with another boy. Hell, she might have had sex with lots of boys. Now there was a thought that brought out actual jealousy, whether it was warranted or not. By the time he got to his room, he had worked up an overwhelming desire to see Anna. Not just on the comscreen, but to really see her in person; to actually be with her.

"Diggy, call Anna." He was taking clothes out of the dresser drawer and putting them in his overnight bag when Anna's face came on screen. "Anna, I'm coming out to

Kremmling to see you." He hardly even looked up from packing.

"What? When?" The look on her face was definitely one of surprise, but James wasn't sure, as he looked up at the screen, whether it was a pleasant surprise, or not.

"I'll leave early and be there first thing in the morning. If the roads are good, that is."

"James, wait...how can you come here? I thought your Dad wouldn't let you."

"He won't, but he doesn't have to know." James' thoughts were in overdrive now. Since he had the new Jeep, James usually drove down home to Castle Pines on the weekends, but he had already told his Mom and Dad that he was going to stay at school this weekend to study. He hadn't bothered to tell them that what he planned on studying was the anatomy of a certain girl from Southern California. "I already told them that I'm not coming home this weekend. They'll think I'm just studying here at school."

"James...James, wait a minute. You can't drive out here early in the morning. It's been snowing in the mountains all day long. Are the passes even open?"

He looked up from the overnight bag at Anna's face on the big screen, not sure about the expression he saw on her dark features; not sure what was written in those deep brown eyes. "Anna, don't you want to see me?" The hurt in his voice was unmistakable.

Anna's beautiful dark eyes softened and lit up. "Oh James, I do want to see you," she said. "More than anything. It's just that I wish you'd let me know sooner. Why don't you wait until next weekend? You can drive out Friday afternoon, and we can spend the whole weekend together."

......•......

Reluctantly, James had agreed to wait until the following weekend to go to Kremmling. After hanging up, though, he had changed his mind. Anna wanted to see him as much as he wanted to see her, he was sure of that. He'd decided that he'd just have to surprise her.

Anna was right about the snow in the mountains. The snow in Boulder, however, had stopped sometime shortly after dark. There was still no light in the east as James unplugged the charger from his Jeep. Anticipation had kept him from sleeping well, which was very odd for James Mendez. He usually slept like a log. At times, the com alarm even had trouble waking him up. This morning, he had bounded out of bed at four o'clock, even though the com was set for five.

*It's gonna be warm today,* he thought. There was a warm chinook breeze already pushing the cold front off to the east. The sky was brilliantly clear, millions of stars like tiny jewels shimmering in the pre-dawn darkness. It wasn't deep dark, the moon was nearly full, but it was just about to set behind the mountains to the west. *Follow that moon,* he thought, as he settled into the autonomous jeep. Instead, he just said, "Nav, take us to the BR Ranch near Kremmling."

James watched, as the map appeared on the screen in front of him. It was centered on Kremlin, Montana, and seemed to be searching for the BR Ranch. "Not Kremlin, Montana; Kremm-ling Colorado". He said, emphasizing the G at the end of Kremmling. The map re-centered instantly on the town of Kremmling, and then a marker pin appeared, looking like some kind of giant pole rising right up out of the location of the BR ranch headquarters about halfway between Kremmling and Silverthorne.

A female voice with a slight British accent came out of a hidden speaker. "Is this the correct destination?" she asked.

"Yes," James said. *Maybe I'll try another voice,* he thought. The British accent had seemed cute when he set it up, but for some reason, he now found it kind of annoying.

The Jeep backed nearly silently out of the parking spot and pulled out onto Highway 36. "There is a delay near the Eisenhower-Johnson Tunnel," the British voice said, "but it is still our quickest route. We should reach our destination by eight-fifteen."

James adjusted the seat to a full reclining position and closed his eyes. "Diggy, wake me up at seven-thirty, and don't let the queen of England disturb me unless it's an emergency."

This time, the answer that came out of the hidden speaker was the familiar voice of his digital assistant. "If the queen of England calls, I'll tell her you are not to be disturbed."

James had to laugh. "Yeah, and don't let the nav-system wake me up, either."

....•.•....

They weren't moving. James pushed the button that raised him up out of his reclined position. It was bright sunlight shining through the bullet-proof glass of the Jeep. He could see that they were somewhere high in the mountains. Snow banks still lined both sides of I-70, but the banks of snow were only about a quarter of what they used to be this time of year. *The snow's going to be all gone in another month,* he thought. *It'll be a long dry summer if the snowpack's already gone by April.* He looked at the nav-screen and found that they were sitting on I-70 about two miles from the tunnel's east portal. The clock on the screen said 7:03. They must have been sitting stationary for quite a while; he had definitely caught some sleep. The Jeep was in the left lane; on the right, there was an autonomous electric semi blocking his view. In front, there was a single SUV and then just empty highway. *Looks like a new Benz,* he thought. Turning to look back, directly behind there was one of the newer autonomous electric buses that were, to a large extent, replacing the electric passenger trains. The buses were now the primary mode of transportation for the masses. At least, for those who could afford a ticket. Over on the eastbound lanes, traffic, what traffic there was, seemed to be moving normally. There wasn't much traffic at all, just a few semis. The only other private transportation that James saw was the Benz parked in front of him.

"Nav, why are we stopped?" There didn't seem to be any obstructions in front of the Benz. There was a red stoplight, presumably there just in case a human driver happened along in an antique vehicle.

"There is a snow removal operation in progress," the Brit voice said. "The delay should last for approximately two more hours, our ETA at the BR Ranch is now ten-twenty."

*Two more hours?* James thought. *How can it take two hours to open up the highway?* "Can't we just go over the pass?" he asked the Nav, referring to the old Highway 6 route over Loveland Pass.

"Loveland Pass is closed, with no planned reopening," was the reply from the navigation unit.

"Diggy, call Anna." James couldn't remember ever calling Anna this early, but he had to let her know he was on his way to see her. He had awakened with the beginnings of a new plan in mind.

"James?" Anna's voice came out of the Jeep's sound system.

"Good morning." He noticed right away that Anna had answered voice only, apparently, she wasn't prepared for James to see her yet. *Like I wouldn't think she was beautiful without makeup,* he thought. "Guess where I am?"

"Umm, how am I supposed to know? Let's see; did you go home after all?"

"I'm waiting on snow removal sitting here on I-70. I should be there by about ten-thirty."

There was a long silence before Anna spoke. "You're coming here - today? I thought we'd decided on next weekend." Definitely surprise in her voice, but, once again, James wasn't really sure that it seemed like a pleasant surprise. "Does your Grandpa know?"

"Nobody knows but you. As a matter of fact, I have an idea – let's not let anyone else know at all. I'm only coming out there to see you, not Grandpa."

"And how are you going to show up at the ranch without Chuck knowing you're here?" She was at least now sounding a little bit intrigued.

"Is it warm enough that you can take Pintada out for a ride, by yourself?"

"Yes, the weather is beautiful, but I can't take Pintada anywhere. She has a new colt. Remember? I told you she was pregnant."

"Oh yeah," now he remembered. "What about Midnight? You said you'd been riding him some, just to keep him in shape."

"Yeah – I suppose I could take Midnight out for a ride this morning, but James..." She didn't get a chance to finish.

James didn't let her finish, all he heard was the part about she could take Midnight for a ride. "You remember that old forest road a half mile or so south of the south pasture? How 'bout I meet you there?"

There was another pause on the line, before she answered, more than a little frustration creeping into her voice. "I haven't been on that road for a long time, James. I'm not sure it's even passable."

"Surely I can get at least a little way off of Highway 9. We can meet about a quarter of a mile in. That way my jeep won't be visible from the highway." He felt the Jeep start to move just as he said it.

"James, I wish you would have let me know sooner. I have a" there was a pause, "I had plans to go into town today."

Oblivious to the undertones of frustration and disappointment in her voice, all James heard was that she'd *had* plans to go into town. Which to him meant only that her plans could now be changed. "I couldn't let you know sooner, I just decided last night. Anna, I need to see you. What do you want me to do, just turn around and go home?"

There was a silence and a barely audible sigh before she answered. "No James, I do want to see you. I really do. I can get out of going to town." Then, in a happier sounding voice, "How soon did you say you'd be here?"

After the conversation ended, Anna sat on the edge of her bed, looking at the picture on the home screen of her com. It was a picture of her and James sitting side by side on Pintada and Midnight. Just another picture of two happy kids, seemingly, without a care in the world. She sat that way for a few minutes before telling her com to call Will. Will wasn't going to like her breaking their date, but deep down she knew that, even though she'd dated him for almost a year, Will had never been anything but a surrogate. She may have given in to physical need and given her virginity to Will, but that twelve-year-old girl in the picture on her com had already known she was in love, way back then.

Having slept most of the way from Boulder, James hadn't noticed the condition of I-70. It had been seven years since he had traveled over the mountains. Maintenance on the old highway wasn't what it used to be. *Good thing it doesn't have to carry the traffic that it once did,* he thought, as barriers narrowed the road down to one lane. The left lane was just gone. A large hole had opened up and half of I-70 had slid down the mountain. He wondered if it would ever be repaired. *Probably not unless this lane goes, too.* It wasn't a very comforting thought, as they passed the gaping hole.

As bad as it was, Interstate 70 proved to be in much better shape than Highway 9 leading from Silverthorne to Kremmling. Being the major east-west corridor for truck freight, I-70 did get some maintenance, but Highway 9, in recent years, was mostly used by just a few farmers and ranchers; and the school buses that carried their children to school in Kremmling or Silverthorne. The potholes and cracked and missing asphalt made it quite an obstacle course for the Jeep's navigation system. As they got to within a few miles of the BR, James had the sudden realization that the nav system was taking him directly to the ranch. For all he knew, it might not even have the old forest road in its database.

"Nav, I want to change our destination, show me an aerial map of this area." It took some study for James to re-orient the lay of the land with his memory. He zoomed in on the BR and struggled to remember all of the places he and Anna had been six years ago. It was easy to make out the buildings that comprised the ranch headquarters. From there, he could easily make out the big meadow to the north. He studied the area on the south side of Spider Creek. The south pasture wasn't nearly as easy to distinguish as the big meadow on the north side of the ranch. It wasn't nearly as big, and much of the terrain of the south pasture looked like the rest of the surrounding area. Finally, though, he spotted the forest road he was looking for. He zoomed in to where the map was large enough for him to touch the spot where the forest road left Highway 3. "This is our new destination," he said. "I want to turn off on this road and stop about a quarter of a mile From Highway 3."

"I am sorry," the British voice said, in a matter of fact manner, "the road you have selected is not in my database."

"I want to go there, anyway. At least get me to the intersection. And change your voice." The accent was suddenly very irritating. "Use the voice of an American man."

"Certainly," the voice was now a man's voice, with no noticeable accent at all. "Our ETA at the intersection is ten thirty-two."

As it turned out, the forest road was completely impassable by vehicle. A large dead aspen tree had fallen across the old road no more than twenty yards from the highway. James had the Jeep back up into the forest road as far as the log and parked it there. Not that getting off of the highway was very important; James had only seen two other vehicles on the road this side of Silverthorne. There were several more fallen logs that he had to go over and around, as he walked up the road. The feelings of anticipation hadn't subsided, but, as he approached the rendezvous, strong feelings of nervousness were taking over. Now that he was this close, doubts started creeping in. Did Anna want to see him, as much as he wanted to see her? What was it that he felt for Anna? Was this true love? He knew that what he had felt for Maddi wasn't love. It had definitely been lust, but it wasn't love. What did sex have to do with love, anyway? If he was truly in love with Anna, and if she was in love with him, would sex change the feelings they had for each other?

He saw Midnight first, but not before Midnight saw him. James came around a bend in the old forest road to find the horse staring straight at him from the shadows of an aspen grove. Midnight's ears were following James' movements as well, and his nostrils were searching the air to ascertain what, or who, it was walking up the forest road.

At first, he didn't see Anna. She was sitting on a fallen aspen at the edge of a small clearing off to the side of where she had tied Midnight to a tree. The hopes and fears that Anna had been feeling, as she waited for James were, if anything, even stronger than the emotions he had been feeling. Seeing him come into view was terrifying and thrilling at the same time. She wanted to run into his arms, at the same time she was afraid to. She wanted nothing more than she wanted to make love to this love of her life. She was also terrified that the act of physical love would diminish or destroy their love for each other.

Anna stood. She started walking toward James. He continued walking toward her. Neither said a word. They came together in the middle of the clearing; their eyes were locked in a silent embrace before they wrapped their arms around each other as their lips met. At that moment, it seemed they had always been together; that they would always be together. Eternity was fully contained in that one moment of holding onto each other, expressing infinite feelings with their kiss.

They made love on a bed of aspen leaves, in the middle of a clearing, in the middle of nowhere. It was paradise. It was heaven on earth. They were, for those fleeting few minutes, at the center of their own universe. They might as well have been the only two people on earth.

The afternoon was gone in an instant. With their clothes back on, James and Anna sat together on the same fallen tree that Anna had been sitting on when James arrived. James had his arm around Anna, and she had her face snuggled against his chest.

"I don't want you to go," she said. There were tears in her eyes; tears of happiness. "I love you, James."

"I love you too, Anna. More than anything. I'll be back before you know it. How could I ever stay away?"

# Chapter 6

THE TRIP BACK TO Boulder had been mostly a blur, with nothing at all worth remembering. James had grabbed a burger in Silverthorne while the Jeep was recharging. He had then slept most of the way to Boulder. He had even slept through the long delay near the west portal of the tunnel.

It was almost four o'clock when the Jeep pulled onto the charging pad at the dorm, and James made his way up to his room. His first thought on entering was that he had left the light on. Then he saw Don sitting in the recliner looking at him.

"Hello James," It was a friendly greeting like they'd just ran into each other on the street somewhere.

"Don, what are you doing here?" An almost imperceptible shiver seemed to run up James' spine.

*What the hell was Don doing here?* He looked at the man sitting relaxed in the recliner. Don always appeared relaxed. He wasn't that much older than James, only in his late twenties, and he and James were about the same size and build. James worked out enough to be well muscled, but nothing like Don. Don's muscles were like steel springs, always tight; and yet, paradoxically, always relaxed. Like the springs of a cocked bear trap, full of tension contained in a misleadingly relaxed pose by the trap's trip mechanism. Don was, among other things, highly trained in self-defense, and James knew that he was also always armed. Don was his father's favorite bodyguard. Strange as it seemed, he was also James' favorite of those who were tasked with protecting the Mendez family. James and Don had always had a rapport that James didn't ever feel around the others. Maybe it was the fact that Don was much closer to his age, or maybe it was just that Robert had tasked Don with protecting his son much more than he had any of the other security personnel. As a result, James had spent much more time with Don than he had with the small army of security that worked for Robert Mendez.

Don smiled. "Well, James, I'm here on orders; your dad sent me." His smile widened a little more. "Course you probably already figured that. Fact is, it's time to go."

James looked at him blankly. *Time to go? Time to go where?* It was then that he noticed that his things were gone. The desk was bare, the picture of Anna was gone from the nightstand by the bed. As he looked around, he could see through the open closet door that even his clothes were gone.

"What do you mean time to go? Graduation is still over a month away."

"Guess you graduated early. Robert wants to see you, in his words, as soon as possible."

*He knew. Somehow, he knew I went to see Anna.* The thought was accompanied by a cascade of emotions. There was a bit of fear, along with dread at the confrontation with his father that was now imminent. But mostly, he felt anger. His father had been spying on him or at least tracking his movements. *How? How had he known?* More importantly, *why? Why had his own father been spying on him? What gave him the right? I'm eighteen years old,* he thought. *I'm an adult. I don't have to do what I'm told.*

"Tell him no. You tell him I don't want to see him, and I want him to stop spying on me. I'm not a kid anymore." The anger was boiling over now. "Never mind, I'll tell him. Assie..." in the heat of the moment he reverted back to his digital assistant's old name, before correcting himself, which only added to the level of frustration. "Diggy, call Dad."

"He won't answer." Don still seemed totally relaxed in the recliner. "You know that. If he was going to simply request your presence, he would have called you."

As the com continued to ring, James knew that Don was right. If his father had meant to simply request his presence, he would have called. Robert Mendez was not much in the habit of making requests. He was much more in the habit of simply giving orders. Orders that were not to be ignored.

"Diggy, stop the call. And what if I refuse to go with you? What are you going to do, kidnap me?" The edge was going off his anger. He was still mad as hell at his Dad, but not at Don.

The expression on Don's face turned cold. He looked at James with an icy stare. "That's not something you want to do James. Look around. All your stuff's already gone. The school won't let you stay, and I'm taking the Jeep when I go. The Jeep's going to Castle Pines, whether you're in it or not."

James broke away from Don's icy stare. The blinds were open, he looked out at the darkness of night. Somewhere in the open land off to the northeast, he could see the flickering glow of distant campfires. *What am I going to do,* he thought? *Join the homeless out there?* Suddenly, the anger was gone. In its place was the beginnings of a plan. "Let's go," he said, as he turned and headed back out the door, without even looking back at Don.

The short trip from Boulder down Highway 36 to Denver was totally unlike any trip that James had ever been on with Don. Neither spoke hardly a word. As soon as they were on the road, Don was on his com texting. James presumed that the messaging was to his father and Don didn't want James to hear a voice conversation. His suspicion was confirmed when Don redirected the Jeep's Nav to take them to the MICI office building downtown. The MICI, which stood for Mendez Investment and Consulting, Inc., was a somewhat unassuming office building in downtown Denver. Other than the security guards and the armor gated entrance to the below-ground parking area, the thirty-story building was much like the other office buildings in downtown Denver. Few people knew that it was the world headquarters for a multi-billion-dollar empire. A financial empire that Robert James Mendez had built from the ground up.

The clock on the nav screen showed 5:03 as the Jeep pulled off of 20$^{th}$ into the drive that led to the underground parking. The guardhouse at the gate was manned twenty-four hours a day. No electronic enabled entrance gate for Robert Mendez. That would never have been secure enough to suit him. As a matter of fact, the gate, as well as the rest of the building's security measures were not connected to Amerinet at all. Anything connected could be hacked.

"Kind of early for Dad to be at work, isn't it?" James asked, finally breaking the silence between them.

"Yeah, it is. I'm not even sure he's here, but this is where he said to bring you."

The guard stepped out of the guardhouse armed with an M4 rifle and stepped up to the Jeep's window. James knew that there were at least two other armed guards stationed in armored rooms, where the two windows above the opening to the underground parking looked down on the drive. Those two windows were one-way bullet-proof glass with openings between them where heavier armaments like armor-piercing rockets could be fired on anything that was sitting in the driveway below.

Don rolled down the window of the Jeep. "Howdy Mike," he said. "How's it hangin'?"

"Don! didn't expect to see you. What? You lowering your standards, riding around in a plain old Jeep?" It was obvious that the guard felt subordinate to Don, and then he leaned in to see James. "And James!" he really didn't expect to see James Mendez. Now Mike was all business. "I'll open the gate."

"Hey Mike, is the boss up there?" Don asked as the guard turned back toward the gate.

"Not sure, but I think so. An airdrone landed up on the pad about fifteen minutes ago. Since nobody bothered to shoot it down, I figure it was him."

The entire top floor of the MICI Building was Robert Mendez' private suite. Totally self-contained, he could stay here full time if he so desired. The elevator that James and Don rode up from the parking garage opened into a reception area where Margie, Robert's personal assistant, would have been seated at her desk during business hours. The semi-circular desk was empty at this late hour, but the door to Robert's office behind the desk was half-way open.

"James, please come in." Robert's voice came over the intercom as soon as James and Don stepped from the elevator. "Don, thanks as always. Please relax in the lounge for a while, if you would."

Don immediately headed down the wide hallway toward the lounge. James, feeling strong trepidation and wishing he were most anywhere else, nonetheless, walked purposefully through the door into his father's office.

Robert Mendez was seated behind the L shaped mahogany desk, but he was turned away from the desk, looking out the huge corner windows at the lights of downtown Denver. He was not a large man. James was a couple of inches taller than his father and had a huskier build. Robert was dressed as he always was, in a tailored grey silk suit. Clean shaven, with his black hair immaculately in place, the only thing missing this late in the evening was his necktie. Otherwise, he looked the same as he always did at work. Right down to the cup of coffee that he held in his right hand. For some reason, the coffee caught James' attention more than anything else. He had the thought that he seldom saw his father without a cup of coffee. For that matter, it seemed like years since he had seen him dressed in something other than a suit.

"James, come in and sit down." Robert didn't even turn to look at his son, just continued looking out the window.

"Okay, Dad. I don't seem to have much choice, do I?" He walked across the plush carpet and sat in one of the chairs across the desk from his father.

Robert finally turned to look at his son. He set the coffee cup down on the desk without taking his eyes off of James. He didn't say anything for a long moment, just looked at his son with what seemed like a longing for something. "Choices," he said. The one word just hung there. "I guess that's why we're here, isn't it? It's all a matter of choices."

"I didn't choose to be here, Dad. Don didn't really give me a choice."

A kind of sad smile came over Robert's features. "In many ways, I didn't choose to be here, either, son. But the choices we've made definitely brought us to this place and time." He swept his left hand through the air, indicating the place they were in. The smile left his face, but the sadness remained. "I guess it's past time for us to talk about the choices I've made in my life. And, more importantly, the choices you have to make in yours."

"I'm beginning to wonder if I really have any choices in my life Dad." Anger was starting to come back to James. "You seem to be making my choices for me."

Robert looked away, his focus seeming to shift off into the distance somewhere. "Maybe none of us have any choice," his voice was soft. He seemed to be speaking more to that distance than to James. Abruptly, he refocused on James, and a strong tone of command returned to his voice. "Have you ever wondered why I never speak of my youth? Or, how I got to be where I am? Have you ever wondered about how I came to marry your mother?"

James hadn't wondered about any of those things. There was no need to wonder. Like anyone else who was as rich and powerful as his father, Robert Mendez' life was an open book, in news and magazine articles, as well as in Wikipedia. Anyone could find out anything they wanted to about Robert Mendez, or so it had always seemed to James. His was the quintessential story of the American dream. Robert's parents had immigrated to the United States from Guatemala in the early 1990s. Unfortunately for them, they had done so illegally. Fortunately for Robert, he was born in Pueblo, Colorado, which made him a U.S. citizen. His father worked as a laborer in the construction industry, while his mother worked at whatever odd jobs she could find. In short, Robert Mendez' parents did whatever they could find to do, just to survive and to provide for Robert and Robert's older sister, Marie.

"Everybody knows your story, Dad. You're famous. What's to wonder?"

"Yes, everybody knows my story," his gaze seemed to wander off into the distance again. "How I was able to overcome the deportation of my family and everything else to become the self-made billionaire that I am today." He looked at James and smiled again. "It's a good story. A good story with a lot of holes. Yes, I was able to work my way through school to learn economics and finance. But the story doesn't say why I chose to study those subjects. Do you know why, James?"

"I guess that was what you were interested in."

"But why?" there was a new intensity in Robert's voice. "Why was I interested in finance? Why was that the choice I made."

In spite of himself, James was now curious. *What was his father leading up to? What was this really all about?* "I don't know. What made you interested in finance? Did you actually control what you were interested in? Seems to me that we don't really control what interests us, only what we do with those interests."

"Exactly!" Robert proclaimed. "I wasn't interested in economics and finance at all. People think I'm a financial genius. I'm not a financial genius. My interest was in power. Pure and simple. When my family was deported, and I was left alone I was the same age as you are now. At first, I was interested in law. After all, it was the law and the people that made the laws that had deported them. At first, I thought that power was in the law and that I should study law and learn to wield that power. But power isn't in the law, James. Money is power. That's what I was really after. If you have enough money, you can control the laws. Without money, legal knowledge will get you nowhere."

James was fascinated, his father had never, in his eighteen years of life, talked to him like this. He had always been rather stern. He hadn't been exactly cold to James, but he wasn't exactly warm, either. He had mostly just seemed distant. James had always, in his own mind, blamed that distance on the fact that Robert's parents and sister had all been murdered shortly after they were sent back to Guatemala. Now, it seemed there was more to it than that.

"So, you decided to study finance to acquire money?" James asked, his growing interest in his father's story obvious.

"No! Not to acquire money, to acquire power. Money is just a vehicle. A means to an end, nothing more." He seemed to grow introspective, and then, in a softer voice, "there is never enough. You can never control everything. No matter how much money and power, you just can't control everything." Once again, he looked off into some unknown distance, leaving James to wonder where his mind was going.

"Is that why you have been spying on me? Are you trying to control me, too? Is that why you have kept me away from Grandpa's ranch?" The feelings James had when he realized his father had been spying on him had morphed from burning hot anger to a cold slow simmering resentment.

Robert turned and looked at James again. He had a sad smile on his face. "No son, I haven't been trying to keep you away from Chuck or the ranch. The Duran girl is the problem."

"What do you mean, problem? Anna's not a problem. I love Anna. You can't keep me away from her anymore. I'm going to go live with Grandpa Chuck. I'm eighteen years old and you can't stop me." James' plan had come into focus. He would simply go live at the BR. He could be with Anna every day. He could learn how to be a rancher and help Grandpa Chuck. His grandfather was getting old and probably needed the help anyway.

The sad smile left his father's face, and his eyes turned cold. "I won't allow it. I won't allow you to throw away what I have built. You will go to Harvard or Yale and learn to take over what I have built. And you will meet someone who is worthy of you to make you forget about Anna. I had hoped that Madison Miller girl would have done it, she's from a good family. A family with power. The kind of family that can add to what I've built. Oh well, there will be others. You will find the right girl at college, just like I found your mother."

Anger welled up again in James. Anger, defiance, and righteous indignation. "Like hell, I will!" He stood up and turned to leave.

"James, if you walk out that door, there won't be any coming back." His father's voice was cold and menacing. "You, Chuck, and the entire Duran family will end up cold and homeless, just like all the rest."

It was a threat. James was half-way to the door when it hit him. It was not an idle threat; the threat was very real. Could his father actually somehow force Grandpa Chuck and the Duran family off of the BR Ranch. As impossible as it seemed, he knew the answer was yes. Robert Mendez probably had the power to make that happen, or did he? He turned back to face his father. At that moment, the only emotion that could describe what he felt toward the man was hatred. He had a sudden realization about his father and mother.

"Did you ever love my mother," he asked, his expression and voice now as cold and hard as his father's. "For that matter, have you ever loved anyone?"

"I love you, son. Your mother may have been a means to an end, but then she gave me you. I love her for that, at least. I love her for giving me you."

"You say you love me, and yet you could throw me to the wolves? Along with Grandpa Chuck? That's a strange way to show love if you ask me."

"I suppose it is, but I won't have you ending up married to a nobody. Squandering away the power that has taken me a lifetime to build. The Mendez family won't ever go backward. If you won't honor your responsibility to all I've built, it'll pass on to someone who will."

*Who?* James thought. *I'm his only son. Who could he possibly leave all this to?* Then it dawned on him – *why should I care? I don't want to be like him, anyway. Besides, he has no one else.* "You're bluffing," he said, with more confidence than he felt. "I'm all you've got."

The coldness in Robert Mendez' voice was chilling. "You have a cousin, James. He lives in the squalor of Guatemala. There is nothing he would like more than to come to America. To inherit this." He held out his hands as if to encompass the whole world. "He would be grateful. He would know how important it is to gather and maintain power. He would know that there is never enough."

James was shocked to his core. He didn't know the man sitting at the desk. The man who was his father. "How?" he finally said. "How can I have a cousin? Your family was murdered."

"Yes, my family was murdered. The whole world knows that. What no one knows is that I had an older brother who was left behind when my family came to America. He, too, was murdered eventually, but not before he produced a son. I have secretly nurtured and protected my nephew, just as I have nurtured and protected you. So, you see James, it is up to you. You are right, I won't stop you if you decide to throw all of this away, but know this - you won't be ruining your life only. You will also be destroying the life of that girl you say you love. Believe me, I will see to that."

They looked at each other for a long quiet moment. James trying to understand how, after eighteen years, he could know so little of his father. *How can I even be his son?*

"Go." Robert broke the moment. "Go and decide. You're right. You're a man now. Your life is yours to decide." He turned back toward the window, and James knew there was nothing left to say. He turned and left the office. His father, who had always been distant, was now a total stranger.

Don was sitting alone in the lounge. Daylight was starting to come through the picture window, where Denver was slowly coming to life at the start of a new day. The windows in the lounge faced to the west, and James could see that sunlight had just reached the tops of the peaks; a warm golden glow, on those snow-capped mountains to the west. His thoughts weren't on the peaks, though. His thoughts were on the Blue River Ranch, off to the west of the peaks. When Don brought him here, he had every intention of telling his father that he was leaving to go live with Grandpa Chuck. Now, he didn't know what to do.

"Am I free to go now?" he said, knowing that Don would already have instructions from his father.

Don didn't look at all surprised by the question. "Yes sir. The boss says I am to return the Jeep. I'm not even supposed to go with you. Looks like you are on your own". He paused, unsure of what to say. "James...I'm sorry."

James wondered how much Don knew, but it really didn't matter. Don may have seemed somewhat like a friend, but that was before. In his other life, the one before today, James had friends. Now, he found himself alone. As the day dawned, he was awakening not to a new day, but to an entirely different world than the one he thought he knew. "Is the Jeep still programmed to my bios then?"

"Of course." There was not a hint of sarcasm in Don's voice. "It's your Jeep."

James glanced through the window at the mountains to the west which were now entirely lit up by the rising sun. The sky was clear except for a few clouds nestled around the top of some of the peaks. He turned and started to leave.

"James," - he stopped. "Be careful out there."

Without so much as even a backward glance, James walked through the door and headed to the parking garage.

"Nav, take me home." His mind in so much turmoil that only part of his thoughts seemed like his own, he was lost in his own head. One basic question kept rolling through his mind in different forms, *what to do? What should I do now? What can I do?* It was never, *what do I want to do?* That was a question he could no longer ask himself. The question of what he wanted to do was no longer relevant. It had been ripped from him by the revelation of who, or what, his father really was.

The number of people on the streets of Denver this early in the morning was astounding. It was obvious that most, if not all, were homeless. Some were wearing little more than rags, while others were dressed quite well. *Newer to the street,* James thought. They were there in droves, going through dumpsters, searching everywhere for any scrap of anything they could find to eat. He remembered something from his childhood as he passed the starving hoards. Back then, it had seemed like every street corner had a resident homeless person with a sign begging for help. This memory was of one incident, in particular. He had been riding somewhere with his mom and dad; must have been five or six years old. They were stopped at a red light, and on the corner next to them, there was a woman dressed in rags with a sign asking for help. He couldn't remember what the sign said. What he did remember was the baby she had strapped to her breast in one of those packs that allows the child to be in front; as opposed to the pictures he'd seen of Native American women with babies strapped to their backs. He remembered his mother had wanted to open the window and give the woman some money. His father had said no. James knew that Robert Mendez hadn't been nearly as wealthy then as he was now, but they had certainly been wealthy enough. As he remembered the scene, he thought he could remember his father saying something like, *We don't give, we take. That's the difference between those who have and those who don't.* Looking back on it now, James wondered if the memory was real, or if he had just manufactured the memory in response to the meeting he'd just come from.

"James! - what are you doing here?" his mother's genuine surprise let him know that she knew nothing of his father's actions. "What's wrong?" she asked, the concern in her voice was reflected in her eyes, as she crossed the room to give her son a hug.

He accepted the hug and held on, grasping for a return to the innocence that had been taken from him. *She doesn't know him any better than I did,* he thought. The thought filled him with sadness. He broke away from his mother. "Why don't you ever go home?" he asked.

The question obviously surprised her. She seemed a bit startled, but then answered simply, "This is my home."

James looked at his mother, searching; trying to see what he may have never seen before. Trying to see, simply by looking at her, what had brought her, and therefore him, to this place in time. Noni Mendez was an attractive woman. She had auburn red hair and blue-green eyes. She was tall for a woman, nearly six feet tall. James had finally grown taller than her only after starting high school. Though his father wasn't there, standing next to her, he knew that she was a little bit taller than him. Noni Pierson had to have grown up wearing cowboy boots. It occurred to him that his mother must have worn boots while growing up on the BR. Everyone who lived there wore boots, almost exclusively. When she became Noni Mendez, the boots became a thing of the past. *His father wouldn't allow it,* he thought. *He would appear short if his beautiful wife was standing next to him in high-heeled boots. Or shoes, for that matter.* He realized he had never seen her in high heels either.

"Don't you ever miss it?" he asked, knowing that she did; knowing that she had to long for her childhood on the old Blue River Ranch.

Noni didn't have to wonder what James was asking if she missed. She thought about all she had lost every day, but she didn't want her son to know. She had played the part far too long to stop now. "Miss what, James?" she asked, looking truly puzzled.

For James, that may have been the saddest moment of that entire evening. The moment when he knew his mother was living a lie. Deep down, he had always known his father was manipulative and power hungry, but the extent of that megalomania had only become clear that night. The sadness of the fact that his mother was being kept from her father and her childhood home, now that he knew the truth, was overwhelming.

"Why, Mother? Do you love Dad that much, that you'd let him keep you from Grandpa?" even as he asked, he knew that was not the case. He knew with a certainty that there was no love left between his mother and his father. As he watched her face crumple and the tears form in her eyes, he felt lost. *Who were these people?* The parents he had looked up to and tried to please his entire life. *How could he not have known how terrible his father really was? How could he not have known that his mother had spent her entire married life subjugating her will to that of his father?*

Seeing that he wouldn't get any answers from his mother, who was now sobbing and covering her face with her hands; he started toward his room to gather his things. "I'm leaving," he said. "I'm going to live with Grandpa."

"No!" he hadn't taken three steps when the exclamation hit him in the back. "James - you don't – you don't understand." The words came hard, between the sobs. "You can't! He won't let you."

"He can't stop me, Mother. I'm eighteen years old, I can do whatever I want."

He heard the sobbing stop and the coldness that came into his mother's voice. "He'll destroy you both."

He turned back to his mother. Her face was now streaked with mascara. She had stopped sobbing as suddenly as she had started. There were no more tears coursing down her cheeks, her lips were set in a firm line and there was a vacant stare in her pretty eyes. "How Mother? How could he possibly make my life any worse?"

Her eyes, that had always provided solace, now stared right past her son, seeing something from another place, or maybe another time. "He'll take the ranch." It was a flat statement, there was no longer any emotion at all in her voice.

James was taken aback. For the second time today, he heard the threat that his father would take away his grandfather's ranch. Land that had belonged to the Pierson family for over a hundred years. "That's crazy mother! Dad doesn't own the BR, Grandpa does. Dad may be rich, but he can't take what doesn't belong to him."

"He controls the oil and gas. He doesn't need a deed to own the BR. All he has to do is shut off the rest of the gas. The land hasn't supported itself for decades. It's the mineral rights that have allowed Dad to live all these years, not the cattle. And besides, he'll take the cattle, too."

Noni Mendez, once a woman who dreamed of a life for her son that was free of her husband's manipulations, slumped into a chair, once again covering her face with her hands. "I'm sorry, James. I am so sorry." Barely above a whisper, the words rang loudly in James' ears as he left the room.

He pulled the com out of his pocket and sat at the desk in his room. He unfolded the com and stared at the picture of Anna that was his home screen. His stare was almost as blank as his mother's had been. He thought about how he had hidden the picture of Anna while dating Madison. He didn't feel shame, it was just a thought. Emotions had left him. Now, there were only thoughts and memories that were almost random. "Diggy, delete the pics of Anna." He couldn't stand to look at her picture now; no more than he could stand to call her and hear her voice. Picking up the com, he pulled up a keyboard and started thumb typing. Dictation would never do. He could no more stand to dictate the words he was typing than he could stand to speak them to her. Instead, he started typing: *My Dearest Anna, I can't see you anymore. I can't explain. You have to forget about me, about us. I can give you nothing but misery, and more than anything else in this life, I want you to be happy.* He looked at the words he'd written for a long time before hitting the send button. "Diggy, block all communications from Anna," he said, as he slumped in his chair and covered his face with his hands, feeling the warm tears flowing freely down his cheeks.

# Chapter 7

D AMN IT, STEVE, THIS is the third one. What the hell am I supposed to do?"

Sheriff Steve Larson looked up at the grizzled old rancher, whom he'd known as long as he could remember.

"Well Chuck, I know it ain't much consolation, but you're not the only one losing stock these days. Wish I knew what the hell any of us is supposed to do."

Chuck Pierson reached up with his left hand, still holding the reins, and pulled the battered old straw hat off his head. He wiped the sweat off his mostly bald head with a huge right hand and replaced the straw hat over what was left of his once jet-black hair. The black hair had about as much gray now as it did black. That and the weathered wrinkles at the corners of his dark brown eyes gave away the old cowboys age. The sparkle of life that was still in those old brown eyes and the tall muscular build attested to the fact that he was aging well.

"It was probably one of those families of refugees coming up from Texas" the sheriff continued. "Some of 'em are so hungry looking they could probably eat that calf raw."

Chuck looked back at the remains of the calf lying in the trampled grass. The predators and carrion eaters hadn't much gotten to it yet, but the sight of circling turkey buzzards is what had led Chuck to ride over here. The calf had one small hole in its head, right between the bigger holes where its eyes should have been. The buzzards had already eaten the eyes for hors d'oeuvres before Chuck arrived. *Shot with a small caliber, probably just a 22 or 22 magnum*, he thought. Probably shot right from the road, which was just beyond the barbed wire fence, no more than twenty yards from where the two men stood.

The calf hadn't even been gutted properly, the only thing missing was the left hind quarter. Undoubtedly hacked off with great haste in case anyone had heard the shot that killed it. The thought that whoever killed it needed the meat much more than he needed that calf alive, didn't do much to relieve Chuck's sense of anger over having it stolen from him. He had a sense that everything he had known in his sixty-five years of living was being slowly taken away, one thing at a time.

"Guess as hot as it's been, it would only be half-raw if they just left it out in the sun for an hour or two," he replied. "Why do you think they only took the left hind quarter?" He pulled out his comphone and looked at the stock ID screen. Sure enough, it showed calf number 1433 right there in front of him. Of course it did; the BR had been implanting the stock ID chips in the right hind quarter of their stock ever since the ubiquitous ID chips replaced old-fashioned branding.

Chuck looked up at the slowly deteriorating, pot-holed asphalt; what was left of old highway 9. It came over a small rise from the south and disappeared around a bend about a quarter mile away to the north, generally following the route of the Blue River, as it meandered its way downstream to a rendezvous with the Colorado. There was a time, no more than twenty years ago when that highway was fairly busy with constant truck and auto traffic carrying all the freight and tourists of a prosperous nation. Now, there was only Sherriff Larson's electric Jeep sitting in the tall weeds at the side of the road. *Even that Jeep's old by now, probably a twenty-three or twenty-four model. I wonder if anybody still drives new cars,* Chuck thought to himself. He knew that some people somewhere must, but he couldn't remember the last time he'd seen a brand-new personal vehicle.

"Whatever happened to this country, Steve? Or the world for that matter? Remember when we were young, and the world was full of promise? How did we come to this?"

Chuck didn't really expect an answer, and he didn't get one.

"Damn, it's hot," was all Steve had to say.

*Damn it's hot, is right, must be the hottest August ever. At least they got enough snow up high last winter that the Blue still has a pretty good stream of water. That's a lot better than last year when it was just a trickle by now.*

"You know Steve, we always put our chips in the right hind quarter, not the left. You suppose whoever shot this calf knew that?"

"Nah, probably just a coincidence, most of these city folks passing through don't even know the stock have chips."

*That's true,* Chuck thought. *But what if it wasn't one of the refugees from the cities?*

"What if it was a local did this? Some of the people right down in Kremmling are hurting some, too."

"They are hurting, but that doesn't make them thieves," the sheriff answered. "Did you ever lose stock before the refugees started coming through?"

"I've always lost a calf or two here and there, a bear, or a lion, but I've got to admit, losing stock to two-legged animals is kind of a new phenomenon."

"That's right, this kind of thing only started when people started emptying out of Texas. That's why I don't think we can blame it on anybody local."

Chuck put his com back in the holster on his left hip and absently reached down to the handle of the gun on his right.

"Guess it really doesn't matter, local or refugee, they better not ever let me catch 'em in the act."

The motion of Chuck putting his hand on his gun wasn't lost on the sheriff.

"Hope you don't plan on doing anything stupid, Chuck. You catch someone, you call me. Let the law deal with this."

·····•·•·····

The big red quarter horse didn't need any direction from Chuck. He instinctively knew when they were headed for home and set out across the big meadow at a nice brisk walk. Chuck sat the saddle like he was born there. He may not have been born in a saddle, but he had spent a good deal of his life sitting in one.

The big meadow, as it was known, was the largest hay meadow on the Blue River ranch, known simply as the BR by the locals. The big meadow covered roughly two hundred acres of gently sloping grassland, nestled in a big bend of the Blue River where it came down from Frisco Reservoir, flowing north to its confluence with the Colorado River. The grass was short and stubbly now, the hay crop all stacked neatly in the big pole barn which wasn't visible from here; hidden, along with the rest of the ranch buildings, behind the rise at the west end of the big meadow.

Chuck could see the rest of his black angus cattle spread out along the river on the north side of the meadow. *At least they're away from the road,* he thought. *Guess we better move them up to the mesa to keep them safe until we're ready to ship 'em.* There had been forty-five of this year's crop of calves that they'd separated from the main herd to send to Pro Foods. The bulk of the herd was still high in the mountains to the west, grazing on the Forest Service lease that had been part of the BR since before Chuck was born.

Chuck found himself in a reflective mood as he approached the crest of the rise where he could see the BR laid out in the valley near the river. "Whoa Red," a slight pull on the reins brought the big quarter horse to an abrupt stop. He leaned back in the saddle, pushed the brim of the old straw hat up with his free hand and scanned the Blue River and Spider Creek valleys, from the north end of the ranch all the way to the south and the canyon that marked where Spider Creek broke out of the mountains. Spider Creek Canyon was about a mile upstream to the west of the BR headquarters. Hidden from view by the old cottonwood trees lining the river, the remains of Chuck's great-great-grandfather's homestead lay in ruins right up against the rock outcropping, where the rugged rock canyon spilled the Spider out into the wide-open valley to join the Blue. *That's where it all started,* he thought, and then, *that's probably where it'll all end.*

Just a touch of Chuck's heels to Red's side and the horse headed toward the barn at the bottom of the hill. Instead of continuing on to the barn, with a light touch of the rein on the side of the horse's neck, Chuck turned him toward the large ranch garden where the entire Duran family was busy picking vegetables.

The Duran family had been part of the BR for nearly as long as the BR has existed. Clyde Duran had lived on the BR his entire life. His father, Ben, was Chuck's dad's foreman when Charlie senior had died of a heart attack up on Buck Mountain back in '99. Ben hadn't lived a whole lot longer, also dying of a heart attack in '07. Chuck was only 30 years old when his dad died, and he was suddenly and totally responsible for the operation of the entire BR.

*Don't think I could have done it without Ben's help*, Chuck thought as he reined up at the gate to the garden. *And now, not without the help of Clyde and his boys.*

The "garden" could have been an entire farmstead for some. It covered the better part of two acres and was entirely enclosed in an eight-foot fence to keep out the deer and elk. Chuck loosely tied Red's reins to the corner post, walked through the open gate and down the rows of tomatoes toward Clyde, who was bent over picking the ripe tomatoes and placing them in an old bushel basket. As he looked over the plentiful crop of tomatoes, Chuck absently thought about how hard it used to be to grow tomatoes this high up. The BR headquarters, at an elevation of nearly 8000 feet hadn't always been the ideal place to grow most vegetables. He had a little inner chuckle as he remembered how his dad, Charlie senior, hadn't believed in climate change.

"Hey Clyde," Chuck said, as he approached the ranch foreman, "you were right about the buzzards, it was another dead calf."

Clyde stretched his back as he turned away from the tomatoes to face Chuck. His long black hair was tied up in the usual single braid that reached to the middle of his back.

Other than the thick black hair, his head was bare to the sun. Clyde never wore a hat.

"Yo Chuck," Clyde answered the old rancher. "Just one, then?"

"Yeah, it was just the one. Shot with a small caliber and the left hind quarter gone. Sheriff thinks it was one of those families migrating through from Texas."

"Could be," Clyde mused. "What do you think?"

"I'm not so sure, could be a coincidence that they only took the one hind quarter...or maybe they knew the chip was in the other, and they didn't want it tracking them. How many people around here do you suppose there are that know we put our chips in the left side?"

Clyde glanced over at his two sons who were still busy with the harvest. "Well, besides those two," he said, lifting his chin toward them, "we've had quite a few young folk from round about help us out over the years. S'pose all those that helped with the implants would remember."

"That's kind of what I was thinking. May not be just coincidence that we seem to keep losing just one hind quarter, and it's always the left. Anyway, we better move the rest of the calves up to the mesa. Get 'em away from the road. Can you and the boys," Chuck always referred to Clyde's sons, Ralph and Cody, as *the boys,* "take care of that this afternoon? I'll see if I can get the shipment date moved up. Maybe we can get 'em to market before we lose any more."

"You bet." Clyde turned to the boys, "Ralph, Cody, saddle up." Then to his wife, Shellie, "Sorry Shel, we'll be back in a few hours."

Chuck looked over the bounty of the garden, "Looks like I better see if we can get some help with this, too. Probably plenty of folks in Kremmling that'd be glad to help pick veggies for a share. Looks like we have plenty and then some. Hate to see it go to waste."

With Red unsaddled, unbridled, and contentedly chomping on some oats in his stall, Chuck headed to the big house. The big house was a large lodge-style home made of logs. Chuck's father had the big house built when Chuck was just a young boy, back when the oil and natural gas royalties really started coming in. Looking down the lane to the old white clapboard ranch house that the big house replaced, Chuck wondered again about the oddity of him living alone in the big house, while all four of the Duran family lived in the much smaller old house. *It was five,* he thought, *till Anna left.*

He had a sudden memory of seeing James, his grandson, walking with Anna, from the old house down toward the river. It had been a warm summer evening, and the young couple out for an evening stroll had reminded him then, as the memory did now, of similar evening strolls with his late wife, Nancy. The joys of young love. *I should have asked Clyde about Anna,* the thought bothered him. *Wonder how she's doing these days.* A movement in the tall weeds at the edge of his vision caught his eye. The movement of the weeds showed where something was scurrying toward the trees. As he watched, an armadillo appeared out of the weeds in a clear patch of ground. *Guess people ain't the only things leaving Texas,* he thought. *Who would've ever guessed, armadillos in Colorado?*

# PART THREE

CHUCK DOESN'T ENTER THE big house through the large front veranda with the massive front double doors. Instead, as always, he walks around the side of the house and in through the mudroom. Seems like the only use he makes of the veranda is to occasionally enjoy a cup of coffee as he watches the sunrise. Of course, drinking real coffee anymore is a rarity, indeed. Mostly, Chuck's morning beverage now is brewed from roasted chicory root.

After grabbing a chunk of roast beef and some homemade cottage cheese, compliments of Shelly Duran, out of the refrigerator, he sits down at the same barstool where he always eats. The bar is all that separates the kitchen from the rest of the huge great room that takes up most of the ground floor of the big house. Chuck always sits on the kitchen side of the bar facing the large comscreen above the fireplace on the other side of the great room.

"Hey Bozo," he says, with a heavy emphasis on the *Bozo*. He still finds simple pleasure in the name he gave to his digital assistant, once the option of selecting your own name replaced the likes of Siri, Alexa, and Google. "News."

The big comscreen flashes to life with a running script scrolling up the screen, as a clear female voice gives the same information, it's as if she's reading the news from a teleprompter. Chuck set up his com this way long ago, finding the videos from the newscast to be too distracting.

*-Yesterday's high of 111 degrees has now been confirmed as a new record for Dallas. The previous highest recorded temperature for the month of November was the 106-degree reading on November 7th of last year. -*

*-On Amerinet, there are rumors of a new flu virus in Europe. Due to ongoing problems with international communications, Colnews can neither confirm nor deny the rumor. There have been no reports of any new virus in this country. The Colorado Department of Public Health has filed a request for information with the CDC in Atlanta. Stay tuned for updates as they become available.*
*-*

*Good luck getting anything out of the feds,* Chuck thinks. He remembers when the whole world was connected by the internet and you didn't have to rely on the government for information about anything. That was before the Great Mid-East war, of course. Before that dark day when the internet went dead to Americans forever. It had taken well over a year to rebuild the cyberinfrastructure and to bring the Amerinet of today online, even though the government had been secretly developing it for decades. *The feds might control it, and you might not be able to find out about Europe,* Chuck muses, *but at least it's secure from cyberwar and other governments. And what about our own government?* he wonders. *Can't even trust Colorado government, let alone what's left of the Feds. What's left of the Feds seems to be more of a problem than ever,* he thinks. *Sure, the military's been cut down to size, but how many that counted on social security are starving? How many can't even afford that crap they call Allpro?* It bothers Chuck immensely that most of the purebred Black Angus beef he raises now goes into the production of Allpro. *Not too many of us lucky enough to still eat this,* he thinks, as he takes the last bite of the cold roast beef. *Course there's always those few; politicians, bankers...I'm sure they're still eating steak.* The thought of bankers eating steak reminds him of his daughter and his never-ending quest to understand how she could have ever married a bankster.

"Bozo, music." As usual, the news tends to just be upsetting. The sound of River Waltz by the Cowboy Junkies fills the room as Chuck finishes chewing his roast beef. *Plenty of dying rivers to choose from nowadays,* he muses. His thoughts turn to memories of his wife Nancy. Hearing her favorite song always seems to bring out those memories. *God, I miss her! If only she'd gone to the doctor sooner.* It's still a bitter haunting thought, even though ten years have passed since Nancy died of ovarian cancer. *Ten years,* he thinks. *Ten years since she died and Noni hasn't been here since. Hell, it's been years since James has even been here. Guess he must have taken after his worthless father.*

Another thought comes to Chuck, unbidden. A saying from his own youth; *life's a bitch, and then you die.* He tries to shake off the melancholy. *Guess I'm just feeling old,* he thinks, as he finishes the last of his lunch.

# Chapter 8

*D*ATELINE, *MAY 17, 2035. The eye of Hurricane Ida is expected to pass directly over Philadelphia sometime around midnight tonight...*

The throwback dateline was what always brought James back to this particular newsfeed. Something about that dateline made him almost feel like he was living in an earlier time; a better time, when the world didn't seem to be falling apart. James was in his secure apartment on the Colorado College campus in Colorado Springs. The clock in the corner of the screen showed 6:47. Almost nine in Washington, he thought. He was getting ready to go to a show at the Fine Arts Center with Julie. Julie was getting ready in the other room.

*The storm, which made landfall as a category 5 hurricane earlier this evening has weakened but is still packing 130 mile per hour winds and torrential rains. Damages to the area around the Capitol are expected to be severe, compounded by high tide, which will occur at 11:31 eastern time. According to a statement released earlier today by the White House, the President, members of Congress and the Supreme Court, as well as all other essential government personnel are riding out the storm in an undisclosed secure location in the DC area. In other news, the familiar voice of the newscaster droned on, as James finished knotting his tie, the army has dispersed a group of rioters, who were attempting to storm the Allpro production plant in Springdale, Arkansas. Army spokesperson, Susan Baker, reports that casualties among the rioters were less than three hundred, with twenty-two army personnel also killed. Warning against further riots, the army cautions that any attempt to subvert food production facilities will be met with lethal force.*

Subvert facilities, what a farce. Knowing the reality; that the starving mobs didn't want to subvert anything, that they only wanted food to eat, just made the melancholy that James had been feeling even more pronounced. What a world, he thought. I'm getting ready to go to a play, while people are starving to death. Fiddling away, while Rome burns.

All of a sudden, James' thoughts were interrupted by silence. The news had gone silent. He looked at the big screen on the wall. The words, **BREAKING NEWS** were displayed in huge letters across the middle of the screen. Just then, the familiar face of the newscaster came back on the air. She was speaking in the same calm voice as always, but she appeared shaken.

*We have just received word from the USGS that a powerful earthquake has been detected in the Atlantic Ocean. Tsunami warnings have been issued for the Atlantic coast from Maine to Florida and the entire Caribbean, as well as the entire western coast of Europe and the northwest coast of Africa. Initial reports indicate a massive earthquake with a magnitude of at least 9 on the Richter Scale. The epicenter of the quake was approximately 1250 miles southeast of Bermuda. We will update this story as news becomes available.*

"Hey Julie," James shouted toward the master bath. "Did you hear that?"

"Hear what?" She stepped out of the bathroom, obviously ready to go. She was wearing a stunning low-cut deep blue gown. Her long blonde curls falling around her shoulders, framing the fine features of her face. Her blue eyes sparkled nearly as much as the diamond necklace that drew attention to the deep cut of the blue gown, and the cleavage exposed at the V of the cut.

As gorgeous as Julie was, James hardly noticed. His thoughts were on the disaster that was unfolding thousands of miles away. "The earthquake! There's been an earthquake in the Atlantic."

Julie looked at James with an expression that seemed to say, so what, what does that have to do with us, before she noticed the truly worried look on his face. She looked up at the newscaster, who now appeared to be actually frightened. She was getting up from behind the news desk, still talking. *We have been told that we have to evacuate the studio here in New York. We transfer you now to our affiliate in Los Angeles.* The camera showed the newscaster being hurriedly ushered away before the feed could be transferred to Los Angeles. Damn, James thought, it's like nature's trying to destroy us. And why not? We've been at war with nature for a long time.

The screen went blank for a moment, and then a different studio appeared with a man seated behind a desk, much as the woman had been in New York. *Good evening ladies and gentlemen,* the man began. He was dressed in a shirt and jacket that looked like they had been thrown on in a hurry. His lack of makeup seemed unnatural on a newscast. James was struck by the incongruity of the fact that a lack of makeup seemed unnatural, while someone made up to the hilt seemed to be normal. *This nation is in the midst of a natural disaster,* he stammered a little, the teleprompter script obviously out of sync, *a series of catastrophic natural disasters that is unprecedented...*

The man's voice droned on in the background. James sat down in one of the leather chairs opposite the comscreen. "Maybe we better not go," he said absently, as he continued looking at the screen.

Julie wasn't about to give up the play she had been dying to see just because of a weather incident on the other side of the country. "What do you mean, we better not go? To the play? We have to go, it's the final performance."

James turned his attention from the screen to Julie. He knew she was emotionally shallow. That was part of what had attracted her to him. That, her looks, and plain old sexual attraction. At the time, he was really only interested in a sexual relationship, with as little emotion involved as possible. James had met Julie Johnson the day he arrived at Colorado College three years earlier. "Do you really think an off-Broadway play is more important than what's happening on the east coast?"

"Of course not. But we can't do anything about the east coast. Besides, hurricanes hit the east coast all the time. People ought to be used to it by now."

Mentally, James shook his head in disbelief. "Did you not hear them say, tsunami?" he asked incredulously. "Do you know what a tsunami can do?"

"They don't know for sure that a tsunami will hit," Julie pouted.

Flabbergasted, James decided to try another tack. "Diggy, is the play still on at the Fine Arts Center?"

There was a very short delay before the response, "No, the play has been canceled due to events on the east coast."

"Fuck!" It was almost a shout, as Julie stormed back into the bathroom and slammed the door.

Guess I probably won't get any tonight, James thought, as he turned his attention back to the newscast on the big screen. *We are getting reports of impassable roads, as people try to evacuate coastal areas. With aircraft unable to take off due to Hurricane Ida, if a tsunami does hit, the loss of life and property is expected to be beyond catastrophic.*

Everything's beyond catastrophic these days, he thought. For some reason, his thoughts turned to his arrival at Colorado College. He had arrived in late May, giving himself a week to adjust before classes commenced the first week of June. Convincing his dad that Colorado College would be better for him than Harvard or Yale had been a challenge. Guess it's a good thing I stayed in Colorado, even if it does mean being in the same state with Dad. James avoided his father as much as possible. He could hardly stand to talk to him on the com, let alone be in the same room with him. In the end, his father had agreed to Colorado College as a compromise for James promising to never see Anna Duran again.

James had arrived in Colorado Springs riding alone in his Jeep, with no escort or security of any kind. It had been a bit of a shock when he saw the perimeter wall that was nearly completed around the campus. There had been a security fence around Colorado One, but it was nothing like the wall that now surrounded the entire campus of Colorado College. This was a thirty-foot-tall structure made of precast concrete panels topped with razor wire. He remembered having a thought when he first saw that wall, am I going to college or to prison? Outside the wall, the City of Colorado Springs had been a total mess. The streets were littered with debris. Most of the old storefronts were either boarded up and vacant or standing empty with broken glass and broken doors. Some of the open doorways he passed had haggard looking people staring out at him. There were a few businesses still open, and they not only had bars on all the windows, they were protected, not by private security people, but by the U.S. military. Some had Air Force troops while others had groups of Army troops standing at the entrance. All were heavily armed. James remembered how strange it had been to see so many military people and not one member of a civilian police unit. Thinking back on it now, he had the thought; military town to the very end.

Like the businesses on the way in, the entrance to Colorado College had been guarded by a group of heavily armed army personnel. With a gate across the road and two armored vehicles for good measure, it had reminded James of news clips from his childhood of military checkpoints in places like Afghanistan and Iraq. He hadn't had any trouble getting through the checkpoint, of course. The sergeant, who seemed to be in command, had simply wondered out loud how the hell James had arrived without any security detail. Once inside the checkpoint, it had been like another world. Colorado College was like a thriving small city inside the vast ruins of a once thriving metropolis. He had pulled into a nearly empty parking lot in front of the apartment building he had been assigned to and had no trouble at all finding an empty charge station. Nearly all of the parking spaces had charge stations, but there were only three other vehicles in the entire lot. Wondering, as he fitted the plug to the port on his Jeep, where all of the cars could be; that question was answered by what he saw coming through the barricade behind him. It was a convoy. At first, it seemed like a military convoy, with a military-style armored vehicle in the lead and another in the rear. But the vehicle in the middle was definitely not military. It was a black stretch limo.

James watched as the convoy pulled up in front of the building, stopped, and two people got out of the limo. He recognized the woman who stepped out of the limo first. It was Senator Jill Johnson. Julie Johnson had stepped out of the limo next. It was the first time James saw Julie.

As he remembered how the convoy had left Julie at the school that day, he wondered, is Senator Johnson in Washington?

His thoughts were interrupted by silence. He realized that the newscast was silent and looked at the screen. It was blank. "Julie," he spoke to the closed bathroom door. No answer. He walked over to the door and knocked. "Julie, is your mother in Washington?" There was still no answer, but he could hear muffled sobs from the other side of the door. He tried the knob, it wasn't locked. He opened the door slowly to give her time to react if she was going to, and then went in.

Julie was sitting on the toilet in just her panties and bra. The fine blue gown was in a heap in the middle of the bathroom floor. She had her face in her hands and was sobbing. Loudly, he noticed, now that he was not on the other side of the door. "Julie, Julie honey," he tried to console her, kneeling and putting an arm around her shoulders. "It'll be okay. They'll protect your mom." Even as he said it, he wondered who he thought they were, and how they, no matter who they were, could protect anyone from the terrible wrath of nature.

·····•··••····

The rising sun shining brightly through the living room window woke James with a start. His neck was stiff from the awkward position he'd been sleeping in, still fully dressed, slumped in the easy chair in front of the comscreen. A commercial was blaring from the com. The same Allpro commercial that seemed to be on the air more than all other programming combined.

**...*it's not just good for you, it's good for America.***

James stood up and stretched. He was hungry and wondered, as he had before, if there was something psychological about the commercial that brought on hunger. Just what the starving masses need, he thought, something to remind them how hungry they are. He walked into the bedroom to find Julie stretched across the bed sideways, still dressed in nothing but the pale pink bikini panties she'd been wearing the night before. She'd taken off the bra, which lay near the foot of the bed. She had obviously cried herself to sleep at some point. There was something about the vulnerability of her lying there asleep on her stomach, nearly naked, that made him horny. Great, he thought, as he rearranged the unwanted erection that was straining uncomfortably against the confinement of his jeans. I'm not only hungry, but I'm horny. Nero fiddled while Rome burned, I'm ready to screw as America ends.

That unbidden thought, as America ends, brought him up short. The erection was gone as quickly as it had materialized. He turned quietly, so as to let Julie sleep, left and went back to the living room. He turned the com volume down, as he turned his attention back to the screen. There was a female newscaster on screen now, and James didn't recognize her any more than he had known the man from the night before. Unlike that man from last night, she was made-up and looked professional in every way, right down to the extremely worried look she portrayed as she spoke.

*...communication with the Federal Government in Washington has not been restored. We have also been unable to reach our New York affiliate. We do know that a tsunami hit the Atlantic coast of the United States at approximately 1:15 a.m. eastern time, but the extent of the damage is unknown. Tsunami warnings for Europe and all other locations have now been canceled.*

Something on the woman's teleprompter caused her to pause and look questioningly off camera to her right. She turned back to face the camera. She was visibly shaken.

*We have now acquired new video that we have reason to believe was captured by someone in Ocean City, Delaware. We believe the footage was being transmitted live as it was shot, otherwise, it would have been lost. No other details are available. The video you are about to see is disturbing, to say the least.*

The scene on the screen was dark and grainy. At first, it was hard to make out anything but a few specks of light. Slowly, it became clear that it was not only darkness obscuring the scene, but sheets of torrential rain as well. There were gaps in the rain as one sheet of rain would pass, with an open gap before the next sheet of rain obscured the view. The view, when not totally obscured, was one of a mostly darkened city, with some buildings lit by what had to be emergency lighting. There was one building, in particular, that really stood out. It appeared to be seven or eight stories tall and must have had extremely good emergency lighting. It seemed like most of the building's windows were lit up. It was hard to make out any detail, but the building seemed to be a block or two from where the videographer was standing. There didn't seem to be any buildings beyond the one that was all lit up, and then, in a moment devoid of any rain, it became obvious why there were no other buildings beyond that one. A beach could be faintly seen on the other side of the well-lit building, with the darkness of what had to be the ocean just beyond. There was sound with the video. The howling of the wind and the driving rain. Then there was another sound, like a roar in the distance. It reminded James of the roar of a jet engine. The roar quickly grew louder, like a jet was coming down a runway toward the camera, and then it seemed like a wall appeared where the ocean should have been. In a matter of seconds, through a long break in the rain, it became obvious what the wall was. James watched in morbid fascination as the wall of water, that was a tsunami wave, completely engulfed the lit up building. The wall of water had to have been at least twice the height of the building it devoured, maybe even three times as tall. It was hard to believe his eyes, the sight was so unworldly. How could something like that be real? The screen suddenly went black and silent.

James stood staring at the dark screen, his mind having trouble coming to grips with the scale of the disaster that had just hit the east coast. No, not hit the east coast; it was obvious that the tsunami had totally wiped out parts of the east coast. Nothing could survive the wall of water that he had seen with his own eyes. The sea walls and levies that had been built over the previous decade in response to rising sea levels might have protected most places from Hurricane Ida, but nothing could protect anyplace or anyone from a tsunami like the one that hit that building. It was as if the earth itself had struck at the heart of America; retribution for the long war man had waged against nature.

It was then he became aware of Julie standing in the bedroom doorway. Her normally pale complexion had gone totally white, accented by the dark streaks of mascara running down her face, like some kind of ancient war paint. She stood stock still with her arms at her sides. The tears had stopped long ago, and now she seemed to be staring almost blankly at the blank screen. She's in shock, he thought, and then; hell, we're probably all in shock. At that moment, he felt an overwhelming pity for her. Had she just lost her parents? Washington wasn't on the coast, had it been spared? Where were her parents when the tsunami struck? He walked over and put both arms around her pulling her in tight. She remained unmoving, unresponsive to the hug.

With his back to the screen, James didn't see the newscaster come back on the air, but he heard her say, I can't. She seemed to be sobbing, as she spoke. With Julie totally unresponsive to his touch, he let her go and turned back to look at the screen. Just as he did so, three men dressed in military uniforms walked onto the set amid some commotion in the background. In what almost seemed to be a choreographed performance, two of the men grabbed the newscaster by her arms and gently lifted her out of her chair. She didn't resist at all as they escorted her off camera and the third military man took her seat.

*My fellow Americans, I am sorry you had to witness the fake news that was just forced upon you. This is an obvious attempt by certain factions in the military to sow doubt and discord among us.*

Fake news? Could the whole thing have been faked? Obviously, it could have, but it didn't feel right. Why James wondered, was someone, who he presumed was a general, at the studio to start with. The news studio would have had military protection to be sure, but a general? He looked at the man again. The four stars on each shoulder definitely screamed general, and it seemed like he should recognize the face, but he couldn't quite place the man.

*Rest assured that the government of the United States is safe and secure. In order to maintain that security, the country has been placed under martial law, effective immediately. All banks and financial institutions, as well as all food production and distribution facilities, have hereby been placed under direct government control. A nationwide dusk to dawn curfew will take effect immediately. Please remain in your homes after dark.*

And what about all of those who have no home, James thought, just as the general let the real bombshell drop.

*In order to provide security and to protect the legitimate government of the United States from the forces that assail us, all broadcast systems and all personal communications will be shut down immediately. Please leave all comms in standby mode in order to receive further updates as they are made available. Thank you for your cooperation. God bless America.*

The screen went blank and silent. The old Yogi Berra saying came unbidden into James' mind; it's like deja vu all over again. "Hey Diggy," he said, knowing there would be no answer. He was remembering that day six years ago when the world went silent. Martial law had gone into effect then, as well; but that time, it had been to restore communications. This time, it seemed to be an effort to squash communications. He turned back to Julie. She was visibly better. She seemed almost relaxed and the color had returned to her face. She wasn't smiling, but the relief on her face was obvious. She had really believed the part about the government being all okay. James didn't. *If the government is all okay,* he thought, *why was a general declaring martial law instead of the President.* It didn't make sense. Hell, none of it made any sense. He wondered, not for the first time, how the world could have changed so much in just the past three years.

He knew it wasn't really just the past three years. His education, here at Colorado College, had truly taught him how much of a bubble he lived in. He had been shielded and protected from reality while attending Colorado One. Sure, he had seen plenty of homeless people, and knew that the world was divided into the haves and the have nots; but he hadn't known at the time just how many have nots there were; and how few there were, like him, that had it all. He had also known nothing of the rebellion against the status quo that had been growing for years. He lost his ignorance, along with whatever innocence he had left, when he took a course titled, THE UNITED STATES – 50 YEARS OF DECLINE. The course was taught by Dr. Mitchell; an aging professor who was nothing, if not a rebel himself. Dr. Mitchell had refused to teach the approved version of history. He had openly encouraged his students to question everything about government, and especially, everything about the elite and the military who controlled that government. It was not an easy task, teaching the elite children of the ultra-upper class to question their right to the status they enjoyed. Dr. Mitchell's course was one of the first classes James had taken, on his arrival at Colorado College. Fresh off the total shattering of his illusions of his father, James had been one of Dr. Mitchell's most avid students.

It had been a strange experience. All of the students who attended Colorado College were part of the elite that Dr. Mitchell questioned, and most who took his course did so just to earn the history credit. Most of the students thought Dr. Mitchell was just an old man, teaching beyond his time. Many wondered how on earth he was still allowed to teach such nonsense at all. They certainly didn't think of their status as anything but a birthright. Those who had been born unfortunate enough to have nothing just needed to get over it. The natural order of things dictated that these few, who had been born to the wealthy elite, were not only entitled to their place in the world; they were required to maintain their elite status, that the natural order should not be broken.

James, on the other hand, had whole-heartedly accepted the premise that there was nothing "natural" about the current "natural order of things". He had enjoyed Dr. Mitchell's lectures so much that he had started meeting with him for one on one conversations, outside the confines of the lecture hall. The meetings and the conversations hadn't ended when the course did. James had continued seeking conversation with Dr. Mitchell whenever he could. It never ceased to amaze James how much Dr. Mitchell knew of things going on behind the scenes. When the "news" had a story about an Allpro shipment being hijacked by domestic terrorists, and how the military would deal with those terrorists; Dr. Mitchell had pointed out the fact that all shipments of Allpro, or any other food, for that matter, were now protected by military convoy. The news story hadn't mentioned any casualties at all. How could that be? Dr. Mitchell – John, as he'd insisted James call him, had not only known the proper question, he had also known the answer. It was through John that James had learned of the growing rebellion in the ranks of the military. James had always known that the military served the Federal Government, just as the Federal Government served those who allowed the politicians to be in office. What he hadn't thought much about, at least not before he met John, was who makes up the military? Through John, he learned that most rank and file military personnel were there because it was their only means of escaping poverty and hunger. It was an unspoken fact: join the Army, and you'll always have enough to eat. You may have to leave home and loved ones behind, starving; but you, yourself, won't go hungry. "How many of those recruits do you suppose there are," John had asked, "who would like to be able to feed the ones they left back home? How many do you think there are, in this day and age, who are truly loyal to the government; or maybe I should say, to those behind the government."

Julie had gone back into the bathroom and James could hear the shower running. He shook his head. *She really does think all is well,* he thought. *She'll soak in that shower for an hour, while the "normal" people in Colorado Springs are rationed to a few gallons per day at most.* He needed to talk to John Mitchell. Everything was definitely not okay. Maybe John would be able to tell him just how not okay things really were. He stepped into the bathroom and yelled loud enough for Julie to hear, "I'm going to see Doctor Mitchell, I'll be back in a little while."

A pleasant "okay," was her only reply, and then he heard her humming a tune. He was shaking his head in disbelief, as he walked out of the bathroom.

# Chapter 9

HE APARTMENT THAT JAMES and Julie shared was in the newest and nicest student housing building. They actually had the entire top floor to themselves. There were four apartments on each level. Julie and James had adjoining apartments, and the other two were vacant. Julie still had a lot of things in her apartment, but they mostly lived in James'. The building was only two stories tall, with a parking garage and storage underneath, but it sat on a hill at the far northwest corner of the campus. With the building on high ground, the big picture window in the living room of James' apartment looked out east over most of the campus of Colorado College. As he walked by the window, he could see the sun rising over the plains to the east, then something else caught his eye. There seemed to be some kind of commotion at the front gate.

The front gate, with the back gate always closed and locked, was the only way in or out of campus. It was about a quarter of a mile away from James' apartment. The gate was always guarded by a military detail of some kind with a couple of armored vehicles which always sat with their guns pointed out at the city. Only now, the armored vehicles were moving. As he watched, four soldiers came out of the guard barracks and piled into the armored vehicles which had pulled up to the entrance gate. The gates swung up out of the way and the two vehicles sped through the opening, turned right on the street out front, and disappeared from view behind the wall that surrounded the campus. The gates didn't close.

Trying to make sense of what was happening, he looked over the rest of the campus. About half-way between where he stood and the front gate was the coffee shop where he knew John Mitchell usually spent this time of the morning. That was where James planned on talking to the old professor. The entrance to the coffee shop faced back toward his apartment building. The front gate wasn't visible at all from there. This time of the morning, the coffee shop was probably the busiest place on campus. The normalcy of students and faculty going in and out of the coffee shop was a sharp contrast to the anything but normal events of the past night, and especially to the abnormality of the gates standing wide open, with no one guarding the entrance at all. Suddenly, he saw another military vehicle come from the opposite direction of the ones that had just left. It was another armored vehicle with some kind of machine gun mounted on top; a man sitting behind the gun was sweeping it from side to side, as the vehicle turned the corner and entered the gate. At first, James thought it must be replacements for the soldiers who had just left, but when another identical vehicle came around the corner, followed by another, he knew something wasn't right. The three light armored vehicles were followed by four army trucks and then five buses, which were also painted army green. The convoy of vehicles didn't stop at the entrance but pulled up to a stop right in front of the coffee shop and the campus grocery that was right next door. Two more light armored vehicles brought up the rear, but they did stop at the gates. Instead of taking up positions with their guns aimed out at the city, however, they stopped, blocking the gates, with their guns aimed at the campus itself. As soon as they came to a stop, troops started piling out of the first bus. They were all armed with assault rifles and fanned out quickly. There must have been at least fifty of them. They were outfitted in full battle gear. It looked like an invasion.

*It is an invasion!* The thought struck James like a physical blow. He watched in horror, as some of the soldiers started rounding up the students and faculty members who had gathered in front of the coffee shop. Other soldiers entered the coffee shop and rounded up those still inside. Other soldiers were fanning out in groups of two or three spreading out across campus. As the soldiers from the first bus were scattering out across campus, more people started pouring out of the second bus. At the same time, the first of the trucks turned and backed up to the front of the campus grocery. The second bus was smaller than the first. Probably no more than thirty people piled out. None were dressed in army fatigues, and none had weapons. At least not any visible weapons. They looked to James like the homeless people or refugees who seemed to be everywhere these days. Some of their clothes looked tattered, and a few weren't even wearing shirts. With the temperature already in the upper eighties, they didn't really need shirts. Unlike the soldiers whose body armor made it impossible to distinguish gender, there were definitely both men and women in the second group. They didn't seem as efficient or orderly as the soldiers, but they did move as a somewhat orderly group toward the truck that had backed up to the grocery store entrance. The truck that had stopped momentarily, proceeded to back right through the large plate glass entrance to the store and then pulled forward. Two of the soldiers, who preceded the civilians, then used the butt of their rifles to smash out any jagged edges of the remaining glass. The civilians, no longer orderly at all, thronged through the broken storefront and disappeared inside. Meanwhile, the soldiers started herding the students and faculty members toward the buses at gunpoint.

James didn't wait to see more. He ran back into the bathroom, where Julie was still in the shower, singing, of all things. "Out!" he yelled. "Get out now!"

"What?" Julie started to say, as he tore open the door and grabbed her. She had obviously finished washing and was just enjoying standing under the running water. *Wasting precious water, as usual*, he thought, as he slammed the water off.

He forced the towel into her hands. "Hurry. Get dressed. We've got to get out of here."

About to protest, the urgency in James' voice cut Julie short. There was a fear in his voice that was contagious. Hurriedly, she wrung some of the water out of her hair and made a few quick swipes with the towel before dashing off to the closet. James, who had headed back out to the living room hollered back at her, "Jeans and a shirt. Comfortable shoes. HURRY!"

As quickly as she could, she got dressed and headed to the living room carrying her running shoes. She found James looking out the front window from a position off to one side. She was shocked to see a gun in his hand.

"Stay away from the window." It was clearly a command, not a request. By now, the soldiers were herding the first group of students and faculty from the coffee shop into the third bus. James thought he could see the pure white-haired head of his old friend and professor, John Mitchell, among the first of those to be forced onto the bus. The back three buses had bars on the windows, obviously some kind of prisoner transport. Just then, one of the students behind Dr. Mitchell must have decided he wouldn't be herded into a prison bus like an animal. He broke free of the group and started to run toward the science building. He hadn't made it more than ten yards when two of the soldiers opened fire; the bullets tearing into his back propelled him forward in a dive to the ground. His legs kicked a couple of times like they were still trying to run, and then he lay still.

Julie, who was sitting on the sofa tying her shoes, herd the gunshots. "James, what is it? What's going on?" she demanded. She was no longer afraid. She was terrified.

James was watching the soldiers, who now seemed to be going building to building, rounding up everyone on campus. He noticed that they seemed to be totally bypassing some buildings and breaking into others, herding the occupants out one building at a time. *How do they know which buildings to break into,* he thought? Then he noticed that each group of soldiers had one person carrying what appeared to be some kind of electronic device with a small antenna, scanning the buildings as they went. Then it dawned on him, the general in the newscast had specifically told everyone to keep their coms on standby. They were tracking people down using the signal from their coms. He stuffed the gun into his pants and grabbed his com. "Where's your com?" he yelled at Julie, louder than he had meant to.

Julie burst into tears again. "I don't know, on the nightstand?" she asked, looking around as if she could see it from her sitting position on the sofa.

James rushed into the bedroom. Sure enough, her com was there. He grabbed it and hurried back out into the living room. Julie had stood up and was standing squarely in front of the window, her mouth agape. As he grabbed her by the arm and pulled her away from the window, he got a glimpse of the front of the grocery. The civilians, who had arrived with the soldiers, were now going in and out of the store carrying its contents out and loading the trucks. They were stealing all the food from the campus grocery. Most were stuffing handfuls of whatever they could find into their mouths as they went. James had to wonder what it would be like to be that hungry.

"Come on," he said, still pulling Julie by the arm. She started following on her own, and he dropped her arm, as he went out the door, looking both ways, up and down the empty corridor. He ran toward the stairwell at the end of the hall, looking back to make sure Julie was running behind him. He burst through the door into the stairwell and took the stairs three at a time. He paused at the first-floor landing just long enough to yell back at Julie to wait here. He charged through the door into the corridor that ran from one end of this floor to the other. The two floors of the building were laid out identically. At the midpoint of the hallway, there was an elevator alcove with a couple of chairs and a table. James, making sure they were both still on and in standby mode, stuffed his and Julie's coms down in between the cushions of one of the chairs. He sprinted back toward the stairwell just as Julie started to come through the door. Not wanting any of the residents of this floor to know he was there, he didn't yell, instead, he waved her back, as he ran toward her.

James looked over his shoulder once to make sure no one had seen him, before silently pushing Julie back into the stairwell and bounding down the stairs to the underground parking and storage area. Julie followed him, silently now, like a lost kitten trying to keep up.

The basement, designed with eight parking stalls seemed strangely empty, with only two vehicles parked there. James had a moment of longing, as he ran right past his Jeep to the other side of the basement. Opposite the parking stalls, there were ten doors lined up across the entire side of the basement. Illuminated by the twenty-four-hour security lighting, the sign on the first door read: Mechanical. The next room was Maintenance, and then there was a storage room for each of the building's eight apartments. James ran straight to the maintenance room and, knowing it would be locked, threw his shoulder into the door trying to force it open. The impact didn't seem to move the door at all, but it definitely hurt like hell. He stood back and tried kicking the door open. That didn't work either. He pulled the gun out of his pants and aimed at the lock, but he didn't pull the trigger. The last thing he needed was for the soldiers to hear a gunshot. *I need a crowbar,* he thought. That's what he wanted to get out of the maintenance room. Looking around he ran down the row of doors to number seven, which was his storeroom. Maybe an axe would work. He had an axe, along with other camping supplies in storage. The storeroom lock was a four-digit code. He punched in the code on the keypad and pushed the door open.

It had been years since James had used any of the camping supplies that he had in the storage room. He had brought all of the equipment with him three years ago when he first arrived at Colorado College. Back then, he had visions of being able to go off into the foothills and mountains to the west on his own. That was before he knew how unsafe it was to venture beyond the confines of the campus. Hurrying, but not wanting to leave something they might need, James rummaged through his things. He grabbed a backpack and looked inside. It was as he'd left it, with most everything needed for a day hike, other than food, still packed up and ready to go. He pulled a jacket and a raincoat out to make more room in the pack. With the temperature hardly ever dropping below sixty anymore, there wasn't much chance of needing warm clothing. On some shelves in the corner of the room, there were some dehydrated food pouches, vacuum sealed mylar bags of jerky, and some similar bags of nuts. Scooping the food into the pack quickly, as well as a six-pack of bottled water, he closed the zipper and slung the pack over his shoulder. The axe was leaning against the end of the shelves. He grabbed it and turned back to the door. *Hope this will work*, he thought.

Julie was standing just outside the door, watching. Her pale complexion was white with fear; her hair, still damp, hung down to her shoulders in long curly strings. She didn't say a word, as James led her, running again, toward the door to the outside stairs that led up to ground level from the basement. The outside entrance to the parking garage came out on the back side of the apartment building, opposite the side that faced the main entrance to the college. James' only hope, as they climbed those stairs, was that none of the soldiers had yet worked their way around behind the building. He poked his head up above the stairwell enough to scan the surroundings.

The security wall, prison wall, as John used to call it, was no more than fifty yards to the west of the apartment. The grounds of the campus were xeriscaped, with red gravel from the stairs to a concrete path that James knew ran around the entire perimeter. There was a space between the path and the wall that was planted with drought hardy shrubs and trees. The width of the area between the path and the wall varied, as the wall was straight, while the path meandered in curves. James had walked that perimeter path with John Mitchell many times. The old professor had loved walking the path, discussing history and current events.

There was no one in sight, but the sounds of the chaos from the other side of campus echoed off the wall. There was a lot of yelling and then some more gunshots. James spoke quietly, just above a whisper. "We have to get over to the wall. There's a space between the wall and the path where we can hide in the brush, ready?"

Julie nodded, her eyes wide with fear. James, carrying the axe in his left hand, grabbed her hand with his right and ran straight toward the wall. Without looking back, he practically dragged her across the path and crashed through the undergrowth. Dragging Julie behind him, he crawled into a small space between the wall and some Mormon tea plants. They had to stay crouched down, the plantings here were only about four feet tall. Julie was whimpering. He wasn't sure, as he looked at her, if it was because of the bloody scratches on her arms, or just the situation, in general. Seeing the scratches from the brush, he could feel how scratched up his own arms were. Ignoring the scrapes and scratches, he peered out through openings in the brush. *So far, so good,* he thought. He still couldn't see anyone. The buildings blocked his view of what was happening on the other side, which meant they blocked anyone from seeing this way, as well.

Taking his bearings, he wasn't sure which way to go. He hesitated trying to remember where it was. He remembered the day John had shown it to him. They had been on one of their usual walks around campus. John had seemed unusually agitated that day. James remembered him saying that it had to end, that a revolution was past due in the United States. "We can't hide behind walls forever," he'd said, gesturing at the security wall, "while the rest of the world falls apart." It had been a frequent topic of discussion. John knew who James' father was, and how he manipulated the strings of power. He seemed to have a true sense that James did not, of just how bad things were on the other side of society. Other than occasionally seeing homeless people and refugees on the streets, James had been sheltered from the economic and climatologic disasters of the previous two decades. His only experiences with "normal" people had been during his trips to the Blue River Ranch. He hadn't argued with John that day, but he hadn't really believed a revolution was possible either. He believed it now.

*It had to be north,* he thought. *It was closer to the northwest corner of the wall.* "Come on," he said to Julie, who was still whimpering softly, "we have to get out."

Walking in a low crouch where the brush was tall enough to shield them, and crawling on hands and knees where it wasn't, they made their way north along the wall. Crawling almost on his belly through a particularly tight spot between the wall and some kind of thorny brush, James came out into a cleared area that was larger than any they had yet seen. Next to the wall, at the edge of the clearing, there was a metal lid, or door, on some kind of underground vault. *There it is.* He had a strange tingle of elation, as he stood up. This clearing was well shielded from view. As he walked across the clearing, memories of John showing him this vault came back, as clearly as if it had been just yesterday.

It had been a hot day the previous summer when John had stopped walking along the path to look around. No one else was out, it was too hot. John had made sure they were alone before saying to James, "Follow me, I need to show you something." Amused, but curious, James had followed as John carefully worked his way through the brush to this opening. "When the time comes," he'd said, pointing at the underground vault, "this is the way out."

"When the time comes?" James had asked.

John Mitchell had gestured at the wall by pointing with his chin. "When that really is a prison wall," he'd said.

Now, looking up at the wall, James remembered how skeptical he'd been at the time. He remembered thinking that maybe his good friend, Dr. Mitchell, had finally lost it. *Guess it wasn't John that went off the deep end,* he thought, *it was the rest of world out there.*

The door to the vault had a hasp type lock with an old-fashioned padlock securing it. James tried using the blade of the axe to pry the lock open. It wasn't working. That's why he had wanted to get into the maintenance room; he'd hoped to find a crowbar. The sound of more gunfire in the distance gave him hope that no one would hear as, giving up on prying the lock off, he swung the axe like a sledgehammer, striking the lock with such force that it not only sprung open, it shot across the clearing, missing Julie by just a few inches.

"I can't go in there," he heard Julie say, as he swung open the lid. "I'm claustrophobic."

*Oh great,* he thought. *Now's a fine time to find out.* "We don't have a choice, Julie. There's no other way." He rummaged in his pack until he found the headlamp stashed in the bottom. The light from the opened hatchway revealed the top of the built-in ladder that descended into the vault. Relieved to see the headlamp batteries still had juice, James shined the light down to reveal the inside of the vault. The concrete walls extended to the floor, which appeared to be a good ten or twelve feet down from the surface. The built-in ladder went straight down the south wall. There were tunnel openings in the east and west walls at the bottom of the vault, with multiple pipes and conduits running from one tunnel opening to the other. The pipes and conduits had valves and control boxes of some kind mounted to the floor and the north wall of the vault. It appeared that all of the utilities were mounted on the north side of the tunnel as well; leaving a space to walk through the tunnel along the south wall.

Julie had backed a couple of feet away from the open vault. She was obviously terrified. Just as James was hoping she was more terrified of the soldiers on campus than she was of the confined space of the vault, loud shouts came from the direction of their building. Someone yelled, "stop or I'll shoot!" They could hear the sound of someone running along the path on the other side of the brush. Then they heard the blast of two gunshots, and something, presumably the runner, crashed into the brush, no more than fifty feet away. James had the sudden fear that he may not have been the only person, other than John Mitchell, who knew about the tunnel. If others knew, they might accidentally lead the soldiers to them.

He jumped up and grabbed Julie, who was actually shaking, and started pulling her to the vault. "Now! We have to go now!" he hissed, in a loud whisper. Julie whimpered, softly at least, as she allowed him to pull her to the opening. Carefully controlling the volume of his whisper, James implored her, "close your eyes, go down by feel. Pretend it's just a ladder out in the open." He helped guide her to the top rung, wishing she would go faster, as she closed her eyes and felt her way down the ladder, shaking and whimpering as she went. As quickly as he could, once Julie had cleared the top two rungs of the ladder, he started down behind her, pulling the hatch lid closed above them. James' foot hit something that felt different from the ladder rungs just as he heard Julie squeal. He'd stepped on her hand. When Julie reached the bottom, she hadn't let go of the ladder but was standing on the floor, holding on and still shaking. Turning his head down, James could see from the light of his headlamp that Julie still had her eyes closed, and seemed to be paralyzed with fear. She had pulled the hand he'd stepped on out of the way, but still held tightly to the ladder with other.

"Julie," he said, as softly and calmly as he could, "you have to let go and back away from the ladder." He could see her shaking her head sideways, still trembling. The ladder wasn't really a ladder, as such, but consisted of individual rungs that were U shaped with the legs of each rung embedded in the concrete wall. The rungs protruded from the wall some four or five inches, and James decided that he was going to have to squeeze past Julie by using the side legs of the rung for a ladder. The fear of being caught, trapped half-way down into the vault was overpowering. Squeezing past Julie with the backpack on wasn't easy, but he finally reached the bottom by literally shoving her sideways. She refused to release her grip on the ladder, and she was still trembling all over, tears were being squeezed out of her tightly closed eyelids. James placed one hand over the hand that held the ladder and wrapped his other arm around her, pulling her in close, he whispered in her ear, "Julie honey, you have to open your eyes. You can do this. Please. You have to do this for me. I need you." The trembling subsided some as he held her close, and after a few seconds that seemed like hours, she opened her eyes, only to be blinded by the light from James' headlamp.

"I can't see," she said, much too loudly to suit James. "Your light's blinding me."

James almost laughed, in spite of himself, as he turned his head, so the light was out of her eyes. The light now revealed the tunnel leading off to the west; straight as an arrow, fading into the blackness beyond the reach of the headlamp's beam. As he gently pulled her clenched hand off of the ladder and pulled her toward the opening he had to wonder where they were going. Not just the location of where they would physically end up, but the where, or what, of a totally unknown future.

# Chapter 10

I T SEEMED THE TUNNEL had no end. It was only about six feet from the concrete floor to the ceiling, not quite tall enough for James' six-two frame, which meant he had to walk in an uncomfortable bent over position. They were slogging through water puddled on the floor in most places, and several times they came to places where there were tees in the largest pipe, which had to be a water line. Smaller pipes would tee off from the mainline and cross the tunnel opening, only to disappear into the concrete wall. There were always valves at these pipe junctions which took up much of the room in the tunnel, making it difficult to squeeze past.

James pulled his right leg sideways off of the pipe he was straddling. This was a particularly tight spot, which he'd had to squeeze through sideways; his back rubbing the tunnel wall, while he was almost bear-hugging the six-inch pipe that protruded from the ceiling to just above the nut on top of the valve. The wall of the tunnel, as well as the pipes and conduits, were wet and slimy. Julie had to be cold. *Hell, I'm cold,* he thought, as he tried to straighten and turn to shine the light for Julie. Straightening too much, he bumped his head, once again, on the concrete ceiling.

"Ouch! Damn it!" he exclaimed, too loudly in the enclosed space. Julie jumped slightly at his outburst shattering the silence. Without saying a word; she hadn't said a word since they entered the tunnel, she started climbing over the obstruction. "Be careful," James whispered, "this is a tight one." He heard the sound of tearing cloth as she slid off the pipe to stand next to him. Her jeans had caught on one of the valve bolts and she'd ripped a hole in the thigh of her muddy wet jeans. A small whimper was the only sound to escape her lips, even though he could see her shivering in the lamplight. James turned back around, in his crouched position, and continued slogging through the tunnel. His back and neck were starting to ache from walking crouched over. *Wish I was only five-six like Julie*, he thought.

Finally, they came to a vault opening in the tunnel similar to the one they'd used to enter. James, telling Julie to wait at the bottom, climbed the ladder and tried to open the hatch. No luck. He braced his feet firmly on the ladder and pushed as hard as he could with his back and shoulders, but the hatch door wouldn't budge. Then, he got lower on the ladder so he could push up with one hand while pounding upwards on the aluminum door with the other. That didn't work either. Not only did it not work, but the pounding definitely made too much noise to suit him. *God damn it! Why didn't I bring the axe? Now what?* he thought as he climbed back down the ladder.

Julie, standing right where he'd left her, still shivering, finally spoke. "We're trapped, aren't we? My God! What are we going to do?"

Hearing her voice, edging on hysteria, James knew he had to soothe her, even if he, himself, wasn't sure what they should do. "We're not trapped, there'll be another opening farther on. One that won't be locked from the outside," he added, hurriedly. He hoped he was right, even as he considered going back for the axe. Deciding against that idea, he stooped down again and headed on through the next section of the tunnel.

After what seemed like another eternity of walking in such a stooped over posture that he didn't know if he'd ever be able to stand straight again, James could see a wall in front of him. He thought maybe they were approaching a bend or a junction in the tunnel when the ceiling of the tunnel suddenly opened up above James' head. It felt so good to stand up straight again, that it took him a couple of moments to notice that this opening wasn't like the other two vaults. It was a round opening, about five feet across. Like the other vaults, there were steps embedded in the wall leading up into the opening. Shining the light up toward the top, he could see that the circular opening narrowed as it rose. It was the inside of an offset cone, with the top of the cone only about two feet in diameter. James had never been inside a manhole, but he recognized one when he saw it. At the top, he could see the rusted bottom of a cast iron cover. At least it wasn't another aluminum hatch opening. He climbed up the ladder and was elated to find that, although it was heavy, the cast iron cover could be pushed upwards. As the cover cleared the rim, the daylight above was blinding, even though he had only lifted it up an inch or so. He lowered the lid back into place. He had no idea where they were. He knew they had to be some distance west of Interstate 25; how far, he couldn't guess. Not only did he not know how far west, but he knew nothing about Colorado Springs over on the west side of the interstate. He was trying to decide if he should go back down and wait for nightfall when Julie's scream echoed loudly around him.

She had obviously seen the daylight shining through the slightly opened lid; for her, the proverbial light at the end of the tunnel. Having the light snuffed out again was simply too much. "Open the goddamned lid!" she shrieked. "I can't stand it." She was already reaching for the step to start up behind him.

His mind made up for him, James shoved the lid up above his head and slid it off to the side. The dazzling blue sky above seemed like heaven. He took another step up, poking his head up out of the hole. He saw nothing. At least not any buildings or sign of people, just an open field of dirt. There were some stubbly grasses here and there, but the drought had decimated what appeared to have been some kind of park or green space.

Once they were up out of the tunnel, the open space didn't provide any cover at all, but there didn't seem to be any need to hide. They were in a low spot with mostly gently rolling red dirt hills surrounding them. Directly west of where they stood, there was a much taller hill with a huge water tank on top. *That's where the water pipe must go,* James thought, looking up at the graffiti-covered tank. He looked at Julie and had to laugh.

"What's so funny?" she asked, clearly offended.

James got his laughter under control, but he was still unable to get over the absurdity of the situation. "You should see yourself," he answered. "You look like a refugee."

Julie did, indeed, look a lot like so many of the refugees and homeless people that seemed to be roaming the streets everywhere; though she was probably dirtier than most. Her blonde hair was all tangled and stringy with streaks of the grime from the tunnel. Her wet clothes, besides having tears from crawling through the tight spots in the tunnel, were filthy. There had been nothing clean or dry in the tunnel they had just escaped from.

"You don't look so hot, yourself," she told him. "What are we doing?" She started shaking again and James knew it wasn't from being cold. She started laughing and crying at the same time. It was hard not to laugh at the site of James covered with grime from head to toe, but she was about to the point of hysteria. "What's happening?" she sobbed. Then, remembering what she'd seen from their apartment; "why were they shooting? They were shooting students! Who are they?" the words came out between sobs.

All James could do was shake his head and mumble, "I don't know." He remembered Dr. Mitchell saying, "when the revolution comes," and he really did know. He didn't want to know, but the truth was inescapable. *What now?* he thought. *What happened to John and all the others that the soldiers had rounded up and loaded into the buses? What was happening elsewhere?* He thought of his family, mostly his mother. Surely, whatever this revolution was, it hadn't affected the Mendez family. His father had never relied on the police and the military; he had his own private army for security. It dawned on him suddenly, *that's the answer. We have to get home to Castle Pines. We'll be safe there.* "Come on," he said, with the same authority he'd used to get Julie through the tunnel. "We can't stay here."

Not knowing exactly where they were, and not knowing anything about the streets on this side of town, James just headed north. As soon as they climbed out of the hollow onto the first rise, city and streets came into full view. He could see what appeared to be a major east-west street about a quarter of a mile to the north. The street seemed to mark the northern edge of the open space they were in. On the other side of the street, there was no more open space, just the urban sprawl of old subdivisions. To the east, I-25 was visible in places and hidden in others. James knew the college was just on the other side of the interstate, due east of where they now stood. He couldn't see any people or any vehicles at all on the streets that were visible from this vantage point, so he decided to just continue heading north. It would probably be easier to just walk along I-25 instead of going across country, but his gut instinct told him that would be a bad idea. If they could walk about twenty miles a day, they should be able to get to Castle Pines in about three days, without using I-25.

Just as they got close to the major east-west street, James heard and then saw, some vehicles coming out from under the I-25 overpass, heading directly toward them. They were army green. It looked like some kind of convoy. His first instinct was to hide, but other than a few scraggly dead juniper trees, which wouldn't hide anything, there was no place at all to hide. Fighting a desire to run, he told Julie to sit down next to one of the dead junipers. He sat beside her, trying to look like a couple of refugees or homeless people. He had a strange thought; *here we are trying to look homeless. Hell, we might be homeless, for all I know.*

The military convoy didn't even slow down. There were four vehicles in the convoy, two armored vehicles and two trucks, like the ones at the college. They had to have seen James and Julie sitting by the side of the road, but they sped on past heading somewhere to the west. James couldn't help but notice that all four of the vehicles were of the autonomous variety. Either Amerinet and all communications had been restored, or the military had only shut down all civilian communications systems. *Probably the latter,* he thought, as he stood up and pulled Julie to her feet.

There were no other vehicles in sight, nor people for that matter, so James decided this would be as good a place as any to get back over on the east side of the interstate. From his memory of the terrain, it seemed that the trek north would be easier if they were a few miles to the east. As soon as they came out from under the I-25 overpass, James knew where they were. The perimeter fence that surrounded Colorado College stretched out to the east, on the south side of the street. They were just about a hundred yards due north of where they'd entered the tunnel a few hours ago. He had a strong desire to follow the wall to the east and then south to the entrance to the college. *What happened to all of those who had been rounded up? What was the situation inside the wall now? Was there anything he could do to help anyone?* With a nod to the old thought that discretion is the better part of valor, he turned north instead of following the wall and headed up the frontage road that ran parallel to I-25.

They'd walked several blocks north passing abandoned, gutted looking strip malls, and one large forlornly empty shopping mall, when they first saw other people. They were approaching what appeared to be another mall or shopping center of some kind, but this one was anything but empty. It was a hub of activity. It wasn't a mall, James noticed, there was a large King Soopers sign above a line of people; actually, two lines of people. *A functioning grocery store?* The thought was as fleeting as it was hopeful. James knew this was anything but normal, as the razor-wire fencing surrounding the large, mostly empty, parking lot came into view.

They were half a block south of the intersection of the frontage road and what appeared to be another major east-west street. The old King Soopers store and parking lot took up most of the next block on the east side of the frontage road. People were coming and going from the old store from every direction but south. James and Julie were the only ones approaching from the south. That's what James thought at first, anyway. Then he noticed, as they got closer to the intersection, that people were walking down the I-25 off-ramp. Looking up at the overpass, he could see a couple of groups of people walking north on the interstate. Everyone, except those crossing the overpass, seemed to be coming to or leaving from the entrance to the old grocery store. There was a good-sized crowd gathered there. Some had backpacks, some were pulling old toy wagons, and some were pushing old shopping carts. Some had nothing but the clothes on their backs. As they got closer, James could see that people leaving the old store were carrying or hauling the old familiar cans of Allpro. Most also had various sizes and shapes of water containers. That seemed to be it, nothing but Allpro and water.

James led Julie diagonally across the intersection to skirt around those who were crowded in front of the entrance to the parking lot. There were at least twenty or thirty fully armed soldiers guarding the only two apparent openings through the razor wire fencing. The openings were only wide enough for people to get through single-file. One was obviously an entrance and the other an exit. A large hand-painted sign between and above the two openings proclaimed in large letters, **EMERGENCY RATION CENTER #108. LOCAL CITIZENS ONLY!** Below that, in somewhat smaller lettering, it advised everyone to have their IDs out and available for the guards.

One of the small groups of people that had come down from the interstate were on the same side of the street as James and Julie. There were four of them, two men and two women; couples James presumed. They were ahead of James and Julie and had stopped directly across the street from the entrance to the ration center. The two men each had a backpack, but not the women. Their clothes seemed tattered and dirty. *They look like they've hiked a long way,* James thought, as they drew near enough to hear some of what the four were saying to each other.

"We need water," he heard one of the women say. "We won't get it here," one of the men answered. "I'm so hungry," the other woman complained.

The group grew quiet when they noticed James and Julie approaching. At the same time as the group noticed them, James noticed that three armed soldiers were coming across the street toward the group. The soldiers got to the middle of the street, the one in front motioned at all of them with his rifle, while the other two flanked him with their guns raised. "Move on," the lead soldier yelled. "refugees aren't allowed here."

"Please," the woman who'd complained of hunger begged. "We're starving."

Seeing them raise their weapons, James was afraid the soldiers would think they were all together and start shooting. "Come on," he said to the entire group, including Julie. "There's nothing for us here." He led Julie right past the other four people and noticed them fall in behind as he passed. *Better than getting shot,* he thought.

They walked along in silence to the end of the block. James looked back to make sure they weren't being followed by the soldiers. The three soldiers had made their way back to the crowd, but now James noticed that there were groups of soldiers everywhere around the perimeter of the emergency ration center. He wondered how many had been killed simply for being hungry or thirsty. He stopped at the corner of the intersection, deciding where to go. His mind made up, he turned to face the group. "I can get you something to eat and some water, but not here; follow me." He turned, and without looking back, continued walking north.

They'd walked due north about a mile before James decided they were far enough from the soldiers to stop. There was a bridge here where the street they were on crossed a mostly dried up creek bed. There were live cottonwood trees lining the creek, which told James that the creek hadn't dried up completely. James was mighty thirsty himself, by then. It was the middle the day and the temperature had to be approaching a hundred degrees.

"Where are you from?" he asked, as he turned to face the group. He noticed that everyone, including Julie, had a look of quiet desperation on their faces. They'd simply followed someone, anyone, who was willing to lead. "I'm James, and this is Julie," he added when no one said anything.

The woman who had begged the soldiers for food was the first to come out of her stupor. "We used to be from Austin," she said quietly. It was then that James noticed how truly emaciated the four people were. They were rail thin, their clothes hanging loosely from their bodies. Their eyes seemed to be kind of shrunken into their sockets, and their lips were all cracked and dry. *They're like walking skeletons,* he thought.

"Can you really get us some water?" It was the man who seemed to be the group's de facto leader. "I'm Ken." His voice was little more than a whisper. He was so dehydrated that he could hardly speak, James realized.

The interstate had veered off to the west away from the road they were on, and they'd crossed over a hill that now shielded them from the activity back to the south. The road ahead went over another hill, shielding them from the north. James looked around carefully, making sure they were alone, before taking off his pack. He reached down into the bottom of the pack and pulled out the six-pack of bottled water that he'd grabbed from his storage room back at the apartment. "This is all I have," he said as he handed a bottle to each of the group. He twisted the top off of his and only took a sip of the water. Each of the four strangers did the same. They very carefully unscrewed the plastic caps and drank a bit of the water slowly, cautiously; allowing it to bath their parched mouths with precious moisture before they swallowed.

Julie, unlike everyone else, was gulping her water down in big swallows. James reached out and pulled the water bottle down away from her mouth. "Julie, there isn't anymore." He said it quietly, but firmly. "We have to make this last."

For just a moment, the defiant look of over-privilege flashed in Julie's eyes, then the predicament they were in came back to her. "What are we doing, James? Where are we going?" The questions were a plea. It was almost as if she expected him to tell her that all was well, and he'd lead her back to the safe life of ease and plenty that she'd always known. Deep down, that is what James wanted as well. We just have to get home, he thought. Dad will have everything under control, once we get to Castle Pines. He kept trying to think positive thoughts about how his father had a private army and didn't rely on the U.S. military for security; how everything would be just fine, once they got back to where that private army could protect them. *Stay positive,* he thought, *just stay positive.* But try as he might, he couldn't dispel the doubts and dark fears lurking just below the surface.

James looked around some more, deciding they should first get out of the sun. He led the group down around the side of the bridge abutment, into the dry creek bed under the bridge. "Let's just wait out the heat of the day right here," he said, as he sat down on the concrete footing of the bridge that made a perfect bench. As the others sat down as well, he fished in his pack and tossed one of the large bags of trail-mix to Ken. "Not much," he said, "but better than nothing. Hope it isn't too stale."

The gratitude in Ken's eyes was heartbreaking, as he very carefully opened the bag, and doled out a few morsels to each of his companions.

The dire situation that they found themselves in must have finally hit home for Julie. She was seated next to James, on the side opposite their four companions. She leaned over and whispered in his ear. "You can't give them our food. What are we going to eat? I'm hungry too, you know."

For a moment, Julie's selfishness angered James, but then he simply felt sorry for her. Like himself, she had never wanted for anything. Everything in her life had always been all about her. She was a lot like his father, he realized; pretty much devoid of empathy. Is that what had attracted him to Julie? Did he somehow love his father, in spite of Robert's lack of empathy? By extension, did he love Julie, precisely because of that same lack of empathy? He thought of his love for Anna. So much different. *Other than mother, perhaps, Anna is probably the kindest person I know.* The thought filled him with regrets. *And what about me, he thought? How could I have been so cruel?*

His thoughts were interrupted by Ken. "We need to get moving," he said, as much to himself as anyone it seemed. After handing out just a few handfuls of the trail-mix, he had very carefully resealed the bag and tucked it into his backpack. None of the others had complained.

"Wouldn't it be better to travel at night?" James asked. "Or at least not during the worst of the heat?"

Rather than answer his question immediately, Ken just looked at James and Julie before speaking. "What are you two doing out here? It's pretty obvious you haven't been on the road."

The question set James back a bit. It must have been pretty obvious that they couldn't have been on the road for long alright, but how much did he want to share? Not only how much did he want to share, but what did he really know? It seemed that some kind of revolution or military coup had taken place, but he really didn't know much of anything for a certainty.

James decided he would be as truthful as he could. These people didn't seem to be any kind of a threat. "You're right, we haven't been on the road. Near as I can tell, we've just escaped being captured by some kind of renegade army unit; or worse. Maybe the entire U.S. military is renegade, or maybe it's like a coup. I just don't know. I..." the sentence trailed off into thoughtful silence.

"So, you two are government of some kind?" the question, which sounded a lot more like an accusation than a question, came from one of the women, who had yet to introduce herself.

Julie started to respond, "We aren't government, but..."

James cut her off, thinking it might be better not to tell them that Julie's mother was a U.S. Senator. "We were at school. They just came and started rounding up everyone at our school."

Julie must have caught the idea from James that it might be better to keep her mother out of this. "They shot some of the students," she said; "Why would they do that? Why would soldiers shoot students like that?" She seemed to be asking James, as much as the rest of the group.

Julie and James now had all four of the stranger's complete attention, and James wasn't so sure that was a good thing. He was getting some of the same vibes of disdain for the privileged that he remembered feeling while talking to that salesman on the train so very long ago. The four had to know that James and Julie were from the privileged class if they were college students in this day and age. They didn't have to know just how privileged, though.

After a few seconds of silent scrutiny, there seemed to be a softening of attitude among the four. "I'm Darrell." The man who hadn't spoken up until now stuck his hand out and James shook it. "The whole world must really be going to hell if they're shooting college students. Thought it was only us." James wasn't sure who the 'us' referred to. Darrell seemed to be referring to more than just the four of them.

The two women then introduced themselves; Chris and Sarah were their names. Sarah had a coughing fit before she was able to get out her introduction, and James noticed that none of the four seemed to be totally well. How could they be? Up until he shook Sarah's hand, he had attributed their apparent lack of good health to the ordeals of walking so far and an obvious lack of food and water. Sarah's hand was actually hot. He realized that she was not only hungry and thirsty, but she was also ill; unless dehydration could cause one to have a fever.

"Are you ill?" he asked. Not that anything could be done about it if she was, it just seemed like the right thing to say.

"God, I hope not." She actually managed a weak smile. "I sure don't want to end up like some of the others we've come across."

"Have you run into people who were sick?" James asked. He remembered hearing something on the com a month or so ago about some kind of rare spring flu virus or something that was going around.

Sarah looked down at the ground and it was Ken that answered. "Not sick, dead. And not just one or two..." he kind of trailed off and seemed to look back in time. "Too many. Way too many."

James decided he should change the subject. "Why did you leave Austin? On foot, of all things?" He directed the question at Ken and could see by the look on his face just how incredulous the question seemed.

"You really have been in a cocoon, haven't you? Do you know anything about the world out here?" Ken gestured just enough to show that 'out here' encompassed pretty much everything.

James could sense some of the earlier contempt returning to Ken's voice. He started to answer with, "Guess our coms," as he instinctively reached to his side, where his com should have been. It was then that he noticed no one had a com. He knew what had happened to his and Julies, but none of the four strangers had one, either. "Guess our coms," he went on, "haven't kept us very well informed."

"Coms!" It was an outburst from Darrell. "Spreading nothing but fucking propaganda for years. You think you fucking rich people hiding behind your walls learn anything about what's going on by listening to all that crap? You think the government or anybody else really gives a shit when most of Miami's underwater? Or Austin bakes so dry that it's impossible to ship enough water to keep people from dying of thirst? Do you think anybody in the government cares one bit about all of the people who are dying? The government in Washington doesn't care about anybody but people like you! Rich kids, protected at college, while the rest of us die of starvation!"

Darrell had come to his feet during his rant and, for a moment, James thought he might have a fight on his hands. But Darrell sat back down after the outburst and bent over with his head in his hands, his elbows propped on his knees. Julie also had her face in her hands, and she was sobbing again. The other three just sat there looking angrily at James. He didn't know what to say. He stood up slowly, and grabbing Julie by her arm, pulled her to her feet. "Come on," he said softly, turning to leave. He spoke louder over his shoulder to the other four, "guess you probably haven't heard about the tsunami that hit Washington."

"Well, I guess chickens do come home to roost," he heard Ken answer. Then the tone in Ken's voice softened. "James, thanks for the food and water. I wouldn't travel at night if I were you. Best to hide out where they can't see you with night vision goggles."

James could hear Sarah having another coughing fit as he helped Julie scramble back up the embankment to the road. He decided to head back to I-25. Maybe it was the best way to go north. That's the route most were walking; maybe there was some kind of safety in numbers. He and Julie just had to get better at blending in.

# Chapter 11

T HEY COULDN'T HAVE TRAVELED more than seven or eight miles before they came upon the first body lying off the side of the interstate. They smelled it sweltering in the heat before they actually saw it. The body was just over the edge of the embankment, sprawled face first with its head down the hill and bare feet sticking up above the edge of the road. James couldn't tell if it was a man or a woman. Someone had obviously stolen the shoes, and the rotting bare feet had already been pecked apart. Some ravens and a couple of magpies flew up away from the body at James' and Julie's approach. The birds didn't go far, settling down a few yards away to wait for the intruders to leave them to their feast.

It was already getting to be late in the afternoon, and the heat seemed unbearable. They'd been walking along the edge of the interstate; working their way around the few stalled vehicles that they came across. James had been surprised by how few stalled vehicles there actually were. He could remember how many vehicles had stalled and plugged the streets and highways when all autonomous vehicles had died the first time the net and GPS went down. It had also seemed strange that the stalled vehicles all seemed to be personal transportation, not the autonomous semi-truck freight haulers that you'd expect to see on I-25. They hadn't been on I-25 for long when that mystery was solved by the first of many military convoys that were the only vehicles still plying the interstate.

They had been walking along the outside edge of the northbound lanes of the road and heard the convoy approaching from behind before they ever saw it. James' first instinct had been to try to hide from the approaching vehicles, but not only was there no place to hide, there was another group of people a quarter mile or so ahead of them, also trudging northward, who didn't seem to be paying any mind at all to the oncoming convoy. So, James and Julie just got further off to the edge of the road and watched the convoy as it passed them by. The convoy had been led by some kind of light armored non-autonomous vehicle, which was followed by some sort of military vehicle that James had never seen before. It looked like some kind of transport truck that, instead of a normal truck bed, had a large dish antenna looking device mounted on the frame. The antenna was pointed back toward the convoy. James noticed that like the armored vehicle in the lead, the antenna truck was also not autonomous. They both had soldiers manually driving them down the middle of the highway. Directly behind them, however, was a string of five autonomous semi-trucks, two freight vans, and three water tankers, followed by two autonomous armored vehicles bringing up the rear. It was obvious to James that the military, or someone, had shut down the GPS and communications systems that allowed autonomous vehicles to function; and then had the means to get autonomous vehicles to use signals from mobile antennas to lead those vehicles wherever they wanted them to go.

*But why?* A real coup or revolution was the only possible answer he could think of. As disturbing as that answer was, it did at least answer the question of what had happened to all of the trucks. What they planned to do with all of the freight, mostly food and water, that they were rounding up was another question.

*With no more convoys approaching, James and Julie skirted past the dead body by walking down the middle of the traffic lanes. They were approaching another exit ramp with a road crossing the interstate on an overpass about a quarter of a mile ahead. The sign above the interstate said* **EXIT 153 Interquest Parkway.** *James wished he could remember more about the Colorado Springs area than he did, but being basically holed up at Colorado College for the past three years hadn't been very conducive to learning what was outside its walls. One thing he did know; they weren't making very good time. The group of people who had been a short way ahead of them when they first started walking along I-25 had left them in the dust. They were now completely out of sight on the other side of the overpass. James was walking a few yards ahead of Julie, wishing she would walk faster, when he heard the sound of her plastic water bottle hitting the pavement behind him.*

He stopped and turned to see Julie standing there with her empty water bottle slowly rolling toward the edge of the highway. "Damn it, Julie, what are you doing? You think there's more water where that came from?"

She just glared at him. "I don't care," she almost screamed. "I was thirsty!"

James took a couple of strides back to Julie, and she cringed like she was afraid he was going to hit her. He didn't say a word; just stepped past her and picked up the plastic bottle and the cap that she had dropped. He took off his pack and put the empty capped bottle inside. Then he took out his own water bottle and, deliberately so she would watch, very carefully took a small sip of his own water. He then returned his water bottle to his pack and put the pack back on, before very calmly saying, "let's go."

They hadn't taken more than a couple of steps when they heard what had to be machine gun fire off in the distance ahead of them. Then they felt, as much as heard, a single loud blast, like a bomb exploding. A black cloud of smoke started rising; it looked to be coming from up the interstate, a mile or so ahead of them. They watched the smoke rise straight up for a few hundred feet, then, catching a breeze aloft, stream off toward the mountains in the west. Next, came the rumbling sound of another convoy of some kind. It was coming toward them from the north; from the location of the explosion. James looked around for a place to hide. For some reason, he had a fear of whatever was heading their way. He grabbed Julie and pulled her into the shallow ditch on the east side of the interstate.

"Down in the ditch. Hurry!" He didn't really wait for her to get down, but instead pulled her.

"Ouch!" her knees hit the gravel harder than James intended. "Goddamn it, James, you're hurting me."

Ignoring her complaints, he ordered her to lie down at the same time as he pulled her on down into the ditch. "Don't move, they'll just think we're more dead people," he whispered as if the people in the approaching vehicles could hear them.

James had positioned himself so he could peer over the edge of the road to get a look at whatever it was coming from the north on the other side of I-25. It wasn't what he thought it was at all. The vehicles producing the loud rumbling weren't in any way similar to the convoys they'd heard and seen before. James didn't know much of anything about military hardware, but he knew enough to see that what was rumbling down the interstate was a convoy consisting of just two tanks of some kind. The lead tank had a bulldozer type blade in front with some kind of large gun above the blade. The second tank didn't have a blade, but it had an equally large gun; the gun on the second tank was pointed back up the highway from where they'd come. The tanks must not have been autonomous since they didn't have an antennae truck leading them. They must have had some kind of connection to each other, though; they continued heading south down the interstate, perfectly maintaining no more than a tank's length between them. As they passed by, James regretted having basically thrown Julie into the ditch. Whoever was in those tanks, they would have probably just ignored James and Julie, anyway.

His knees hurt where they had hit the gravel. Looking down, he could see that the knees of his jeans were bloody. Then he looked at Julie. She was now sitting up, holding her bent knees in her hands. She was crying, and when she reached up to brush the tears away, her hand had blood on it, as well. He sat beside her and put his arm around her shoulder.

"I'm sorry, Julie. I didn't mean to hurt you. I was trying to protect you." He pulled her close and she didn't resist; she just started sobbing harder. "When I heard the explosion, it just freaked me out. How are we supposed to know what or who's safe, and what isn't?" he tried to soothe her.

"God, I'm scared," she managed to get out between sobs. "Where are we going? What are we going to do?"

For several minutes, James just held her, letting her sob it out of her system. Then, when the sobbing stopped, he got a bag of the trail mix and some jerky out of his pack and offered some to her. "We just have to get home," he said. "We'll be safe there."

The trail mix was stale, and the jerky had long ago passed its sell by date, but both of them were hungry enough that it was definitely better than nothing. James offered Julie some of his water to wash down the nuts and dried fruit. She accepted, and very carefully only drank about half of what was left in the bottle. That left James a couple of swallows and then they were officially out of water. He rummaged around in his pack to see what else he had. It had been so long since he had used the pack that he couldn't remember what was in it. He felt something that was fairly bulky in its own nylon bag. Pulling it out, he remembered it. It was an old-fashioned water purification pump. He carefully put the water purifier back in his pack, relieved that maybe they could find some water after all. All they had to do was find a stream or pond that hadn't dried up, and they could refill their water bottles.

The sun was getting pretty low in the western sky. James gave Julie a hug and asked her if she was okay to walk some more. They both had sore knees, but managed to start walking again, headed toward the smoke that was still rising from something a mile or so up the interstate.

The smoke had all but died out completely by the time they got to the scene of destruction. It looked like it had been a convoy of some kind in its own right. There were the blackened remains of what appeared to be one of the light armored vehicles they'd seen earlier, along with one of the antennae carrying vehicles, but what really caught James attention, was the remains of the third vehicle in the convoy. It was an autonomous armored stretch limo, like the one his dad preferred to travel in. There wasn't much left of the limo. It looked like it had been hit with some kind of armor piercing projectile that had then exploded, blowing it open from the inside out. Another light armored vehicle had been bringing up the rear. It hadn't suffered as much damage as the others, but it was full of holes. James surmised that it must have been hit by the machine gun fire they'd heard. The bullets must have been armor piercing as well. All of the vehicles had been pushed into the median, between the two halves of the interstate. *Must be what the dozer blade on the tank was for,* James thought. He had a strong foreboding feeling, as he stopped to ponder the scene of destruction. Other than the light armored vehicles appearing to be military, this could have easily been the kind of secure motorcade that his father usually traveled in.

Julie silently surveyed the scene as well. It was hard to tell what her thoughts might be. She had to be thinking about her mother, James concluded. Her mother had, no doubt always traveled with a military escort. Their silent reverie was shattered by two fighter drones that screamed overhead no more than fifty feet above them. The roar of their engines hitting James and Julie a few seconds after the drones were already gone. It couldn't have been more than a few more seconds before they heard two explosions from the south, back toward Colorado Springs. There was no way to know for sure, but James had a feeling that the drones had just taken out the two tanks they'd seen earlier. He had the unsettling thought that it really was some kind of revolution. There wasn't much doubt left that some part of the military was now pitted against some other part. *Dr. Mitchell was right,* James thought. *The revolution he predicted must be happening.* He wondered again what had happened to John Mitchell, and the other students and faculty from Colorado College.

The sun was starting to drop behind the mountains to the west and Ken's words came back to James. *What had he meant about it not being safe to travel at night?* It didn't seem to be safe to travel, period; but he now had a nagging feeling that they needed to take cover somewhere. A short way ahead of them, he could see some cottonwood trees on either side of the interstate; a meandering line of trees stretching out to the east and the west that had to be a stream, or at least a creek bed. He didn't say anything at all to Julie, just started walking again. He had made up his mind to get off of I-25. He had decided that they should follow the creek line to the east; maybe they could find some water and a place to hole up for the night.

# Chapter 12

T HEY REACHED THE OUTSKIRTS of Castle Rock at mid-morning on their fourth day of walking. They had worked their way north on back roads and old highways on the east side of I-25. It had taken longer than James thought it would, but they had continued to hide every night. James was never sure what or who it was that they were hiding from, but he decided it was better to be safe than dead. There had been the sound of explosions off in the distance every day. *Must be what it's like in a war zone,* James had thought, before realizing that they actually were in some kind of a war zone.

Fortunately, there had been plenty of places to fill their water bottles. As they crossed mostly dried up streams and creeks, there always seemed to be a few pockets of water, even in the creeks that had completely dried up. Finding food was another matter, though. They had finished the last of the jerky and trail mix by nightfall of the second day. Neither James nor Julie had eaten anything for a day and a half by the time they got to Castle Rock. They had passed by several farms and seen quite a few people, but no one was willing to share any food. Some were probably as hungry as James and Julie, and the rest were jealously guarding whatever food they had.

It seemed that the people out away from the cities had all banded together into groups that were protecting whatever supplies and meager farm crops they might have. Every time James and Julie passed one of the farms where the groups were gathered, there would be a number of armed people guarding their perimeter. None of them actually threatened James and Julie with violence, but they also made it abundantly clear that they should just keep moving. The farms and houses that weren't protected by armed guards had all been totally abandoned by people and animals alike. James had searched a couple of the empty places, looking for something to eat, but the places he searched had already been stripped bare of pretty much everything.

Julie's cough was getting worse. James stopped walking when he heard the hacking rasp of her cough too far behind him. It seemed like she had been getting slower and slower, as her cough got worse. He had first noticed that she seemed ill yesterday afternoon. She had spent the previous night snuggled up to James, shivering, even though the temperature didn't drop below about eighty degrees. *I'm not feeling the best, either,* he thought, as he turned to wait for Julie to catch up. He felt light-headed and weak. It seemed like his whole body ached. If he hadn't started coughing a little bit himself, he would have just blamed it on hunger and exhaustion; but it was beginning to feel like descriptions he'd heard of the flu or something. He didn't understand how they could have the flu; everyone he knew, and especially everyone at Colorado College, had received the universal flu vaccine. The flu was supposed to be something from the past, like small-pox or polio, or some of the other diseases that had been eradicated years ago. *So, if it isn't the flu, what is it?*

"Are you okay?" he asked Julie when she caught up to him.

"I don't know," she said. "I've never felt like this before." She was overcome by another coughing fit before she could say anything else.

James took his pack off and got out some water. He offered her the water, thinking maybe it would help relieve her cough. She took a few sips of the water, which did seem to bring her some relief.

"You don't need to save water now," he told her. "It's only a few more miles." He looked around at the houses that now lined both sides of the street they were on. Most looked deserted, but there were a few, here and there, that looked like they might still be occupied. *Maybe I should see if anyone will give us something to eat,* he thought. *Not very likely,* he decided. He thought about searching through the abandoned looking places, but that, too, seemed futile. All of the places he'd searched before had turned up empty.

He decided that it wouldn't hurt to try one of the houses that looked occupied. Feeling the weight of the pistol that he still carried stuffed into the waistband of his jeans, the thought occurred to him that anyone in any of those houses was probably armed, and he probably better make damn sure they didn't think he was a threat. He took the pistol out of his pants and stuck it in his pack. He took another look around, and not seeing anyone anywhere, told Julie to wait here by the pack.

"Where are you going?" she asked.

"I just want to see if anyone's home," he replied, and headed across the street toward an older brick house that still had all of its doors and windows intact. He walked straight up the sidewalk to the front door, with just a tinge of fear that someone might just shoot first and ask questions later. He stood in front of the door for a moment, listening. The only sounds he could hear were the scattered sounds of birds in the immediate neighborhood. There were no sounds at all coming from the house. He rapped his knuckles on the old wooden front door and waited. The house remained totally silent. Knocking harder and louder at the door, he yelled, "anyone home?" Still no answer.

Pondering just what he should do now, he reached down and tried the latch. The door was locked. He didn't dare break in, there was probably someone on the other side of the door with a gun, just waiting to blast anyone who might try that. He had just decided that it was no use; that no one was going to help them, and started to turn away when he heard what sounded like a moan coming from inside the house. "Hello," he shouted. "Can you help us?" More silence was the only answer he got from inside.

James looked both ways, up and down the street, wondering if anyone had heard him. Wondering, for that matter, if there really was anyone on this street at all. Julie, who had now sat down on the curb where he had left her, was the only person in sight. He decided to go around to the back of the house. He walked around the side of the house to where he'd seen a gate in the fenced back yard. Inside the gate, the back yard was nothing but dirt. What had once been a lawn had dried up long ago. The front yard had been covered with gravel at some point, in an effort at landscaping, but the backyard had simply been allowed to die out and return to bare dirt.

The fence was about halfway from the front of the house to the back, so, as he walked past, James tried looking in the side windows on the inside of the fence. The windows on this side were completely covered with some kind of drapes, just as the windows on the front side had been. He started getting a whiff of a bad smell just as he went through the gate, and coming around the back corner of the house, the smell just about gagged him. He recognized the smell from the corpses they'd walked by on their way up from Colorado Springs. Just as he realized what the smell was, he saw the source. The house had a covered concrete patio that was raised up above the yard by a couple of feet, probably at the same level as the floor of the house. The corpse was sprawled down the steps leading up to the patio. It appeared to be a man. Thankfully, it was lying face down, so James didn't have to look at whatever was left of the face.

He heard another moaning sound, and, trying to ignore the corpse as much as possible, walked around the body to investigate. The back door of the house was standing ajar with swarms of flies buzzing in and out. James could see what must have been hundreds of them crawling all over the dead man. The moaning sound was definitely coming from inside the house. James wanted to go in; maybe he could help someone. Maybe he could find something to eat. The thought of something to eat, combined with the smell coming out of the house and off of the dead body lying on the stairs, caused him to wretch. He heaved and lost what little bit of water he'd just had to drink. There was nothing else to throw up. *I can't.* The thought turned him back away from the patio. *What could I do to help, anyway?* He dry-heaved some more as he stumbled back around the corner of the house and headed back across the street. *We can get home,* he thought. *We don't need any help.*

James knew they would have to cross I-25 in order to get home to Castle Pines. He was dreading that part, wondering if they should wait until nightfall to try to sneak across in the dark. That wasn't going to work. He was helping Julie every step of the way now. He held her left arm around his shoulder and had his right arm around her waist as they trudged up the deserted four-lane street toward the I-25 interchange. When they got close enough to see the interstate, James was surprised to see a few vehicles traveling across the overpass. As they got closer, he was even more surprised to see that it wasn't just military convoys like they'd seen back at Colorado Springs. Though there weren't nearly as many vehicles as there should have been, it seemed to be somewhat normal traffic; mostly trucks, but one or two passenger vehicles as well. They definitely had military escorts, but he couldn't see any of the vehicles with dish antennas. He had the sudden realization that Amerinet and the GPS and communication networks must be back up and functioning.

*Damn – wish I had my com,* he thought, as they got closer to the interchange. The interchange was barricaded off with military personnel and various armored vehicles and tanks blocking the entrance to I-25. There were also freight vans and water tankers parked under the overpass bridges. There was a banner of some kind above the barricades, but James couldn't make out what it said. When they got closer, he could see a group of people walking down the exit ramp off of I-25 headed toward the military encampment. At about the same time, he was able to read the banner. It said:

### U.S. ARMY - REFUGEE AID STATION.

"Look! We're safe now." His voice was hoarse, and the words were followed by another cough. A deep rasping cough was the only reply he got from Julie.

So, the country was still functioning. James was so relieved at first that he failed to notice that all of the army personnel were wearing masks. When he did notice, he was shocked to see that they weren't just some kind of filter masks; everyone was wearing a minimum of what looked like full-fledged gas masks. Many of the troops were not only wearing gas masks but were covered from head to toe in white hazmat suits. Wondering just what would cause the soldiers to be wearing hazmat suits, James half-dragged a stumbling Julie toward the checkpoint entrance to the aid station. *Damn, that's gotta be hot,* he thought, as he approached the fully covered soldier at the entrance.

The soldier at the checkpoint was a woman, her voice muffled by the hood and full-face mask she was wearing. "Where are you from?" she asked, temporarily barring their entrance to the aid station. "Do you have some I.D.?"

Normally, James would have used his com for identification, and he felt a bit of panic that the soldier wouldn't help them; then he remembered his billfold was in the bottom of his pack. Unlike the military units that had attacked the college and seemed to be running Colorado Springs, James had an immediate trust of the troops at this aid station. Without knowing how he knew, he just knew that these people were regular army, and they were definitely not part of whatever revolutionary force it was they had escaped from. "I'm James Mendez," he told the soldier, as he took off his backpack. Another cough wracked his chest before he could add, "and this is Julie Johnson." There was no recognition in the eyes of the soldier, as James handed her his autonomous vehicle operator's license. "Robert Mendez is my father, and Julie is the daughter of Senator Jill Johnson."

The soldier looked at the ID, then back at James and Julie. Her eyes got wide as she realized they truly were who he said they were. "Come with me," she said, motioning another soldier to take her place at the check station. She led them back into the center of the camp, which was quite a bit bigger than James had first thought. There were tents and trailers set up underneath the overpass bridges of I-25, with more temporary barracks, tanks, and all kinds of armored vehicles stretching out into the flat area on the west side of the interchange. She led James and Julie to a large white trailer that had a big red cross on the side. The inside of the trailer looked like an old-fashioned doctor's office on one end, but the rest of the trailer looked like something out of a bad apocalyptic movie. There was a hallway going down one side of the trailer with hospital beds lining the other side. James quickly counted the beds; there were twenty, and all but two were empty. The two closest to the office each had people in them. Both patients were wearing oxygen masks and had IV drips set up beside them.

The soldier bent down to tell the woman at the desk something, and James noticed that this woman, who was obviously a doctor, wasn't wearing a mask at all. The doctor stood up and started around the desk just as James felt Julie go limp, leaving him to support her full weight. A nurse, who was wearing a mask, saw Julie faint and rushed over to help. "Get her to number three," the doctor ordered leading the way and pulling the cover down from the third bed. With help from the nurse, James was able to get Julie onto the hospital bed, before having a coughing fit himself that left him feeling dizzy and lightheaded.

"You better take this bed," the doctor told him. He sat down on the bed next to Julie's.

He watched as the nurse and doctor worked together getting an oxygen mask on Julie and some kind of IV drip started into her arm. The two hardly spoke, but their movements were smooth and coordinated; a choreographed routine that they had obviously practiced many times.

"What's wrong with her?" he asked the doctor while suppressing a cough.

Finished with Julie, at least for the time being, the doctor turned to James. "She's been infected with V1, I'm sure, and so have you, I think," she told him. The questioning look in his eyes let her know that he had no idea what she was talking about. "It's a virus. A very dangerous virus that I'm sure you have never heard of. Now, let me look at you." With that, she pointed a thermometer into his ear. "Only a hundred and one," she said, almost to herself, as she attached the device to his left index finger that would tell her his pulse rate and blood oxygen levels.

"V1 is extremely contagious and very deadly," she told James, as she studied the monitor by the side of the bed. "The government has been suppressing any information about the virus to prevent panic. We think it came here from Europe, but some CDC scientists are speculating that it is some kind of ancient pathogen that was released by the thawing of the permafrost in Siberia." She turned from looking at the monitor and looked at James. "You should know that this virus, V1, has a very high mortality rate." She kept her voice perfectly flat, studying his eyes for reaction to what she had just said.

The nurse brought a glass of some kind of thick orange liquid and handed it to James. No one had to say anything, his hunger was overpowering. He drained the glass slowly, letting it soothe his throat as it filled his shrunken stomach.

It tasted of orange juice and medicine. Had he not been starving, he would have thought it undrinkable. As it was, it seemed delicious.

"She'll be alright now, though?" he asked as he set the glass on the bedside table. "Now that she's getting treatment."

The doctor sort of slumped and almost imperceptibly shook her head from side to side. "I'm not sure," she told him honestly. "Maybe if we had the right antiviral... all we can do now is treat the symptoms and hope for the best."

It suddenly occurred to James that Julie wasn't the only one he should be worried about. He already felt better after drinking the orange concoction, but the doctor had said that he, too, had been infected. And what about the doctor, herself? "Why aren't you wearing a mask, like the others?" he asked her directly.

"I seem to be immune," she said, studying James to gauge his reaction. "Not just me," she said. "I believe you are also immune. I should say, I believe our immune systems are somehow able to fight off the virus." She seemed to focus somewhere beyond James. "I don't know why. If only..."

An alarm went off on the display that was above the first bed in the room. The doctor jolted out of her reverie, turned and, along with the nurse, went over to that bedside. She reached up and turned off the alarm. The nurse methodically removed the oxygen mask from the patient's face and the IV from her arm. There was nothing urgent in their movements; just the same routine they had practiced far too many times before. The doctor pulled a com out of a pocket in her uniform and spoke a few words into it, while the nurse pulled the sheet up over the patients face. James watched silently as they carefully rolled the dead young woman up in the sheet that had been covering her.

Two soldiers dressed in hazmat suits came through the door with a stretcher, and without saying a word, rolled the sheet wrapped body onto the stretcher and carried it out. The doctor still had a kind of faraway look in her eyes, and James could see through her face mask that the nurse was crying.

"Was that one of the refugees?" he asked, without really directing the question at either one of them.

"No," the doctor answered, "that was Shandy. She was a nurse. We've stopped trying to save any of the refugees."

James looked around the room; at the doctor and nurse who seemed to both be in a mild state of shock, at Julie lying on a hospital bed with an IV drip and an oxygen mask, at the only other patient, a middle-aged man who was also wearing an oxygen mask and had an IV drip beside his bed. Both patients were unconscious. "What about him?" James asked gesturing toward the other patient. "Is he a soldier, then?"

The doctor seemed to snap out of it and looked at James with a sad smile. "No," she said, "not a soldier. That's Tom. Doctor Thomas Welch. He's in," she corrected herself, "he was in charge of this facility."

The nurse's shoulders were shaking as she looked down at the unconscious doctor. Her silent sobs betraying the depths of her grief. James felt her grief. He was becoming overcome with grief, himself; not wanting to admit the truth that he knew instinctively. He looked at the doctor and asked, "Does anyone recover?"

The doctor looked down at the floor, and quietly said, "Just a few, you and me."

James' mind was racing. The doctor had said that Julie needed an anti-viral that obviously was not available.

Maybe his dad could get some. "Call my father, maybe he can get you some of the anti-viral drugs."

The com in the doctor's pocket buzzed. She listened to it for just a few seconds, then placed it back in her pocket. "That was Captain Rogers. They've been trying to reach your father since you arrived. They can't get through."

James started to protest, "what do you mean, they can't get through? Who did they talk to? Let me borrow your com, they'll let me talk to him."

The doctor was shaking her head as she took the com out of her pocket and offered it to James. "Have it call the MICI home office," he told her, knowing that it would probably only obey her commands. She did as he requested and handed him the com. James put the com to his ear and listened for the fake ringing sound that was a carryover from the age of the telephone. The com clicked like it was starting to ring, and the line went dead. *What the hell,* he thought. James took the com away from his ear and looked at it like maybe he could figure out what was wrong if he stared at it long enough. *Why did I leave my com?* He berated himself. If he only had his com, he could call home or even Robert's personal com. It was impossible with a stranger's com, though. Even if he knew the right number or code, neither of his parent's coms would allow incoming calls from unknown sources.

The doctor reached out and gently took the com out of his hand. "It probably wouldn't make any difference anyway," she said. The resignation in her voice was chilling.

"What do you mean it wouldn't make any difference?" James almost yelled at her, frustration starting to get the best of him. "You said they need an anti-viral." He looked at the two patients; one a doctor that he didn't know, and Julie. Julie who had let him lead her here to this place. She'd trusted him to take care of her. He knew that she loved him in her own way, and he couldn't help but feel love for her as well. Love, and a responsibility to protect her.

The doctor looked away from James and said simply, "Dr. Welch had an anti-viral." She went on to explain that they had arrived at this camp with several doses of an experimental anti-viral drug that they thought would combat the virus. At first, they'd used it on the refugees that came in sick. It seemed like it was working, so they sent out an order for more. It was just about then that the world turned upside down. The tsunami hit Washington at just about the same time as the revolution hit the military. The first of the refugees they'd treated with the anti-viral had seemed to get well, only to relapse within a couple of days. All had died. Even though the doctors and nurses had all followed proper protocols, they too, began to get sick.

Dr. Martin had been one of the first to start feeling ill. She'd tried to hide it from the rest of them. She said it had affected her much like it seemed to be affecting James. She'd had a mild fever for a couple of days and felt a little weak and light headed, but then it had passed. Then it hit Dr. Welch. Knowing that they had no alternative, even though it hadn't saved anyone yet, they administered the last dose of the anti-viral to him. Just like the others, he seemed to get well but then relapsed two days later. He'd been lying here in a coma since yesterday. "He'll be gone before nightfall…" she trailed off into silence.

The muffled sound of a cough broke the silence, and James was startled when he realized that it wasn't Julie or Dr. Welch. It was the nurse that had been crying. The sound of her coughing was muffled by the mask she wore. James had a sudden overwhelming desire to flee, to just get away. *This was no aid station; it was a death camp. But what about*

*Julie?* He couldn't just leave her here. He had to get help. "I'll go for help," he said as he stood up to leave.

The nurse sat down on the bed where another nurse had just died and slowly reached up and removed her mask. Her face was still streaked with tears, but she was no longer crying. She'd resigned herself to her fate. "There is no help," she said softly.

At first, Captain Rogers had been reluctant to give James any assistance at all. After getting one of the soldiers who was posted outside the infirmary to take him to whoever was in charge, James had asked for a ride into Denver to try to find his dad. The captain had told him that the rebels had hit Denver pretty hard, and there wasn't much left of the downtown business district. It seemed that the rebel's main purpose had been to attack the centers of business and finance; to hit the wealthy elite establishment as hard as they could while doing as little damage as possible to the lower rungs of society. James had the uneasy feeling that the Captain was somewhat ambivalent about the rebellion; that he sympathized with the cause, even if he couldn't bring himself to support it openly. Captain Rogers had also been concerned about the number of troops that were deserting. It seemed that everyone wanted to get away from the camp, as if getting away would do them any good. He'd finally relented and agreed to have a trusted lieutenant drive James the few miles to his parent's home in Castle Pines.

The lieutenant, dressed in a full hazard protection suit, didn't seem to want to talk at all as he "drove" James out of the camp. They were in one of the autonomous light armored vehicles, so the lieutenant didn't really drive the vehicle; he simply told the vehicle where to go. It was a pretty secure system. Once the vehicle was assigned to the driver or vice versa, the vehicle would only function on the driver's commands.

Looking out through the small horizontal slits that served as the only windows in the vehicle, James noticed that there didn't seem to be as many soldiers as when they'd arrived, just an hour or two earlier. *If they're deserting that fast,* he thought, *the camp will be empty in no time.* He was musing on that as they left the camp, headed north and west. What he saw next was the most shocking thing he'd seen in the last few days, maybe the most shocking thing he'd ever seen. They were passing a large pit that had been recently excavated just a short way from the camp. There were a couple of military dump trucks backed up to the edge of the pit. At first, James couldn't tell what they were dumping into the pit, and then he realized they were bodies. All kinds of dead bodies; still dressed in whatever they'd been wearing when they died. Some were obviously refugees or homeless people, but there were others, as well. There were even what appeared to be soldiers among the bodies; still wearing the hazmat gear that had not protected them. As they passed the pit, the scope of the crisis hit James like a sledgehammer. There were bodies piled on bodies. Hundreds, maybe thousands. It was like nature had given up on humankind and decided to just wipe the species off the face of the earth. *And why not,* he thought. *How many species have we driven to extinction?* The rest of the short trip to the place in Castle Pines that he'd always known as home was a time for silent reflection. It seemed that mother earth or nature had declared war on mankind. But then again, it was really the other way around. Man had long ago declared war on nature. He thought about how fast, in the greater scheme of things, man had destroyed so much. He knew from his studies of recent history how people had been warned a long time ago of the consequences of their actions. One of the things that had most interested James about the effects of climate change had been how much faster devastation had hit than the scientists of the late twentieth and early twenty-first centuries had predicted it would. Twenty years ago, they had predicted at most a few feet of sea level rise by the end of the century. In the twenty short years since those predictions, the great ice sheets had melted much faster than predicted. Sea level was more than a meter higher now than it had been at the dawn of the twenty-first century.

James' musings on man and nature were interrupted by the lieutenant. "Shit!" The exclamation was muffled by the hazmat mask and hood that completely covered the lieutenants head. The vehicle came to a sudden stop as the muffled voice continued, "nav-net's down again. I knew we should have used one of the antique Humvees. Shit," he exclaimed again for emphasis.

James, looking through the small window, recognized the familiar neighborhood. They were only about a half mile from home. He could faintly hear some kind of communication coming through the lieutenant's hood. The hazmat suits had coms built in. At least coms are still working, he thought. "I'll walk the rest," he told the lieutenant, who was listening closely to whatever was coming through his com. The lieutenant seemed to ignore him, so he pulled the emergency exit latch and pushed the gull-wing door up and out of his way. He stepped out, closed the door and started walking as fast as he could up the hill toward home. He had one driving thought, *Julie will die if I don't get her better treatment than what they have at that aid station. Dad's doctors will surely have the right anti-viral. If?*

*If...?* The thought was left hanging as he got to the top of the hill.

The view from this spot had always been one of James' favorites, especially at night. From this point most of the greater Denver area filled the vista to the north; the high-rise buildings in the distance marking downtown Denver, itself. James stopped and stared, having trouble comprehending what his eyes were seeing. The high-rise buildings of downtown Denver were gone. All that he could see were a few wisps of smoke still rising from where downtown Denver should have been. From this distance, he could only imagine what the piles of rubble must look like where the skyscrapers had once stood. The MICI building had been one of those skyscrapers that were no longer there.

# Chapter 13

THE MENDEZ ESTATE WAS surrounded by a rock wall, whose purpose of providing security was expertly camouflaged by the sheer beauty of the stonework. It had been constructed by true artisans using a massive amount of native stone. The only opening in the twenty-foot-high wall was where the split driveways accessed the property. There was a large guardhouse between the entrance and exit drives with wrought iron looking gates across both. The gates were designed to look like oversize ornamental wrought iron, but they were actually constructed of very heavy-duty steel. The gates and the guard house were only about half as tall as the wall, but James knew the guard house was always manned, with at least six people who were armed well enough to defend it against any attack, even an attack by a tank.

As he approached, James could see the sun glistening off of the one-way bullet-proof glass wall of the guardhouse that faced the road. He expected to see the door in the side of the guardhouse, which was inside the gate, opening at any moment. Surely, they wouldn't recognize him in his current state. Protocol required one guard to come out into the open to confront any approaching stranger, while the others manned the armaments that would be aimed at any potential threat. Knowing the guns that would be aimed at him through the small openings in the façade gave James a little bit of a chill as he approached the gate.

He walked right up to the gate and still no one came out of the guardhouse. Now that he was this close, he could see through the steel bars of the gate that the door into the guardhouse was slightly ajar. A shiver of fear ran up his spine. "Hey!" he yelled. "It's James. Anybody home?" The eerie silence that answered filled him with more foreboding than anything he had ever experienced.

There was no way to open the gates manually from the outside. The estate had its own electric power, generated by wind and sun, and enough battery backup to get through any period of non-generation, but there had never been a mechanism to activate the gates from the outside. Security concerns had trumped any inconvenience of not being able to control the gates from the outside, and the entrance was guarded around the clock; until now, that is. *Now what?* James looked at the gates and yelled as loud as he could at the empty driveway that led through the trees toward the house. None of the buildings of the estate were visible from here, but his voice should carry that far. He yelled again. Still nothing. He looked the gate up and down and started climbing. He remembered that Robert's chief of security had wanted to electrify the gates, but his mother had put her foot down. "It's too much like a prison, already," he remembered her saying. *Good thing she got her way that time,* he thought, as he reached the top and swung his leg over to the other side.

"Hold it right there." James froze, one leg on one side of the gate and one on the other; astraddle the big iron bars like the gate was some kind of mechanical horse. He looked up to see a man with an assault rifle coming toward him from the edge of the trees along the driveway. It was Don. "Don, thank God; it's me, James."

Don helped James get down off of the gate. They looked each other up and down. Don looked like he always had, clean shaven, muscular, well dressed; but now his clothes and hands were dirty. The main difference James noticed, though, was the haunted look in Don's eyes, as he grabbed James and gave him a bear-hug.

"Goddamn, James. It's good to see you." He let go of the hug and held James out at arm's length. "You look like hell."

James tried not to breathe. Don shouldn't be touching him. He pushed Don away and turned his head before saying, "Don, I'm contagious. Back away – please. It's terrible."

Don's response was not to back away at all. Instead, he laughed. There was a kind of madness in his laughter that shook James somewhere deep inside. "You think you're the only one?" he got out between his laughter. Laughter that now seemed to be only about half laughter and half crying. "Where do you think the others are?" he asked, motioning toward the guardhouse. "They're dead! That's where they are James. They're all dead. I just finished burying Sam. He was the last one. Hell, I buried them all."

Don got himself under control and retrieved the assault rifle from where he'd leaned it against the side of the guardhouse. "Come on," he said, latching the guardhouse door. "Boy, is Noni going to be glad to see you."

His mother was alive. A wave of relief swept over James. "What about Dad?" he asked, as they hurried up the drive towards the house.

Don stopped so he could look at James to give him the news. "We honestly don't know for sure; but James, I'm afraid he's gone. He was at the office when the missiles hit. At least that's where he was last I knew. I'm sorry James."

The news didn't really surprise James, but it shocked him, none the less. Don started walking again. "That's why your Mom is going to be so glad to see you," he added as if to get James to hurry. As they hurried to the house, Don told him that his father had known something was going on between different factions in the military establishment. He'd received a warning of some kind from one of the defense contractors that a substantial minority of people throughout the military were talking about taking the country back from the wealthy. Robert's source had feared that it would come to some kind of violence, if not full out revolution. So, he'd sent Don and a security detail to go to Colorado Springs to get James. The security detail had been headed south on I-25 less than a mile north of the Castle Pines Parkway exit when their convoy of autonomous vehicles died, and the missiles started hitting Denver. It was extremely lucky that they were as close to Castle Pines as they were. They'd abandoned their vehicles and made their way home on foot. "Some of them were already sick, though," Don said. Then, almost as an afterthought, "sick with what? What kind of sickness kills so many people so fast? Was it some kind of germ warfare? What the hell is it?"

James didn't have a chance to respond. They were walking again and had reached the front of the house when Noni Mendez came running out the front door. She must have been watching through the window. There were tears in both their eyes when James and his mother threw their arms around each other and just held on tight. Words were unnecessary, and the silent embrace lasted long enough for Don to walk over and sit down on the step.

The mix of emotions was overwhelming for James. The utter relief of finding his mother okay mixed with the sorrow of finding out that his father was probably dead. On top of the sorrow at the loss of his father, he had a profound sense of guilt. Over the past several years, James had come to believe that he hated his father for so thoroughly controlling his life. Now he felt guilty. His father had only ever wanted what was best for him, how could he have rejected that? And now, there would never be a reconciliation. His father was gone; gone forever. So much was gone; so many people who were now gone forever.

Still holding his mother as tight as he could, his thoughts turned to Julie. She wasn't gone. At least, not yet. "Mother, do you know if Dr. Yew is...is still alive?" It seemed so strange to be asking if a fixture of their lives was still among the living. Dr. Yew had been the Mendez family doctor since before James was born. And Dr. Yew was not just an ordinary family doctor. He was a leading research physician, with connections to everything from the Mayo Clinic to the Centers For Disease Control. If anyone would know of anything to help Julie, it would be Dr. Yew.

Noni Mendez let go of her son and held him out where she could look at him. "James, are you sick?" The question was edged with fear that went way beyond concern.

"No, not me," he answered quickly to relieve her anxiety. "I mean, I have been. Some. But I think I'm immune. It's Julie. Julie's the one who's..." he couldn't bring himself to say dying, "sick. She needs some kind of antiviral." Even as he said it, he had another concern. "What about you Mom? Are you okay?"

"I'm fine, James. At least I think I am. For some reason, whatever it is, it spared me. Me and Don." She looked away, as she added, "everyone else is gone. I'm afraid Dr. Yew

Ignore that.

might be gone, too. We tried to get him the day before yesterday when Sam and the others got so sick. We left messages on his com, but he never called back."

"We have to find him. Is the com working?" James was already ushering his mother back inside as he spoke. He went straight to the kitchen. He was still so hungry and thirsty that he was filling a water glass and looking for food, even as he commanded the house com to call Dr. Yew. There was no response from the house com. He tried again, as he rummaged through the kitchen grabbing some cheese and crackers. Still nothing.

"That's odd," Noni said. "I was just talking to Dad a few minutes ago."

"Damn! The net's down again," James managed, between mouthfuls of cheese and crackers. "Is Grandpa okay?" He hadn't thought about Grandpa Chuck much lately. Thinking about Grandpa Chuck and the BR always led to memories of Anna; memories and feelings he tried to avoid. Memories and thoughts that were triggered, even now, by simply asking about his Grandpa. Sure, he was worried about Grandpa Chuck, but he really wanted to hear that Anna was okay. Thinking about Anna invariably led to more feelings of guilt. And now the guilt was double. He still felt terrible guilt for the way he'd discarded Anna's love, and now he felt another guilt for even thinking about Anna while Julie was dying in Castle Rock.

Noni told James that Grandpa Chuck had said he was fine, and that as far as he knew the sickness, whatever it was, had not even affected the western slope. He hadn't been to Kremmling in over a week, but everyone had seemed fine last time he was there.

Noni didn't mention Anna at all, but her words lifted a terrible weight off of James. *Maybe this sickness was local.*

*Maybe the whole world isn't dying. There's still hope.* The feelings of hope for his grandpa and for Anna compounded his feelings of guilt over his relationship with Julie, and his feelings of grief, or guilt for a lack of grief, for the death of his father.

"I have to go." It was Don; the flat statement interrupting James' thoughts. "I have to get to Kansas City."

James remembered that Don was from Kansas City. He remembered him taking a few vacations to go back and spend time with his family.

"I have to know," Don went on. "I have to know, one way or another."

"I understand," James told him, and true understanding of just how much Don had sacrificed to look after his family hit James hard. Don was a friend as much as a Mendez family employee. How hard it must have been these past few days, protecting Noni while wondering about the well-being of his own mother.

"Have you heard anything from them?" James asked.

"Not since last week." Don seemed to be searching his memory, as he answered. "I tried calling as soon as the com came back online, but nothing. And now, coms out again. Who knows when, or if, they'll come back online?"

Torn between wanting Don to help him with Julie, and wanting to help Don find out about his own family, James decided the Mendez family had asked way too much of Don already. "You better take one of the old manuals," James told him, referring to the manually driven, non-autonomous, vehicles in Robert Mendez' private collection of automobiles. Don deserved anything James could give him.

Robert Mendez had been, among other things, a longtime collector of automobiles. The collection was housed in a long, low, warehouse that was architecturally designed to resemble an old-time riding stable. It was the largest building on the estate, and Noni had nicknamed it the car barn. The collection inside the car barn included everything from a fully restored Model T, to a 1964 Corvette, to the newest electric autonomous Rolls Royce.

Knowing that the only chance he had of saving Julie was to get her to a much better medical facility than the refugee aid station, James was as anxious to get going as Don was. He ushered Don out of the house, and they walked to the car barn together.

The new Rolls Royce had been delivered less than a month ago, and James was seeing it for the first time, as he and Don walked into the ornate, immaculately clean warehouse. The Rolls was a real beauty, but without the Navnet available for autonomous navigation it was basically little more than a sculptured work of art.

"Too bad you can't take the Rolls," James told Don. "Looks like she would have been a great way to travel."

"I wouldn't take that car even if I could," Don answered. "That's your Dad's favorite." James couldn't help but notice that Don had spoken of his father in the present, instead of the past.

"Take any of them you want," James said. "He owed you that. We owe you that."

Don decided that he'd better stick to one of the EVs since he had no idea if he'd be able to get gas or diesel anywhere between Denver and Kansas City. He ended up choosing the 2021 Rivian pickup. With its extra battery pack in the bed, it was probably the only one in the collection with enough range to get to Kansas City without recharging. Finding a functional charge station along the way was as questionable as finding gas or diesel.

"Don, I don't know how to thank you," James stuck out his hand to shake. Don grabbed his hand and pulled him into a hug.

"Thank me for what, James? I was only doing my job."

*Only doing his job,* James thought, holding up his hand in a final wave, as the Rivian eased out the door. Both men knew they would probably never see each other again. Don had always done so much more than just "his job". James had the disheartening thought that losing Don might be worse than losing his own father.

James liked Don's choice of the Rivian pickup but decided he would rather take the other Rivian anyway, the SUV. He had to find medical help for Julie. Too many were lost, he wouldn't let the disease claim her, as well. He decided that he would have to take his mother with him, instead of leaving her there alone. Even if they couldn't find Dr. Yew, they'd surely be able to find help at the University Hospital in Aurora.

At first, Noni didn't like the idea of leaving the security of the estate. She especially didn't like it when James wanted to leave the front gate open because there was no way to open it from the outside. James acquiesced and had to climb over the gate from the inside, after parking the Rivian on the outside and closing and locking the gate. He'd just have to climb back over to open it, once they got back.

It was an eerie drive back to the refugee aid station at Castle Rock. The autonomous armored vehicle that had brought James home was still parked at the bottom of the hill, but there was no sign of the lieutenant. That's what was eerie, there was no sign of anyone. At least not until they got to I-25. The first body they came across was on the edge of the on-ramp. They saw several more on the short four-mile drive to the aid station. James couldn't help but wonder how many they didn't see. They had to work their way around several stalled or abandoned vehicles, both civilian and military; how many of them had dead bodies inside? How could there possibly be so much death? The first living person they saw was a single man walking north over on the other side of the interstate. He was wearing some kind of military uniform, but from this side of I-25 James couldn't tell the branch or the rank of the man. It did seem kind of strange that he wasn't in the military hazmat gear that everyone had been wearing at the aid center. Just as James was about to get to the aid station exit ramp, two antique Humvees came out of the on-ramp and headed south down the interstate. *How many? How many people had the ability to fight off the disease that seemed to be killing nearly everyone?*

It had only been a couple of hours since James left the refugee aid station, but the place had changed dramatically. The hustle and bustle of an active military operation was gone. The entire aid station seemed mostly deserted. With the Navnet down, the trucks and armored vehicles were stalled and stranded all over the place. One of the dump trucks that had been collecting the dead was parked where it had dumped its last load of bodies, its bed still up in the air. The dozers that were supposed to cover the bodies sat still and lifeless behind the huge piles of earth that had been excavated to make the burial pit. The outside temperature display on the Rivian dashboard showed ninety-seven degrees, and the smell of those rotting bodies was overpowering, even with the windows up and the AC keeping the interior of the Riv at a comfortable seventy-five. James switched the AC to recirculate the interior air, but the smell was already inside.

"My God!" Noni exclaimed when she saw the burial pit. She had known it was bad, but the sheer scale of the unfolding tragedy hadn't hit her until then. She put her hand over her mouth and simply stared in shock and horror, not even noticing the tears that were running down her cheeks.

James pulled up to the medical trailer where he had left Julie. He had to get her out of there. That was the thought that drove him. He had to get her out of this place of death. He had to get her over to University Hospital. Even as he thought about it, he had the near certainty that University Hospital would be as lifeless as this camp. *Surely not. Surely, there's a proper hospital functioning somewhere. Surely, someone, somewhere has a treatment for this terrible virus or whatever it is.*

He found Dr. Martin seated at her desk in the medical trailer. She was sitting stock still staring out the window at the stillness of the camp. "Where is everybody?" he asked her, heading toward the row of beds where Julie and the nurse were still the only occupants.

He heard Dr. Martin mumble, "gone", as he saw Julie in the bed where he'd left her. Her face was still covered with the oxygen mask and the IV was still attached to her arm, but something was wrong. She was totally still. He glanced over at the nurse in the other bed. She, too, was still and silent. Then he looked up at the displays of the life support mechanizations and realized they were turned off. The screens were black and as silent as the bodies lying in the beds below them. It hit him like a train; Julie was dead. She was gone. The form there in the bed no more Julie than the dead body of the nurse that lay in the other bed. He collapsed onto the bed next to Julie's dead body and wept. *How could he have failed to protect her? How could the world be like this? So much death. So much death.* He was overwhelmed by guilt. Guilt for failing Julie, guilt for living such an elite life, and guilt for being alive at all. That was the gist of his despair. *How could he be alive, while almost everyone else was dead and dying?*

James didn't know how long he sat on the bed and wept, but finally he managed to rouse himself up from despair, like a drowning man surfacing for air. He wiped the tears off his face and decided that he still had to get Julie out of here. Even if it was only her dead body that remained, he wouldn't leave her here to rot. He pulled the oxygen mask off of her face and pulled off the tape holding the IV in her arm. It seemed odd, but when he pulled the IV needle out, there was practically no blood. A single small drop oozed out of the hole in her arm. That was it. He pulled the bedsheet over her head and wrapped her up in it as best he could. Then, he stooped down and lifted her cold body up, draping her over his shoulder like a sack of seed. He was shocked by his lack of strength. After the hungry trek from Colorado Springs and the ravages of the disease, he knew that Julie couldn't have weighed over a hundred pounds, but the last few days had taken a toll on James as well. He felt weak, but not so weak that he couldn't carry Julie's dead body.

As he passed Dr. Martin on his way out, she was still just sitting, staring out the window. She seemed almost catatonic, but then, just as he was stepping out the door, he heard her say, "He killed himself, you know."

James stopped in the doorway. "Who? Who killed himself?" he asked, thinking he already knew the answer.

"Captain Rogers," she answered. "Why would he do that? He was one of us. He was immune. Why would he kill himself?"

Knowing Dr. Martin didn't expect an answer, as if there was an answer, James went down the steps and gently placed Julie's body in the cargo compartment of the SUV. As he pulled away, Dr. Martin was still staring aimlessly out her window. He wondered what would become of her; more importantly, what would become of any of them. *What would become of the few who survived?* He looked at his mother, and the question became even more pronounced. She was sitting silently, staring straight ahead, seemingly at nothing, with the same near catatonic look on her face as the one Dr. Martin had.

"Mother," James desperately wanted someone to not be lost, "I want to bury her at home. Is that okay?"

The question did seem to snap Noni out of her reverie, at least somewhat. "That's fine James," she said, as if they were discussing a normal everyday decision about a simple matter. Then she added, "let's go get your father. We should bury him at home, too."

James didn't really think they had much chance of finding Robert's body, but instead of heading straight home, James drove toward downtown Denver. The soldier they'd seen earlier was still walking up I-25, and since he was the only other living person in sight, James decided to stop and talk to him. The soldier had a rifle slung over his shoulder, and though he seemed a little worried about the Rivian pulling up to a stop beside him, he didn't reach for his gun. That seemed like a good sign. The soldier was walking on the left shoulder of the highway, so James just rolled down his driver's side window, wondering what to say. Nothing that would have been normal even a few hours ago seemed appropriate. He was about to say, need a lift, but decided that seemed like a strange question. *Of course, he needs a lift. He's walking, isn't he?*

"Where you headed?" was the best James could come up with.

The soldier was a young man, about James' age and build. The uniform he was wearing was desert camo, and James could now see that he was a member of the U.S. Army. But James had no idea what rank the soldier was; just a private, he presumed, though he wouldn't know a private from a sergeant without being told. The soldier looked around like he wasn't sure any of this was real. "Guess I don't know exactly," he said. "Just away, I guess. I don't really have any specific destination in mind."

Noni sat quietly staring straight ahead as if the soldier didn't even exist; almost as if the vehicle were still moving along the highway, and she was watching where they were going. James decided that with so few people left alive, it would be best if those who were, helped each other out. "Want to go with us?" James asked. "I'm James Mendez, and this is my mother, Noni."

"Where are you going?" the soldier asked. "And why would I want to go?"

He had an instant liking for the soldier. "Guess I don't really know where we're going either, in the long run," he said. "But in the near-term, I could use some help finding my dad. We'd like to take him home for a proper burial."

"Finding one dead person among so many seems like a pretty tall order," the soldier replied. "You plan on looking at every dead body out here." The motion of his head indicated that he basically included the whole world in the "out here."

James could have almost laughed at the absurdity of the situation. He felt like he should wake from an apocalyptic nightmare and find that none of this was real, but he knew that wouldn't happen. It was an apocalyptic nightmare, alright, but he wasn't dreaming. It was real. "No," James said, "we're pretty sure we know where he died. Don't think it was the sickness that got him. Think it was the bombs."

"Missiles," the soldier corrected him. "It wasn't bombs, it was missiles. That asshole, General Korliss, and his stupid rebellion. Like we needed another civil war. Like America wasn't already screwed." It was obvious that he had not been one of those who had rebelled. He looked around some more, deciding. "Guess I might as well," he said. "Not like I've got other things to do." He opened the passenger door behind James and climbed in. "Corporal David Ortiz," he introduced himself, then added, "guess the corporal doesn't mean much anymore. Just call me Dave." Then, "you collecting dead people?" he asked, looking at the sheet wrapped body behind the seats.

James explained about Julie as he resumed driving toward the MICI building. He told Dave where they expected to find Robert's body, and Dave told him that he was wasting his time. The army had already pulled out any survivors and casualties that could be found without heavy equipment to dig through the rubble. "Are you really Robert Mendez' son," he asked. He obviously found it ironic that circumstances had led him from poverty to the army to riding in the same vehicle with one of the richest people on earth. But then circumstances were nothing like they used to be. Nothing at all.

Noni, who hadn't said a word, seemed to snap out of it, at least momentarily. "He is," she said proudly, as if being rich and powerful had any meaning left in this new world.

They were only able to get within eight blocks of what was left of the MICI building. The destruction of the downtown area of Denver had been total. Here at the edge of the devastation, some buildings were still standing, and others had collapsed or partially collapsed. Scattered debris blocked the streets. Farther in toward the center of the destruction, the scattered debris became mountains of rubble where skyscrapers had once dominated the skyline. They hadn't been able to find Robert Mendez, of course. After seeing the mountains of rubble, and having no idea where his body might be buried underneath it all, they hadn't really even tried. Noni had insisted that they look, so they had climbed over and around and through the rubble to the place where the MICI building had once stood, and James and Dave had made a show of digging through the rubble by hand. The futility of the effort was so obvious that they had only moved a few pieces of the rubble before making their way back to the SUV, and heading back to the Mendez Estate.

·····•·•·····

Dave patted down the last of the dirt on Julies Grave. James was leaning on his shovel, looking over what had once been his mother's flower garden, but was now a makeshift cemetery. No wonder Don had been dirty and exhausted, James thought, looking at the six other graves where Don had buried the rest of the security detail by himself. He was glad that Dave had agreed to help bury Julie. It had been a lot of work, even for the two of them.

"Do you want to pray, or something?" Dave, who was now also leaning on his shovel, asked.

"Pray for what?" James answered. "Pray that there's a God somewhere that can fix all of this? Do you believe in God, Dave? What kind of God would allow this to happen?"

"Yeah, not exactly the rapture that my folks expected, is it?" Dave said, looking up at the clear evening sky. "Guess it's Armageddon alright, but I don't think the righteous were spared any more than anyone else."

James wondered how many people, righteous or otherwise, actually had been spared. They had seen a few more living people on their way back to the estate from downtown Denver, but not many. James hadn't stopped to talk to any of them. What good would it have done? Did anyone who was still alive know why they didn't get sick and die along with everyone else? Did anyone have any idea how a virus or bacteria or whatever "it" was could have wiped out everyone in the span of just a few days? It was incomprehensible.

"So, your parents are religious?" James asked, just to make conversation.

"Were," Dave answered. "My parents were religious. Extremely religious. Or, at least, that's how I remember them. They were killed in the border riots of twenty-six." He grew pensive for a moment, then; "Kind of ironic, isn't it? I've spent most of the last two years keeping people just like them from coming across that same border. Guess it doesn't really matter anymore though, does it?"

There wasn't much that did seem to matter anymore, as James thought about it, but he still couldn't help but wonder how all of this destruction could have come about in such a short amount of time. "So, were you clear down at the border when the - the sickness hit?" he asked.

Dave didn't answer right away, he seemed to be thinking pretty hard. "I guess I don't really know when the sickness first hit. Thinking back on it, I'm not sure anyone knows. Six days ago, our unit was ordered away from the border. Our new mission was to set up a quarantine station on I-25 at Castle Rock. They outfitted us in hazmat suits that we were supposed to wear full time, and we were to stop everyone and anyone coming north. Anyone coming from the south was to be placed in quarantine. They had special doctors set up to check everybody out. None of us knew what the doctors were looking for. Not until people started dying, that is." He trailed off, deep in thought again. "Once the first refugees started getting sick and dying, we didn't mind the hazmat suits anymore. But then, soldiers started getting sick, too. Soldiers that had been sealed in those suits just started getting sick and dying, just like the refugees. Jesus, even the doctors started getting sick. Guess that's when I first realized how bad it was. When the doctors and nurses started dying right along with everyone else."

"Did they say what it was? What it is?" James still just could not understand.

"No one ever said. At least, no one ever said for sure. They just called it V1. Thinking back on it, I'm sure none of those doctors or anyone else really knew for sure. At first, the word was that it was some kind of biological, like maybe germ warfare or something." Dave had a little bit of an incongruous grin as he continued. "People started talking about that old Stephen King story, The Stand. Don't know if you've read it or not, but I heard one of the guys say we were probably going to be okay as long as we didn't hear the sound of Randall Flagg's boots." Dave actually chuckled a little at that memory. "Anyway, Captain Rogers put that theory to bed. He told us that it was definitely not germ warfare. He said it was some kind of new virus or something. The thing that didn't make any sense to me, was how a virus, any virus, could spread fast enough to kill everyone in just a few days."

That was the very question that kept playing through James' mind, over and over. "Yeah," he said. "It just doesn't make any sense, does it? How the hell could it hit everyone all at once?"

"I did get a chance to ask Doctor Welch that very question," Dave continued. "You know what he told me? He said they figured it didn't infect everyone all at once, it just seemed that way. He said the CDC was working on the assumption that the virus had been infecting people for quite a while and then just lying dormant. Just being carried around like herpes or something, with no symptoms at all until something triggered it. He said that's what they were really trying to figure out. What triggered the virus, and how it happened to everyone all at nearly the same time. Guess if they could have figured it out, they'd also know why it didn't trigger in people like us."

James thought about it. *What if it was just delayed in some people? What if it was still going to strike them all dead, just like the rest, but triggered at a different time.* Even as he felt the fear of the possibility, he felt that he knew that wasn't the case. He somehow instinctively knew or thought he knew, that people like him and Don, and Dave, and his mother, were somehow immune from V-1, whatever it was.

"Anyway," Dave was still talking, "I don't think they ever figured it out. Kind of funny isn't it. Killed them all before they ever figured out what it was that was doing the killing. Course it might not have got them all. Might be someone still trying to figure it out somewhere, but they sure as hell aren't in Castle Rock, Colorado."

# Chapter 14

I T HAD BEEN ALMOST two months since the great dying, as
James had come to think of that week in May when
the world had ended. Or, at least the world that anyone
had ever known had ended. It was early in the morning
and the temperature on the patio thermometer hadn't yet
hit a hundred. With a slight breeze, and shaded from the
early morning sun, it was comfortable enough that James
and Dave were finishing up their breakfast on the patio.
They were eating bacon and eggs; the last of the eggs,
as a matter of fact. They probably wouldn't be finding
any more, not unless they ventured out into the country
somewhere to find some chickens. The eggs they were
eating this morning had been liberated from a Whole
Foods refrigerated warehouse right after the great dying.
There may have still been eggs in that warehouse, but
they would surely be totally rotten by now. The power
grid, communications networks, and pretty much all of
modern infrastructure had died along with the people
who operated and maintained it. James wondered how
many self-sufficient places like the Mendez estate were still
functional. They still had electric power and most of the
conveniences that went with it. They were definitely better

off than most of the other survivors they'd seen on their foraging runs into what was left of the city. There seemed to be more survivors than James had originally thought there were. He and Dave had discussed it quite a bit and their best guess was that the great death had probably killed somewhere around ninety-nine percent of people on the eastern slope. If that guess was close, somewhere between thirty-five and forty thousand people would have survived in the Denver greater metro area. They had no way of knowing about the rest of the world, but, since there was no evidence to the contrary, they had decided that the survival rate was most likely about the same worldwide.

Surviving the great death was actually the easy part. That was simply the luck of the cosmic draw. The great death, or V-1, or whatever you wanted to call it, had killed most people while sparing just a few lucky survivors. How lucky it was to be a survivor was somewhat questionable. Continued survival after the great death wasn't very easy for people who had only known the structure and convenience of modern civilization.

"We need to get more water today," James broke the silence of the morning. The electricity on the Mendez estate might still be flowing, but the water was not. The taps had run dry less than a week after James and Noni had brought Dave back to the estate. No one knew if there was a broken main, or if the treatment plant had shut down, or what caused the city water to stop flowing. Hell, James didn't even know where the water came from. It had just always been there when he turned on the tap. Not anymore, though.

"Think we can find any closer, or do you plan on going back out to that water train in Commerce City?" Dave asked, referring to a whole train of water tankers they'd found stalled on the tracks.

"Guess it wouldn't hurt to look, but we probably better just do our looking on the way up to Commerce City, don't you think?" James was worried about conserving diesel in the old water truck that Dave had got rigged up to haul water. Dave had been a real godsend that way. Where James was not that mechanically inclined, Dave seemed to be able to make just about anything work.

When the water pipes went dry, James had been ready to panic, but Dave had simply said, "let's go find some water". And they did. First, they found an old antique Western Star ten-wheeler with a water tank that still had the words, **Potable Water,** printed on the side. The old truck was parked out in the back lot of an Aurora City shop. There hadn't been anyone at all anywhere around the shop, so Dave and James had just broken into the yard and then into the shop. Not only did they find the truck, but they also found all of the hoses and tools that Dave said they'd need. The old truck wouldn't start, of course, but Dave found an old battery charger in the shop that would work off of the Rivian's 110-volt outlet. The fuel tanks on the old water truck were nearly full and the diesel hadn't gone bad, which meant that the City of Aurora had been using the truck fairly recently. James couldn't imagine why they would have been using it at all. Not with all of the electric trucks at their disposal, but he was sure glad that they had. Not only did Dave know how to get the old truck going, he knew how to drive it. James wouldn't have had a clue. It had also been Dave's idea to look for one of the water trains that had been used to transport water from the Great Lakes. All in all, James and Noni probably wouldn't have known how to survive without Dave's help; or at least they wouldn't have been surviving in such relative comfort.

The morning breeze shifted from the southwest to the north and brought with it the stench of death from Denver. The smell of rotting human corpses was always in the background, but sometimes, when the wind was right, it was almost overpowering. That was the worst part of going into the city whenever they had to get water or more food from the abandoned stores and warehouses. James thought about how much food there was available; enough canned goods and non-perishables to last a lifetime, especially if you wanted to eat Allpro. There were warehouses full of the stuff. What had been stored to feed many millions of people for a week or two, was enough to feed the few thousands of survivors for a very long time. That was especially true since the survivors seemed to be abandoning the city. The number of people that James and Dave saw on their outings had steadily diminished over the past couple of months. They had seen people leaving the city going every direction over that time span. Some traveling alone, and some small groups of two to six people traveling together. They had stopped and talked to many of the people they ran into on their "shopping" trips. It was interesting to James that everyone seemed eager to talk and no one seemed the least bit interested in stealing from anyone else anymore. He wasn't sure if that was simply because almost anything anyone could want was available for the taking, or if it had to do with the fact that there were so few people left anymore that hurting anyone else who had survived was simply unthinkable. Though most of those leaving the city were leaving on foot, Dave and James had both been surprised to come across a few others in vehicles of various sorts as well.

Dave finished the cup of instant coffee he'd been nursing and turned his gaze from the mountains toward James. "You know James, I've been thinking about leaving." He said it thoughtfully, not stating that he was leaving, but putting the thought out there to start a conversation.

"Why?" James obviously found the thought a little absurd. *Why would anyone want to leave, when they had everything they needed right here?* At least they had enough to survive, that is.

"I don't know," Dave continued, "Guess it seems like I can't just stay holed up here forever. The great death might have missed me, but death is still going to find me sometime." He paused, thinking about it, then added; "You know, I'm not a religious man, but something keeps coming back to me from the bible. That part about going forth to multiply and replenish the earth." He chuckled under his breath. "Maybe I'm just horny, but I think I need to go forth and do my part."

James laughed out loud. *Dave was horny. How could any twenty-one or twenty-two-year-old man not be?* He had to admit he was horny himself, but not just horny; he was finding himself dreaming and thinking about Anna more and more. *Did she survive? If so, where is she now?* He'd been thinking more and more about leaving, also; maybe talking his mother into heading out to Kremmling. He thought about Noni now. He wasn't at all sure that she would be willing to go anywhere. She didn't do much of anything anymore but sit and stare into space. Whole days would go by that she hardly even got out of bed. James was worried that she was going to simply sit there and waste away.

"Maybe we can find some women in town to bring back here," he said, more to get his mind off Anna and keep the conversation going than anything else.

"Maybe..." Dave mused. "But there's more to it than that. I think I want to head north. Maybe Montana, or even up to Canada; get away from the heat...the heat and the smell," he added as another blast from the city hit the two of them.

"Damn, you'd think it would go away, wouldn't you?" James got up as he spoke. It was too hot and too smelly to sit on the patio anymore. The air conditioning inside the house not only kept the heat at bay, but it also held the stench down to a minimum as well. "Let's go get some water. If you're really thinking about leaving, maybe you better teach me to drive that thing," he said half-jokingly, referring to the old water truck.

James didn't think that Dave would really leave, or maybe he just couldn't imagine not having Dave around, but he figured it would be a good idea to learn to drive that old water truck, anyway. He'd never be able to learn to do everything that Dave had done to make the estate as livable as it was, but he could certainly learn to drive an old diesel truck. He was thinking about how handy and mechanically able Dave was, as they disconnected the hose from the water truck that Dave had rigged up to supply water to the house using gravity. With the truck parked on top of the landscape mound in the middle of the circle drive, the hose that was connected to the outside faucet supplied actual running water to the house. With so little head pressure, it may have only been a trickle, but it was running water, nonetheless.

Driving the old Western Star wasn't as hard as James had thought it would be. It had power steering and an automatic transmission, which Dave had said was rare in a truck this old. The hard part to get used to was the physical size of the thing; learning where the right side of the vehicle was on the road seemed especially trying. It didn't help that you couldn't simply drive down a road or a street to get where you wanted to go. Getting anywhere required working your way around stalled vehicles, all kinds of trash and debris, and the occasional dead body rotting in the sun. It was a slow trip getting anywhere, let alone clear over to the train in Commerce City. With James learning to drive, and Dave following in the Rivian, they didn't get to the train until midday.

The air conditioning didn't work in the old Western Star, and James felt like he was sitting in a pool of sweat by the time they got there. He steered the old truck toward the spot where they'd got their last load of water a few weeks ago. It was a low point alongside the railroad tracks, where the rails were built on a raised embankment crossing over an old natural drainage. The drainage didn't look right, as James eased the truck down the slope to get low enough to use gravity to fill the truck from the tank cars above. He didn't remember the drainage channel having any sign that water had actually run down it at any time in the near past. Now, it looked like a significant stream had run through the box culvert under the train at some point. It wasn't that it was wet, it was dry as a bone, but James had to stop to keep from driving into a channel that was about a foot deep. It looked like the channel had been formed by too much water rushing through the drainage, headed downstream toward the South Platte River.

James punched the yellow diamond-shaped button on the dash and heard the reassuring sound of the air release that set the truck's brakes. It was only after he climbed out of the cab that he saw what had caused a big enough flow of water to cut a channel in the old drainage bottom. Below the center of every one of the water tank cars, sitting on the rails above, the railroad embankment had a ditch cut in the bank, where the valves had been opened and the precious water had flowed down into the drainage. At first, he couldn't quite believe he was seeing what he thought he was. He scrambled up the rail embankment, Dave, who had parked the Rivian right behind him, was already at the top of the bank looking at the open valves on the nearest car.

"Son of a bitch!" Dave exclaimed. "What the..." he trailed off, as he looked up and down the tracks at the other water tankers that had also been emptied.

"How... who?" James stammered, as he reached the top of the embankment and realized that the water was gone. "Who would do something like this?"

"Jesus! Fuck!" Dave was not at a loss for words. "It's fucking insane! This is just fucking insane." His voice calmed a little as the scope of what he was seeing hit home. "It is insane. It had to have been a crazy person. No one in their right mind would have drained these tanks."

*Dave's right, of course,* James thought. *No one in their right mind would have wasted all of that water.* It hadn't dawned on him until then that some of those who survived the great death might be insane, or evil, or both. Of course, simply being a survivor caused some insanity. It seemed to James that his mother was proof of that. Noni may have been wasting away out of grief, but she wasn't evil. This; this wasting of water for no apparent reason was purely evil. *What kind of person would do such a thing? How could someone that survived the great death even think about wasting the water that was needed to survive?*

Dave walked down the line of cars, checking each one as he went. James just stood there watching, knowing that whoever had done this hadn't done it half-assed. He knew Dave wouldn't find any water left in any of the tank cars. He made his way back down the slope, thinking about what they should do now; wondering if they could find another source of water where they'd be able to fill their tank. Thinking about what they should do, if they couldn't. Thinking about how fucking hot it was. The temperature had to be over a hundred and ten degrees. He climbed into the air-conditioned comfort of the Rivian to wait for Dave to come back.

"What now?" Dave asked as he took his place in the passenger seat. He'd only checked about a dozen cars before deciding it was no use.

James had been trying to decide *what now?* ever since he crawled into the Rivian. "Damn, I don't know," he answered. "I'm kind of wondering if you might be right about leaving. Even if we can find another source of water, how do we know it'll be there next time?" He had a thought, even as he asked the question. The South Platte was just about a quarter of a mile away over on the other side of the tracks. He put the Riv in reverse and backed out of the drainage. They'd have to go down the tracks a little to find a place to cross, but James decided that they needed to see if there was water in the river. Maybe they could find some kind of pump and a place where they could pump water straight out of the river into the water truck. Dave could probably figure out how to do it.

Seeing the mostly dry riverbed was probably even more of a disappointment than finding all of the water gone from the train had been. Knowing that they'd been in an extreme drought for at least the past decade didn't make looking at the dried-up river any easier. The riverbed wasn't completely dry. There were a few small puddles where whatever small amount of water that was still trickling through the gravelly bottom pooled on the surface.

"Maybe we could dig enough of a hole to pump water from," Dave said, apparently picking up on James' thoughts. "Take a pretty good hole, though. Wonder if we can find a backhoe or something to dig with?"

James shrugged. He wasn't feeling exactly optimistic about anything. Dave could probably find a backhoe and a pump, and rig the whole thing up to get water, but James knew that he couldn't. It struck him that he and Noni had only been able to go on living at home the way they had because of Dave. It wasn't a good feeling; the realization that the easy life he'd been handed on a golden platter had left him so ill-prepared for the world they now inhabited. He took a deep breath, exhaled and said, "You're right about leaving Dave. We should get out of here. Get away to the country somewhere." He looked around. "This is nothing but a dead city. The great death killed a lot more than just people, didn't it?"

··········

There was still a couple of hundred gallons of water left in the four-thousand-gallon tank, so James parked the water truck back in its place on top of the berm, and he and Dave reconnected the hoses to enable the use of that remaining water. It was late in the evening by then and the sun was just starting to drop behind the mountains to the west. With the sky totally dry and devoid of clouds, it would be another in a long line of bland, unremarkable sunsets. For some reason, James was thinking about how sunsets had seemed a lot prettier when he was young.

Dave had taken the Riv to the car barn to charge it back up, and James expected to find Noni sitting in her favorite chair in the living room. He had made up his mind, and he wanted to tell her his plan right away. His plan was to take her and enough supplies to get them there, and to make the journey to Kremmling. He hoped they would find Grandpa Chuck alive and well; and, truth be told, he wanted nothing more than to find Anna. Maybe they could talk Dave into going with them, maybe not. It didn't really matter anymore. What really mattered was getting away from the dead city, and James and Dave must not have been the only ones who thought so. Today's outing had been the first time that they had failed to see another living human being. Everyone, it seemed, had already deserted the death and the rot; all that was left of the once thriving Denver Metro area.

"Mom," he yelled when he didn't find her in the living room. No answer. He looked in the kitchen, no one there. "Hey Mom, we're home" he yelled a little louder, heading toward her bedroom. He thought he heard a moan coming through the open door, and hurried into her room.

Noni was there, in her king size bed. Her face was as white as the sheet that was pulled up to her chin. As white as that part of the sheet, that is. Much of the sheet wasn't white at all. It was dark red and wet; soaked in blood. Noni was lying in a pool of blood. She was moaning in pain and there was a fear in her eyes that James would never forget.

He rushed to the side of the bed and fell to his knees. "Mother...mother," he didn't know what to say. His mother was obviously dying. *Why?*

"Don't cry son," her voice was weak. James hadn't even realized he was crying at all. "It's the cancer. I'm sorry James, I should have told you. Ovarian cancer. Same as killed Mom...was supposed to have a hysterectomy, but then...but then Dr. Yew...gone. All gone. So sorry, James. So sorry."

"It's okay, Mom. It's all okay." James was on the verge of sobbing.

"No!" her voice was suddenly much more forceful than seemed possible. "It's not okay. Shouldn't have let him..." the words were getting softer, trailing off. "Shouldn't have let your father keep you from Anna...oh James...I'm so sorry...so, so sorry." She gasped in a sudden intake of air and then lay still, her eyes opened wide but now devoid of life.

···········

Early the following morning, Dave helped bury Noni out in the flower garden turned cemetery. "I'm leaving," he told James after the last shovel full of dirt was placed on the grave.

"I know," James said flatly. He was totally drained of emotion and exhaustion was weighing him down. He hadn't slept at all in more than twenty-four hours, and his thoughts were random and scattered. "You should take the Riv," he told Dave.

"What will you do? Now, I mean. Now that your mother's gone. You should come with me."

"No," James answered slowly. "No, I'm not sure what I'm going to do now. Maybe go to Kremmling...should have taken her to Kremmling." He gestured toward his mother's fresh grave with his chin.

James had talked enough about the BR Ranch and Kremmling that Dave knew what he meant. He also knew that James hoped to have loved ones still alive out there. James had broached the subject of all of them going to Kremmling a couple of times, but Dave had always shrugged it off. He hadn't told James how hard it was to be there with two people who still had each other when everyone he had ever loved was gone. He hadn't ever told him how much harder he thought it would be to live among even more family members. He didn't want to live with a loving family that he could never be a part of. No, Dave had made up his mind that he would go north. Somewhere, someday, he would find his own love. It was time to start his own family; a new family, a new life, in a strange new world.

······

James woke suddenly. It took him a moment or two before he realized where he was. He was stretched out in his recliner with a light blanket covering him. He pushed the button, the recliner raised him to an upright sitting position. Memory streamed into his consciousness, leaving him, once again, empty and alone. He remembered sitting down in the recliner after he and Dave had finished burying Noni. He remembered sitting there and thinking. It was fairly early in the day when he'd sat down. It was now dark. The house was totally dark, with the light of the moon through the big picture window casting an eerie glow on his surroundings. He didn't know how long he'd been asleep, but it must have been near midnight, judging by how high in the sky the moon seemed to be. Dave must have covered me, he thought, remembering that he didn't have a blanket when he'd sat down. He pushed the blanket off and stood up. Walking as quietly as he could, so as not to awaken him, he went down the hall to Dave's room. The door was open, and the moonlight fell on an empty bed in an empty room. He'd done it, then; Dave was gone. With no need to be quiet anymore, James strode back to the kitchen. He was hungry. It didn't seem right to want to eat, but his body seemed to be on autopilot, as he opened a can of Allpro and started filling the emptiness in his stomach. That, at least, was one emptiness that could be filled.

# Chapter 15

J AMES WAS CARRYING HIS third cup of instant coffee, sipping
it as he walked out to the car barn. The Rivian was gone.
*Good for him,* he thought. He was glad that Dave had taken
the Riv. Where James was headed it probably wouldn't have
been much use, anyway. He'd given it a lot of thought and
based on how badly clogged the streets and roads were in
Denver, he didn't think there was much chance that any of
the roads leading over the mountains would be passable
by car. If Dave headed north and stayed out in the plains,
he could probably take the Riv off-road to get around the
stalled vehicles that would inevitably block the way. That
was most probably not the case for one who was headed
west over the mountains. Every route over the mountains
that James could think of had stretches of road along rivers
and through canyons where there were drop-offs on one
side and cliffs or steep mountains on the other. Just a
couple of stalled autonomous trucks or cars would render
those stretches of road impassable by car or truck. No, he
wouldn't take any of the cars or trucks in the warehouse, he
would ride to Kremmling on his old motorcycle.

James hadn't been on the old Zero for at least five years, so
he needed to get it charged up and ready to go. He plugged it

in and checked the tires, glad to find that they still held air. They were low on pressure, so he started the air compressor, found a tire gauge and aired them up. While he was getting the bike ready, he was remembering how angry his mother had been, when his dad had allowed him to have a dirt bike on his fourteenth birthday. She'd ranted and raved for a full day about how dangerous motorcycles were. She'd been right, of course. He had to smile at the memory of how much angrier she had become when he crashed for the first time. Fortunately, he had never been seriously injured, just a few scrapes and bruises, but no broken bones.

Thinking about Noni was mostly what he'd been doing, so the memory of her fear of motorcycles was just one more thread in the tapestry of the memories of his mother. He wished that he had taken her to Kremmling as soon as they'd buried Julie. She had deserved to see the BR Ranch again before she died, whether or not Grandpa Chuck was still alive. James had a feeling that Chuck was alive. He also had the same feeling regarding Anna, only stronger. He imagined what that reunion would have been like. Riding the Zero up the ranch lane from Highway 9, with his mother on the back. The mental image made him laugh out loud, in spite of his grief. There was no way in hell that he could have ever talked Noni into riding to Kremmling on the back of a motorcycle.

The backpack seemed too heavy, but James was sure it would be alright. He'd already pared it down to what he thought he might need. He would just have to get used to it. He wasn't even packing his own water. He had figured out a way to tie two jugs of water onto the sides of the bike. That should be plenty to get him up into the mountains, where he was sure he'd be able to get all the water he needed. He had the same water purification filter in his pack that he'd carried from Colorado College. The gate was still closed, Dave had gone to the trouble of locking it up and climbing over when he left. *Probably no need for that now,* James thought, as he went in the gatehouse and opened the gate for the last time. He'd left the power on and the air conditioner running, just like he intended to return. Maybe someone would find it like that, maybe not. Eventually, the systems would all break down or malfunction and the Mendez Estate would be as dead as the people buried in the flower garden behind the house. He pulled through the ornate open gate, stopped and turned for one last look, before pulling out of the drive onto the roadway, headed for an unknown future at the Blue River Ranch.

..........

Even though he coasted all the way down the west side of Loveland Pass, the Zero ran out of juice just about a mile west of the old Keystone Resort. James hadn't planned on being able to get all the way to the BR on the bike, it was simply too far for the Zero's range. He had thought it would be close, but there were just too many stalled vehicles abandoned all along I-70. Working his way around, between, and through the dead cars and trucks had drained the Zero's battery pack faster than he'd anticipated. Plus, he'd decided to not even try to get through the tunnel, and the route over Loveland Pass added, not just extra miles, but extra uphill miles.

The old Keystone Ski Resort had been mostly abandoned years before the great death. Like all ski resorts in Colorado, it had been the victim of multiple factors. Not the least of which was the end of heavy winter snowpack and the overall lack of water for making snow. That, and the lack of skiers, as the world's economies had all nose-dived over the past decade or so. James had fond memories of snowboarding down the slopes that were still the dominant feature of Keystone Mountain. The lifts were still there, hanging above the green open slopes surrounded by what was left of the forest; as many brown dead trees as green. *It's kind of a minor miracle,* he thought, *that the whole place hasn't already burned. Probably won't be much longer before a lightning bolt from a dry mountain thunderstorm hits the right tree and ignites a firestorm that will take it all out, just like the other side of Loveland Pass.* It seemed like he'd already seen more burned forest than live trees. Even the living forests were, like this one, more than half dead already.

James dropped the Zero on its side at the edge of old Highway 6. He left the water jugs, along with the bike, and started off toward Dillon on foot. From now on, hiking on foot, he would only be able to carry what water he had in the bladder in his backpack. That would do. It wasn't that much farther to the Blue River Ranch. The mountain streams and rivers didn't flow like they used to, but he was sure that he would be able to find enough pools and trickles to keep the bladder supplied with filtered water. He stopped and looked back at the dirt bike laying on the ground at the side of the road. It was the last of it, the last of his old life. He turned and started walking briskly west, the backpack and the old .300 Weatherby that was slung over his shoulder seeming to get heavier as he thought about all the miles that lay ahead.

The sun was about to go down by the time James got through what remained of Dillon and Silverthorne. He remembered hearing about the wildfire that had burned through most of the area, including the twin communities, back in 2030. There wasn't much that had been rebuilt after that. There was no need. The tourism and ski traffic that had caused the towns to boom in the last half of the twentieth century was gone forever. He was pretty well exhausted, and he knew that he probably hadn't even covered ten miles yet. He hadn't seen another living person since Georgetown, and those two people he only saw from a distance. They had appeared to be working a garden on the outskirts of town, over across the valley from the interstate. There was plenty of wildlife. The great death virus or whatever it was didn't seem to affect any animals other than humans. Of course, there was no way he could know that for sure. For all he knew, it might have wiped out all primates, or pigs for that matter, but he didn't see any indication that it had been at all harmful to the fauna that was native to the Rocky Mountains.

He had been pleasantly surprised to find that there was still some water in Dillon Reservoir; not much, but there was a stream of water still flowing on down the Blue River. That was a really good sign. If there was water flowing down the Blue here, there would still be water at the BR. James was feeling pretty exhausted, though he knew he'd only walked ten or twelve miles. As much as he wanted to get there, he knew he couldn't just keep walking all night. It had to be at least another twenty miles to the ranch. Maybe, with a good night's rest, he would be able to do the rest tomorrow. As he walked, watching for a good place to camp for the night, he saw a wisp of smoke rising from behind a clump of trees on the other side of a small hill. At first, he feared it might be a wildfire, it was just beyond the line that marked the boundary between what had been destroyed by the big fire of 2030 and the forest that had been spared. James marveled at the mysterious way some forest had been spared and some had been utterly incinerated. As he followed Highway 9 on around the hill and got close enough, he decided it had to be a cooking fire. There was the unmistakable smell of some kind of roasting meat in the air.

Once he got around the small hill, some very old ranch buildings came into view. The ranch had to have been there long before there was ever a Dillon Reservoir or a Keystone Ski Resort; long before there was ever an interstate highway running through Silverthorne. Just to look at it, James would have guessed it to be as old as the Blue River Ranch. It was probably homesteaded at about the same time as his great-great-great-grandfather had settled the Blue River Ranch, twenty miles or so down the valley. *Had to have been some hardy people that staked out this area,* he thought. *This might have been the BR's closest neighbors back then.* Back in the 1800s, this high up, the winters would have been terrible. James had skied both Keystone and Breckenridge as a youngster and had learned enough history from visiting the local museums to know how much different the area's climate had once been. It was hard to believe how much the climate had changed in just the past fifteen years, let alone the past hundred and fifty. James was contemplating those changes as he walked up the short lane to the ranch house.

The cooking fire was on the backside of the house, so James walked on toward the old barn instead of walking up to the door. On the backside of the house, in an open area of bare ground, there was a man turning something on a spit that had been improvised over a rock-lined fire pit. James couldn't tell what the animal was, but it smelled delicious.

"Hello," he called out, trying not to startle the man too badly.

The man did kind of jump, obviously startled more than James had intended, but he seemed friendly enough when he turned toward James and said, "Howdy do. Sure wasn't expecting anybody walking up on me like that." He turned back to the house and hollered, "Hey Jack, Rita, we've got company."

A young blonde woman came out of the old-fashioned wooden screen door, followed by another dark-haired man. The woman was about James' age; the man probably eight or ten years older than James. Both seemed as happy to see another living person as James was to see them.

"Come on in," the man who had been tending the barbecue said. He walked out toward James. They met at the edge of the dried-up lawn. "Jack Thompson," the man said, extending his hand to James. "And that's my brother Ray, and Rita McKendrick," he added, as they shook hands.

James introduced himself and shook hands with Rita, who had followed closely behind Jack, and then he walked over to shake Ray's hand and see what was cooking. Ray had taken over the cooking spot at the fire, vacated by his brother Jack. At first, James couldn't tell for sure what was cooking; his first guess was that it was a small deer, maybe this year's fawn, but it seemed too fat and stubby. Ray informed him that it was lamb. He said there were quite a few sheep roaming around the mountains, but he didn't know for how long. "Figured we better salvage some while we can," Ray told him. "Before the bears and lions get 'em all." He went on to tell James how they had gathered a small flock that they had grazing somewhere off a ways to the west. "Connie's watch tonight," he added, explaining that there were actually four of them living on this old ranch, but someone had to tend to the flock.

It turned out that Connie was Rita's sister, and it didn't take long for James to realize that these two surviving brothers had somehow found two surviving sisters, and the four of them were starting over together here on this old abandoned ranch.

"So, what brings you here to our humble abode?" Ray asked. "We haven't seen many people since – since..." he didn't have to finish the sentence.

"Since the great dying," James finished it for him. "That's what I call it, anyway."

"Yeah, the great dying. Guess that's as good as any. What the hell was it, anyway? We've been trying to figure it out ever since everyone died."

James told them what he knew, which wasn't much, but at least they were a little relieved to hear that it wasn't some kind of biological, or germ warfare.

"Were you guys living here before?" James asked, even though he was pretty sure that was not the case.

Jack answered. "Oh no, Ray and I are both from Glenwood. We just had to leave after – after most everyone died. It's a terrible thing to lose your family. How 'bout you, where are you from?"

James was relieved for some reason that none of the three had apparently connected him to Robert Mendez. Of course, why would they, Mendez was a fairly common name. He decided to keep it that way, no reason for them to know his true past. Nothing from his previous life seemed to matter anymore; maybe that was best. "I'm from Denver," he told them, "headed for my Grandpa's ranch down by Kremmling. Guess I had to get out of Denver, same as you having to get out of Glenwood. Just wasn't anything to stay for." He went on to tell them how it seemed like most everyone that survived had already left the rotting city.

They wanted to know if he'd walked all the way from Denver; why they hadn't seen more people from the city up this way, and on and on. He told them it seemed to him like most of those who had survived had headed north; that he would have headed north, too, except for the chance that he hoped to find family still alive on the BR Ranch.

Jack, Ray, and Rita were all sympathetic and told him that they hoped he would find his Grandpa alive, but James could tell they didn't really think he would. They invited him to join them for an evening meal and even invited him to spend the night in the hayloft of the old barn instead of trying to find a place to camp. How could he refuse? Other than Dave and his mother, James had hardly talked to another person in more than two months. It was good to listen to other people's stories, even if the stories just confirmed that the great death had probably hit everywhere, not just on the eastern slope of Colorado.

Jack and Ray had grown up in Glenwood and were both still living there when it hit. James had the feeling, as he listened to their life story, that they had come from a locally powerful family. He couldn't recall ever hearing anything about the Thompson's of Glenwood Springs, so they must not have been in the same class as Robert Mendez, but then, who was?

The Thompson brothers had apparently been the owners of several car dealerships on the western slope. The family business their father had started had done well enough that they were pretty well off, even after most people could no longer afford to buy cars. Ray and Jack had both been married and lost their wives to the great death. Jack had also lost a two-year-old son. His younger brother Ray didn't have children. Like James, the pain of their loss was still really strong. He wondered how much the passage of time would be able to ease pain like that.

Rita was crying by the time Jack finished telling James about losing his wife and two-year-old son. Ray put his arm around her and held her, as he asked James, "What about you? How did Robert Mendez' son end up out here with us lesser folk?"

*So much for anonymity.* "Didn't think you knew," James said.

"I didn't know for sure, just a hunch. Mendez Investments handled a lot of our family's money over the years. I never met Robert personally, but I thought I remembered him having a son named James. I take it the great death, as you call it, didn't spare the ultra-wealthy, either."

"No," James began, "it didn't spare anybody. Just us. I mean just the few of us, like you guys, who were immune - somehow. How, or why we didn't die too, I guess we'll never know. Kind of makes you feel guilty, doesn't it? Living, while everyone else dies." He went on to tell them his whole story, from that day back in May when he and Julie had fled Colorado College, right up to the present. When he got to the part about the death of his mother, Rita went from weeping to outright sobbing.

"We had to bury our mother, too," she got out between sobs. By then there were no dry eyes left at the table. There was a catharsis in sharing each other's stories of death and grief, and the men prodded and encouraged Rita to open up and let it out. She told them about her and her sister, Connie, growing up on a sheep ranch outside Montrose. She was twenty-two and Connie was a year younger. Their father had died of a heart attack four years ago. The two of them had been helping their mother run the ranch when *it* hit. They'd buried their mother in the yard, just like James had done, but they hadn't left immediately. At first, they'd thought they would just keep on living as they had. Neither of them had ever known anything different. They'd lived on the ranch outside Montrose their entire lives. Both had lost boyfriends that lived in town. Rita had actually gotten engaged just a couple of weeks before it happened.

"You know, IT was just the final blow," she said. "We didn't leave her any choice."

The men exchanged some questioning glances. "Who?" James asked. "Who didn't you leave any choice?"

Rita gave him a look that said he should know exactly what she was talking about. "We!' she said emphatically. "We – the human race. We didn't leave her any other choice. Mother Nature. Don't you see? Mother Nature – Mother Earth; call her God if you want to. Whatever you want to call her, IT was the only option left. We declared war on nature long ago." Rita had gone from a grieving young woman to a priestess delivering a sermon. "The Anthropocene they called it. Call it what you want, it was a war against nature. And you know the funny part? The funny part is we killed ourselves. Somehow, it was forgotten that we are also nature. If you look at Mother Earth and everything she contains as a living entity, mankind was like a cancer. IT, the great death, as you call it," she said, looking at James, "was just an immune response. Nothing more than a cure for a disease."

All three men stared at Rita silently. James could tell that Ray and Jack were as stunned as he was. Rita, having delivered her sermon, looked right back at them, like she was waiting for a rebuttal. None was forthcoming. He didn't know what the other two were thinking, but James thought Rita made a good argument. Problem was, he didn't believe in God; did that mean he didn't believe in nature? How can you not believe in nature? It's everywhere. It's all around us. And then the thought hit him, *it is us. We are nature. She's right about that, for sure.*

James needed to change the subject. "How did you guys all meet up?" he asked, to no one in particular.

Jack was as ready for a change of subject as James was. "I guess Connie and Rita just kind of saved us." He smiled at the memory. "Ray and I decided we couldn't stay in Glenwood. It was mainly the smell that got us. Living in Glenwood, you get used to the smell of the sulfur water, but I don't think you can ever get used to the smell of so many dead people. There were way too many dead for us and the others that survived to bury or deal with at all. Some of the others left before we did. They headed out different directions...wonder where they ended up? Anyway, after about a month of no comms, and nobody coming to the rescue, we decided that Glenwood must not have been the only place hit by IT. So, we decided to head east, thinking maybe IT might not have hit as hard on the eastern slope. We thought maybe some of the big hospitals might have been able to save more than survived in Glenwood...you know, we used to have a pretty good medical system in Glenwood." Jack looked into the distance, his mind obviously off on a tangent.

"We figured the canyon would be totally blocked," Ray picked up where Jack had left off. "So, we put on our backpacks; Jack and I have always been avid hikers. Anyway, we just started hiking toward Denver. We were just about to Vail when Connie and Rita rode up behind us. Their dogs like to scared us to death."

"Not exactly what Connie and I expected to find, when we left Montrose," Rita actually laughed, obviously back from her pseudo-religious rant. "Of course, we didn't really know what we were going to find. We just knew the sheep ranch wasn't going to cut it anymore." She laughed again. "And here we are raising sheep again. But at least we've got help," she added, putting her arm affectionately around Ray.

It was obvious that these two brothers and two sisters had, for want of a better term, mated up. James wondered about human nature. In the face of the death of so many people, instinct drove men and women together. The sex drive was a powerful instinct. Maybe the most powerful of all. These two couples had come together, not through love, but through the instinctual desire to mate, to procreate, to ensure that the human race would continue. They might come to think of it as love if they hadn't already, but love was just an emotion, probably just a tool used by an age-old instinct.

James was roused out of reflection by Jack rejoining the conversation. "Yeah, don't know where me and Ray would be now if Rita and Connie hadn't come along. Probably not raising sheep in the middle of nowhere." It was Jack's turn to laugh now. "Course I guess every where's the middle of nowhere anymore."

Eventually, James heard the whole story. Connie and Rita had set out from Montrose on horseback hoping to find somewhere, anywhere that hadn't been devastated by IT. James still preferred *the great death*, but IT was the only way the others referred to the virus or whatever it was. They'd ridden to Grand Junction first, but had headed toward I-70 through Palisade after the smell on Orchard Mesa turned them around. By the time they caught up to Jack and Ray, after passing through Rifle, Glenwood, and the lesser towns along the way, their only hope was that the devastation was contained to the western slope. In truth, they'd given up hope. If there was any functioning government left in Denver, some kind of help would have already arrived.

When they came upon Jack and Ray, the four of them had seemed to come to a nearly instantaneous mutual decision to go on together. They'd ridden doubled up the rest of the way to this old ranch outside Silverthorne. Much like James, the four of them had been looking for a place to camp for the night, when they came upon the ranch buildings. They'd found the corpses of an old man and an old woman in bed together in the master bedroom. Deciding that the old couple deserved a decent burial, they had dug a grave out back and buried them by moonlight, together, in the same grave. It had seemed like that was what the old couple would have wanted. The old house had three bedrooms, and the four had decided that a real bed would feel too good to pass up after several nights on the ground. Nothing was said explicitly about it, but James deduced that they had coupled up that very first night on the ranch. By the next day, they had decided there was no use going any further. Presuming the old couple that they'd buried were the owners, and being sure they wouldn't mind, Ray and Rita, and Jack and Connie had decided to start a new life on the old ranch. It had everything they needed, a well with an antique hand pump for drinking water, the Blue River flowing by for the livestock and a huge garden that had been planted in the spring. The neglected garden had taken quite a bit of work, but Rita said they would get enough vegetables to get them through the next winter. The green salad that they'd served with the lamb had made the shared meal the best James had eaten in months.

The four talked well into the evening before Ray decided it was time for bed. He told James that he was welcome to sleep in the master bedroom, but they'd burned the bed that they found the old couple in. James declined, opting to spend the night in the hayloft of the old barn. A reasonably soft bed of old hay sounded better than a hardwood floor. He also figured there would be a better breeze through the large hayloft doors than there would be through the windows and screen door of the old ranch house.

·······

After a surprisingly good night's sleep, James was still enjoying the cool early morning stillness when he heard the barn doors open below him. The horse in the stall directly beneath where he was laying, neighed a welcome home to the other horse that was being led into the barn. The sun had just come up over the mountains to the east, casting bright streaks of light through the cracks in the sides of the old barn. James quietly watched through the spaces between the boards of the loft floor, as the young woman that had to be Connie, took the saddle off of the palomino she'd brought into the barn, and led him to the stall next to the other palomino. Connie was as blonde as Rita, but she had longer hair flowing down her back from beneath a western style straw hat. James couldn't see her face, but he could see that she was a very well-built young lady. The skimpy shirt and tight jeans gave that away immediately.

James felt a stirring in his pants at the sight of such a sexy young woman and thought about his reaction. *What is it that makes me horny at just the sight of a sexy stranger,* he wondered? He ignored the horniness and rolled over to speak down through the hay opening in the loft floor. "You must be Connie," he said.

Connie, startled by the sound of James rolling over, was looking up at him, as he spoke. When she looked up, her face was lit up by a spot of sunshine coming through a knothole in the side of the barn. The effect was that of a spotlight, and she truly was beautiful. She smiled up at him, and said, "I am, and who might you be?"

James introduced himself and told her that he'd already met the others the night before. She crossed over to the ladder into the loft and climbed up. James crawled out of his sleeping bag and pulled on his jeans to cover his obvious sexual interests before her head poked up through the hole in the floor. He was standing shirtless facing her as she turned toward him. Connie looked him up and down; he could actually feel her eyes as they momentarily stopped on the bulge that his jeans could not conceal. Her blue eyes quickly met his, and her face had a definite blush, as she glanced away, and walked over to push some loose hay down through the opening into her horse's manger.

James could do nothing but watch spellbound as she bent over to push the hay. His eyes were fixed on the curves of her butt displayed by the tightness of her jeans. His own jeans felt even more confining by the throbbing they contained. His desire was so irrational that it scared him. *How can I want somebody this much? I don't even know her.*

Connie turned back toward James and walked straight to him. Her face was flushed, not the blush of embarrassment that he thought he'd seen before but flushed with what must have been the same desire he was feeling. Her face was basically fixed, trancelike. She was neither smiling nor frowning. She didn't say a word, as she reached down with both hands and started unbuttoning the jeans he'd just put on. They couldn't get each other's pants off fast enough, as they fell to the sleeping bag. It was over before he knew it.

*God, I haven't been that fast since that first time with Maddy,* James thought, as he rolled over and quickly started getting dressed.

They got dressed without saying anything to each other at all. James helped her get some hay out of her long blonde hair, as feelings of guilt hit him in waves. He was only a day's hike from Anna. How could he have possibly done what he just did? Anna, who he knew he would always love like no other. Why? Why had he done this thing? And what about Connie? It didn't matter whether or not it had been purely sexual instinct. It didn't matter that he didn't know her at all. In just a matter of minutes, he had developed feelings for her that were as hard to explain as the instant sex they'd just shared.

"I'm sorry," he finally said. "I know you're Jack's woman. I – we had no right."

"I am not Jack's woman," she answered defiantly. "I'm nobody's woman but my own." Then she smiled at him. "Besides, I'd say I'm the one that fucked you, remember."

James hurriedly finished dressing. He had an overwhelming desire to get out of there. He didn't want to face Jack and Connie together. He was afraid of what would be revealed for all to see. "I have to go," he said.

"Go where?" she asked, with a mischievous grin. "Where is there to go? You could just stay here with us."

The thought was horrifying to James. Not that he could say he had no more desire for Connie, but rationality had returned. He was afraid of all that he now knew instinct could compel. He was afraid that if he didn't leave, and leave right now, Jack would probably feel the need to kill him. It was not a comforting thought, but a stark realization that did not bode well at all for all the people who had survived the great death. When civilization dies, the ancient instincts of the caveman return. How would people deal with those instincts? The drive to procreate so strong that a man might be willing to drag a woman by her hair back to his cave to give him babies. Could the rational mind overcome instincts that had been laying mostly dormant for all these thousands of years? It was a question that didn't even need an answer to be terrifying.

# Chapter 16

T HE SUN WAS SETTING in the west directly in front of
James as he walked up the gravel lane from Highway
9 toward the Blue River Ranch Headquarters. He was
exhausted. Knowing one could walk twenty miles in a day
wasn't the same as actually doing it. His legs ached, and
his feet were sore. Every step was one more step too many.
When he got to the top of the rise between Highway 9
and the Blue River Ranch, and the ranch buildings finally
came into view, the sight didn't give him the lift he'd
expected. There was no sign of anyone. The big meadow
that stretched away to the north was brown and dying from
lack of irrigation. The grasses that should have been knee
high were thin and short. There would be no hay crop to cut
and gather this year.

To the south of the BR ranch buildings, where it was
visible, James could see water flowing in Spider Creek;
water that he knew was normally used to irrigate the huge
hay meadow. A feeling of dread came over him, as he
stopped and took in the apparently lifeless scene. He was
almost afraid to go on; afraid of what he was going to find.
What if he'd come all this way only to find everyone dead?
Steeling himself against the dread, he continued on down

the lane toward the big house. He was still a couple of hundred yards from the house when a dog started barking and he finally saw movement. A black and white border collie bounded off of the veranda and started running toward him, but stopped instantly when a man's voice yelled, "Blackie! Stay!"

Chuck Pierson stepped off of the veranda with a rifle in his hand. He carried the old 30-30 carbine loosely in one hand; the barrel pointed at the ground. He walked out to where the dog had stopped in its tracks and continued on toward James. Blackie fell right in step at his heel. James, as tired as his feet and legs were, started running toward his grandfather.

"Well, I'll be..." was about all Chuck could get out at first. James hugged the old man tight without saying anything at all. Blackie stood right behind Chuck, his tail wagging.

"Didn't think I'd ever see you again," Chuck said, with tears in his eyes. "Look at you, all grown up...didn't think I'd see you again," he repeated. "Least not in this life, anyway. Your Mom?"

James didn't have to answer. The look in his eyes told Chuck that his daughter hadn't survived. "Was it the sickness?" Chuck asked.

Crying, James shook his head no, and said, "cancer. She survived the sickness. Cancer killed her. Same as Grandma."

The tears in Chuck's eyes dried up, as he almost imperceptibly shook his head yes. His jaw was set, and he had a faraway look in his eyes. He'd already done his grieving. "Come on son," he said. "You must be exhausted." He turned and started walking back toward the house.

James walked beside him, with Blackie now running ahead of them. Chuck could feel the question, as he noticed

James looking around as they walked. "They're all gone," he said, in response to James' unasked question.

James felt like his heart skipped a beat. "Anna?" it was a one-word question.

"Don't know, son," Chuck could feel his grandson's pain. "She was away at school."

James dropped his pack on the floor and leaned his rifle up against the wall before collapsing into the easy chair on the veranda. Chuck went into the house and returned with a large glass of water for each of them. James was hungry, but he had a greater hunger for information than he did for food. The two men spent the next several hours sharing all they knew about loved ones who were no longer there, the great death, and general catch-up. It had been nine years since James and Chuck had sat and shared each other's company on this veranda. To say the world had changed in those intervening years would have been such a gross understatement that neither man even commented on it.

James couldn't help but notice how old his grandfather seemed. Just the toll that age takes on everyone would have been enough, but Chuck had aged far beyond his sixty-eight years of living. His once jet-black hair was now totally white, along with the full beard on his face. James had never known his grandfather to wear a beard, he thought, as he stroked his own. Maybe everybody quit shaving after the great death. Chuck was still lean as ever, maybe more so, and he had the weathered look of one who has spent a good deal of their life doing hard physical work. Other than the white beard, the main features of aging that James noticed were the wrinkles and weakened look of Chuck's neck; and the back of his hands, where the skin seemed thin and stretched despite the wrinkles.

"You really loved her, didn't you?" Chuck said, as James stared at the unfathomable number of stars in the totally dark sky.

"I do love her," James answered, unwilling to put Anna in the past tense. "Where did she go to school?" He had the thought that he might just go wherever it was to find her.

"Oregon, of all places. She followed that worthless Will Donovan to Oregon. They got engaged, you know. What happened James? I know about your secret visit a couple of years ago. I also know you broke her heart. Didn't do much for my feelings either, when you didn't even stop in to say hi."

The pain of ending his relationship with Anna came back to James like it was yesterday. "It was Dad," he said.

"Figured as much," Chuck told him. "Your mother half-assed let me know, but she wouldn't ever openly say anything bad about the son of a bitch. Never understood why she always backed that man, even when she knew it was wrong."

"It was you, Grandpa." James had to tell him. "He would have taken the BR and evicted you. She couldn't let him take this away from you. She didn't have a choice." James paused, the silence between them broken only by the sound of coyotes yipping somewhere off in the distance, and the gentle sound of water running lazily over the rocks of Spider Creek. "You know," he continued, "it took most of my life to learn about my father; to learn what he really was. By the time I knew he was a psychopath, it was too late. Too late for me...for me and Anna."

Chuck didn't say anything for a while. He just took in a deep breath and let it out in a sigh. They sat in silence for several minutes, listening to the soothing sounds of the

Colorado night and looking at the milky way stretching across the starlit sky.

Chuck finally spoke. "Don't blame yourself, son," the tone of his voice saying the rest, that there was always plenty of blame to go around. "Besides, maybe Anna's still alive. Just before the comms died, she told Clyde she was headed home. Maybe she'll show up here, same as you. You must be starving," he added, as he got up out of his chair with a groan.

·····•·•·····

The morning sun shining through the open window brought James back from a deep dreamless sleep. It seemed like he ached all over. His legs hurt so bad that he didn't even want to stretch, let alone get up. It took a little bit to get oriented before he remembered where he was and the conversation with his Grandpa from the night before. He caught the smell of wood smoke drifting up through the open window. Wood smoke and something else; bacon. The smell of frying bacon! He forced his aching legs to carry him over to the open window and looked out. He couldn't see the source of the smoke from this window, the breeze was carrying it around the house from the back. He could see the old house that the Duran's had lived in looking the same as it always had. The huge garden they had always raised didn't look any different than he remembered it, either. In his mind's eye, he could picture the scene as it had been nearly nine years ago; the last time he stood at this window looking out. *Grandpa's been working the garden,* he realized. It wouldn't have looked nearly as good, otherwise. He closed the window and pulled the blinds to block out the morning sun. Better to keep as much of the daytime heat out as possible.

Chuck was bent over the raised fire pit on the patio when James walked out the back door of the house. The old man was frying eggs in a huge cast iron skillet to go with the bacon James had smelled. The fire pit had been turned into a wood grill with the addition of a steel mesh grate over the top. There was an old antique speckled blue enamel coffee pot boiling beside the skillet.

"Still eating bacon and eggs, I see," James greeted his grandfather.

"Not for long, I'm afraid. This is the last of the bacon," Chuck answered. "Grab your cup, coffee's ready."

The patio table had been set for breakfast for two. James grabbed both cups and carried them over for Chuck to fill. The steaming brown liquid had a woody nutty smell that wasn't like any coffee James had ever had before. "What is this?" James asked as he took a sip.

"Chicory," Chuck answered. "Been drinking the stuff for years now. You didn't expect real coffee, did you?"

The chicory beverage had a flavor that was reminiscent of coffee but was definitely not the same. Pretty good, James thought. "Not bad," he told Chuck. "Where'd you get it?"

"Chicory root. It's everywhere. Surprised you've never heard of it." Chuck looked around and pointed to a patch of wild blue weeds growing just past the gravel of the yard. "There," he said pointing at the weeds. "Those blue flowers, right there."

James was struck again by the thought that he had a lot to learn to live in this strange new world. He had to learn to live as his ancestors had lived. The technology that had been the foundation of all James had ever known was all either gone or going fast. His Grandpa cooking over an open fire was a perfect example.

As he ate the bacon and eggs that was the best breakfast he could remember having in a very long time, he asked Chuck why he didn't use the electric range in the kitchen. It seemed to James like the house had plenty of PV panels. As it turned out, the PV panels weren't the problem. Chuck's system didn't have enough battery capacity to always use the electric range. "Better to make sure the freezers keep working," Chuck told him. "Wish there was more of this bacon in there," he added. "We don't have any pigs, guess I wouldn't know how to make bacon, anyway. Got plenty of chickens, though. Don't guess we'll run out of eggs."

*The freezers will stop, too,* James thought. *None of it's going to work forever. Hell, even the solar panels won't work forever. Not only that,* he thought, *Grandpa's not going to be here forever, either.* He decided that he needed to learn as much from Chuck as he could about how to live without technology. He was sure Anna would be home soon, and he was starting to dream of having children and living here on the BR as his forefathers had done; without the aid of any modern technology.

"I sure am glad you're here, son," Chuck told him. "It's been a might lonely around here, waiting. Figured I was waiting and hoping for Anna to show up; didn't have much hope of seeing you or your mom again. Sure am glad I was wrong."

"Me too, Grandpa. Glad you waited. How long do you think it'll take Anna to get here?"

"Don't know, James. It's a damn long walk if she had to walk all the way." Chuck looked away from James, but not quick enough to hide the doubts that lay beyond the old man's dark brown eyes. "Guess now that you're here," Chuck changed the subject abruptly, "to help me, we should get that electric range out of the kitchen and put my great-grandmothers old wood cookstove in there. Always wondered why Dad kept that old antique stored out in the shop. Guess now I know."

..........

It turned out that a lot of the old antiques that had been stored on the Blue River Ranch over the past hundred years would be worth much more than the modern marvels that had replaced them. From the draft horse harnesses, to the pedal-powered grinding wheel and blacksmith forge in the old shop, to the horse drawn implements that were weathering away in the scrap heaps behind it; Chuck and James filled the days with re-learning the old ways. Having grown up on the ranch and living there his entire life, it was much easier for Chuck than it was for James, but James learned more and more every day. The one constant to everything he learned was just how much physical hard work was involved. It was hard work from sunrise to sundown every single day. The days went by one after the other, and not a day went by that James didn't think this was the day that Anna would be home. The ranch truly did become home for James, as he started losing track of time.

..........

They'd started putting up the hay crop from the mesa meadow just a couple of days after James' arrival. That had been interesting, to say the least. There hadn't been enough diesel left in Chuck's storage tank to complete the harvest using the modern implements, so they had to use a team of Belgian draft horses for part of the work. Chuck had always kept draft horses as a hobby, even using them to sometimes pull an old sled to feed cattle in the winter. To put up this year's crop of hay, Chuck had decided to do the cutting and raking with the horses, saving the diesel to power the tractor and baler. The cutting and raking worked out okay, after a lot of work in the shop getting the old horse-drawn sickle bar mower back into working condition; but the diesel ran out before they finished baling. It didn't take long for James to understand how much of an improvement baled hay had been to the old method of stacking using a horse-drawn buck rake and pitchforks. Bucking hay bales onto a wagon wasn't easy, but a lot more hay could be moved and stacked in a day than could be done the old-fashioned way. The baled hay was put into the hayloft of the log barn using an electric motor-powered hay elevator, but the loose hay they had to put up in stacks right in the field. The mechanism for lifting loose hay into the hayloft using a horse and ropes and pulleys was long gone. Chuck had commented that next year they would have to either rebuild a system to do that, or they would just have to not stack hay in the loft. Despite the hard work, James had really enjoyed learning how to harness up and work the draft horses.

Too much time had gone by with no sign of Anna. He had stopped counting days, but James was starting to drive himself crazy. He was finding it hard to concentrate, or even think about whatever task was at hand. His thoughts were constantly on Anna, wondering where she could be. He had tried not to even discuss it with Chuck anymore. He didn't want to hear any negative thoughts. Anna had to come home. She just had to. He kept thinking he should go look for her, but where? It was over a thousand miles from

Kremmling to Eugene, and the multiple possible routes of travel made the odds of finding her incredibly slim.

"I have to go," he told Chuck. They were in the process of harvesting winter squash in the garden. "I need to go find Anna."

The statement caught Chuck by surprise. He set the two butternut squash gently down in the wheelbarrow. He wasn't surprised that James had been pining away for Anna. That wasn't a well-kept secret. He was surprised that his grandson would even be considering just heading out toward Oregon with about zero chance of ever finding anything, let alone Anna.

"How you gonna do that son? She might not even be alive," he tried to be as gentle as he could. "Pretty strong odds she didn't make it, you know."

"She did make it! I know it. She's out there...somewhere. She should have made it home by now."

"I hope she's alive, too, James." Chuck was as lonely as anyone. "But hope doesn't make it so. I wish your mother was still alive, and your grandmother. God, I miss Nancy." Chuck paused, trying to find the right words. "We just have to go on living as best we can James."

"You call this living?" the anger in James' voice stung the old man as much as his words. "What are we doing, Grandpa? Why are we just holed up here like we're the last people on earth? We aren't you know. You haven't even left the ranch, have you? Since, since it happened..."

There was pain in Chuck's voice as he answered, "Yes, yes I have left the ranch. After I buried the Durans, I rode over to the Crowley place and buried John and Martha. Then I went on down to Smith's and buried the whole family, all four of them." The memory of having to bury all of his neighbors was obviously hard on Chuck. He looked off into the distance. "I didn't go any farther, James. Guess I was just too tired of burying people."

James' anger and frustration gave way to pity. He couldn't be angry at Chuck, he felt as sorry for his grandpa as he did for himself. But this life was hardly worth living. This really wasn't living, at all; it was merely, and barely existing.

"We can't just go on like this, Grandpa," his voice was soft and even. "Life isn't worth living if this is all there is."

Chuck looked down at the ground and stroked his white beard in thought. The sorrow in his eyes was painful when he looked back up at James. "You're right, son. This isn't living. Tell you what, let's finish getting the squash into the cellar, and I'll ride into Kremmling with you tomorrow. Might be somebody there; somebody to give us a better idea of...of the odds."

It was obvious to James that Chuck didn't think Anna was alive. *She has to be,* he thought. *Grandpa's wrong. He has to be wrong. I'll find her. I won't stop at Kremmling. I'll keep going until I find her, or...or...*

James was up before dawn; truth was he'd hardly even slept. Hope and doubt had waged a war in his head all night long. He couldn't wait for daylight, *bound to be enough juice in the battery for just the kitchen light,* he thought. As quietly as he could, he got the fire going in the cook stove and got the pot of ground chicory started. By the time chicory finally started simmering, he figured he had enough heat to fry some eggs. *Eggs again.* James would never have believed he would ever get tired of eggs, but with the chickens laying more than two people could ever possibly eat, they ate more eggs than any other food.

Dawn was finding its way through the open kitchen windows by the time the six eggs were turning white in the old cast iron skillet. Chuck came into the kitchen wearing only his jeans and an old white undershirt. He went straight to the kitchen sink and washed his face and hands with cold water, not even bothering to use any of the warm water from the teapot that was always on the back of the stove.

"You okay, Grandpa?" James asked. Chuck seemed pale and he wasn't moving with his usual morning vigor.

"I'm fine son," he said, as he slumped into the chair at the end of the table. "That coffee ready?"

James poured a mug of the chicory coffee and set it on the table before flipping the eggs. He poured himself a cup while the eggs finished cooking, and gave each of them a plate of eggs before sitting down at the other end of the table. Chuck hardly moved. He held the coffee mug in one hand, with the mug and his elbow resting on the table. He was looking down at his eggs. Besides the pallid look of his skin, James thought his breathing wasn't quite right. He seemed to be taking slow deliberate breaths, as he stared at the plate of eggs. James couldn't tell if he'd even drank any of the coffee.

"Grandpa, you don't look so good. You sure you're okay?" What had been mild concern was turning to fear. What if his grandpa was really sick? What would he do?

Just as James was on the edge of panic, Chuck seemed to snap out of it. "I'm fine," he said, as he straightened up in his chair and took a sip of the chicory coffee. He set the mug back down and started chopping and stirring his eggs with his fork.

*What a relief,* James thought, as he dove into his own pile of eggs; morning hunger overcoming the monotony of the same old breakfast. James wolfed down his breakfast, getting more and more anxious to start out. He was still torn between the need to go find Anna and the fear that he never would. The fear that she was gone forever, that he would end up living here alone for his whole life gnawed at him. He fought that fear with hope. He had to believe. *She has to be alive,* he told himself. *She's out there, somewhere. She has to be. I'll find her alive, just like I found Grandpa.*

He looked up at his grandpa. Chuck was eating much slower than James. Slower even than normal. He seemed to be pushing eggs around on his plate more than putting them in his mouth. "Listen, Grandpa," James told him, as he got up and carried his plate over to the sink, "you don't have to go if you don't feel like it. Why don't you just stay here and rest? I'll ride into town and find out what I can. I promise I'll be back tonight." It would be a long hard day to ride all the way into Kremmling and back, but as much as he wanted to just strike out toward Oregon, he didn't want Chuck to have to make that ride if he was sick.

"I'm fine," Chuck told him, for at least the third time. "Go get our horses saddled up while I clean up breakfast. If we're going to ride all the way to town and back, we better get started."

James hesitated, but only for a moment. He was driven by a relentless hope, and equally as relentless fear that just wouldn't let go. Already dressed in his riding clothes, he headed out to the barn to saddle up Red and Midnight.

With the horses ready to go and tied up in the barn, James walked back toward the house. It seemed like Chuck should have been out by now. "Hey, Grandpa," he hollered from the mudroom on his way to the kitchen, "you ready to go?" He stepped through the kitchen door and froze.

Everything was almost the same as he'd left it. The chicory coffee pot was still steaming on the wood-burning stove, as was the large hot water tea kettle. Chuck's coffee mug sat on the table, still more than half full. His plate still had most of the pile of eggs drying in place, but the fork was laying upside down and sideways off to the edge of the table. Some egg had splattered out onto the table where the fork had fallen. Chuck wasn't exactly seated at the table. It looked like he'd dropped his fork and pushed himself back away from the table. But he never got up. He was slumped down in the chair, his hands dangling down below the arms of the chair that held him in place. His head was lolled forward with his chin resting on his chest; his dead eyes forever staring straight down. James' mind seized up. He stood there staring, knowing with certainty that his grandfather was dead, yet comprehending nothing. He was lost.

# Chapter 17

T HE SOFT GLOW ON the eastern horizon slowly brightens and the world suddenly springs to life, as the sun seems to leap over the peaks to the east. *Already quite a ways south,* he thinks, seeing the sunrise, and he wonders what day it is. James isn't even sure what month it is. *Must be October. Doesn't seem like October, I don't even need a jacket.*

James is sitting on the bench directly behind the headstones of the Pierson family cemetery. He has been sitting in that same spot since the sun dropped off the western edge of the world yesterday evening. He has to pee, but his body seems frozen in place. Standing and stretching only makes the necessity more urgent. He looks around as if someone might see him if he just opened his fly and pissed right here. *Wouldn't be respectful,* he thinks and walks over behind the three big Blue Spruce trees that his great grandfather planted behind the cemetery some seventy or eighty years ago.

*What now?* The thought seems strange. *His grave needs a cross. Why? Who's ever going to see it? I'm the only one left. Why me? What now?* He is back sitting on the bench in exactly the same place where he spent the night. He looks up from the earth that he finished mounding over the grave just before sunset last night. The sun has climbed a little way up the cloudless sky. That totally clear, deep blue sky that seems unique to the Rocky Mountains.

*I should be hungry.* It seems like a strange thought, even though he has had nothing to eat since yesterday morning.

*Why should I eat? To live?* He almost laughs. *They're all gone.* His eyes scan the markers of the final resting place of the sons and daughters of the Blue River Ranch. The markers vary from the old granite headstones of his great, great, great grandparents to the four simple wooden crosses where Chuck had buried the Duran family just six months ago. The four Duran family graves with their simple wooden crosses are arranged with a space between two sets of two crosses.

*Grandpa left a spot for Anna,* he thinks. *Mother should be buried here too. Not where I left her, back in Castle Pines. I should have brought her.* He thinks back to the journey from Castle Pines. *Could have been done, I could have brought her body.* He has a memory flash from childhood of one of Grandpa Chuck's favorite shows, Lonesome Dove. An image of the wrapped-up body of Gus McCrae draped over the back of a horse being carried back to the spot in Texas where he wanted to spend eternity.

*What's the point? They're all dead. Dead is dead. I'm alive. Why? Why am I still alive?* His eyes are a little blurred, but not crying, there is a kind of lump, almost a pain in his throat. He is barely conscious of the .357 revolver that he is holding in his lap.

*Why not Julie? I loved Julie, why shouldn't she be here? She should be here, but you didn't bring her. Anna should be here, too. You loved Anna more than you ever loved Julie, but you ran out on her. You ran out on Anna, and you left Julie to rot in that hell hole. At least I buried her with Mother. You should have buried them here with Grandpa.*

He doesn't really even notice that he is raising the big revolver as he argues with himself. It's more like it moves of its own volition. He looks again at the space where Anna should be buried. *Who'll bury me?*

A movement catches his eye. There, down in the valley below, on the lane leading from old Highway 9 up to the ranch. At first, it doesn't register, then he realizes it's a horse. A horse with a rider coming up the lane toward the ranch. Too far away to tell for sure, the rider seems to have long black hair, it seems to be a woman. A lone rider coming up the road to the BR.

*Looks like Anna. Can't be Anna, Anna's dead. Dead with the rest of them. But it looks like Anna. You must be hallucinating. But it looks like Anna. You know it can't be Anna, Anna's dead.*

The big revolver, which seems to move with a life of its own, as he argues with himself, stops and hovers, suspended in mid-flight, the end of the barrel just inches below his chin.

·····•·•····

**Somewhere high overhead, the chilling sound of an eagle's scream pierces the quiet stillness of the Colorado morning.**

# THE FLIGHT TO BLUE RIVER

## Thermals Of Time - Book Two

# Dedication

**For Casey**

**No one, other than her mother, has so profoundly affected my life.**

# PART ONE

In the beginning, our beginning, Mother Earth gave us life. Mother Earth is not Planet Earth. Mother Earth is the life-giver, from which all life springs.

Mother Earth gave life to all living things. To plants and animals, to birds and fish, and even the planet itself. Did you not know that this planet is a living thing?

When Mother Earth gave the first humans life,

she could not know that
humans were like a virus.
She could not know how
fast we would multiply
and how far we would
spread.

Mother Earth gave us
life, and in turn, we
brought death to so
much of what once
was good. Other life
vanished. The corals
and fish in the sea;
on land, animals and
plants beyond count, and
wondrous birds in the
air. All diminished or
extinct. Even the great
eagles no longer soar
where once they were
king.

Know you this, Mother
Earth will defend the
life of this planet. Man's
reign will end, and the
eagles will return. In
time, balance will once

again be restored to this
world. — *Mystic Martin
2030*

# Chapter 1

T HERE HAD ONLY BEEN two weeks to go until the end of the semester, just a month to go until her twenty-first birthday. That's when the world ended. At least the world Anna had always known came to a sudden halt. Not only her junior year at the University of Oregon but basically the United States Of America, as she'd always known it, came to a sudden unexpected end.

Anna was testing a newly modified storage battery at the lab, where she'd spent a great deal of time over the past three years. Majoring in electrical engineering, she spent more time doing hands-on work in the lab than she spent studying theory in a classroom. It was getting late, but she was just about finished with this round of testing when she felt the com vibrate in her lab coat. Will was onscreen as soon as she pulled the com out of her pocket.

"You better come home," he said, without so much as a hello. The look on his face accentuated the concern in his voice.

"What's wrong?" It was all too obvious to Anna that something terrible must have happened.

"People are dying," was not the response that Anna expected.

Will worked at the McKenzie-Willamette hospital while doing his pre-med studies at the University of Oregon. He'd worked there since he and Anna arrived in Eugene three years ago. People always died at McKenzie-Willamette. So, why was Will so agitated?

"What do you mean, people are dying?" she asked.

"At the hospital," Will managed to get out, before coughing.

"I'm just about finished," she told him. "I should be home in an hour or so."

"You don't understand," Will told her before being wracked by a severe fit of coughing.

*He doesn't look well,* Anna thought, noticing that Will seemed too pallid, and there were beads of sweat on his forehead.

"Are you alright?" she asked, even though the answer was obvious.

"Not so good," Will managed to get out between spasms of coughing. "Hurry," he said, and her screen went blank.

Tendrils of fear were working their way through her thoughts as she hurriedly started shutting down the battery test. *What was that all about? Will is obviously sick, but he seemed just fine when we got up this morning. What did he mean, people are dying at the hospital?*

When Anna got home to the duplex they had lived in for the past three years, she found Will sitting in front of the comscreen in his favorite chair. He was wrapped up like a mummy in a blanket that he must have dug out of the back of the closet. There was a newscaster on the comscreen talking about some hurricane and an earthquake somewhere, but Anna didn't pay much attention to the com. Her attention was focused on Will.

How could he stand to be wrapped up like that? It felt like it must be eighty degrees in their apartment.

She hurried across the room and didn't even need to touch his forehead to feel the heat coming off of him. *My god, he's burning up,* she thought. He seemed to be asleep.

"Will, wake up!" she shook his shoulders. *I need to get him to the hospital,* was her first thought. Then, *he just came from the hospital.* A moan and a cough were the only responses from Will.

*That fever will kill him,* she thought. She rushed into the bathroom and started filling the tub with cold water, as cold as it would get anyway. With high temperatures averaging around a hundred degrees lately, water from the tap was not that cold. She added a binful of ice from the ice-maker to the water. Then she ran back to Will and pulled the blanket off of him. She gently slapped his face trying to get him to wake up. Another moan was all she got for her efforts.

Will weighed about a hundred and seventy pounds to Anna's hundred and twenty, but Anna was a strong girl. You don't grow up on a ranch working cattle with a family of men without developing quite a bit of strength. Reaching under his arms and wrapping hers around him, she was able to drag him to the tub and literally drop him into the water. Even that didn't wake Will up. She had to quickly pull him back to a semi-seated position to keep his head above water. Then she faced a real quandary. She wanted to do more, though she didn't know what. Her com was back on the table in the other room, but who could she call? Will's words, "people are dying," came back to her, and she was gripped by fear. Was Will dying? Was everyone at the hospital already dead? What the hell was it?

Anna coughed, and a new fear hit. *Do I have it, too?* She didn't feel sick, but then Will had been perfectly fine less than twelve hours ago. *And now he's dying.* That thought shook her into action. She couldn't leave Will's side, she had to hold onto him so he wouldn't just slide under the water and drown.

"Raven," she yelled at her com. Anna had always called her com Raven, after the ability of the large black birds to communicate over long distances. "Raven, call the hospital." Not hearing any response from her com, she yelled, "Raven, maximum volume!"

"Which hospital?" her com asked from the other room.

"McKenzie-Willamette," she yelled back.

After what seemed like an eternity, her com informed her that no one was answering. "Call PeaceHealth," she yelled back.

After not getting through to either one of the hospitals and no answer from 9-1-1, Anna was at a loss. More than that, she felt lost. She looked at Will through tears she hadn't realized were in her eyes and could tell that his breathing was getting shallow and ragged. *This can't be happening.* The thought was a vain protest. Anna knew without a doubt that it was happening. Will Donovan, her fiancé, the man she'd followed to Oregon and lived with for three years, was dying, and there was absolutely nothing she could do.

......•.•....

Anna wasn't sure if it was the sunlight streaming through the window or the noise of the newscast coming from the comscreen that woke her up. As soon as she was awake, the events of the night before came rushing back into her consciousness. Her deep brown eyes were red and swollen from crying. She couldn't have been asleep for long, but the sun was high enough in the sky that it had to be mid-morning. Her neck was stiff from sleeping with her head on the arm of the sofa. The big comscreen on the living room wall was still on with an unfamiliar female newscaster who started sobbing on air.

A newscaster sobbing while live on the air was unexpected enough, but she really got Anna's attention as she uttered the words, *"I can't."* Anna's attention was riveted to the screen as a couple of military looking people basically picked up the well-dressed woman who had been broadcasting the news, and escorted her off-camera. A third man dressed in a much fancier military uniform took the woman's place in front of the camera. Anna didn't know much about military insignia, but she knew by the four stars that this man was some kind of general or something. She listened, almost spellbound, as the man spoke.

*My fellow Americans, I am sorry you had to witness the fake news that was just forced upon you. This was a blatant attempt by certain factions in the military to sow doubt and discord among us.*

Anna had slept through the news of the hurricane and the tsunami hitting the northeastern United States, so she had no idea what the general was talking about. But at least it momentarily took her mind off of Will, lying dead in the bathtub. The general continued:

*Rest assured that the government of the United States is safe and secure. In order to maintain that security, the country has been placed under martial law, effective immediately. All banks and financial institutions, as well as all food production and distribution facilities, have now been placed under direct government control. A nationwide dusk to dawn curfew will take effect immediately. Please remain in your homes after dark.*

The general onscreen now had Anna's total and undivided attention.

*To provide security and to protect the legitimate government of the United States from the forces that assail us, all broadcast systems and all personal communications will be shut down immediately. Please leave all coms in standby mode in order to receive further updates as they are made available. Thank you for your cooperation. God bless America.*

The screen went dark and silent practically before the general finished speaking. Anna sat and stared at the screen. What was that all about? She realized she was probably in shock, but that couldn't be driving her total lack of comprehension. What the hell was going on? Then she coughed and realized she didn't feel one hundred percent well. Fear gripped her again. Did she have what Will died of? She didn't really want to go back into the bathroom, but she had to pee.

She tried not to look at Will, but she couldn't help herself. It was strange, but he mostly just looked peaceful. Like he'd just decided to take a nap, fully clothed, reclining in a bathtub full of tepid water.

*I need to call his mom,* she thought, and then remembered what the general had said about all personal communications being shut down. Returning to the living room, she grabbed her com just as another small coughing fit took hold. Now she wanted to call 9-1-1 for herself, but the words "NO SERVICE" were prominently displayed on the screen. She felt a chill. Grabbing the blanket that she'd pulled off of Will last night, she snuggled into the same recliner where she'd found him and wrapped the blanket around herself. *Guess I'm exposed, I'm probably going to die,* she thought. In all the years of her young life, Anna had never been as scared as she was right at that moment.

..........

The room was dark. Anna felt like she was being suffocated. It was the blanket that had her wrapped up like a mummy. *I'm alive.* The thought seemed strange until she remembered sitting in the recliner, thinking she was going to die.

She threw the blanket off, whatever fever she'd had earlier was gone. She didn't even seem to have a cough. She wondered how long she'd been asleep. Judging by the fact that it appeared to be the middle of the night, she must have slept for at least twelve hours. She was hungry. *How long has it been since I had anything to eat?* she wondered. The events of the past couple of days were fresh in her mind, but it was like she woke up in a different world than the one she went to sleep in.

Other than thinking it would be nice to have a shower, she paid Will's body in the bathtub little mind as she used the toilet and then washed her hands and face. She undressed and gave herself a sponge bath, occasionally glancing at Will in the mirror. *I have to contact the authorities,* she thought. *Maybe they can get in touch with Will's mom.* Since Will didn't have a father, and he was an only child, it seemed extra crucial that his mother should know of his death. *Why?* she wondered. *Do I just want someone to share my sorrow?*

Anna took one last look at Will and let the overwhelming sorrow wash over her once again before turning and walking out of the bathroom. She went to their bedroom and had a hard time deciding what to wear. She had no idea what she was dressing for. It certainly wasn't going to be just another day at school. She ended up in khaki shorts, a light chambray shirt, and her light hiking boots. She decided on the light hikers after remembering how most forms of transportation stopped working the last time the internet went offline, back at the start of the Great Mid-East War. It was a couple of miles to the police station, but Anna was used to hiking. Hiking had always been one of her and Will's favorite activities. During the past two years, the two of them had hiked trails all over the state.

Back in the kitchen, she threw a couple of frozen waffles into the toaster and waited impatiently for them to heat up. Looking at the glowing orange wires down in the toaster, she was once again amazed at the simplicity of the technology that had toasted bread for well over a hundred years. Anna had been fascinated by technology for as long as she could remember. Especially electrical technology. While most people from her generation were more into electronics and computers, Anna was fascinated by electricity itself. Fascinated by all the different methods one could use to produce electric power, and by the incredible multitude of uses for that power once it was made available. That's why she had decided to study electrical engineering. She loved figuring out the way things worked and how to make things work better.

After eating the waffles in a hurry, and checking her com one more time, Anna stuffed a couple of protein bars into her pocket and stepped out into the hot midday sun. The duplex was on a quiet street, but there was absolutely no one in sight in either direction as she looked up and down the road. It seemed not just quiet but eerily silent. On a whim, Anna decided to see if Cheryl and Jasper were home. Jasper and Cheryl lived in the other half of the duplex.

Anna knocked on the door and waited. She couldn't hear any sound from inside at all, so she banged on the door even harder. Still nothing, so she turned and started walking toward the police station. The intersection with Gilham Road was only about a quarter of a mile away, so it didn't take long to get there, but she didn't see a single vehicle pass through the intersection as she walked toward it. When she got to the intersection, it was easy to see why. Autonomous vehicles were stalled out, blocking the road in both directions. *Just like what happened during the Great Mid-East War,* she thought. To the north, nothing was moving as far as Anna could see. There were a couple of people several blocks to the south. They seemed to be walking away from her, headed in the same direction she was.

Anna started walking faster, thinking she might catch up to whoever it was on the road ahead of her. It seemed really strange that they were the only people in sight. She was just over a block away from Cal Young Road when the couple ahead of her stopped walking at that intersection. As Anna got closer, it became clear that the two people were a man and a woman, probably middle-aged or older, from the look of them. When she first saw them, the couple had been walking side by side. By the time they got to the intersection with Cal Young, the man was obviously supporting the woman and helping her walk.

As Anna got close to the elderly couple, two more people on an electric scooter came toward them from the east. The scooter was making its way west along Cal Young Road, mainly by staying on the sidewalk that wasn't blocked by dead autonomous vehicles.

*Damn, wish I could have borrowed Jasper's scooter,* Anna thought. Not that she minded walking, but she could have made it to the police station that much quicker.

The scooter stopped next to the man and woman, and Anna noticed that the younger looking man who was sitting on the back of the scooter was actually the one doing the driving. The other passenger was another man who was slumped over in front of the driver. The driver was holding the front passenger, who was unconscious, in place.

"I'll come back for her as soon as I get my dad to PeaceHealth," Anna heard the scooter driver tell the older man who was supporting the woman on the sidewalk. The scooter pulled away just as Anna came up behind the elderly couple.

"Let me help," Anna told the man, who she could now see was quite old. He was probably at least in his seventies, and he was now totally supporting the woman. The old lady, apparently the man's wife, seemed to have fainted or lost consciousness.

"Thank you," the old man said, as Anna grabbed the other side of the old woman and took some of the weight off his straining arm.

"Let's set her down here on the grass," Anna told him, gently pulling the couple over to the manicured grass along the side of the walk.

The old man didn't resist as Anna helped him gently ease the old woman to a lying position on the soft grass. He held the woman's hand as he and Anna knelt on the ground beside her.

"Thank you," the man said again. "She's my wife," he added, stating what was already apparent to Anna. "She's sick," he said, still not telling Anna anything that wasn't already obvious.

The old woman was burning up just like Will had been, and she seemed to be having trouble breathing. Having watched Will die, Anna knew that the old woman didn't have more than a few minutes left to live. A strange emotional coldness came over Anna. She felt detached. Detached from herself, detached from reality. Part of her felt pity for this poor old man who was about to lose his wife. Part of her was so drained of emotion that she couldn't feel sympathy for anyone, not even herself.

*I'm in shock,* Anna thought. *We must all be in shock. At least those of us who are still alive, that is.* That thought really shook her. She remembered how the man and woman had been walking side by side when she first saw them less than an hour ago. And now, here she was looking down at a dying woman. What the hell was it? What kind of sickness or disease could kill people so quickly?

"I'm sorry," she told the old man. "I lost my fiancé."

Anna looked the old man in the eye, and she could see that he knew his wife would die. "What is this?" he asked. "How can everyone just be dying? If this is a nightmare, why don't I wake up?"

*And why are the two of us alive, and not even sick?* That was the burning question in Anna's mind. "Have you been sick?" she asked the man.

"I was a little bit under the weather when I got home last night," he answered. "But Sandy was fine. Now look, she's," he paused, not wanting to say the words. "She's dying," he managed to get out.

*It has to be some kind of virus or something,* Anna thought. *But what virus or sickness can spread and kill this fast?* As if cued by the thought, the old woman lying on the ground drew in a ragged, rattling breath and just stopped breathing.

"No!" the old man cried. "Not Sandy. Why?" He covered his face with his hands, sobbing, and sat down on the grass, next to his dead wife.

Anna stood and looked up and down the streets in every direction. There was no one. *Are they all dead?* When she left the duplex, her only thought was to get to the police station because she couldn't dial 9-1-1. She needed an ambulance or a mortuary or someone to come and take Will's body away. That's what happened to dead people. Someone came and took them away. *What happens when the dead outnumber the living? Outnumber the living? What if it's just him and me?* She looked at the old man sitting in the grass, sobbing.

Just as despair was about to incapacitate her, Anna saw a movement out of the corner of her eye. She looked up and saw a motorcycle weaving around and between the stalled out vehicles on Cal Young Road. The motorcycle was coming toward them, and as it got closer, she could see that it was one of Eugene's motorcycle cops. *Thank god!* The feeling of relief was almost overwhelming. The police were still on duty.

The policeman stopped his motorcycle at the curb, took off his helmet and looked at Anna and the old man like he must be looking at ghosts. He looked like a ghost himself. His face was ashen.

"They're all dead," the policeman said, seemingly to no one. He, too, was obviously in a state of shock.

"Who's dead?" Anna asked, not really wanting to know the answer.

The policeman looked at her like she'd just asked a ridiculous question. "All of them," he answered.

"All of who?" Anna asked.

"The station," he said simply. "Everyone at the station is dead."

Anna looked from the policeman sitting on his motorcycle to the old man sobbing on the ground beside his dead wife. She looked up at the clear blue sky, and then back down at the totally quiet city street. She started to turn around, then stopped and turned back toward the policeman.

"Where are you going?" she asked him. But the real question in her mind was, *where am I going?* There was obviously no reason to go on down to the police station. Was there a reason to go anywhere? If so, where? No sooner had the questions gone through her mind than she knew the answer. *I have to get back to the BR. Back to my family.* Thoughts of the Blue River Ranch, and her family, as always, were immediately followed by memories of James Mendez.

*They have to be alive,* was the only thought in her head as she turned away from the policeman and started walking back the way she'd come, oblivious to anything else the policeman might have said.

Anna was about half-way back home before she saw another living person. This one was a woman in her backyard with a shovel digging a hole. From the street, Anna couldn't see the hole in detail, but she knew without a doubt that the woman was digging a grave. Maybe more than one grave, for all Anna knew. *Guess I better bury Will before I go,* she thought, and she didn't bother to talk to the woman at all.

Digging a hole in the small backyard of the duplex was harder than Anna would have thought. It had taken her a couple of hours worth of hard labor in the hot afternoon sun to dig a big enough hole to be a shallow grave for Will. She leaned on her shovel and looked at the neighbor's backyard on the other side of the white vinyl fence. *What about Jasper and Cheryl,* she thought. They must be dead, too. Logical thinking was beginning to overcome the emotional freefall that she'd been in for the past two days. She looked at the other back yards all neatly lined up side by side, facing another row of back yards across the alley. There was no other living soul in sight. *Jesus! How many dead people are there?* She looked back at the other half of her duplex. *Can't bury them all,* she thought, as she headed inside to drag Will's body out to his final resting place.

············

Anna knew she was within ten or fifteen miles of Bend when the scooter battery finally gave out. She'd taken Jasper's electric scooter after breaking into their side of the duplex and finding both him and Cheryl dead. As she parked the scooter off the edge of the road, she remembered how Jasper and Cheryl had been when she discovered their bodies. They were in their bed. It appeared that Cheryl had died first, and Jasper had laid down beside her and wrapped his arm around her dead body. Anna had simply left them lying together in that eternal embrace.

With a backpack full of supplies strapped to her back and her pistol in the holster on her hip, Anna started walking toward Bend. There weren't nearly as many vehicles stalled out on Highway 20 as there had been near Eugene. None at all, as far as she could see, on this particular stretch of highway. The way she was dressed, with the full backpack and wide-brimmed trekking hat, she would have looked more at home in the evergreen forests that lined both sides of the road than she did walking down the paved shoulder of the highway.

The few vehicles that had stalled out on Highway 20 didn't block the road here like they did in more congested areas. Most had simply stopped in the lane they were in when the navigation systems went down, so the other lane was open. A human-driven vehicle could simply go around the stalled cars and trucks without ever leaving the pavement.

Anna had at least part of a plan brewing in the back of her mind. As many people as there were dead, she figured she could "borrow" someone else's non-autonomous vehicle and drive it however far it would go on the charge in the batteries. Then, she'd simply have to "borrow" another one and continue on. Seeing how open the road was once she got away from more populated areas, she decided she would try to stick to less-traveled roads and less populated areas. Having grown up on the Blue River Ranch near Kremmling, Colorado, sparsely populated areas with roads less traveled should feel a lot like home.

With the sun just starting to go down behind the mountains to the west, Anna decided that the next order of business was to make camp for the night. She knew she could get to Bend before dark, but the Oregon woods offered a feeling of comfort and security that another dead town could never match. She climbed the grass-covered embankment on the side of the road and disappeared into the woods.

# Chapter 2

F INDING THE FIRST VEHICLE to borrow had been really easy. Anna hadn't even walked all the way to Bend before deciding to start taking a look at some of the farms she was passing by. Some of these places looked like they'd been prosperous for decades. Nice farms that had probably been owned and operated by multiple generations of the same family. She picked a farm about halfway between Tumalo and Bend. It had a large old red brick farmhouse that was only about a quarter of a mile back from the highway. Actually, she didn't pick this particular farm so much as Katy picked her.

The dog started barking at her before she even got to the lane that led up to the house. All black except for a white patch around its right eye and a white star in the middle of its chest, the dog looked like some kind of cross between a poodle and a border collie. It would come no closer to the highway than the fenceline that marked the farm's boundary. As Anna approached the drive, the dog kept coming out toward the road and barking. It would come to the edge of the property, look at Anna, bark a couple of times like it was trying to tell her something, and then turn and start trotting back toward the house. Then it would stop, turn to look back at Anna, and trot back out to the end of the drive to bark at her some more.

*It's like he's trying to tell me something,* Anna thought. She started walking toward the dog, who immediately turned and started trotting back up the lane. The dog ran a few yards up the drive, stopped, and looked back. Seeing that Anna was still following, the dog turned and went further up the lane before stopping, and once again looking back. *He's making sure I'm following.* Anna had grown up around some excellent stock dogs, and she recognized a smart dog when she saw one.

"Good dog," she said, by way of encouragement. The dog said nothing, just turned and padded on up the lane.

With Anna following, the dog went straight up to the back door of the farmhouse, raised a paw and scratched at the door. It whined or whimpered a little as Anna caught up. There was an expression of sadness in the dog's brown eyes. Anna reached down and patted the wooly fur on top of the dog's head. "It's okay," she said as she scratched behind the dog's ears and looked at the black leather collar around its neck. There was a metal tag on the collar with the dog's name, Katy, engraved on it. "So, you aren't a he at all, are you?" Anna said as she continued petting the dog.

Katy looked from Anna back to the door and scratched at it again. "Okay, okay," Anna said as she first knocked loudly on the door, and then when there was no sound at all from inside the house, she reached down to turn the doorknob. To her surprise, the door wasn't locked. Anna had no more than pushed the door open a crack when Katy knocked the door out of her hand and bounded into the house.

Anna followed Katy and found herself in an old-fashioned mudroom that led into a homey kitchen. She could hear Katy whining further on into the house.

Following the sound, she walked into a spacious living room. Katy was sitting on her haunches in front of a large sofa, whining at the obviously dead woman stretched out under a blanket. The woman couldn't have been dead more than a day. Anna was surprised to see that she was quite young, probably just a few years older than herself. For some reason, she'd envisioned nothing but old people living in this old farmhouse.

Anna found another body in the master bedroom. A man who was probably the dead woman's husband. The man had obviously died before the woman downstairs, and the smell of death permeated the air in the bedroom. Anna closed the bedroom door and went back downstairs in a hurry.

·····•··•·····

That had been the day before yesterday. "Well, it looks like time to start walking again," Anna told Katy, as the old F-150E came to a stop on the edge of Highway 26 just east of Vale, only a few miles from the Idaho border. The old electric pickup truck that she'd commandeered at Katy's farm had done well. Over three hundred miles before the battery died. At that rate, it would only take a couple more vehicles and a few more days to get home.

Katy had come with Anna, of course. If it was Katy's farm, since Anna didn't know the dead people's names, then the truck, which she found in the old metal shop, must have also belonged to Katy. The dog certainly seemed at home in the passenger seat with her head hanging out of the open window.

Katy pulled her head back inside and looked at Anna. Why are we stopping? She seemed to be asking. "Out of juice," Anna answered the unspoken question as she reached over and scratched behind Katy's ears. "Hungry?" she asked. Katy didn't answer. She just pricked up her ears and tilted her head slightly. Anna wasn't sure if it was a questioning look, or if the dog was simply turning her head into Anna's scratching fingers. One thing Anna was sure of was that Katy really liked being scratched behind the ears.

Anna stepped out of the truck with Katy right behind her. She opened the back door and grabbed one of the cans of Allpro that she'd stashed behind the driver's seat. The Allpro had also come from Katy's farm. Anna had found what looked like a lifetime supply in the massive pantry of the old house. Using the spork from her backpack, Anna scooped about half of the Allpro into Katy's bowl, which she'd also brought from the farm. Then she poured some water into the other half of Katy's two-sided bowl.

Katy lapped up some of the water and just looked at the Allpro before looking up at Anna. With a sporkfull of the Allpro already in her mouth, Anna had to laugh. She swallowed the Allpro and said, "Not very good, is it?" to Katy, who kept looking down at the bowl of Allpro then back up at Anna with a questioning look on her face. "Guess I'm not sure that it's real food either," Anna told the dog, as she threw the half-full can of Allpro into the back of the truck.

Katy looked extremely grateful as she scarfed down the half of a protein bar that Anna gave her, before dumping the Allpro out of the dog's bowl. There wasn't enough room in Anna's pack for Katy's bowl, so Anna rigged a way to tie it on. She was glad to have Katy's company, but she didn't want to share dishes with her.

This part of the world was truly farm country. They were in a broad flat valley of fields full of the spring greenery of young crops. As they started walking toward Idaho, Anna couldn't help but wonder at the vagaries of climate change. What made this part of the western U.S. so much wetter than most of the parched land? Maybe it was just close enough to the Pacific Northwest that it got spillover moisture. Whatever it was, Anna knew that it wasn't much farther south or east in either direction, before she'd get to the real drought-stricken parts of the country. The last time she talked to her folks, they'd told her there had been practically no snow at the Blue River Ranch during the previous winter. As Anna walked along, with Katy right beside her, she wondered if her parents and brothers were okay. Her dad had seemed so happy when he heard that she was coming home soon. That was back a few days ago when she and Will had been planning on going home for a visit at the end of the trimester. Not in her wildest nightmare would she have dreamed she'd be going home this way, crossing a dead and dying land. Going home alone, with Will dead and buried back in Eugene.

There was an emptiness in Anna's heart where Will used to be. A hollowness inside where something had been carved out. Maybe it wasn't just Will. Maybe it was the overwhelming loss of everything. Life, as she'd always known it, was gone. What about her mom and dad? Her brothers? What about Chuck Pierson, who was more like a grandfather to her than just her dad's employer? And what about James? *God damn you, James!* The thought was unbidden and shocked her. *Why? Why did he do it? How could he just cut it off like that? And why can't I stop thinking about him?*

Anna shook her head and reached up to brush the tears from her eyes. She hadn't even realized she was crying until she stumbled and almost tripped on a rock at the edge of the road. Wiping her eyes with the back of her hand cleared her vision, but she knew she had to get her emotions under control. Yes, the man she had agreed to marry was gone. And yes, she had loved Will. But as she thought about it, she came to a sobering realization. Losing Will wasn't as bad as losing James had been. She'd lost James a long time ago, whether he was alive or not. And now, here she was trudging along toward Idaho, hoping against hope that she would find him again. Hoping to find him and hating him all at the same time. Hating him for leaving. Hating him for the fact that she wouldn't even be here if he hadn't broken her heart in the first place.

Katy, who was a few paces ahead, stopped suddenly and forced Anna to look up from her wandering thoughts. The dog's ears were pricked up, and she had her full attention focused toward an intersection that Anna could see about a quarter of a mile ahead. A sign on the shoulder of the road told her they were approaching the Oregon Highway 201 junction. At first, all she noticed was a couple of stalled vehicles right at the intersection. Then she saw what had caught Katy's attention.

There was one car, from here it looked like an older Tesla, that was pulled off on the right-hand shoulder of the road. Anna noticed that the driver's door was open just as a woman stepped out of the car and stood up. Anna had been looking down, not paying any attention, but Katy must have heard the car door open. Anna wasn't close enough to tell for sure, but it looked like a young woman. She definitely had long blonde hair that she was pushing away from her face as she turned and saw Anna. The woman waved, and Katy's tail started wagging. Anna raised her hand and waved back.

Anna picked up their pace, almost running. It had only been a couple of days, but it would be so nice to talk to another living human.

"Hi," the girl yelled as she reached down to pet Katy, who had run on ahead.

"Hi," Anna said as she got close. "God, it's good to see somebody else alive." The woman was definitely young. Probably even younger than Anna.

"Oh my god! It really is." The blonde girl was almost giggling as she reached up and grabbed Anna by both arms. "I'm Heather," she said. Her blue eyes were glistening with tears, and Anna couldn't tell if it was joy or sorrow.

"I'm Anna," she said and realized there were tears in her own eyes, as well. Heather had a huge smile on her face that matched the one she knew was on her own. She put her arms around the total stranger, and they stood hugging each other in a silent embrace.

Katy barked, and Anna pulled herself away from Heather. She looked down at Katy, who seemed to be wanting a hug too. "And this is Katy," she said as she stooped down and did give Katy a hug.

# Chapter 3

A S THE THREE OF them, Anna, Heather, and Katy, walked south on 26 toward Nyssa, the two young women were eagerly sharing their life stories. Sharing simple human companionship was such a treat that they practically forgot to even look for their next vehicle. Anna learned that Heather was a year younger, just twenty years old. She had been going to school at the University of Washington in Seattle when the sickness hit. Now, much like Anna, she was trying to get home to learn the fate of her own family. Home for Heather was Pocatello, Idaho. Deciding to travel together didn't actually even require a decision. Anna figured they might have to split up before they made it all the way to Pocatello. Or maybe not. Depending on what route she decided to take, Pocatello wasn't much out of her way at all.

Walking and talking, they'd covered about five miles when Anna spotted an old Tesla Cybertruck parked in a driveway just off the road. Nyssa was just down the road, but there was no guarantee that there would be anything available there. "Let's try that one," she told Heather, pointing toward the truck.

"What if there's somebody there?" Heather asked. Having driven her own Tesla all the way from Seattle, "borrowing" someone else's car still seemed a lot like stealing to her.

"Guess we'll find out," Anna answered as she started walking up toward the front door of the house.

After ringing the doorbell and waiting, knocking as loudly as possible and waiting some more, then ringing the doorbell again, there was still no answer. Anna tried the door, but it was locked.

"What now?" Heather asked. She'd stood back off the edge of the porch watching nervously while Anna pounded on the door.

"Well..." Anna walked past Heather letting the word hang in the air. She walked up to the Cybertruck and found it locked as well, which did not surprise her at all. The truck was still plugged into a wall charger, so it probably had a full battery. She continued on around to the back of the house with Heather right on her heels.

Banging on the back door was as futile as knocking on the front door had been. All of the racket on the outside was answered by dead silence inside, and Anna was pretty sure that dead was the operative word. She looked around for an easy way to break into the house. All they needed was the fob that would grant them access to the Tesla.

Heather watched with trepidation as Anna grabbed a rock from the border of a flower bed and used it to shatter the glass window that made up most of the top half of the back door. A siren immediately started going off in the house. The burglar alarm was deafening, but Anna was undeterred. She calmly used the rock to break out the shards of glass that were still sticking out of the frame where she wanted to reach inside. Anna reached carefully in through the broken window and unlatched the door.

Heather was looking around wildly like she expected the police to show up at any minute.

The wailing siren was really deafening inside the house. Fortunately, Anna didn't have to go far. She spotted the cute brass basket on the wall as soon as she stepped inside. It was hanging just inside the door with a couple of car fobs and some other keys filling the small basket. The control for the alarm was directly below it, a flashing red light keeping time with the siren. Anna grabbed both of the fobs and got back out of the house as fast as she could. The blaring siren was a lot easier on the ears once she was back around the corner of the house.

She tossed one of the fobs to Heather, who had preceded her back around the house. Heather had to pull her hands down away from her ears to catch the fob that Anna threw her way. It turned out that Anna would only have needed one of the fobs. They were identical; apparently, one for him and one for her. She pushed the unlock button, and the truck's lights flashed. As she disconnected the charge cord and closed the charge access door, she thought of something that she'd noticed inside the house. There'd been a light on in the kitchen. The old farmhouse didn't have any solar panels or a wind turbine, and there hadn't been any sound of a generator before the burglar alarm drowned out everything else.

*The power grid must still be live here,* she thought. For Anna, who was well on her way to becoming a full-fledged electrical engineer, the fact that the grid was still functioning raised some interesting questions. Were there people somewhere still alive at some of the power grid control centers, or were the computerized systems still working autonomously? Probably the latter, she decided, as she put her backpack and Katy in the back seat of the

Cybertruck. As bad as her ears were ringing, she could only imagine what Katy must be feeling. She waited for Heather to deposit her suitcase in the back and get in before pulling out of the driveway and heading south. The rolling bag that Heather had pulled all the way from her car, along with Anna's backpack, didn't leave much room in the back seat for Katy, but the dog didn't seem to mind.

Through the ringing in her ears, Anna heard Heather ask, "what if somebody comes back for this truck?"

Anna looked over at her and then back at the road before answering. "Guess they'll just have to find another one," she said.

·····•·····

The bridge was blocked. Anna looked it over. Two autonomous freight haulers had apparently both shutdown as they met each other right in the middle of the Highway 26 bridge across the Snake River. They'd both tried to pull over to the shoulder as they coasted to a shutdown. The result was that the two semis were sitting diagonally on the bridge, blocking not only the travel lanes but the shoulders as well. Having a bridge blocked only a couple of miles from where they'd "borrowed" the Tesla was not a good sign.

"Guess we could go back up to I-84 in Ontario," Heather suggested.

Anna thought about it, but it didn't seem like a very good idea. If Highway 26 was blocked, a highway as busy as I-84 was probably impassable. She didn't know the area very well, but she made up her mind to keep working their way south, figuring there had to be another bridge across the Snake River somewhere upstream. At the end of Nyssa's main street, she turned left on State Highway 201. At first, with the highway headed back due west, she thought maybe she'd made a mistake.

"Do you know where this road goes?" she asked Heather.

"Not really," Heather said, "but it seems to be going the wrong way to me."

Anna was just about to turn around when she saw a highway sign stating, **Adrian 12**. "Do you know Adrian?" she asked.

Heather thought for just a second before answering. "I'm not sure, but I think Adrian is another little town on the Snake River. I don't see how, though," she added, "since we're headed away from the river."

Looking up the road, Anna thought she could see that it was going to turn to the south, so she continued on. With a few jogs, the road did indeed continue mostly south, and there were very few stalled vehicles to go around. Katy was whining, so Anna stopped the truck and put her backpack and Heather's suitcase in the back. Katy obviously needed more room to stretch out. As Anna was reaching in to get her pack out of the backseat, she noticed some kind of atlas sticking up out of the pouch on the back of her seat. It was an ancient topographic atlas of Idaho. Anna instantly realized what a treasure such an atlas was. Now that coms and GPS enabled watches and all of the other technological marvels of the 21st century were gone, old fashioned printed maps were worth their weight in gold.

Finding that atlas was really lucky. How hard it might be to get through Boise had been worrying Anna for a while. After studying the maps, she and Heather agreed to just keep following the Snake River south and east all the way upstream to the crossing near Hammett. That would put them almost halfway between Boise and Twin Falls before hitting Interstate 84.

The Highway 78 bridge just east of Hammett was wide open, and they crossed old U.S. 30 in downtown Hammett right at dusk. Just north of town, there was a wide sweeping curve to the east just before 78 got to the I-84 on-ramp. As they rounded the bend and the interstate came into view, something wasn't right. There was a semi parked across the road blocking the entrance to the interstate. Not only that, but there was a small group of people standing in the middle of the road in front of the semi.

*Shit!* Anna thought. They were now close enough to see that there were four men, all wearing orange jumpsuits, and all four were armed with rifles.

"Fuck!" Heather screamed as Anna cranked the wheel hard to the right, and they bounced down the highway embankment, crashing through low scrubs of brush and busting through an old wire fence. At the bottom of the embankment, a two-track road followed along the edge of an old irrigation canal. All four wheels of the Cybertruck gained purchase as Anna swerved onto the half-ass road and avoided driving straight into the ditch. The canal ran almost parallel to the interstate heading east, and Anna didn't waste any time once she was on the canal road. Katy, who wasn't buckled in like Anna and Heather, was doing her best to keep from bouncing all over the cab, as Anna floored it, and the Tesla nearly flew down the rutted old canal road.

Anna only stayed on the canal road for about a quarter of a mile before slowing just a little and turning back across a sagebrush-covered flat toward the interstate. Bouncing Katy clear up against the roof one last time, she pulled back up onto the interstate and stomped on the throttle, heading east.

The interstate wasn't as totally devoid of vehicles as the backroads had been, but Anna only had to zig and zag around a few cars and trucks.

"The charge might last longer if you slow down a little," Heather said as they slid a little bit sideways coming out of a tight spot between two autonomous freighters.

A glance at the speedometer showed they were traveling at over a hundred miles an hour. Another quick glance in the rearview mirror didn't show any sign of pursuit, and a quick look at Heather staring straight ahead with both hands latched firmly to the oh shit handles convinced Anna to ease up on the throttle. Heather's face, light-skinned to begin with, was definitely a whiter shade of pale.

Anna, with their speed slowed to a more manageable level, studied the road behind for any sign of anyone who might be following them. "Sorry," she told Heather. "I just kind of freaked out."

Heather was starting to relax her grip on the grab bars and feeling a little better about riding with a madwoman behind the wheel. "Guess I totally forgot about the prisons," she said. "What the fuck do you suppose those inmates were up to?"

"Don't know," Anna replied, "but it sure didn't look like they were up to anything good. What do you mean, prisons? How many prisons are there?"

Heather finally let go of the grab bar and gave Katy's head a pat where it was sticking up between her and Anna's seats. "I don't really know," she answered. "I just remember that most of Idaho's prisons are in the Boise area. Even Idaho's own super-max is somewhere south of Boise. We must have slipped right past it."

That little bit of news didn't make Anna feel good at all. She wondered how many evil people had survived. *Probably about the same percentage as decent people,* she thought. *If ten percent of the population was basically evil, then ten percent of survivors probably are as well.* It was definitely not a very comforting thought.

Working her way slowly around another semi and a tanker stalled just underneath an overpass, Anna's thoughts were interrupted by what she saw ahead. They'd just come by the second Glenn's Ferry exit, and it was probably a good thing they weren't running along at a hundred miles per hour. Interstate 84 used to cross the Snake River a quarter of a mile or so ahead of them. Now, the interstate ended at a ragged hole where the bridge used to be. There were blasted remains of what looked like some kind of military vehicles on both sides of the missing highway.

From this point, where Anna had stopped to try to make sense of the scene before them, one couldn't see down into the river, but she guessed there were probably more remains of military vehicles. It reminded her of scenes from old war movies. Some kind of military convoy had apparently been blown up. For some reason, the memory of the general taking over the newscast a few days ago came to mind. The general who had replaced the newscaster to inform the world that all communications were being shut down. In Anna's mind, the picture of that general saying, "God bless America," followed by the image of a blank comscreen momentarily replaced the scene of destruction before them.

The westbound bridge had also been hit by the bombs or missiles, or whatever had destroyed the eastbound side. The other bridge wasn't totally destroyed, but it was definitely impassable.

"What the hell?" Heather said, just as Anna decided she didn't need to see any more. She pulled down into the grassy median and up onto the westbound lanes on the other side. Nervously scanning the horizon for any sign of the convicts, she headed back toward the west. Not for long though. Just as Heather was wondering what Anna had in mind, she took the exit to Glenns Ferry. Instead of turning left into town, Anna turned right onto old U.S. 30 and punched it.

For a little over a mile, the girls rode in silence. Each lost in their own thoughts. Anna continually watched the rearview mirror, but she didn't see any other vehicles moving anywhere. The old highway made a curve around a hill that blocked any view of where they'd been.

"Do you know where this road goes?" Anna asked, even though Heather didn't seem to know this part of Idaho any better than she did.

"Other than King Hill, I guess not," Heather answered. They'd both seen the road sign stating that it was four miles to King Hill.

"Check the map," Anna told Heather. She really wanted to check it herself but didn't want to stop. Not with some kind of prison gang somewhere behind them.

While she was driving, Anna glanced at Heather thumbing through the pages of the topo atlas. It was pretty obvious just from a few passing glances that Heather had no idea how to use the old paper maps. Not too many people did, of course. With the built-in nav screens in vehicles, not to mention the self-driving capability of most cars, people's understanding of printed maps had atrophied over the years.

*Thank God Dad taught me how to read maps,* Anna thought. There wasn't much to the community of King Hill, but she decided to use what there was to get off of the highway long enough to figure out what route they should take to get to Pocatello. She turned left onto Idaho Avenue after checking the rearview one last time to make sure no one was following them. It was getting pretty dark under the old trees that lined both sides of Idaho Avenue, and Anna couldn't help but notice that there was no artificial light anywhere. The streetlights weren't coming on at all. She wondered if the entire grid was finally down, or if it was just here.

After just a couple of blocks going north, Idaho Avenue made a sweeping curve to the east, and Anna pulled off onto a tree-lined driveway where she knew there was no way they could be spotted from old U.S. 30. "Let's take a look at the map," she told Heather, as she clicked on the other overhead light.

Heather handed the atlas to Anna, but instead of just studying it herself, Anna spread the book open on the console between them. While Katy seemed to watch with rapt attention from the backseat, Anna gave Heather a quick lesson in using the old topographic atlas. They decided they would avoid the interstate for as long as they could. Some of the back roads that Anna planned on using would be gravel or even dirt, and it might take quite a bit longer to get to Pocatello than it would otherwise, but they would be on U.S. 26 and Idaho State Highway 24 most of the way. Remembering the state of disrepair that Highway 9 was in back home, Anna figured that 26 and 24 probably hadn't had the best of maintenance over the past few decades either. And the lesser roads she planned to take from Minidoka to American Falls might be in terrible shape.

Anna was glad the vehicle they'd found was a Cybertruck. *If we can make it in anything,* she thought as she backed out of the driveway, *this should work.* As she pulled back out onto Highway 30, her thoughts turned to another abandoned road and another time. The bittersweet memories of meeting James on a dirt backroad a few years ago were as fresh in her mind as if it had happened yesterday. The wondrous joy she'd felt making love in the woods was followed, as always, by the terrible pain of the next day's text message. Anna could still recall word for word the last she'd heard from James Mendez - *My Dearest Anna, I can't see you anymore. I can't explain. You have to forget about me; about us. I can give you nothing but misery, and more than anything else in this life, I want you to be happy.*

# Chapter 4

T HE MORNING SUN WAS just bringing light to the eastern sky as Anna was jolted awake. Heather was driving, trying to carefully work her way across another washed out section of some old gravel road somewhere north and east of Lake Walcott. Katy was whining in the back seat. *Probably needs to pee,* Anna thought. *So do I.*

"Let's take a break," she told Heather. "Katy and I need to get out." It had taken them all night to drive just a couple of hundred miles. The roads had been worse than Anna feared. Especially after they turned off of U.S. 26. The whole world's infrastructure really had been going to hell over the past several decades. *Good thing we had passenger trains,* Anna thought, remembering how she got from Kremmling to Eugene in the first place.

After squatting beside the road to relieve herself, something that Anna was obviously a lot more comfortable with than Heather, Anna rummaged around in her backpack for something to eat. She still had Allpro and some of the protein bars that she'd brought from Eugene, and they'd liberated a couple of gallons of bottled water from an old country store in Shoshone. Finding some more food in the abandoned store would have been good, but the place had mainly been stocked with Allpro. Since she already had more in her pack than she'd ever want to eat, Anna passed on acquiring any more of that particular delicacy.

The Allpro did taste better this morning. Even Katy wasn't turning up her nose at it. *Must be pretty hungry,* Anna thought, meaning all three of them, based on the way Heather seemed to be shoveling down her share.

After breakfast, such as it was, Anna started driving again. She figured they had to be getting close to American Falls as the scenery started changing from mostly barren low rolling hills to old leveled agricultural fields that were now just as barren as the hills and flatlands surrounding them. Unlike the area around Bend, this area was far enough east that it was definitely in the grip of the drought that was plaguing most of the western and southwestern United States.

"This country is starting to look familiar," Heather said. She was really looking the country over, seeing familiar terrain from an unfamiliar back road that she'd never been on.

The terrain didn't look much different to Anna, except for the dried up circular fields and what looked like mostly abandoned run-down old farmhouses and outbuildings. The farm fields were like giant crop circles in a desert. The remains of pivot irrigation systems still strung out across many of the old parched fields. Decaying pipes and machinery waited for an era that would never come again.

Anna noticed that the road seemed to be improving dramatically, just as she caught the glimmer of water ahead. Looking off to the southeast, she could see giant wind turbines in the distance. *Back to civilization,* she thought. *Or what used to be civilization.* The thought was accompanied by mixed emotions. What would they find when they got to Heather's home? Looking over at her blonde traveling companion, Anna could see that Heather was probably even more anxious and nervous than she was.

The automatic braking system kicked in hard before Anna even saw him. The boy darted out from behind a mostly dead hedgerow lining a driveway. He jumped in front of the truck, frantically waving his arms up and down for them to stop. Anna slammed on the brakes. A totally unnecessary habit, as the Cybertruck was already coming to an abrupt halt. The boy, who appeared to be no more than twelve or thirteen years old, ran around to the driver's side of the Tesla as soon as he saw that it was stopping.

"Please help me," the boy was pleading as he came to Anna's open window. He was a sandy-haired boy with freckles, and Anna could see the tears in his eyes and the desperation on his face. "Please," he begged again, "my mother's sick. She's so sick."

It wasn't just desperation on the boy's face. Anna could see that he was also in shock. She had the realization that the sickness, as she'd come to think of it, must have hit this area later than it did Eugene. She tried, but couldn't even remember how many days it had been since she'd buried Will. The recent past, from Will's call asking her to come home from the lab, to right now was just kind of a blur. *I was in shock, too,* she thought.

"Get in," she told the boy, as her thoughts turned to her own family and her youngest brother, Cody, who wasn't much older than this boy. Maybe the sickness hadn't even hit Colorado. Maybe she would get home to find the Blue River Ranch just as she'd left it. Even as she had the thought, she knew instinctively that would not be the case. She looked at Heather as the boy was crawling into the back seat with Katy. Anna didn't know Heather that well, but she knew her well enough already to see that she was torn between sympathy for this boy and a desire to just get home to her own brothers. Any kind of delay this close to home had to be really tough for Heather.

The reason the boy was in shock was evident as soon as they stepped into the living room of the old farmhouse. There was a dead man, obviously the boy's father, on one half of the L shaped sofa, and a dead girl, who was probably the boy's younger sister stretched out on the other half.

"In here," the boy said, leading them right past his sister and father like they weren't even there.

The moaning sounds from the bedroom that the boy led them to told Anna how sick his mother was before she even saw the woman. It was like Will all over again. The woman was all wrapped up in blankets on the bed. Before even getting close, Anna knew from the ashen dry look of the woman's skin that she was burning up from fever. She also knew that the comatose woman on the bed was beyond any help that anyone could offer.

Anna heard Heather sobbing behind her and knew that was not what the one person here who could still use their help needed. Not that she blamed Heather for losing control of her emotions. To get this close to home, after hoping against hope to find home untouched, and then to see this, the same sickness that she and Anna had fled, was just too much.

Anna took the boy's hand and asked him to show her where to get a cloth and some cold water. Knowing that the woman would be dead soon was no reason to do nothing. She could at least go through the motions of trying to help. Bathing the fevered forehead with cold water was not for the sake of the dying woman, but for the sake of the boy.

·····•·•·····

Jeremy, that was the boy's name, said he didn't want to pray anymore. He said he'd prayed enough already; that he'd prayed and prayed, but they all still died. Anna was exhausted, and she had blisters on her hands from digging the three graves in Jeremy's back yard. She found that she was disappointed in herself for growing so soft over the past couple of years in Oregon.

Heather was even more exhausted than Anna. She hadn't grown up doing a lot of hard physical work like Anna had.

Burying Jeremy's parents and his sister hadn't been the first option after his mother succumbed to the sickness. At first, Jeremy had insisted they drive into American Falls to the Mormon church that the family attended. He'd hoped to find the Bishop and make arrangements for funerals. What they'd found in American Falls was about the same as what Anna had found in Eugene that first day. A few survivors wandering around in shock, but not much else. There was no one at the church, so Jeremy directed them to the Bishop's house. They'd knocked on the door, rang the doorbell and pounded on the door some more. Jeremy wanted to go inside when no one answered, but Anna led him back to the truck. She was pretty sure of what they would find inside.

It was getting dark by the time they finished burying Jeremy's family, and as much as Heather wanted to get home, they decided to spend the night in the old farmhouse. After a few nights on the road, it would be good to sleep inside a house for a change.

Anna, who was most definitely in charge by now, rustled up a pretty good meal of fried eggs and Allpro before they discussed any sleeping arrangements. After a meal that was mostly eaten in silence, Anna decided to boil the other dozen eggs that she found in the refrigerator so they could take them along when they hit the road tomorrow. The power was already out, so the eggs would just end up spoiling anyway. Fortunately, the cookstove was such an antique propane burner that it didn't require electronic ignition.

"Will you stay with me?" Jeremy asked Anna.

The question just came out of the blue, and she didn't have a ready answer. She'd been thinking about what to do about the twelve-year-old boy, but she hadn't figured it out yet. She couldn't just leave him here alone to fend for himself.

"Well," she answered, "I was hoping maybe you could come with us. Don't you think that would be best, Heather?" she asked, trying to get Heather involved in this too.

"I think that's a great idea," Heather answered, and Anna could feel the empathy toward Jeremy that was shared by the two young women. "We can all go home to my house," she added. "My brother, Scott, is just your age. You guys will get along great."

Even as she said it, Anna could see the worry on Heather's face and feel the concern growing deep inside her own being. What if their brothers didn't make it? What if they found their own families dead or gone along with most everyone else? It was a thought that Anna refused to let stay in her mind. She was relieved when Jeremy brought her back to the here and now.

"But this is home," he said. "I've never been anyplace else."

Anna bent down to his level to look him in the eye. "We can't just leave you here, Jeremy," she told him. "We need to stick together now. We'll stay here tonight, and then tomorrow we'll head out together. Please say you'll come with us." She had no intention of leaving such a young boy all alone, but it would be much better if it was his decision to go with them.

He searched Anna's eyes before answering. "Okay," he said finally, "guess I don't have any reason to stay here anymore, do I?"

# Chapter 5

H EATHER DROVE THE REST of the way to Pocatello. She was up before sunrise, refreshed even though she didn't really sleep that much at all. She was so anxious to get home that she wouldn't let Anna fix them any breakfast other than the eggs she'd boiled the night before. Heather didn't even want to give Jeremy time to pack anything, but Anna wasn't about to force him to leave home with nothing but the clothes on his back. As it turned out, Jeremy didn't have a lot more than the clothes on his back anyway. Still, his family was doing better than many before the sickness hit. They had a home and, based on what she saw in the kitchen, plenty to eat, which was more than most people had.

As Heather wound her way around and through the stalled traffic on I-86, Anna was surprised to see a couple of vehicles making their way in the opposite direction over in the westbound lanes. Anna had never been to Pocatello before, so she kept looking for any signs of prosperity, wondering if the people here had fared better than anywhere else. It was disappointing to see that was not the case. The few businesses Anna could see from the interstate seemed dilapidated and just flat worn out. They all had the obligatory bars on the windows if they had windows at all, and, though no one was in sight right now, Anna could imagine the armed security guards that must have stood watch when the businesses were open. Most would have also had at least one armed guard posted in the store or shop at night.

Heather worked her way around and through Pocatello, avoiding the interstates, which were jammed with a lot of disabled cars and trucks. They were almost out of the city at what Anna thought had to be the very southeast end of Pocatello when Heather pulled to a stop in front of what must have been the most affluent neighborhood in this part of Idaho. "That doesn't look good," she said as she saw the gates to the gated community standing wide open.

Anna didn't even have time to respond before Heather drove through the gate and wound her way down a totally deserted looking winding street with mega-mansions from another age on either side. Heather turned into a long winding driveway that led up a slight grade to one of the most imposing old homes.

*My god, Heather's rich,* Anna thought, then corrected herself, *was rich.* Being wealthy didn't mean much now, but the imposing antebellum-style house that they were parking in front of reminded her of James. Not that this house was really that big. It was designed to look bigger than it really was. It was like a miniature version of some grand old southern mansion. Anna used to dream of seeing the Mendez estate in Castle Pines, but that was not to be.

There was no sign of life, and Anna feared the worst as she opened the back door to let Katy out. Katy was off and running just as soon as her feet hit the ground, so many unfamiliar smells assailing her from every direction, that she seemed to have a hard time deciding what to explore first.

Jeremy got out and looked all around, obviously in awe of this place that was so much different from the home he'd always known just a few miles down the road. This didn't just seem like a different home to him; it seemed like a different world. As if he'd just stepped out of the Tesla onto the surface of a different planet entirely.

As the other three took in their surroundings, Heather literally bounded up the wide front steps and attempted to just open the front door. It was locked. Almost frantically, she punched her code into the keypad and heard the comforting click of the door unlocking. Pushing the door open and stepping through in one motion, she was lucky she didn't get shot. Inside the house, she came face to face with the business end of a shotgun. At the other end of the gun was the oldest of her younger brothers.

"Jesus Tom, you just about scared me to death," Heather exclaimed, as Tom lowered the gun.

He not only lowered the gun, he just let it drop to the floor before throwing his arms around his older sister. That's how Anna and Jeremy found them when they got to the top of the stairs. Anna couldn't see Heather's face. Her back was to the door. She could see the face of the boy that was hugging her, though. The resemblance to Heather was amazing, right down to the natural blonde hair. What Anna really noticed, though, was the swollen red eyes. She knew the tears coursing down the boy's cheeks weren't tears of joy, and her heart went out to both Heather and her brother.

An intense longing to see her younger brothers, Cody and Ralph, came over Anna. She remembered the last time she'd seen them, standing at the depot waving goodbye. That was a couple of years ago. *That's how I'll always remember them,* she thought. *The train car's window framing them like a picture.* She felt the tears on her cheeks and realized she wasn't just missing her brothers, she was mourning. *No! They're still there. They're still alive. I'll see them again soon.*

··········

Anna woke up early as usual. Not wanting to wake the others, she lay quietly in bed thinking. She'd been here at the Smith home for a week now. Strange how she hadn't known Heather's last name until they'd arrived at her home. Anna could imagine that last names wouldn't matter as much as they used to, now that so much of the human population was gone. She wondered, once again, how many people had survived the sickness. Did any of her family survive? Maybe the sickness hadn't even hit Kremmling or the BR at all. Pocatello seemed to be about a week behind Eugene, as far as the sickness was concerned. Heather's mother and little brother, Scott, had both died the day before they got here. Why did the sickness kill so many, yet spare a few? What determined who lived and died? It didn't seem to be genetics, or was it? If it was in one's genes, why did Scott and Mrs. Smith die, but not Tom or Heather? And what about Mr. Smith? Tom didn't know what had happened to their father. Mr. Smith had been away on some kind of business trip back east when the world stopped. Tom, and now Heather, had both resigned themselves to the fact that their father had probably been either a victim of the tsunami that hit the east coast or the sickness that was wiping out everyone else.

Anna crawled out of the comfortable bed and slipped quietly over to the window of what had been Heather's parent's bedroom. The master suite was on the top floor, with a large picture window providing a view to the east. An orange glow was just beginning to light up the sky above the mountains. Anna wanted nothing more than to head off into that rising sun. To hit the road for home, to find whatever awaited her at the Blue River Ranch. Looking down on the large backyard that ended at the edge of the Portneuf River, she knew that she couldn't leave. Not yet, anyway. She couldn't just leave the others here alone to fend for themselves, and they didn't want to go with her. Anna had become the leader of their little tribe because she was the most capable, but none of them, not even Jeremy, wanted to follow her to Colorado.

After burying Heather's mother and brother, it had been a hectic week getting the Smith home set-up to be as self-contained as possible. The house already had a large enough array of solar panels, but the PV system was designed to just feed power into the grid. There was no battery backup, and the PV system was designed to just shut down if the grid went down. The grid had gone dead the day after they got to Pocatello. Anna had spent most of the last week scrounging tools, batteries, controllers, and other components to convert the PV from a grid-tied system to a totally off-grid system.

Heather and Tom hadn't been as much help as Jeremy, but they tried, and Anna tried to teach them all everything she possibly could. Neither Heather nor Tom seemed to have much mechanical ability, but Jeremy, even though he was only twelve years old, showed real promise. Anna found herself wondering if it had something to do with growing up on a farm instead of in the city.

*Just one more major project,* Anna thought, as she looked down at the small creek that they called the Portneuf River. The small stream was a mere shadow of what the river had once been before the mega-drought. *It may not be much, but at least it's water.* Anna turned away from the window, got dressed, and headed downstairs to start the day. Today she would go back into Pocatello to find a pump, a pressure tank, pipe, and the rest of what they would need to turn the running creek into running water for the Smith house. The city water had stopped flowing before Anna and Heather got to Pocatello, and packing water from the creek one bucketful at a time was a real pain. The water would still have to be boiled before drinking, but there was nothing she could do about that. First, she'd get them running water; then, she could head out for Colorado.

..........

Anna pulled the Cybertruck up to the large detached garage, and Jeremy got out and ran around to plug it in. The wall charger was now powered solely by the PV system, and it drew a lot of juice, but keeping the Tesla charged up was one of Anna's priorities. She damn sure wanted a full battery whenever she could finally head for home.

The bed of the truck was filled with everything that she and Jeremy had picked up for the water system. Most of it, they'd gathered up at the old Home Depot store, which someone else had broken into long before Anna and Jeremy arrived. It had been somewhat eery finding their way around the darkened store and carrying what they wanted back out to the truck. Birds were flying around inside the store, and Anna had found herself jumping every time she heard one of them make a strange noise. Who else might be foraging at Home Depot? As it turned out, they didn't see anyone else at the store and only a handful of people anywhere along the way back and forth.

Anna could hear voices coming from the backyard as she carried the pump toward the gate in the privacy fence that separated the yard from the driveway. She stopped abruptly at the gate, hearing a voice she didn't recognize. It was a man's voice, definitely not Heather or Tom. Setting the pump down quietly, Anna was about to turn back to the truck to get her gun, when the gate opened.

"Looks like you can use some help," a man that Anna had never seen before said. He was probably ten or fifteen years older than Anna, not as old as her dad, but not young enough to be part of her generation either. Seeing the startled look on Anna's face, he held out his hand. "I'm Richard," he said, as Anna shook his hand, "and you must be Anna."

"Richard lives just down the road," Heather explained. She and Tom followed Richard out of the gate and grabbed as much as they could carry from the Tesla while Richard picked up the pump and carried it into the yard.

..........

The installation of the water system took a lot less time and was much easier with Richard's help. Richard had been an excavation contractor before the sickness. When it came to plumbing and waterworks, he had more experience and expertise than the rest of the group combined. With his help, it only took another five days to get the water system installed and functioning properly. Richard had even gone so far as to get one of his battery-powered electric backhoes from his old business to help. They used the backhoe to dig a sump in the creek to pump out of, and to bury the waterline underground so it wouldn't freeze next winter.

Richard had more or less invited himself to not only work with the little group to get the waterline installed but to move into the big house with them. His wife died from the sickness, and, being childless, he didn't have much reason to stay home. The group had canvassed the neighborhood to see if there were more survivors, but they didn't find any. After getting the water system up and running, Richard had suggested that, since they had the backhoe, maybe they should bury the neighbors who'd died. Or, at least the ones closest to their house. It was a pretty gruesome task by the time they got started. Some of the neighbors had been dead for well over a week by the time they got to them. But they persevered, broke into houses, and buried all of their closest dead neighbors. Using the backhoe to dig the graves, the project only took a couple of days. Not only did they bury their neighbors, but they also liberated a pretty overwhelming supply of food stocks from their neighbor's pantries and storerooms.

Anna had been in Pocatello for fifteen days, and each day the desire to get home to Colorado grew stronger than the day before. Her desire to get away from Idaho was also fueled by awareness of another problem that was starting to develop. With two young women at the sexual prime of their lives now living under the same roof with one sexually mature man, and no other potential sexual partners around, personal relationships were bound to become strained.

*I have to leave today,* Anna thought, as she lay in bed fighting against a strong desire to just go crawl in bed with Richard. *Why am I so damn horny? What is it about death that brings out such strong sexual desire in people?* Anna knew it wasn't just her. She couldn't help but notice the way

Heather looked at Richard. It was only a matter of time before Richard would be ready to move beyond grieving for his wife. Only a matter of time until Richard felt the same sexual attraction that both she and Heather did. And then there was Heather's brother, Tom.

Yesterday, Anna caught Tom masturbating in the garage. At fifteen years old, he was probably still a virgin, but his young body was as physically ready for sex as it was ever going to get. Having younger brothers herself, Anna was not at all surprised that Tom would be masturbating. What did shock her was her own reaction. She had to force herself to look away, to give the young man the privacy he deserved.

Even now, lying in bed as the sun was rising in the east, Anna was picturing young Tom standing in the garage. She fantasized about what it would have been like if she had just walked in and introduced him to real sex.

An orgasm sent tingling sensations from her head to her toes. She hardly even realized she was masturbating, as she dreamed of taking the virginity of a fifteen-year-old boy. *I do have to get out of here,* she thought, as she crawled out of bed and stepped over Katy, who was sleeping peacefully on the floor, oblivious to the activity in Anna's bed.

# Chapter 6

ANNA TOOK HIGHWAY 30 from McCammon, Idaho, to Interstate 80 near Little America in Wyoming. She was starting to get worried about finding another vehicle to "borrow". Having wasted a couple of hours and several miles of the Cybertruck's range looking for a replacement vehicle in Kemmerer, the day and driving range were both getting shorter as she approached Little America. Anna and Katy had left Pocatello early that morning after very emotional goodbyes with the four friends they'd left behind.

"What do you think, Katy," she asked the dog, who was curled up in the passenger seat, apparently tired of looking out the window at the barren desert that southwest Wyoming had become. "Should we check Little America, or just go on to Rock Springs?"

Katy raised her head off of her paws and looked at Anna as if to say, "you're asking me?" Anna checked the range again, she still had about 75 miles of range left. Plenty to get to Rock Springs, but that was about it. Anna didn't even have to look at a map to know they would run out of battery somewhere between Rock Springs and Wamsutter. Being just a few hundred miles from home, Anna knew this part of the world much better than she knew Idaho. This part of the world had been empty and barren forever. Southwestern Wyoming was one of the few places in America to remain nearly unchanged for at least a hundred years.

*Better check,* Anna thought as she took the Exit 68 offramp. She hadn't found a useable vehicle in Kemmerer, would Rock Springs be any batter? From I-80, she couldn't tell if the old Little America parking lots had any cars in them or not. The trees that had been carefully nurtured to turn Little America into an oasis were mostly dead now, but they still blocked the view from the highway. Based on how empty I-80 was, she didn't have very high hopes as she pulled under the overpass and headed into the iconic travel stop.

There were a lot more vehicles than Anna would have guessed at Little America. Even stranger than there being quite a few semis of various sorts and several cars, trucks, and SUVs, there were a couple of military vehicles of some kind parked over in one corner of the truck lot. She drove slowly through the auto parking lots looking for suitable transportation to replace the Cybertruck that had served so well. Her nerves were on edge, with the military vehicles reminding her of the blown-up bridges back in Idaho. Staying as far as possible away from the military trucks, Anna cruised the auto parking area, her senses on high alert. Even Katy sat up straight in her seat with her head out the window, testing the air with her nose.

Anna didn't need a nose like Katy's to take in the overriding smell of death in the air. It seemed extra strange that there didn't seem to be a single living person in the whole area, just that insidious smell of decaying human flesh. The vehicles all seemed to be of the autonomous variety, and Anna was just about to give up when she spotted a car off by itself, parked behind the old restaurant. At first, she couldn't tell what it was, it looked old, older even than the Cybertruck. As she got closer, she realized it was a Chevrolet Bolt. *God, I haven't seen one of those for a while,* she thought. She parked the Tesla and got out to take a closer look. A Bolt would never have been her first choice, but, seeing the cord running from behind the building to the charge port on the car, it might be her only choice. Anna had no doubt that there wouldn't be any power flowing through that cord now, but maybe the car had been fully charged before the power died.

Katy, freed from the confines of the truck, took off on her own while Anna walked up to the Bolt and tried the door. It was locked of course. *Now what?* The fob for this one car could be on a dead body anywhere. It was odd, though. There weren't any dead people just lying around. She'd seen some bodies in some of the cars in the parking lot, and she was sure she'd smelled more than she'd seen, but there weren't any just lying around. *Maybe someone's still alive.* Anna suddenly had a strong sense that there were more than just dead people left at the Little America travel plaza. For some reason, that wasn't a comforting thought.

Wishing Katy wouldn't have gone off exploring, Anna grabbed her old .40 caliber Smith and Wesson handgun out of the console of the Tesla. Her dad gave her the gun for her sixteenth birthday. He also made sure she knew how to use it. The weight of the gun belt wrapped around her waist gave her a little better feeling as she walked around the corner of the restaurant. The Bolt was probably one of the employee's cars. If that was the case, the owner was most likely inside the building, either dead or alive.

As she came around the front of the building, she caught a glimpse of Katy running between a couple of semis out in the truck parking lot. She hollered, but the dog kept going, seemingly intent on something other than Anna. The entrance door to the restaurant was standing wide open, blocked that way by a rock someone had placed in front of it. A little chill went up Anna's spine. Were there still living people here? If so, what kind of people?

Walking through the open door, Anna just about gagged. Based on the smell, the only people in the restaurant were dead people. The horrific sight inside left Anna no further hope of finding anyone alive. There were at least eight decomposing bodies in the restaurant's booths. It looked like they had just laid down in the booths and died. Another woman's body was sprawled out on the floor with flies and maggots crawling in and out of her gaping mouth and nostrils. The sight and the smell were too much. Anna bent over and wretched up the last of the protein bar she'd eaten an hour or so ago.

She turned and rushed back out into the open air. She couldn't do it. She'd just have to find another car. There was no way she was going to search those dead bodies for a key fob. She'd just have to find something at Rock Springs.

The unmistakable loud crack of a gunshot stopped her instantly. It sounded like it came from over behind the semis where she'd last seen Katy. Anna froze. She couldn't see anyone or anything besides the trucks that had been parked out there all along. She pulled the slide back and let it go, jacking a shell into the chamber of the gun that was in her right hand. The pistol had almost magically jumped from her holster into her hand. Grabbing the gun and cocking it had been a nearly instantaneous reaction, made without any conscious thought at all.

*Who shot the gun? Why?* She was pretty sure that it wasn't aimed at her. A quick look around let her know there was no place very close to hide even if she wanted to. Why should she hide? Just because someone shot a gun didn't mean anything. The sound of gunshots was a fairly common occurrence anywhere in the rural mountain west.

"Hey," she yelled as loud as she could. "Who's shooting?" Her yell was answered by silence. The fact that no one answered scared Anna more than the gunshot had. "Katy, here Katy," she yelled as she took off running back toward the Tesla. Coming around the back corner of the building, Anna froze. Someone was looking in the window of the Cybertruck. It was a man dressed in some kind of desert camo military uniform.

The man saw Anna at just about the same time she saw him. He also saw the gun in her hand that was now aimed directly at him.

"Whoa," he said, raising his hands above his head. He was a large man, but he didn't seem to be armed. "Easy ma'am," he said with a definite southern accent. "Just looking's all, no need for weapons."

Anna lowered the gun as the absurdity of the situation struck her. Here they were, two of the few people left alive in the whole area. Why would anyone want to harm anyone else now? *Then what about the gunshot?* With that thought, Anna started to raise the gun again, but it was too late. She felt the blow to her head that knocked her to the ground and had the fleeting thought that it must have been someone else shooting the gun. Her world faded to black as she lost consciousness.

# Chapter 7

I T WAS A NIGHTMARE like nothing she'd ever had before. She was tied down somehow, laying on her back. Her arms were stretched out to her sides. She struggled to free a hand to push the man that was on top of her away. Her legs were spread wide apart, held that way as securely as her hands. She could feel the man thrusting as she struggled and squirmed, unable to escape. She felt the man shudder as he thrust hard one last time.

"My turn," she heard a voice say, and Anna regained full consciousness, realizing it wasn't a nightmare at all. At least it wasn't a sleeping nightmare. This was really happening. She was being raped. Worse, she was being gang-raped.

"Sure," the man said as he crawled off of her. It was the same man that had been looking at the Tesla. She could see him much better now. As he buttoned up his pants, Anna looked up at his face. He was older than her, probably in his thirties. She couldn't help but notice, as she had before, that he was a big man. When she had seen him from a distance, she could tell how large he was, but now, close up, she could see how muscled he was as well. He had close-cropped blonde, almost white, hair. She felt totally consumed by hate as she looked into his pale blue eyes. Eyes that screamed crazy. Here was a truly insane man.

He smiled down at her. "Go ahead, Curt," he said. "Get some while you can. She's a real keeper." He looked up apparently at someone named Curt, who wasn't visible to Anna. "After this, though, she's all mine, understand?" "Sure Sarge," Curt said. He must have understood, alright. She watched in horror as he stood over her and pulled down his pants before kneeling between her legs. Through blurred vision, she saw that Curt was smaller in every way than the other man. "Don't cry," he said, "you should enjoy this as much as me." Anna didn't even have to see Curt's eyes to know that he was as crazy as the first man, the one called Sarge.

Anna had pulled into the Little America parking lot in the early afternoon. It was late in the day by the time the man named Curt crawled off of her. Anna could feel the earth beneath her back. She could feel that she was totally naked, stripped, and staked out on the bare dirt. She could feel the ropes biting into her wrists and ankles, and the scrapes and scratches where her back, and especially her butt, had been ground into the hard dirt. She had been concentrating on feeling all of those abrasions to avoid feeling what was happening to the rest of her body. Now that the men were finished with her, she just hurt all over. She could feel the sun burning her naked body even this late in the day.

"Now what?" she heard the man called Curt ask. Then she saw Sarge come around from behind her to stand between her outstretched legs. She was afraid that he was going to rape her again, but this time he just raped her naked body with those crazy pale blue eyes.

"You're mine now. You understand?" he said.

Anna, almost involuntarily, shook her head yes. She understood that she had no other choice.

"Cut her loose. Put her with the others," Sarge told Curt. Then he looked back down at Anna. "You run, I'll kill ya. Understand?"

Anna nodded her understanding again, as she felt Curt cutting the rope loose from her left wrist. She did understand. She understood that she hated these two men like she had never hated anyone before, especially Sarge. She understood how much she'd like to cut Sarge's throat to watch him bleed out and die. But she also realized that she would have to bide her time and wait for the right opportunity.

Curt let her get dressed, except for her shoes. She'd been wearing her light hikers when they stripped her, but he told her to carry them. Apparently, he was afraid she'd make a run for it if she had shoes on. *Not much chance of that,* Anna thought. *Not with him holding a rifle on me. And not with my head throbbing like this.*

Curt forced her to walk ahead of him while he trained the rifle on her back. He directed her toward the back corner of the lot where the military vehicles were parked. Thankfully, he'd let her put her socks back on. The scorching asphalt still burned the bottom of her feet, even through the socks. He forced her to walk between two semis that seemed out of the way. Coming out from between the two trucks, she saw why the man forced her to come this way. Katy was lying dead in a pool of blood in front of one of the semis. The dog that had been her closest companion for weeks, a gentle thing that would never hurt anyone, had been killed for no reason by the man walking behind her. As tears filled her eyes, she heard the man laugh. *I'll kill him, too,* she made a silent vow to her dead friend.

Anna kept on walking. She wouldn't give the crazy sonofabitch the satisfaction of seeing her grief. He herded her to one of the military vehicles that she hadn't really noticed before. It was like nothing she'd ever seen. It was an armored truck with obviously extreme off-road capabilities. The cab had no windows at all, just slots that were probably more to shoot through than to see out. The truck had to either be autonomous, or else it had to have cameras projecting the road ahead on a screen for the driver. The cab wasn't what really caught her attention, though. The truck had an enclosed bed that was about thirty feet long, and probably ten feet tall. There was a row of window-like openings about a foot high all down the side, just below the roof. The windows were covered, not with any kind of glass, just vertical bars. It was like a mobile armored prison or jail cell, with no insignia to identify which branch of the military it belonged to. The only symbol of any kind that might help identify the truck was three black crosses painted on the side of the cage. The three black crosses looked like they had been painted on the side of the truck by hand. Other than the three black crosses on the sidewall, what really grabbed Anna's attention was on the roof. The entire top of the truck was covered with solar panels that were angled to capture the maximum amount of solar radiation. Without being able to get a better look, it appeared to Anna that they were somehow mounted with some kind of tracking system to keep them always turned toward the sun.

Curt didn't allow Anna any time to study the PV system but forced her to the back of the truck. Stepping around the back corner, trying to stay on the shaded part of the hot asphalt, she was confronted with the fact that this wasn't so much a mobile jail cell as it was a cage. The entire back of the van box was open to the elements. Open that is, except for the solid steel bars running from the floor to the ceiling with a barred door right in the center. Anna watched as Curt touched a button on the side of the van, and a set of steps silently slid out from under the door and lowered to the pavement.

"Stay back or your dead," he yelled at the back of the truck as he pushed another button. Anna heard the click of the locks unlatching, and the cage door automatically swung inwardly open. "Get in," he said, waving the barrel of the gun at her.

Walking up those steps and into that cage was as hard as anything Anna had ever done. Part of her wanted to just make a break for it and accept the bullet or bullets that would bring an end to the nightmare. In the end, it was hatred, plain and simple, that kept up her will to live. She had to live. At least long enough to kill these two monsters.

The interior of the cage on wheels was dim but not dark. There was plenty of light from the row of barred windows along the top of each side and the barred open end of the cage. There were three other people, all women, sitting on built-in benches at the front end of the steel cage. Besides the benches, the only furnishings in the van were another small bench near the door of the cage and a bare mattress lying on the floor against one side. The little bench at the rear of the mobile cell was only big enough to accommodate one person, and it had a round hole in the seat. It was obviously a toilet. Anna heard the cage door lock behind her as she walked toward the front of the van. Even with the ventilation provided by the barred openings, the late afternoon heat was stifling. The outside of the truck was painted in light-colored desert camo, but the heat coming off the steel wall that had been facing the sun all day was still intense.

The first two things Anna noticed about the three other inhabitants of her cage was they were all women, and they were all darker-skinned than she was. As she got close enough to see their eyes looking at her, she noticed that they all had a vacant hollow stare. It reminded her of pictures she'd seen in history books of prisoners of war, or the images of Nazi death camps. Anna was shocked to see that one of the women wasn't a woman at all. She was just a girl, no more than thirteen or fourteen years old. She appeared to be Native American, and, if possible, her stare was even more vacant than the other two.

"You been raped yet?" was the first thing any of the three said. It was the one that appeared to be the oldest. She was a Black woman, who Anna guessed to be about thirty. The question seemed like a strange thing to ask, but it let Anna know that all three of them had also been raped, even the young girl.

Anna sat down on the floor against the sidewall of the van a few feet from the others before answering. She knew she didn't really need to respond, the answer had to be written all over her face. "Yes," she answered simply, "two of them."

The woman sitting between the Black woman and the girl was probably about Anna's age. She seemed to be Latina, but darker-skinned than most. She looked at Anna with that vacant stare that wasn't quite as empty as it appeared. "Just once?" she asked.

Anna wasn't sure she understood the question. She'd just told them there were two of them. "There were two men," Anna answered. "Both of them raped me." She held out her wrists toward the other three, thinking maybe the rope burns and cuts could make them understand.

"Just once?" the Chicana girl asked again, incredulously. Anna just stared at her, wondering if she had lost her mind or something.

"There's only two of them," the Black woman said. "What Sonia wants to know is if they both only raped you once. Those are the horniest two crazy sonsabitches I have ever seen. Shit, they took turns a couple of times on poor Jasmine there. Made us watch while they did it. Poor girl hasn't spoken since."

Anna looked over at the young Native American. The look in Jasmine's eyes was especially haunting. She looked like the caged animal that all of them had become. Anna felt so sorry for the young girl that it helped push her own trauma to the back of her mind.

"I'm Anna," she said softly to the girl.

"What is your tribe?" Jasmine asked Anna to the utter surprise of the other two women. With Native American ancestry from both her mother and father, Anna did look more native than a lot of the people on tribal rolls, but she had never been listed on any tribal roll that she was aware of. She didn't even know from which, or from how many tribes she was descended.

"I don't know," Anna said, and she wished she did know. It had been a long time since she'd felt that longing to know her ancestry. Probably not since junior high school when others called her Pocahontas. The nickname, meant to bully or shame her, had just the opposite effect. Anna wore the nickname proudly. No one had called her Pocahontas for a long time. Probably not since she had insisted the would-be bullies call her that all the time. Since then, she'd had the derogatory, injun, thrown at her a few times, but not many.

"I am Shoshone," Jasmine told her with pride. And Anna could see how genuinely proud the girl was of her own ancestry.

"I'm Flo," the Black woman said, jumping into the conversation. "And in case you haven't noticed, I'm a Black woman. Since I've been in this cage the longest, guess I should fill you in. The first thing you need to know is these ain't no ordinary crazies. No, Sarge and Curt are both some special kind of crazy. They're white supremacists, for one thing. They seem to think if you don't have lily-white skin, you ain't good for anything but killing or fucking. The only reason we're alive is for fucking. Those assholes actually think they're breeding us. They think they're going to raise their own crop of slaves. Can you believe that shit? What kind of person plans to use their own children for slaves?"

Anna and the other two listened while Flo told her story. Apparently, Flo hadn't told this entire story to either of the other two before now. She said that she'd kind of lost track of time, but that she'd been taken about two weeks ago. She and her husband, Ben, had both survived the sickness when it wiped out most of the rest of Sacramento. They'd been on foot, crossing Interstate 80 on the outskirts of the city when they saw the truck heading east on the shoulder of the freeway. Flo and Ben had thought it must be some kind of U.S. military or National Guard coming to help survivors, so they waved their arms and waited for the oncoming vehicle. Flo paused for a bit, with a mixture of emotions ranging from anger to grief playing across her face.

"They shot Ben before they even got to us. Don't know if it was Sarge or Curt. I heard the impact of the bullet hitting Ben in the chest, and the thud as his body was driven to the ground. I didn't understand. Ben was just dead on the ground with a pool of blood starting to form around him. I didn't understand..." Tears were forming in Flo's eyes, and for a moment it seemed that she couldn't go on. "One more dead nigger. That's the first thing Sarge said when he got out of the truck." Flo was finally able to continue. "At first, I wondered why they didn't just kill me too if they were trying to wipe out Black survivors. It didn't take long to figure that one out, though."

She said they didn't rape her right then, but threw her in the cage and headed east. It was when they stopped somewhere by Truckee that they dragged her out of the cage, and Sarge ordered her to strip while Curt held a gun on her. When she didn't comply immediately, Sarge hit her in the face so hard that it knocked her flat. "Now, take off your clothes, or you're a dead woman." He'd told her.

Flo had another short breakdown before continuing. "Should have just let them kill me," she said softly.

There seemed to be some kind of catharsis in talking that Anna somehow triggered in the other three. Why they hadn't told each other before, Anna couldn't guess, but they seemed to be telling their stories for the first time.

Sonia was next. When Flo fell silent, she told them how she had been taken near Elko, Nevada. Like Anna, Sonia was a ranch girl. She'd grown up on a ranch on the Humboldt River west of Elko. Unlike Flo, the sickness left Sonia totally alone. The rest of her family had all died within two days of each other. Where Sonia lived had been pretty well removed from the rest of the world. Her dad had been some kind of prepper isolationist. From what Sonia said, it sounded like her father had been prepared for almost anything. Anything except the sickness that wiped out everyone that is. She'd been homeschooled her whole life. Occasional trips into Elko were her only contact with outsiders. When everyone else in her family died, she hadn't known what to do. There was never a com of any kind on the ranch, so she had no idea that it wasn't just her family. Not until she got out on Interstate 80, that is.

She was headed into Elko to get help when she encountered Sarge and Curt. Sonia had been driving her dad's old Chevy pickup but got stuck when she tried to go around some semis that were stalled in the middle of I-80. Her dad's old truck was just two-wheel drive, and she high-centered in a washout on the shoulder of the interstate. That's when she first saw other dead people. Other than her family, that is. Walking toward Elko, she'd come across a dead man and woman lying in the median in the middle of nowhere. She was pondering the dead couple and all of the stalled autonomous vehicles on I-80 when she saw the camouflaged military truck working its way slowly up the shoulder of the interstate toward her. "I thought they would help," she said and fell silent.

No one spoke for a while. All four women seemingly lost in their own thoughts. Then Jasmine said, "I was a virgin. It wasn't supposed to be like that. It hurt so bad," she sobbed.

Anna got up and sat down beside the poor girl. She put her arm around Jasmine and held her while Jasmine cried on her shoulder.

"What do they want?" Anna asked, as much to herself as any of the other three. "I mean other than fucking and, apparently, trying to raise slaves. Are they collecting sex slaves, or what?"

Anna didn't really expect an answer, so she was surprised when Flo answered, "You got it exactly right. They want slaves period, not just sex slaves. That first time, when Sarge was raping me, he told me I should feel honored. Honored because I was going to bear him lots of slaves. It seems, from what I've overheard, that some crazy white supremacists had a plan to overthrow the government and take over the old south. They call themselves *The New Army Of God*. They plan on turning back time to their good old days when white men ruled, and people of color were nothing but slaves."

The question that immediately popped into Anna's head was why they hadn't just enslaved Flo's husband instead of killing him. She posed the question to Flo, whose answer was as crazy as the two lunatics that had captured them. "They don't think they can trust any modern men of color to yield to becoming slaves. So, they figure they'll just breed their own slave stock. What I can't figure out is what they plan on having slaves do. Pick cotton? I do know Sarge and Curt, at least, plan on breeding us all just as fast as they can. Like I said, I never knew men that could fuck as much as those two can." Flo leaned close to the others then and whispered, "Wouldn't they be disappointed if they knew my birth control implant will last at least eleven months or so."

Anna felt the truck start to move as she had the thought, mine will last even longer. It wasn't much, but there was a little comfort in the knowledge that at least she couldn't get pregnant. That probably wasn't the case for poor Jasmine, who was still sobbing on her shoulder. Anna guessed that it was also probably not the case for Sonia. Sonia hadn't said so, but Anna had the feeling that Jasmine wasn't the only one who had been a virgin. It was impossible to imagine a worse way to lose one's virginity than to be raped by two crazy men. *Guess I should be thankful. At least it wasn't my first time.* The thought didn't provide any comfort at all. If there was one thing Anna didn't feel, it was thankful.

# Chapter 8

"**W**HAT IF NOBODY'S THERE?" Anna could hear the two men talking outside the cage. It was Curt's voice asking the question.

"Somebody's gonna be there," she heard Sarge answer. "You think we're the only two motherfuckers that survived this shit?"

It had been about a week since Anna was taken captive. From the snippets of conversation she'd overheard, she knew that Sarge and Curt were members of some kind of white supremacist group. Flo had called them The New Army Of God, but Anna never heard Sarge or Curt use that name at all. Whatever they called themselves, they were imbedded in the U.S. Army and Marines. Apparently, they hadn't been as successful in the Air Force, Navy, or Space Force; but Curt and Sarge seemed to look down on those branches of the military as much as they looked down on people of color. From conversations Anna had overheard, this group of white supremacists had all agreed to meet up in Kentucky after staging a revolution to take out the United States Government. The plan was to begin with Kentucky and start a whole new nation. A new white-ruled slave state, based on the model of the old Confederate

South. Curt and Sarge talked about killing niggers and Mexicans with relish. They, not just Sarge and Curt, but the movement they belonged to, planned to exterminate any people of color that couldn't be assimilated as slaves. The movement's planners obviously didn't count on the sickness doing so much extermination for them, but that was something no one could have predicted or planned. In actuality, the sickness had probably killed as many members of The New Army Of God as it did anyone else. *I hope it killed them all,* Anna thought, even though two of them were still very much alive.

After traveling every night for the past six days, Anna had no idea where they were, other than a long way east of where they started. It was getting light enough to really see the surroundings through the bars at the back of the truck. They were definitely in a much greener place than any she'd seen since western Oregon. They were parked on the outskirts of what seemed to be a small town somewhere, maybe Nebraska or Kansas. Anna had never been east of Colorado before, so the terrain was totally unfamiliar. Through the bars, she could see that they were parked next to a bridge. There was an old sign on the bridge that filled her with longing and memories. The sign on the bridge read, **The Big Blue River**. How she longed to be back at the Blue River in Colorado. The longing to be back home was at least as intense as the dread of what she knew was coming next.

Sarge and Curt followed the same routine every day. Every night, as soon as the sun went down, they traveled for about four hours. Anna figured that must be how long the batteries lasted on a full charge. Then, they'd stop somewhere, usually in, or close to a town of some kind. Wherever they stopped, they'd wait out the rest of that night and the following day. Anna was sure they remained stationary all day, every day, in order for the PV panels to recharge the batteries. Apparently, the solar tracking mechanism couldn't function while they were in motion.

For the four captives, the growing light didn't bring the promise of a new day. It brought the promise that one or two of them would soon be fucked again by Sarge and Curt. It wasn't so much rape anymore, as it was simply being fucked. None of the women resisted at all, resistance was futile and only made it worse. All they could do was endure. What Flo had told Anna that first day about Sarge and Curt being the horniest two men she'd ever known was definitely right. Anna couldn't understand how or why the two men started off each day by fucking one of the women, but they hadn't missed a morning yet. She used to think her fiance, Will, was horny, making love to her at least three or four times a week. Not that she'd had anything against that. Anna enjoyed making love with Will as much as he did, maybe more. There was nothing enjoyable about being fucked by one of the monsters she could hear talking outside the cage, though. Not that Curt ever got another chance to fuck her. No, Sarge may have been crazy, but he was definitely in charge, and he was true to his word. Anna was strictly his own private property. Curt always got his choice of any of the other three.

"I'm going to let you go first this morning," Anna heard Sarge tell Curt as the two men came around to the back of the cage. "Pick whichever one you want. As long as it isn't Anna," he added quickly.

Flo looked questioningly at Anna. "Now that's a first," Flo whispered, having obviously overheard the two men's conversation as well as Anna had. Anna wasn't sure if Flo meant that this was the first time Sarge had allowed Curt to go ahead of him, or if she meant it was a first that one of the women was off-limits to Curt. It may not have been as noticeable to Flo as it was to Anna that she was Sarge's favorite.

"Damn, I don't know, Sarge," Curt said, looking through the opened door to the cage. "What I'd really like is some white pussy for a change."

"Save that for the sisterhood," Sarge told him. "There'll be plenty of white women once we get to Kentucky. True Aryan women worthy of being wives. Those are the women we need to bring back our glory. We can rebuild the Aryan race later. Right now, we have to make colored babies." It wasn't clear how many white women of some sisterhood Sarge expected to find in Kentucky, but it was clear that whatever cult they belonged to expected white power to retake control of the world.

"S'pose so," Curt answered as he walked into the cage. "You, Jasmine, get your tight little Indian cunt over here."

Jasmine didn't even hesitate. Her spirit had been completely broken. The young woman was pulling off her clothes as she walked to the mattress that was never used for sleeping.

The women were always fucked right there in the cage in front of the others. That bothered Anna as much as the act itself. She always made herself look away, usually at whichever man wasn't doing the fucking. Whoever that was, he'd invariably be holding his rifle pointed at the other three women while mostly watching the sex being performed by the other. Like dirty old men at a peep show, Curt and Sarge watched each other fuck with rapt attention.

*I wonder if the other women watch when Sarge fucks me?* Anna wondered absently, staring straight at Sarge through the bars. Sarge, of course, wasn't staring back at Anna. He obviously had other things on his mind. The rifle was pointed at the three women in the front of the cage, but his eyes were fixed on the activity on the mattress. *He's probably trying to decide between me or seconds on Jasmine,* Anna thought. She hoped Sarge would choose the young girl and leave her alone this morning, and then she was ashamed of herself for wishing that on anyone.

The sounds coming from the mattress and the intent look in Sarge's crazy eyes told Anna that Curt was about to finish. Then Sarge's head exploded, followed by the reverberating sound of the blast of a high-powered rifle. That was followed immediately by another blast from the gun that was falling from Sarge's dead hands.

Everything seemed to happen at once. The blast that blew up Sarge's head knocked him instantly to the ground. Curt jumped off of Jasmine and headed to the open door, but he wasn't fast enough. Anna tackled him from behind as he was running down the stairs toward the rifle he'd left at the back of the cage. Anna didn't even hear the sound of the gunshot that had been meant for Curt. She was totally unaware that she'd saved Curt from the same sniper that killed Sarge. The focus of her whole being was to get to the rifle before Curt did. He was still scrambling to get back to his feet by the time Anna grabbed the gun. She pulled the trigger the first time, hitting him in the chest as he turned toward her. That first shot no doubt killed him, but Anna pulled the trigger again and again, the dead man's body bouncing each time another round tore into it. It still wasn't enough. Anna turned the rifle on the lifeless form of Sarge lying on the ground and emptied the rest of the magazine into his dead body.

She heard Flo telling her, "it's okay Anna, they're dead," as she came back to the now from the murderous rage that had taken her outside the confines of time. Anna let the gun slip slowly to the ground as the red blur of rage slipped from her vision, and she turned back to face the other women. Flo was standing at the top of the stair, looking down at her. Jasmine was naked, sitting up on the filthy mattress with the faraway stare of someone in total shock. And then there was Sonia. She hadn't moved from the bench at the front of the van. She was right where she'd been when the violence erupted, only now she was slumped down with her head bowed forward, her chin resting against her chest just above where blood was spreading from the little hole right between her breasts. The reflex action of Sarge's trigger finger had claimed one life, even in death.

# Chapter 9

"**A**NOTHER COUPLE OF THESE assholes came through here about two weeks ago." The Black man was answering Anna's question about how he'd known from a distance that Sarge was not just some kind of active duty military. "They shot my brother in law and were about to rape my sister, but I got them first. It wasn't just no count assholes like these that served in the Marines, you know. I was a sniper back in my younger days."

From what Anna had just witnessed, he must have been a good one. Having just killed a man herself, she couldn't help but wonder how different it must have been to kill someone in a war. To kill people that you had absolutely nothing personal against. Anna was still shaking, almost sick from the adrenaline that had overwhelmed her just a few minutes ago. She literally felt sick to her stomach. Sickened as much by the strength of rage and hatred that had festered inside her for the past week, as by the knowledge that she'd just taken a human life.

"Well praise the lord, that's all I gotta say. Hallelujah and thank you, Mr.?" Flo didn't even give the man time to tell her his name before throwing her arms around him in a bear hug embrace.

"Daniel Day," the man said, extracting himself from Flo's embrace. "Just call me Danny," he added, looking up into the cage and then quickly averting his eyes from Jasmine's naked young body.

Jasmine was still standing at the top of the stairs in the open cage door, staring at the scene below. Her blank detached stare was unlike anything Anna had ever personally seen before. Anna was reminded, once again, of pictures she'd seen in history books of the prisoners who were freed from the Nazi death camps at the end of World War Two. It was a look of total shock and disbelief, wondering if what they were seeing was even real.

Seeing Jasmine in such straits focused Anna's mind back away from the rage and the killing of just a few minutes before. She shook her head, as if to clear out cobwebs, and climbed the stairs to help Jasmine. With neither of them saying a word, Jasmine allowed Anna to lead her back to where she'd dropped her clothes. She just stood there, staring down at the little pile of clothes until Anna reached down and gave her panties to her. Jasmine dressed herself, but only as Anna handed her clothes to her, one piece at a time.

"It's been a long time since I've seen one of these," Danny was telling Flo as Anna led Jasmine down the stairs out of the cage. He was looking at the mobile prison.

"Where'd it come from?" Flo asked.

Jasmine had a firm grip on Anna's hand like she was never going to let go. Anna looked at the Black man that had killed Sarge with one shot. He was even bigger than Sarge but older. Anna guessed the man must be about the same age as Clyde, her dad. He had the rifle that had killed Sarge slung over his shoulder. It was a high-powered hunting rifle with a scope, not a military rifle at all.

Danny, still looking over the mobile jail cell that had brought them here, said, "They used them for prisoner transport in the desert back in the day. I thought they'd all been destroyed." He looked at the three recent inmates of the mobile cage. "Where do you think they got it?" he asked the women.

"Must have been somewhere in California," Flo answered. "They killed my husband and took me in Sacramento. I figure they must have come up from LA or somewhere else in southern Cal. Where they got this thing, though, I couldn't say."

Danny absently pushed one of the buttons on the side of the van, and the cage door slowly swung shut and locked. "I'll be damned," he said. "Ya'all been in that cage all the way from California?"

"Just Flo," Anna answered. "Jasmine here is from Idaho, and they took me in Wyoming. I'm Anna," she added, realizing she hadn't even told him her name. "Where are we, anyway?" she asked.

"Blue Rapids, Kansas," Danny replied, looking at the women with a new sense of wonder. "All the way from California," he seemed to mutter to himself while looking at Flo. "All the way from California in a cage." A renewed look of hatred came over him as he looked past the women at the two dead men behind them.

Anna, holding the hand of the youngest victim, thought of the other prisoner who'd shared their cage. None of them deserved what Sarge and Curt had done, but Sonia, especially, didn't deserve to die. They were all survivors, up until just a few minutes ago. Even the two men that she'd gladly kill again if she could. There was something flawed about the human race. It seemed like the sickness had wiped out most of humanity. How could anyone who had survived the sickness rape and kill other people? How did anyone get to be like Sarge and Curt?

"Do you have a shovel I can borrow, Mr. Day?" Anna asked.

Danny, mistaking Anna's intention, said, "No way we're burying these sonsabitches," he said. "They don't deserve to be buried. No, we're gonna put these two out with the ones that killed Ned. Let the buzzards have at 'em."

"Not them," Anna said. "I need to bury Sonia. She didn't deserve to die. She deserves a decent burial, Mr. Day."

"Don't you worry about her," Danny said. "And please, just call me Danny. Me and the boys, we'll bury the other young lady, just like we have so many of the townfolk."

..... ..... 

Danny Day and his two sons had buried most of the people that had once been their neighbors in Blue Rapids. And they'd done it the hard way, hand-digging so many graves that adding one for Sonia was no problem at all. True to his word, Danny drug the bodies of Sarge and Curt out into a field south of town and left them there to rot. Maybe buzzards could get some good out of them, after all.

There were more survivors in the little old town of Blue Rapids than Anna would have guessed. Members of four different families had all survived the sickness. But none of the families had survived intact, and of the survivors, only three, Danny and his sister, Doris, and a man named Lucas were very much older than Anna.

..........

"We need to find a bigger inverter," Anna told Charlie. Charlie was Danny's oldest son. He and his younger brother Noah were the only two of Danny's five children that survived the sickness. He was just a year younger than Anna, and though he wasn't nearly as well educated, he had an innate mechanical aptitude that was amazing.

Sometime between the death of most of the town, and that day nearly a week ago when Danny's marksmanship facilitated an end to Anna's nightmare, the eight remaining survivors of Blue Rapids, Kansas, had all banded together. There had been nine survivors, before Doris's husband had been killed. Like a long line of Black men before him, Doris's husband was murdered simply for being Black. For Anna, it was disheartening to know how much racism had survived the pandemic. The Blue Rapids survivors had formed into a sort of tribe, or extended non-biological family, and taken up residence in a large, ancient farmhouse on the edge of town. The old house was made out of cut limestone that must have come from a quarry somewhere nearby.

The farmhouse and surrounding farm had always been the home of the youngest of the survivors. Amelia was a toddler with blonde hair and bright blue eyes who wasn't old enough to have any idea what had happened to her family. When Anna asked her how old she was, the girl just said, "Four," and held up four little fingers for emphasis.

The other members of the Blue Rapids clan were an older man named Lucas, and two women, Valentina and Olivia. Valentina reminded Anna of Sonia. She was a Chicana woman in her mid-twenties. Besides little Amelia, Olivia was the only other anglo in the group. Olivia, like Anna, had just recently turned twenty-one years old.

It was mid-afternoon, and the entire group, all eleven of them, were in the basement waiting out the hottest part of another July day. The basement was one of the main reasons the clan had taken up residence in this old farmhouse. Not only did they find a lot of food stored in that basement, but it was cool down there, even though it was well over a hundred degrees outside.

"I need to go potty," Amelia interrupted Anna and Charlie's discussion of the PV system they were trying to get up and running.

"I'll take her," Olivia said, getting up out of the old plastic lawn chair and taking Amelia by the hand. Going potty meant climbing the old wooden stairs to one of the two bathrooms on the main floor. Thanks to Charlie, the old house actually had some running water. Though it hadn't been used in decades, he had been able to tap into the old well out behind the house. The remains of the windmill that had once been used to pump water from the well were of no use, so Charlie had rigged up a solar-powered pump to get water from the well to the house. The only problem being the pump was too small to supply much water, and it had no battery storage, which meant the running water was only available when the sun was shining. Anna made it her mission to get the Blue Rapids clan set up with all the power they'd need. Not just to have full time running water, but to power the air conditioner. Sitting out the worst heat of summer in a basement that was really just a cellar was not how anyone wanted to spend their time.

"I've looked, Anna," Charlie told her. "There just never was much solar power here in Blue Rapids."

Anna had looked through the town enough to know that Charlie was right. They weren't going to find what they needed here. As bad as she hated the thought of leaving the security of this place, she knew they were going to have to look elsewhere. But she had no idea where to start looking. She really didn't even know where in Kansas Blue Rapids was located.

"Are there any bigger places anywhere near here?" she asked.

Charlie didn't answer immediately. He seemed to not want to answer the question. Finally, he said, "Manhattan. Guess we're going to have to go to Manhattan." It was easy to see that Charlie didn't want to go to Manhattan at all.

Anna knew that Manhattan, Kansas must be a reasonably large city since it was home to one of Kansas' major universities. Still, she had no idea where it was in relationship to Blue Rapids.

"How far?" she asked.

"I don't want you going down to Manhattan," Danny said, before Charlie even had a chance to answer. "We can live without electricity if we have to."

Danny was the leader of this little clan, and Anna didn't really want to go to any city of any size anyway. Growing up in rural Colorado, and seeing how much worse everything seemed in the cities she'd been to, even before the sickness hit, she was afraid of how dangerous cities might be now. It didn't dawn on Anna that Manhattan was probably no bigger than Pocatello. There was nothing rational about her fear of a strange city. After the ordeal she'd been through, Anna was mostly just scared, period. How many other white supremacists or others like them were there? Being surrounded by this Blue Rapids clan of basically decent people, couldn't erase the fear of others. The only thing she wanted anywhere near as much as the security she felt in this clan was to be back home in Colorado with her family. And she had a new fear now. She feared more and more that she wouldn't find her family alive. Seeing how few people had survived, and how no families had survived intact, she had accepted the fact that she would probably never see all of her family again. Would she see any of them? Would she be better off just staying here and becoming one of this new clan? A tribe of survivors.

Anna's thoughts were interrupted by Charlie. "Maybe we can find something up at Marysville."

Anna had no more heard of Marysville than she had Blue Rapids. "Is Marysville very big?" she asked.

"It has a Walmart," Danny answered, which was really not much of an answer at all.

"Four or five times as big as Blue Rapids," Charlie clarified. "And probably twenty times as well off," he added. "At least they were a lot better off before the sickness hit."

"How far is it?" Anna asked, thinking they might have to put the rolling cage back together again to drive to Marysville. Anna and Charlie had already started dismantling the hated vehicle to make use of its PV collectors, tracking system, and batteries.

"It's only about twelve miles up the road," Charlie said.

Anna figured a twelve-mile hike to get to Marysville wouldn't be a problem, but carrying an inverter back, if they found one, would be. They'd already told her they were pretty sure there were no usable vehicles in Blue Rapids, but Anna really didn't want to put the old military prisoner transport back together. The solution, she decided was to walk to Marysville and find not only an inverter but a vehicle to use to haul it back. Danny and Charlie agreed with her plan, but it was too hot to head out right away.

After debating whether they should do the trek after the sun went down, or wait until tomorrow, they decided to head out well before dawn in the morning.

It was easy walking on old Highway 77. The nearly full moon in a totally clear sky illuminated the potholes in the old asphalt. *Better shape than Highway 9,* Anna thought, remembering how broken up the old highway in front of the Blue River Ranch had become. Charlie and Anna were walking side by side, headed north in the middle of the old southbound lane, facing into the non-existent oncoming traffic. Not only was there no traffic on the old highway, it didn't look like this road had ever had much traffic. They walked about two miles before they saw any vehicle of any kind.

There was some kind of old abandoned factory or something on the west side of the road. The hulking remains of the large metal buildings had been visible for at least a half-mile before they got to it. For the longest time, it seemed like the old highway was going to run right into the ghostly factory. There was an old autonomous electric delivery truck of some kind parked half in and half out of the main drive into the old plant. The way it was parked, it looked like its navigation had cut out at the exact instant it was turning in to the place.

"What's that?" Anna asked Charlie, pointing at the old factory.

"You mean the truck or the old gypsum plant?" Charlie asked.

"A gypsum plant," Anna mused out loud. "I thought Gypsum was the only one."

Not knowing anything about the town of Gypsum, Colorado, Charlie didn't know what Anna was talking about, so he tried to clarify. "They used to make wallboard, you know, sheetrock, back in the day. Course it's been at least ten years since it shut down."

"Last I knew, the one back in Gypsum, Colorado was still operating," Anna told him. "I guess not anymore, though."

On a hunch, Anna turned off of the highway and walked around the stalled delivery truck into the main driveway entrance to the old factory. She was wondering why a delivery truck would have been headed into a place that was obviously abandoned.

"Where are you going?" Charlie asked, following Anna. "I thought we were going to Marysville."

"Just want to check it out," Anna said over her shoulder.

"Well, I don't think there's anything to see here," Charlie told her, hurrying to catch up. "It used to be something to see, though. I don't remember much about it, but Pop says the day they shut this plant down was the day the town of Blue Rapids died."

Charlie was telling her all about how most everyone that lived in Blue Rapids, including his dad, had been employed at the gypsum plant back then. Anna was half-listening, but mostly wondering why a factory that had been closed for at least ten years still had a perfectly maintained ten-foot chainlink fence around it. With razor wire on top, no less.

There was a wide gate across the main, or maybe the only entrance to the plant. It was as tall as the fence, and it too was topped with razor wire. The gate was one of those that rolled sideways to open, actuated by an electric motor. On the side the gate opened from, there was a small guard shack. It seemed typical for any kind of factory or business. It had one-way glass windows that would allow someone inside to see out, but no one to see in. The glass was also no doubt bulletproof. There was a steel door on the side of the guard shack. Anna was surprised when she pushed down on the latch, and the door opened.

Her surprise turned to shock when she looked over the interior of the guardhouse. There were two comfortable looking chairs in front of a control panel that had way too many switches and buttons for merely opening and closing the gate. The bright green and red electric diodes and a brightly illuminated display screen were what really caught Anna's eye.

*This place has electricity!* She thought. *How?* The display screen above the control console was split into six windows, each with a different view from security cameras that were in and around the facility. The cameras would have allowed someone in the guardhouse to monitor the entire perimeter of the old factory.

"Jesus. What is this place?" she heard Charlie ask behind her.

Anna didn't answer, but then Charlie probably didn't really expect an answer anyway. As she looked from the monitor and console to an open trapdoor in the floor on the other side of the small room, she too wondered, *what kind of place is this?*

# Chapter 10

ANNA WAS WEARING HER old .40 S&W on her hip, and Charlie was carrying the M4 that he'd taken from Sarge's dead hands, but it was still spooky going down into the tunnel below the guardhouse. Charlie insisted on going through the trap door first. Anna followed, once Charlie reached the floor, which was about ten feet below the guard shack.

There was a tunnel opening in the wall on the side away from the steel rungs of the ladder. The tunnel was about three feet wide and seven feet tall. It had smooth concrete walls, floor, and ceiling, and was amazingly well lit. There was a row of LED lights down one side of the ceiling. Orienting herself with what she'd seen from the outside, Anna thought the tunnel headed straight toward the big steel building that she'd seen from the road.

The tunnel ran too far into the distance to see what was at the other end. "What the hell do you suppose this is?" Charlie asked.

Anna was beginning to have an idea of what it was, but she wasn't sure. "Only one way to find out," she answered, and started into the tunnel. Charlie didn't even object to letting her lead the way.

It was a good two or three hundred yards to the other end of the tunnel, and it seemed like they were going slightly downhill the whole way. Near the end, but not quite to it, there was a thick vaultlike steel door standing wide open, just like the trap door had been at the guardhouse. If that blast door had been closed and locked, it would have taken some powerful explosives to blow it open. It would also, no doubt, bring the whole tunnel down. *Good thing it's open,* Anna thought. *But why? Why is this place not all sealed up?* She took her pistol out of the holster and jacked a round into the chamber before going on.

On the other side of the open blast door, Anna and Charlie found themselves in a small room or chamber. The only light in this room, which was about ten feet square, came from the LEDs of another control console of some kind on one side of the room. There was another door in the wall opposite the red and green glow of the console.

Charlie, who had let Anna lead the way through the tunnel, insisted on taking the lead once again. He walked over to the closed door and turned the knob. With Anna right behind him, he walked through the door and stopped. "What's in there," she asked, trying to see into the darkness beyond Charlie.

"It's pitch black in here," Charlie answered, "I can't see a thing."

Anna reached around to the wall inside the door, feeling for the switch she was sure would be there. Sure enough, her fingers found a switch and flipped it.

"Holy shit!" Charlie exclaimed. He stepped further into the room, and Anna followed into what looked like some kind of brightly lit underground warehouse. It was huge. The wall adjacent to the door had a rack of some sort of assault rifles that looked a lot like the one Charlie was carrying. There were metal ammunition boxes on the floor beneath the guns. Probably enough ammo for a small army. Starting about twenty feet away and going straight back into the room as far as they could see, there were rows of industrial shelving. The shelves were filled with all kinds of supplies. From the door, Anna could see case after case marked Allpro. Another rack was full of toilet paper, of all things.

In the corner off to her left, there was the cage of a freight elevator that was big enough to accommodate the small forklift parked next to it. The elevator had to be how all of those supplies had been lowered into the room. Next to the freight elevator, there was another door. Anna headed straight for that door while Charlie wandered off toward the stacks of food and supplies. Before she even opened the door, Anna was now absolutely sure of what she was going to find on the other side.

She'd heard of rich people building bomb shelter bunkers in some pretty weird places, like abandoned missile silos, but she never would have expected to find one beneath an abandoned factory. This particular shelter must have either been built to support multiple families or one huge family. On the other side of the door to the warehouse storeroom, Anna walked into an industrial kitchen, complete with two separate electric cooktops and two full-sized electric ovens and a massive side by side commercial refrigerator freezer.

Just as Charlie came into the kitchen from the warehouse, Anna walked through the next doorway into a massive great room or hall. It was about thirty feet wide and fifty feet long. At the end near the kitchen, there was a long dining table with seating for up to sixteen people. Beyond the dining table was a room with enough easy chairs and sofas for the sixteen diners to relax after dinner. There was a giant entertainment screen of some kind high on one wall of the great room with rows and rows of old-fashioned paper books beneath it.

At the far end of the great room, a hallway led between two doors. One marked Men and the other Women. Anna walked right past those facilities and into another room that was just about as large as the great room. This was the last room, the sleeping quarters. There were eight beds inside half wall cubicles along each of the sidewalls. In the center of the room, there were an additional eight smaller cots. The whole thing looked like some kind of luxurious barracks, but a barracks, nonetheless. It gave Anna the heebie-jeebies. She couldn't imagine being locked in this place for any length of time, no matter who was here with her.

"You check the men's, I'll check the women's," she told Charlie, who was just walking into the sleeping quarters. There was no one but the two of them in the whole place, neither living nor dead.

The bunker may have been empty, but Anna still couldn't wait to get out. She led Charlie, who was pretty much speechless, to the freight elevator back in the warehouse-sized storeroom. Inside the cage of the elevator, there were no buttons, just a single lever about waist high near the door. The lever was in the middle of its slot. Anna closed the cage door and lifted the handle to the top of the slot. The large elevator was amazingly quiet as it lifted them skyward.

Anna guessed that there must have been at least twenty feet of earth between the ceiling or roof of the storeroom and the surface. It was getting light as they came to a stop above ground. At the surface, the elevator came to a stop inside the remains of the old gypsum plant. The sun had yet to come up, but the glow from the eastern sky was enough to illuminate the interior of the giant old building. It was more like an enormous courtyard now. The roof was gone as well as parts of the surrounding walls. Much of the floor space was covered with an array of solar PV panels. The panels were mounted on short pedestals with tracking mechanisms to follow the sun. They were all facing due east, waiting for the morning's first rays of sunlight.

"Guess we don't need to go to Marysville after all," Charlie said. "Bound to be everything we need right here."

*And then some,* Anna thought, as she made her way past the solar panels to the other end of the factory. She couldn't help but notice that the south wall of the old factory had mostly been demolished, but not the other three walls. Even the lower half of the south wall had been left intact. Enough of the wall remained to shield the existence of the solar panels from outside view.

At the far end of the factory, there was a smaller building that was still intact. It had pre-cast concrete walls and a steel man door. "This has to be the battery and control room," she told Charlie, as she tried the steel door. It was locked. The first locked door they'd come to in the whole place. Anna looked at the numeric keypad on the wall beside the door and wondered how hard it would be to guess the right code. Nearly impossible, no doubt. There had to be another way in, though. This was just a man door. If the kind of equipment she was looking for was on the other side of that wall, it would have been taken in through a much larger doorway. "Come on, let's look outside," she said, leading the way back to the overhead shop door near the elevator.

Just outside the shop door, on one side, there was a trailer that looked like a temporary construction trailer. On the other side of the door, an old F-250 pickup truck was parked facing the factory wall. Anna and Charlie walked around the old Ford truck and down the length of the building to another overhead door that Anna knew had to lead into the battery room. There was another keypad next to that wall, but no other way to open the door. This part of the old factory seemed to be completely intact. There were no windows in the concrete walls. *Probably vented through the roof,* Anna thought.

"If we had some tools, we could probably break in," Charlie said, but Anna was starting to think along a different line. She was still trying to wrap her mind around the bigger picture, and she kept coming up with more questions than answers. Who had left the doors unlocked, allowing her and Charlie access in the first place? Why? Why had they left the guard shack open? Would they be back?

Suddenly she had an idea. She walked back to the construction trailer without saying anything to Charlie. She walked right up the metal steps and opened the door. Somehow, she'd known it wouldn't be locked. The stench that came out of the trailer was unmistakable to everyone who had survived the sickness. It was the smell of rotting human flesh. Anna forced herself to go inside, Charlie didn't follow. Inside, she found exactly what she'd known she would. This was not a construction trailer at all. It was living quarters. With a bedroom at each end, it had been living quarters for at least two people. One of whom, though no longer living, was still there. This trailer was where the guards had lived. It was permanent housing for full-time security guards, for a never used shelter.

*The other guard, or guards, must have left the guardhouse open,* Anna thought, *wonder if they planned on coming back.*

*Not likely. They would have locked the door if they expected to be back.*

Turning to go back outside, Anna saw a keyring hanging from a hook beside the door. She grabbed the keys and went straight to the Ford pickup. Judging by the thick layer of dust that covered the old truck, it hadn't been driven in a long, long time. It was a pleasant surprise when the old internal combustion engine fired up almost as soon as she turned the key. Anna knew that the propane tank in the bed of the truck was probably the main reason it was still able to run. If it had been gasoline or diesel powered, the fuel most likely would have gone bad long ago. The people who built this place had really planned for the long term.

Anna hit the switches to open all of the side windows of the old truck. The air in the cab was so stale she could hardly stand it. There was no telling how long it had been since anyone else had been inside. Looking out the open driver's side window, Anna saw a huge propane tank that she hadn't really noticed before. *Must be at least ten thousand gallons,* she thought. *A lifetime supply for this one old truck. Then again, maybe whoever owned this place planned on bringing some more propane-powered vehicles.*

"Wait," Anna told Charlie, who was just crawling into the passenger seat. She turned off the ignition. "Let's lock this place up first."

Anna explained what she had in mind to Charlie as they took the elevator back down into the storeroom. Anna went straight to the control room at this end of the tunnel. She figured that one of the guards had got sick and died. With no coms and no way to know what was going on, the other guard, or guards had abandoned their post.

"Why didn't they take the truck?" Charlie asked.

"And why didn't they lock up?" Anna answered his question with another question. Both were questions with no logical answer.

She found the switch and turned on the control room lights. The long desk had a computer console and a large monitor at one end, and several loose-leaf style books standing up on a shelf at the other. Anna randomly pushed a key on the computer keyboard, and the monitor flickered to life. It had the same camera views that they'd seen on the screen in the guardhouse. She looked over at the books at the other end of the desk. Each of the loose-leaf binders had a label on the spine. They were maintenance and operations manuals for the entire shelter. There were two large manuals marked **PV System**, another marked **Appliances**, but one small loose-leaf was the only one that really mattered to Anna at the moment. It was marked **Security**.

Reading through the manual as quickly as possible, Anna discovered that the various keypads throughout the complex were programmable from this main control room computer. Both the trap door in the guardhouse and the blast door at this end of the tunnel could also be remotely opened and closed using this computer. Anna and Charlie studied the manual together. They closed and locked the tunnel doors. Then they cleared any existing access codes in the outside keypads and put in two new ones. Each of them chose a code they could easily remember.

They left the elevator open and walked around to the entrance gate to make sure the codes they'd programmed into the keypads worked. The door on this side of the guardhouse was locked, but Anna's code did indeed open the door. She relocked it, and Charlie tried his. Both codes worked perfectly. With Anna staying inside the guardhouse just in case, Charlie went out the other door and locked it behind him. His code worked just fine on that door also.

It was mid-morning by the time Anna drove the old Ford truck through the gate and waited for Charlie to close the gate and lock the guardhouse door behind him. The odds of one of the owners making their way to this shelter from wherever were pretty slim, but wouldn't they be surprised if they did get back here only to find they couldn't even get in.

# Chapter 11

ANNA RECHECKED ALL OF the connections for the umpteenth time, closed up the breaker box, and started flipping the switches on the control panel. The dials and gauges came to life, indicating that the system was working.

"You did it!" Charlie exclaimed. He grabbed Anna and gave her a celebratory hug.

"We did it," Anna said, pulling back away and looking into his eyes.

The two of them had been working together all day, every day for the past few weeks. They'd put together a solar electric system that would provide all the power that the farm, as everyone was now calling their little commune, could ever need. And they did it without using anything from the bomb shelter at the old gypsum factory except the old Ford pickup that they borrowed to haul the components from Marysville.

After discovering the gypsum factory shelter, Charlie and Anna had locked the place up and took the pickup back to the farm. They'd both wondered if maybe the Blue Rapids Clan should just move to the shelter and forget about living at the farm. It may have been the easiest way for the group of survivors to go on surviving, at least in the near term. But none of them, Charlie and Anna included, much liked the idea of living cramped up in a bunker underground. Of course, Anna had no intention of living in Kansas at all, so she refrained from the decision making process.

The whole group decided that they didn't want to move to the gypsum factory, but they also agreed not to steal anything from there if they didn't have to. Danny didn't want to take anything just in case the rightful owner or owners eventually showed up. Anna didn't think that was very likely, but she agreed with the rest of them that it might be wise to just keep the place intact as a backup plan, should they ever need it. Danny, who was, after all, the group's real leader, finally agreed that they could at least "borrow" the old Ford pickup truck. Charlie and Anna had used the old pickup a lot. They had made multiple trips to Marysville to obtain all of the components and supplies they needed. Fortunately, they hadn't needed to go anywhere besides Marysville.

Looking into Charlie's eyes that were as deep a shade of brown as her own, feelings that Anna had been suppressing oozed to the surface. Working side by side, she'd come to admire Charlie's capabilities and his intellect. She'd also found herself admiring his athletic body more and more as he worked shirtless through many a hot afternoon. After the ordeal with Sarge and Curt, Anna had been pretty sure she would never be interested in sex again. Now, as her lips met Charlie's, her body was more than just interested in sex. It was a yearning that couldn't be suppressed. Not just a craving for sex, but for that deepest sharing of human companionship. It was not a desire to share with just anyone. She wanted to give herself to Charlie, and she wanted Charlie to be hers. Was she falling in love with this man?

Anna pushed herself back away and looked into those dark brown eyes again. "What about Olivia?" she asked. It wasn't much of a secret that Charlie and Olivia sometimes slept together, just like everyone knew that Danny had been sharing his bed with Flo. The way the world was anymore, it just seemed natural that people would seek out love and companionship wherever, if not whenever, they could.

Charlie lowered his gaze. "I don't know," he said. He shook his head slightly, "I guess I just don't know." He looked back into Anna's eyes. "I know it's not right, but I want both of you. I can't help it." He started turning away, before almost whispering to himself, "I love both of you."

Anna watched Charlie walk out of the garage that they'd converted into the battery and control room. She found herself thinking about polygamy. *Is that what we're coming to?* She wondered. Discounting Lucas, who was probably too old, and Amelia, who was definitely too young, the Blue Rapids clan consisted of six women and three men. Anna couldn't help but wonder if that ratio held true for survivors everywhere, or just here. If men had succumbed more readily than women, the odds of finding her family intact back on the Blue River Ranch were slim. *Slim to none,* she admitted to herself. *And what about James?* A wave of sorrow washed over her. Not for James. James was still alive. She wouldn't let herself think otherwise. No, the grief she felt was for her family. No matter how much she tried to suppress it, she couldn't rid herself of the feeling that some of her family, if not all, were gone.

Watching Charlie walk away, she had the thought that maybe she should just give up on the idea of ever going home. She looked at Charlie and thought about what it might be like to just live here for the rest of her life with this new "family" that she'd found in Blue Rapids. Could she genuinely love another man, other than James or Will, or was love what she really felt for Charlie? That she felt lust was undeniable, but love was not so easy to pin down. *And what about Olivia?* She thought, asking herself the same question that she'd just asked Charlie. *Can I love Charlie and share him with Olivia? I like Olivia, but could I be happy as a sister wife?* It was a question Anna had never ever considered. Growing up on the Blue River Ranch, she had always just dreamed of marrying her childhood sweetheart, James, and raising a family on the ranch. Just like her parents before her. And now, here she was considering a life as a sister wife in Blue Rapids, Kansas. *Another BR*, she thought absently, just as Charlie yelled back at her, "Come on, let's check out the air conditioner."

Anna wasn't really surprised when Charlie crawled into her bed that night, and she didn't tell him no. She just moved over to make room and asked, "does Olivia know?"

"She does," Charlie answered as he wrapped his arm around her.

*I'll talk to Olivia tomorrow,* was Anna's last thought of the other woman before succumbing to thoughts of only one thing. The feeling of Charlie's naked skin pressing against her own washed away any notion of resisting the desire that was coursing through her body. At that moment, that desire was all there was. At that moment, her entire being existed for just one thing. She pulled Charlie over on top of her as much as he got there by his own motivation. Anna and Charlie lost themselves in each other, in the eternity of that one brief moment in time.

·····•··•·····

It was still early in the morning. The sun had only been up for an hour or so, but it was already getting too hot. Anna and Olivia were pulling more of the never-ending supply of weeds that always tried to take over the garden. They were working side by side, with only the row of corn stalks between them.

"Do you ever feel jealous?" Olivia asked.

Anna stood up, stretched her aching back, and looked around. She and Olivia were the only ones working here in the northwest corner of the enormous garden. The garden had been planted too late in the year, but it was better than no garden at all. Anna searched her feelings. *Do I ever feel jealous?* She asked herself, echoing Olivia. She could see the sun glistening off Charlie's naked back, where he was hoeing a row of okra a few rows over, oblivious to the conversation between the two women he slept with.

"I guess I really don't," Anna answered. And it was true. "How about you?"

Olivia stood up and stretched as well before answering. She, too, looked over at Charlie then turned to look at Anna.

"Not anymore, I guess," Olivia said. "I have to admit, though, I was at first." She laughed. "I actually cried that first night when he told me he was going to sleep with you. Funny, if you'd have told me a year ago that I was going to be sleeping with Charlie Day, I'd have thought you were crazy. Let alone, sharing him with another woman."

Anna hadn't thought about it much, but now she wondered if Olivia had feelings for Charlie before the sickness. The two had grown up together right here in rural Kansas. Or had they? Come to think of it, Olivia had never told Anna where she lived before everybody died. Charlie had shown her the little place a few blocks over where the Day family had lived, but Olivia never talked about where she lived before. As a matter of fact, thinking about it now, Anna couldn't remember Olivia ever talking about before at all.

"Did you and Charlie, I mean before?" Anna asked.

"Oh, God no," Olivia laughed. "If my parents knew I was sleeping with Charlie Day, they'd roll over in their grave. You have noticed that he's Black and I'm white?" she asked sarcastically. She brushed a lock of her long blonde hair back up under the sunbonnet that she always wore and laughed again. "Of course, that doesn't mean I didn't have my fantasies."

"So, you did know Charlie. Before I mean?" Anna asked.

"Knew of him, more like it," Olivia answered. "My parents mostly kept me away from the Black folk and the poor white trash here in town."

Anna and Olivia both went back to weeding while Olivia told Anna all about the life she'd lived before. Anna was astounded. She never would have guessed that Olivia was from a wealthy family that didn't actually live in Blue Rapids but on an estate south of town. Olivia had never attended the public schools that Charlie went to. Hers had been a life of boarding schools and high society.

As Olivia talked about the boarding schools she'd attended, Anna thought of James Mendez, and how she used to wish she was at Colorado One with him, instead of the dilapidated old public high school in Kremmling. She thought of James and, once again, felt the tug of a love that she knew would never die. *I may not be jealous of sharing Charlie with Olivia,* she thought. *But how would I feel if it was James?* That was followed by other thoughts. *Why do I keep trying to compare Charlie and James? James is just a glorified memory. I don't even know what kind of man James grew up to be. I love Charlie Day. He's kind, intelligent, and great in bed. At least when he's in my bed and not hers.*

"Hello there," someone yelled from out on the road. It was a strange man's voice, and the yell brought Anna and Olivia, as well as the rest of those working the garden instantly to their feet. Anna had her hand on the gun she wore on her hip before she even knew she'd reached for it. Before she realized that anyone who meant her harm wouldn't have just yelled hello.

It wasn't just a single man out on the road in front of the garden. It was a whole group of people. There were two men, three women and a couple of children. Everyone working in the garden put down their tools and headed out to the road. Having strangers in their midst was the most exciting thing to happen in Blue Rapids since Danny Day shot Sarge.

The group of strangers consisted of one Black man and a Black woman, one white man, and two white women. The children, one boy and a girl, both belonged to one of the white women. Other than the mother and her two kids, the group was entirely unrelated to one another, but they had quite a tale of how they came to be traveling together in a group.

Some of them had come all the way from Hopkinsville, Kentucky, near Fort Campbell. As Anna listened, she realized that had to be where Sarge and Curt had been headed. Apparently, some kind of revolt in the military had hit Fort Campbell about the same time that the sickness did. Ben and George, the two men, had been friends since childhood. George, the Black man, told how Ben, his white friend, had saved him. It seems Ben caught wind of how white supremacists were taking over Fort Campbell and planning to enslave or kill all the Black people. By then, both men's families had died of the sickness.

"I didn't really have a choice," Ben said. "I could have joined them, been one of the ruling whites in the community, but I'd rather be dead and buried with my wife."

Melissa and her two children, Damon and Sarah, had been Ben's neighbors. Ben had helped Melissa bury her husband, and when he decided to escape what was coming to Hopkinsville, she chose to go with him. The four of them had fled in Ben's original Mach E Mustang in the middle of the night, stopping only long enough to pick up George, who lived on the other side of town.

Ben told them the Mustang had about fifty percent charge when they left Hopkinsville, and they'd only made it a couple of hundred miles before running out of juice somewhere just outside St. Louis. They'd walked the rest of the way, picking up the other two women, Poppy and Kathleen, along the way.

"Where are you headed?" Danny asked the group of strangers.

"Reckon we don't rightly know," George answered, and Ben, who'd done most of the talking up to now, shook his head in agreement.

"We've just been heading north and west to get as far away from that Fort Campbell bunch as we can," Ben said. "Don't know how much farther we can go," he added. "All this walkin's kind of hard on the little one." He reached down and gave the little girl a gentle pat on the head.

"You go much farther west, you're likely to run out of water," Anna told them. "I haven't seen it for myself, but from what I've heard, what used to be the great plains, is mostly just a great desert now."

"Maybe we should just go north." It was Poppy, the Black woman, who hadn't spoken at all up until then.

"Well, for now, why don't you come in and have lunch with us," Danny invited them in. "Get out of this heat and take a load off."

Everyone but Anna headed to the house. Spending the hottest part of the day in air-conditioned comfort had become the normal routine in Blue Rapids. As the others walked toward the house, still talking, Anna gazed to the west. Against her will, she had an uncontrollable longing to cross that great unknown. She needed to know the fate of her family. And yes, she still had an undeniable longing to find James Mendez.

# Chapter 12

T HE OLD SMITH PLACE, as Danny and Charlie called it, was the nearest neighbor to the Farm. The two houses were less than a quarter-mile apart. It hadn't taken much convincing to get the refugees from Fort Campbell to stop walking and take up residence at the old Smith place here in Blue Rapids.

*People are herd animals, just like horses.* Anna, for some reason, had been thinking about Pintada and the other horses back home at the Blue River Ranch in Colorado. She was sitting in the living room of the Smith house, enjoying the first cooling breeze from the old window AC unit that she and Chalie had installed. Getting the Smith house set up with its own PV and water system had been difficult. The former Smith house didn't have a well, so they had to run a water line all the way from the farm. It had taken Anna, Charlie, and George at least three weeks. It would have taken even longer if it had been just Anna and Charlie. George had once been head of maintenance at a processing plant back in Kentucky. He was old enough that Charlie and Anna did most of the physical work, but his expertise, especially with the water system, was invaluable.

Nobody really kept track anymore, but Anna figured it had to be mid-September or so. Satisfied that the Smith house was now ready for occupancy, she went back outside to the battery shed where George and Charlie were monitoring the system controls.

"AC's working great," she told the two men. "All good in here?"

"Finer'n frog hair," George answered. "Let's tell the others we can move in." He was obviously excited at the prospect of being able to get out of the Farm. The big old limestone house, totally adequate for nine, had seemed tiny and cramped with sixteen people all living under one roof.

It was barely lunchtime when Anna, George, and Charlie finished testing the systems. The entire clan spent the rest of that day getting the newcomers situated in their new abode. It was quite a relief for everyone involved. Now, near midnight, Anna lay awake in her bed, unable to sleep. Having a bedroom to herself seemed strange after sharing it with Melissa and her two children for the past three weeks or so. Anna found that she was missing their company. She especially missed Damon and Sarah, the two children. Anna had enjoyed their company more than she could have imagined. Children had a way of giving one hope for the future. *I want children of my own,* she thought, and the realization startled her. The desire to have children was accompanied by another longing. Charlie hadn't shared her bed since the others moved in. Now, Anna found herself resenting the fact that he'd apparently chosen to spend this night with Olivia instead of her.

She got up, walked over to the window, and pulled the curtains open. Her bedroom was on the second floor, and her window faced west. Anna stood at the window, looking out across the moonlit night to a place she couldn't see. She looked out toward home and thought about her past and her future. Anna found it odd that she hardly thought about Will at all. It made her sad somehow that she didn't miss Will like she missed James. It just didn't seem right. She'd spent years with Will. They'd shared everything, and yet the one man she really missed was James Mendez. Maybe that was it. Maybe it was the mystery of James. By the time Will died, there was hardly any mystery left at all.

As Anna got back in bed, she knew it was more than that. You don't get to choose who you love, or why, or for how long. What Anna knew, as she tried to go to sleep, was that the physical yearning she felt could have been partially satisfied by making love with Charlie, but she had a deeper longing. It was an insatiable desire that could only be satisfied by finding James; by exploring the mysteries of love interrupted. He has to be alive. He has to be alive, was the mantra that finally put her to sleep.

"Where's Sarah?" Amelia asked. Amelia and Sarah had been nearly inseparable at the Farm. The two girls, one four and the other five, had become more like sisters than friends. Now, with Sarah living at the Smith house, Amelia was somewhat lost.

"She's at home. We can go see her after breakfast," Doris told the little girl. Danny's sister Doris, more than most others in the group, had taken on the role of mother for the young orphan girl.

Breakfast without the group from Kentucky seemed strange to Anna, too. It seemed odd that a house with nine people still in it could feel as empty as the Farm did this morning. *It's the kids,* Anna thought. It was the lack of the two other children that made the Farm seem so quiet.

"Sarah lives here," Amelia said. "Here's home. I want her to live here with me."

*Is this home for me too?* Anna thought. *Amelia should live with Sarah. Where should I live?*

After breakfast, it was Anna and Olivia's turn to clean up. Everyone else was already out taking care of morning chores. Even old Lucas was out sitting in the yard watching Sarah and Amelia happily playing together. The two little girls were indeed inseparable.

"I'm pregnant." Olivia didn't even look up from the sink as she said the words. Her voice betrayed very little emotion. Maybe just a touch of fear, more than anything else.

Anna didn't know how to respond. "Are you sure?" she asked.

Olivia said she was pretty sure she was pregnant. She told Anna that she hadn't been on any kind of birth control and that she had now missed two periods.

"Are you happy?" Anna asked.

Olivia looked at Anna and just sort of had a meltdown. She smiled and started crying all at the same time. "I should be happy," she stammered. "I am happy. It's just, it's just...it wasn't supposed to be this way. I was supposed to be married. I was supposed to live in a normal family, in a normal world," she sobbed.

Anna took Olivia in her arms, letting her sob on her shoulder. The two women really had become sister wives in all but name. "I'm happy for you," Anna told her. "And I'm happy for Charlie, too." She found that her own eyes were wet with tears. "I'm happy for all of us," she said. "It's good to bring new life into this world – this world that has seen so much death."

That was the moment when Anna made up her mind to leave. In reality, the decision to leave had been made before she ever decided to stay. But at that moment, the decision to leave crystallized in her mind. She'd spent the past three months with this group of people who had become like a second family to her. She loved them all, but she knew she had to leave. It was time to search for what had been left behind in another life. Anna had to know the truth about a love she'd carried for as long as she could remember. Her love of James was like a slow-burning ember in her heart. It might flicker at times, but it could never be extinguished.

········•·•······

It took several days to get ready to leave. Charlie took her to Marysville in the Farm's old propane-powered Ford to find some mode of transportation. Finding a suitable vehicle wasn't an easy task. It seemed like most people in this part of the world hadn't been driving electric vehicles at all, let alone non-autonomous EVs. In the residential areas of Marysville, they found nothing but antiques as old as the Ford truck they were riding in. The biggest problem was, all of the old antiques they found were either gasoline or diesel powered, and most looked like they hadn't been driven for a long, long time. Most people in Marysville had probably just been relying on the various forms of mass transit for many years before the sickness hit.

They did find one good thing, though. Clear out on the southeast edge of Marysville. Anna and Charlie were just about to turn around to search another area when they saw a man standing in front of an old farmhouse holding a rifle in front of him. The man didn't raise the rifle or seem threatening at all, so Anna didn't even reach for her own gun. Instead, Charlie and Anna stopped and got out of the truck and walked up to the man with their hands in the air. "You can put your hands down," the man told them. "It's good to see others still alive." The man introduced himself as two women, and a young boy came out of the house behind him.

Besides those four people, it turned out that a whole clan had taken up residence in that farmhouse and the one next to it. There were eight of them altogether, and they seemed to be living together, much like the group back in Blue Rapids only without the modern comforts of electricity and running water. Charlie was so excited to find a group of neighbors living just twelve miles away that Anna didn't think she was ever going to get him to stop talking so they could resume their search for transportation. As it turned out, the time spent visiting was time well spent. Probably for everyone. Charlie promised the Marysville group that he would come back to help them set up their own PV and water systems, and for their part, the Marysville group told Anna where she was most likely to find a vehicle. There was a manufacturing facility in Marysville that had still been actively producing farm equipment when the sickness hit. Not that farm equipment was going to do Anna any good, but the owner of the business had also been somewhat of a collector of cars and trucks.

..........

Sure enough, they'd found an old Tesla Model Y at the manufacturing plant. The old SUV had less than a quarter charge when they found it, but they also found a wall charger in the same metal building that housed the small collection of mostly antique vehicles. Back at the Farm, it only took a couple of hours to get the wall charger wired up and charging.

Now, with the car fully charged and ready to go, it was hard to say goodbye. It was early morning, but the entire Blue Rapids clan had gathered to see Anna one last time before she left. Everyone, except maybe the children, knew this was probably more than a temporary goodbye. Anna knew she would most likely never see any of them again.

She hugged each and everyone and wished them all the best. When she came to Charlie last, he held her tight and whispered in her ear, "I love you Anna. I hope you know that."

The road was blurred with tears as she drove away. *I love you, too, Charlie,* she thought. *Like I loved Will before. Why is it never enough? Damn you, James Mendez!* She cursed to herself as she headed west on Highway 77. The Blue River Ranch was no longer Anna's destination. No, Anna had decided that if home is where the heart is, the BR might no longer be her home. She wiped the tears from her eyes and tried to focus on the road. The road that now led to a place Anna had never been. In time, she would return to the Blue River Ranch, but first, she was going to Castle Pines.

# Chapter 13

A NNA DIDN'T KNOW MUCH about Kansas, but she figured the shortest route to Castle Pines, Colorado would be to travel due west as much as possible. Although in what seemed like a previous life, she'd never been any farther east than Limon, she knew Colorado geography well enough to easily find her way to Castle Pines once she crossed the state line.

Expecting the plains to be dry and actually seeing it with her own eyes were two very different things. It was hard to believe how fast the terrain changed from farms and fields that were drying up in the early autumn heat to a near-desert that had dried up years ago. Anna knew enough American history to know that this part of the country was once the breadbasket of America, if not the world. Now it reminded her of far western Utah or Nevada. It really was a desert. And it wasn't just the countryside that had dried up. The towns along the way had all been abandoned long before the sickness.

It was already the middle of the afternoon, and Anna had driven less than a hundred miles. The roads out here, mostly just secondary routes back in the best of times, were crumbling and decayed to the point of being nearly impassable in places. She could tell by the trees that she was coming into another town. *Probably another ghost town,* she thought. Most of the trees were no longer green but looked like ghosts themselves. Dried up and dying, just like the country surrounding them. Some of the trees still had a few green branches, but most were merely death still standing.

The faded sign at the edge of town said Jewell City Limits, but that meant nothing to Anna. It might as well have said Timbuktu. Anna wished, once again, that she had an old fashioned paper map to figure out where she was. She knew she had been traveling mostly due west on an old Kansas highway numbered 148, and that she wasn't too far south of the Nebraska state line. Other than that, she could have been anywhere.

Jewell was definitely a ghost town. It looked like no one had lived there for at least ten years. After driving past the abandoned homes and businesses, Highway 148 came to an abrupt end at a T intersection. Anna looked at the old dead traffic light swinging in the wind. She turned on the air conditioning, which she'd been using as little as possible to conserve motive power for the car. *God, it must be a hundred twenty degrees out here,* she thought. A quick glance at the touchscreen told her it was actually just one hundred seventeen outside. She scanned the road north and south, trying to decide which way to go. There was a sign directly across from where she sat that said I-70 was sixty-one miles south, or U.S. Highway 36 was eight miles north. Anna decided, as much as she hated losing the sixty miles, she might be better off going south to I-70. She had no way of knowing if Highway 36 would be in any better shape than Highway 148 had been. Interstate 70, on the other hand, had always been the main east-west route across both Kansas and Colorado. As soon as she was headed south, she switched the air conditioning off again and opened all of the windows. She was afraid the Tesla wouldn't have enough battery to get to Colorado, and she knew that getting stranded out in the middle of this desert would probably be fatal. She took another drink of hot water from the jug she had in the passenger seat and decided if she could stand to sweat out the rest of the day, she'd drive the rest of the way after dark.

It must have been about midnight when the Tesla finally ran out of battery and came to a stop. Interstate 70 had been surprisingly easy to travel. Other than working her way around a few stalled semis and even fewer passenger cars, the worst part was the drifts of sand and dirt that had blown across the highway. It was a good thing the old Model Y had all-wheel drive, or she probably wouldn't have been able to make it. As luck would have it, the moon was nearly full, so Anna hadn't even needed to use the headlights. Not that the lights would have shortened her range much anyway, not like the air conditioner, but Anna had conserved all she could. Still, she was just west of Burlington when the car came to a stop.

*At least I made it to Colorado,* she thought, *even if it does look just like Kansas. What now?* She was somewhere about halfway between Burlington and Stratton, so she strapped on the backpack that she'd prepared before leaving Blue Rapids and started trekking west. She was pretty tired, having been awake for a good eighteen hours by then, but she figured if she had to walk, she better walk at night. She didn't want to end up like the remains of others she'd seen scattered along the interstate. People that had probably died of exposure when their autonomous vehicles shut down in that great desert.

She'd only walked a mile or so before she came across another one. The corpse was so far gone that Anna couldn't even tell if it had been a man or a woman. She wondered as she passed by if the poor soul had died of exposure or the sickness. No one would ever know. She thought about how many had died. *Must be hundreds of millions just here in America,* she thought and wondered if anywhere on earth had fared any better.

The moonlight was bright enough to make out a sign beside the highway that said it was sixty miles to Limon. Anna knew she was in good enough shape that she should be able to walk at least twenty miles a day, or night more likely. With the night more than half gone already, she decided that she would hike to Stratton and then find someplace to shade up and wait out the heat of the day. Maybe, in Stratton, there would even be another vehicle she could use. As she walked past another desiccated corpse on the shoulder of the road, she doubted that would be the case.

·····•·•·····

Anna's feet and legs ached. It was getting harder and harder to keep putting one foot in front of the other. Unable to find a vehicle in Stratton, she had hiked at a bruising pace all night, every night, for three nights in a row. The sun had already been up for a couple of hours, but she had to keep going. She could see Limon off in the distance, maybe three miles away. It was already getting hot, and it had been at least four hours ago that Anna drank the last of her water. She knew she had to get to Limon and find some water, or she would die. She would just be another one of the dead people scattered along the old interstate highway.

There was no sign of life at the travel stop and charging station on the north side of the interstate, but Anna approached the place with extreme caution. There hadn't been any indication of anyone at Little America, either. There were a few autonomous semis plugged into the row of truck and bus chargers, but only one car at the car charging stations. It was one of the newer autonomous Volkswagens, so she was out of luck as far as finding transportation.

Though she was dying of thirst, Anna carefully explored the entire perimeter of the building with her gun in hand. She even looked inside all of the vehicles in the parking lot. Satisfied that she was the only one there, at least on the outside of the building, she studied the interior of the store through the glass front with bars on the windows before going inside. She pushed the unlocked entrance door open and checked between the aisles and behind the counter before relaxing at all.

The interior of the travel store smelled terrible, but it wasn't the smell of dead people. It was the smell of rotten foodstuffs. The shelves seemed fully stocked, and an overstuffed mouse scampered out of Anna's way, as she went straight to what had been the refrigerated section at the back of the store. Through the glass doors, it appeared that no one had taken anything out of that section, either. Anna put her gun back in the holster on her hip and grabbed one of the glass bottles of water. She drank slowly at first, knowing that too much, too fast would make her sick. The warm water tasted like heaven. It was so soothing to her parched lips and throat. She pulled the bottle away from her lips, realizing that she'd guzzled over half the bottle. *Go slow,* she told herself. *It'll make you sick.*

After filling the plastic bladder in her backpack with water, and stuffing it full of non-perishable food, mostly Allpro, Anna found a real treasure back in one corner of the store. It was an old folded up paper map of Colorado. Not only did it have the state's roads and highways on one side, on the other, it had street maps of the state's major cities. Anna had been wondering since starting this journey how she was going to find the Mendez place in Castle Pines. She still remembered the address from the cards she'd sent to James years ago, but knowing an address and finding it without a map were entirely different things.

She sat outside the store, her back against the wall in the shade on the north side of the building, and studied her newfound treasure. After debating the pros and cons, she decided that she would only follow I-70 to Highway 86 and then take 86 to Castle Rock. From there, she could follow I-25 north to Castle Pines. She decided that she'd search Limon first in hopes of finding a vehicle to borrow. The thought of walking another eighty miles was not very pleasant. She knew she could do it, probably take four full nights of hiking, but finding something to drive would be so much better. *Even an old bicycle would be great,* she thought, as she painfully stood up and stretched.

It didn't take much searching through Limon to tell it had been mostly abandoned before the sickness ever hit. Limon, like most places in eastern Colorado and western Kansas, had shriveled and died along with the Ogallala Aquifer. As the water dried up, so did the town. A train of the familiar blue water tankers sitting on the tracks at the edge of town told Anna where Limon's water had come from in recent years. What she couldn't figure out is why there seemed to be no people in Limon at all, neither living nor dead. There were just a few houses in Limon that appeared to have been recently inhabited. Those were the ones Anna searched. Invariably, the houses looked like someone had just left for the day and failed to return. From rotten food in refrigerators to dirty dishes in sinks, the homes appeared to have been abandoned all at once. Some had beds neatly made, and in others, the bed, or beds, were unmade, like people had been in too big of a hurry to make up the bed before leaving.

*Where did they go?* She wondered. Anna was about to the west end of town, and the heat was getting unbearable. It was the middle of the day, and she'd been on her feet for a good eighteen hours. She decided to shade up and get some sleep before continuing her trek west after nightfall. She'd all but given up on finding any kind of transportation.

The house she was walking past looked a lot like the others that she'd already explored. The front of the house faced south, so Anna, after knocking on the door and getting only silence for an answer, walked around through the side yard to find a place in the shade. She was delighted at what she found on the north side of the house. There was a covered patio with lawn furniture, including a chaise lounge with the cushions still intact. That lounge chair looked more inviting than anything Anna had seen in days, but before she stretched out, she decided to check out a shed in the back corner of the yard. Inside the shed, she found not only a bicycle but an electric bike. Even more surprising, the battery had nearly a full charge.

It was the middle of the night when Anna woke up. It took a moment to remember where she was. She'd awakened from a nightmare. In the dream, she was riding a strange horse up the lane to the Blue River Ranch, but the ranch was gone. It wasn't just gone, it was as if it had never existed. It was the strangest thing. The lane from old Highway 9 was still there just as she remembered, but it led to nowhere. Where her home and the other ranch buildings should have been, the lane just disappeared into the trees that lined Spider Creek. The thought, *you can never go home again,* came unbidden to mind and filled her with dread.

# Chapter 14

ANNA WAS ONLY ABOUT five miles out from Limon, riding west on the eastbound side of I-70 when she saw the lights. At first, she couldn't tell what or where the lights were. The lights came into view some distance ahead as she topped a gentle rise. Anna stopped immediately, putting her feet down, standing stationary astraddle the bike, she could tell that the lights weren't moving. It was definitely artificial lights on the ground, not stars or something stellar just above the horizon. As Anna studied the lights, she thought she could make out some kind of building off to one side. It looked like it had to be a large building or group of buildings fairly close to I-70. Anna could feel the tiny hairs on the back of her neck stand up. Something about artificial light in the middle of nowhere was frightening.

Wishing she didn't have to, Anna rode slowly toward the lights. As she got closer, she could see they were spotlights shining on an object or objects that weren't yet clearly visible. She knew what the lights were shining on before she could clearly make out the crosses. The three black crosses, even though illuminated by the spotlights, didn't stand out much against the midnight sky. But there they were, three large black crosses. The biggest cross in the middle must have been at least forty feet tall, with the two on either side no more than half that.

Anna wanted nothing more than to turn and flee. The Modern Times Church compounds with the three black crosses in front had never bothered her before. Before she'd been kidnapped and raped by men who'd painted the same three black crosses on the side of a military prisoner transport truck, that is.

She got off of the bike and pushed it along the edge of the highway, staying as far away from The Modern Times Church compound as she possibly could. She kept the bike between her and the church as she walked, like the bike was some kind of talisman that could ward off evil. It truly was a compound, not just a single building, and like the rest of the Modern Times Church compounds that Anna had seen, it was surrounded by a tall wrought iron fence. Now that she was close enough, she could see the dim glow of other lights inside the compound. The place obviously had its own electrical power.

*Are people in there?* she wondered. *Maybe that's where the people from Limon went.* Not that she had any intention of finding out one way or another. The compound was built on a hill on the opposite side of I-70 from Highway 86. Seeing she was at the onramp from Highway 86 to eastbound I-70, Anna jumped back on the bike and accelerated as fast as she could up the ramp. The little e-bike only had a top speed of about thirty, but Anna was going almost too fast to make the turn onto 86 at the top of the ramp. She was watching her rearview mirror as much as she was watching the moonlit road ahead, willing the bike to go faster as she sped past the sign that said it was forty miles to Kiowa.

Anna couldn't shake the feeling of fear. It was with her for the rest of that ride. The ride ended when the e-bike's battery went dead just before she made it to the small abandoned town of Kiowa. Having to dodge potholes big enough to swallow both her and the bike, and traversing stretches where the road was just gone, it took the rest of the night to make it that far. In the early light of dawn, she could see the remains of the small town no more than two miles away. Pedaling the e-bike without any battery assist seemed harder than walking, so she dropped the bike off the shoulder of the old road and started walking toward the buildings in the distance.

Since leaving Blue Rapids, Anna had passed through and passed by many towns, both large and small. Now she found herself afraid of the little old ghost town ahead of her. There was no sign of anything to fear. Certainly, no black crosses or compounds that she could see. Looking back over her shoulder every few steps, Anna knew she wasn't really afraid of what was in front of her. It was what lay behind that was so terrifying. Was the Modern Times Church evil, or had some evil people just commandeered their religion? *Evil in the name of God?* She wondered. *How much evil has been done in the name of God?*

..........

The smell was overpowering at first. The closer Anna got to the city, the worse it was. Especially when the wind blew out of the west. It took a few hours for Anna's nose to become desensitized to the terrible smell of death that grew stronger as she made her way through the ever denser suburbs and slums approaching the city. It was mid-morning, getting hot already, and Anna was exhausted. She'd walked all night after spending a restless day in the shade of an old barn on the edge of Kiowa.

Anna knew it was only another two or three miles to Castle Rock, and she had a decision to make. Should she keep going, or find someplace to sit out the heat of the day? She was coming up on what looked like a major intersection. There was some kind of old warehouse on the south side of the road that was tall enough to make a large area of welcoming shade. She sat down with her back against the warehouse wall, had a sip of precious water, and studied her map. Using her finger for a scale, Anna figured it was about ten more miles to the Mendez address in Castle Pines. It seemed odd that she hadn't seen another living human for so many days in a row. It was especially strange as she got closer to the Denver metro area.

She didn't have to see the bodies to know the area around the warehouse was still densely populated, now with dead people. The smell told her all she needed to know about that. Anna wasn't exactly hidden, but she felt like hiding, just in case there were people around who were still alive. *Don't be so paranoid,* she told herself. *It wasn't just evil people that survived the sickness.* She found herself thinking about the good people she'd left behind in Blue Rapids. One man in particular. *I should have just stayed there,* she thought. *There's nothing here but death.* Sitting in the shade of the warehouse trying to decide what to do, it wasn't the fear of being seen, but exhaustion that finally won out. Anna bowed her head and closed her eyes. It was dark when she opened them again.

It was too dark. The sky was full of stars, but the moon was not yet up. Somewhere in the distance, Anna heard the unmistakable yipping of a pack of coyotes. Their cries only adding to the eeriness of being in a totally dead, totally dark cityscape. Deciding she could see well enough to walk by starlight, and knowing she just needed to get to I-25 and then follow it north to Castle Pines Parkway, she stretched her aching legs and set off.

The quarter moon came over the horizon behind her as she walked. By the time she got to I-25, it cast a ghostly light on the surreal scene before her. It looked like some kind of field base for the army had been plopped down under the highway overpass. She could see the remnants of some sort of banner hanging from the overpass above the camp, but she couldn't tell what the banner said. The only part she could still make out was a red cross. *At least it isn't three black crosses,* she thought. Whatever the camp was, it was as dead and quiet as the rest of Castle Rock. Silent except for the coyotes anyway. The coyotes were much closer now. It sounded like they were just on the other side of the interstate, somewhere over on the west side of the abandoned army camp. There was a slight breeze out of the west that carried not only the yapping of the coyotes but the overpowering smell of a lot of rotting flesh.

From the top of the overpass, Anna could see the source of both the stench and the howling coyotes. Less than a quarter-mile to the west, a large pit had been excavated. The heavy equipment that had been used to do the excavating was all still sitting around the perimeter of the pit. There was even a large dump truck with its bed up in the air. It sat there next to the edge, frozen for all time in the act of dumping bodies of the eternal dead. Anna didn't want to get one step closer to that pit. In her imagination, she could see the tangled mass of bodies in the bottom of that hole. She had no desire to see them with her eyes.

Interstate 25 was totally clear of vehicles, which seemed surprising considering the amount of traffic that had once flowed north and south. There were a few vehicles pushed off to the side of the road and abandoned. There were none of the autonomous freight trucks that Anna would have expected. And the only people she saw were the remains of a few bodies scattered along the shoulder and in the median.

As she started walking west on Castle Pines Parkway, Anna had a small problem. She couldn't remember the map well enough to know the twists and turns to get to Castle Lane. She couldn't even remember which street she needed to take from Castle Pines Parkway, and there wasn't enough light to read the map by moonlight. She seemed to remember thinking that she would be on Castle Pines Parkway for at least two or three miles before heading south on...? Not being able to remember the name of the street was frustrating, but she was sure she'd remember it when she saw it.

Anna could feel the excitement building up inside. She was less than five miles from the Mendez residence. As she walked, she imagined the reunion that was now only an hour or two away. *They'll all be asleep,* she thought. *The guards probably won't even let me in the gate.* James had told her enough about the Mendez estate to know it was walled in and protected by a private army. She hadn't given that fact much thought up to now. *Damn it! I need to wait until daylight,* she decided, but her pace picked up instead of slowing.

North Briar Road. The name of the street where she needed to go south popped into her head long before she got there. North Briar Road climbed at a steady grade, as it wound its way up the hillsides. The road was empty until coming around a curve, Anna saw a vehicle in the road ahead. She froze as soon as she what it was. It was some kind of military vehicle that looked both armored and armed. It was just sitting there stopped in the middle of the road. Fear gripped her. Anna didn't know what it was, and she wasn't sure she wanted to find out.

Hoping she hadn't been spotted by anyone, she retreated back around the bend in the road and climbed up into a thicket of dead brush to hide. She found a bare spot in the brush to sit down and rest and to ponder her next move. She considered working her way through the brush up past the military vehicle. She listened intently, but only the night sounds of animals disturbed the stillness. It would be daylight in a few hours. She stretched out on the soft earth to rest.

The ground that she woke up on didn't feel anywhere near as soft as it had when she laid down. She had no more planned on falling asleep than she'd planned on running into the Army, or whatever that vehicle was. The sun wasn't up yet, but it was definitely light. She stood up, stretched, and brushed the dirt off as well as she could before putting her pack back on. She sucked the last few drops of water out of the hydration bladder. It was barely enough to moisten her throat, let alone quench her thirst. *James will have water,* she thought, remembering how close she was to the Mendez Estate.

The armored vehicle was still there, exactly where she'd seen it last night. Anna peered at it through the brush. *Abandoned?* She wondered. At least it didn't have any black crosses painted on it. She approached the vehicle cautiously and walked right past, breathing a sigh of relief that it truly did seem to be abandoned. From the way it was covered with dust, it had probably been sitting right there for months. *What was the army doing up here in the first place?*

She wondered as she made her way up the hill to Castle Lane.

It was just a few hundred yards up the hill to where Castle Lane ended at the gated entrance to the Mendez Estate. Seeing the rock wall that James had described, and knowing she had made it to his home was the most wonderful feeling Anna had experienced in a long time. The feeling was extremely short-lived, though. The massive wrought iron security gate was standing wide open.

No one challenged her as she walked up to the guardhouse. She stopped just long enough to open the unlocked door and look inside. It was empty. She walked on up the driveway around the curve to where the house came into view. The mansion was pretty much as she had always imagined it would be. Robert Mendez, James' father, was, after all, one of the richest men in the world. The only thing that seemed totally out of place was the water truck sitting on top of a landscape berm in the center of the circular driveway. Seeing the hose running from the truck to the house, buoyed Anna's emotions once again. Someone had arranged a backup source of water for the place, which meant they'd survived the sickness.

She was so excited that she practically ran the rest of the way up the steps to the big double front door. She pushed the doorbell button and pounded on the door as loudly as she could. After waiting as long as she could stand to wait, she reached down and tried the latch. To her surprise, the door was not even locked. "Hello," she yelled into the open doorway. There was no answer. She walked into the large foyer and hollered some more. Still no answer.

Instead of going further into the house, Anna went back outside. As she was running up the steps to the house, she'd noticed an open door on the large stable looking building that she knew, from James' description, had to be the car barn. James had told her that his mother called it that, much to the chagrin of his father. Thinking James might be out there in the car barn, she hurried to the open door, hollering as she went, but getting only silence in return. The automobile collection inside the car barn was absolutely astounding, but that's all there was. There were only cars and trucks, with no sign of anyone or anything else inside the vast warehouse. Anna made her way back to the house and found her way to the kitchen. She could hear a faint humming noise that was coming from the refrigerator. She flipped on a light switch, and sure enough, the place still had power. Remembering how thirsty she was, she tried the tap at the kitchen sink. The water that came out was a little bit rust-colored and definitely warm. It must have been from the steel tank on the water truck, but it tasted wonderful to Anna.

*Someone must still be living here, please let it be James,* it was almost a silent prayer. A prayer to whom, Anna couldn't say. She was about as non-religious as a person can be. *Maybe he went somewhere in a vehicle from the car barn,* she thought. *That would explain the barn door being left open. Maybe he's just out scavenging supplies or food.* She looked in the refrigerator. There wasn't much there, so she opened the door to the pantry. The pantry seemed pretty well stocked. Not only was there plenty of AllPro, there were a lot of other canned goods and non-perishables. She'd looked in the refrigerator, now she checked out the freezer. The freezer was stocked even better than she would have guessed. It was full of frozen meats and frozen vegetables. There was even a tub of chocolate ice cream. Anna couldn't remember the last time she had eaten chocolate ice cream or any ice cream for that matter.

*So, I'll just wait for him to come home,* she thought, slipping out of her backpack and hanging it on one of the barstools. She found a bowl and a spoon, having decided to treat herself to some of the ice cream. *James won't mind.*

The ice cream was good but not as good as the ice cream of her memory. Of course, that was homemade, and this was not. A thought nagged at her as she finished the bowl of ice cream. *What if it isn't James that comes home.* Anna felt, as much as heard, the air conditioning unit kick on. *Must be getting hot already,* she thought, and decided to check out more of the estate before it got unbearably hot. That's when she found the graves.

It had obviously been a beautiful flower garden back when it had water. Now it was obviously just a cemetery. *Eight graves?* She wondered. The graves were all unmarked, and they were all relatively recent burials. Anna could tell that one of the graves was a little bit newer than the other seven. *Who's buried here?* That was the troubling question. *And who did the burying? It had to be James,* she thought. *James must have buried...buried who? His mom and dad? That's only two. Who else? Security guards? A maid, housekeepers?* There were too many possibilities to even think of them all. Anna went back inside to wait for James. No use wondering about it, James would be able to tell her everything as soon as he got home.

········

A week passed, then ten days. Every morning, Anna knew this would be the day that James would come home. Every night, she went to bed disappointed. Disappointed and lonely. She'd enjoyed the comforts of the Mendez mansion just about as much she could stand. It had been totally wonderful at first. Especially having a shower with hot running water. Even if it was just barely a trickle of hot water. Second only to the shower, was the luxury of sleeping in a bed in air-conditioned comfort, something Anna hadn't had the pleasure of experiencing since she left Blue Rapids.

Over the past ten days, Anna had thoroughly explored and examined the entire Mendez estate. She'd been amazed at the totally self-contained power systems on the estate and disappointed to find that the water truck had no more than a hundred gallons of water left. Maybe he's out looking for water, she'd thought, when she discovered that the water tank was nearly empty. That had been ten days ago. Now, Anna had a decision to make. There was no longer enough water in the tank for it to even come out of the kitchen faucet.

*What if he doesn't come back?* She wondered, as she finished the last of the ice cream that she'd decided to have for breakfast. *I can't just wait here forever. Soon I'll be out of water. What then?*

It was time to go home. Time to give up on the dream she'd nurtured for so long. The dream of finding James Mendez alive in Castle Pines. Anna knew she'd actually made up her mind yesterday. Last night, she'd plugged in one of the old Volkswagens out in the car barn. She had her doubts about being able to drive all the way to the Blue River Ranch, even with a full charge. She'd developed a planned route to avoid the mountain passes as much as possible by first working her way north along the eastern edge of the Denver metro area. She thought she'd be able to make her way around the north edge of Fort Collins to Highway 287 north to Laramie. From there, she'd just take the old secondary highways down through Walden and on down to Kremmling.

Just one more thing to do before setting out for home. For a moment or two, she just stared at the blank piece of paper and the pen poised in her hand, ready to write. What did she want to say? What if someone besides James finds the note? Finally, the pen started moving, the words appearing on the blank page:

*Dearest James,*

*I've waited for you to return for ten days. I'm just about out of water, and I can't wait here any longer. When you find this note, I'll still be waiting for you, but I'll be waiting at our secret place. Please come to me soon.*

*I love you,*

*Anna*

# Chapter 15

ANNA DIDN'T EVEN LOOK back as she drove out of the gate and started down the hill. She wondered again at the meaning of the army vehicle that would no doubt be sitting in the middle of the road for eternity. She made her way around a curve to a point where the view opened up to reveal the entire city of Denver laid out to the north. That view did bring her to a stop. It had been dark when she'd come up this road, so this was her first view of downtown Denver. Now, in the distance to the north, where downtown Denver should have been, there was nothing but a scene of destruction. It looked like the city had been bombed. She stared at the ruins, trying to make sense of it all. *What the hell happened here?* It was a question that would probably never have an answer. At least, not for Anna.

It took longer to skirt out around the eastern side of the city than Anna had anticipated. She had to make her way around stalled vehicles of all sorts and dead bodies that by now, all looked pretty much the same. There really wasn't much left of the dead but the smell. Ravens, magpies, and buzzards were still feasting on some, most had already been picked clean.

Anna had previously decided to avoid all of the major highways, but seeing how clear and open E-470 looked, she decided to give it a try. It was not just open, it was eerily so. There was not a single stalled vehicle of any kind. It was like someone had cleared it completely of all vehicles. Then, at Pena Boulevard, E-470 was just gone. The interchange ramps and bridges had been blown into piles of rubble. Not only that, but the wreckage of a bunch of military vehicles was scattered throughout the debris. It looked like some kind of convoy had been bombed while crossing the overpass. *Did we have a war?* The question brought to mind the bombed-out bridge across the Snake River back in Idaho. Then she had an even scarier thought. *Was it some kind of germ or biological warfare?* It would make some kind of sense out of the terrible toll the sickness had taken. *How could anything else have killed so many, so quickly? But why not me? Why did any of us survive?*

She was still wondering, still trying to make sense of it all, when she finally got to Highway 287 on the northwest side of Fort Collins. In all that way, she hadn't seen a single living person. Highway 287 wasn't clogged with abandoned vehicles, but it wasn't completely empty either. She had to cross the median several times and use both the northbound and southbound travel lanes. She had just worked her way around a stalled semi when she saw the sign that said Walden, with an arrow pointing to a left turn. Anna had forgotten about Cameron Pass, now she stopped and pondered it. It would be a lot shorter than going all the way up to Laramie and then back down to Walden. If the road was open, that is.

She searched her memory for the only time she'd ever been over Cameron Pass. It had been many years ago when she was just a girl. Her dad and Chuck Pierson had let her ride along on a trip to a ranch on the east side of the pass. She seemed to remember the purpose of the trip was to look at a bull. She couldn't remember now if Chuck had bought the bull or not. What she was really trying to remember was the pass itself. If her memory was accurate, it seemed like Cameron Pass wasn't carved into the mountainside like Berthoud or Vail. From what she could remember, even if the travel lanes of Highway 14 were blocked, she could probably get by on the shoulder or in the borrow ditch. It had already taken longer to get here than Anna thought it would, so she decided to take the shorter route to Walden.

Anna had traveled just over a mile when she saw the green trees that lined the Cache la Poudre River and the old sign that let her know she was on Poudre Canyon Road. Knowing the highway might easily be blocked in a river canyon, Anna decided to keep going anyway. If her way was blocked, it wouldn't be that far back to Highway 287.

She couldn't have been more than five miles up the canyon when she saw them. At first, she couldn't believe it. It had been so long since she'd seen another living human being that she doubted her own eyes. As she got closer, it became clear that there really were four people working in a garden about halfway between the highway and the river.

It was two men and two women harvesting the fruits of a long summer's labor. It reminded Anna of the Farm and those she'd left behind in Blue Rapids. There was absolutely nothing threatening about the four people. They must have felt the same about Anna. They all stopped what they were doing and waved frantically, like they were afraid she wouldn't see them.

The four were already walking toward the road before Anna could even get the car parked. She walked down the shoulder of the road and met the group at the fence that protected their garden. It was a six-foot fence, meant to keep deer from harvesting their precious crop of vegetables.

"I can't believe it!" the first man to reach the fence said. "I was beginning to think we'd never see another soul coming up that road again. I'm Steve."

Steve was short, not even as tall as Anna. He had long sandy blonde hair and a full beard to match. He looked to be around thirty years old. Steve introduced the other three, Mary, Claire, and Mike, before Anna had a chance to say anything.

"I'm Anna." She introduced herself, noticing how strange it was that surnames didn't seem to matter anymore. "It's been a long time since I've seen anyone. Anyone alive," she added. "Are there more?"

"Not here." It was the redhead, Claire, that answered Anna's question. "Just us four, but there's another group a few miles up the canyon. Don't know beyond that, been months since we've seen anybody else besides Josie's bunch."

Claire was probably the oldest of the four, maybe thirty-five or forty. She looked stout and not very feminine. She was the apparent de facto leader of this little family.

"There's seven in Josie's clan," Mary, the youngest looking of the group, added. Mary was a pretty girl. She had long black hair and dark skin. She was built and looked a lot like Anna. If a person didn't know better, they might have mistaken Anna and Mary for sisters. It seemed to Anna that Mary spoke with more of an affinity for Josie's clan than the rest of the group.

Mike, who looked to be in his mid-twenties, didn't say anything. He just kept staring at Anna, looking her up and down in a way that made her feel uncomfortable.

"Well, come on in," Claire said. "Driveway's just up the road. We'll meet you at the house." Without waiting for a reply, she turned, grabbed Mike's hand, forcing him to follow, and walked away.

"It's lunchtime anyway," Mary said. "Please join us." Then she and Steve turned together and followed Josie and Mike.

Anna could hardly refuse. As much as she wanted to get home, she'd been too long without human companionship to pass up the opportunity to visit with others. Besides, they might know whether or not Highway 14 was passable all the way to Walden.

Claire's clan, as Anna thought of these two couples, had quite a little homestead going. The old house that they occupied had belonged to Claire before the sickness. She'd been a widow, living alone for several years before everyone else died. Her husband had died of cancer some years before the sickness. The others had joined her one at a time after the sickness destroyed their world. As Anna listened to their stories, and she shared parts of hers, she found it fascinating that so many of those who survived the sickness were all doing basically the same thing. Banding together in small groups and relearning to live much as their ancestors had decades or even centuries before. Claire's clan seemed to be reasonably happy living with practically no modern conveniences at all. They did have running water, but it was just water piped directly out of the Cache la Poudre River. They boiled the water before drinking it or using it for cooking. There was a well that used to supply the house with water, but without electricity to power the pump, Claire's clan was stuck with water out of the river.

Claire's clan had a wagon and a couple of horses to pull it. Anna couldn't help but wonder why they didn't just go down to Fort Collins to get PV panels and equipment to supply their own electricity. *Guess none of them knows how,* she thought. As they shared the most wonderful lunch of fresh greens that Anna had eaten since leaving Blue Rapids, she had the thought that she could help them set up an electrical system. *Maybe I can come back and help them later,* she told herself, dismissing any ideas about staying with the group any longer than lunch.

Lunch was long enough for Anna to get a lot of information from Claire's clan. All but Claire, herself, had been living in the Denver area in their previous lives. Anna learned how bombs or missiles had destroyed Denver just before, or at the same time as the sickness was killing everyone. No one knew who, where, or why the city was attacked. Strangely, no one seemed to want to talk much about life before the great dying. Perhaps it was too painful to remember. It was something Anna could relate to. She didn't tell them anything about how she ended up in Blue Rapids, Kansas, either. Some memories are best left buried.

Mike had been the first to stumble into Claire's life. Like the others, he had been fleeing the city that was so full of death that it had become unbearable. Like the others, he had no idea where he was going, just away. Claire had invited him in when she'd seen him walking up the road. He stayed and became Claire's lover before Steve showed up. Steve had been invited to stay with Claire and Mike a couple of weeks later. He had decided instead to just keep heading up the canyon.

That's where he found Josie's clan and Mary. Mary told Anna about Josie's clan, which had the same problem as the group Anna had left behind in Blue Rapids, too many women or not enough men, depending on how you wanted to look at it. There were only two men and five women in

Josie's clan. There had been six women before Steve came along and eventually convinced Mary to go back down the valley to Claire's. Apparently, it hadn't taken too much convincing. One of the only two men at Josie's was Mary's older brother.

*Is it love, or just instinct or necessity that still drives men and women together,* Anna thought. Steve and Mary really did seem to be in love. Mike and Claire, not so much. Anna could definitely feel the lust in Mike's stare when he looked at her, and she felt sorry for both Mary and Claire. It was evident to Anna that Mike wanted Mary more than he wanted Claire. *This group is not going to last,* Anna realized with a sadness that surprised her. As an outsider, she was probably the only one who could see it. As an outsider, she knew there was nothing she could do about it.

No one in Claire's clan knew for sure whether the road to Walden was open or not. Anna was the first person they'd seen on the road for a couple of months. Claire said she'd seen a few other vehicles go by back when the exodus from the cities first began. She figured the road must have been open at that time because she didn't see any of them come back down.

Anna thanked them for the lunch and the information and told them she hoped to come back and visit one day. Mary gave Anna directions to Josie's place and asked her to stop in and say hi to her brother. Anna said she would, even though she knew she wouldn't. As she drove away, her thoughts were on human nature and what the future would hold for the few people left in this old world.

It was getting late in the afternoon when Anna saw the sign that said Rand, with a left turn arrow. Highway 14 was heading almost due north at that point, and she knew the geography of this part of Colorado well enough to know that cutting through to Rand and then on down to Granby would cut a lot of miles off her trip. The Volkswagen was already down to less than half of its battery capacity. She looked at the old Colorado map just to make sure, then decided to take the old county road to Rand. She wished it was earlier in the day, but Highway 14 had been a pretty slow go. Like most secondary roads in the state, it was pretty dilapidated from lack of maintenance. That was another point in favor of cutting through to Rand. The old county road might be in better condition than the state highway.

Anna didn't make it to Rand. Her luck ran out before the car's battery pack did. She came to a point where a windstorm had blown several large dead trees over, blocking the road completely. From the looks of it, the road had been blocked and unused for a long time. The sun was setting, and Anna didn't know what to do next. She was pretty sure she was closer to Rand than to Highway 14, but if she turned around, based on the battery gauge, she might well end up running out of juice farther away from home than she was now. Studying the map, Anna figured it was less than eighty miles from where she sat right now to the Blue River Ranch. Eighty miles would be no more than four days walking, so she decided to just spend the night in the car and start walking at daybreak. Now that she was up in the mountains, it wouldn't be too hot for hiking during the day.

It was too cold to sleep. It had been so long since Anna had been in the mountains at night that she hadn't really considered how much cooler it was than the lowlands. She didn't even have a long sleeve shirt, let alone a jacket or a coat. Thinking it might be nice to have a fire, she rummaged around in her pack for the lighter she knew was there.

When she got out of the car, though, she decided it was probably only an hour or two until daylight. She must have slept more of the night than she thought. It wasn't a full moon, but it was definitely light enough to see where she was going. So instead of building a fire, Anna hoisted the familiar pack to her shoulders and set off at a brisk walk.

As light filled the eastern sky, Anna realized just how much she'd missed the mountains. Hiking in the Colorado high country made her feel like she was already home, not just on a journey to get there. Coming around a bend in the road, the forest gave way to a large fenced pasture on one side of the road. The five horses grazing in the meadow saw Anna at least as soon as she saw them. The horses had been at the back of the pasture near a small stream that ran through one corner. They came running across the meadow toward Anna as soon as they saw her.

If there was one thing Anna knew well, it was horses. She could tell at a glance that these were fine animals. Especially the red Quarterhorse gelding that was in the lead. *They act like they haven't seen people for a long time,* Anna thought as she walked over to the fence to meet the herd. She held her hands out over the fence, fingers curled into a fist with palms down. The big red gelding reminded her of Chuck's horse at the Blue River Ranch. He timidly sniffed her hand and allowed her to reach up and rub his forehead. Then he stuck out his nose toward her face. Anna exhaled through her nose right at his nostril as she scratched behind his ear.

"What's your name big boy?" She asked, as the other four horses jockeyed for position to get some of her attention.

From where she was, Anna couldn't see any ranch buildings or a house, and she hadn't passed any yet. So, she started walking along the fence line with the horses shadowing her, like she was the pied piper or something. She crested a hill and could see the ranch buildings laid out about a quarter of a mile away. The meadow was cross-fenced at the crest of the hill, so the horses could no longer follow. As she hurried toward the ranch, one of the horses neighed loudly behind her. She was pretty sure she knew which horse it was.

Anna was reasonably sure she wasn't going to find anyone alive on the ranch. She knew she was right as soon as she walked around the corner of the old ranch house and saw the remains lying on the ground with a revolver lying next to it. There wasn't much more than a skeleton left of the man, but the revolver on the ground and the missing part of his skull told the story. He was lying next to a grave. Anna guessed he'd probably buried his wife before killing himself. *Did he kill himself because he was sick, or just because of grief?* Anna wondered.

She would never know why the rancher had killed himself, but she did know taking horses and tack from a dead man wouldn't be stealing at all.

# Chapter 16

ANNA WAS CURIOUS as to whether anyone was still living in Granby, but not curious enough to ride the three miles into town to find out. Instead, she headed west as soon as she got to the intersection with Highway 40. She was getting so close to home, she could hardly stand it. One minute she was filled with dread over what she might find, the next minute, she was consumed by hopeful anticipation.

This was her second day of riding Red Two, which was what she decided to call the horse that she'd "borrowed" from the dead rancher. By the time she found a bridle and saddle, caught Red Two, and saddled up, it had been late morning yesterday before she even got to Rand. She'd left the gate to the pasture open, and the rest of the horses had followed Red Two for a few hours before getting sidetracked by some extra good grass to graze on. Anna rode as far as the old Denver Creek Campground before stopping for the night. It was hard to believe how sore she'd been after eight hours in the saddle. A few years ago, it wouldn't have bothered her at all.

Anna had awakened this morning even more stiff and sore than when she'd crawled into the bedroll the night before. The bedroll had also been "borrowed" from the old ranch. She'd even found a nice warm lined denim jacket that fit well enough to keep out the early morning chill. Now, after a couple more hours in the saddle, her rear end had gone from being sore to mostly just being numb.

Anna stopped and dismounted to stretch her sore legs and to take off the jacket. It was probably just eight or nine, but the morning sun was already plenty warm to shed that layer. Anna tied the coat behind the saddle with her backpack and bedroll. *Should have grabbed some saddlebags,* she thought. The backpack wasn't a very good substitute for real saddlebags. It was pretty awkward and hard to get tied on securely behind the saddle. Windy Gap Reservoir was low, but it did still have some water in it. Anna led Red Two to the water's edge and allowed him to have a good long drink before mounting up and heading west along the shoulder of Highway 40.

It was disappointing and foreboding to ride through Hot Sulphur Springs without seeing anyone at all. In Byers Canyon, several autonomous semis had all stalled out at once, completely blocking Highway 40. "Good thing I've got you instead of that stupid Volkswagen," Anna told the horse, as she made her way past the stalled vehicles.

She wasn't surprised at all to not see anyone in Parshall. Parshall had pretty much been a ghost town for as long as Anna could remember. But Anna was getting worried as she made camp on the bank of the Colorado River just outside the old town. Having not seen anyone or any sign of a living soul since Poudre Canyon, she was becoming fearful of what she might find in Kremmling tomorrow.

............

Anna didn't make it all the way into Kremmling. Seeing the town of Kremmling again, as she came through the last little cut and around the curve that brought the old airport into view, filled her with such elation that it brought tears to her eyes. She pulled Red Two to a stop, and just sat there for a moment drinking in the sight of her old hometown. From there, with the nearest buildings still a mile away, Kremmling looked just as she'd remembered it. All except for the lack of any vehicles moving on Highway 40, that is. As she got a little closer, she could even see a tiny wisp of smoke rising from somewhere on the other side of the airport. *Probably someone's morning cookfire that hasn't gone out yet.* The thought that someone in Kremmling had a fire was absolutely thrilling. Somebody was still alive in Kremmling.

She was trying to figure out where exactly the smoke was coming from. Maybe even the Donovan's. Maybe Will's mother had survived. Their house was definitely in that general direction. The Donovan house was below the hill just off Highway 9. Anna was just about to the airport when she absently looked over at the old Bureau Of Land Management office on the north side of the highway. What she saw there made her involuntarily jerk back on the reins so hard that Red Two almost reared and immediately started backing up.

The old BLM office building looked much as it always had. The difference that instantly chilled Anna to her core was in the parking lot. The flagpole that had always stood in front of the entrance was gone. In its place, there were three large black crosses. The one in the center was taller than the two that flanked it. Just then, the front doors swung open, and two men walked out. Anna could tell that they saw her at the same time as she saw them. She didn't wait to see more. Spinning Red Two like he was chasing a bolting calf, Anna kicked him just enough to put him into a full gallop headed back east along the shoulder of the highway.

Anna kept trying to look back, but at full gallop, it was hard to see whether or not anyone was following. In the fleeting instant that Anna saw the men come out of the building, she had also noticed a couple of vehicles in the parking lot. *We need to get away from the road,* she thought, but it was almost a mile to where the airport security fence ended, and she was able to get away from the highway. She turned Red Two down toward the Colorado River and eased him back into a walk. He was a damn good horse, but a mile at full gallop had taken a lot out of him. Anna scanned the terrain back to the west, back toward Kremmling, as they headed south toward the river. There was no sign of pursuit of any kind, but she kept a head swiveling lookout all the way down to the river and all the way to the other side. The river was pretty low, and it was easy to find a place to cross. What she hadn't counted on was the fence on the other side. *Damn, what I wouldn't give for some wire cutters,* she thought, as she turned the horse to follow the fenceline downstream toward the Highway 9 bridge. It was less than twenty miles up that old highway to the Blue River Ranch. Less than twenty miles to home.

It wasn't too far downstream to where the fenceline came to a corner, and the fence went due south. Anna knew that if she followed it, she'd hit the county road in no time. The county road she could follow to Highway 9, that she could then follow home. There was a problem with staying on roads, though. If anyone was looking for her, the roads were the most likely place to search. There was a thick growth of trees and brush dead ahead. Anna took another good look around and made up her mind. She got off of Red Two and led him along a game trail that led into the thick brush. She wanted nothing more than to get home, but she decided to just hide out for the rest of the day and head up Highway 9 after dark. She found an opening with plenty of grass for Red Two, tied him up with a rope, and took off the saddle and bridle. Then she stretched out on the grass to rest and think.

Was she crazy to be so paranoid every time she saw a Modern Times Church? They'd never seemed evil before, but then she really didn't know anything about them. They'd just seemed like another crazy religious sect before Little America. Before the three black crosses painted on the side of Sarge and Curt's rolling slave cage. But, unlike Sarge and Curt, the two men she saw in Kremmling weren't wearing uniforms, and they weren't armed. At least they weren't carrying rifles. Then again, Sarge had seemed unarmed and innocent when Anna first saw him.

There had never been a Modern Times Church in Kremmling or anywhere else on the western slope that Anna knew of. She was sure the first she'd ever heard of it was in Eugene. How did there come to be one in Kremmling? Maybe it wasn't the same, but thinking about it, the one in Eugene had just seemed to spring up after she had arrived. Perhaps they were popping up all over the country during the past couple of years. She was absolutely sure that she had never heard of The Modern Times Church before Eugene. It was tempting, now that the adrenaline rush of fear was gone, to just ride back into town and confront the place, to find out for herself what it was all about. She ultimately decided to just get home to the

BR. Maybe her folks could tell her something about the mysterious church. *If they're still alive,* she thought, and immediately regretted even having the thought that her parents might be dead. More than that, deep down, she felt that her parents were both gone. She'd been trying to deny that feeling for months, but it just wouldn't go away.

··· ·· ·· ·· ·· ···

Other than a noticeable lack of use, the lane from Highway 9 to the ranch looked just as Anna remembered it. The sun had just come up in the east behind her, bathing the buildings of the Blue River Ranch in a bright morning glow. Anna was finally home. After riding all night, after unimaginable months of yearning, she was finally home. She felt an entire kaleidoscope of emotions all at once. The incredible feeling of finally being home was tempered by the fear that she might be the only one. There was no sign of life from any of the buildings up ahead. Somebody had survived after the sickness, though. There was no other explanation for the hay crop having been put up in the big meadow. The sickness had killed everyone in the spring, and the hay wouldn't have been put up until summer. *Then where is everyone,* she wondered.

About halfway up the lane, not seeing any sign of activity, worry settled in a little deeper. The piercing sound of an eagle's scream high overhead startled her. Then she saw movement. It was Blackie, Chuck's dog. The Border Collie came running toward her from the big house, letting out a bark at nearly the exact same instant that another sound, much louder, punctuated the quiet morning stillness. It was a gunshot. Red Two, Anna, and Blackie all seemed to freeze at the same time, as the sound of that single gunshot echoed around them, and a flock of birds took flight from the trees behind the old homestead.

# PART TWO

# Chapter 17

**W**HAT THE HELL! SHE thought. Anna grabbed the pistol on her hip without even realizing it. Then, without drawing the gun, she dismounted and scanned the area. It sounded like the shot came from up behind the old homestead, maybe from the area of the old family cemetery. *Who's shooting?*

Blackie ran up to Anna, with tail wagging wildly. It was amazing how a dog instantly recognized someone that it hadn't seen for almost two years. Anna knelt down and didn't so much pet Blackie, as she embraced the old dog. "What's goin' on, boy?" she asked, still looking up toward where the shot had been fired. She still couldn't see anyone, but, oddly enough, she didn't feel threatened at all. The sound of firearms being discharged had always been a normal part of life on the ranch.

Then she heard a shout. A man's voice, sounding almost hysterical. "Hey! Hey! Hello!" The shouting was coming from where she'd heard the gunshots.

"Hello," she yelled back. She didn't recognize the voice. She was pretty sure it wasn't her dad or Chuck, or either one of her brothers. She started walking toward the sound, leading Red Two, with Blackie running on ahead.

She'd taken just a few steps when she saw what looked like a crazy man come running out of the trees behind the big house. He was waving a gun in the air as he ran toward her. Tears filled her eyes. She dropped the reins and started running to meet the mad man as soon as she recognized him.

Anna and James ran into each other's arms and held on for dear life. Tears were streaming down both of their faces, and Anna was sobbing when she finally pushed away.

"You bastard!" she sobbed. "I hate you! How could you? Why?"

James knew exactly what Anna was asking. He'd asked himself the same thing over and over again and hated himself for the same reasons that Anna did. How could he have just dumped her the way he did? How many times had he thought about the things he could have done - should have done? Having just come within inches of killing himself, James' emotions were as wild and mixed up as Anna's.

"I love you Anna. I love you more than anything," he was able to get out past the lump in his throat.

"If you love me so much, why didn't you ever come back? Never even so much as a call."

Anna's sobbing was tapering off, but the sorrow and pain in those deep brown eyes was almost more than James could bear.

"Please Anna, don't hate me. I had to. He made me do it. It was my dad. It...He...I did it for you and Grandpa. Oh Anna, I'm so sorry."

James looked down at the ground, unable to look at the hurt in Anna's eyes. When he looked back up, the pain was still there, but there was also questioning in those eyes. Eyes that James had feared he would never see again.

"What does Chuck have to do with this?" The sobbing had stopped, but Anna's tear-filled eyes still held the pain that she'd carried for the past three years. "And what do you mean, it was your dad?"

"He made me stop seeing you. He would have taken the ranch. He would have ruined Grandpa...and your whole family."

As soon as he mentioned Anna's family, James regretted that he would be the one who had to answer the question in her eyes.

"They're gone Anna. All of them are gone now. It's just us. We're all that's left."

James never told Anna that the shot she heard had missed his head by mere inches when the gun discharged accidentally. He never told her that if she hadn't shown up when she did, the pulling of the trigger wouldn't have been an accident at all, and the bullet would not have missed. He never told her how close she came to being the sole survivor on the Blue River Ranch.

········

Anna placed the wildflower bouquets on each of the graves and remembered her family. The family that was gone forever. These would be the last flowers of the year. It was either late fall or early winter, she wasn't sure which, but the nights had been getting cold, and the days were definitely getting shorter. There had been a heavy frost that morning. Down at the ranch, she could hear James splitting wood. He'd been at it for hours. *Better get down there and help him stack it,* she thought.

The past month or so, since Anna had been home at the BR, was mostly just a blur. She and James had never once left the ranch. There was so much that needed to be done to get ready for winter. James was willing and able to provide a lot of help, but he still had a lot to learn about living on the ranch and caring for the animals. He was learning, though. Grandpa Chuck had taught him a lot, and he was happier than seemed possible. Anna had to admit to a real feeling of contentment, herself. Other than the grieving that she still felt every day, she was happier than she'd ever been. She couldn't say that life with James was exactly as she'd imagined it would be, but then nothing was as she'd imagined it. No one could have ever imagined the world after the sickness, or the great dying, as James called it.

As she walked down the path from the cemetery to help James stack wood, she thought about all they'd accomplished in such a short time. The immediate pressing concern had been making sure they were ready for the winter ahead. Using the old wood-burning cookstove to boil the jars to can tomatoes and beans had been like working in a foundry. The stove heated the house so much that James and Anna were forced to sleep in the old house on canning days. Sleeping with James in the bedroom from her childhood was strange. Some mornings, it almost seemed like another age. It would take a moment or two to fully wake up and realize she wasn't a kid anymore. To reckon with the reality that, other than James, she was alone in her childhood home.

Anna figured she could probably stand to use James's great-great-grandmother's cookstove through the winter, but come spring, she planned on going somewhere to find enough solar components and storage batteries to upgrade the system. By the time summer rolled around next year, Anna planned to have the electric range back in the kitchen and to have air-conditioned comfort to sleep in.

Thwack! The maul stuck in a particularly large block of fir that was probably too green. "You might need to use a wedge for that one," Anna told him, as she came around the corner of the woodshed.

The woodshed was about halfway between the big house that she and James now occupied and the older original ranch house that she'd grown up in. It was really just an oversized loafing shed, big enough to hold all the firewood that two families would need to get through the winter. Both households had always relied on wood heat to keep the winter at bay. Unlike most of the other ranchers in the area, Chuck Pierson had never made the switch to natural gas.

"Do we have enough yet?" James asked as he rubbed the back of a gloved hand across his forehead to wipe away the sweat that was about to drip into his eyes.

Anna looked at the nearly full woodshed and the pile of split wood scattered around the chopping block. "Plenty," she told him. "That would have been enough for both of our houses."

"Good," James said, "then that damn maul can just stay right there."

Blackie, who'd been resting in the shade a safe distance from the flying pieces of firewood, suddenly jumped up and let out a single bark. The fur on his back was standing up, as he looked out toward the highway. James and Anna both turned to see what had aroused the dog's attention. Two people on horseback were coming up the lane. They were still way out by the highway so Anna couldn't be sure, but it looked like a man and a woman.

"Blackie, stay!" Anna commanded the dog as she reached down to her hip for the gun that wasn't there. She'd stopped wearing the pistol on her hip once she finally felt securely at home.

"Looks like we've got company," James said as he started walking out to meet the riders. Even from a distance, he felt like he should recognize the two people. As they got closer, and James got a better look at the woman's long blonde hair, he knew who they were. Anna and Blackie followed James out to the barn to meet them. "Hello, neighbors," James greeted the couple as they dismounted.

"Anna, this is Jack and Connie," James did the introductions. "They're two of the neighbors from up by Silverthorne that I told you about," he explained to Anna. "At least I guess you're still up by Silverthorne?" he asked, directing the question at Jack. James may have told Anna about the two couples near Silverthorne, but he hadn't told her everything about his encounter with Connie. Now, he didn't want his body language to reveal that particular little secret.

"Still there." Connie smiled as she answered the question for Jack.

"Just the two of you?" Jack asked, and Anna and James both knew the rest of the unspoken question. Did anyone else survive the sickness?

"My grandpa died after I got here," James told them. "Think it was a heart attack, but I'm not sure."

There was no need for Jack or Connie to say they were sorry or offer condolences of any kind. Everyone had lost so many loved ones that words were unnecessary.

James couldn't help but steal a glance into Connie's blue eyes. Her wistful smile brought the memory of their short intimate encounter in a hayloft immediately back to mind. James had told Anna about staying with Jack and his brother, and Connie and her sister, while on his way from

Castle Pines to the BR. He hadn't told her about the early morning sexual encounter he'd had with Connie, though. From Jack and Connie's demeanor, James was pretty sure that Connie had also kept that little secret to herself.

"Please, come in and have lunch with us," Anna told the two. "You must be pretty tired from such a long ride." She intuitively knew there was more about Connie than James had told her, but she also knew how much she had never told James. She'd told him some about being taken captive by Sarge and Curt, but, other than the fact that she'd been raped, she spared him most of the details. She hadn't told him about sharing Charlie with Olivia either. As a matter of fact, she hadn't told him much at all about Charlie. Some things are just better kept to oneself.

They put Jack and Connie's horses in the old log barn with some fresh hay to munch on. Then, they all four went into the big house to share lunch with someone other than each other for a change. Talking with someone other than James made Anna realize how much she missed other people. It was especially nice having another woman to talk to. And it wasn't just Anna. All four of them seemed to really enjoy each other's company. Seeking out someone besides Ray and Rita to talk to was the main reason that Jack and Connie had ridden all this way. *People are like horses,* Anna thought. *We truly are herd animals.*

James was having similar thoughts himself. The awkwardness he'd first felt at seeing Connie again gave way to a pleasant feeling of companionship with both her and Jack. *No wonder ancient humans always seemed to live in clans or tribes,* he thought. As much as he loved Anna and wanted to always be with her, it was clear that he'd missed contact with others. It was something that he'd never admitted to himself. He, too, was a social animal. He remembered telling Grandpa Chuck that what they were doing without Anna wasn't living, it was just existing. It wasn't until now that he admitted to himself that Anna wasn't enough either. He had always thought she was all he needed. Now, he knew the truth. They could survive together with no other human contact, but it wouldn't really be living. To really live, not just survive, people need people. Looking across the great room at Anna and Connie sitting on the sofa chatting like old friends, James knew that everyone in the room had similar feelings.

"So, what are you planning to do with all the cattle?" Jack's question broke through James' introspection. Jack was obviously referencing the herd of forty-seven Black Angus in the big meadow. When James and Anna had gathered the herd and brought them down from summer grazing in the high country, Anna had been disappointed that they'd only found forty-seven head. "Used to be thousands," she'd told him, and James had wondered what they were going to do with forty-seven, let alone thousands.

"Damn good question. Guess we're just raising a bunch of big grass-eating pets." James answered. "You guys still raising sheep?"

Jack laughed. "Yeah, I'm kind of like you. How many sheep do four people need? I think the thirty-some head we've got is a little too much. I mean, how much lamb can a person stand to eat?"

James couldn't help but laugh, too. As far as he was concerned, he'd rather have beef any day. "Kind of strange, isn't it?" he asked. "Do you think there are people who could use some beef or lamb. Or wool, for that matter. If there are, how would we ever know? More important, how would we ever get it to anybody that needed it?"

James and Jack's conversation was interrupted by Connie. "We better get going Jack, it's going to be dark before we get home."

Neither James nor Jack had noticed how the time had flown. It was already mid-afternoon. "Why don't you guys just stay tonight and ride back tomorrow?" James asked, adding, "We've got all kinds of room. Two houses worth."

"As much as we'd like to take you up on that offer," Jack answered, "we better take a rain check. Ray and Rita would be out looking for us for sure."

"Thank you so much for the hospitality," Connie was telling Anna as they walked out onto the veranda. "I'm so glad I got to meet you."

"Likewise," Anna told her, "wish you didn't live so far away."

"Me too," Connie said. Then, as she took a last look around, "wish our place was this nice."

As Jack and Connie saddled up and started to head home, James and Anna promised to pay them a visit soon.

"I think we should ask them to come and live here," Anna said, seemingly out of the blue. She and James were just finishing what had been a quiet evening meal of beefsteak and fried potatoes. Both had been mostly lost in their own thoughts all through dinner.

"You mean Jack and Connie?" James asked as if she could have been talking about anyone else.

"I mean all four of them," Anna answered. "They can live in the old house. Sounds to me like it's a lot nicer than where they live now."

James didn't know what to say. The idea of having other people around was appealing, but what would Anna do if she found out about that morning in the old hayloft with Connie. What would Jack do? Probably just as important, if they all lived on the same ranch, would it ever happen again? James already felt like that one encounter in the hayloft had been a betrayal of Anna, could he keep it from happening again? He remembered Connie's words that morning, "I'm the one that fucked you, remember." What if she wanted to fuck him again? It hadn't felt at all like that today, but still, he had to wonder.

"I liked them, and I'm sure I'll like Ray and Rita too." Anna's voice pulled James back into the conversation. "Besides, Connie's going to need all the help she can get. She's pregnant, you know."

James didn't know and trying to not show total shock, he asked as casually as he could, "how pregnant? I mean, when's she due? She didn't look pregnant."

"She thinks she's two or three months along," Anna answered, looking obliquely at James as she added, "can't be more than three months. That's about how long she said she and Jack have been together."

# Chapter 18

ANNA WAS AMAZED AT the warm weather. It seemed like it had to be at least October, maybe even November, but you'd never know it except by the bare aspens and bare, brown cottonwood trees. They'd been riding since just after daybreak, Anna on Pintada and James on Midnight. Each of them was leading another saddled horse behind. James was leading Chuck's old horse, Red; and Anna, Red Two. It had only been a few days since Connie and Jack had been to visit the BR, and now Anna and James were riding up Highway 9 to repay that visit. The two other horses were gifts. When James told Anna that their closest neighbors only had two horses between the four of them, she insisted that they share. There was still a whole herd of horses on the Blue River Ranch. Hell, anymore, there were damn near as many horses as there were cows.

"Do you still think it's a good idea?" James asked, even though he knew what Anna's answer would be. They had talked about it incessantly since Connie and Jack's visit. Anna wanted to share much more than just the two horses. She really did want to share the entire Blue River Ranch.

"You know I do," Anna told him. "Don't know if they'll think it's a good idea, though. Guess all we can do is ask."

"What if they do move into the old house, and then we find out that we don't really get along?" James, himself, wasn't even sure why he kept questioning the idea, but he couldn't seem to stop.

Anna just rolled her eyes and kept riding. She was no longer concerned at all with whether or not asking the others to move to the BR was a good idea, she was thinking about the logistics. Not so much the logistics of getting them moved, but the logistics of the living arrangements once they moved in. The old house that Anna had grown up in didn't have a wood-burning cookstove, just an electric range. It was the same problem that she'd been wrestling with since getting home to the BR. The PV system at the Blue River Ranch was just not adequate. It had only been set up to be an emergency backup for the grid, not the primary power system for the entire ranch.

Maybe she needed to move up the timeline for installing adequate PV power. If the weather stayed this mild, there was no need to wait until spring. Anna knew she was more than capable of putting in a system that could supply all the power the ranch would ever need. She'd proved her capabilities to herself back in Blue Rapids. What she didn't have were the components necessary to build such a system. Where could she find PV panels, batteries, and inverters? And how could she get them home? There were plenty of components down on the front range, but that was a long way to haul stuff in a horse-drawn wagon. Anna was still pondering that dilemma when she saw the wisp of smoke rising from near the old white farmhouse that had to be where Ray and Rita, and Connie and Jack lived.

It hadn't been clear to Anna when James and the others had tried to tell her where the four were living, but now she recognized the old Johnson place. It saddened her to realize that Mr. and Mrs. Johnson were the old couple who the four had buried in their own backyard. Jim and Sarah Johnson had been friends of her parents for as long as Anna could remember. Now, they were all gone. The Johnsons, her parents, so many people just gone. *We're still in shock.* The thought came to her that those who had survived the sickness would probably be in at least a mild state of shock for the rest of their lives. *Why me?* She thought. *Why James? Why the four who are now living in Jim and Sarah's house?* And then she had a much more disturbing thought. *Why did people like Sarge and Curt survive the sickness?* If there was any kind of God anywhere, how could kind, gentle people like Jim and Sarah die while scum like Sarge and Curt were allowed to go on living?

"I don't know," Ray was saying. "I mean, we're all set to spend the winter here. We've got enough canned vegetables put up, plenty of firewood, and god knows we've got plenty of mutton to eat."

"I'm not sure we're even going to have winter," James said. He'd let Anna put the proposal to the other four, and now the whole group was discussing it. It seemed like everyone except Ray was all for it as soon as Anna asked if they'd like to live on the BR. "Besides, we can hitch up the wagon and haul everything you've got down to the ranch," he added.

"Ray, they've even got electricity," Rita added to the argument for the move.

"Well, that might be a little bit of a temporary problem," Anna said. "We don't have enough power to cover everything. Especially on cloudy days. Mostly, we don't have enough battery storage capacity."

Anna went on to explain that the old house they were offering had plenty of electricity for lighting and most things, but not enough to always power the electric range. She told them that she'd planned to add power next spring, but maybe they could do it sooner.

"Guess electricity would be nice," Ray argued, "but do we really need it? Rita and Connie made candles out of tallow, we've got the old wood-burning cookstove. Granted, this old house is small, but we've got plenty of room for the four of us."

"We don't!" Connie exclaimed. "We don't have plenty of room. Ray, I'm pregnant." She looked over at Jack, whose expression left no doubt that it was news to him. "I'm sorry, Jack, I should have told you sooner. We're going to have a baby, and I don't want to have it here."

Rita walked over and put her arm around her sister's shoulders. It was pretty clear that she already knew Connie was pregnant. "We're going to live at the BR," she said flatly to Ray and Jack. "If you want to come along, that's fine. If not, that's fine, too."

..........

The six of them rode along behind the herd of sheep. The four people weren't really herding the flock. Connie and Rita's dogs did most of the herding, keeping the sheep moving along at a good steady pace. Anna hoped the sheepdogs, Mutt and Jeff, would get along well with Blackie, who James and Anna had forced to stay back at the ranch. After Rita's ultimatum made up Ray's mind, the group had decided to get the four moved as quickly as possible. Just because they hadn't had any snow yet, didn't mean they wouldn't get any at all.

After the decision was made yesterday, Anna and James had spent the night in the same hayloft where James had slept before. Early the next morning, before daylight, he even got lucky again. Only this time, the roll in the hay was with Anna instead of Connie. That was a good six hours and at least as many miles ago.

James had never followed a herd of sheep before. It was a lot different than herding cows. When the sheep were bunched close together, they seemed to move in waves. Looking down at the backs of the herd was like looking into gently rolling waves on the ocean. Once, he was so mesmerized by the waves of moving wool that it made him feel seasick. Now, he knew better than to stare down at the swirling mass. *Guess it makes sense to get the herd moved first,* he thought, wondering if cattle and sheep could share the same pasture, or if they'd have to keep them separate.

"Can they stay in the big meadow with the cows?" he asked Anna, who was riding next to him. "Or will we have to keep them separate?"

Anna laughed. "They'll be fine with the cows," she told him. "It's the dogs I'm wondering about. Blackie's pretty used to having the run of the place all to himself."

Anna couldn't help but notice that Jack had hardly said a word since Connie told all of them that she was pregnant. He was even riding by himself, keeping his distance from everyone else. The other five were bunched up riding along together talking, but Jack was on the other side of the right of way, bringing up the rear a few horse lengths behind the others.

"What's with Jack?" Anna asked no one in particular. "Seems like he should be excited about being a father."

"He's just afraid." It was Connie that answered. "He already lost a son and a wife to the sickness. He'll come around, I'm the one that should be afraid."

"Jack will be alright," Ray joined in. All of them talking quietly enough that the conversation wouldn't carry back to Jack. "And you're right, Connie. You should be afraid. Much as I'd like for Rita to have a child, I'm afraid of what could go wrong. It's not like there's a hospital or even a doctor around. Or even a midwife for that matter."

That pretty much shut everyone up for a spell, and they all rode along lost in their own thoughts. Anna couldn't help but look at James. *I want to have his baby.* It was something she'd known, if only instinctively, since before the first time they made love. The instinct to procreate in this time of so much death was something that nearly everyone must be feeling, but Anna knew it was more profound than that. It wasn't just that she wanted to bring new life into this world, she wanted to have their baby, his baby. *Does he want it, too?* she wondered. *It doesn't matter. At least not as long as I have this implant in my arm.* She tried to guess how much longer the implant would prevent her from becoming pregnant. She'd had the implant for almost three years, which meant it was about due for replacement. *What happens if I just leave it in there? Probably not a good idea,* she thought. But how was she going to get rid of it? Like Ray said, there wasn't a doctor around anywhere. At least none that anyone knew of, and she couldn't hardly cut the damn thing out herself. She felt the small lump under the skin on the inside of her left arm. *I'll get Connie or Rita to cut it out.*

"Does it seem like there are more eagles than there used to be?" Rita asked, opening up a whole new subject for conversation. She was looking up, and the others followed her gaze to where two golden eagles were riding the thermals high above.

"Guess I haven't noticed," James was first to answer. "Do you think there are more than there used to be?"

"Don't know, really." Rita laughed. "It's just something Sam told me once. Sam was my fiancé before." She didn't have to say before what. "He'd been going to that new church in Montrose. I think they called it the Modern Times Church or something like that. Anyway, he said the church was founded by some kind of modern-day prophet who predicted that some kind of plague would end the reign of man on earth, and then the eagles would return." She laughed again, a sad short laugh this time. "Guess he was right about the end of man, wonder if he's right about the eagles. It doesn't seem to me that we've ever had any noticeable shortage."

The question of whether or not there were more eagles now than before, hardly even registered for Anna, but the mention of the Modern Times Church immediately caught her attention. "Did it have three black crosses?" she asked. "The church, I mean. The church in Montrose," she added, seeing the blank look on Rita's face.

"Matter of fact it did," Rita answered. "Don't they all have the three black crosses?"

James knew why Anna was so interested in the Modern Times Church, but Anna hadn't told the rest of them. As she gave Ray and Rita the bare outlines of her ordeal with Sarge and Curt, and the three black crosses on the side of the transport cage, Jack rode up to draw even with the rest of the group. He must have overheard some mention of the church. Anna didn't go into detail about being raped, but she said enough to leave no doubt. She also told them about the seemingly fantastic plot to basically start a new confederacy.

"That can't have anything to do with the Modern Times Church," Jack said. "At least not the church that I knew. I only went to a few of their meetings. But the church in

Glenwood, and the people who went there, were nothing at all like that."

"So, what was that church all about?" Anna asked. "It seems like it just sprung up everywhere, all at once."

"I guess that's true," Jack said. "The one in Glenwood couldn't have been there more than a year or two when my wife talked me into checking it out. Looking back on it, I think it was just a product of the times. On the other hand, that Mystic Martin sure did hit the nail on the head."

"Mystic Martin," James laughed. "What's a mystic martin?"

"The prophet. That's what he called himself. I know, pretty weird, right? Weird or not, though, he did prophesy the end of the world, or at least the end of the world we used to know." Jack sounded sold on the guy.

"Hasn't pretty much every religion predicted the end of the world?" James asked. "What makes this Mystic Martin so special?"

"Well, like I said, I only went to a few meetings myself, so mostly I only know what my wife told me. I can tell you it did seem different than any other church I've ever known anything about. For one thing, they didn't seem to have any belief in a god or gods at all."

Anna was spellbound as Jack told them what he knew about the Modern Times church. The three black crosses had nothing to do with the cross or crosses that had always been a symbol of Christian religions. Rather, he said, the black crosses represented three ages of man. The first cross on the left, less than half as big as the middle cross, was for humankind's early development when we were more in balance with the rest of the world. The big center cross represented the modern age, from about the time of the industrial revolution to recent times. A period of time when humans, or humankind, outgrew the entire planet. Dominating and destroying the natural world that had nourished life in the earlier ages of man. And the third cross, "have you noticed it's even smaller than the first?" he asked. "The third cross is now, I guess. Mystic Martin apparently didn't just prophesy the end of the world, he predicted when it would end."

"Wait a minute," James interjected. "Are you telling me this Mystic Martin not only predicted the great dying, but when it would happen?"

Jack laughed. It was good to see him laugh. He'd been so morose since Connie told him she was pregnant. "Well, when the tsunami hit the east coast before anyone was even sick, my wife told me this is it. Martin's right, she told me. The end time is here." Jack's demeanor grew sullen again. "Before she died, she wanted me to take her to that church. She was too sick by then. Maybe I should have taken her anyway."

The entire group became introspective and rode on in silence for a while before Anna had to ask Jack another question. "Did Mystic Martin have anything to say about what happens to us now? I mean, the ones of us that are left."

"He said we would return to the old ways of community, that people weren't meant to live separate lives, but should always be part of a community."

"I guess we're doing the right thing then," James said, "forming our own little community."

"I need to go to Kremmling," Anna said.

# Chapter 19

I T WAS EERILY STILL and silent, like a soundproof blanket had covered the world. Anna got out of bed quietly, hoping to let James sleep. She didn't open the curtains on the bedroom window but instead slipped quietly downstairs for a look outside at the foot of new snow covering the ranch. *Guess we won't be going back to the old Johnson place today,* she thought. *Won't be going to Kremmling, either.* She looked out at the giant, softly falling flakes of snow. It was just starting to get light, but it was snowing so hard that she couldn't even see the old house just a couple of hundred yards away. What an unexpected wonder. She tried to remember the last time she'd seen this much snow. It had to have been years and years ago.

"Looks like a fairy tale, doesn't it?" James startled her. She hadn't even heard him slip up behind.

"It does," she said. "It's been a long time."

James put his arm around Anna's shoulders, and they stood side by side, gazing in wonder as the flakes started to get smaller and taper off. The old house slowly materialized as the snowfall ended. James could see a light shining from one of the windows. That seemed as odd as the snow. The old house had been dark and empty for as long as he'd been living in the big house. *It must be half a year now.* The thought took him back to a much earlier time. A time when he and the world were both so much younger. A time when the woman standing beside him was just a girl who lived in the old house that was now occupied by new residents.

It was chilly. "Guess we better build a fire," James said. He pulled Anna into a tight warm hug and held her briefly before letting her go and crossing over to the kitchen side of the great room to get a fire going in the cookstove. "Hard to believe it's cold enough for a fire to actually feel good," he told Anna. "Especially as warm as it was yesterday."

The clouds had been building, and the temperature dropping yesterday evening while they put the sheep in with the cattle in the big meadow. It was dark by the time they got the four newcomers somewhat settled into the old house. Now, Anna could see a wisp of smoke rising from the chimney of the old house. *Good thing we made sure they had firewood,* she thought.

The snow completely stopped falling by the time it was fully light. All six of the newly created Blue River clan traipsed out through the snow to throw some hay to the sheep and cattle. Fortunately, they didn't even need to hitch up the wagon to haul the hay. They just had to use pitchforks to throw it over the fence from one of the loose stacks that James and Chuck had put up a few months ago.

"Should we haul some hay to the horses in the north pasture?" asked James. Caring for livestock in winter was one more thing that James had yet to learn. Anna, Rita, and Connie all told him no at about the same time.

"The north meadow wasn't mowed," Anna told him.

"The horses can paw through the snow to plenty of grass," Rita said.

413

Feeling the warm sun on her face, Connie added, "Snow'll be all gone by this evening, anyway."

The exchange brought out an irony that was mostly lost on the men, but not the women. This little band of people was made up of three men who were less knowledgeable than any of the three women when it came to surviving in this new reality.

By the time they were finished feeding, the sky had begun to clear, and the sun started melting the snow at a phenomenal rate. True to Connie's word, by nightfall, the BR had changed from a winter wonderland to a muddy mess.

The windows were all wide open in the big house. Cooking the group's first dinner together on a woodburning stove in what was now, temporarily at least, a communal kitchen had completely overheated the entire house.

"We have got to get enough power to stop using this damn thing," Anna said, referring to the stove that was still putting off way too much heat. "I think I know where to get enough batteries for storage. There are two semis stuck in Byers Canyon that have more than enough battery capacity. Getting the batteries out and getting them home might be tough, but the real problem is going to be finding PV panels and controllers, and inverters, for that matter."

"Why go all the way to Byers Canyon?" Ray asked. "Plenty of trucks on I-70, and it's a lot closer."

Anna had already guessed there would be trucks on I-70. She had another reason to go in the other direction, though. What she really wanted was to find out who and how many had survived in Kremmling. Now that it seemed like the Modern Times Church was not a threat, she really wanted to find out if any of her friends from town had lived through the sickness. There was even a chance that Dr. Ming was still alive. Or, maybe one of the nurses from the clinic.

"What about the solar farm up by Frisco?" Jack asked. "Could we get any components from there?"

Anna didn't know anything about a solar farm near Frisco. "What solar farm?" she asked.

Jack said the power company had installed a large array of PV panels just outside Frisco three or four years ago. He didn't really know anything about it, other than that it was visible from the interstate, and some of the few rich people that still maintained mountain homes up by Breckenridge had complained mightily when it went in. The *"not in my back yard"* crowd didn't want a solar farm detracting from the mountain views.

Anna was considering the possibility of being able to get parts from a commercial solar installation when a downdraft forced a puff of smoke from the cookstove. *Definitely worth checking out,* she thought. Then she had another thought. *If there were still summer homes for the wealthy near Breckenridge, wouldn't some of them also have PV systems?* Thinking about wealthy people's homes led to another thought. *There might even be a usable vehicle and charger we could borrow.*

..........

It was quite a procession that made its way up Colorado 9 from the BR to the Johnson place the next day. James, who was extremely grateful that Chuck had taught him to drive the team of draft horses, and Jack, who'd never been on a horse-drawn wagon before, were in the seat of the old wagon. They were led by three border collies, who seemed to know exactly where they were going. Four horseback riders, three women and one man, followed along behind at a leisurely pace.

There was not even a trace of yesterday's snow left, but the tops of the peaks were still white in the distance. The plan the group had put together was to spend the night at the Johnson place and then, tomorrow, while the other four loaded up the wagon, Anna and Connie would ride up to Frisco to see what they could find in the way of PV power supplies. James hadn't liked the idea of two women going off alone, but Anna had patted the pistol on her hip and pointed out that Connie had her trusty old 30-30 rifle in her saddle scabbard.

It was a long round-trip ride from the old Johnson place to Breckenridge and back, so Anna and Connie set out before sunrise. Jack was right about the abandoned semis on I-70. The two women ran into the first of them as soon as they got past the burnt-out remains of Silverthorne. They stopped, and Anna studied the first one to see what she thought it would take to get the batteries out of the truck. One thing she didn't want was to come all the way back from the BR to steal batteries and find that she hadn't brought all the tools needed to do the job.

Satisfied that she knew what tools to bring when they came back for the batteries, she and Connie rode up the interstate to where they could see the PV array off toward where Dillon Reservoir used to be. What was left of Dillon Reservoir was a lot more ruinous to the picturesque beauty of the scenery than the solar farm had ever been. What had once been a large lake was now mostly bare ground with little pools of water remaining in the very lowest areas. Anna could remember seeing the reservoir full of water once when she was very young. In her mind's eye, she could still see the sailboats in the distance. Boats that hadn't been on that lake for at least ten years now. *Guess Denver doesn't need any water now,* she thought, remembering her dad telling her that all of that water wasn't even enough to satisfy the needs of the capital city. The concept of there being enough people to drink Dillon Reservoir dry had been unimaginable to her three or four-year-old self.

They had to cut through the fence that surrounded the PV farm, but Anna had planned on that. She had brought both wire and bolt cutters. Jack was definitely right. It wasn't the largest solar farm by any means, but there were enough PV panels to power a small town. And better yet, they were less than five years old. In use, they should last another twenty-five years or so. Anna had the thought that if she could get them all and store them away somewhere out of the sun, she'd have a lifetime supply of panels and then some. Of course, storage would still require batteries, but there was a lifetime supply of those in the trucks on I-70.

"Will they work?" Connie asked.

"We can make these panels work just fine," Anna answered. "If we can find the rest of what we need, that is. Do you know if there is, I mean was, any kind of electrical supply places anywhere around here?"

"Sorry," Connie laughed. "I'm not from around here. Not only that, I don't know much at all about electricity. After the power went out, I figured we'd just have to live like my great-great-great-grandparents did. You know, before electricity."

"Kind of tough, isn't it? Living like our ancestors did."

Connie really laughed at that. "Why do you think I was so anxious to move to the BR?" she asked. "After a couple months at that old Johnson place without any power or running water, I was ready to go anywhere." She looked thoughtful for a moment before continuing. "At first, I thought going back to the old ways might be a good thing. I mean, look at how badly we screwed up the planet with all of our modern conveniences."

Anna smiled. "Guess we did really blow it, didn't we? It's ironic that just about the time we finally stop killing nature with fossil fuels, nature finally gets around to killing most of us."

"Yeah, as much as I hate to admit it," Connie said, "the world's probably a better place without so many people in it." She rubbed her hand on her tummy, where new life was now growing. "What will life be like for our children? I mean, won't they have to learn to live without all of this?" She pointed at the rows and rows of solar panels.

Anna thought about it before replying, "Not if I can help it. We may not be able to manufacture any more of these, but we can certainly use what's already here."

"I'm glad you can," Connie said, as she started to get back on her horse. "Thanks Anna. I don't know where we'd be without you."

Anna, holding the reins of Pintada in one hand, didn't mount up, but looked up at Connie, who was already in the saddle. "Does Jack know?" she asked. Connie didn't answer, though she knew what Anna was asking. She blushed a little as Anna held her gaze. The answer was plainly written in Connie's blue eyes. "It's okay," Anna finally said. "I don't think James knows either. I mean, he may wonder, but he doesn't know the baby is his."

"I'm so sorry, Anna." Tears welled up in Connie's eyes. "I didn't know you. I didn't know anything. It just happened. It..." she looked down and mumbled, "I'm sorry."

"I'm not," Anna said the words with such truth of conviction that it surprised her as much as it surprised Connie. "The men don't need to know," she added, as she stepped into the stirrup and mounted Pintada. "Sometimes the men don't seem to know much, anyway."

Connie couldn't help but laugh through her tears. Anna crowded Pintada close enough to Connie's horse to reach over and give Connie a hug. "We can help each other raise James' children," Anna said. "I plan on having his children myself someday, you know."

Connie hugged Anna back. "My baby could be Jack's, you know. It was only that one time with James. Oh Anna, it'll never happen again. I promise."

Anna let go of Connie and looked into her eyes. "You probably shouldn't be making promises like that. Never's a long time. We can't know the future any more than we can know for sure who's baby you're carrying. Let's just promise each other to make our shared future as good as it can possibly be."

"That I can promise," Connie answered. "I'll help any way I can, but you'll have to tell me how."

"First thing, let's see what we can find in Frisco and Breckenridge," Anna said over her shoulder, as she rode back toward the highway.

They didn't find much in Frisco. Anna found it especially odd that there didn't seem to be anyone alive, or even any indication that anyone had survived in Frisco. It seemed like since there'd been some survivors almost everywhere else, why not here? The grocery stores didn't even look like they'd been ransacked at all. There were a few human remains scattered around, but they'd been dead so long that scavengers had pretty much picked the bones clean.

"Shouldn't we get back?" Connie asked when Anna turned toward Breckenridge instead of heading back to the interstate. It was already late morning, and a good half day's ride back to the Johnson place.

"Guess we should," Anna answered. "But something isn't right here. Let's just take a quick ride up to Breckenridge first."

About a mile up the road toward Breckenridge, Anna struck gold. There was a huge building supply store that not only had lumber but all kinds of electrical and plumbing supplies. The store had all of the breakers, switches, wire, and everything else Anna would need to put together a good power system. *Sure wish I had that old propane-powered truck that me and Charlie found in Blue Rapids,* she thought. She'd found everything they could possibly need. Everything except something to haul it all back to the BR. *Maybe we can find something in Breckenridge.*

Something was still bothering Anna as she talked Connie into continuing on up toward Breckenridge. It was the way people's remains seemed scattered in the wrong places. Like most of them had died outside instead of sick in bed. A few dying outside seemed reasonable, but there were definitely more than just a few. She was pondering the question of why so many were outside when the three black crosses came into view. Anna stopped Pintada, and Connie, who'd been riding side by side, continued on a little before stopping and looking back at Anna.

"What's wrong?" Connie asked.

Anna forced herself to relax the reins and gently nudge Pintada with her heels to start walking again. "Sorry, those three crosses still freak me out," she answered as she caught up, and the horses started walking side by side again. "Guess I just need to get over it." She forced a laugh. "What's one more old abandoned church?"

"That church kind of creeps me out, too," Connie said. They were just passing by the driveway that led up to the church's parking lot. "Something about the way it just sprang up everywhere all at once. It always seemed like a cult or something to me. Guess most religions are basically just cults, though."

Before Anna could respond, the peace and quiet of the valley were shattered by a girl's scream from inside the Modern Times Church. Then a girl's voice yelling, "You can't. She's too little! I won't let you." The girl sounded hysterical.

Anna was off of Pintada in an instant and had her pistol in her hand practically before she realized it. Connie was almost as quick to dismount and pull the 30-30 out of the saddle scabbard. Then, a man's voice yelled, "give me back my gun. I'll kill you, you little bitch."

The sound of two gunshots followed in quick succession and then another scream. Anna was running toward the front door of the church when the door opened, and a man stumbled out, clutching his abdomen. He looked more deranged than anyone Anna had ever seen. Sarge and Curt both had crazy eyes, but this man made them look sane. His hair was sticking up in every direction, the blood spilling out between his fingers was only adding to the filth of the chambray shirt. But the eyes were what Anna would never forget. They were the craziest eyes she had ever seen. Having obviously been shot, fear in his eyes would have been normal, but not the wide-eyed total insanity that was so obvious. The man almost made it to the first step of the porch before falling face-first down the steps. If he wasn't dead before he fell, the way his head hit the concrete walk at the bottom of the stairs surely would have killed him.

As the man fell away, Anna was face to face with a young girl pointing an assault rifle at her. The girl was almost as filthy as the dead man had been. Her stringy long blonde hair looked like it hadn't been washed in ages. She was wearing some kind of dirty denim dress that might as well have been a sack. She appeared to be a pre-teen, or maybe in her early teens. The girl's pale blue eyes weren't crazy. They were just terrified. The tears streaming out of those eyes were leaving trails through the layer of dirt on the poor girl's face.

Anna lowered her pistol. She couldn't have shot the girl if she wanted to. "She's too little," the girl mumbled, as she too lowered the weapon in her hand and let it drop to the floor. "I couldn't let him fuck her too. She's too little," she said between sobs, as she sank to her knees and then just kind of folded over frontwards.

Anna holstered her pistol and rushed up the stairs, thinking maybe the girl was wounded. "Are you hurt?" she asked as she knelt beside the girl. The girl, head down, just continued to sob. Anna put her hand on the girl's shoulder, as a younger girl came out of the door and knelt down to hug and hold the first girl. The younger girl was at least two years younger than the first girl, who was obviously her older sister. Both girls were sobbing.

"You saved me, Misty," the younger girl sobbed. "You really did it. You saved us. He won't ever kill anybody else. Not ever again."

Anna looked up from the two sobbing girls to see Connie standing over the dead man. Connie's normally pale complexion had turned pure white. She backed away from the body on the sidewalk and bent over and wretched. "Jesus, the smell!" she got out between heaves.

The stench was definitely overpowering. Anna wasn't sure how much was plain old body odor and how much was the blood and guts spilling from the dead man's body. She gently lifted the two girls to a standing position and led them back inside the church. If there was anyone else there, they would surely have made themselves known by now.

Inside the church, the first thing Anna noticed was the lights. The church had electricity. "Is there anyone else here?" Anna asked the two girls. The girl's sobbing had subsided, but they were probably both in shock. Anna didn't really expect an answer, the building just seemed empty.

"Just us now," the younger girl surprised Anna by answering. "He killed the rest."

They were in what must have been the main meeting room of the Modern Times Church, but it seemed more like a business conference room than a chapel. There was a small stage with a podium at one end of the room, with two rows of long tables and cushioned chairs filling the rest of the space. The tables and chairs had once been arranged so that seated people could face each other across the tables or turn sideways to face the podium. Now, the room was a total mess. Some chairs were still in place at the tables. Some were laying scattered about like they'd been knocked over and left. Some were even broken. The tables, chairs, and walls were riddled with bullet holes, and the brown stains of old dried blood were everywhere. Anna looked around at the scene of what must have been a massacre. A massacre that had happened quite a while ago. *Where are the bodies?* She wondered. Then she noticed the dried streaks of blood on the floor, all leading to a closed door at one side of the room. Anna decided she had no desire to see what was on the other side of that door.

"Can we go home now?" It was the older girl, the one named Misty. Her voice was totally flat, with no emotion.

Anna looked at the girl's blank stare and could not imagine the trauma and horror these two young girls must have been through.

Connie, who'd followed the others into the church, took Misty's hand and started back toward the entrance. "Sure," she told the girl, "let's go home."

Anna took the younger girl by the hand and followed Connie and Misty. "I'm Anna," she told the younger girl. "What's your name?"

"Mandy," the girl answered. "Mandy Carlisle."

"Well, Mandy Carlisle, where is home?" Anna asked, as they walked toward the two horses that were patiently trying to graze on some old grass at the side of the road. Not an easy feat with a bit in their mouth and reins dragging along the ground.

"Up there," Mandy said, pointing in the general direction of Breckenridge.

"Have you ever ridden a horse?" Anna asked.

"Oh sure, that's how we got here, but our horses ran off. Can we really go home?"

It was heartbreaking for Anna to tell Mandy she'd take her home, knowing that for Mandy, there would never really be any going home. At least not any kind of home the young girl had ever known before.

Mandy didn't do much talking except to give directions, and Misty might as well have been mute. Anna mostly thought about the trauma these two girls must have endured. Being a rape survivor herself, she could not imagine what it must have been like for Misty, who must have been raped repeatedly by the crazy man. And poor Mandy, the insane bastard was apparently going to rape a girl that hadn't even reached the age of puberty. How Misty had been able to get the gun and kill that man, they might never know, but if any man ever needed killing, it was the one they left lying face down in front of the Modern Times Church.

It was a mostly silent ride for a couple of miles up Highway 9 before Mandy directed them to take a paved driveway that disappeared into the trees on the west side of the highway.

"Are your parents alive, Mandy?" Anna knew the answer before she asked, but she needed to get it out in the open. She knew they'd have to take the two girls back to the BR. There was no way she could stand to leave them here alone.

"Mom died," Mandy answered, and then got quiet again.

"He killed him." It was Misty, not Mandy, that continued to answer. "That's what you want to know, isn't it? He killed our dad just like he killed the others."

"Who was he?" Connie wanted to know, or maybe she just wanted Misty to keep talking; to get her out of the dark place she was in.

Neither Misty nor Mandy answered right away. They seemed to be lost in thought for a few moments before Misty said, "I don't think he was from here. He just showed up at the church. He just walked in with that gun and, and..." She burst into tears again.

Everyone fell silent again, except for the sobs coming from Misty. They rode around a bend in the driveway and came upon three horses grazing at the side of the drive. All three were saddled with rope halters on their heads but no bridles.

Mandy saw the horses at about the same time as Anna did. "Peanut!" she squealed. "Look, Misty, it's Peanut."

One of the horses was a buckskin with a dark mane. *That one has to be Peanut,* Anna thought. The other two horses were white. All three were pretty animals, but the saddles they wore were twisted and dirty. *How long have they been trying to rub off those saddles?* Anna couldn't help but wonder.

Misty raised her head and stopped sobbing as soon as she saw the horses. The nearly instantaneous change that came over her was so profound it was amazing. Anna couldn't help but smile at the sight. Here was a girl who loved her horse as much as Anna loved Pintada.

"Which one's yours?" Anna asked.

"Cloudy," Misty answered. And then she even smiled. She didn't even wait for Connie to stop before swinging her leg up over the horse's rump and sliding to the ground.

Anna stopped Pintada to let Mandy off, and watched as the two girls walked right up to the horses. The horses seemed to be as happy to see the girls as the girls were to see them.

"We should have brought the bridles," Misty said. She took hold of a halter in each hand and started leading the two white horses up the drive. "We should have known the horses would come home," she told her little sister, who had a grip on Peanut's halter, and was following alongside.

Anna almost laughed out loud. It was hard to tell if Mandy was leading Peanut, or if Peanut was pushing her along. The phenomenal change that came over the two girls made her think about the power of love. Not just between people, but between people and animals. She reached down and patted the side of Pintada's neck and remembered how much she'd missed her horse when she was away at college.

The driveway, which had been climbing steeply, worked it's way around a switchback and then, after a short straight stretch and another curve, came out on the cleared top of a hill. There was an impressive looking house at the end of the drive, an even more impressive barn and corrals off to one side, and a large metal shop on the other. Misty and Mandy led the horses straight to the barn as Connie and Anna followed.

With their own horses tied up loosely at the hitching rail in front of the barn, Anna and Connie helped the Carlisle girls get the other three horses unsaddled and into stalls. Mandy seemed to want to get to the house, but Misty, just as Anna herself would have been, was intent on caring first for the animals. Like any good old-fashioned horse barn, this one had a hayloft. Anna helped Misty break a couple of hay bales and throw the hay down through the openings into the horse's troughs. Then, back down on the ground floor, to Anna's amazement, Misty opened the spigot on a yard hydrant and, using the attached hose, filled a water bucket in each stall. Must be a well, Anna realized. But, also power for a pump.

"I'll put them out in the paddock later," Misty said. "After I have a chance to clean them up."

Following Mandy and Misty toward the house, Anna glanced back over her shoulder at the barn and saw the source of electric power. The entire south-facing gambrel style top of the barn was covered with a solar roof. *Must be storage batteries somewhere,* she thought, and made a guess that the large metal shop contained some kind of battery room.

Connie and Anna were both surprised when the two girls didn't go straight into the house but walked around the side to the back yard. There, for a moment, they stood silently, with heads bowed at an obvious grave in the back yard.

"It's our mother," Misty explained. "This is where Dad buried her."

"Do you have any other family?" Connie asked.

Misty put her arm around her little sister, as she answered. "No, I guess just me and Mandy live here now." Then she looked up at Connie. Almost pleading, she asked, "Do you want to live here with us? We have lots of room," she added.

Connie and Anna both smiled at the invitation. "We'd love to," Connie answered, "but we already have a home."

"And we have other people waiting for us," Anna added. "It's a long ride, and we have to get back before they get worried about us. But you can come, too."

"I don't want to go," Mandy practically screamed. She ran to the back door of the house and disappeared inside.

"We can't stay here alone, can we?" Misty said. The forced maturity of one so young was heart-wrenching.

Fighting to hold back her own tears, Anna knelt down in front of Misty and took hold of her hands. She looked up into the face of the girl who was so much older than her years. "No," she told her, "you can't stay here alone. But I promise you can come back. When you're a little older, you can come back here to live if you want to."

Misty bent down and gave Anna a hug. There were tears in both their eyes, but Misty was no longer sobbing. The young woman and the even younger girl, who had both been through so much, just held each other in a silent embrace for a long time.

Finally, Anna stood up. "It really is a long ride," she said. "We better get started."

"We should take my Dad's truck," Misty said. "We can load the horses in the trailer." Anna and Connie both stared at the girl in shocked surprise. "If you can drive it," Misty added.

# Chapter 20

ANNA WOULD LIKE TO have seen the look on James' face when he came out of the Johnson place and saw a truck with a horse trailer coming down the road. It was probably about like the look on hers when they opened the shop doors at the Carlisle place, and the truck and trailer were sitting there side by side. Both the truck and the trailer were plugged in, and both were fully charged and ready to go. Anna had never seen a truck-trailer combo like this one, but it didn't take long to figure out that they were truly designed to work together as a unit. The combination vehicle was like a small electric semi-truck with massive battery capacity. There was not only a huge battery compartment under the fifth wheel and cab of the power unit, the entire floor of the four-horse trailer housed a separate battery pack. When Anna first pulled the truck out and connected it to the trailer, the combined indicator gauge said it had over a thousand miles of range.

It was just a thirty-minute drive instead of a three-hour ride on horseback, but it was still late afternoon when Anna parked the truck at the Johnson place. Anna and Connie had allowed Mandy and Misty to have baths and change clothes while they put four horses in the trailer and got ready to go.

"Well I'll be damned," James said by way of greeting, as Anna climbed out of the driver's seat. He wasn't sure what to say when the back doors of the truck opened, and two young girls got out, one on either side of the truck.

Anna gave James a quick hug and then stood back and introduced him to Mandy. Meanwhile, Connie was introducing Misty to Jack, Ray, and Rita over on the other side of the truck.

"Misty and Mandy are going to come live with us," Connie announced to the group.

"Just for a while, though," Misty was quick to add. Anna had promised the girls that someday they would be able to go back home. She hadn't said how many years away someday might be.

Anna put her hand on Mandy's shoulder and said, "someday, these young women want to go back home to Breckenridge. They have an absolutely beautiful home, and I promised them they could go back. Who knows, they have such a nice setup there, I might want to go live with them myself." She winked at James and gave Mandy's shoulder a slight squeeze.

Mandy looked up at Anna and smiled. "Really," she said hopefully. "You might come live with us."

Anna smiled down at her. "Maybe," she said. "Someday."

The thought had actually crossed Anna's mind that the Carlisle place was, in some ways, set up better than the BR. It was already comfortably self-contained, with plenty of power and well water. As Anna had checked it out, she'd realized that the Carlisle place had never been on the grid to begin with. So, when the lights went out most everywhere else, nothing changed at all at the Carlisle residence. The problem, though, was it was just that, a residence. There was no pasture or even a garden. Mandy and Misty's parents must have been quite wealthy to own and maintain a place like that, but it was only self-contained as far as water and power were concerned. Food, for both the people and their animals, had to be imported instead of grown on-site.

Anna had thought about the Carlisle home a lot while driving from Breckenridge. The vehicle she was driving was nearly perfect for the BR's needs. The only thing that could have made it better would have been all-wheel drive. But then again, as rare as winter snow was anymore, maybe that wasn't even a factor. Anna's first thought regarding the truck was that she should move some of the electrical systems, including the chargers for the truck and trailer, from the Carlisle home to the BR. She'd already changed her mind by the time they got to the Johnson place. No, much like she'd left the bomb shelter intact back in Blue Rapids, leaving the Carlisle place intact was a better option. It was less than forty miles from the BR to the Carlisle place. Anna would just have to charge the truck and trailer there when needed. With a fully charged range of well over a thousand miles, it wouldn't need to be charged very often. When it did, she and James and the two Carlisle girls could just spend a night or two there instead of at the BR.

Right now, what was needed was getting people, horses, and a wagon load of possessions back down to the Blue River Ranch. The group had previously planned to spend another night at the Johnson place before riding home tomorrow. Having the truck changed all that. The old horse-drawn wagon was already loaded up for the trip back, but there was no good way to pull it, other than with the team of draft horses. So, they decided to put the two Belgians in the Johnson barn, and make two trips with the truck to get the people and the other horses on down to the BR before nightfall. Tomorrow, Anna would drive James back up to get the horses and wagon.

··········

With the Carlisle truck to transport components, and the entire Blue River clan pitching in to help, it took about a month to complete the power system on the ranch. Anna even had extra PV panels, batteries, and other components safely stored in the shop before ending the solar salvage runs to Frisco.

During that time, Connie's pregnancy was starting to show, and Anna was becoming more and more envious. It was strange how she could shrug off not being jealous of Connie for having sex with James, but couldn't help being envious of her pregnancy. The desire to have her own baby was growing faster than Connie's belly.

"I have to go to Kremmling," Anna told James. They were still lying in bed, basking in the afterglow of morning lovemaking. She leaned up on one elbow and looked at James. "Maybe the doctor's still there. I need to get this stupid implant out so we can have a baby."

James smiled up into Anna's bright brown eyes. "Thought you said we could cut it out right here," he said. "How hard can it be?" He reached over and felt the tiny lump on the inside of Anna's arm.

"I suppose we probably could, but we need to find out about Kremmling. I need to know who's still there."

The sounds coming from downstairs told the two lovers that Misty and Mandy were already up. Caring for the two young girls had turned out to be no trouble at all. Misty, aged by trauma, was so much more mature than her twelve years of age. She not only did most of the caring for herself, but she also took care of her little sister, too. The only indication of the PTSD that the young girl was undoubtedly suffering was the occasional breakdown into uncontrollable sobbing. Anna would hold her and try to comfort her through those times and, once the anguish passed, Misty would seem rejuvenated and energized once again.

Anna, who had sat up on the edge of the bed, thinking she should get downstairs to help the two girls fix breakfast and then deciding that Misty was fully capable, twisted back around to look at James. "It's not just me, you know," she told him. "Connie's going to need someone, too."

James had wondered about the possibility that he might be the father of Connie's baby, but he thought that possibility was known only to himself and Connie. Like most men, he had no idea what a powerful force women's intuition could be. Besides, the odds of that one encounter making Connie pregnant seemed pretty slim. "What if the doctor in Kremmling didn't survive?" he asked.

"I don't know," Anna answered. "What I do know is that no one on this ranch has any experience delivering a baby. Even if Dr. Ming is dead, there might be somebody in Kremmling to help. We know some people are still living there."

"Two people. You only saw two men, and they were coming out of one of those churches that seem to be home to some really crazy people. What if they're like those two you ran into in Wyoming? Besides, Connie isn't going to have her baby for a few months yet. Maybe we should wait a while before we risk going to Kremmling."

Anna stood up and started toward the door. "I'm going to Kremmling," she said over her shoulder. "I hope you'll come with me."

It was a cold day. *It has to be about Thanksgiving,* thought Anna, as they got closer to Kremmling. She wished she had kept track of time so she'd know what day it was, but then again, what difference would it make to anything. She could see wisps of smoke rising above the hills before they even got to the point where Kremmling came into view.

"Looks like somebody's there," James said.

"More than I would have guessed," Rita added from the back seat. "That's at least four separate fires."

There were four of them in the truck, Jack and Connie had stayed home with Misty and Mandy. All four were armed, even though Jack tried to convince them there was nothing sinister about the Modern Times Church. Even Misty agreed with him. Apparently, the Carlisles had been members of the Modern Times Church. When she'd finally opened up to Anna about her ordeal in Frisco, she said the crazy man she'd killed was a total stranger to the members of the Frisco Chapter of Modern Times. Misty had no idea where the man had come from, or why he killed everyone but her and Mandy. That was just one more mystery that would never be solved.

As they topped the rise in the highway where Kremmling and the Colorado River Valley came into view, all four of them were wondering the same thing. How many people were living in Kremmling, and what kind of people were they? By the time they got to the Colorado River Bridge, Anna could see that like before, at least one column of smoke was rising from the southwestern part of Kremmling where Will's mother, Sharon, lived. *First stop, Sharon Donovan's house,* Anna thought.

Seeing that smoke really was rising from the chimney of the ancient white clapboard four-square where Will grew up, brought Anna wildly mixed emotions. She had always loved her potential mother-in-law at least as much as she'd loved her potential husband. Sharon Donovan was a strong-willed, independent woman that Anna looked up to from the day they first met. The great joy Anna felt at the thought that Sharon had survived was tempered by the sorrow of having to be the one to tell her that her only son was dead.

When Anna stopped the truck and stepped out in front of the Donovan house, and Sharon Donovan came out of the front door, Anna didn't have to say a word for Sharon to know that her worst fear had been realized. Anna rushed through the gate in the old white picket fence that surrounded the Donovan home. Sharon met her in the middle of the yard, and the two embraced and held each other while Anna's companions got out of the truck. When Anna gently held Sharon Donovan at arm's length and really looked at her, the effects of the great dying, as James called it, were obvious. Sharon Donovan was not a large woman. Anna stood nearly a full head taller than Sharon, but now, it seemed like she had shrunk even more. Her short sandy blonde hair had turned totally white, and she looked much older than Anna knew her to be. It was like Sharon had aged twenty years in the two years since Anna last saw her.

Sharon wiped at the tears in her eyes with the back of her hand and said, "Come on in, it's too cold to be standing around out here. Why are you all carrying guns?" she added, seeing that Ray and Rita both had rifles, and James had a pistol.

"Long story," Anna said. "Let's talk inside." Ray, Rita, and James put their guns back in the truck following Anna's lead as she unstrapped the gun belt around her waist and placed it in the console. Then, they all followed Sharon Donovan into her home.

"I wanted to come and tell you sooner," Anna told Sharon, referring to Will's death, "but when I came into town and saw two guys come out of that church with the three black crosses, I just kind of freaked out. I'm so sorry, Sharon."

Sharon looked at Anna, perplexed by what she'd just said. Then she looked at Anna's three companions, who were seated across the room on the sofa, to see if there might be a clue there as to why two men coming out of a church would cause Anna to freak out. The small living room was arranged with the sofa and the two easy chairs that were occupied by Anna and Sharon in a sort of semi-circle, all facing the woodburning stove that was throwing out way too much heat. The only information Sharon could take in from looking at the three people sitting on the sofa was that all three were too hot.

"Maybe you should open that window behind you," Sharon told them before turning her attention back to Anna. "Why would a couple of guys coming out of the church freak you out?" she asked.

Though Anna dreaded reliving the traumatic experience again, she told Sharon, without going into too much detail, about being kidnapped and held in a cage with three black crosses painted on the side. She was careful not to say anything about being raped, and she skipped entirely the time spent in Blue Rapids. Having never told James about her romantic entanglement with Charlie, she wanted to just avoid the subject of Blue Rapids altogether.

"You poor girl," Sharon said, rightly guessing that Anna had left much out of the story of her long journey home. "I wish he could have been buried here," she said, completely changing the subject. "We buried everyone, you know, the whole town. Put 'em all in one huge grave. It was quite an undertaking," she rambled on, looking at the three on the sofa. "Will should have been buried with the others," she finally trailed off into silence, looking off into a distance that no one else could see.

Anna allowed Sharon a few moments of silence before bringing her back to the present. "Sharon, how many people survived here in Kremmling?"

"Well, let's see." Sharon seemed to be counting them off in her head. "I guess fourteen right here in town, if you count the kids. There's the Schumachers, Richard, Jean, and their daughter Sam. Then there's Donna Farris."

"Mrs. Farris?" Anna interrupted the recital of names. "Mrs. Farris is still alive?" Mrs. Farris had been Anna's high school biology teacher. *She has to be at least seventy-five,* Anna thought.

"Yes, she is," Sharon answered. "She taught you and Will both, didn't she?" Sharon didn't even wait for an answer before starting, once again, to list the names of Kremmling's survivors. "Then there's Johnny Garcia. God bless Johnny. If it wasn't for Johnny, well Johnny and Richard, if it wasn't for them, we'd be packing water out of the river instead of having it come right out of the tap. Sure is a good thing the town switched over to solar power and that wind turbine for the water and sewer plants. You know, it was really controversial when we did that." Sharon was getting sidetracked again. "Wish we would have taken the whole town off-grid, so I could have electricity. The natural gas quit working, you know."

Anna couldn't stand it anymore. "What about Dr. Ming?" she asked. "Is Dr. Ming still here?"

"Oh yes, Dr. Ming's still here." Sharon looked askance at Anna, and then at the three on the couch. "Are you sick, dear?" she asked Anna.

"It's my sister," Rita answered before Anna could respond. "My sister, Connie. She's not sick. She's pregnant."

"Is Dr. Ming at his clinic?" Anna asked.

"He's probably at the church," Sharon answered, like everyone should know that not only was Dr. Ming usually at the church but which church that might be.

Sharon agreed to ride to the church with them since it was almost lunchtime, anyway. "I've never seen a truck like this," she said, while Anna was trying to figure out what lunchtime had to do with the church.

"Which church?" Anna asked, as she started to pull away from Sharon's house.

"You know, The Modern Times Church," Sharon answered. "Where the Bureau Of Land Management office used to be."

To everyone but Sharon's surprise, there were two vehicles parked in front of the Modern Times church. Anna recognized one of the vehicles as being Sherriff Larson's old Jeep, but she didn't recognize the pickup truck that was parked next to it.

"Is Sherriff Larson still alive?" Anna asked. Sharon hadn't said so earlier.

"Oh no," Sharon answered, "he's buried with the rest of them. Richard usually drives the old jeep now. It's kind of like our public transit system. Guess he won't have to pick me up today, though," she added, as Anna parked next to the Jeep.

"What about the pickup?" James asked, stepping out of the truck with his revolver in hand.

"That's Johnny's truck," Sharon answered. "Well, it is now. You won't be needing that here," she said, seeing the gun in James' hand.

James hesitated before putting the revolver in the console with Anna's gun. "Why don't you two wait here for just a minute," James said to Ray and Rita, who were both holding their rifles between their knees. They both nodded their heads, letting James know they understood what he was saying.

As soon as James and Anna followed Sharon into the church, it was apparent what being almost lunchtime had to do with anything. The smell of cooking food greeted them in the foyer, and in the main room, the room that would have been a chapel in most old churches, tables and chairs were set up for dining. There was no one in the dining hall, but voices could be heard coming from an open double doorway that obviously led to a kitchen.

"Need some help?" Sharon asked through the open doors as she led James and Anna into the kitchen. "We have guests for lunch."

There were four people in the commercial style kitchen, which, like the dining hall, was brightly lit by overhead electric lights. The two men were leaning against a counter, talking, while two women were apparently doing all of the work. As Anna and James walked in behind Sharon, the only person Anna recognized turned away from the large pot that she'd been stirring.

"Oh my god!" the little old gray-haired woman exclaimed. "Anna Duran!" She didn't even bother to put down the spoon in her hand before rushing across the kitchen to hug Anna.

Anna hugged her back, careful to avoid the dripping spoon. "Hi, Mrs. Farris," Anna said to her favorite high

gation">439

school teacher. "It's so good to see you...to see you..." Anna's voice trailed off, and Mrs. Farris continued the thought.

"To see me alive?" she smiled. "It is amazing, isn't it? And stop calling me Mrs. Farris. Mr. Farris has been dead for twenty years now. This is a new life. I'm just Donna from now on, okay?"

"Okay, Donna," Anna answered, though it felt really strange to call her old teacher by her given name.

"Anna, do you know Samantha?" Donna asked before Anna could say anything else. Then she proceeded to make introductions all around.

"And this is James Mendez," Anna gestured toward James standing uncomfortably in the doorway. "He's my..." once again, Anna was at a brief loss for words as she glanced at her once future mother-in-law.

"It's alright, Anna," Sharon told her. "I know Will's dead."

"I'll get the others," James said, backing out of a somewhat uncomfortable situation.

"Where is Dr. Ming?" Anna asked, after James left the room.

"Probably in his office," Johnny Garcia was first to answer. Then, after seeing the puzzlement on Anna's face, "down the hall, last door on the left."

"Guess I better go round up the others for lunch," Anna heard Richard Schumacher say as she headed down the hallway to find Dr. Ming.

··········

Anna felt the bandage on the inside of her arm, where Dr. Ming had removed the implant. She thought about all they'd learned in Kremmling. James was driving home. Ray and Rita were mostly silent in the back seat; everyone lost in their own thoughts. Besides the gift of having the implant removed, Anna clutched another treasure in her lap. A gift from Dr. Ming. It was a calendar. A real multi-year calendar, with the days all marked off right up to today, which Dr. Ming had assured her was the third of December. Her guess that it was about Thanksgiving had been pretty close after all.

Anna pondered the fact that there was nothing sinister at all about the Modern Times Church. Quite the opposite, in fact. The truth about the Modern Times Church, as told by the Schumachers, was that it was indeed founded by a man who called himself Mystic Martin. Mystic Martin founded the church to respond to the end of mankind's reign on earth. He had apparently foreseen the sickness that would wipe out most of mankind, and his followers built churches that, using modern technology and renewable energy, had only one purpose; sustaining those who lived through the great dying. The Modern Times Church had pretty much nothing at all to do with religion. Calling it a church was the easiest way to ensure tax-free status and to use America's freedom of religion laws to accomplish things that would have otherwise been impossible. Each chapter, as they called their individual groups, built their own building. Or, as in Kremmling, repurposed an existing building, with some guidance from the church, which was headquartered in California. The standard features of all of the chapter houses, besides the three black crosses, were renewable energy production and storage, a water well and septic system, a good supply of non-perishable food, and a community meeting place.

The Kremmling Chapter of the Modern Times Church had, since the sickness, truly become the center of the community for the survivors. Being the only place in town, besides the water plants, that was totally self-contained, it had become the community kitchen, gathering place, and doctor's office. Dr. Ming had moved what he could of his practice because the old health clinic didn't have any electrical power.

Over a wonderful lunch of homemade stew, Anna had been discussing with Dr. Ming the possibility of getting power to the old clinic. Johnny Garcia, overhearing their conversation, had asked, "Why not the whole town?" Johnny, it turned out, had been Kremmling's water utilities supervisor before the sickness. He had some ideas about using a large PV array that was up by Wolford Reservoir to supply power to the whole town. Since most places in Kremmling had relied on natural gas for heat and cooking, and natural gas was no longer flowing, converting to electricity seemed like a perfect idea. If it could be accomplished, that is.

Anna had been impressed by Johnny Garcia's intelligence and resourcefulness. The only problem was, he had very little expertise when it came to electricity. Water and sewer systems were his domain, and he was the first to admit that he didn't know enough about electrical power systems to put his ideas into practice. Anna had promised to check out the feasibility of making his dream a reality when she next came down to Kremmling.

Anna absently fingered the bandage on her arm again, thinking about the fact that it was likely she would soon be pregnant. The thought was thrilling, but the thrill was tempered by what Dr. Ming had told her. When Anna told Dr. Ming she wanted to have a baby, he responded with a question. "Did you notice Lisa Smith?" he'd asked. Anna had noticed the quiet young woman sitting at the other end of the table at lunch. Lisa looked to be no more than a few years older than Anna, and Anna couldn't help but notice that she hardly ate a thing and didn't join in the conversation at all. "She lost a baby boy a little over a month ago." Dr. Ming said. When Anna mentioned that was well after the sickness had killed everyone else, Dr. Ming went on to explain that Lisa had given birth to a healthy baby boy right there in his office. The child seemed perfectly fine for three days before coming down sick. Really sick. Within a single day, the child went from being totally healthy to dying of the exact same symptoms that killed everyone in the great dying. "That baby died of V-1 just like everyone else," Dr. Ming had said. He didn't know how that was possible, and he didn't have a lab to prove it, but he was absolutely sure that was the case.

*What if we're it?* Anna thought, still fingering the bandage on her arm. *What if we're the last? What if babies can't survive?*

# Chapter 21

J AMES CAUGHT A MOVEMENT out of the corner of his eye. It was mid-morning, February fifteenth, according to Anna's calendar. He and Jack and Ray were feeding the mixed herd of cattle and sheep. He had just stabbed his pitchfork into the loose stacked hay for another load to throw over the fence when the movement out on Highway 9 caught his attention.

At first, when he looked up, he wasn't sure what he was seeing. He stared, not quite believing his eyes. "Hey Ray, do you see that, or am I hallucinating?" he asked. Ray was working closest to him on the same side of the stack. Jack, working on the other side of the stack, couldn't see the strange object coming up the highway.

"Jack, come here," Ray said, sticking his pitchfork in the ground and rubbing his eyes as if to clear away an illusion.

"What the fuck is that?" Jack muttered, coming around the haystack to get a view.

It looked like a crane coming up Highway 9 from Kremmling. A crane that was being followed by some kind of car pulling a small RV. It seemed strange that only the top half of the crane was visible behind a slight rise, while most of the SUV style vehicle and towed trailer behind it were visible clear down to the top of the wheels. It created the illusion of some kind of large off-road crane being followed by a car and trailer that were floating in the air.

As the men watched, the crane came up out of a dip, and the illusion was shattered. It was indeed a relatively large off-road crane, but it was pulling two separate trailers behind it. One looked like some kind of flatbed without much on it. The second trailer carried the SUV and RV camper. *Looks like a Rivian,* James thought. *Looks like Dad's Rivian. No, can't be.* He was headed back toward the house with the other two right behind him before the crane even turned off the highway and started up the lane to the BR.

"Thought maybe I should return your car," the man said as soon as he climbed down out of the crane.

Jack and Ray watched as James ran up to the stranger and grabbed him in a bear hug. "Dave Ortiz," James said, stepping back away. "How the hell did you ever find me? And what the hell is that thing you're driving?"

"This, my friend, is how you travel anywhere you want to go in this day and age." Dave gestured toward the crane. "It's a Link-Belt 9045 E. You find something blocking your road, you just move it out of the way. You wouldn't believe how many roads I've opened up between here and Montana. And finding the Blue River Ranch, that was easy, once I got to Kremmling. Some guy in a Jeep with a sheriff's star on it gave me directions."

"Must have been Richard Schumacher," James said. "He isn't really a sheriff, you know."

"Yeah, I figured that. He told me that him and some guy named Johnny could sure use some crane work, but I told him it would just have to wait. I told him I had a long-overdue appointment at the Blue River Ranch."

James looked from the crane to the two trailers behind it, and then he saw a door swing open on the RV trailer. Two women stepped out of the RV onto the deck of the second trailer. Jack and Ray also saw the women get out of the RV, but neither one of them had any idea why James burst into laughter. He slapped Dave on the shoulder and stopped laughing long enough to say, "Mission accomplished, I see. Looks like that replenishing the earth thing might be working out for ya." One of the women who got out of the RV was obviously very pregnant.

"Not mine," Dave said over his shoulder as he hurried back to help the pregnant woman down off the trailer.

By that time, everyone on the BR had gathered around Dave and the two women. Introductions were made all around. "Feel like I already know you," Dave told Anna, shaking her hand. "James used to talk about you a lot."

The two women with Dave were Charlene Dixon and Rachel Cosgrove, both from Billings, Montana. Connie and Charlene immediately started discussing and comparing their pregnancies. Charlene said she figured she was due in about a month, so Connie was a month or so behind.

Anna listened to the conversations around her, but the engineer in her couldn't help but study the way the electric crane and trailers were set up. The first trailer was a flat-bed, at least forty feet long. The crane just had a pintle hook, so the trailer was attached by using a fifth-wheel dolly. But the solar PV system that was built on the deck of the flatbed is what was really fascinating. The entire trailer was covered with PV panels mounted flat on top of a steel box that was about a foot high. The box undoubtedly housed an enormous bank of storage batteries.

"How much storage capacity?" Anna asked Dave. "That looks like a huge battery pack."

"Ten actually, it's ten separate battery banks. Makes it easier to charge." Dave was obviously proud of the crane and trailer set-up. "Five thousand kilowatt-hours altogether. Plenty of storage, but she could sure use a lot more PV. Guess I should have added another trailer full of panels."

"You add much more to that train, you'll have to put it on rails," James said, hearing Dave and Anna's conversation. "Don't see how you can turn it around as it is."

"Good point," Dave laughed. "Takes about forty acres. How big did you say this ranch is?"

"Way more than forty acres, but don't be getting in a hurry to turn it around. Let's get inside out of this damn wind." The wind wasn't really that cold for February in the Colorado mountains, at least not by historical standards. The temperature was probably right at freezing, but Mandy and Misty were neither one wearing coats.

There was a lot of space in the great room of the big house, but it felt pretty cozy with eleven people gathered together. As the warmth from the woodstove chased away the chill from being outside, the people inside sort of separated into two groups. The women, all but Anna, gathered around the woodstove on the large L-shaped sofa, while the men and Anna were seated at the dining table. Mandy and Misty gravitated toward the two pregnant women on the couch.

Anna caught herself trying to listen to two separate conversations at the same time. Charlene and Rachel were both from Montana, and Connie and Rita were comparing how recent history had unfolded in Montana compared with Colorado. With Misty and Mandy listening attentively, the four women were trying hard not to re-traumatize the two young girls.

"What I can't figure out," Anna heard Rachel say, "is why V-1, that's what Dave says it's called, why did V-1 kill so many more men than women. From what I've seen, I bet there are over twice as many women now as there are men." *She's right,* Anna thought. *It was the same in Blue Rapids. More women than men.* She looked around the room at the four men and seven women, counting Misty and Mandy. At Blue Rapids, there had been six men and nine women before she herself left, and in Kremmling, there were seven women, four men, and three children. Two girls and a boy.

"Our mom got sick, but not Dad," Mandy volunteered, catching the gist of the conversation. "He didn't get sick, the devil killed him."

That brought the conversations on both sides of the room to a momentary standstill until Misty, giving her little sister a disdainful look, said, "I told you, Mandy, that man was not the devil. He was just a really bad man."

"Well, Misty killed the devil." Mandy was mostly undeterred until she saw the look her sister gave her. "Okay, Misty killed the really bad man. He wanted to fuck me like he did Misty, but she stopped him."

"Shut up Mandy, you promised not to tell." Misty burst into tears and ran down the hall to her room. Anna got up and followed her without saying a word.

"That sounds like some pretty bad shit," Dave said quietly to the table.

"Ain't that the truth," Jack told him. He lowered his voice even more, to try to keep Mandy from hearing. "That crazy son of a bitch that Misty shot, not only killed their dad, near as I can tell, he killed everyone that survived in Frisco and Breckenridge."

James, shaking his head and bringing his voice back up to the level of normal conversation, said, "Anna ran into some evil guys, too. Guess V-1 or whatever you want to call it, spared the bad right along with the good."

"Yeah, there were some in Montana, too," Dave told the group. "Called themselves The New Army Of God. Near as I can tell, the main tenant of their religion, if you can call it a religion, is white supremacy. Guess they're the main reason we didn't stay in Montana."

"Well, I don't think the crazy SOB in Frisco was anything but that," Connie said. "Just a totally insane loner. I don't think he had anything to do with any new army of god, or any other army. Or God, for that matter."

The men didn't realize that Connie and the other women over by the stove were even listening to their conversation. James, knowing much more about Anna's ordeal than the others, wanted to know more about the white supremacists. "How many were there?" he asked. "White supremacists, I mean."

"Not that many," Charlene said. There was only one conversation going on in the great room now. "I'd guess no more than fifteen or twenty at that church outside Billings. Wouldn't you say, Dave?"

"Yeah, sounds about right," Dave answered.

Based on the size of the surviving population in this part of the world, fifteen or twenty people at one church seemed like a lot to James. "Jesus, is everybody in Montana a white supremacist?" he asked.

"Oh, hell no," Dave said. "They're just a small minority holed up at that church. But I'm afraid they're the leftovers from the ones that started the revolution. I guess my biggest fear is that more like-minded followers of General Korliss will get together and really start some trouble."

The main thing that James heard was the part about fifteen or twenty people being just a small minority. "How many people survived in Montana?" he asked, hoping maybe there were places less ravaged by V-1 than Colorado.

"They're not from Montana," Rachel spoke up. "The New Army Of God, I mean. I never heard of it until after everyone died, and strangers started moving in."

Rachel, Dave, and Charlene went on to explain that Montana, at least the Billings area that Charlene and Rachel were from, hadn't fared any better than anywhere else during the great dying. Most everyone that Charlene and Rachel knew before had died. Rachel and Charlene, even though they were both from Billings, had never even met until they ran into each other on the road as they were leaving the city. Billings may have been small compared to Denver, but there were way too many dead people for the survivors to deal with. So, most everyone that survived just left.

Rachel and Charlene hadn't walked that far from Billings when they came across a couple of other women and a man digging graves in a field near the Yellowstone River, just outside of Park City. Glad to see others still alive, Rachel and Charlene stopped to visit and ended up staying. They helped the other three, none of whom were from around there, bury the farm family that had all died in the big old farmhouse. Then the five of them took up residence. That was just a few weeks after the great dying. Apparently, more and more people found the Park City area appealing over the months that followed.

"I wasn't the only one headed north," Dave said. "By the time I got there, must have been at least a hundred people living in and around Park City. Gotta admit it was a pretty nice spot. Far enough from Billings to escape the smell, but close enough to acquire almost anything a person might need. That's where I got my crane."

"I'm not sure any of them were from Montana," Charlene added, in reference to the people who settled in Park City. "I think the men, and it was just a few men to start with, that moved into that old church up toward Billings, were from California or Arizona."

"They got there before me," Dave said. "Probably no more than four of five people there until they put those three black crosses out front. Those crosses were like a magnet to attract scum."

"Wait." Anna came back into the room just in time to hear about the three black crosses. "You mean they were part of the Modern Times Church?"

"No, you missed the first part," Dave answered. "They call themselves The New Army Of God, and their crosses are different."

"What do you mean different, you said three black crosses?"

"You know, the crosses are just different. The Modern Times Church has the one large cross in the center that's really more like a T. The New Army Of God's crosses are all the same size and all definitely cross-like."

Anna's mind flashed back to the crosses on the mobile cage she'd been enslaved in. They were definitely the same size. *So Sarge and Curt didn't have anything to do with The Modern Times Church,* she thought. It was a huge relief. All this time she had thought there had to be a connection, but there wasn't. "So, there's nothing wrong with The Modern Times Church," she mumbled, as much to herself as anyone.

The others looked questioningly at Anna before Dave continued his narrative. "More and more people kept coming up to Montana from all over, like it was the promised land or something. Most just seemed like normal people, but a few fell in with that church. They basically turned it into a compound. Put up a wall around the whole place with armed guards at the gate."

"Do you know if they had any women?" Anna asked.

"I did see a couple of women coming and going from the place," Rachel said. "I guess some women must have joined them."

"No," Anna clarified, "did they have any kidnapped women? Any slaves?"

"Not that any of us would know about," Charlene answered. "They would never have let any of us through the gate. Like we'd ever want anything to do with any of them anyway."

"They had a big sign out front," Dave explained. "It said, white is might, white is right. Don't know if they had any slaves, but I know they didn't think us people of color were good for anything else."

"What about the rest of the community? I mean, you said this Army of God was just a minority. Was the whole community racist?" James asked.

Dave laughed. "Most of the rest of the community looked just like us. And the ones that looked like Connie and Rita there, they didn't want to have any more to do with the New Army of God than we did."

James looked over at the contrast between the four women seated by the stove. Connie and Rita with blonde hair and blue eyes were the only purely white looking women in the room. Charlene had dark ebony skin and kinky black hair, and Rachel was one of those women whose ethnicity is hard to distinguish. She may have been Native American or Hispanic, or Asian for that matter. She was definitely not white, though. "But you said you left because of the New Army of God. Sounds to me like that group of Nazis was way outnumbered, why leave?" James asked Dave.

Dave seemed to look for the answer somewhere off in space before he said, "They're like cancer. That little compound is just the early stage. Just a small tumor now, but they're insidious. Eventually, the cancer will grow enough to destroy that community. Remember me telling you about General Korliss' rebellion in the Army? It started the same way. Just a small group to start with. But once that cancer metastasized, the whole country was screwed."

"I thought they were all back in Kentucky," Anna said. "The New Army Of God, or whatever they call themselves. I didn't think we'd ever have to worry about people like that out here."

"Don't think we do," James told Anna. "I think we're all pretty safe right here." Then to Dave, "I'm glad you're here. I hope you and Rachel and Charlene will stay. If not with us, at least close."

Charlene gave a little gasp and put her hand on her belly. "Hope it's just a kick," she said.

"Maybe we should take you into Kremmling to see Doctor Ming," Anna told her. She didn't tell anyone that she wanted to see Dr. Ming herself. She didn't want to tell James she was pregnant until she was absolutely sure, herself.

# Chapter 22

*WHAT WE REALLY NEED is a computer wizard,* Anna thought. She was studying the computer-controlled switching systems at the large solar array near Wolford Reservoir. Dave and Johnny were there with her. As was James, who seemed unwilling to let her out of his sight once he found out she was pregnant.

Dave, Charlene, and Rachel had been living with James and Anna for two weeks now. The big house at the BR, with five full bedrooms, had initially been built for a much larger family than had ever lived in it. It was not, however, designed for multiple families under one roof. With five adults, one pre-teen and one teenage girl, all living there now, the big house didn't seem so big anymore. Not that it felt uncomfortable. That was one of the strange aftereffects of the great dying. Having multiple family units all living together seemed more normal now than each family living in separate homes.

This was the second trip to Kremmling since Dave's arrival at the Blue River Ranch. It had been two weeks since Dr. Ming told Anna that she was definitely pregnant, and he told Charlene that she was due any time now.

*Wonder why Sharon and Mrs. Farris still live alone. It seems like they'd be better off together.* Anna's mind was wandering. She focused back on the problem at hand. "If we can figure out how to bypass all of these remote computer controls," she told the guys, "we don't have to move any of this."

"Guess I'm not much help when it comes to computers," Dave said. "Wish I was."

"Another one of my weaknesses, too," Johnny added. "Give me pipes and valves and filters, and I'm your man. Computers, forget it."

"Don't look at me," James added, "my experience with computers is minimal at best."

The Wolford Reservoir solar farm was much more than Anna had expected. Not only was it an extensive array of PV panels, it also had a utility-scale battery bank. The system was big enough to power a lot more than just Kremmling, and there was enough storage to make it through many days without sunshine. Best of all, it was already tied to the grid that had fed Kremmling power before everything shut down. And not just Kremmling. If Anna could figure out how to do it, she could isolate it from the overall grid and convert it to a smaller area-wide network that could feed electrical power to Kremmling, and even the BR. *We could probably power up Granby and the whole Fraser Valley,* she thought. *Wonder if there's anybody over there.*

"Have you had any contact with anyone from Granby?" Anna asked Johnny. Maybe, just maybe, someone from Mountain Parks Electric had survived. And, just as important, the computers that controlled this whole system would be located at Mountain Parks Electric in Granby.

"Can't say as we have," Johnny answered. "I tried to drive over there once, right after everything went down, but

Highway 40 was blocked by a couple of dead semis in Byers Canyon, and the old county road from Parshall over to Hot Sulphur Springs hasn't been passable for years."

"What's in Granby?" James asked.

"Mountain Parks Electric," Anna told them what she'd been thinking. "The computers that control all of this. And maybe, someone that knows something about the Mountain Parks Electric system."

"Only one way to find out," Dave said. "Let's go get my crane and open up that canyon."

Back in Kremmling, any plan to go pick up Dave's crane was put on indefinite hold. They had left Charlene with Dr. Ming for a thorough check-up. When they got back to his office, Charlene was in labor.

"Don't know how you did it," Dr. Ming told them, "but you got her here at exactly the right time. Of course, this being her first baby, and since she just started early labor, it's probably going to be a while."

Since Dave was the only one who knew anything about his crane, and he wasn't about to leave Charlene alone with Dr. Ming, the power project was put on the back burner. Anna and James agreed to make the run back up to the BR to pick up the things Charlene would have brought with her, had she known this was going to be anything more than just a checkup.

The old Rivian SUV was really proving its worth. It was a lot more nimble at missing the potholes in Highway 9 than the Carlisle's truck. What would have been at least an hour's drive in the truck took only about forty-five minutes in the Rivian.

Rachel insisted on going back to Kremmling with them, so she could be with her "sister," Charlene. This caused a little bit of a row because Mandy wanted to go, too. For reasons unknown, Mandy had become almost instantly attached to Rachel. It was like the ten-year-old girl had picked Rachel to be a surrogate for her dead mother. And Rachel had been more than willing to fill the role. Separating the inseparable wasn't easy, but Rachel finally convinced Mandy to stay with Misty. She gave the young girl a hug and told her, "If you need anything, Connie will be right next door."

"I had a little girl once." The statement from Rachel, who was riding in the backseat, came out of the blue. "Think that's why I'm getting so attached to Mandy."

Anna turned half around in her seat, shocked to hear that Rachel had once had a child. "You didn't tell us you had a daughter," Anna said.

"I haven't told anyone," Rachel answered. "Not even Dave or Charlene. I don't know why I'm telling you." She had her face turned away from Anna, looking out the side window of the car as she spoke. "Guess I just wanted to forget about Amy. Seemed easier. It doesn't work, though. You don't ever lose a child, you know. Once you give birth, that child will be with you forever. Even if your baby only lives for a year. It probably wouldn't have mattered if she'd only lived for a few minutes. I think it must be the nine months before the child is born that does it. You just can't forget someone that you carried around inside your own body for that long. I sure hope Charlene's baby will be okay." She trailed off into silence without ever turning to look at Anna.

"I'm sorry," Anna said. It seemed there wasn't much else to say. "Sorry you lost your daughter."

Rachel turned away from the window to look at Anna. There were tears in her eyes as she said, "I need to tell Dave myself. Please don't tell him and Charlene."

James and Anna both promised to keep Rachel's secret. By the time they got back to Kremmling, Rachel's tears had all dried up, and she was back to being her usual self. *How do we just go on living with so much loss?* Anna thought, and then she looked at James. She put her hand on her lower belly, where she knew his child was growing inside her. *It's hope. As long as we live, there's hope. Right up to the end, we just go on hoping for a better future.* She watched Rachel hurry through the door of the Modern Times Church. *If we ever lose that...if we lose hope, that will definitely be the end.*

·····•·•····

"Anna, wake up." It was James, gently shaking her. *What a strange dream,* she thought. She'd been flying. Vast reaches of the earth, opening up below her. She was somewhere over the plains, soaring toward mountains in the distance. Flying was effortless. It was as though she didn't have a body to propel through the sky. Just an ephemeral self that had only one goal. She had to reach those mountains in the distance. The mountains were home. It was time to return home to the mountains.

*Where am I?* she thought, seeing the strange surroundings come into focus. Then she remembered. "Guess I fell asleep, huh?" she said to James.

He was smiling. "It's a boy," he said. "Charlene has a new baby boy."

Anna sensed that it was very early in the morning. The windows of the Modern Times Church looked out on a dark world. Inside the building, the LED lights in the lounge area where Anna had fallen asleep had been dimmed to a soft glow. She stood up and stretched. Anna and James were the only ones in the lounge. She headed down the hall toward Dr. Ming's office, with James right behind her.

Dr. Ming's office in The Modern Time Church building actually consisted of several rooms that had once been offices for the BLM. One of the offices had been set up to be a small maternity ward. Dave and Rachel were already there, of course. Dave and Dr. Ming on one side of the bed, and Rachel on the other. Everyone in the room looked happy. Everyone except Charlene, who simply looked exhausted. She held the swaddled newborn close to her breast. The baby was asleep. "We should let them rest," Dr. Ming said to everyone and to no one in particular.

"Is the baby healthy?" Anna asked Dr. Ming once they were back out in the hall. Dave had stayed in the room with Charlene and the baby. Instead of leaving with the others, he just sat down in the easy chair that was next to the bed.

"Mother and child both seem perfectly healthy." Dr. Ming answered. Then looking directly at Anna, "Lisa's baby was born healthy, too."

"Who's Lisa?" Rachel asked.

"Lisa Smith." Dr. Ming answered. "She had the first baby born here, after, after, you know. Anyway, that was a couple of months ago. Lisa's baby seemed perfect for three days."

"And?" Rachel asked.

"On the fourth day, Lisa's baby developed a terrible fever and the other symptoms of V-1. There was nothing I could do."

# Chapter 23

FOR ANNA, THE ROAD through Byers Canyon was filled with both hope and fear. She hoped they would find the means to switch on the power. But there was a fear now that Anna took with her everywhere. Like tinnitus, never drowning out other sounds, but always present just beneath the surface, Anna constantly carried the fear that the baby growing inside her would end up like Charlene's, and Lisa Smith's before that. Charlene's baby only survived two days before the sickness took it. Anna couldn't imagine carrying a child for nine months, only to have it die two days after birth.

Today was the twenty-fifth of March. Charlene's baby boy had died exactly two weeks ago, on the eleventh. Anna looked over at James, who was riding in the passenger seat. *Is he afraid, too,* she thought? He hardly ever let her out of his sight even though she was barely two months pregnant. Protecting her from any harm that might befall her during pregnancy was one thing, but no one could protect their baby from an invisible disease that wouldn't even make itself known until after the baby was born.

Anna's mind wandered back to the private talk she'd had with Dr. Ming after Charlene's baby died. That talk was as much at the root of her fear as the death of poor Charlene's infant son. Anna had pressed Dr. Ming to tell her what he knew or even what he guessed could be causing newborn infants to suddenly die, apparently of V-1.

"I'm no virologist or epidemiologist," Dr. Ming had said. "But then, even the epidemiologists couldn't understand V-1." He'd rummaged around in a file cabinet by his desk and brought out a single sheet of paper. "This is the last report I got from the CDC. I barely got it printed before the coms went down. Guess it's a good thing I'm old-fashioned, or I probably wouldn't have printed it at all."

Anna read the report and then re-read it. Some of the medical and scientific terminologies didn't mean much to her, but the gist of the document was that the CDC basically didn't know much more than anybody else. The best scientific data on V-1 at the time of the report suggested that it was some kind of totally new, previously undetected virus. The previously undetected part was the key to its lethality. Apparently, nearly everyone in the world carried the virus in their system and had for some time. No one knew if it was months or years. The scientists didn't know how long ago humans were first infected with V-1, nor did they understand why it suddenly turned lethal at the same time all over the world. What they did know was that it killed more men than women. The data suggested that V-1 could possibly kill ninety-nine percent of humans on earth, and up to seventy percent of the one percent remaining would be women.

"But what about the babies?" Anna had asked after reading the report for the third time. "Why does it kill the babies?"

Dr. Ming's answer was basically no answer at all. "The scientists who wrote that report were probably gone by the time any babies were born. And, even if any of them are still alive and able to continue their research, how would they ever disseminate the data?"

Anna looked at the report again before asking Dr. Ming, "What do you think? What could have made a virus so lethal? And why babies?"

Dr. Ming had stared off into space, searching his own mind before answering, "I wish I knew, Anna. I really wish I knew."

Coming out of Byers Canyon into Hot Sulphur Springs, Anna's thoughts turned to Charlene. She wondered how long it would take the poor woman to recover, if ever. It wasn't just Charlene, either. Dave just wasn't the same as before. He took it as hard as if he really was the father. Dr. Ming tried to tell them they should try again. That those who were still in their reproductive years needed to keep having children. Without babies, if no children could survive, our species was doomed to extinction. He was right, of course. Anna knew that what he said was true, but the intellectual knowledge of the truth didn't override the purely emotional fear of the possibility of losing a child.

It wasn't just Anna that feared for an unborn child. Connie, who was due in a month, hadn't been herself since Charlene's baby only survived two days. She was going crazy, trying to figure out a way to keep the same thing from happening to her baby. When she asked Dr. Ming if he had any ideas, he told her to pray if she was a religious person. "How could anyone still believe in God?" she'd asked Dr. Ming. "Any God. What kind of god would allow so much death?"

There had been no sign of anyone at all in Hot Sulphur Springs where they left Dave's crane. They left the crane after Anna assured them Highway 40 was open from there to at least Windy Gap Reservoir. The road was as empty as Anna remembered. Driving past Windy Gap, a mostly dried up lake that had once been a wetland bird's paradise, Anna thought about all that had happened in the past five or six months. It seemed impossible that less than six months had passed since she rode Red Two down this stretch of highway. Her thoughts turned to all of those who were gone. The family she'd hoped to find at the BR. The grief in finding they were all gone. *At least I found James,* she thought. *His baby has to live.* She unconsciously put her free hand on her belly again. *He just has to.* And then she was struck by the way she assumed the baby was a boy.

"What the hell is that?" Anna's thoughts were interrupted by Dave's exclamation from the back seat. He was reaching up between the seats, pointing toward Granby.

Anna and James both looked where he was pointing. It was something shimmering in the mid-morning sun, something in the sky. As they watched it rising higher above the hills, all three realized it was some kind of airplane.

"Now there's a sight I never expected to see," James said.

"Guess there's at least one person alive in Granby," Anna added.

Dave was studying the plane as it made a wide circle and headed back toward where it came from. "Looks like an old Eviation, or maybe a Sonex," he said. "Pretty small, whatever it is. Probably just a two-seater."

"So, you think it's an E-plane?" Anna asked.

"That'd be my guess," Dave answered. "There might still be some good av-gas around, but I'd have a hard time trusting it. And it definitely wasn't big enough to be one of those commercial hybrids, if any of those are even still flyable."

Just after crossing the Colorado River bridge near the Fraser River confluence, Anna saw the people before she saw the garden. There were most definitely survivors in Granby. It looked like there were at least twenty or thirty people working in what had to be the biggest garden Anna had ever seen. What was once a hay meadow or pasture had been converted to food crops for people, not animals. *A community garden,* Anna thought. *Like the one in Kremmling, but at least five times as big.*

The garden, more like a truck farm than a garden, had an eight-foot fence built all around the perimeter to keep out deer and elk. There was a parking and hitching area adjacent to the garden. Surprisingly, there were two electric vehicles parked near the open gate to the garden, along with about fifteen horses tied up to hitching rails. The people, most of whom had been bent over planting or pulling weeds when Anna first saw them, were all standing and staring at the Rivian as Anna pulled into the parking area. The scene reminded her of a prairie dog colony with the animals all standing at attention, studying an intruder, ready to sound the alarm, and dive into their holes if the intruder proved to be dangerous.

"I believe this is the most people I've seen in one place since the great dying," James said.

"Most since Montana, anyway," Dave said, leaning up from the back seat to get a better view.

"Nice garden, too," Anna mumbled as she glanced at the clock on the dashboard. Almost 10:30 if the old clock was still accurate, and already eighty-two degrees according to the thermometer. *Not even April, and it'll probably hit ninety today.* The thought was anything but comfortable. Anna remembered her mother telling her they used to not plant most things until the end of May or even early June to avoid a killing frost. *Now, they'll start harvesting in early June. If they don't run out of irrigation water first.*

Everyone in the garden headed toward the gate as Anna, James, and Dave got out of the Riv. Having a strange vehicle pull into their little parking lot had to be a novel experience.

A dark-haired woman wearing an old beat-up straw hat was in the lead and seemed to be the de facto leader of the group. She wasn't a young woman, the wrinkles in her dark brown skin attested to that. She had the look of one that has never been a stranger to hard work outdoors under a scorching sun. The bent and wrinkled straw hat on her head matched the woman perfectly. Both had a lot of wear written all over them.

"Hello strangers," the woman said, as they all met at the gate. "Been a while since we've seen anybody but us around here. I'm Ruth Aguilar, and this," she gestured with one arm at the rest of the people gathered behind her, "is the Granby gardeners." She laughed. "Least they're learning to be gardeners."

The group of people crowded around Ruth were, for the most part, younger than her. The group seemed to be about two-thirds women and one-third men. A few of the women were really just teenagers, and two boys were even younger than that.

"Hi Ruth," Anna, as usual, took the lead, "I'm Anna Duran." She took the woman's calloused old hand in hers and introduced James and Dave. "We're from the Blue River Ranch south of Kremmling. Well, I'm the only one originally from the BR," she clarified. "But James and Dave live there now."

"So you must be Clyde Duran's daughter. Well, I'll be. I can see a little resemblance, but you must take more after your mother. Is Clyde," the old woman hesitated. It was still difficult to ask who had died.

Anna shook her head. "No, I'm the only one of my family that survived."

"What about Chuck, is he still with us." Ruth Aguilar seemed to know a lot about the people of the Blue River Ranch.

James answered that one. "No, Chuck was my granddad. He survived the...the great dying, but then he died. I think it was a heart attack."

"Well I'll be," Ruth said, again. "You must be Noni's son then. Noni?"

"She's gone, too," James answered the one-word question. "Died of cancer, just like my grandmother." The woman hadn't asked about James' dad, so he didn't volunteer any other information.

"How do you know the BR?" Anna asked.

"Oh, I imagine everybody that grew up in these parts knows something about the Blue River Ranch. Guess I did know Clyde Duran and Noni Pierson better than most, though. We all went to school together over in Kremmling." For just a moment, Ruth seemed to stare back in time. "Doesn't even seem like the same world now." Then, coming back to the present, "What brings you young folks over to Granby after all this time?"

After Ruth heard about the possibility of getting electric power back up and running in the valley, she was more than happy to help. And it wasn't just Ruth. The Granby gardeners, as Ruth had called them, were about as excited as any group of people Anna had ever seen. One of the women said that her husband had worked in IT for Mountain Parks Electric before, but he got sick and died along with everyone else. "Liz might help, though," the woman said.

"Who's Liz?" Anna asked.

Ruth answered before the other woman had a chance. "Liz is the one person in this valley that'll be going hungry if she doesn't stop tinkering with that stupid airplane long enough to help with this garden."

"Liz was a lineman for MPE," the other woman added.

"Line person," a man standing near the front of the group said. "Liz wouldn't like being called a lineman."

"Like I give a rat's ass what Liz would or wouldn't like," Ruth told the man. "Come on," she said to Anna, "I'll take you to her."

On the drive to the Granby airport, Ruth gave Anna, James, and Dave a quick overview of the status of Granby and the nearby surrounding area. Other than a few people who were too old to help with growing food and Liz McClure, the Granby gardeners were all that remained of the living in Granby itself. Apparently, there were a few people up in Fraser and a few more in the Grand Lake area, and no more than a dozen scattered out on the ranches in between. As seemed to be the case everywhere, more women in Granby survived the sickness than men.

"How'd you get lucky enough to have two men?" Ruth asked Anna with a wink.

They told Ruth about the other people now living on the Blue River Ranch, and the people who were still living in Kremmling. Ruth was especially interested in Dr. Ming. Apparently, no one with any kind of medical background had survived in Granby. When Dave told Ruth about Charlene's baby dying, she became visibly upset. "I'm sorry," she told Dave. "Same thing happened to Yvette a couple of months ago. She had a fine baby boy. All on her own. No doctor, no midwife, no nothing. The baby seemed as healthy as a horse for a couple of days. Then he just got sick and died. It's like that sickness that took everybody is still here. Still here, just waiting to kill off anybody born to replace those who are gone." Everyone was silent for a moment before Ruth brightened and said. "They'll be glad to know there's a doctor in Kremmling, though. Three of the other women back there are pregnant, and the rest of them are trying their damndest to get that way." She laughed out loud. "I'd be tryin' too if I was just a few years younger."

Anna hadn't told Ruth that she herself was pregnant, and decided not to. Instead, she switched to the subject at hand. "Do any of you have electrical power?"

Ruth laughed at that. "Mostly just horsepower," she said. "Oh, there are some places around with solar power. That's what keeps those EVs you saw charged up. Just pull through the gate there." The gate through the security fence at the Granby airport was standing wide open. "And then there's Liz, here," Ruth continued. "She's got more solar working here at the airport than anywhere else I know of. Even more than at the Modern Times Church. At least, I think she has more."

The drive through the gate led between a couple of hangars. "Liz'll be in this hangar on the left," Ruth said. Anna turned left as she came out onto the apron in front of the hangars. Sure enough, the big doors on the front of the hangar were wide open. The cavernous space inside would have been adequate for a much larger plane or several small ones, but there was just one little airplane sitting near the back of the vast space.

Anna stopped just outside the hangar door, and a woman stepped around from behind the lone airplane as everyone got out of the Rivian.

"Well, well," the woman said, seeing Ruth get out of the passenger side. "You come to drag me back to the farm?"

Ruth refused to take the bait. "No, I think we may have found a better project for you. This is Anna, James, and Dave from Kremmling, and they have an idea you might be interested in."

Liz McClure introduced herself since Ruth had failed to do that part. "What kind of an idea would I be interested in?" she asked, the skeptical look on her face suggesting she probably wasn't really interested in much of anything. Other than her airplane, that is. She was obviously interested in that.

Anna wasn't the only one to pick up on Liz McClure's attitude. "Is that a Sonex?" Dave asked, walking toward the little plane.

"Sure is," Liz told him, as she fell in step beside him. "Restored it myself."

"Really?" Dave sounded impressed. "Don't think I've seen one of these since I was a kid."

Liz looked at Dave with a little more interest than she'd shown before. "You a pilot?" she asked.

"No, my dad was. Took me up in one of these babies once. I must have been seven or eight years old at the time. Thought I wanted to be a pilot after that." Dave took his eyes off the little plane and smiled at Liz. "Never worked out, though."

"How do you get enough power to charge the batteries?" Anna asked, taking advantage of the opening Dave had created.

"Panels on the roof." Liz pointed up at the ceiling without ever taking her eyes off Dave.

*Uh-Oh,* Anna thought. *Dave has definitely got her attention.* Liz McClure seemed a little older than Dave, but not much.

Probably in her late twenties or early thirties. She may not have been the most attractive woman in the world, nor even in the hangar, for that matter. But the coveralls she was wearing and the disheveled hair that she ran a hand over masked some hidden charms. Charms that were now directed at Dave.

Interestingly to Anna, Dave seemed interested in Liz as well. *Jesus, that's all he needs. Like two women aren't enough already.*

"What about the grid? Couldn't we get at least part of the grid online?" Anna asked.

Liz finally broke eye contact with Dave to look at Anna. "Grid's dead," she said. "Dead as all those people that used to keep it going."

"Well, Anna here thinks we can resurrect it," Ruth told the younger woman. "Seems like that'd be a lot more valuable than tinkering with an old airplane all the time."

Ruth didn't really like Liz, and the feeling was reciprocated. That was evident to all. Dave broke the tension once again. "Seems to me we should be keeping technology alive as much as we can. Airplanes included. Otherwise, we'll all be living in caves before you know it."

*Is it even possible, though?* The question triggered by Dave's statement hit Anna hard. *Can we really keep technology alive?* And then, another even more profound question, *should we?* After all, it was modern technologies that got the world into this mess in the first place. It was nearly ninety degrees in March, and the mega-drought in Colorado showed no signs of easing anytime soon. *But it's not like we want to burn any fossil fuel. And there are hardly enough people left to make much of an impact on the climate, anyway.* She put her hand on her lower belly, conscious of the other life growing there. Aware of the desire, of the need, to bring new life into this dying world. *But what if new life can't survive in this world?* She forced the question and the fear out of her mind. *First things first, let's get some electricity flowing in this valley again.*

···········

Working together without any computer experts among them, they decided the best solution was to eliminate Mountain Park Electric's centralized computer control system. After their somewhat inauspicious first meeting, Liz McClure proved to be invaluable. Not only Liz but her little airplane, too. They couldn't eliminate the system's computer controls without some new switching gear. Switching gear that was nowhere to be found locally. Liz, however, knew of a warehouse in Casper, Wyoming, of all places, where she figured they could acquire the necessary gear.

After discussing the range of the airplane, the size and weight of the switches, and whether flying to Casper was better than driving, Dave agreed to fly up to Casper with Liz to get the switches. Instead of a two-day trip by Rivian, it was no more than a three-hour roundtrip flight.

Anna and James were waiting at the Granby airport when the little plane came into view. Seeing that silver speck in the sky was a huge relief. Seeing Dave and Liz together after they exited the plane, Anna found herself wondering how well Rachel and Charlene were going to take to sharing Dave with a new sister wife.

"You two seem pretty happy," Anna said. "I presume you found the switches."

James just looked at Dave and shook his head. What else the two had found was just as evident to James as it was to Anna. "So, do we need to make room for another woman at the BR?" James teased his friend when they were far enough away for Liz not to hear.

"No," Dave chuckled, "but I might need to spend some time over this way once in a while."

"Maybe you can take flying lessons," James told him.

Liz, who had just walked around the plane with Anna, heard that last part. "I think that's a great idea," she said. "I'd love to teach you to fly, Dave."

............

Anna watched as Liz tightened the last connection. It was the first of April. *Sure do hope we're not all April Fools,* she thought. The two women were alone at the Wolford solar farm. James had reluctantly agreed to go back down to Kremmling with Dave. The two men, along with Johnny Garcia and Richard Schumacher, were tasked with watching for problems when the power was switched back on. They'd taken every precaution they could think of to prevent any potential issues. But the power had been off for nearly a year, no one could know what might happen when it was suddenly switched back on. It took several days, but the residents of both Kremmling and Granby had gone from building to building shutting down all of the master switches or pulling the main fuses on every house or business from Kremmling to Fraser.

The four major substations that connected the local grid to the high voltage transmission lines had all been disconnected from the overall electrical grid. All that remained now was throwing the right switches in the proper sequence.

"Have they had enough time?" Liz asked, wondering if everyone was in place in Kremmling. Ruth was supposed to have a detachment in Granby doing the same thing as the men in Kremmling. Watching for any little problems with the power to keep any minor issues from becoming a catastrophe. With no fire departments or fire trucks, an electrical fire would definitely be catastrophic.

"I think so," Anna answered. "Go ahead."

"Oh no. This is your idea; you get to do the honors."

"May have been my idea," Anna said, "but we couldn't have done it without you. Let's do it together." Anna grabbed Liz's hand, and they threw the first switch together. As Anna started to guide Liz's hand to the second switch, Liz stopped her. She pulled Anna's hand back away from the switch.

"Boy, would I have been fired for that. Back in the day, I mean. First safety rule, don't touch anyone else while you're working with live power, and always assume the power is live." Liz pulled Anna back away from the switchgear. "Let me do it. No point in all three of us getting fried," she said, looking pointedly at Anna's belly. Liz threw the rest of the switches herself, while Anna watched from a few yards away.

With no indication of any problems on their end, both women jumped in the car. Anna and Liz were giddy with excitement, anxious to get down to Kremmling to see the results of their handiwork.

"I really envy you, Anna," the statement was totally out of the blue. They were about half-way back to Kremmling. "I'd give just about anything to have Dave's baby."

"You and a couple other women I know," Anna answered. "You do know about the others, right?"

"Honestly, I don't care. Actually, I'd like to meet Rachel and Charlene. From what Dave says, I think I'd like them. What about you? I mean you and James. What if he decided to up the odds of fathering children? There are plenty of women that would jump at the chance, you know."

Anna did know. The more she saw of this new world, the more obvious it became that the imbalance between the number of men and women would require major structural change to the old status quo. Monogamous pairs of people just didn't make sense when women outnumbered men by at least two to one.

"I don't know," she told Liz. "I honestly don't. I do know that Dave living with two women at the same time is probably more normal now than the way the rest of us on the BR are living. I mean three apparently monogamous couples in a world where there seems to be at least twice as many women as men isn't very sustainable, is it?"

Liz laughed. "I know it's not working that way in Granby," she said. "Hell, I think Ruth even gets laid once in a while."

"What about you Liz, were you married before?"

"Way before. I got married when I was twenty-two, divorced two years later. I've been a free agent ever since. Up until the sickness, anyway. Dave's the first since my last boyfriend died. Just never could see much in any of the men that survived in Granby. That's why I was working so hard getting my plane ready. I haven't told anyone else this, but I was just about ready to leave Granby when you guys showed up. If you'd waited another day or two, you wouldn't have found anything but an empty hangar at that airport."

"Why? I mean where would you go?"

"I don't know for sure." Liz turned her head to look out the side of the Riv, thinking about the question before answering. "Probably just somewhere north. I just knew I had to find somewhere that I wanted to live." A slight smile played across her face as she turned back to Anna.

"That's not exactly right. I had to find someone to make living worthwhile. Someone to make me want to bring new life into this nearly dead world."

"Maybe there is such a thing as fate," Anna told her, though she was having trouble believing it herself. "Maybe things do happen for a reason."

"Maybe," Liz said. "Tell you one thing, though. When it comes to having Dave's baby, I am definitely not leaving that up to fate. Working hard to bring that about myself," she laughed.

Anna laughed with her and then drove in silence for a spell before saying, "None of them have made it, you know. None of the babies born since the sickness have lived."

Liz's only reply was to stare silently out the window, and Anna drove in silence. Both women lost in their own thoughts. One hoping to beat the odds with a baby on the way. One who wanted nothing more than a chance at those odds herself.

# Chapter 24

I F ANNA HAD A religious bone left in her body, she
would have been praying. It would have been a
simple prayer, please God, let Connie's baby live. She
was sitting in a comfortable chair in the waiting room
of Dr. Ming's old clinic. With electric power for the
equipment all restored, the clinic was a much better
healthcare facility than the Modern Times Church in the
former Bureau of Land Management building. The clinic
even had an ultrasound machine. A couple of weeks ago,
Connie had been the first person since the power went
out to know the sex of her baby before it was born.
Connie was giving birth to a baby girl.

James was sitting next to Anna. Ray and Rita were sitting
on the other side of the waiting room, and Jack was back in
the delivery room with Connie, Dr. Ming, and Lisa Smith.
Dr. Ming had convinced Lisa, who had once worked in a
dental office, to be his assistant. Being sixty-four years old,
Dr. Ming knew the little community would need someone
to provide care after he was gone. There wasn't much
chance of a trained healthcare professional showing up
in Kremmling ever again. He would just have to teach

someone else everything he could in whatever time he had left. Lisa was the someone he'd chosen.

Anna sat with her hands resting on the slight bulge of her belly. It was both comforting and frightening to feel the changes happening to her body. Random thoughts swirled around inside her head as she waited. *Would the baby growing inside her survive? Would Connie's? If the babies did survive, what would their world be like?* It was a question that had always plagued expectant parents, is it right to bring new life into this world? For Anna, before the great dying, or V-1, or whatever one wanted to call it, the answer had been a resounding no. The pre-plague world was not a world fit for a child, not for any child.

Now, bringing new life into this new world was what she wanted more than anything. *Is it just instinct?* She thought. *Is it just our species' drive for survival?* She looked at James, sitting next to her asleep in his chair. *Is that what love is, too? Just another way for ancient instincts to drive procreation.* Somehow, it didn't seem right that reasonable, rational humans could be manipulated by instincts that predated us as a species. *Right or wrong, that's the way it is.* The realization was a little bit unsettling. Were human beings no different than any other species of animal, driven by instincts that could even overpower our supposedly much larger brains? There was no stronger drive than the drive for survival. Not for the survival of the individual, any individual, but the survival of homo sapiens. The continuation of the species was what really counted.

Anna looked across the room at Ray and Rita, who were also both asleep in their chairs. They'd been waiting for a good twelve hours now. The window above Ray and Rita showed the glow of first light beginning in the east. *Wonder why Rita hasn't conceived yet?* The question in Anna's mind sparked another thought. *One of them must be infertile.* That, in turn, brought another realization. *They'll both have to try with other partners.* The instinctual drive to procreate would allow nothing less. *Emotions such as love and jealousy don't stand a chance. Not against the unrelenting instinctual need to bring new life into this world.*

Anna's thoughts were interrupted by the sound of a door opening. Dr. Ming stepped into the room with a big smile on his face. The others all awoke at the sound of the opening door, and Dr. Ming told them mother and baby were both doing well. He said they could go back for a brief visit, but it would be best if just two at a time went back to the small maternity ward.

"Do you think it will be different this time?" Anna asked, after Ray and Rita left the waiting room.

Dr. Ming and James both knew exactly what she was asking. A slight frown momentarily furrowed Dr. Ming's brow before the smile returned. "Where there's life, there's hope." He answered.

............

It was the third of May. A day like no other in anyone's memory. Today, one week after giving birth, Connie and baby Michelle were coming home to the BR. Anna was so excited she could hardly contain herself. Michelle, born into some kind of plague-infested world, was alive and healthy. Dr. Ming, who had resisted letting the baby out of his sight, finally relented. If she didn't get sick in that first week, she was probably immune. None of the other babies had survived more than four days. Besides, if the baby did get sick, there was likely nothing he could do about it, anyway.

James and Anna were sitting on the veranda, watching the sun climb above the hills in the east. James had a cup of the chicory root brew that he still called coffee. Anna was sipping a glass of water. The hot chicory beverage that James enjoyed every morning didn't seem to go too well with morning sickness. Rita had left before dawn. She'd taken the Rivian into Kremmling to pick up Connie, Jack, and baby Michelle. Ray was somewhere out above the north pasture guarding the flock of sheep. The herd was a lot smaller now than it had been a week ago. Last week, while everyone was in Kremmling with Connie, a bear had torn through the flock of sheep.

Anna had heard stories of bear attacks on sheep before, but the carnage was worse than she could have imagined. When a bear gets into a herd of sheep, it doesn't just kill one or two of the sheep to eat. It kills as many as it can and just leaves them lay. Fresh mutton isn't what the bear is primarily after. The dead sheep and lambs are just the raw ingredient of what the bear really wants. A meal of mutton isn't fit for a bear until the dead sheep's carcasses are fly-blown and crawling with maggots. The maggots are the delicacy that bears crave, not the mutton.

Everyone's first instinct had, of course, been to kill the bear when it came back to feast on rotting mutton. Oddly enough, Rita, who grew up raising sheep, was the one that talked them out of it. "Probably a sow with cubs," she'd said. "What are we going to do with all these sheep, anyway?"

*What are we going to do with the sheep and the cattle?* Anna wondered. *Leftovers from a world that no longer exists.* She thought about the vast number of animals the world had once required to feed and clothe billions of people. *How many animals, from chickens in chicken houses to pigs packed together like sardines, had perished along with the billions of people?* That was another sobering thought. The world, once home to many billions of humans, was probably now inhabited by no more than a few million survivors. There were possibly fewer people scattered around the globe now than had inhabited any one of the world's largest cities before. *How many eons have passed since this old world contained so few people?*

*How many of the cows and calves will come back down from the high country this fall?* They had just let the cattle wander off toward the mountains on their own this year. The older cows and bulls had made the trek year after year until it was just part of their nature. The new calves just followed their mothers. The calves were most susceptible, of course. Most of the cows, and probably all three bulls would be back down by winter. But some of this year's calf crop would end up feeding non-human predators. *Kind of a strange relationship,* Anna thought. *People and cattle. Without people needing meat and dairy, cattle don't really have much of a place in this world.* The BR herd that had wandered up to the high country was about ten times as many cattle as everyone on the BR and in Kremmling combined could ever possibly use. Granby had their own old outlying ranches supplying them. Anna was sure that was the case all over the west. There were no doubt some people somewhere that could use some beef or dairy, or wool, but there was no way to find them, let alone get the products to them. *No, in this new world, just as well allow the non-human predators to have most of the livestock.*

"Looks like Dave's back," James said, interrupting Anna's thoughts.

She looked out at Highway 9. It was indeed the Carlisle's truck and trailer coming up the road from Kremmling.

"Dave's back," Anna hollered at the screen door.

Charlene and Misty came out to watch the truck coming up the lane. Rachel and Mandy were with Dave and Liz in the truck. Charlene hadn't taken to having a third "wife" in Dave's little family quite as well as Rachel had. Mandy, who hardly let Rachel out of her sight, had insisted on going along to get Liz's things from Granby. They had been gone for a couple of days. It was quite a project to dismantle the PV system and charging apparatus for the Sonex plane, but Liz wasn't about to leave the airplane in Granby.

"Can I stay here?" Misty asked as the truck came up the lane. Dave was in the process of moving his family up to the old Carlisle place above Frisco. He'd already cleared a long straight section of old Highway 9 between Frisco and Breckenridge to use as an airport for Liz's plane. There was a big barn just off the highway that they planned to convert to a hangar and charging station.

"I thought you wanted to go home," Anna said.

Misty sat down next to Anna. "I like it here with you," she said. "I did want to go home, but not anymore. I don't think I want to live with Dave's family."

"I know what you mean," Charlene said from behind them. "Don't get me wrong. Dave's been good to me, but I kind of like it here myself."

"What about Mandy?" Anna asked Misty, trying to ignore Charlene's input. Anna had a feeling that Charlene wasn't so much leaning away from Dave as she was leaning toward James. "You know Mandy's going wherever Rachel goes."

"I know," Misty answered. "But I'm almost a grown woman now. Mandy needs someone to take care of her. I don't. Besides, it's not that far. I can go visit whenever I want. Please. Please let me stay here with you."

James got up and started back into the house. "Looks like I better get some more chicory brewing," he said, totally ignoring the women's conversation he had just overheard.

Dave looked out toward Kremmling again. "Thought they'd be right behind us," he said. Dave, Liz, Rachel, and Mandy had stopped at Dr. Ming's in Kremmling, and Jack had told them that Connie and the baby were just about ready to leave. Now Dave was anxious to get on up to Frisco. "Dr. Ming said he just wanted to give the baby one more quick checkup."

The whole group had just finished a breakfast of lamb chops, fried potatoes, and awkward conversation. James and Dave, each with a cup of chicory in hand, walked out toward the fully-loaded truck and trailer.

"You know I haven't, with Charlene, I mean," James told Dave. The two men were by themselves out by the truck.

Dave laughed at the change of subject, or maybe just to relieve some tension. "You're not the only one. Far as I know, Charlene hasn't had sex since long before she lost her baby. Now, I think she's afraid to get pregnant again."

"Well, I just want you to know that I had nothing to do with her deciding to stay here, that's all."

"Yeah, I know," Dave said. "Guess there's no more understanding women now than there ever was." He laughed again. "Difference now is, each of us has a lot more of 'em to not understand."

James couldn't help but laugh at the absurdity of the truth in that statement. How could anyone reasonably expect relationships to be the same now as they were before? With the entirety of the only society they'd ever known now gone, how would the survivors, and more importantly the children of the survivors, reorder this new world. *What will life be like for our children?* It dawned on

James that that question was one that every parent who ever lived had probably asked themselves. That and, *how do we make this a better world for our children?*

"Here they are now." Dave motioned with his chin at the Rivian that was turning up the lane to the BR.

"The power went out in Kremmling," was the first thing Jack said as he and Rita got out of the car and scrambled to help Connie out with the new baby. "Dr. Ming's office went dark right in the middle of the exam. Couldn't have been more than five minutes after you left," he told Dave.

The entire house emptied out as soon as the Rivian came up the lane. There may never have been another group of people so excited to see a newborn baby come home. Everyone was crowded around Connie and baby Michelle when Rita asked, "Where's Ray?"

With everything else going on, no one had noticed that Ray hadn't returned from his overnight sheep guarding duty. Usually, he would have been back home shortly after daybreak. The sheep were reasonably safe from predators during the day.

As Rita asked the question, she looked off toward the north pasture, to where they had moved the herd. Anna, with her back to the north, seeing a look of horror come over Rita's face, quickly turned around. A horse was walking slowly up the path toward the barn. Anna instantly recognized Red Two. His head was down, dragging the reins from the bridle along the ground. He wore a saddle, an empty saddle where Ray should have been sitting.

# Chapter 25

NO ONE WOULD EVER know what caused Ray to fall or be thrown from the saddle. As Rita said, "he never was a very good rider." It didn't take them long, following Red Two's tracks, to find him. He was lying flat on his back, his head next to the bloody rock that had smashed the back of his skull on impact.

It was so hard to believe that he'd been killed by a freak accident. After surviving the great dying to come to such an end seemed so unfair. *Fate,* thought Anna. *Was it just his fate? Are we all just fated to who knows what?* She thought of the life growing inside her. A life that seemed so much more precious now after the loss of another man. Anna was sure the child she carried was a boy. She would bear a son. The world needed men. How could fate deny her the chance to bring one into the world? *There is no rhyme or reason to fate,* she thought. And the thought frightened her. What if humankind was fated to simply fade away? To simply become extinct like all the other species driven to extinction by a human race that would, in the end, destroy itself.

Anna and Liz were almost to Kremmling. Just the two of them, alone in the Rivian. It was just after noon. They'd left everyone else at the BR, grieving, after burying Ray early that morning. Ray was the first person buried in the ranch cemetery that wasn't related to the Piersons or the Durans. It was just over twenty-four hours ago that the joy of a new baby on the ranch had turned to sudden sorrow. Both Anna and Liz would have preferred to be back at the ranch, but they had another responsibility. The two of them had brought electricity back to Kremmling, and the two of them knew it was up to them to keep the power flowing.

"What if we weren't here?" Liz asked. The question seemingly coming from nowhere. "I mean, what happens when we can't keep the power on anymore?"

It was part of a question Anna had asked herself many times. *What happens to him,* she thought of her baby, *when all of the old technologies are finally gone?*

"Guess people will just have to go back to the old ways," she told Liz, wondering *what old ways?* even as she said it.

They stopped and picked up Johnny Garcia at the water plant before going on out to the Wolford Reservoir solar farm. Liz and Anna agreed that, of all the people in Kremmling, Johnny would be the best bet to learn the power system.

As it turned out, other than learning what breakers and switches to check if it happened again, Johnny didn't get much of a lesson on this trip. It took about fifteen minutes to get the power back on, but Anna knew it wouldn't always be so simple. For the first time, she really thought about how hard it was going to be to teach the children of this world everything they needed to know to keep the power flowing.

Back in Kremmling, after dropping off Johnny at the water plant, they stopped at Dr. Ming's office for Anna to have a quick check-up and to give him the bad news about Ray.

"Do you think the power is going to be reliable now?" Dr. Ming asked Anna. "I mean if I was trying to do some kind of emergency surgery or something..." He just let the "or something" trail off into the ether.

"We need to get you some emergency backup," Anna told him. "If any place needs it, this clinic does. We need to salvage some batteries and find an inverter and controller, so you have at least a couple days' worth of battery backup."

"Sure hope you can get it set up quickly, this place is about to become a full-time maternity ward. Jackie Adams from Granby is due in about two weeks, and there's two more over there that aren't far behind. I just hope V-1 is finally behind us now. Before Connie's baby, I was starting to think the human race would just go extinct."

On the way back to the BR, Anna and Liz decided they would have to get Dave to clear old Highway 40 all the way from Granby down to I-70 and then I-70 on into Denver. It wasn't just electricity that the clinic needed. Dr. Ming would also run out of medical supplies someday, just as the people of the valley would eventually run out of other things. Baby clothes and diapers being high on the list of things that people would need if procreation continued at its current pace. The old Walmart stores in Granby and Frisco wouldn't supply what everyone needed for much longer. No, they would have to start making salvage runs down to Denver. The metro area could provide most everything they needed for a long, long time to come. *But not forever* was the thought that lodged in Anna's mind. *Someday, it will all be gone.*

··········

*Just barely over a year ago.* In retrospect, it didn't seem possible to James how much had transpired since the last time he was at the Mendez estate in Castle Pines. "I should have buried her at the ranch," he told Anna. They were standing in the old flower garden turned cemetery, paying respects to Noni. Like most spaces in the Denver area, dryland weeds were taking over the old garden. There was one giant tumbleweed growing right on top of Julie's grave that James found particularly troubling. "That's Julie's grave," he said, pointing out where he and Dave had buried his last girlfriend.

In the month just past, James had told Anna all about Julie and the other women he'd known. He even told her about the sexual encounter that he'd had with Connie. He was surprised when Anna told him she already knew about that. In turn, Anna told James all about Charlie Day and about being a semi-willing participant in a polygamist relationship in Blue Rapids.

"Did you love her?" Anna asked.

"I guess I did. But not like I love you."

"Strange, isn't it?" Anna thought out loud. "Love, I mean. Love, lust, sex. What was it that brought about monogamy as an ideal? It certainly isn't the norm in most of the animal world."

James thought about it before replying, "I don't think it's natural for humans either." He laughed. "People may have preached monogamy, but I don't think very many ever truly practiced it. At best, the old norm was serial monogamy. One sex partner at a time, but any number of sex partners over time."

"Guess that's true," Anna laughed. "Doesn't seem like it makes much difference, does it? I mean, what's the difference between having multiple partners over time or having them all at the same time."

James put one arm around Anna and placed his other hand on her swelling tummy. "Well, at least with one at a time," he said, "you always know who the father is."

"Come on," Anna said, "let's go see what we can find."

Dave and Liz were waiting for James and Anna inside the Mendez house, where it was a little cooler. In the year that had passed, the uninterruptible power supply of the Mendez estate had finally stopped working, but it was still cooler inside than out. This was the first supply trip since Dave finished opening the road. The four of them had driven the Carlisle truck and trailer down early that morning.

"We could probably fix the power," Anna said when she and James were back inside.

James took one last look around the home he'd known for most of his life. "Why bother?" he said, "I don't think I'll ever be back." With that, he turned and left home for the very last time.

With a trailer full of supplies, some medical, but mostly baby clothes, shoes, boots, and an inordinate amount of disposable diapers, they turned onto Highway 40 from I-70 just as the sun was going down.

"Wonder if there's still anyone in Georgetown?" James asked. He told the others about seeing a couple of people there from a distance, way back when he'd first made the trek from Castle Pines.

"Guess next time we should run up there and see," Dave said. In the past month that they'd spent clearing the highways enough to make this trip, they hadn't seen anyone between Fraser and Denver. That trend had continued today. Searching and salvaging through a metro area the size of Denver without seeing another living soul really brought home just how isolated their little community was.

As they made their way around the switchbacks on Berthoud Pass, Anna wondered if isolated communities like Kremmling-Granby and Blue Rapids would survive. *Can our species even survive?* It was a question she'd been thinking a lot about. The recent births at Dr. Ming's clinic provided hope. The two women from Granby had both given birth to healthy baby girls, neither of which showed any sign of V-1, or whatever the sickness was that had taken all the earlier babies. There were now three new baby girls in their little community. *But no boys* was the thought that made Anna wonder about the survival of the species. *We need more men,* she thought. *We need you to grow up healthy,* she silently told the baby boy growing inside her womb.

# Chapter 26

T HE THERMOMETER ON THE dashboard read 112 degrees. It was the twenty-eighth day of August. Anna was due in about six weeks, and she was totally miserable. The unrelenting heat wave gripping the valley would have been bad anytime, but the heat made being eight months pregnant almost unbearable. James was driving, and the two of them rode mostly in silence. The weekly trip down to see Dr. Ming was routine now. After the ultrasound confirmed what Anna's intuition already knew, that she did indeed carry a baby boy, Dr. Ming was as concerned about the health of Anna's baby as anyone. There had been two more births in Dr. Ming's clinic during the past two months. Another totally healthy baby girl and one baby boy that lived for only three days. Four baby girls born in the valley and no baby boys.

The valley had also recently lost another one of the older men. One of the men from Granby had died of an apparent heart attack. The longterm viability of the entire Middle Park community seemed more and more in peril, and Anna was becoming ever more fearful for her unborn son. As her due date approached, she found herself wishing she could just keep her baby secure in her womb, safe from a world of dying men and boys. *Maybe we really are doomed,* Anna thought. Looking down at not much more than a trickle of water as they crossed the Colorado River bridge didn't help her state of mind at all.

"That's different," James said as he parked next to a strange old SUV parked in front of Dr. Ming's clinic. It was definitely a different vehicle than any they'd seen in the valley before.

The strange car put both James and Anna on edge. Who was it? *Probably just one of the Granby bunch,* Anna thought. *The Granby Gardeners,* she corrected herself, remembering Ruth's name for that community. *Who knows how many old cars might be hidden away somewhere?* She found herself taking her pistol out of the console anyway. Having the old S&W.40 in her bag gave her a feeling of security, warranted or not.

There was, as it turned out, nothing threatening at all about the two women sitting in the waiting room. Women that neither James nor Anna had ever seen before. One was Black, and the other either Latino or Native.

"Where are you from?" Anna asked after the two women introduced themselves. *Strange question,* she thought as soon as the words left her lips. *Where are you from before? Or, where are you from now?*

"We came here from Montana." Constance, the large Black woman, said. Constance and the other woman, Mary, were both in their mid-twenties. Other than age, the only common physical trait shared by the two women was the fact that they were both females. Constance was a big woman in every way. Not obese by any means, just exceedingly large. Mary, on the other hand, was a petite, extremely attractive young woman. Where Constance was over six feet tall, Mary was probably no more than five-four.

Constance was probably north of two-hundred pounds, while Mary would be lucky to go much over a hundred.

"Dr. Ming said we would be welcome to stay here in Kremmling," Mary said. "Even after Lenore and our baby can leave." She looked at Constance before adding, "if we want to stay, that is."

"We have some friends that came down from Montana," James had to think for a second to remember where in Montana. "Somewhere close to Billings, Park City, I think."

"Wow, that's where we were," Mary brightened. "Guess it's still a small world after all."

"Too small," Constance said. "Too small for the likes of those trying to take over Park City. Dr. Ming says none of those New Army Of God people are around here. Is that true?"

James and Anna told the two that no one in the area had anything to do with the New Army Of God. They also assured them that Dr. Ming was not the only one that would welcome them into the community. Everyone in Middle Park would be glad to see them stay.

After James and Anna's reassurances, the two women really opened up and shared their story. The three women had fled increasing persecution in Park City. Apparently, The New Army Of God was growing and starting to take over the entire Park City area. And they weren't just taking over land and property. They were trying to make what Mary said they called "a whites-only paradise" in Park City.

"That New Army of God bunch is trying to drive people of color out of the area. And it isn't just Black people like Constance," Mary told them. "It doesn't matter what color you are if you aren't lily-white."

"If you ask me," Constance said, "they don't want us out. They want us to be slaves. Just like before the Civil War.

Think they're some kind of superior beings just because they're white."

"They want you to be slaves," Mary told Constance. "They just want to kill those of us that are sexually diverse." After looking at James and Anna to gauge their reaction, she continued. " I guess that was the final straw, the lynching," Mary looked down, remembering the horror. "When we found Scott hanging from that overpass, we knew we had to leave."

"Poor Scott," Constance said. "He had the misfortune of not only being Black but also being gay. Guess there isn't much worse than a gay Black man, as far as the New Army Of God's concerned."

Anna's own memories of her encounter with The New Army Of God were too painful. She had to change the subject. "Is Lenore pregnant then?" she asked.

"She was," Mary said, glad to talk about something else. "Now we have a baby boy. Daniel. Born right here two days ago."

Anna couldn't help but notice the ring that Mary fidgeted with as she spoke. "Is Lenore your partner?" she asked.

"We're married," Mary held up her hand to show off the ring. "Been married for three years now. Kind of a strange concept anymore, isn't it? Marriage, I mean. Almost as strange as a couple of lesbians having a baby." She looked for any signs of disapproval on James and Anna's faces before laughing and adding, "Me and Lenore wanted to have a child before - you know before," she paused before continuing, "anyway, we always planned for one of us to have a child using a sperm bank. The problem was, we could never agree on which one of us would actually get pregnant, but then," she paused again. "After - I mean now, it just seems like we need all the babies we can get. I tried to get pregnant too, but Lenore got pregnant first. Guess I still want to get pregnant myself someday," she confided. "Not that I relish sex with a man." She looked directly at James. "No offense," she said.

James laughed. "None taken," he answered.

Anna knew exactly what Mary was feeling as far as her desire to have a child, it was that same maternal instinct that seemed to afflict almost every woman that survived the great dying. The drive to reproduce so the species would survive was something common to all women, regardless of sexual orientation. She had the thought, *for men, it's probably not much different now than it's ever been. Wonder how much they understand about what it is that drives them to do or say damn near anything to get laid.* Anna looked at James, then she turned back to Mary, and asked the question that was foremost in her mind, "Is the baby healthy?"

"He is," Mary answered, but she had a concerned look on her face. "At least he was. What's going on around here?" she asked. "Why did Dr. Ming make me come out here just because Daniel had a little touch of fever?"

Anna's heart dropped. *Not another one, please not another one,* she thought. Anna didn't want to be the one to have to tell Mary about the other baby boys that had all died shortly after birth. Even more than that, she didn't want to know herself. But how could she not know? How could she just unknow what she already knew? How could she maintain the belief that the baby she carried would be okay when another baby boy was probably dying right now back in the maternity ward. Anna couldn't help it, she burst into tears.

Mary's expression changed from concern to bewilderment, and finally to fear as James started trying to explain, "It's just that baby boys haven't made it yet. They just..." he was saved from having to continue by Dr. Ming opening the door and stepping into the waiting room.

Anna didn't need to hear the sounds of a woman sobbing back in the maternity ward to tell her what the look on Dr. Ming's face made all too clear. Dr. Ming walked over to Mary, who stood up and was looking at the door. The closed door that had now shut out the sobs of her lover.

"There was nothing I could do," he said softly, but not too softly for Anna and James to hear.

# Chapter 27

T HE GOLDS AND REDS of autumn were almost gone. The aspen trees were nearly bare, the whole world fading into the drab grays and browns of winter. Anna walked the lane from the house out toward Highway 9, James by her side. This daily walk out to the highway and back was the only exercise she had allowed herself lately. The baby was due any time now. The baby was the only thing that mattered. The depth of Anna's worry about the upcoming birth, and the health of the baby, was as deep as any ocean. She couldn't stop thinking about it.

The horses, cattle, and sheep were all in the big meadow now. The hay crop had been put up months ago. *Wonder why we bother,* Anna thought about the hay. She tried to remember the last winter with enough snow to keep the animals from being able to just graze their way through until spring. *October seventh, I've been back here for just about a year now.* Anna spent a lot of time thinking lately. She thought about the events of the year just past. The first year of a new world on the Blue River Ranch, and the year before that, when the old world came to an abrupt end.

The pain in her lower back seemed worse than usual today and walking more difficult. They were less than halfway out to the highway when she felt something different, a pain that seemed to radiate from her lower back and spread through her swollen belly. She gasped and stopped walking, her hands holding her stomach, which seemed harder and tighter than usual.

"Anna, are you alright?" the concern in James's voice matched her own anxiety.

Having never experienced childbirth before, Anna couldn't be positive, but she was pretty sure. "I think it's time," she said. "We better turn around."

James carefully pulled her left arm up over his shoulders and reached around her back with his right hand to give her support and help her walk. He led her not to the house, but straight to the metal shop building where the Rivian was all charged up and ready to go. With Anna securely buckled up in the passenger seat, he pulled away from the shop and only stopped at the house long enough to run inside and grab the bag that was packed and waiting.

"It's time," he told Charlene and Misty, who were sitting at the bar having a snack. No one was in sight over at the old house, and James didn't want to take time to figure out where they were. "Charlene, why don't you come with us now. You can drop us off at the clinic and bring the Riv back for the others. Misty, tell the others where we went." The calm, collected demeanor James displayed was utterly at odds with the chaos swirling through his mind.

The emotional storm hidden behind James' façade wasn't lost on Charlene. She jumped up immediately. "Better let me drive," she said.

As Anna was helped into Dr. Ming's clinic by James on one side and Charlene on the other, she wasn't sure which was more terrifying, the fact that she was about to give birth, or the harrowing race from the Blue River Ranch to Kremmling that she'd just experienced. *Should have just driven myself,* she thought.

Lisa was seated at what had once been the receptionist's desk at the clinic, studying what was undoubtedly some kind of medical textbook. Dr. Ming's school of medicine was in full swing. Seeing Anna being helped through the door, Lisa leaped to her feet and grabbed the wheelchair that was always sitting near the front desk.

"Dr. Ming's at the church," Lisa told Charlene, as they eased Anna into the chair. There was no reason to specify which church. "Please go get him." She wheeled Anna back to the delivery room with James firmly in tow.

···•··•·····

"I want to call him Alpha," Anna said, as she rearranged the cover over the new baby boy that was nursing at her breast. "He's the first. The first baby boy to survive. The first male child to inherit this new world."

Dr. Ming was filling out some kind of birth certificate form that he'd dug up from some archive somewhere. He looked up at James for affirmation. There was no way for Dr. Ming to know James and Anna had already been over this too many times to count. From that first ultrasound showing Anna's baby was a boy, James had wanted to name him Charles, after his grandfather. Anna's early choice was Clyde, after her father. They'd considered Charles Clyde, but Anna always seemed to balk at naming her son Charles. James didn't know why. For him, Charles was his grandfather and his great grandfather before that. That the name might remind Anna of Charlie Day didn't even occur to him. Yesterday, he had been as surprised by the name, Alpha, as Dr. Ming seemed to be now.

"I wanted to name him Charles," James told Dr. Ming. The way he said it, Dr. Ming could see that James had already given up on that.

"Maybe we should just leave the name blank for now," Dr. Ming said. "He is just barely two days old."

Anna knew what Dr. Ming was saying. Maybe it would be better to not give the child a name for a week or so. If the child didn't survive, it might be easier to bury a nameless child than one who had a name. Like a child was meaningless until it was given a name.

"His name is Alpha," Anna said, firmly but without malice. "Whether you write it down or not." Then she looked from Dr. Ming to James. "I'm sorry James, I just can't name our baby Charles." She looked up at the ceiling, remembering another Charles. Not Chuck Pierson, but Charlie Day back in Blue Rapids. Olivia would have had Charlie's baby by now. Anna hoped it was a boy. She hoped her Alpha wasn't truly the first. She hoped that another baby boy had already survived back in Kansas.

"Alright, Anna," Dr. Ming asked, "what about the surname, Mendez, or Duran."

"Pierson or Duran," James stated firmly. "I won't have my child named Mendez."

Anna and Dr. Ming both looked at James. Anna knowing why James didn't want Alpha named Mendez, Dr. Ming, not understanding at all.

"None," Anna said. "Alpha is just Alpha. I don't think surnames from the past have any meaning anymore. The old world is dead. Just Alpha is good enough for this world." She looked down at her baby boy, who had stopped feeding.

Dr. Ming stopped writing. "I guess you're right," he said. "There's probably no reason for a birth certificate, either. Look at how many have died without a death certificate.

I guess I'm just too old for a totally new world. Alpha, I hope you can make a better world than the one we did." He put down the pen and reached over to gently place his hand on the back of the newborn's head. Dr. Ming's hand nearly recoiled of its own volition before he could steady it. The hand that had touched hundreds of babies during a lifetime of medical practice was much too sensitive to miss the telltale signs of the beginning of a fever.

# APOCALYPTIC WINDS

## Thermals Of Time - Book Three

# Dedication

For Sadie and Atticus(once they're old enough)
May the Thermals Of Time be kind

# PART ONE

Tomorrow arrives on wings of the past
Riding the thermals of time
What came before comes once more
The fall before a climb
Yesterday and tomorrow are one
Time an endless illusion
Future past and the endless now
No more than mass delusion

# Chapter 1

ROBIN CHECKED THE PLACEMENT of the explosive charge one last time. It wasn't that she had less trust in her team than she did anyone else, but Robin hadn't risen to her leadership role at such a young age by trusting people. She trusted no one. At least no one other than Helena Hunt.

Satisfied that the charge would be enough to blast the door open without destroying everything inside, Robin followed the thin wires around the earthen berm to the backside of the building. The other four members of her team watched as she carefully pulled the battery out of her front shirt pocket and removed the protective cover. Batteries were a very precious commodity. *Maybe we will find some more inside,* Robin thought as she held the bare end of one wire tightly to the negative post on top of the small battery. The blast that went off the instant she touched the other bare wire to the positive post didn't seem as loud as it should have been. Before investigating though, Robin replaced the cover on the battery and put it back in her pocket, securely stashing it away behind the patch with the three black crosses.

It was a relief to see that the steel door had indeed been blown open with minimal damage. As a matter of fact, the only visible damage, other than the twisted metal door, was to the brass sign embedded in the concrete at the entrance to this bunker-like underground building. The date at the bottom of the plaque, 2025, was all that was still legible. *Built clear back in twenty twenty-five?* Robin thought. *God, that was twelve years before I was even born.* She didn't give much thought to the rest of the plaque that had been destroyed by the blast. The part that had the three letters, CDC, at the top.

"Get the coolers," Robin ordered her team. Probably more abruptly than she should have. After all, these women were soldiers, all members of the New Army Of God. They all wore the same uniform as she did, with the same insignia, a single patch with three black crosses. This was no slave labor salvage crew. One of those slave labor crews had found this place outside the old city of Memphis and reported it back to Fort Campbell. Which was why Robin was now stepping through the partially opened door into what looked like a dark underground cave. She was thinking it might be a wasted mission as she let her eyes adjust to the dim light coming through the partially opened door. She wished she could have gone with the rest of Helena's troops to someplace called Brookfield in the old state of Missouri. Robin was a firm believer in New Dixie. She enjoyed nothing more than raiding places that had yet to be assimilated, places where the others, those that weren't white, were still free. Being a free person of color was against New Dixie's laws and against the will of God. Absolute rule by God's pure white race was simply the way the world was meant to be.

Robin could see well enough to take a few more careful steps into the darkness. She seemed to be walking downhill into a dark tunnel. Just as she was about to reach the limits of the available natural light, she was momentarily blinded by artificial light flooding the entrance tunnel and the vast room beyond. There were no motion sensors in Fort Campbell. It was almost like magic, the way the lights in the lab came on all by themselves.

Helena was right! But then, when had Helena ever been wrong? Robin remembered the look on Helena's face when she first heard of this place. Helena became interested as soon as the salvage crew described finding a huge solar array behind an underground building, a building they couldn't break into. When the salvage crew's nearly illiterate leader described the sign with the letters CDC, Helena was downright excited.

Robin knew that Helena wanted to come herself, and she would have if the raid on Brookfield wasn't imminent. As Robin walked into the underground lab and heard the sounds of her team coming through the tunnel behind her, she felt immense pride that Helena had trusted her with this vital mission. Seeing all the vials and racks of test tubes in the refrigerated glass-fronted cases, Robin knew missing the initial raid on Brookfield was worth it. Besides, if they hurried, she would complete this mission to collect drugs and medicines and still be able to get to Brookfield in time to get in on some of the action.

"Okay," she told her team, "everything in these refrigerated cases must be loaded in the coolers as carefully and quickly as you can. We need to make sure everything is kept cold. Do not leave these cases or our coolers open any longer than absolutely necessary. And remember, this is not a normal salvage operation. Everything in these refrigerated cases is as precious and rare as anything ever brought back to New Dixie. If Helena is right, and we know she is, these drugs and medicines will save countless lives."

Robin walked away as her team started carefully packing the coolers. She was thinking about the route she should take back to Fort Campbell and how fast she could get there and then on to Missouri. Maybe she could still make it in time to get in on some of the initial fighting. Her thoughts were interrupted by the sound of glass breaking on the concrete floor. She turned to see all four members of her team staring down at the broken test tube and spilled liquid on the floor. All four of them had the same look of fear on their faces as they watched her walk over to the broken glass. Robin knew as she bent down and picked up the biggest piece of the broken glass, the one that had the paper label holding it intact, that none of them would confess to dropping the test tube. Her anger faded a little. It wouldn't do any good to try to punish the whole group. Besides, it was only one small vial out of so many others.

"Get back to work," she ordered the team. "Let's finish this up."

Robin turned the piece of glass in her hand so she could read the label. The writing on the label didn't make any sense at all. *Probably not even important,* she thought as she looked at the single letter followed by a series of numbers: ***V1-203601/10.***

# Chapter 2

C HARLENE LOOKED AT THE group outside the gate. She could see them from three different angles on the monitor, but this wasn't the first time she'd seen this particular group of refugees. Unlike everyone else she knew, Charlene had dreams or visions. Charlene's visions, though infrequent, were quite accurate most of the time. Charlene couldn't foresee the future, though she wished she could; mostly, she could see a lot more of the now or the recent past than most people. A couple of days ago, Charlene had seen this particular group of people trekking toward Blue Rapids in one of those visions.

In some ways, Charlene's visions, though accurate, were incomplete and frustrating. She saw actual events as they happened or as they had happened, but what she saw was only bits and pieces. Sometimes, it was hard to put the vision in context. It was like reading a paragraph or two from the middle of a book without knowing what came before or what comes after.

She had seen this group of people and knew they were coming to Blue Rapids, but that was all she had seen. Where did they come from? And why were they headed to Blue Rapids? Were they fleeing the New Army Of God or merely seeking a new place to live? Maybe they were escapees from New Dixie.

Like most of those who came before, this group was mixed, but almost entirely women and children. In Charlene's vision, there was only one man in the group. Just one dark-skinned older man and five women. Two of the women had skin lighter than Charlene's, while the other three were as dark as old Danny Day. The nine children in the group were a mixed bag, both by age and skin color. None of the children were male. That really would have been something. The young girls in the group seemed to range in age from about five to the oldest, who was probably in her early teens. Charlene knew from her studies of the before that girls and boys used to be born in near equal numbers. Not like now. Now there were no baby boys, or so it seemed.

What really caught Charlene's attention now as she looked at the screen was a second man who had not been in the vision. *What does it mean?* She wondered. Why had she not seen this man before? He was a young man, probably about Charlene's own age, which meant he was either very young when everyone died, or he was the only male Charlene had ever seen that might have been born after that great dying. His white skin, blue eyes, and red hair seemed out of place in the predominately mixed-race group of people.

"What do you think?" asked the older woman sitting in front of the monitor.

By way of answer, Charlene leaned over, pushed the button, and said, "I'll be right out" into the microphone.

"More refugees," she said to the woman sitting in front of the computer screen. "I think we better put them up in Marysville. Let Sarah know they're coming. I'll go welcome them to our little community." *Another young man will be more than just welcome,* she thought.

This little office in the bunker beneath the old gypsum plant was the technology and communications center of the growing Blue Rapids-Marysville community. As Charlene walked through the open blast door, leaving Kahina sitting in front of the monitor, she found herself once again in awe of everything Kahina had accomplished.

Charlene was just a baby when Kahina came to Blue Rapids. There weren't nearly as many people in the community then. The population had grown exponentially in the twenty years since, from just a few survivors to hundreds of people living in all of the old communities surrounding the old town of Marysville, Kansas. What started out as the Blue Rapids community was now centered twelve miles to the north in Marysville.

Like many before her, Kahina had been fleeing the ravages of the great dying when she came to Blue Rapids. Unlike any before or since, Kahina was a technological wizard. In the before, she had been an IT contractor for the Department Of Defense.

Charlene had no personal knowledge of the old DOD, of course. Or any other personal knowledge of the times that older people referred to simply as *"the before"*. Charlene was born after the before. Everything she knew about the before she'd learned from her elders and from books. Olivia, Charlene's mother, and Charlie Day, her father, instilled a love of learning and taught her to read at a very young age. They also taught her the most important lesson of all. They taught her that she had the ability to learn. They were the ones who introduced Charlene to the Marysville library, where she first learned to educate herself.

It was Kahina Khan, though, who continued to teach Charlene about all of the old technologies from the before. It was Kahina that first introduced a young Charlene to the old university library in what had once been Manhattan, Kansas. Kahina not only maintained and built up all of the computer and communications systems the Blue Rapids community depended on, but she also taught Charlene how to put knowledge to use in the physical world. Kahina taught her how to actually make the computer and communications systems work. Just as her father had taught her how all of the community's various power and water systems worked.

Leaving Kahina sitting at her desk, Charlene walked briskly up through the tunnel that, other than the freight elevator, was the only way in and out of the bunker she called home. Charlie Day discovered the bunker beneath the abandoned gypsum plant more than twenty years ago. Charlie didn't live in the bunker, though. He and Olivia, Charlene's mother, still lived with a group of people in the old stone house over on the other side of Blue Rapids. The place that had been Charlene's childhood home.

Climbing up through the trap door, Charlene exited the guard shack through the door that led directly to the group of newcomers gathered outside the gate. Some of the newcomers were armed, but Charlene didn't feel threatened.

"Are you Charlene?" It was one of the lighter-skinned women that stepped forward and asked the question.

"I am." Charlene walked up to the woman and held out her hand. "And what is your name?"

"Kimberly, but everyone calls me Kim." Kim firmly gripped Charlene's offered hand. "Charlie said we could find you here. He said you could help us."

Kim was the apparent leader of this little band of refugees, though the group didn't seem to have any organized structure. She was an older woman, probably about the same age as Charlie and Olivia, which meant she had been one of the few who survived the great dying. Charlene wondered how well these people would assimilate into the more organized Marysville community. That was always a consideration when newcomers arrived, especially those newcomers who seemed to already have a dominant leader. There was always the question of whether or not they would fit into the loose power structure of the Marysville community.

"I think we can help," Charlene said, looking over this group of people in person for the first time after seeing all but one of them in her vision. "Are you just passing through, or are you looking for a place to settle?"

"Well, I guess I don't really know. Mostly we're just trying to get away from the Narmy," Kim said, using the common slang for the New Army Of God. She may have seemed like the leader of this band of refugees, but she obviously didn't have a long-term plan.

"I don't know about everyone else, but I'm looking for a new home."

It was the young man with red hair and blue eyes who had been absent from Charlene's vision. Kim, with a look of total surprise on her face, turned back toward the group. Charlene also looked at the redhead, really looked at him, for the first time. He was tall and muscular. He was lighter-skinned than anyone else in the group but dark enough that his skin color didn't seem to fit the red hair and bright blue eyes. Those eyes were what really grabbed Charlene, though. As their eyes met, the connection seemed like a lot more than just eye contact.

"What's your name?" Charlene asked the young man.

"I'm Jackson." The man seemed suddenly hesitant to offer more information as he turned his bright blue eyes back to Kim.

Was there a conflict of authority? Charlene couldn't help but wonder. Everyone else in the group seemed to defer to Kim.

"Where are you from?" Charlene directed the question at Jackson, but he looked from Kim to Charlene, and then back at Kim, apparently deciding to let Kim do the talking.

Kim dropped eye contact with Jackson and turned her attention back to Charlene. "We're from what used to be Brookfield, Missouri. At least all of us here but Jackson. He joined up with us somewhere around old Saint Joe." Kim paused, trying to remember, then turned back to Jackson. "Where did you say you were from?" she asked.

"I was living down around Sedalia," Jackson answered, "before the Narmy came."

It struck Charlene as odd that he didn't say he was from Sedalia, but he'd been living down around Sedalia. What did that mean exactly?

"We had a nice community in Brookfield," Kim interrupted Charlene's thoughts. "At least until the Narmy came. We'd heard they were expanding their territory, but we thought we had good enough defenses to keep our little community safe." Kim looked down at the ground, remembering the terror. "They came at night," she continued. "Killed our sentries and just started rounding up the rest of the community. Don't know what they did with everybody else. We were able to escape in all the chaos. It still seems odd that they didn't track us down, us being on foot and all. Guess they just wanted our place, not us."

"They probably just didn't care about women escaping," Jackson said. "They've got more women than they know what to do with. And Solomon here's probably too old to do them any good anyway. No offense Solomon," he told the old Black man.

"And what about you?" Charlene asked. "Why did you leave Sedalia?"

"I escaped." The look in Jackson's eyes told Charlene that he didn't want to say more, but she wanted, no, needed, to know more.

"You mean the New Army Of God took Sedalia, too?" she asked.

Jackson looked down and then back up to make eye contact. "It was more than a year ago when they took Sedalia."

Charlene glanced at Kim and the rest of the group. Jackson now had everyone's attention. This was apparently the first any of them had heard this much about Jackson. Jackson kept those blue eyes focused on Charlene, though, and she could feel his pain.

"They made me join them," he said quietly. "That's what they do. If you're a white woman, you can either join them if you're lucky or die if you're not. If you're a white man, you have the choice of joining willingly or becoming a sex slave. They don't take any white people for normal slaves. Apparently, that's against their religion."

As Charlene stared into Jackson's eyes, she caught a brief vision of him surrendering to the Narmy. He was lined up with several other white people, mostly women, held at gunpoint by a group of uniformed women with assault rifles. The people of the Narmy were all women, except for one crazy-looking man who was their obvious leader. All wore some kind of military-style uniform with no insignia except for a patch of three black crosses. She could hear in her mind the crazy man, who was the apparent leader of the Narmy group, coldly asking, "Will you kneel before the crosses? Will you join us?" She could feel the fear that coursed through Jackson as he, along with a couple of the other prisoners, took a knee and knelt before the man. She could feel his helpless rage as he looked down at the ground, and the Narmy opened fire on those prisoners who hadn't knelt.

And then it was over. The vision ended as soon as it began. It was almost as though Jackson had opened his mind to her for just a moment and then closed it abruptly. *Too much pain,* she thought.

Charlene had seen the three black crosses before, then as now, only in visions. She hoped she would never see those three black crosses in person, but she knew from previous visions that the Narmy was slowly but surely expanding New Dixie to the west and north. She knew that one day the people of her community would come face to face with the same evil that Jackson and Kim and all the others had fled. It was only a matter of time. *We need to prepare,* she thought, not for the first time. If only she could convince the rest of the Marysville community.

Charlene broke eye contact with Jackson to focus on the whole group. "Are you hungry?" she asked. Charlene turned toward the closest security camera without waiting for an answer and told Kahina to have Noah bring the bus around. "And tell whoever's cooking today there'll be sixteen newcomers for lunch," she added.

As with those who came before, the people of the community would feed and house the newcomers up in Marysville. They'd then let each of them decide whether or not they wanted to stay and join the community or move on. In the past, most, but not all, had decided to stay.

...........

For some reason, Charlene had a hard time getting Sedalia out of her mind. She knew Sedalia had once been the home of the Missouri State Fair. Of all the trivial things Charlene had learned about the before, it seemed odd that it was one of the few things she knew about Sedalia, Missouri. Why did Jackson say he'd been living in Sedalia? Where was he from, if not Sedalia, and why did it matter? The most important thing to know now was that Sedalia had been taken by the Narmy. Sedalia and Brookfield both. Both were now part of New Dixie.

Charlene could see where both places were located on the map in her mind's eye. With something akin to a photographic memory and total recall, she carried a complete atlas of the old United States around in her head. As an overlay on that map, she could see New Dixie. With every passing year, the map of the territory claimed by New Dixie and controlled by the Narmy grew closer to Marysville. Expanding mainly to the west and north, New Dixie, if not stopped, would be bigger than the old Confederate States in no time at all.

The Narmy didn't really have any choice about which direction they could expand. New Dixie may have fashioned their state based on the old Confederate States of America, but occupying the same territory was out of the question. Much of that territory was underwater now, and much of the rest was too hot and humid for anyone to even survive there.

"Have you ever been to Sedalia, Missouri?" Charlene asked Kahina.

The two women were sitting in one corner of the great room of the bunker they called home. It was late afternoon; two of the bunker's other residents, Damon and Amelia, were starting to prepare the household's evening meal in the kitchen at the other end of the large room. The other inhabitants of the bunker had yet to return home for the evening.

"Not that I can remember," Kahina answered. "But then, my memory doesn't work like yours." She smiled at Charlene, thinking how she had never known anyone else whose memory worked like Charlene's. "Unless there is some kind of military installation there, probably not."

"I wonder why the Narmy would invade a place like Sedalia?" Charlene asked. "I don't know much about the place except that it used to be the home of the Missouri State Fair. That, and it's where Jackson said he was living when the Narmy came."

Having watched Charlene's meeting with the newcomers on the monitor, Kahina had to wonder if Charlene was interested more in Sedalia or in the young man named Jackson, but she didn't bring it up. "Well, you know more about Sedalia than I do." She didn't have to say it, but Charlene knew more about anything and everything than anyone Kahina had ever known. As Kahina watched Charlene pondering Sedalia, she was in awe once again of the knowledge contained in the younger woman's head.

"Did anything happen in that area of Missouri during the Civil War?" Kahina asked. She knew that Charlene had taken a particular interest in that part of old American history. Kahina had watched her studying that history the first time she took her down to Manhattan. On that first trip to the Manhattan library, Kahina first witnessed Charlene's unique ability to acquire knowledge.

"Confederate forces captured Sedalia on October fifteenth, 1864."

Kahina wasn't surprised that Charlene knew such an obscure bit of trivia. She knew that Charlene remembered everything she ever saw in a book. Kahina remembered watching in awe as Charlene devoured books at the Hale Library on the old KSU campus in Manhattan.

That would have been seven years ago. Kahina remembered talking Charlie into taking them down to Manhattan after one of the scavenger crews brought back a few books. The scavengers reported finding a huge building that was completely full of books. It was still a wonder to Kahina that the university library had remained mostly intact more than twenty years after the great dying. Kahina could still see the way Charlene's eyes lit up when they first walked into that cavernous building. It reminded her of how she felt when her parents took her to Disneyland so many years ago. The sparkle in Charlene's eyes had been something to see, and then she started reading.

Charlene didn't exactly read, though. Not like everyone else anyway. Watching Charlene acquire knowledge was an amazing thing. She would open a book and simply start turning the pages, just about as fast as a person could turn one page at a time. She didn't seem to even scan the pages. It was more like her eyes were a camera with a fast shutter speed. As Kahina got used to watching the process, she imagined hearing the click of a shutter every time Charlene turned a page. Click – turn the page, click – turn the page, one after another. Charlene didn't read books. She consumed them. She read everything and anything at the rate of about a page per second.

Coming back to the present, Kahina had a thought, "God, you don't suppose they're trying to recapture all the territory the old Confederacy had before, do you?" she asked.

"No, probably not." Charlene shook her head. "I doubt they even know the history of Sedalia. Or much history at all, for that matter. The Narmy is just taking whatever they can. They'll be here one of these days."

That wasn't what Kahina wanted to hear, but she recognized the truth of the statement when she looked at the faraway look in Charlene's eyes. She, too, knew it could only be a matter of time. Would it be a year, ten years? Maybe even decades, but one day New Dixie's boundaries would expand to take in Marysville.

"Count me out for dinner," Charlene hollered across the room to Damon and Amelia. "I'm going up to Marysville to eat with the newcomers."

"Me too," Kahina yelled, before telling Charlene, "I'll go with you."

# Chapter 3

K AHINA WAS DRIVING THE Chevy Bolt that was at least five or ten years older than Charlene and still working just fine. Like so many of the old electric vehicles of a bygone era, it didn't have that many miles on the odometer. Especially not considering its age. This was the same car that Kahina had driven to Blue Rapids in the year after the great dying. Now, as she drove toward Marysville, Kahina was thinking about that trip from Wichita so long ago.

She'd been visiting her parents in Wichita when the world ended. Kahina was working on a Department Of Defense project in Arlington at the time. She had taken a couple of weeks off to be home with her mother, who was dying of cancer. *Guess we shouldn't have worried so much about cancer,* was the thought Kahina had, as she remembered those terrible few days. Kahina's mother and father, along with most everyone else, died of V-1 within hours of each other. Kahina would never know for sure what happened to her husband and the two sons she'd left back home in Arlington, but she'd seen the footage of the tsunami that hit Delaware. She had always assumed that the tsunami, not V-1, took her husband and children. Kahina did get sick when her parents died. She remembered thinking the virus was killing her, too. In the days that followed, after burying her parents in their own backyard, she had often wondered if it was even worth it to go on living.

*That's what I was looking for when I left Wichita, a reason to go on living.* She glanced over at Charlene, who had become that reason. *Over twenty years ago,* she thought, remembering when she'd climbed into this very same vehicle, her father's Bolt, and headed north. She didn't have a destination in mind and knew that she wouldn't get much over two hundred miles away from Wichita, but she had to go somewhere.

The Bolt had been just about out of juice when Kahina drove into Blue Rapids and saw a group of people working in a garden. They invited her to stay, and she'd been there ever since. She glanced over at Charlene again as she remembered those early years in Blue Rapids. Charlene was the reason Kahina had stayed. Even as a young girl, Kahina knew there was something extraordinary about Charlene. Now, here she was, all grown up with abilities like no one else Kahina had ever known. Kahina was about to ask Charlene what she hoped to learn from the newcomers, but stopped short when she saw the trance-like state that had come over her.

·····•·•····

It was an office at the New Army Of God headquarters in Fort Campbell. The older man seated behind the ornate desk was General Korliss. The younger man flanked by two members of his own personal security detail was Clint Davis, who preferred the title of Commander. Charlene didn't know how she knew all of this. It was just how the visions were—a knowing without understanding how she could possibly know. The important visions, like this one, were similar to the old movies that Kahina loved to watch back in the bunker, except the visions were total immersion, instead of just scenes on a big screen.

General Korliss wore a dress uniform that proudly displayed the four stars on each shoulder. He was older than Charlene would have thought, probably in his mid-seventies. His sharp hazel grey eyes seemed a perfect match for his short-cropped grey hair. He had the look of an older man who worked hard at staying in good physical condition, and he exuded authority.

"What do you mean, we don't need to keep expanding?" the younger man almost yelled at General Korliss.

"Just what I said, Clint." The older man spoke calmly, ignoring the agitated state of the man on the other side of the desk. "We both wanted a New Dixie. Now we have one. Why keep spreading out into unknown territory that we don't need?"

The calm demeanor of General Korliss seemed to infuriate Clint Davis even more. Here was a man who was seldom calm. The contrast between the two men was striking in every way. Clint Davis had long, wild black hair and a bushy full black beard. He wore a uniform that had to be a replica of a Confederate general's uniform. With General Korliss in his modern dress blues and Clint Davis looking like a younger General Lee, Charlene could almost have been watching a scene from an old Civil War movie. Of course, if it was a Civil War movie, all of the soldiers would have been men, not just Clint Davis and General Korliss. Clint Davis was flanked by a female soldier on either side.

"I would appreciate it if you would address me as Commander Davis." The younger man seemed to be trying to contain the rage that was obvious behind his dark, crazy eyes. "I am a direct descendant of President Jefferson Davis, and by God, I am the rightful leader of New Dixie."

General Korliss stood up slowly. He was a tall man, towering over Clint Davis, who wasn't short by any means. The general leaned down with his fists on his desk to be at the same eye level as Davis.

"You listen to me, Mister Davis," General Korliss kept his voice under control, just slightly overemphasizing the word, mister. "I led the New Army Of God to victory over the old United States Government. I won't have what I fought for my entire life destroyed by fanaticism. New Dixie doesn't need more territory, and we damned sure don't need any more slaves."

Clint Davis didn't interrupt General Korliss, but Charlene could see the rage building inside of him. *Can't the old man see it?* She wondered. It was obvious to her that Davis was about to erupt.

It must have been evident to Korliss also; as he spoke, a side door opened, and another woman entered the room with an automatic rifle pointed at the young commander and the two women who were obviously his personal guards. Apparently, General Korliss had his own personal guard as well.

"Do you know what doomed the old Confederacy?" General Korliss went on without missing a beat. "No, you obviously don't," he answered his own question. "It was greed. Greed and mismanagement. That and plain old-fashioned cruelty. Cruel masters cause rebellious slaves, Mr. Davis, it's not the other way around."

Clint Davis' face, what could be seen of it through the beard, had grown deep red. His jaw was clenched tightly shut, his crazy eyes mere slits. General Korliss leaned even closer to the volcano that was about to erupt.

"Now, Mr. Davis, I am not going to try you for treason. I am going to allow you and your people to go back to Alabama. You can even run the place however you want. But you need to stay in Alabama. Don't you ever threaten me or New Dixie again. If you do, I will personally see you hung. And I'll let your own slaves do the hanging. Do you understand, Mr. Davis?"

Clint Davis moved faster than Charlene would have thought possible. In what seemed like one instantaneous motion, he had one of his own bodyguards between himself and the woman who had entered through the side door. General Korliss's bodyguard was firing multiple rounds into the poor woman Clint Davis was using as a shield even as Davis grabbed her gun. He swept the dead guard's gun up in a deadly firing arc, hitting General Korliss's bodyguard first in the leg, then the abdomen, chest, and finally in the head before the woman could even fall. The gun in Clint Davis' grasp was aimed right at General Korliss by the time the two men's dead personal bodyguards hit the floor.

"Now, it's your turn to listen to me, you son of a bitch," Davis snarled at the General. "And listen good. These are the last words you're ever going to hear. Your problem is you're fucking weak. That's what doomed the old Confederacy. Too many of the Rebels were just too fucking weak."

Davis was now yelling to be heard over the sounds of a gun battle that had erupted outside. His surviving bodyguard, who Charlene knew was named Helena Hunt, went to the door and looked out at the fighting taking place between the General's and the Commander's forces.

Satisfied that the coup was going as planned, Helena turned back to watch the execution of General Korliss.

"Before you die, old man," Davis was yelling, "I want you to know that your dream of a New Dixie will be realized. But we are going to have it all. We won't be satisfied until the whole fucking country is New Dixie, like it should have been two-hundred years ago."

General Korliss tried to reach for the sidearm he mainly wore for decoration, but he was too old and far too slow. His hand was barely off the desk when the single bullet from Davis' rifle tore through his heart.

..........

"Did you know a General Korliss back in the before?" Charlene asked as she came back from the vision.

"I knew of him," Kahina answered. "I never met the man personally, but I suppose everybody that worked with the DOD knew of him. I don't think many of us believed he was actually trying to overthrow the government. At least not until we saw him on the com after the tsunami. Why do you ask?"

"He's dead." It was a simple statement of fact, not a question.

"Yeah, I figured as much. Not too many of us lived through that great dying. What did you see?"

"He survived V-1. Clint Davis shot him."

Kahina parked the Bolt in front of the community center in Marysville. In the before, the old brick building had been the home of the High School. Now, it was the central hub of the growing Marysville community. There were a few individual vehicles in the school's parking lot, along with the three buses that served as public transportation for anyone who lived in the outlying areas. The three electric buses had all been salvaged from Kansas City many years ago.

"Who is Clint Davis?" Kahina asked as she pushed the power button to shut off the Bolt.

"He calls himself Commander Davis. I think he is now the leader of the Narmy and New Dixie. Him and a woman named Helena Hunt," Charlene added, realizing the woman may have been more than just a bodyguard. What I just saw was a coup. General Korliss must have been the founder of New Dixie."

"That makes sense," Kahina said, as much to herself as Charlene. "If Korliss survived the great dying and he was already putting together a revolt...yeah, I can see him leading those who longed for a return to the glory days of the old south."

"Korliss had everything he wanted and then some," Charlene said. "I don't think he liked the way New Dixie turned out in the end. I think he had regrets about all of the people like us that had been killed or enslaved. I don't think New Dixie was what he envisioned back before the revolution and V-1."

Charlene stared straight ahead, gathering what she'd felt instead of seen in the vision. "Clint Davis is insane," she said flatly, turning toward Kahina. "He wants to turn the whole world into the old Confederate States of America. And that woman with him, Helena Hunt, I think she must be his second in command. I'm not sure what she wants, but I'm sure it isn't good."

# Chapter 4

*P*RETTY BIG CROWD, CHARLENE thought as she walked into the cafeteria with Kahina. There were probably thirty people in the room. It was nothing like the number of students that the cafeteria had been designed to feed, but more than typically showed up for the evening meal.

"Word gets around fast, doesn't it?" Kahina said. There were usually no more than ten or fifteen diners at the cafeteria on any given night.

"Yeah, guess it's only natural for everyone to want to meet the newcomers." *Especially when there are men among those newcomers,* was Charlene's unspoken thought.

Sure enough, almost all of the locals who had come out to dinner were women. Of course, with at least three or four women for every man in the entire community, there were always a lot more women than men. That disparity was especially noticeable tonight, though. As Charlene looked around, she noted that her father, Charlie, and his brother, Noah, were the only male members of the community in attendance. Her uncle Noah was always there. He drove the bus from Blue Rapids every day.

The other two buses, one from Frankfurt and one from Waterville, were both driven by young women. Charlene could see that Emma and Harper, the two bus drivers, were already trying to stake an early claim on Jackson. They had him sandwiched between them at the end of one of the long dining tables. *He's going to be kind of hard for those two to share unless he's willing to split time between Waterville and Frankfurt. He might be worth it, though,* she thought, as she looked him over on her way to the buffet.

Charlene couldn't help but wonder why her father was having dinner here instead of back home in Blue Rapids. "Hi Charlie, didn't expect to see you here this evening," Charlene said as she walked past him with a tray full of food.

"Yeah, I had a little argument with Pop. Decided to just get out of the house for the evening." Pop was Charlene's grandfather, Danny Day.

Danny Day was the patriarch of the entire community. A strange thought struck her as Charlie talked about arguing with Danny – *must be odd to be the patriarch of a matriarchal society.* Charlene loved both her father and grandfather, but she knew from books and Kahina's movies how different family arrangements were now than back in the before. Charlie Day had lived the first twenty years of his life in the before. It was hard to imagine the changes he'd witnessed in the years since. That way of life had ended forever before Charlene was even born, and the changes her father had seen were nothing compared to everything old Danny Day had witnessed in his long life.

Charlene grew up living in the same house with Charlie, Danny, and Noah, but the family relationships in that household were unlike anything from the before. Everyone who lived in that house was family, though not necessarily biologically related. Most of her extended and non-biological family all still lived together in that same big old house where she grew up. Out of that entire family, Charlene's relationship with her mother, Olivia, was the only one that even remotely resembled family relationships of the past. Charlene had seven half-sisters that she knew of, all fathered by Charlie Day. While Charlene was Olivia's only child, her half-sisters were from three different mothers.

"Seems like you two are always arguing about something," Charlene told Charlie as she set her tray down on the next table over, the table where Emma and Harper had Jackson trapped. Charlene chose to sit directly across the table from Jackson. Kahina, on the other hand, decided to have a seat at Charlie's table.

"So, what were you and your dad arguing about?" she heard Kahina ask Charlie. Charlene didn't hear the answer but instead focused her attention on Jackson and the two young women seated on either side of him.

"I see you've met Emma and Harper," Charlene addressed Jackson as she nodded at the two women in turn. "Let me guess, Emma wants you to settle in Frankfurt, and Harper is trying to get you to Waterville?" She smiled at the other two women before looking directly into Jackson's bright blue eyes and asking, "what about the women you came here with?"

Jackson glanced down the long table to where the rest of the newcomers sat together in a group before answering. "No, none of them have any claims on me," he replied.

Charlene wondered why not. Why wasn't at least one of the women in that group mating with such an unusual and attractive man? And why did Jackson seem so aloof and apart from the rest of those newcomers who all sat together as a group at the other end of the long table? Noah and several of the local women were having their evening meal with the group of newcomers. More than one of the newly arrived women already had their eyes on Noah. It was easy to see they were interested in having more than just a dinner conversation with Charlene's uncle. *Good luck with that,* Charlene thought, knowing that Noah was already mating with at least three other women. Aside from the women who were bound to be disappointed by Noah, a couple of the newcomers already seemed just as interested in two of the local women. With men so inaccessible, turning to other women for companionship was totally natural.

*He's lost someone,* Charlene thought of Jackson. *He's afraid to lose another.* It was odd to feel like she already knew this total stranger. It wasn't so much a knowing, as it was a connection. How could that be? Did he feel it, too?

"Was there more than one in Sedalia?" Charlene asked.

The two other women looked questioningly at her. They apparently didn't know where Jackson was from, but they immediately grasped what Charlene was asking, as did Jackson.

"There were two," Jackson answered, and Charlene could feel the pain that was evident in those bright blue eyes before he looked down at the table.

"I loved them both," he murmured to his plate.

Jackson looked up at Charlene with tears in his eyes, and she knew what had happened.

"They wouldn't submit to being slaves, would they?" She asked, already knowing the answer.

Jackson wiped the tears from his eyes and looked into Charlene's before answering.

"He killed them both. It was the Commander himself. He killed them with that long sword he wears. He said nigger bitches weren't worth wasting a bullet on."

Of the three young dark-skinned women sitting at the table, only Charlene knew the derogatory term's full historical context. Emma and Harper had no idea what the word nigger meant or where the name came from. Like most born after the before, they knew very little of the history of the old United States.

It wasn't the word nigger that most caught Charlene's attention, though. "You said the Commander, was it Commander Davis?" she asked.

"How do you know about Davis?" Jackson was obviously surprised. "I'd never heard of him before they attacked Sedalia. We thought General Korliss was in charge of New Dixie."

"Davis killed Korliss. I saw it."

Emma and Harper weren't surprised by Charlene's statement. Everyone in the Marysville community knew about Charlene's visions, but Jackson didn't know what to make of it.

"How?" he asked. He searched Charlene's dark brown eyes for answers. Not just to the question of how she could possibly know anything about General Korliss and Commander Davis, there was a more profound mystery here. Why did he feel such a strong connection to this woman he'd never met?

"I see things," she said simply, staring right back at him. "Things that I know are real. I don't know how or why; I just know things."

Seeing disbelief in Jackson's eyes, Charlene smiled.

"Davis was wearing the uniform of an old Confederate general. He has long, wild black hair and a full bushy beard. His hair and beard are really black, as black as mine. But it's his eyes that really grab your attention. Dark, narrow-set eyes that scream crazy. Clint Davis is insane. All you have to do is look at the man to know he is evil incarnate."

Jackson's eyes grew wide as Charlene described the man that had killed Elena and Nora in Sedalia. The man that had forced him to join the Narmy and do things he could never forgive himself for doing.

"When did Davis kill General Korliss?" Jackson asked, even though he had an idea that he already knew the answer.

"I don't know, I just saw it in a vision while we were driving over here. It had to have either happened as I saw it or sometime in the past. I never see the future. I wish I could."

"It was in the past," Jackson said, no longer skeptical of Charlene's ability. "It had to have been before they attacked us at Sedalia. That's why General Korliss didn't keep his word. He had promised us that we could live in peace outside the border of New Dixie. General Korliss said there was plenty of room for us to coexist. Then, out of the blue, Commander Davis and that woman of his, Helena Hunt, attacked us a little over a year ago. He said he didn't give a damn what General Korliss said, that General Korliss was no longer the leader of New Dixie. He didn't tell us Korliss was dead. Guess he didn't have to."

"That makes sense," Jackson's account added context to the vision Charlene had earlier. "Before Davis killed Korliss, they were arguing about expanding New Dixie. Korliss wanted to stop the expansion, to stop the killing, but not Davis. Clint Davis wants to rule the whole country. He thinks he's fulfilling the destiny of his ancestor. The destiny Jefferson Davis was denied."

Now, all three of the people across from Charlene had questioning looks on their faces. Sometimes she forgot that not everyone knew the ancient history of the old United States.

"Jefferson Davis was the President of the Confederate States Of America during the civil war two hundred years ago," Charlene explained. "Clint Davis claims to be a direct descendant, but I don't think he is. Even if he is descended from Jefferson Davis, he obviously doesn't know much about the man. Jefferson Davis may have owned over a hundred slaves, but he wasn't much of a leader. Even if the Confederacy had won the civil war, Davis would have probably been forced to turn the presidency over to Robert E. Lee."

Charlene could see that neither Jackson nor Emma or Harper had any idea what she was talking about.

"Well, I don't know anything about Jefferson Davis," Jackson admitted, "but Clint Davis isn't much of a leader either. You're right about one thing though, he is definitely insane. Not only him but all those around him. They don't really care about anything but killing everyone who won't join them and anyone they can't dominate. The Commander's personal guards are the most sadistic people you can imagine. They don't need a reason to torture and kill. They do it because it gives them some kind of pleasure."

Jackson dropped his eyes back down to the table, remembering things he wished he could forget. Memories that would haunt him for as long as he lived. Memories of the terrible things he'd seen others do and the things he'd been forced to do himself.

Charlene could feel his pain or at least some of it. She couldn't see the memories that were causing him so much pain, but she could feel the guilt within him.

"You only did what you had to do, Jackson," she said softly.

Jackson jerked his head up in surprise. Did she know? Had she seen the things he'd done?

"No," she answered his unspoken questions and smiled. "I haven't seen, but I can feel the agony you're feeling right now. You have to stop running away, Jackson. You can run from Davis and Hunt, but you can't run from yourself."

As Jackson looked into Charlene's eyes, searching for salvation, tears ran down his cheeks, and he could hardly speak.

"I don't deserve to live with decent people," he said. "I should have died with Elena and Nora. I couldn't save them; I was a coward to save myself."

Charlene sensed that Jackson needed to stop wallowing in self-pity. Instead of following that path any further, she pushed herself back from the table.

"I think there is plenty of good in you, Jackson," she said as she stood up. "I think you can do our community a lot of good, too. The gods know we can use more men around here. I hope you'll stay. Look around the area, see if you think we're right for you. But don't let Emma or Harper drag you back to either of their lairs just yet."

That brought a scowl from both of the bus drivers.

"Damn, Charlene, you make it sound like we're black widow spiders or something," Harper said.

Charlene picked up the tray of food that she'd yet to touch before replying, "I just think he needs to see his options before agreeing to be claimed, that's all."

"Yeah, and you probably want to do the claiming," Emma chimed in.

Charlene didn't rise to the bait but addressed Jackson instead; "We have a community meeting right here tomorrow night. I would like you to join us if you will."

Not waiting for him to answer, Charlene turned and joined Charlie and Kahina at the next table over.

"What, exactly do you think he wants?" Kahina was asking Charlie.

Charlene took a bite of the roast vegetable medley that, along with fried chicken, was this evening's community meal. The freshly harvested vegetables were delicious.

"The same thing he's always wanted, I guess," Charlie answered. "He wants everything to be like it was when he was my age."

*Not really,* Charlene thought, knowing instantly who Charlie and Kahina were talking about. *He wants things to be the way he believes they were when his parents were young.* Tom Abernathy was a few years older even than Danny Day. The old-timers, the few who survived that great dying before Charlene was born, all longed for their youth. Charlene wondered if she, too, would dream of her youth when she was as old as them. *They don't really long for the reality of earlier times,* she thought. *They long for the illusions of those times.*

"He thinks we shouldn't be living like a bunch of socialists and communists. He wants to live the way Americans always lived before."

"What about you, Charlie?" Charlene joined the conversation. "You remember the before. Was life better then than it is now?"

"It was for some, but not many." He pointed at the plate of food Charlene was busy devouring. "Most of us didn't eat nearly this well back then. I guess for old Tom Abernathy and people like your mother's family, times were better then. You should ask Olivia what she thinks."

Charlene already knew what her mother thought. Olivia once told her that back in the before, she had felt just as trapped by her family's wealth and social status as people like Danny and Charlie Day were trapped by poverty and racism.

"I'm pretty sure that Olivia doesn't share much common thought with Tom Abernathy," Charlene said. "If she did, she'd probably be going to that church of his."

Besides running the same dairy farm up north of town that he grew up on, Tom Abernathy was the preacher at the only old-time Christian church in the whole area. The Abernathy family was definitely unique in the Marysville community. Rachel, Tom's daughter, who was at least fifty years old, still lived with her parents in the same old farmhouse the Abernathy family had called home for over a hundred years. Living in the same home with her parents wasn't unusual, but the fact that it was, and always had been, just the three of them living together was different. As far as Charlene knew, old Tom Abernathy had never allowed himself to be taken by any woman other than his wife, Ginger. And Rachel, for all anyone knew, might be the world's oldest living virgin. It wasn't just old-time capitalism that the Abernathy's wanted to revive. More importantly, it was old-time religion and a monogamous family lifestyle.

Kahina laughed. "Kind of crazy how many people listen to that old man preach every Sunday and then go home to live in a completely different reality than what he's preaching." She thought about it before adding, "I guess it was always like that though, back in the before. The world was full of hypocrites back then. Preaching about loving neighbors and sharing with the needy on Sundays, then cheating the needy and their neighbors out of everything they could during the rest of the week."

There was a bitterness in Kahina's voice that seemed totally out of character.

"Were you religious?" Charlene asked.

Kahina was thoughtful for a moment. She seemed to be looking back in time before answering.

"I don't think I was ever religious. My parents made me and my brother go to church, but I don't think either of us ever really bought in. Not sure my parents did either. Going to church on Sunday was just what people did in Wichita, Kansas. Seems like everybody at the church we went to was so worried about being ready for the rapture and the next life that they mostly forgot about living in this one."

Kahina looked around the cafeteria before adding, "Guess Armageddon didn't turn out quite like they thought it would."

Neither Charlie nor Charlene chose to reply. They were both lost in their own thoughts. Both thinking about the way things were and the way they used to be, thinking about how different everything was now.

*How are people meant to live?* Charlene wondered. She thought about the structure, or the lack of structure in their little community. The way people lived now was so much different than anything in the before. Nothing was the same now as then. The before was so much different in every way that it seemed impossible to compare the two lifestyles. Charlene only knew the before from books and the old DVD movies that Kahina loved to watch. Try as she might, she couldn't see how the world she grew up in could ever be anything at all like that old world.

The only social structure Charlene had ever known was what existed in the now. How could the idealized nuclear family life of the old times even work in a world with so many more women than men? If every man mated only one woman, most of the world's women would never be mated at all. *We need more men.* That thought was never far from Charlene's mind.

And what about economics? In the Marysville of today, there was no such thing as money, let alone capitalism. How would the community survive if everyone didn't pitch in and do whatever they could for the good of the community? Charlene was sure that if everyone was just looking out for themselves and striving to "get ahead" like they did in the before, it would be nothing but a disaster.

Charlene looked at her father, who was lost in his own deep thoughts. "What specifically does Tom Abernathy want?" she asked.

Charlie came back to the here and now from wherever his mind had wandered. "He wants to stop, in his words, just giving all of his dairy products to the community. He thinks we should set up some kind of barter system where everyone trades for everything."

"How the hell would that work? Instead of the scavenging teams that go to Kansas City and Omaha, would each of us have to go do our own scavenging? And what about people like Kahina here? How much milk would the work that she does be worth?"

It was apparent something had touched a nerve, but sometimes Charlie didn't understand the depths of his oldest daughter's thoughts any more than anyone else did.

"It's not me, Charlene," he said apologetically. "I'm just telling you what Tom said. I figure it's best you know now, so you have some time to think about it before the community meeting tomorrow. Tom and Rachel are going to bring it up in front of the whole community."

*Guess that's about right,* Charlene thought. *Between Tom Abernathy's insanity and what I intend to propose, this will probably be a meeting to remember.*

Finished with her dinner, Charlene got up and started to carry her tray back to the kitchen for clean-up. When she turned around, Jackson was sitting alone at the table behind her. Emma and Harper had moved down to the other end of the table with the rest of the newcomers.

Jackson was still deep in thought, but he watched Charlene get up and looked her in the eye when she turned around.

"Thank you," he said the instant he caught her eye. It was a simple statement that acknowledged what he had come to know over the course of just a few hours. Charlene was the actual leader of this community, whether she knew it or not. If such a thing existed, she was first among equals.

"Don't thank me," Charlene smiled. "I think Amelia did most of the cooking."

Jackson stood up and followed Charlene to the drop-off bin for dirty dishes. "Can I help with clean-up or anything?" he asked as he set his dirty dishes in the plastic tub.

"Not tonight, but if you stick around, you'll get plenty of opportunities to help in the kitchen. We all end up with kitchen duty sometimes."

Charlene started to turn back toward Kahina and Charlie but stopped and looked at Jackson. "Let's go for a walk," she said.

"Okay." There was a slight hesitancy in his answer, and Charline could see the question in his eyes. Was he being "claimed," as Emma had said?

Charlene smiled. "No, nothing like that," she laughed. "At least not yet anyway."

It was definitely a tease, but Jackson couldn't help but think that being "claimed" by Charlene might not be bad at all.

Charlene just turned, and Jackson followed as she headed to the door. She stopped and asked Kahina for the fob to the Bolt. "Can you ride the bus with Noah if I'm not back soon?" Charlene asked the older woman.

Kahina smiled knowingly as she handed over the fob, and Emma and Harper both simply glared at Charlene as she walked out the door with Jackson in tow. *Guess everybody thinks the same thing,* was the thought that Charlene carried outside. *Wonder what Logan's going to think about this?* She smiled to herself. *It might be good for him to be reminded that he doesn't have any claim on me. That we, the women, do the claiming, not the other way around.*

Charlene and Jackson walked side by side in silence to the end of Walnut street before Charlene headed north. They continued on for a couple blocks before Charlene finally broke the silence.

"First things first. I didn't ask you out here for sex. Don't get me wrong, it's nothing against you, but I do already have one man that I share with Stacey. It would hardly be fair for me to claim another. Not with so many women without a man at all."

Jackson laughed. It was the first time Charlene had heard the young man laugh. He had a rich, joyful laugh that was surprising coming from the serious sad man that she'd seen in the cafeteria. Charlene felt a sudden desire for more than just conversation but refocused on why she brought Jackson out here.

"How safe do you think we are?" she asked. "You've been around the Narmy. Do you think they will ever come here to take over our community like they took over Sedalia?"

Jackson stopped walking, and Charlene stopped and turned to hear his answer with all of her senses, not just her ears.

"I don't think, Charlene. I know absolutely that it's just a matter of time. It isn't a question of if the Narmy will claim this community for New Dixie; it's just a question of when. The only question is how long it will take them to get here. They don't just claim men like you do. They make slaves out of anyone that seems worth keeping alive and kill everyone else."

"What can we do? Can we defend ourselves, or better yet, negotiate with them?"

Charlene could see the darkness come over Jackson's bright blue eyes in the waning daylight, like a thunderhead in a clear blue sky.

"There is no negotiation with Commander Davis and Helena Hunt. You know that as well as I do. If General Korliss is really dead, negotiation is out of the question. No, the only way to stop those two is to kill them. If you want to protect this place, you're going to have to raise an army of your own. One that's capable of fighting the Narmy. From what I've seen of the people here, that isn't going to happen."

"Why not?" Charlene asked. "We have guns, plenty of them."

Jackson laughed out loud again, but it wasn't a joyous laugh. *How can she know so much and still be so naïve?* he thought.

"It takes more than guns," he said gently. "It takes organization and leadership to build an army. It takes people who are willing to die for a cause. I'm not seeing that here."

"You could help us, Jackson. You know how they will attack when they do. You can help us prepare, so we'll be ready for them when the time comes."

A sad smile came across Jackson's face as the sights and deeds he wanted to forget flashed once again across his mind.

"I'm sorry, Charlene, but you seem to have a mistaken perception of who I am. I'm not some kind of hero for escaping the Narmy. I'm a coward. Plain and simple. If I wasn't a coward, I'd be dead. I wouldn't be here at all."

Charlene looked into his eyes, trying to see what had led him here to this place and time.

"You and everyone who'll go with you should just leave," Jackson continued. We all need to keep moving until we find the right place and enough people to join together to fight the Narmy. It's going to take a real army to defeat the New Army Of God."

"We can't just leave. There are too many of us who are too old and too young. Besides, where would we go? Why isn't this the right place? We aren't anything at all like New Dixie. I do know that much."

"That's the problem, Charlene. The only way to beat the Narmy is to be more like them. It's going to take a real army to repel them, not a handful of old people with guns and young people who have never even been in a fight at all. Where are you going to find an army like that?"

Charlene thought about it. She'd already been thinking about it, but she didn't have an answer.

"Where is it any better?" she asked. "Where do you think you're going to find a better place with the right people to fight them?"

Jackson wondered why he hesitated to tell her everything he knew. "There's a place somewhere that Davis and Hunt are already worried about. One day, I overheard them discussing it. Wherever it is, the Narmy had some kind of outpost there until the other people rebelled and forced them out. From what I gathered, the people there are already forming their own new country with some kind of real government organization. I don't know where it is, just that it's somewhere far away from New Dixie. When we first stopped here, I kind of hoped we'd found it."

"Maybe you have found it, Jackson. Maybe we just need to build it. I don't know much about anywhere but here, but I know of at least two other communities nearby that are at least as big as this one. One's about sixty miles south, and the other's only about forty miles north. Maybe we can all join together to form some kind of regional government and build our own army."

"Those are some pretty big maybe's," Jackson said. "Too big. Think I'll just keep heading north. Here's a maybe for you – maybe you should come with me. You and whoever will come with you," he added quickly.

Charlene didn't offer an immediate response. She could imagine running away with Jackson. At the same time, she couldn't imagine ever abandoning her family and the Marysville community.

"Will you at least come to our meeting tomorrow night?" she asked. "Come and tell the community what you know of the Narmy and New Dixie."

"That I can do. It's not like there's a big rush to move on. It'll be a while before the Narmy gets here."

Jackson was already thinking about what he would tell the Marysville council about his time with the Narmy, and more importantly, what he would leave out. Charlene, for her part, was remembering a phrase she'd once read that was attributed to somebody named Horace Greeley; *Go west, young man, go west and grow up with the country.*

# Chapter 5

THERE WERE MORE PEOPLE in the cafeteria than Charlene had ever seen at a community meeting. As she made her way to an open seat next to Danny Day, Charlene was thinking about the first time her mom brought her to one of these meetings when she was just seven years old. Back then, nearly everyone within about a thirty-mile radius of Blue Rapids attended the meetings that used to be held in the old Valley Heights School building about halfway between Blue Rapids and Waterville. The population of the entire area couldn't have been much more than fifty people, though. Now, the much larger Marysville High School cafeteria was nearly filled up. In the fifteen years since Charlene attended that first meeting, the entire area's overall population had at least tripled, maybe quadrupled.

*We should probably do a census,* Charlene thought as she bent down and gave her grandfather a hug. She recognized everyone in the cafeteria, but not everyone who lived in the area was in attendance. *We really do need some kind of representative organization.* Up to now, community meetings in Marysville had been nothing more than a monthly get-together. It was a place where anyone who wanted could come and discuss whatever issue they might have. In recent years, very few people had been showing up for the meetings most of the time. Tonight, there were at least a hundred. As Charlene looked over the crowded cafeteria, with people all gathered in small groups, she wondered how to have a meaningful discussion with so many people all talking at once.

Before sitting down, Charlene looked around to make sure Jackson was in attendance. She spotted him sitting a few rows back, once again sandwiched between Emma and Harper. When they made eye contact, the look on his face seemed to say, help, get me away from these two. Charlene just smiled in answer before taking her seat.

"Can you believe how many people showed up?" Charlene asked Danny as she took a seat next to her grandfather.

"Yeah, Charlie warned me. Said he expected some trouble out of old Tom Abernathy. That old man's been a troublemaker his whole life."

Charlene found it amusing to hear Danny call Tom an old man. She knew Tom was a little older than Danny, but not much.

"He must have been working on this for a while," Charlene said. She hadn't realized until right then that what was happening was a sort of insurrection. The Marysville community had never had any kind of official organization or government. Since the great dying, Danny Day had been the unofficial leader of the Blue Rapids and the greater Marysville community. In recent years, a small group of younger people, including Charlie Day, Kahina, and Charlene herself, had been filling that role more and more.

"You better get this thing started," Danny told her, "before he does."

Charlene understood then that Danny was abdicating. If he hadn't already turned his leadership role over to Charlene, he was doing so now. She stood up and looked out over the crowd.

"Hello, neighbors." Charlene had a strong voice, but it obviously couldn't be heard over the din of the dozen or so other conversations that were buzzing in the room.

Suddenly, there was the deafening shriek of the loudest whistle Charlene had ever heard. Instant silence in the cafeteria followed as Charlene saw Jackson take the two fingers that had facilitated that whistle out of his mouth. Emma and Harper both had their hands over their ears. *That may have really deafened them,* Charlene thought.

"Thank you, Jackson," Charlene started again. "I don't think we can have much of a meeting with everyone talking at once."

Charlene saw Tom Abernathy stand up on the other side of the room. *Here we go,* she thought before he even interrupted her.

"You're right, Charlene. We can't all talk at once, but we're all here tonight to talk about one thing, and I'm guessing it isn't the same topic as whatever you usually discuss among yourselves."

If there was one thing Tom was not, it was subtle. His insinuation that Charlene and Danny's group were running the show without any input from the rest of the community was plain enough for everyone to hear.

"You might be surprised, Tom, about what **we** want to talk about." Charlene emphasized the "we" just enough to make sure everyone knew she wasn't speaking only for herself.

A murmur went through the crowd as Charlene continued, "Since you already have our attention, why don't you tell us what's on your mind?" Like there was anybody in the room who didn't already know what was on Tom's mind.

Charlene sat back down, yielding the floor to the old dairy farmer. *Might as well get this over with,* she thought.

"Well, as most of you already know, I'm not real happy with the ways this community has changed over the past twenty years." There were a few muted chuckles in the crowd. Even Charlene had to smile at the understatement. "My family's dairy farm has been supplying this area's dairy products for more than a hundred years now. My great-great-grandfather started the dairy, and it has always been owned by my family, not the community. Now, I know everything changed when most everybody died, and I know times weren't always so great before, either. But at least we owned what was ours, and we could sell it for whatever we could get. Now we don't get anything except a share of what everybody else does. My family here deserves more. We want to trade our products for what they're worth. Since money doesn't mean anything anymore, I think we should set up a barter system. A fair system where people can get what they earn, not whatever they're given."

A murmur went through the crowd as Tom paused. Danny stood up next to Charlene.

"What you want, Tom Abernathy," Danny's voice boomed across the crowd, "is a return to the inequality that gave your white family that dairy farm and gave my Black family most of nothing." There was no disguising Danny Day's anger or his contempt for Tom Abernathy.

The murmuring in the crowd grew into a near roar, with everyone talking at once again. *Time to get this back under control,* Charlene thought. She stood up just as Danny sat back down in disgust. Charlene was able to catch Jackson's eye, who, as if some silent signal had passed between them, raised his fingers to his mouth once again. This time Emma and Harper both had their ears already covered before the painful blast silenced the room.

Charlene smiled at Jackson before looking out over the crowd that was probably no more than fifteen percent white, or what people used to call white. *Why are old ideas of race still an issue at all,* she thought? She loved and respected her grandfather, but she knew from her study of history that division based on race had to end, and it had to end now.

"You and Danny both have valid points," Charlene was looking directly at Tom, who was still standing. "This community does need to change, but I don't think anyone here would want things to be the way they were when you and Danny were young, or would you?"

"We had a good life when I was young," Tom was defiant. "This was a great country back then. A God-fearing country, where a man could raise a family and live a life dedicated to the glory of the Almighty."

Danny stood up abruptly beside Charlene. "It was a good country for you!" he yelled. "Not for most of us. While you were struggling to defend the glory of your God, most of us were struggling to just survive. If you like the old ways so much, old man, you should just go live in New Dixie."

Tom Abernathy's face grew red as Danny yelled. Seeing his bright red face beneath long white hair, Charlene couldn't help but think of what a snowcapped volcano might look like just before it erupted. The analogy was an accurate one as far as the erupting part was concerned. It was easy enough to see that Tom was about to go off.

"You'd like that, wouldn't you? You, you," Tom sputtered, searching for the right insult to hurl back at Danny. "You sonofabitch. Then you could have my dairy. That's what you really want, isn't it? You already act like you own everything. If we'd just leave, you could have it all, couldn't you? Well, you can't have it. We're not leaving, and we're through giving away what's rightfully ours."

As Tom stopped yelling at Danny, and the two men stared at each other across the room and across a lifetime, Charlene saw her opportunity. "Many of us here," Charlene was now addressing the entire room, "don't understand what Tom and Danny are arguing about. How could we? We weren't even alive back then." Speaking clearly and calmly, she was slowly able to pull the crowd's attention away from the two old men who were shooting daggers at each other with their eyes.

"And most of you who lived through the great dying," Charlene continued, "seemed happy with our communal way of life, up to now at least. It was, after all, you who built this community when I was just a young girl."

The crowd in the cafeteria was not the entire population, but it was definitely representative of that population. Very few had been residents of the area before the great dying, probably no more than ten percent. At least half of the people in the room had come to Marysville to escape either the Narmy or climate catastrophes. The rest were either brought to the Marysville area as very young children or, like Charlene, had been born here.

"I, for one, feel incredibly fortunate to have had the opportunity to grow up in this community. To have been raised in a village such as this. But Tom is right about one thing. We do need to change. Our community is indeed threatened, but not by our way of life. Internal conflicts like this one between Tom Abernathy and Danny Day might tear us apart if we let them, but we face a much greater threat. That threat is the New Army Of God. We, as a community, have to prepare to defend ourselves."

Charlene paused to let everyone absorb her words. She could see some nods of agreement and some looks of skepticism in her audience.

"How can the Narmy be a threat? They're clear back in New Dixie." It was Camila Romero asking the question. Camila had arrived with a group of refugees from Kentucky about fifteen years ago.

"The borders of New Dixie have grown since you left Kentucky, Camila," Charlene patiently explained. "As a matter of fact, the Narmy is intent on expanding those boundaries everywhere. Even here. It's not a question of if the Narmy will attack us; it's a question of when."

A few more people were shaking their heads in agreement, but there was still plenty of skepticism in the crowd.

Charlene could see Kim and five of the other members of the newest group of refugees all sitting together at the back of the room. They were all shaking their heads vigorously in agreement.

"I don't know if you have all had the chance to meet the newest members of our community," Charlene said. "At least I hope they stay and become part of the community. Kim, why don't you and your group stand up and introduce yourselves and tell us what brought you to Marysville."

Kim stood up immediately. Some of the others were more reluctant. Kim was already introducing herself by the time the rest of her group got out of their chairs. Jackson didn't stand at all. He apparently didn't consider himself part of Kim's group. Kim allowed the others to introduce themselves and didn't acknowledge Jackson at all. Obviously, she didn't consider him to be a part of her group, either.

"We came from Brookfield, Missouri," Kim told the crowd after the others had introduced themselves. "We had a nice little community there. Smaller than this community, but similar. We knew of New Dixie and the Narmy, but we figured we were far enough away that we didn't need to worry about them. We were wrong. When the Narmy came, they killed most of us and took others for slaves." Kim almost broke down but kept going. "As far as I know, we are the only ones who escaped." She gestured to the group around her. "We've been running ever since. Trying to get far enough away to feel safe again."

"And do you?" Kathleen stood up as she asked the question. "Do you feel safe here in Marysville, now that you're so far away from New Dixie?"

Charlene hadn't expected that. Kathleen was like an aunt to her. Before there was even a Marysville community, Kathleen was one of the earliest refugees to arrive in Blue Rapids. She had been part of the very first group of refugees to settle in Blue Rapids after the death and devastation of V-1. That was before Charlene was even born. Now, Kathleen was apparently taking the side of the skeptics.

"I'm not sure," Kim answered. "It seems like we have come a long way; I'm just not sure it's far enough."

"What do you think, Jackson?" Charlene asked. It was time to exploit the opening created by Kim's doubt. "Please stand up," she added. Then to the crowd, "For those of you who don't know, Jackson arrived with Kim's group, but he is from Sedalia, Missouri."

Jackson stood up and looked around at everyone whose attention was now focused his way.

"I'm not actually from Sedalia. I was living there when the Narmy came. We had already escaped from New Dixie once. Me and," Jackson hesitated at the painful memory. "Me and two slave women. I was born in Jonesboro, Arkansas, which was part of New Dixie from the beginning. Guess it was only natural for Arkansas to be part of New Dixie since it was also part of the old confederacy. We lived in New Dixie, but my mother hated being part of it. She made sure I knew about the great Civil War that had freed slaves long ago. I was only ten when my mother died. To this day, I still thank her for teaching me about the evils of slavery. For teaching me that all people, regardless of skin color, deserve my respect."

Jackson had everyone's undivided attention now. Even Charlene's. He was the first person any of them knew who had actually been born in New Dixie. He stood silent for a moment, seemingly lost in thought, before continuing.

"Elena and Nora were much more to me than just slaves. They were..." Jackson paused, searching for the right words, the pain of his memories written plainly on his face for all to see. "I loved them both," he finally said. "So I helped them escape. We made our way to Sedalia. Like here, the good people in Sedalia welcomed us to their community. They said they had an agreement with General Korliss, who you may or may not know, was the founder of New Dixie. General Korliss had promised the people of Sedalia their autonomy. He told them New Dixie had all the land and people it would ever need. That, even though they lived just outside the borders of New Dixie, they could live however they wanted to live. The people of Sedalia felt safe. When the Narmy attacked, they couldn't understand why General Korliss had broken his word. What none of us knew until Charlene saw it in a vision is that General Korliss is dead. The Narmy and New Dixie are now led by Commander

Clint Davis from Alabama. He personally led the attack on Sedalia, and he won't stop there. You," he paused to look around, making sure everyone knew they were included, "are no more safe from the Narmy here than we were in Sedalia. Clint Davis is insane, and he plans to conquer the whole country for New Dixie."

Complete silence overwhelmed the cafeteria as Jackson's statement sunk in. Tom Abernathy, along with Kim and Danny Day, all sat back down, leaving no one but Jackson and Charlene standing looking at one another. After an extraordinarily long few seconds, a small voice broke the silence. The soft voice seemed loud in that totally silent room.

"What are we to do then?" It was Emma, who was still seated looking up at Jackson standing beside her. "Run away?"

Jackson smiled down at her. "You can," he said directly to Emma, but he was obviously talking to the whole room. "You can run, but you can never run far enough. Clint Davis won't stop until somebody stops him."

"Then I guess we better stop him." It was Danny Day's voice booming out over the cafeteria again. Charlene hadn't even noticed that he had stood up beside her. "Won't be the first one of those sonsabitches I've had to kill."

Jackson had to smile at the large Black man with the totally white hair. Here was a man who would be willing to take on the whole Narmy. *If this community had a couple of hundred more like Danny Day, only much younger, they might have a chance,* Jackson thought.

"It'll take an army to stop Davis," Jackson said, "Not just you and a handful of people with guns."

"Then we'll build an army," Charlene said. It was the opening she'd been waiting for. She looked out over the crowded cafeteria. "Won't we?" she exhorted the crowd.

The response was mostly a disappointing murmur of people talking to one another, not an overwhelming show of support for the idea. Tom Abernathy stood up again and waited for people to notice.

"I don't believe it," he said, as the crowd slowly turned their attention in his direction. "Oh, I don't doubt this young man's word about what he saw. But I don't believe the Narmy is ever going to come this far north. Why would they? How do we even know General Korliss is really dead? Just because Charlene had one of her visions?" Tom's contempt for Charlene's visions wasn't lost on anyone.

"We don't need an army. We need to have faith in God instead of Charlene's visions." Now Tom was in full preacher mode. "Pray to the Almighty, pray and repent of your sins. Pray for salvation, and pray for guidance. Pray for a vision from God," he looked straight at Charlene, "instead of listening to the voice of darkness. God will protect us." his voice was booming now, "Yea, though I walk through the valley..." was as much of the old biblical psalm as he got through before the crowd erupted.

Charlene looked on in disgust as friends and neighbors were all arguing with each other. She could hear bits and pieces of arguments from all over the cafeteria; "religion caused nothing but trouble before"; "how are we supposed to fight an army?"; "what about barter? That's what we're here to talk about."

Jackson looked at Charlene as he was raising his fingers to his mouth once more. She just shook her head, no, and headed for the door. *How can we build an army?* She thought. *We can't even organize a meeting.*

It was a warm, muggy evening once Charlene was out of the air-conditioned comfort of the cafeteria. Too warm to cool the anger she was feeling. Anger at Tom Abernathy for disrupting the meeting. Anger at the community for being so obtuse. And then she realized she was mostly angry and disappointed in herself. She had the thought that the fireflies flitting and dancing through the darkness were better organized than the people of Marysville, and that was as much her fault as anyone else, maybe more. Charlene turned and walked back into the noisy cafeteria.

Inside, people were still talking and arguing in groups. Charlene didn't see anyone still sitting down except old Danny Day. He was sitting next to her empty chair with a look of disgust on his face that matched what she was feeling. Charlene didn't go back to her chair. She walked straight across the cafeteria to the stainless steel counter at the far end of the room. She climbed up on the counter and looked down on the crowd.

A few of those arguing among themselves watched Charlene climb up on the counter. Others turned to see what those few were looking at. Jackson, who had been on the verge of following Charlene outside, was one of those who watched her climb to the top of the counter. Charlene looked at Jackson and nodded almost imperceptibly.

The loud shriek of Jackson's whistle silenced the crowd once again. Those who hadn't yet noticed that Charlene was standing on the counter now looked her way.

"Faith without works is dead. Is that not one of the major tenets of your religion, Tom Abernathy?" Charlene didn't yell, nor did she speak softly, but she had everyone's attention.

"Well, yes it is, but," Tom started to answer.

"No buts, Tom." Charlene cut him off before he could start sermonizing again. "The time for faith without works has passed. We must start working to better organize this community, regardless of New Dixie and the Narmy. Look around this room. Do you see what I see?"

Most people glanced around at each other before turning back to Charlene with puzzled expressions. Charlene gave them a few seconds to think about it before continuing.

"There are too many of us to continue living without some kind of organization."

Some in the crowd, including Tom Abernathy, immediately started to protest.

"No!" this time, Charlene did yell. "Chaos is not going to rule. Sit down, or get out." She pointed at the door. "Tonight, we decide our future. Everyone here can have a say in deciding that future, but not if we're all talking and yelling at the same time."

Charlene definitely had everyone's attention. Most quickly took a seat. Some hesitated, then sat down. Tom Abernathy, his wife, Ginger, daughter Rachel, and a few more of his dedicated followers remained standing. Tom's face turned red again, and Charlene could see a burning hatred in his eyes as he stared at her.

Abruptly, Tom turned and stormed out without saying a word. His followers were right behind him, but Charlene couldn't help but notice the apologetic look on Rachel Abernathy's face before she turned and followed her father out the door.

"Okay," Charlene said, "now we can have a civilized discussion." She looked around the room. "Camila, you look like you have something to say. Why don't you stand up and speak your mind?"

The first organized meeting of the Blue Rapids-Marysville community proceeded smoothly from that point on. Camila surprised Charlene by being the first to volunteer to fight the Narmy. Danny Day, who, as a young man, had been a U.S. Marine, agreed to lead the Community Militia that had over two dozen volunteers by the time the meeting concluded.

Charlene left the meeting with a feeling of hope that their community would continue to prosper and grow. That they would be ready for the Narmy when the time came. What Charlene couldn't know were the dark thoughts in Tom Abernathy's mind as he drove home that night.

# Chapter 6

*M*AYBE TONIGHT'S THE NIGHT, she thought. It seemed to Charlene that she had been trying to get pregnant forever, even though she hadn't started until she was sixteen years old. Still, that was almost six years ago. She waited until everyone in the bunker had gone to bed before getting out of her own bed and padding across the room to Logan's curtained cubicle.

Logan Parscale was just four years older than Charlene. He was the same age as Amelia, who was like an older sister to Charlene. Amelia was the only original inhabitant of the limestone house that Charlene was born in. She and Logan had both been orphaned by V-1. Logan and Amelia were the two youngest people that survived the great dying in the Marysville community. While Charlene grew up in the same house with Amelia in Blue Rapids, Logan was raised by a foster mother over in Frankfort after his family all died of V-1. Though Frankfort was only about twelve miles east of Blue Rapids, Charlene hadn't met Logan before Stacey offered to share him. Stacey was ten years older than Charlene and six years older than Logan.

The sound of soft snoring told Charlene that Logan was sleeping, but she didn't hesitate to wake him up. Some things were more important than sleep. And, with so few people in the world, nothing was more important than making babies.

"Stacey?" Logan murmured as he woke up and turned over to face the woman who'd crawled in bed with him.

"No," Charlene answered, just slightly perturbed. Logan had no way of knowing which, if either, of the two women who usually shared his bed would be doing so on any given night. That was always decided by Charlene and Stacey, just as the other six women who lived in the bunker decided how and when to share the other two men. Kahina, though she'd lived in the bunker longer than anyone else but Charlene, was the odd woman out. As far as Charlene could tell, Kahina had given up on sex before she ever got to Blue Rapids.

"It's my turn tonight," Charlene said as she snuggled up against Logan's warm body.

Instead of kissing her, Logan rolled over to face the wall, stating his rejection as loudly as if he'd yelled at her to get out of his bed.

Undeterred, Charlene pressed her naked body against the bare skin of Logan's back and put her arm around him.

"What's wrong, Logan?" she murmured, gently playing her fingertips up and down his abdomen.

Logan grabbed her hand before it could get much lower than his navel.

"You don't want me," he said. "I saw the way you look at that Jackson guy. Why don't you just go crawl into his bed and let me go back to sleep?"

*He's jealous,* she thought, but she couldn't deny the truth of what caused that jealousy. If she had a choice of Logan's bed or Jackson's tonight, which would she choose?

"Don't be silly," she whispered, kissing the nape of his neck and rubbing her breasts against his back. "I'm trying to have your baby, Logan. That's what I want more than anything."

*It's true,* Charlene told herself, *I do want a baby more than anything,* even as she realized it wasn't necessarily Logan's baby that she wanted. She felt Logan start pushing her hand below his navel and the need for talking temporarily gave way to a more primal instinct.

"Why do you think you haven't got pregnant yet?" Logan asked. "It's been three years now."

The warm glow Charlene always felt after sex was fading as she lay on her back and stared at the ceiling. Logan, lying beside her staring at that same ceiling, was right there beside her, but she may as well have been alone. She couldn't deny that she enjoyed sex with Logan, but she didn't feel connected to him at all.

*Four years,* she thought, annoyed that Logan didn't seem to know how long they'd been lovers. *Lovers? Were they really?* Logan was the only man Charlene had ever had sex with, but that didn't mean she was in love with the man, at least not like being in love in the classic sense. Not like she'd read about and seen in Kahina's old movies.

"I don't know," was the best answer she could come up with. *Why can't I get pregnant?* It was a question that bothered her more and more. Was she infertile for some reason? She had normal, regular menstrual cycles and always tried to have sex with Logan at the most optimum times to conceive. Yet here she was, barren after four years of trying. "Maybe it's just not meant to be," she said.

"Well, it can't be me," Logan said, and Charlene could feel his insecurity. She understood that his inability to make her pregnant felt like some kind of threat to Logan's masculinity.

"No, it isn't your fault, Logan. The girls you've fathered with Stacey are proof of that." *Or are they?* She wondered, even as she said it.

It was true that Stacey had two daughters, but was it true that Logan was the father? Come to think of it, neither of Stacey's daughters bore any striking resemblance to Logan. Charlene didn't know of Stacey taking any man other than Logan, but what did that prove? With no DNA testing like they had in the before, and with so many women sharing so few men, how was anyone to know who their father was? Maybe Stacey had another man sometimes. Perhaps more than one.

"Well, maybe you should try another man, anyway. Maybe it's something about us. Maybe it's the combination, not just you."

Charlene could feel how painful it was for Logan to suggest she try another man. He truly was in love with her in the old-fashioned sense, and it hurt her to know that she would never reciprocate that kind of love. She found herself wondering if he was in love with Stacey, too. She hoped so. It seemed to Charlene that Stacey had always been in love with Logan, even way back when Stacey first approached Charlene about moving into the bunker to share him. It must have been hard for Stacey to offer her man to Charlene. But it would have been totally unrealistic for Stacey to expect to keep Logan all to herself, not with so many women and so few men in the world.

Charlene sighed. "I don't think so, Logan. I think it must be me, but I don't know why. Maybe this time it worked. At least it's fun trying," she added, as she kissed him on the cheek. "Sleep well," she said and crawled out of his bed to return to her own.

·····•·•····

"Now that's a barn!" Jackson exclaimed as the Abernathy Dairy came into view. The main barn had been built at least a century ago and perfectly maintained by generations of the Abernathy family. Charlene had seen the old dairy so many times before that it seemed entirely unremarkable to her. The barn looked the same to Charlene as it always had. *Guess I just kind of took it for granted,* she thought, seeing how much the barn impressed Jackson. *We probably take way too much for granted in this old world.*

"Thank you for staying," she said to Jackson, who was riding in the passenger seat. She wanted to make sure he didn't feel taken for granted.

It had been a week since Tom Abernathy stormed out of the community meeting in Marysville. Kim and most of the others who came to Blue Rapids with Jackson left the day after that meeting. Jackson had agreed to stay. "I'm tired of running," he'd told Charlene. "If you think you can organize your people to fight, I'll stay and help." She still remembered his cynical smile as he added, "You're going to need all the help you can get."

"Are those radio antennas on top of the barn?" Jackson asked as Charlene drove right by the entrance to the dairy. The words, **ABERNATHY DAIRY,** were prominently displayed in a large metal arch fifteen feet above the gravel drive that led straight back past the old house to the barn.

"Yeah, I think so. I seem to remember somebody saying something about Tom being into amateur radio back when he was young."

Not much more than a mile or two north of Abernathy's dairy, Charlene had to leave the highway for the first time. The people of Marysville had cleared all the old roads that connected the various hamlets that made up their community, but roads beyond that were nearly impassable. Between the rotting vehicles that were still sitting where they were abandoned over twenty years ago and the weeds, and even trees growing up through the crumbling pavements, travel outside the community was slow and tedious.

"Do you think it still works?" Jackson, who'd been lost in thought, asked.

"Tom's radio? I have no idea. Whatever radio equipment he has would have to be about as old as he is. Why?" Charlene had a hunch that she might know the answer as soon as she asked the question.

Jackson proved her right. "That's how they communicate. The Narmy uses old ham radios to communicate over long distances, and old CB radios to talk to each other locally."

Charlene was concentrating on working her way through the tall weeds and brush that had taken over the right of way on the side of the road. She had to use the bar ditch to get around what was left of two semis blocking the highway. *Good thing we have this truck,* she thought. She was driving an old Lordstown Endurance that one of the salvage crews had found in Kansas City. Having drive power to all four wheels was critical once anyone ventured outside the area where the roads had been cleared.

"Do you think we could use Tom's old radio to intercept their messages?" Charlene asked. The possibility had her on the verge of turning around and going straight back to Tom's dairy. *We can stop on the way back,* she thought.

"It might be possible," Jackson answered. "If you can get that crotchety old man to let us try."

The need to concentrate on offroad driving forced the idea out of Charlene's thoughts for a short way until they got back to a more open stretch of highway. She and Jackson were on a mission. They were headed to Beatrice, Nebraska, to see if they could form an alliance with the people living there. Salvage crews from Marysville had made contact with the people of Beatrice a few years earlier. From the salvage crew's reports, it seemed the Beatrice community was probably similar in size and makeup to Marysville. Jackson had convinced Charlene that they needed more people, not just better organization, if they wanted to defeat the Narmy. If they could persuade the people of Beatrice to join them, the next step would be to get Highway 77 cleared and get some communication set up between the two communities. With less than fifty miles separating Beatrice and Marysville, getting the highway cleared wouldn't take more than two or three weeks if they worked at it from both ends.

"Maybe someone in Beatrice has a ham radio, too," Charlene said, as much to herself as Jackson. "Maybe we can use old ham radios for our communications." She thought it might be easier and faster than trying to get Beatrice tied into the telecommunications system that Kahina had cobbled together from Marysville's old landline telephone network.

"Guess that might be possible," Jackson answered. "But if we can listen to the Narmy, wouldn't they be able to listen to us?"

He was right, of course. Charlene didn't even bother to answer. She was thinking about the meeting ahead. They needed to get Beatrice on board with their plan in a hurry.

Then they needed to travel down south to Turtle Creek, where there was another smaller independent community. If they could get enough people together who were willing to fight when the time came, they could build their own state. She was thinking of all the obstacles to making that vision a reality. Organizing what amounted to a new government from scratch wouldn't be easy. It would take time. *The one thing we don't have,* she thought.

It took longer to get to Beatrice than Charlene thought it would. They left Marysville just after daybreak and didn't get to the south edge of Beatrice until after midday. It would take a lot of work to get Highway 77 cleaned up and ready for easy transportation between their two communities.

Charlene had never been to Beatrice, but she wasn't surprised at how much bigger than Marysville the city had once been. She knew the population of Beatrice had been around fifteen thousand in the before. Much of the small city was now no more than ruins and, based on the scant information that she and Jackson were able to get out of the first people they talked to, less organized even than Marysville.

That first group of people was made up of five women working at harvesting corn from a field on the edge of town. The women didn't appear to be armed, so Charlene and Jackson left their weapons in the Endurance before walking out into the field. The five women were extremely friendly, especially toward Jackson, which confirmed what Charlene already knew. The shortage of men wasn't just a Marysville anomaly; it was probably the same everywhere. Friendly though they were, the only thing Jackson and Charlene learned from the women was that Beatrice had no community structure or a government of any kind. The women told them their best bet was to talk to Betty at the center. At first, Charlene thought the women must be referring to the center of the city. She asked for clarification, and the woman told her to go all the way through town to the Center, out on the north side. "You can't miss it," she said. "Used to be a Walmart."

Getting help from the residents of Beatrice didn't seem too promising as Charlene and Jackson made their way through town. It was only about five miles from the cornfield to the Center, but it took the better part of a half-hour to get there. The people of Beatrice hadn't even cleared Highway 77 through town. Driving through Beatrice was like going through a maze. You had to take one side street after another, past a mixture of a few houses that were obviously occupied and many more that were falling down or slowly being dismantled.

As Charlene worked her way through the maze of side streets, Jackson wondered where all the people were. Then, turning a corner to get headed north again, there was a group of young girls playing with a ball in the center of the street. As soon as the kids saw the car, they scattered like a flock of birds, running as fast as their little legs would carry them and disappearing behind some of the houses.

"Strange reaction, don't you think?" Charlene asked.

"I'm not sure what to think. They seemed pretty wild to me." Jackson, like Charlene, was starting to think their trip was a total waste of time.

Several blocks east of Highway 77, a couple of blocks north of where the children were playing, they came to an intersection with Highway 136, and things started looking up. Highway 136 was clear and open in both directions as far as they could see. The street they had been traveling north on ended at 136. Knowing they were well east of Highway 77, Charlene turned west and drove the mile or so to what had once been the main intersection in Beatrice. Instead of immediately turning north on 77 toward the Center, Charlene stopped in the middle of the intersection and got out of the truck.

"Why do you suppose they've only opened the highways to the east and west?" she asked.

"And north," Jackson added, looking at the four lanes of Highway 77 headed north between the abandoned, windowless brick buildings of old downtown Beatrice.

On the south side of the intersection, no one had bothered to remove any of the abandoned cars and trucks and weeds growing through the crumbling pavement. To the east, west, and north, the highways had not only been cleared of old vehicles, but the roads were mostly clear of weeds as well.

*Guess we just need to find Betty,* Charlene thought as she climbed back in the truck. The reason the women had called the old Walmart store the *Center* was evident as soon as the old blue sign out front came into view. Someone had gone to the trouble of painting over the word **WALMART** and the **SUPER** from **SUPERCENTER,** leaving just the one word, **CENTER,** clearly legible at the bottom of the faded blue sign.

Betty, or at least Charlene assumed she was Betty, was a somewhat older woman, probably somewhere around fifty, Charlene decided. She was sitting in an old rocker just inside the glass doors that opened automatically as Charlene and Jackson walked up to the entrance. *They definitely have electricity here,* was Charlene's first thought as she walked into the brightly lit, air-conditioned interior of the Center. *Maybe not that friendly, though,* was her second thought when she saw the shotgun that Betty had resting across her lap. Not only was the woman in the rocker armed, but there were also two more armed guards stationed on either side at the back of the foyer.

Charlene and Jackson were both wondering about the wisdom of leaving their guns back in the Endurance when the old woman spoke. "Welcome to the Center. Since you two are obviously new around here, we better get the rules straight. You don't get to look at the merchandise until you show me what you have to trade. And I hope it ain't produce. We've got enough fresh produce going to rot already."

*It's like an old-time trading post,* Charlene thought. *Like way out west in the 1800s.* Charlene suddenly knew a lot more about Beatrice than she did before. Here was a community that was totally unlike Marysville. A community that was held together by barter instead of shared labor and shared rewards. A community along the lines of the one Tom Abernathy had proposed.

"You must be Betty," Charlene said. "Some women south of town told us we'd find you here."

"I am, and anybody could have told you where to find me," the old woman laughed. "I'm always here. Have been for better'n twenty years now." She paused, studying Charlene and especially Jackson before asking, "And who might you be?"

"I'm Charlene, and this is Jackson. We're from Marysville down in Kansas."

Betty seemed surprised. "Long way to come for tradin'," she said. "We don't trade men, just so you know," the old woman added, looking Jackson up and down again.

Charlene could feel more than see that the two armed guards, who were both much younger women than Betty, couldn't seem to keep their eyes off of Jackson either.

"Oh no," Charlene said, taking Jackson by the arm in a show of affection, if not possession. "I would never trade Jackson. We're not really here to trade at all."

"Well, if you ain't here to trade, what brings you all the way from Marysville?"

Jackson, who hadn't said a word, spoke up before Charlene could answer. "Are you the leader of this place, or do we need to talk to someone else?"

Betty seemed taken aback by the brusqueness of the question. "Well, if you're talking leader like government or something, like in the before, there ain't no such thing. I've run this Center since just after everybody died, and I guess it is kind of the Center of the Community, but we don't have no government. Don't need one, don't want one. People around here just live their lives however they want. They grow most of their own food and teach their own kids whatever they want them to know. The damn government's what ruined the before, you know. Course, you two are both too young to know anything about that, I suppose."

Charlene, seeing the conversation headed off the rails, spoke up. "We're here to ask for your help, Betty. We're here to ask your community to help us. Our hope is that we can join our communities together to help each other."

"Help each other how?" Betty asked. "Can't see that we need any help around here."

"You will," Jackson said flatly. "When the Narmy comes, you'll need all the help you can get."

Betty's eyes opened wide. She had at least heard of the Narmy.

"What do you mean?" she asked, "Why would the Narmy come here? From what I've heard from travelers passing through, the Narmy is hundreds of miles from here. They've got their New Dixie. Why would they have any interest in little old Beatrice, Nebraska?"

Jackson related his story of the takeover of Sedalia, and Charlene told of her vision of Clint Davis killing General Korliss. By then, they not only had Betty's attention, but the two guards were now standing on either side of Betty's chair raptly listening to every word.

"Do you really think they'll come here?" Betty asked after Charlene finished her story.

"I know they will," Charlene said.

"Have you seen it?" one of the guards asked. She was about Charlene's age and apparently had no trouble believing Charlene capable of visions.

"No, I'm sorry," Charlene explained. "for some reason, my visions are never of the future."

"How do you know?" Betty asked. "Maybe what you saw was in the future." She was obviously much more skeptical of visions than the young guard. "Or maybe, you just have a really wild imagination, and it never even happened."

"You can believe whatever you want," Jackson said, "but what I saw, I saw with my own eyes. I was with the Narmy for a year before I could escape. I know Helena Hunt and especially Commander Davis will never stop until someone stops them. They won't be satisfied until all of you are either dead or slaves."

Since Jackson was the only person there who wasn't obviously Black or mixed, Betty and the two guards knew the "you" Jackson referred to were all people of color. As the truth of what he was telling them sank in, Betty sat back in her chair and seemed to stare off into the distance.

"We don't have many men around here, not anymore." Betty finally said, returning to the here and now.

Charlene laughed. "We don't either," she said. "Guess it's going to be up to us women."

"Yeah, guess it always has been – truth be known," Betty agreed. "I don't see us being able to get people together until tomorrow, though. You two want to stay the night or come back then?"

"We better get back home, or we'll have people out searching for us," Charlene didn't hesitate, though she knew it would be near midnight by the time they could get back to Marysville. "Maybe you should set up a meeting for the day after tomorrow if you think that's possible."

"Can't guarantee we'll get everybody, but I'll get as many as I can to be here at midday, day after tomorrow."

············

It was too late to stop at the Abernathy Dairy by the time Charlene and Jackson got back, so Charlene drove right by. The Lordstown Endurance was nearly out of battery anyway. The range indicator turned orange just as they passed the dairy. *Not going to be enough to get to Blue Rapids,* she realized. *Just have to put it on the charger at Marysville.*

The old high school that had been converted to a community center in Marysville had the most PV power and storage capacity of anywhere in the entire area. It truly was the hub of the whole community. Six charge stations had been set up in the parking lot. Only one was in use as Charlene and Jackson parked next to the old Tesla 3 that Sarah usually drove.

"Looks like I'll have to take the Tesla down to Blue Rapids," Charlene said, but somewhere between Beatrice and Marysville, another idea had planted itself in her mind.

*I really could just stay here,* she thought, as she watched Jackson connect the charge cord to the Endurance.

It was one of those warm summer nights when there is something almost magical about the light of the full moon. Charlene watched that magic moonlight play across Jackson's face as he plugged in the car, and a yearning that had been building since she first saw him became almost overwhelming.

"Or," she said, "I could just stay here with you."

Charlene was standing right in front of Jackson as he straightened up from plugging in the car. They were almost, but not quite touching, at least not physically touching. Charlene and Jackson were somehow connected in a realm beyond the physical. The intense feelings passing between them like lightning bolts were more potent than simple touch could ever be.

"I'd like that," was all Jackson said as they melted into each other's arms.

# Chapter 7

TOM ABERNATHY MADE HIS way slowly down the old stairs that led to the basement. It was actually more of a cellar than a finished basement, but he had set up a radio room down here over fifty years ago. Tom was in high school when he first became interested in amateur radio, and it had been his favorite, if not only, hobby. Most of the basement was used to store canned goods now, but the radio room full of the old equipment was still there, way back in the corner farthest away from the stairs. It had been twenty years since the radio was last used. Tom had tried to contact someone in the first few weeks after the great dying, but no one ever answered.

As he had for the past week, ever since that disastrous meeting at the community center, Tom was pondering the likelihood of whether or not the old radio equipment would still work after all these years. If the radio worked, would anyone answer now, or was he just wasting his time? As he walked past the Mason jars full of fruits and vegetables, carrying the vacuum cleaner that he would need to remove twenty years' worth of accumulated dust, the irony of what he planned to do didn't even occur to him. The fact that he wouldn't have power for the radio if not for help from the community that he was about to betray never entered his mind.

The Abernathy dairy farm had a few PV panels and a small wind turbine offsetting a little bit of grid power back in the before, but that was all. It had taken Charlie Day and his electrification crew to install enough power to supply the entire dairy. They were the ones who installed enough PV panels and batteries to run the milking machines and other equipment. Equipment that included the radio setup with which Tom now hoped to contact New Dixie or the Narmy. Unlike Jackson and Charlene, who were passing by the entrance to his dairy on their way to Beatrice at that very moment, Tom didn't know the Narmy used ham radios to communicate. Tom had no way of knowing whether or not anyone in New Dixie possessed or used any amateur radio equipment at all, but he intended to find out.

........

When Charlene first woke up, she was surprised to find a man in her bed. Then she remembered it wasn't her bed at all. The sunrise shining through the window gave Jackson's long red hair a fiery glow. He was still sleeping on his side, facing away from her. *Another first,* she thought as she quietly got out of bed. Jackson was only the second man ever that Charlene had gone to bed with. He was the first she'd ever awakened with. In the four years that she had been sleeping with Logan, Charlene had never once actually slept all night in his bed. As she quietly got dressed, Charlene found herself wondering what a child fathered by Jackson would look like. Would it have red hair and blue eyes, or the black kinky hair of Charlie? Maybe black straight hair like her own, with blue eyes. Perhaps blonde hair like her mother's, with her own dark brown eyes. Eyes that she had inherited from Charlie and Danny Day. Charlene knew it wasn't her most fertile time of the month, but she found herself wishing it was.

She quietly made her way out of the classroom that had been converted to one of several dormitory rooms in the old school. She was hungry but decided to wait until she got back down to the Blue Rapids bunker to eat anything. Last night, she'd called Kahina and promised to be home for breakfast.

"Well, tell me," Kahina said. The two women were alone at one end of the massive dining table in the bunker. Other than Logan, who was monitoring the computer desk while Kahina ate breakfast, Charlene and Kahina had the bunker mostly to themselves. Some of the younger girls were playing over in the far corner of the great room, but the adults were all gone for the day.

"Tell you what?" Charlene smiled coyly at the older woman. Kahina was old enough to be Charlene's mother, maybe even grandmother, but the older woman was more like a sister to Charlene than a mother. She was the best friend Charlene ever had. Charlene was comfortable confiding secrets with Kahina that she would never have discussed with anyone else, not even her own mother.

"You know, is Jackson going to move in here with us now?" Kahina prodded.

Charlene laughed. "Maybe he will. I haven't asked him, though."

Kahina could see a sparkle in Charlene's eyes that wasn't there before. "Wow, he must be terrific. You look smitten."

Charlene thought about last night. "It was really different," she said. "Different from Logan, I mean. Is this what love feels like, Kahina? You know, love like in the old novels and your old movies."

"Maybe," Kahina said. "Maybe you are in love. I have only been in love like that one time, and it was so long ago it's hard to remember what it feels like. Everything was so much different then."

Kahina gazed back through her mind's eye at a time before, remembering when she was Charlene's age. Remembering Evan and remembering falling in love. She met and fell in love with Evan while they were both going to school in Austin. They got married just after graduation. Evan's parents, who were capital W white Texans, never fully accepted their new mixed-race daughter-in-law, but Evan loved her as much as she did him. Kahina had to disengage from those memories. She would never get over the loss of Evan and her two sons. In her heart, she was sure they had perished along with everyone else, but in her mind, the question of whether or not they survived would haunt her as long as she lived.

"So much different then," she repeated, coming back to the present. "Might as well have been another world, instead of just another time. It wouldn't even be possible now. I mean falling in love and living your whole life with one man. A man you don't have to share with anyone else. At least I'm fairly certain I wasn't sharing Evan with anyone else."

Kahina had told Charlene a lot about Evan, the two children, and her life before. In the years that Charlene had known the older woman, she had never known Kahina to sleep with a man, even though she'd had plenty of opportunities.

"Is that why you never take a man?" Charlene asked. "You're still being true to Evan?"

Kahina smiled a sad smile. "Guess so – I've been true to Evan for almost fifty years now. Probably no need to change at this late date. Besides, I can't even imagine sharing a man with another woman, let alone more than one other woman."

Charlene laughed. "Pretty hard not to share now. What with so few men and so many women. I think it's even worse up in Beatrice than it is here. You should have seen the way the women up there were looking at Jackson."

"Do you think it's natural?" Kahina asked. "You know, for people to live the way we do now. God knows you've read enough and seen enough old movies to know how it was before. Which do you think is a more natural state of affairs for the human species, the before or now?"

Charlene didn't answer quickly; she contemplated the question for a minute or so, searching back through the books she'd read on human evolution and psychology.

"Both," she finally said. "I think the human species is the most adaptable animal to ever live. In earlier times, it took several centuries and many different religions trying to preach monogamy before it finally took hold. Then, that all changed, literally overnight. People adapt. People always adapt."

"Well, you better take me to Beatrice next time and leave Jackson here. Otherwise, you may be adapting to sharing him with a lot more women than you might like."

"Oh, I don't mind sharing. The strangest thing, though, is how I find myself wanting to have a child with Jackson instead of Logan."

"I see," said Kahina with a knowing smile.

·····•·•····

Something felt strange as Charlene and Jackson drove under the Abernathy Dairy arch and headed up the lane. It felt like they were trespassing in enemy territory or something. *It's just that cantankerous old man,* Charlene thought. She wondered how much of what she felt toward Tom Abernathy was a direct result of growing up in the same house with Danny Day. As long as Charlene could remember, the two old men had harbored nothing but animosity toward one another.

"What is it between Danny and Tom Abernathy?" Jackson asked. The enmity between the two old men hadn't been lost on Jackson or anyone else who was at that meeting last week.

"It's all from the before. I don't know the whole story," Charlene started to answer and realized she didn't really know any of the story. She laughed. "Actually, I guess I don't know any of the story. I just know that Danny has always pretty much despised Tom. And apparently, Tom must feel the same way about Danny."

"Yeah, that was pretty obvious. How have they even been able to work together?"

"They haven't. Up until last week, I don't remember the two ever even speaking to each other." Charlene thought back over all of the community meetings she'd attended in the past. Last week's meeting was the first one she could remember where both men were present at the same time. As she thought back over all those community meetings, she could only remember Tom being in attendance one other time. And Danny Day, who was nearly always there, had stayed away from that meeting.

"But what about the community meetings? They seemed plenty eager to argue with each other at the last one," Jackson said.

"I was just eleven years old the last time I remember Tom Abernathy joining one of our meetings. Rachel has always attended the meetings without him. Sometimes Ginger would come too. But never Tom. Other than preaching at his old-time church every Sunday, Tom Abernathy is pretty much a recluse."

Charlene had already told Jackson that Rachel, Tom's daughter, mostly took care of the dairy's day-to-day operations. So it didn't seem strange that she would handle the family's interactions with the rest of the community.

"Kind of strange, isn't it," Jackson asked, "that the entire family survived from the before?"

"The whole family didn't survive," Charlene answered as she parked the Endurance in front of the big dairy barn. "Tom and Ginger had two other children besides Rachel. Two sons, who were Rachel's older brothers. One of the boys died right here, but apparently, no one knows for sure what happened to the other. He wasn't here. Must have died somewhere else."

Charlene didn't say more. Rachel Abernathy walked out of the barn door to greet them. Rachel was a bit of an enigma herself. Charlene knew Rachel much better than she knew Rachel's parents, but that wasn't saying much. Rachel occasionally attended the community meetings, and she coordinated getting other community members to help with the dairy's day-to-day operations. Other than that, Rachel just seemed to keep to herself. She was about the same age as Charlene's father, Charlie Day, which would put her somewhere in her forties. Her sandy brown hair was streaked with gray. She definitely looked older than her age. *Why didn't she ever take a lover?* Charlene wondered. As far as Charlene knew, Rachel had never had a man in her life at all. Other than her father, that is. *No, it can't be,* Charlene decided, discarding the thought that incest could play a role in the relationships of the Abernathy family.

"Hi Rachel," Charlene greeted the older woman, then, "you remember Jackson - from the meeting."

Jackson had walked around the front of the truck and shook Rachel's hand. "Guess we didn't really get introduced before," he said.

"What brings you two out this way?" Rachel asked just as Tom came around the corner of the barn.

"They're probably here to see if we'll join their little militia," Tom said, having obviously heard Rachel's question. "Well, the answer is no," he added emphatically before anyone could respond.

"Actually, that's not why we're here," Jackson spoke up, thinking maybe the old man wouldn't have the animosity toward a stranger that he did toward Charlene. Even as he said it, Jackson had the distinct impression that Tom Abernathy would be more open to him than Charlene, not because he was a stranger, but because he was white. It was shocking to realize that old Tom Abernathy was a racist, but there it was, plain and simple. "We're here because of those." Jackson pointed up at the large antennas on the roof of the barn.

Tom turned to see what Jackson was pointing at. "You mean the antennas?" he asked. "What about them?"

"Radio antennas, aren't they?"

"Used to be," Tom answered, "mostly just lightning rods now. Haven't been used since long before God sent the plague."

Charlene wondered about the meaning of the sharp look that passed between Rachel and Tom as Jackson asked, "Do you think it still works, the radio, I mean?"

"Don't even have a radio anymore," Tom looked back at the antennas to cover his lie. "Probably ought to just get those old worthless things off the roof."

Watching Rachel's reaction to Tom and Jackson's exchange, Charlene couldn't help but wonder why Tom was lying and what he was lying about.

"Too bad," Jackson was saying. "We'd hoped to maybe listen in on the Narmy."

"There you go again, spouting bullshit about the Narmy." Now the old man was using anger as a shield. "I tell you, the Narmy is nothing to worry about. Not here, anyway. It's like I told you all at the meeting, if you would just come and pray with us and put your faith in God, you wouldn't have to worry about all this nonsense."

Tom turned back toward the barn. "Come on, Rachel, we've got work to do," he said, letting everyone know this meeting was over.

It wasn't a request, it was an order, and Rachel obediently followed her father back into the barn, leaving Charlene wishing she could talk to Rachel alone. *Maybe I can catch her in town,* she thought as she got back in the truck. *She definitely isn't going to say anything around Tom.*

"Why lie?" Jackson asked as soon as they headed back down the lane. It wasn't just Charlene that had noticed.

"Good question. And what exactly is he lying about? Do you think he still has a radio and doesn't want us to know for some reason?"

Jackson thought about the question before answering. "I hope that's all there is to it," he said. "Do you know if anyone else might have an old amateur radio lying around?"

"Not that I know of around here. Maybe tomorrow we can find out if anyone in Beatrice has one."

"Probably a good idea," Jackson said. "In the meantime, what would you think about posting one of our sentries here at the dairy just to keep an eye on things?"

At Jackson's insistence, and with Danny Day's approval, the first order of business for the newly forming militia was to put sentries on all roads leading into the community from the south and the east. As bad as Charlene hated the idea of spying on anyone from the community, she could see the wisdom in the suggestion. What was Tom hiding? Had he been communicating with other people somewhere? Is that where he got the idea that they needed a return to some kind of barter? And then she had a horrifying thought, *maybe he's been talking to them. What if Tom's already communicating with the Narmy.* She was on the verge of turning around to confront Tom to find out if he had contacted New Dixie or the Narmy when Kahina's voice came over the old CB radio. It was hard to make out everything through the static, but she clearly heard "to the bunker" as she adjusted the squelch.

Before they got back to Marysville, Charlene was able to get through to Kahina on the CB. It wasn't an emergency at all. Sophia, who was the sentry on duty just south of Waterville on 77, had called in to report a couple of apparent refugees that she was bringing up to Blue Rapids. Even though there was no rush, Charlene hurried to get back to Blue Rapids. Not just to be there to greet the newcomers, she wanted to talk to her grandfather. It was time to find out about Danny Day and Tom Abernathy. Time to learn what transpired between those two old men in the time before V-1.

The two women that Charlene and Jackson met at the gate to the bunker seemed to be in worse shape than most who made their way to Blue Rapids. They were both Black women; one looked to be in her teens and the other around thirty years old. The older woman was apparently too weak to even stand without the support of the other.

"Can you help us?" it was a plea from the teenager.

"We need to get them out of this heat," Charlene said as Jackson moved to help the teenager support the older woman.

It had never been done before, but Charlene decided to take the two women straight down into the bunker instead of taking them to the community center in Marysville. Thinking it wouldn't be easy to get them down through the trap door inside the guardhouse, she led them around to the freight elevator at the back of the old gypsum plant. It took Jackson on one side and the young stranger on the other to practically carry the older woman from the gate to the elevator.

"Wow," was the first thing out of Jackson's mouth when they stepped out into the vast underground storeroom. "What kind of place is this?"

"I think they called it a bomb shelter back in the before," Charlene said. "Charlie and a friend of his found it before I was even born."

The rows of industrial shelving were just as full of food and supplies as they had been when Charlie first saw them over twenty years ago, only now, instead of case after case of Allpro, most of the food had been produced locally. Some of the supplies stored in the warehouse were still being salvaged from the old cities, but the community was becoming ever more self-sufficient.

Jackson was even more impressed when Charlene led them into the great room than he had been by the underground storage warehouse.

"Welcome to our bunker," Charlene said, smiling at Jackson to let him know she was talking to him as much as to the two strangers.

Charlene helped get the two women seated at the big table and then handed each a glass of water. "I'm Charlene," she said and introduced Jackson as she grabbed some sourdough bread and honey for the two emaciated women.

"I'm Ember, and this is Mya," the younger woman said as she hurriedly spread honey on one of the slices of bread for Mya.

"Thank you, thank you," seemed to be all Mya could say. Her voice sounded as weak as her body looked.

Ember didn't fix any of the food for herself or even have a drink of water until she was satisfied that Mya was drinking and eating. "Thank the gods we found you," she said then, after taking a drink of water. "Don't know how much farther Mya could have gone."

"How far have you come?" Jackson asked.

Ember had to swallow her first bite of bread and honey before she could answer. "We escaped from Council Grove. That was five days ago. Been running and hiding ever since."

"You better take it easy on that food," Charlene told both women. "It doesn't look like you've had much to eat between here and there." Then she turned to Jackson. "Let's let them eat," she said. "I have something to show you."

Charlene led Jackson back out through the storeroom into the command center, where Kahina was listening to a lot of static on the CB radio. You couldn't say Kahina was surprised that Jackson was in the bunker, even though very few people who lived in the Marysville area had ever been down there. No, she had been expecting Jackson to become a resident. As she'd watched on the monitors, what had surprised her was that Charlene had brought the other two women down into the bunker. Jackson was one thing, total strangers another.

"Do you think that's wise?" Kahina asked Charlene. The two women knew each other so well that Charlene knew immediately what Kahina was asking.

"They were starving." That was all Charlene had to say by way of justification. "That's not important, though. Kahina, they escaped from Council Grove. That's less than a hundred miles from here."

"Damn, he's moving faster than I thought," Jackson said. He had never heard of Council Grove and didn't know it was so close. "If Davis is already within a hundred miles of here, we're running out of time. We need to get that arsenal I saw on the other side of that wall into our people's hands right now." Jackson referred to the rack of military rifles and the cases of ammunition stored in the bunker, presumably by whoever built it.

Despite the seriousness of the situation, Charlene couldn't help but smile at Jackson's use of the phrase "our people." She was glad that he already felt like part of the community. As for the arsenal in the storeroom on the other side of the wall, it was only a couple dozen old assault rifles and enough ammunition to last a lifetime. *A lifetime can be pretty short when people start shooting each other,* Charlene thought.

"Maybe we have more time than you think," Charlene told Jackson. "If the Narmy has just taken over Council Grove, won't they take some time to consolidate their gains before hitting anywhere else?"

Jackson thought back to when the Narmy took Sedalia and realized that Charlene was probably right. Davis and his troops had spent the better part of a year in Sedalia by the time Jackson escaped. If they spent even a few months in Council Grove, it might be enough time for Marysville to prepare.

Kahina, Jackson, and Charlene agreed to stick to their security plan with one modification. They had planned on trying to recruit help from a community down on Turtle Lake as well as the one in Beatrice, but Turtle Lake was too close to Council Grove. Davis and his troops might not move north to Marysville for a while, but taking Turtle Lake would probably be part of consolidating their holdings at Council Grove.

Leaving Kahina the task of contacting Charlie and Danny to distribute the assault rifles and ammunition, Charlene led Jackson back out into the bunker's living area. Ember and Mya were still sitting at the table, looking better already. Charlene was pleased to see that they hadn't eaten enough to make themselves sick. The honey was perfect for getting some blood sugar back into their systems as quickly as possible.

"Thank you," Mya said again, this time with some of the strength back in her voice. "I don't know how we can thank you enough."

"Well," Charlene said, "you can tell us what you know about the Narmy. I presume that's who you escaped from."

"It is," Ember said.

"But first," Charlene interrupted, "wouldn't you two like to get cleaned up? No offense, but neither one of you smells that great."

That brought a smile to both women's lips and even a small laugh from Ember. "That would be wonderful," she said.

Jackson and Ember helped Mya get to the entrance to the women's showers, but Mya had already gained enough strength to walk in on her own. After Charlene got Ember and Mya situated with everything they needed in the women's shower, she came back out to find Jackson exploring the sleeping quarters.

"Would you like to move in?" she asked, "we have some empty beds."

Jackson smiled and searched her eyes before wrapping his arms around her. "Are you claiming me?" he asked.

The twinkle in her eyes said more than words as she asked, "Do you want to be claimed?"

A long deep kiss was the answer to both of their questions.

# Chapter 8

S HE KNEW IT WAS Jackson on top of her making love, but Charlene was somehow in another place or another time. Not only that, she was with another man. It was like a vision, or maybe a dream, but not like any vision or dream she'd ever had before. The man who was making love to her was no one she'd ever seen. Unlike Jackson, with his red hair and blue eyes, this man was dark. Not as dark as Charlene, but he had light brown skin and dark brown eyes. She could feel her fingers entwined in his long black hair. He was incredibly handsome, and Charlene knew somehow that he primarily owed his chiseled features to Native American ancestry.

She felt a shuddering orgasm run through the man's body even as it ran through hers. Then, suddenly she was back in the present, and it was Jackson who was lying spent on top of her.

Jackson moved off of Charlene and lay on his side, looking at her in the bunker's simulated moonlight. Charlene looked up at the nightlight in the ceiling that was made to look like a full moon. She had installed that light in the ceiling right after moving into the Bunker. Without it, the darkness was so complete that a person could only find their way around by feel.

Charlene looked back at Jackson and wondered about the dream-vision she'd just experienced. The actual experience of making love with Jackson was completely wonderful all by itself. Why had her mind created a fantasy right in the middle of it? Or had it, what if it truly was a vision? If it was a vision, it would have to be of the future, and that was something that had never happened before. *Why can't I see the future?* She wondered. *And why can't I see whatever I want? Why do I only see random things that have already happened?*

"You seem pretty lost in thought," Jackson whispered. He didn't want to disturb the other people nearby, who were sleeping or making love in the other cubicles.

"Just enjoying the afterglow," Charlene deflected. She snuggled close against him and closed her eyes. "You know, normally I would go sleep in my own bed," she murmured in his ear, "but I think I'd rather sleep right here if it's okay with you."

"It's perfect," was the last thing Charlene heard before sleep took her.

..........

"Do you really think he's lying about not having a radio?" Kahina asked. Charlene and Kahina were just passing by the Abernathy Dairy. They were on their way to Beatrice for the meeting Charlene had scheduled two days ago. Jackson was left behind to help Danny with the arming and training of the volunteers. At least that's what Charlene told Kahina when she asked her to come along on this ride. Kahina couldn't help but wonder if Charlene was just taking her advice, keeping Jackson away from the Beatrice women.

"I'm pretty sure he was lying about something, but I don't know what," Charlene answered. "And I don't know why he would lie to us. Maybe Danny's right. He said Tom was, is, and always will be nothing but a goddamned racist. Those are his exact words. Danny figures he wouldn't share his radio with us even if he had one, just like he doesn't want to share anything that comes from his dairy."

"He'll probably join them." It was Ember who was riding along in the back seat. Charlene brought Ember along to fill in for Jackson. It seemed like a good idea to have a firsthand witness who could tell the people of Beatrice about the horrors the Narmy inflicted on other communities.

"There were a few old white people like that in Council Grove," Ember continued. "Mya said there were a lot of people like that before. She called them closeted racists. When the Narmy came, it was like they had just been waiting for the opportunity to join up."

"That's why Danny and Jackson decided to have someone watch the dairy full time now," Charlene said. "Danny has no doubt that Tom Abernathy would much prefer being part of New Dixie to being part of our own little community."

As she made her way around the blockages on Highway 77, Charlene wondered if they could possibly get the road cleared and easily passable in time. That led to wondering how much time they had. How long before the Narmy decided that Marysville should be a part of New Dixie? Would it be months or years? Surely, they had at least a couple of months to prepare. *Plenty of time, if they'll join us.* Charlene felt like the fate of Marysville was dependent on the people of Beatrice. She simply had to convince them to join forces.

The parking lot at the Center in Beatrice wasn't as crowded as Charlene had hoped it would be. Old folding metal chairs and a few plastic ones had been set up in front of the old Walmart entrance doors. The chairs were in rows facing a plastic table that was obviously where Charlene was expected to make her pitch. Charlene couldn't help but notice there were about as many empty chairs as those that were occupied. Apparently, Betty had counted on more people showing up than actually came. Or maybe more people would show up. It wasn't quite midday yet.

Betty had locked up the trading post and was already seated at one end of the table when Charlene, Kahina, and Ember joined her. Charlene did a quick count as she walked from the truck to the table. There were just thirty-one people in the rows of seats. The chairs were set up in six rows of ten, leaving twenty-nine seats available. The people that were there were clustered in groups, talking among themselves.

"Will others show up, or is this it?" Charlene asked Betty.

"Don't know," Betty answered, "seems most of the people around here don't think we need to be worrying about what's happening way down in Kentucky and Missouri."

"They took Council Grove," Ember said, "that's where I'm from."

Charlene, who hadn't yet introduced Ember, did so and then, seeing the questioning look on Betty's face, said, "It's down in Kansas, no more than a hundred and fifty miles from here."

Betty was shocked to know the Narmy was that close, but it still seemed like quite a distance. "Closer than I thought," she said, "but I'm not sure it'll seem very close to these people. Don't know if you've noticed or not, but the most common form of transportation around here is by horse-drawn buggy. In these parts, we don't have very many modern vehicles like the one you're driving."

"We don't have that many either," Charlene said, "but I bet the Narmy isn't using horses and buggies."

"No, the Narmy didn't come to Council Grove on horses," Ember said. "They came in a bunch of different electric vehicles. From old pickups like Charlene's Endurance to some kind of armored personnel carriers. Some of their armored vehicles even had machine guns and cannons."

Ember's mention of military vehicles was an opening for Charlene to ask Betty a question she'd been wondering about, "Do you know if anyone from your community has been to Camp Ashland?"

The expression on Betty's face told Charlene that she probably didn't know any more about Camp Ashland than she did Council Grove. "Camp Ashland was a National Guard base back in the before," Charlene explained. "It's about halfway between Lincoln and Omaha. I read about it in a book," she added before Betty could question her about the source of her information. "Anyway, I've been wondering if there might still be some useable military equipment stored up there."

Another group of five women showed up while Charlene and Betty were talking. Two of them were in a buggy with the other three on horses. The new arrivals tied their animals at the long row of hitching racks at the north edge of the old parking lot. Kahina, remembering the time before V.1, couldn't help but smile at how preposterous it would have been to find hitching racks at a Walmart store.

"I guess we better find out," Betty said. "I personally haven't even heard of Camp Ashland, but maybe someone has. As soon as those five get over here, we can go ahead and get started. It's already past noon, and this may be all the people we get anyway."

The word of what this meeting was about had already spread throughout the Beatrice community, so Charlene didn't need to start at the beginning. Betty introduced her to those gathered as, "the woman from Marysville that you've already heard about."

"Where's that man you had with you before?" one of the women yelled from the front row before Charlene had a chance to say anything. Charlene recognized her as one of the women she and Jackson had encountered on her first visit to Beatrice. Looking out at the gathering, Charlene realized something else. Most of those gathered were there primarily because they'd heard about Jackson, not because they had any fear of the Narmy or New Dixie.

Of the forty people there, counting the five newcomers and Charlene, Kahina, and Ember, only five were men. The rest were women. They were primarily young women, from teenagers to some who might be in their thirties. Besides being young and women, the other thing that most of those gathered had in common was that very few were white, or what used to be classified as white. Most appeared to be various shades of mixed race. Charlene could only see three women and one man in the crowd with blonde hair. Some of the darker people in the crowd might have been as white as those four blondes were, but you couldn't tell it by looking. *Would the Narmy consider those with darker skin and hair to be white?* Charlene wondered. *Probably not.*

Charlene used the woman's question as a starting point. "He's preparing our people to fight off the coming invasion," she answered the woman directly, then addressed the rest of the crowd. "That's why we're here. An invasion is coming, and we need your help to fight it off. The

Narmy is expanding New Dixie. If we don't want to be a part
of that, we need to join together to defend ourselves."

Murmurs went through the crowd, and Charlene could
feel the disbelief in the air. She introduced Ember and
asked her to relate a little bit of what had happened
in Council Grove. The murmuring subsided, and those
gathered listened respectfully to Ember's narrative of the
Narmy swooping into Council Grove and taking over. The
young woman broke down only once when she related how
her man, one of the few men in Council Grove, had been led
off as a slave while she watched from a hiding place.

"But mostly, they just killed people," Ember told the
crowd. "They killed anybody that wasn't white or that
wouldn't be a useful slave. From what I saw, they seemed
especially intent on killing women. There must not be any
more men in New Dixie than anywhere else. I figure they
would have killed me, too, if Mya hadn't got me out of
there."

"So why would they come here?" a woman shouted from
the back row. "Seems to me they've probably got all the
slaves they could ever need by now. And if it's men they
want for slaves, not women, they'd sure as hell be out of
luck here." That brought a slight chuckle from most of the
crowd.

"They do," Charlene jumped into the conversation. "They
do have more slaves and more territory than they could ever
possibly need, but that's not the point. The man who leads
the Narmy is insane. He doesn't just want enough for New
Dixie; he wants it all. He won't be satisfied until the whole
country is part of New Dixie. He wants to rule everywhere.
Clint Davis is on a mission to take over all of what used
to be the United States. He thinks it's his destiny to fulfill
the dream of his ancestor, Jefferson Davis. He wants New

Dixie to be what the old Confederate States Of America only dreamed of being."

"How do you know?" the blonde-headed man in the back row yelled. "How do you know what some guy that's over a hundred miles away might want? What makes you so sure the Narmy didn't have a good reason to attack those people in Council Grove? Maybe the people from Council Grove brought it on themselves."

*Another one* thought Charlene. The blonde man was definitely old enough to have lived in the before. *Probably a closeted racist back then, just as much as he is now.* Charlene was just trying to figure out the best way to respond when an old Ford F-150e pickup came flying down Highway 77 from the north. The truck was going so fast it barely made the turn into the parking lot before screeching to a stop not fifty feet from the gathering.

"What the hell is Zack doing?" was Betty's response to the interruption.

What both Charlene and Kahina noticed most about the old pickup was the huge antenna that was fixed to the back bumper. It was about ten feet tall. Kahina recognized it instantly as a mobile amateur radio antenna.

The driver of the truck was clearly an extremely old man. He was nearly bald on top of his head with snow-white hair hanging straight down to his shoulders on the sides and back. He had a scraggly white beard and was stooped and bent. Climbing out of the truck as quickly as his old bones would allow, he hurried toward the table just as fast as his crippled legs would carry him.

"Zack, what's wrong?" Betty asked. Everybody there seemed to know Zack, and based on the crowd's reaction, this was nowhere near normal behavior for the old man.

"It's too late," the old man wheezed, trying to catch his breath.

"Slow down, Zack," Betty said as she stood up. "Here, sit down. What's too late?"

Zack sat in the offered chair, and before he could say another word, Charlene could feel a knot forming in the pit of her stomach.

"This," Zack said, pointing at the crowd. Then he looked directly at Charlene and said, "You're too late. I just heard it on my radio. The Narmy's already in Marysville. Some guy named Tom..."

Charlene didn't hear the rest of what Zack was saying. It appeared almost like she fainted to those who were close enough to see it. She slumped down in the chair with her eyes closed. But Charlene hadn't fainted at all; she felt the trancelike state overcome her as the vision played in her mind.

A man who was seated in some kind of moving vehicle was staring straight into her eyes. It was the same man from the sexual fantasy-vision she'd had last night while making love to Jackson. She felt the same strong sense of connection to the man that she'd felt last night. But this time, there was nothing sexual about that connectedness.

"Come west," the man said. "It's time for us to be together," he added as the vision faded. The fading vision left Charlene faced with a terrible reality. She knew without a doubt that her home was no more. She knew without even hearing it from Zack that Tom Abernathy had been in contact with the Narmy. Tom had let Davis know that Marysville's people were trying to raise an army to resist him.

Clint Davis was insane, but he wasn't stupid. He knew the best time to attack a resistance movement was before it had a chance to form. What Charlene couldn't know was what happened to all of those she loved. Her mother and father, Danny, and even Jackson who had escaped the Narmy once already. What had been their fate as Marysville fell?

As the knowing and not knowing left a gaping emptiness inside, Charlene had a thought she regretted as soon as it entered her mind; *they'd be better off dead. Better to die than to live as a slave.*

# PART TWO

# Chapter 9

T HE COM ONLY HAD to ring once to jolt her awake. It was a habit that Colonel Angela Montoya had honed to perfection over a career spanning a lifetime in the Air Force. She was one of those people who is fully alert the instant they wake up.

"What is it?" Angela asked without so much as first saying hello. There was no need for pleasantries. The face on Angela's comscreen was Charlotte, who was on duty monitoring radio traffic at the former New Army Of God compound.

"We've picked up some chatter from a newcomer," Charlotte answered. "He seems to be trying to contact New Dixie or the Narmy."

Angela didn't need to hear more. She was already getting up from her recliner before she told Charlotte, "I'll be right there," and abruptly cut off the call.

It was a short drive from Laurel to what had been the New Army Of God compound just up the road toward Billings. Angela and her army of women had driven those affiliated with the Narmy from their community a couple of years earlier, and now the Montana Militia, as they called themselves, used the former Narmy compound for their headquarters.

Unlike when the compound had been under the control of Narmy wannabes, the gates were standing wide open, and the three black crosses were long gone. With no flags, signs, or insignia of any kind, the sprawling complex seemed totally out of place, sitting in the middle of what had once been an agricultural field.

Angela glanced at the clock on the screen of the Hummer before pushing the power button. It was almost eight o'clock at night. There was no one in sight as she parked in front of the main building and got out of the truck. It wasn't unusual for the compound to seem deserted. No more than a handful of militia members actually lived in the barracks at any one time. As she walked up the steps to the entrance, Angela looked up at the massive radio antennas on top of the building. Those antennas, or more precisely, the radios connected to them, were the reason Angela had decided not to destroy the compound entirely. The radios were monitored twenty-four hours a day, every day. Angela didn't know if the Narmy would ever try to come this far north and west, but the Montana Militia would be forewarned if they did.

Charlotte didn't bother to salute or even get out of her chair, even though Colonel Angela Montoya was the supreme commander of not only the Montana Militia, but the Midpark Militia as well. Angela insisted that no one call her colonel and that no one ever saluted her. She didn't want the joint militias to ever be anything like the U.S. military had been before. She insisted on an informal chain of command and a relaxed atmosphere instead of a rigid system of rules and norms.

"Whoever it was, he hasn't been back on the air," Charlotte said as she removed the headphones from her ears and hung them around her neck. "This is a transcript of what we picked up earlier." She handed a sheet of paper with just a couple of handwritten lines to Angela.

*This is Tom Abernathy in Marysville, Kansas. Does anyone copy? I am trying to contact New Dixie. Repeat. If you can hear me New Dixie, please acknowledge.*

*This is Tom Abernathy in Marysville, Kansas. I have critical information for New Dixie. Repeat: My name is Tom Abernathy, and I have important information for New Dixie.*

"And no response?" Angela asked, handing the page back to Charlotte.

"Nothing yet. But he's not on a frequency they normally use. I don't know if there's anyone in New Dixie monitoring this frequency at all."

Angela, who had been a radio and satellite communications specialist in the Air Force, had configured this radio command center to simultaneously monitor as many frequencies as possible. The Narmy used a system of switching frequencies on a schedule, and Angela didn't want to chance missing something if they made an unexpected change.

"What about the Narmy, anything new from them?" Angela asked. "Are they still in Council Grove?"

"Yes. It sounds like they have Council Grove totally under their control now. I don't think they met near as much resistance as they had anticipated. Commander Davis is making plans now to hit a small community further north at a place called Tuttle Creek Lake." Charlotte hesitated before adding. "I looked at the maps. It's only about sixty miles from Tuttle Creek Lake to Marysville, Kansas."

"So, you think this Tom Abernathy knows the Narmy is headed their way?" Angela asked.

"Seems like if he did, he would have been on the radio before now," Charlotte started to answer.

"Unless," Angela interrupted, "he doesn't know. Maybe he has other reasons for contacting New Dixie. He didn't try to contact anyone in particular. Maybe he doesn't even know how close Davis' forces are."

"We could answer," Charlotte said.

Angela was having the same thought. They could answer Tom Abernathy, pretending to be from New Dixie. What kind of information could the man be trying to get to New Dixie, anyway? What could be so important? It was tempting to answer. To break the protocol of total radio silence just this once. But what if someone in New Dixie was monitoring this Tom Abernathy and just not responding?

"It isn't worth it," Angela told Charlotte. "We can't risk letting the Narmy know we're monitoring their radios. Just keep listening. Maybe..."

Charlotte cut Angela off with a wave of her hand. She had apparently heard something through the headphones. Charlotte swiftly turned to switch the radio from headphones to the speaker.

*"Repeat, this is Commander Davis of the New Army Of God. Come in, Tom Abernathy."* There was no answer.

"Is it the same frequency?" Angela asked.

Charlotte shook her head yes and seemed on the verge of saying something when she heard a now familiar voice on the radio.

*"This is Tom Abernathy..."*

# Chapter 10

A LPHA KNEW IT WASN'T a dream, but it was an exceedingly strange vision. He saw a young girl in a library that reminded him a little of the old Norlin Library in Boulder. The girl was probably in her mid-teens, and he felt an immediate connection to her that was different than anything he'd ever felt toward anyone. Somehow, he knew the vision was of a time in the past, and he wondered how old the girl was now. Alpha was twenty-two years old, and for some reason, he felt the girl was probably about his own age.

Spellbound, Alpha watched the girl going through a history textbook. You couldn't say she was reading the book any more than he read books himself. She was just turning the pages at a rate of about one per second. It was precisely how Alpha acquired knowledge, but he had never seen anyone else *reading* like that.

There was another woman in the vision. She was much older; she could have been the girl's mother or grandmother, but somehow, Alpha knew the two women weren't related.

"We better get back, Charlene," the older woman said, just as the young girl turned the last page in the book.

*Charlene, her name's Charlene,* he thought, and then realized that he already knew the girl's name before the older woman, *Kahina,* even spoke it. *How can I know their names?* That was the strangest part of all. He did know their names. He knew their names just as he knew the reality of their existence. Alpha didn't know where Charlene and Kahina were, but he knew when. This was a vision of the past. His visions were never of the future, only the past or the present.

"Are you okay, Alpha?" he heard his father ask. James had accompanied Alpha here to the Central Library in Denver just to see if the old building was still standing. Unlike his father, who had been here as a boy long before the great dying, this was Alpha's first trip to what had once been the largest depository of knowledge in Colorado. Alpha had spent a good part of the past several years in the old Norlin Library on the CU campus in Boulder. He had greatly expanded his knowledge at Norlin, but it wasn't enough. It was never enough. Alpha's thirst for knowledge was unquenchable.

The vision faded like a comscreen turning black, and Alpha opened his eyes. "I'm fine," he said, returning his attention to the book that was open before him.

"It was a vision, wasn't it?" his father asked.

Alpha didn't bother to stop turning pages as he answered, "Yes, but it wasn't important." He knew it was a lie, even as he said it. He knew the vision was extremely important; he just didn't know why.

Anna, Alpha's mother, had tried to explain his visions away as dreams or daydreams when they first started happening. Or at least when he first realized that what he'd seen was a vision and not just a dream. That was six years ago now. He was sixteen at the time. He may have had visions before then, but if he did, he never realized what they were. The visions didn't come to him often, and when they did, Alpha usually saw simple things that didn't have much impact on anyone. During the past six years, he'd seen things as mundane as a salvage crew from Midpark finding another usable Tesla in a garage in Lakewood. The only thing remarkable about that vision was that Alpha was at the Blue River Ranch, and in his mind, he watched the finding of the old Model 3 in Lakewood as it happened.

Alpha continued absorbing knowledge from the textbook, *Genetics: From Genes to Genomes,* one page at a time, while another part of his mind was thinking about his first truly important vision. The one he had back when he was sixteen years old.

Other than content, that first vision was a lot like those he'd had since. He saw scenes that played across an invisible screen in his mind, like a comscreen that was big enough to fill his entire consciousness. When the visions took over, Alpha was not just viewing the scene, though. It was more like he was transported to the actual time and place of whatever he was witnessing.

In that first vision so long ago, he'd seen three women holding guns on a man they had cornered in some kind of dead-end alley between two buildings. The man was white, middle-aged, dressed in an old military uniform with a simple insignia of three black crosses on the chest. Alpha knew the symbol was that used by the New Army Of God. He had heard of the Narmy long before the vision, but he knew very little about them. The three women who had the man cornered were dark-skinned, but only one seemed Black. She was the oldest of the three and their apparent leader. Alpha stopped reading and replayed that very first vision over in his mind, like watching a movie that he'd already seen before.

"You dumb fuck," the older Black woman said to the man, "what did you think was going to happen? You think we're going to just let you keep killing off what few men there are, just cause they're not white like you.?"

"It's God's will!" the man shouted at the woman, who Alpha suddenly knew to be ex-military herself. "We will have dominion over this world." The man was obviously delusional. There was nothing sane about this man. He had crazy eyes staring defiantly out of a full beard. His long blonde hair was a matted, tangled mess. One look at his wild eyes was all it took to know that he truly was insane.

"You'll have dominion over shit," Colonel Angela Montoya told the man. "You don't know how much I want to blow your crazy fucking head off right now. So, just shut the fuck up and get down on your knees." It had been weird the way Alpha suddenly knew the woman's name. That was still one of the strangest things about his visions, knowing the names of people he'd never seen before.

"Never!" the man yelled. "I'll never kneel for..." that was as much as the man got out before Colonel Montoya fired a single shot from the automatic rifle that hit the man in his right kneecap.

"Shit, Angela, I thought you told us not to kill any of them," Scarlett said as the man hit the ground.

Scarlett and Zoe, the names of the two younger women popped into Alpha's mind, as did the name of the man rolling around on the ground in agony. He was Forrest Becker, the self-appointed leader of the Narmy in Montana.

"I didn't kill the sonofabitch, but I probably should," Colonel Montoya said. "Wish we could just kill 'em all."

"We all do," Zoe said, "but we need them."

"All we need is their sperm," Montoya answered, "and I'm not sure this motherfucker's sperm is even worth saving. I know I wouldn't want to have any baby of his, would you?"

Angela Montoya looked like she was probably too old to have anybody's baby, but Scarlett and Zoe did appear to be of prime childbearing age. They both vehemently shook their heads no in answer to Angela's question. It was apparent that the thought of having sex with Forrest Becker totally repulsed all three of the women.

"That settles it then," the older woman said. "We'll just have to find some more men, bound to be some somewhere." She raised her rifle and fired once more at Forrest Becker, who was on the ground writhing in pain. Forrest Becker's body twitched a couple of times and stopped moving as blood and brains spread out from the gaping hole in his head. That was where Alpha's first vision ended.

Six years ago, when Alpha told Anna the details of that vision, including the part about Montana and the names of those he saw in the vision, she told him it was just a dream. A dream based on stories he'd heard from the many refugees from Montana who had settled in Midpark. Anna had no doubt why he dreamed of the man named Forrest Becker. Stories of his atrocities had been told by many of those from Montana. When Alpha had asked Anna how he knew the women's names, she didn't have a good answer, other than that his mind had just made them up in the dream. Four days after Alpha told his mother about that vision, Colonel Angela Montoya, Scarlett, and Zoe drove an old Hummer into Midpark. After that, neither Anna nor anyone else ever doubted Alpha's visions again.

The ringing sound of his com brought Alpha back to the present. It was Anna telling them that they needed to get home. Another group of women had just arrived in Midpark from Montana. As Alpha stuck the com back in his pocket, he thought about how important Angela Montoya had been to Midpark. If not for her, that com in his pocket would be nothing but a worthless piece of plastic.

Angela Montoya was responsible for the communications that now connected everyone in Midpark and Montana. Having served as a satellite communications specialist, Angela knew how to reactivate the satellites that the coms relied on. Alpha, himself, had played a role in bringing back communications. Still, without Angela, it never would have been possible.

Once Angela reactivated the satellites, it had been up to Alpha to program or reprogram old com handsets to securely link them to those satellites. It was an ongoing project that Alpha had undertaken when he was only eighteen years old using the knowledge he gained, not from the CU library in Boulder, but from manuals they'd discovered at an old Motorola facility in Fort Collins. After Alpha was able to reprogram those first coms, he successfully trained a few other people to also do the programming. Coms had been everywhere before the great dying, so it wasn't hard for salvage crews to find all the handsets anyone could ever need. Now, virtually everyone who lived anywhere in what some now called Midpark State could have one. From Frisco, Colorado, to Laurel, Montana, personal communications were now as easy as before the great dying.

As Alpha thought about his most recent vision, the one of a girl named Charlene, he had a feeling that she would be as important to Midpark's future as Angela Montoya had been to its recent past. With those thoughts of a mysterious girl named Charlene as a distraction, Alpha took one last look around at the destruction inside the old Denver Central Library. He hadn't found everything he was looking for, but he had learned some more about genetics, which was currently his main focus of study. Who knew what might still be found in the piles of books that were scattered everywhere? This old library had been hit a lot harder by scavengers than the one in Boulder. Books and the remains of books were lying about all over the place.

"It's still worth saving," Alpha told his father as they exited the building.

"This library will take a lot more to save than Norlin did," James stated the obvious.

James agreed with his son about the need to preserve as much knowledge as possible. He just wasn't sure they could get enough volunteers for the full-time job of restoring and maintaining this huge old library. Not only would they need people to do the restoration, but a security detail would have to be posted here full time to protect it. *It's a wonder it hasn't been burned to the ground already,* James thought, seeing the ashes and partially burned books that someone had used for a campfire just a few feet from the main entrance. Not that anyone James knew personally was likely to do such a thing, but who knew what people that weren't citizens of Midpark might do. *Citizens,* James thought to himself, amazed at the transformation that had occurred in just over twenty years.

What had started out as a handful of survivors in Colorado's Middle Park area had grown into an organized state. Communities from Colorado had joined with survivors in Montana to organize themselves into the State of Midpark. *Why?* James wondered. *What drives people to form communities and to join together to create a state with a common government?* Granted, the government of Midpark wasn't much more than a council of representatives from the different local communities. Still, it was a more authentic form of representative democracy than the old United States had been back in the before. Midpark, Colorado, and the Park City-Laurel area of Montana, the two main areas that made up Midpark State, were represented on the council by people who were chosen by their respective communities.

*People join together mainly for self-protection and self-preservation,* thought James, answering his own question. *Banding together in complex groups is what has allowed the human species to survive.*

The old battery-powered military vehicle that brought them to Denver was parked just outside the library's main entrance. Misty, who was about ten years older than Alpha and one of the original residents of Midpark, was stationed on guard at the front of the vehicle. Scarlett, who first came to Midpark with Colonel Montoya, was stationed at the rear. Both women carried the same M4 rifles that James and Alpha had. Both the armored vehicle and the weapons they all carried had been salvaged from Fort Carson in Colorado Springs. Though she couldn't be seen, Misty's sister, Mandy, was in the machine gun turret on top of the armored vehicle.

Seeing the armored vehicle and armed guards reminded James of the security details his father always traveled with back in the before. He thought about how privileged his youth had been as the son of a billionaire. It seemed odd now, the way the world was back then, back before V-1 erased that world forever. From where they were standing, in front of the old Central Library of Denver, James could see the hole in the skyline where his father's office building had once stood. He couldn't see the overgrown pile of rubble, all that remained of that part of old downtown Denver, but he knew it was there. *Someday, if we don't protect it, this library and all it contains will be gone, too,* James thought as he climbed in behind the wheel.

As he drove out of Denver, James thought about the three female guards that were with them. He thought about how strange it was that he and Alpha had guards accompany them everywhere. He never would have imagined that he and his son would be as valuable as they were now. But then, twenty-two years ago, when Alpha was born, who would have believed his son would be the only male child born in Midpark since the great dying. Not just Midpark proper, either. As far as James knew, Alpha was the only male child born anywhere after the V-1 pandemic wiped out most of humanity.

··········

*Not quite like the free-love dream of some hippie from a hundred years ago,* Alpha thought as he performed his part in the fertility ritual. *But then love has nothing to do with it. Free or otherwise.* Alpha wasn't sure he believed in old-time romantic love at all. He'd read plenty about love in books from the before, both in fiction and in psychological works, but he doubted he'd ever really experience it. What Alpha was doing with Maci wasn't making love at all. It wasn't really even for enjoyment, though he couldn't deny the physical pleasure he got from the sex.

Maci was one of the latest group of women who'd been sent to Middle Park from Montana to conceive. Alpha didn't know where the fertility ritual originated, but, like Maci, it came to Midpark from Montana. The fertility rites weren't native to Midpark, but once introduced, were embraced with religious fervor. Nearly all the women of childbearing age and most men in Midpark participated in the rituals. Midpark women traveled to Montana to mate with those men, and women from Montana came to Midpark. Alpha didn't really believe in any of the rituals' pseudo-religious aspects, but he had to admit it was an effective way to diversify the gene pool as much as possible.

The ritual tonight was performed as it always was. While Alpha stood by and watched in silence, Maci was bathed by the two young attendants. The attendants were always girls in their early teens who were deemed too young yet to produce a child. The two girls toweled Maci dry before leading her to the fertility alter and applying the sacred oils. The fertility alter was nothing more than a fancy decorated bed. Maci wasn't that much older than the two attendants and had been an attendant herself before reaching the childbearing age of sixteen. This was her first time to travel to Granby from Park City to mate, though she had been through the same ritual twice before in Montana. As she felt the oils being rubbed into her body and listened to the chant of the priestess who stood at the head of the bed, Maci prayed to the Goddess that this would be the time. Her two previous attempts to conceive a child had failed. Now she prayed for not only a child but a male child. She had her eyes closed tight as she felt the warmth of the oils being massaged into her breasts and then down her stomach. By the time the attendant's fingers rubbed the oil between her legs, the orgasm was almost instantaneous.

The attendants backed away and stood at attention on either side of the bed as the priestess at the head of the bed finished the chant:

*Gods and Goddesses of fertility*
*We most humbly beseech thee*
*Bless this union of man and woman*
*That a male child be born into this world*
*That all be well*
*So mote it be*

Watching the ritual unfold never failed to arouse Alpha. By the time the attendants stepped back to the side, he was more than ready to do his part. Now, as the attendants and the priestess looked on, the culmination of the ritual was imminent. Alpha was inside the ritual, inside of Maci, and then, suddenly, it wasn't Maci at all. It was Charlene, the girl from the vision before, but she wasn't such a young girl anymore. Alpha knew he was physically having sex with Maci, but at the exact same time, he was spiritually entwined with Charlene. What he couldn't know as his body shuddered in orgasm was that somewhere far away in northern Kansas, Charlene was looking up at him from her own orgasmic vision at that very same moment.

# Chapter 11

ALPHA TOOK A SIP of the hot chicory brew that he always enjoyed when visiting his childhood home. He and Anna were the only two people still sitting at the breakfast table. James and the other women and girls who lived in the big old house on the Blue River Ranch were already out working on their daily chores. Alpha had moved into Granby when he was sixteen years old, but he drove up to the ranch for breakfast with his extended family at least once a week. He'd made the early morning drive today specifically to discuss his recent visions with his mother.

"You know I don't like those stupid sex rituals," Anna said. "Like trying to resurrect some kind of pagan ritual will do any more good than those who pray to some old Christian God."

Alpha had waited until he had his mother alone to tell her about the visions of Charlene. *Guess I should have skipped some of the details,* he thought.

"I know you don't, mother. Sorry. It's just that there's something different about Charlene. I don't know what it is. Both times that I've seen her, I've felt something I can't explain. It's like we have some kind of special connection, but how can that be? I don't know anything about her. I don't even know where she is."

If it had been anyone but her son talking about a girl he'd seen in a vision, Anna would have just attributed it to a vivid imagination. But this was Alpha, not just anyone. His statement that he had some kind of special connection with this Charlene sparked memories of what she'd felt for James when she was just a young girl. *Maybe old-fashioned love between a man and a woman is still possible,* she thought.

Anna smiled at her son. "Maybe you're in love with a girl you've never even met. Love's a pretty mysterious thing, you know." *Extra mysterious in this day and age,* she thought. When she was Alpha's age, she never would have believed she could still be in love with James while occasionally sharing him with three other women who all lived in the same house. Or that she would also have had other men besides James since Alpha was born.

Alpha laughed. He'd read plenty to know what the idea of love was like in the before. He couldn't imagine feeling that kind of love any more than he could imagine the concept of monogamy. No one Alpha knew of practiced monogamy. The idea of one man married to one woman had died along with most of those who practiced it before he was even born.

"What if I do fall in love someday? I mean, how would I even know? It seems like if I was going to fall in love, I already would have. You know, with at least one of the girls from the fertility rites."

"That's where you're wrong, Alpha. Love isn't just about sex. That's what I hate the most about those damn rituals the women from Montana started. The ritual takes any chance of real love out of the equation. You don't even meet those girls. You don't get a chance to know them at all. You might just as well be a stallion breeding every mare that comes in heat. Do you think stud horses and mares, or bulls and cows, feel anything like love while they're breeding?"

"I know you're right about the rituals, Mom. That's why I've decided to stop. The women that turned sex into a form of religion may have had good intentions, but it's going to take more than praying to any God or Goddess to save us from extinction."

After last night's vision of Charlene, Alpha had decided he was through participating in the ritualistic sex that had taken over Midpark. His mother was right about the rituals being worthless, especially for procreation. Her analogy was spot on. The men who were participating were no more than breeding stock. And in his case, Alpha was a really poor excuse for a stallion or a bull. He may as well have been a gelding or a steer. In the past six years, he'd had sex with more girls than he could remember, and, as far as he knew, he was yet to make any of them pregnant. *Maybe that's it,* he thought. *Maybe Charlene's the girl who's meant to have my baby. There's no such thing as meant to,* he corrected his own thought, *but perhaps Charlene is genetically compatible with me in a way that none of the others are.*

"It has to be genetic, you know. The reason that no one has any male babies," Alpha said, "I think that virus, V-1, did something to people's DNA that makes a woman's body reject any fetus that has a Y chromosome."

Anna thought about it before answering. "If that's the case, how do you explain your even being here having this conversation?"

Alpha had been asking himself that same question for a while now, but instead of answers, he just kept running into more questions. "That's a mystery," he said. "But that's just part of the mystery. Why do you think I'm the only child you ever had? Why has James been unable to father any more children? I know he's been trying. You both have for at least twenty years now. Don't you think that's just as mysterious?"

Anna had given at least as much thought to her inability to conceive as Alpha obviously had. She and James had discussed it over and over again for twenty years, but they were no closer to solving that mystery now than they'd ever been. In desperation, the two of them had each tried other partners over the years. James had even tried participating in the fertility rites a few years ago. Truth be known, that's what Anna hated most about those sex rituals. Now, after twenty years of trying, James and Anna had come to the conclusion that they must both be sterile. The other three women who lived in the big old house had all given birth to daughters, but only after taking partners other than James. The other men Anna had tried mating with had all fathered multiple daughters with other women, but not with her.

*We all had such high hopes.* Anna remembered back to when baby Alpha's fever broke, and he didn't die. Everyone in Midpark had celebrated, especially Dr. Ming. Everyone had thought Alpha would be the first of many, not the only boy out of countless baby girls. Now, twenty-two years later, without another single male child, desperation was setting in on the community. In the twenty-two years since Alpha was born, the population of women had exploded while that of men slowly dwindled away. The community harbored a growing sense of fear and despondence. A feeling that they were witnessing the end of the human species. Women, especially the younger women, were turning to any kind of prayer or potion that came along. Some of the potions actually ended up killing some of the girls who took them. But people were willing to try anything and everything in their desperation. Nowhere was it more evident than in the fertility and sex rituals that had spread from Montana and were now the rule rather than the exception.

"I had a miscarriage once after you were born." Before now, Anna had never told her son about the miscarriage she'd had just eighteen months after his birth.

*Why is that important?* Alpha thought, but for some reason, that information seemed of the utmost importance.

"Was it another boy?"

"I don't know for sure, Alpha, it was much too early. But I think it was. I always knew you were a boy. Somehow, I knew, and I had the same feeling about your brother." The word brother wasn't a slip. Anna did know. In that moment of recollection, she knew the child she'd lost would have been Alpha's younger brother.

"Did you ever have any more? Miscarriages, I mean." *And why haven't you told me this until now?* he thought.

"No, I only had the one miscarriage. I never did conceive again after that."

"Are you sure?" Alpha's mind was racing. "Maybe you conceived but aborted so early you didn't know. What about the other women? The older women. The ones who survived V-1, did they have miscarriages?"

After hearing the sudden intensity in her son's voice, Anna knew he was on to something, but what? She searched her memory.

"Yes," she said slowly, remembering. "Miscarriages were quite common in those first few years, but so was infant death. I don't know how many babies were born, only to die in a few days. We always thought it was just V-1."

Alpha jumped up from the table. "That's it. I have to get back down to the old cities."

"Oh no you don't!" Anna followed Alpha out the door. "Not by yourself. You know the rules. You're far too precious for that."

*You have no idea,* Alpha thought as he hurried out the door. He had to round up an escort to take him down to Denver.

·····•··•····

They were making their way around one of the slide areas on the east side of Berthoud pass when the vision hit. As fast as the vision came on, it was a really good thing that Alpha wasn't doing the driving. One second, he was looking out the side window at the gaping hole where three-fourths of old Highway 40 had slid off the mountain, the next second, a war movie was playing in his mind.

A group of about twenty light-skinned women with mostly blonde or brown hair had a smaller group of dark-skinned people lined up at gunpoint against the side of an old gray limestone house. Alpha didn't know where that house was, but he felt that it was a long way east of Colorado. It was a lot greener than anyplace Alpha had ever seen before. The white women with assault rifles all wore the same military-style uniform, consisting of khaki pants and short sleeve khaki shirts, all with the same emblem of three black crosses over the left front pocket. There were no other markings or insignia denoting rank on any of the women.

Alpha knew he was seeing the Narmy in action for the first time. The New Army Of God had never made it to Midpark, but plenty of people who knew of them had. Forrest Becker and his group who'd been overthrown in Montana had considered themselves a part of the Narmy, but that was an extremely loose affiliation. From what Angela Montoya said, that affiliation had consisted of nothing more than a few shortwave radio communications between Montana and New Dixie. The reinforcements from New Dixie that Forrest Becker and his followers had counted on never made it to Montana.

Most of the ten people who were being held at gunpoint were Black women. There was one woman, though, who was at least as white as any of the Narmy women. There were also two Black men. One seemed middle-aged and the other very old. The old Black man, *Danny Day,* his name suddenly popped into Alpha's mind, was severely wounded. He wasn't standing against the wall with the others but was slumped to the ground with his hands held over his abdomen. The entire front of his shirt was soaked in blood.

A man climbed out of an old, armored personnel carrier parked behind the troop of Narmy women and walked briskly up to stand between the Narmy women and the people lined up against the wall. Clint Davis; Alpha knew this man's name as well. He also knew that Clint Davis was the commander of New Dixie, the leader of the Narmy.

"Please help him," the only blonde woman lined up against the wall said. Her name was Olivia; Alpha suddenly knew most of the people's names in the vision playing in his mind. Olivia was pleading for someone to help Danny Day. "Please, he's just an old man," she begged, with tears streaming down her face. She had to know the futility of begging for mercy from someone as insane as Clint Davis.

Clint Davis wasn't carrying an assault rifle like the women in his troop. He was armed with an old-fashioned revolver in a holster on one hip and what looked like a cavalry sword in a scabbard on the other. He started to reach for the revolver but then, seeming to think better of it, pulled the sword from its sheath and in one practiced swift motion, plunged it through Danny Day's heart.

"He's just a dead nigger now," Clint Davis said to Olivia as he swiftly pulled the sword out of Danny's chest and put the point under her chin. "And you're even worse, you nigger loving..."

Charlie, who Alpha knew was Danny's son, had been standing at the end of the line. "No," he screamed at that instant and rushed toward Davis. Several quick shots rang out from the Narmy women hitting Charlie in both legs, driving him to the ground almost right at Davis' feet.

With a quick thrust, Clint Davis drove the point of his sword straight up under Olivia's chin all the way through her brain. Just as quickly, before the weight of her dead body could even start to fall, he jerked the sword out of her head and thrust it into Charlie Day's back.

Watching the scene unfold, Alpha was filled with sorrow. Anna had never told him about her time in Blue Rapids or any of these people, yet he knew he was watching the murder of people his mother had once loved.

"You stupid son of a bitch!" It was Helena Hunt. "I told you we need the men alive," she screamed at Commander Davis, and Alpha knew in that instant that Helena Hunt, not Clint Davis, was the real leader of this troop of women. Probably the actual leader of New Dixie itself.

"And I told you we don't need no niggers," Davis yelled back at her. "Who do you think you..." that was all Clint Davis got out before the single shot fired from the rifle held at Helena Hunt's hip blew the top of his head off.

"I should have done that a long time ago," she said to no one in particular. The other women in her troop, obviously shocked at what they'd just seen, watched as

Helena switched her rifle to full auto and mowed down the seven other people, all women, who were lined up against the wall. She coughed as she changed her rifle back from full auto. "He was partially right, though," she said calmly. "We don't need any niggers that can't produce sperm."

The Narmy woman closest to Helena suppressed a coughing fit of her own to ask, "Does that mean we're not taking any more slaves?"

"I guess it does," Helena answered. "We've already got way more slaves than we need anyway. What we need are some men who can make babies that aren't female."

Alpha knew many things as he watched the vision play out. He knew that Helena Hunt wasn't insane like Clint Davis had been, but she was just as evil and ruthless, maybe even more so. Alpha was now also convinced that the lack of male babies wasn't just a Midpark and Montana phenomenon. He knew that Helena Hunt probably started out as a true believer in the superiority of a purified Aryan race. Unlike Commander Davis, though, she knew being Aryan wouldn't matter at all if homo sapiens as a species became extinct. Without male babies, or unless women somehow learned to reproduce asexually, it was just a matter of time before humans would be as extinct as the Dodo bird. What difference would it make if the last woman left alive was Black or pure white?

Alpha's vision suddenly switched to another scene. He watched an old man named Zack get out of a beat-up old pickup truck and shuffle as fast as he could toward the table where Charlene was seated with two other women in front of a crowd of people. Alpha heard Zack tell them all that they were too late, and Alpha knew in that instant that he'd just witnessed the execution of both Charlene's mother and father. Alpha felt the sense of fear and loss come over Charlene. He knew what she feared was the loss of her entire community. He also knew the unnamed sense of loss she felt was even greater than that fear. Charlene refused to acknowledge the loss of her parents even though she could feel it with her entire being.

Suddenly, there was a shift in Alpha's perception. Instead of watching the scene as an outside observer, Charlene was there with him. Just as in the sexual vision before, they were, for the briefest moment, together in the same vision. "Come west; it's time for us to be together," he heard himself tell Charlene, and the vision ended as abruptly as it had begun.

# Chapter 12

THERE WASN'T MUCH MORE to be learned from the old books at the Denver Central Library. *I need a lab, not a book,* Alpha thought as he closed the copy of **DNA Sequencing Protocols** that he'd just finished reading. After devouring dozens of books, Alpha's theory was coming into focus. Most, if not all, of the people who had survived the V-1 virus were genetically incapable of producing male offspring. And the daughters of those survivors carried the same genetic mutation that had infected their parents. The virus had somehow altered people's DNA. Of that, Alpha was absolutely sure. What he needed was a functioning genetics lab to sequence DNA. He needed to not only find the mutation, he needed to figure out how to reverse it. First, he had to find a genetics lab that could be restored. In some of the scraps of medical journals that were still in the old library, Alpha had come across references to genetic research work being done at the CU Anschutz Medical Center. Since it was just a few miles away, he decided to start there.

As Michelle, who was driving the restored electric Hummer, made her way slowly across the ruins of Denver toward the CU Anschutz medical campus in Aurora, Alpha was deep in thought. He had no idea what kind of condition the old medical research facility was in now, but it probably wouldn't be good. Besides wondering about what it would take to repair and rejuvenate the genetics lab, the same questions rolled over and over through his mind. *What about me? If everyone's DNA was changed, what about my mother? Or was it James? Was it a change in the X chromosome or the Y? Or maybe both sex chromosomes had been altered by V-1.* Alpha knew the answers had to be hidden somewhere in the roughly nine-hundred genes of the X, or the fifty to sixty genes of the Y chromosomes, but how was he ever going to find those answers? And would he be able to undo the genetic damage to people in time?

Most of the buildings that made up the CU – Anschutz campus were at least still standing, but other than that, things didn't look promising. The grounds were completely overgrown with dryland weeds and shrubs, and there were just a few shards of glass left in most of the ground floor windows. Most of the windows on the buildings' upper floors still had glass, but with ground floor windows all broken out, the old buildings were probably now home to countless birds and other animals. Alpha had been in on enough salvage operations to know how much of a mess birds could make in an abandoned building.

Once he started looking through the buildings, it was worse than he thought. Not only were the facilities full of rats and birds, and who knew what else, scavenger crews had hit these buildings hard. It looked like it had been a long time ago, but there wasn't much left now but mostly empty buildings with some scattered debris left here and there. Alpha didn't think anyone from Midpark or even Montana had done the scavenging, *probably that group from Trinidad,* he thought. There were rumors that a group of survivors lived somewhere down in the areas around Trinidad and Raton.

It didn't take Alpha long to decide that he was just wasting time looking any further at Anschutz, and time was the one thing he didn't have. He'd just have to go to plan B, which was the animal genetics research lab he'd read about up at CSU in Fort Collins. Maybe, it had been spared the scavenging crews that had gutted Anschutz. Fort Collins would have to wait until tomorrow, though. The sun was just about to drop behind the peaks to the west as Alpha and his guardians made their way back to the Hummer.

"Look at that," Michelle said and pointed at a vehicle coming toward them. Michelle was driving the Hummer north, working her way around rusting vehicles and other debris on what had been the southbound lanes of old I-225.

The sight of another vehicle coming toward them, one that no one recognized, put everyone in the Hummer on instant alert. In all of the excursions Alpha had been on, he had never encountered anyone who wasn't from Midpark or Montana.

"Shit! I knew we should have brought the armored," Misty said, referring to the armored personnel carrier that was being repaired back in Midpark. Along with Michelle, Misty and Mandy had once again drawn security detail to protect Alpha. Though no one had ever had to actually protect Alpha from any kind of threat before, the three women were clearly on edge.

On the other hand, Alpha didn't feel any threat at all from the old electric pickup truck that was getting closer. "Stop!" he commanded Michelle. "Keep your guns down." He added as Mandy was starting to raise her rifle.

Michelle complied with the order to stop, but the doubt and fear of the unknown was apparent on all three women's faces. All three were deadly serious about their duty to protect Alpha at any cost.

"These people are nothing to worry about," Alpha said calmly.

"You've seen it?" Mandy asked, evidently assuming that Alpha had seen this in a vision.

It was not that he had seen any such thing, but Alpha decided it might be best to just let the three women think he had. Instead of answering the question, he opened the door and stepped out on the highway, leaving his assault rifle in the Hummer. As the pickup came to a stop in front of him, he could see that the bed was piled high with a multitude of miscellaneous items.

*Scavenging crew,* Alpha thought. There were two women in the front seats and three more in the back. The three in the rear seat were crowded to the middle staring in wonder through the windshield. The front seat passenger was riding shotgun, literally. Alpha couldn't help but notice the two barrels of an actual shotgun pointed at him over the top of the dash. The driver opened her door and climbed out of the truck. She seemed to be unarmed. That was encouraging. *Now the two of us just need to keep our companions from starting a war,* was Alpha's thought as he studied the other women.

"My name's Alpha," he said. "Think you can get her to stop pointing that gun at me?" he gestured with his chin toward the girl holding the shotgun.

"Ariana, I told you to put that thing down," the young woman who had been driving told her passenger. Alpha couldn't help but notice that the driver was younger than any of the other four. She was probably just about his own age. Despite being junior to the other women in age, she seemed to be in charge. The passenger lowered the shotgun as the woman turned back to Alpha.

"I'm Luna," she introduced herself. "Ariana didn't mean any harm. It's just that this has never happened before." It was an apology and an explanation all in one. *Wow, is that an understatement,* she was thinking. She'd been on more scavenging missions than she could remember, but she'd never run into another group of scavengers, let alone a man. She was so intent on studying Alpha from head to toe that she hardly even noticed his companions getting out of the Hummer.

Alpha couldn't help but stare at Luna as hard as she was staring at him. He had an instant attraction to this young woman that seemed so different than anything he'd ever experienced it was almost frightening. It was similar to the feelings that accompanied his visions of Charlene, but not quite the same. The young woman standing before him was tall. Nearly as tall as he was with long blonde hair and striking blue eyes. *Love at first sight?* He thought. *It can't be. That's just a fantasy from the before.*

"You must be from," Alpha started to say, at the same time as Luna said, "Are you from the mountains?" They both laughed.

All of the women from both vehicles were now standing in the middle of the road, so Alpha introduced his three companions. "And yes," he said, we are from Midpark."

The three women with Alpha and the four with Luna were still armed, but at least they were all pointing their guns at the ground. Luna introduced her four companions and confirmed Alpha's guess that they were from the Trinidad area. Tensions eased as introductions were made, but Alpha couldn't help but feel the other's eyes on him as he focused on Luna.

"Been scavenging?" Alpha asked and, feeling the stupidity of the question, quickly added, "Looks like a pretty good haul."

Luna didn't answer right away. She didn't really answer at all. After thoroughly looking over the three women, and especially Alpha, who felt like her eyes were looking into him, not at him, she said, "It's true then. I was right. We'd heard other survivors were living up in the mountains, but I haven't been able to convince the council to let me investigate." She went on to explain that she knew it had to be true when she saw that Interstate 70 west of Denver had been cleared of abandoned vehicles. "How many of you are there?" she asked.

"I don't know exactly," Alpha answered, "maybe a thousand or more between Midpark and Montana. If you count all the children, that is."

"Wow," Luna said, surprise as evident on her face as it was on her companions'. "And men?" she asked the question that had been utmost on her mind since Alpha stepped out of the Hummer.

"Not enough to share," Misty jumped into the conversation. Her mission was, after all, to protect Alpha.

"It's okay, Misty," Alpha said, knowing full well how volatile she could be. "There are forty-three men left between Midpark and Montana." He may not have known the total number of women and girls, but the dwindling number of men was never far from Alpha's mind. "And you?" he asked. "How many men are there in Trinidad?"

Alpha didn't need to hear it to know the answer to his question. The disappointment at hearing how few men there were in Midpark was evident on the faces of all five women from Trinidad. None, more so than Luna. "Only five," she said, looking down at the pavement between them. "Five men and a couple hundred women and girls. I hoped," she looked back up into Alpha's eyes. "When I saw you, I hoped it wasn't the same. Tell me, you don't have any baby boys, do you?"

Now it was Alpha's turn to look down at the pavement. "No," he said, "as far as we know, I'm the only man alive who was born after V-1."

Alpha didn't even have to look up to feel the wonder in the women from Trinidad.

"You were born after?" It was the older woman, Ariana. There was more than amazement in her voice. The question almost had the tenor of worship.

"There's hope then," Luna didn't precisely ask, and it wasn't exactly a statement. She'd never heard the term V-1, but she knew what Alpha was saying. She knew that at least one male child had been born and survived after the death of the old world.

Alpha looked into her eyes once again. "Not much; there's not much hope if I'm the only one."

The sun had dropped behind the mountains to the west, leaving the most beautiful orange glow in the clouds hugging the tops of the peaks. Luna could feel how strongly her companions wanted to kidnap this man who seemed like he might be the answer to their prayers. She could feel how much she herself had the same desire and more. Luna had never felt a stronger desire for a man than she did right at that moment.

The shrill ringtone of Alpha's com startled everyone. Especially the women from Trinidad, who watched with sheer fascination as he took the com out of his pocket and saw Jada's face onscreen. Jada coordinated and presided over the fertility rituals in Midpark. For some reason, the fact that she was already wearing the High Priestess headset angered Alpha before the woman even spoke.

"Where are you?" Jada asked without even bothering to say hello. "The girls from Montana are here."

"No." Alpha's flat one-word statement shocked his three guardians as much as it did Jada.

"What do you mean, no?" Jada asked.

It wasn't that Alpha didn't want to try once again to make a baby, but for the first time in his life, he wanted to try with a woman of his own choosing and, looking up from the screen at Luna, he knew who that woman was.

He looked back down at the screen. "Just that, Jada. I'm through with your rituals."

Jada's protestations were cut short as Alpha touched the end call button on his com.

"How?" Ariana, who was old enough to remember coms from before, was stunned.

Alpha didn't even bother to answer Ariana's question. Ignoring everyone else, he looked into Luna's eyes and asked, "Can I come with you to Trinidad?"

Luna was even more shocked by the question than she was at seeing a working com for the first time. And she wasn't the only one in total shock. Mandy, Michelle, and Misty were nearly apoplectic. Especially Misty. She started to raise her rifle, then lowered it back down as her shoulders sagged. Who would she shoot, Alpha?

"Alpha, you can't," Misty pleaded. "We can't let you go to Trinidad."

"Sorry," Alpha said, never taking his eyes off of Luna. "Can the four of us come to Trinidad with you? I can't seem to go anywhere without my three guardian angels."

"We don't have enough juice," Misty said, grasping for any argument she could think of to stop them from going with these strange women. "The battery will never get us all the way to Trinidad and back to Midpark. We don't even have three hundred miles of range left."

"We can charge you up once we get there," Ariana said. "It's only about two hundred miles."

··········

Old Interstate 25 was remarkably clear of abandoned vehicles all the way from Denver to Trinidad. However, it was evident that clearing the interstate had not been the work of the Trinidad group as soon as Michelle followed the old pickup truck down what had once been an onramp. The US 160 bypass and 160 itself were totally cluttered with rusting hunks of old vehicles. Alpha absently wondered who had cleared the interstate as Michelle carefully followed Luna along the shoulder and through the old highway's bar ditch. The well-worn two-track route on the edge of Highway 160 was distinctly visible in the glow of the Hummer's headlights. It was definitely a route well worn by years of travel. *Do they ever scavenge to the south or just to the north?* Alpha wondered.

The clock on the Hummer's dash, which may or may not have been accurate, said ten forty-four as they left 160 and skirted around the east side of Trinidad. The clock had to be close, and the outside thermometer read one hundred ten degrees.

"Sure hope they have air conditioning," Mindy said.

Alpha had to agree with the sentiment. *How could anyone stand to live here,* he thought. After following backcountry roads that were barely worthy of being called roads for another hour or so, Alpha understood that the people of Trinidad didn't live in Trinidad at all. During that time, the route they followed climbed steadily into the high country that straddled the old Colorado-New Mexico border while the air temperature slowly fell. By the time they followed Luna's pickup into what Alpha could only think of as a compound, the air temperature was down to ninety-one degrees.

The Trinidad compound sat on what looked in the moonlight like some vast plain reaching forever into the darkness. They'd been winding their way through a sparsely wooded area for the last several miles. As near as Alpha could tell from the faint moonlight, very few of the juniper trees in the old forest were still living. The area was mostly just covered with the skeletal remains of what had once been a forest.

The darkened buildings that made up the Trinidad compound sat about a quarter of a mile out into that open plain and were clearly visible in the moonlight as they drove out of the ghostly forest. Not that he would have expected any artificial lights to be on anywhere this time of night, but Alpha couldn't help but wonder if these people even had electricity. Then he remembered Ariana saying they could charge the Hummer, and as if to emphasize the point, two floodlights on the roof of the massive central building sprang to life. *Motion sensors?* Alpha wondered.

"Wow, not what I expected," Michelle said. *Not what any of us expected,* Alpha thought.

With the floodlights adding to the moonlight, Alpha could tell that the Trinidad compound had been some kind of ranch back in the before. Probably clear back in the twentieth century. It didn't appear to have been a working cattle ranch like the old Blue River Ranch in Midpark, but some kind of guest ranch where wealthy people came to play. The sort of place Alpha knew had been fairly common at the turn of the last century. The wealth gap back then made such a diversion possible for many middle and upper-class people.

The huge central building with the floodlights on top was not enclosed but mostly open on all four sides. It had once been a large, covered horse arena. There were half a dozen electric pickup trucks of various makes parked in a row along one end of the arena with one open parking space between two of them. Luna didn't pull into what must have been the usual parking place for the truck she was driving. Instead, she parked behind one of the trucks right next to it. Ariana got out of the passenger door and motioned for Michelle to pull the Hummer into the open space. Sure enough, there was a charger mounted on a post where they parked.

"I still don't know about this," Misty said.

Alpha was feeling more sure about it than when he first made the decision to come here. "Too late now." He pointed at the range indicator showing a mere thirty-one miles of range left. "Better let them know we're here," he added, referring mainly to his mother. When he'd called from Aurora to tell Anna what he was doing, she had neither approved nor disapproved, but she made him promise to let her know as soon as they made it to Trinidad.

Anna's face was onscreen nearly before Alpha finished placing the call. "Thank goodness, I was beginning to worry," she said. "Where are you?"

"Well, I guess we're at Trinidad, but what they call Trinidad isn't the old city." Alpha's recollection of old Colorado maps was as complete as everything else stored in his memory. "I would guess we are actually in New Mexico."

"But everything's okay?" Anna seemed more worried than Alpha thought she'd be.

"Everything's fine," he said, holding up his com so Anna would be able to see the charger in front of the Hummer. "Get some sleep. I'll call back tomorrow morning."

Ariana was already plugging the charger cord into the Hummer as Alpha and his three companions got out of the car. Five of the other vehicles were already plugged into their own charge stations.

"Six chargers, you must have quite a power system." Alpha broke the awkward silence as the two groups of people stood looking at each other once again.

Ariana smiled. "I used to be a solar installer – before, and Chelsea was a full-fledged electrician." Chelsea had to be someone that Alpha and the others had yet to meet. None of Luna's companions had been introduced with that name.

"Will you share your seed?" Luna was looking right at Alpha as she ignored the small talk to get to the heart of the matter.

Alpha was just a little surprised at the frankness of the question. *Not more sex rituals* was his first thought. He didn't say a word but stood there probing the depths of Luna's incredible blue eyes. He felt a strange attraction to this woman. It was like they were connected somehow, though he had never seen her, not even in a vision, until just a few hours ago.

If Alpha was mildly surprised by the blunt question, his three companions were aghast. Mandy and Michelle were speechless, but not Misty. "I told you no! We don't have enough men, either." Truth be known, Misty was hoping to have another chance to mate with Alpha herself. It had been a long time since she'd been allowed to mate with anyone, let alone Alpha.

"But you have no sons." Luna broke off eye contact with Alpha to speak directly to Misty.

"What does that have to do with it? You don't either." Like everyone else, Misty wanted more than anything to produce a male child. Like every other woman in Midpark, she hoped to be the one to do just that. She wholeheartedly embraced the fertility rituals, participating as often as Jada would let her. Daughters were all she had to show for her efforts. Two young girls from different fathers back home in Midpark.

"She's right, Misty," Alpha interjected. "It's genetic. We have to try. We have to find the right combination to produce male children. If we don't, we're doomed. You know that as well as I do."

Alpha may have been using reason to persuade Misty, but, as he looked back into Luna's eyes, the desire he felt to "share his seed" was at an instinctual level so much deeper than logic that he may just as well have been a wild animal instead of a man.

"I would like to share my seed with you," he said, trying to sound as pragmatic about the whole thing as Luna seemed to be.

"Not with me, Alpha. I'm sorry, it's not my time." Luna glanced up at the half-moon above and counted in her head. "It is still four days until my time starts." The look in her eyes told Alpha that she was as sorry as he was that it was not her time.

"My time should be perfect right now," Gianna spoke up. She was the only one of Luna's companions who hadn't spoken a word before now.

Alpha looked from Luna to Gianna. She was a short heavyset woman with short dark hair that looked like it had been chopped off with a butcher knife. She was probably ten years older than Alpha. To say he didn't feel the same animal magnetism toward Gianna as he did to Luna would have been an incredible understatement.

"We discussed it on the way here," Luna said. "Gianna is the only one of us who is ready to share. Will you share your seed with Gianna?"

Gianna was holding hands with another of the Trinidad women, Louisa, and Alpha realized she had no more sexual desire for him than he did for her. It was easy to see she would much prefer having sex with Louisa, or any other woman for that matter, but she was willing to try to conceive a son for the sake of humanity. Knowing as he did that mankind's only hope for survival was finding the right combination of DNA, either through natural sex or genetic modification, could he do any less?

He was still dreading the thought of some kind of sex rite when he looked back at Luna and said simply, "I will."

It was a sad smile that Luna gave Alpha. She was happy that he would share his seed and sad that it couldn't be with her.

"How many can you share with?" she asked him. "There are others who are fertile now. They are sleeping, but we can wake them."

The question should have been expected, but Alpha was once again surprised by the pragmatic way these Trinidad women treated sex. Caught off guard, he had to think for a moment about the fertility rituals that he'd participated in back home. He had successfully mated with as many as three different women in one night. Of course, his potency must have diminished drastically after the first. It was only natural. In Alpha's case, though, successful and potent weren't even the right words. Mating could hardly be deemed successful when none of the women he had mated with had ever become pregnant.

"Just one is best," he said, "but there is something you need to know. I have never fathered a child, let alone a son."

Now it was the Trinidad women's turn to be surprised. Luna looked at him in wonder, and Gianna just looked relieved as she asked, "Do you have the old man's sickness like Marco?"

Alpha couldn't help but laugh out loud. He didn't need to know who Marco was to get the gist of the question. "No," he said, "the equipment works just fine; I just haven't produced any children. Not yet anyway," he added, looking directly at Luna.

"We have to try," Luna said, looking from Alpha to Gianna. "We must keep trying."

"What about us?" Michelle said, speaking up for all three of the Midpark women. "Do we get to try with your men?"

"Is it your time? Any of you?" Luna asked. The simple question and the way it was asked informing Michelle that the people of Trinidad considered the seed of men to be the most precious of all resources. It was a resource that was not to be wasted on anyone who was not at the most fertile time of her cycle.

"No," was the only honest answer Michelle could give.

"It's settled then," Luna was resigned to the necessity of what had to be. "Tonight, Alpha will mate with Gianna. If you wish to come back when it is time, we will share our men's seed with you." She looked back at Alpha. "Will you share with me when it is my time?"

"I will," he answered. He, too, was now convinced that this was the way it had to be. He would do whatever was necessary to save the human species. Tonight, he would mate with an unappealing stranger in an effort to expand the gene pool through sex. As soon as possible, he would study that gene pool in a lab to learn what had gone wrong with human DNA.

..............

Alpha needn't have worried about any fertility rituals in Trinidad, other than mating with a woman who had no more sexual desire for him than he did for her, that is. There had been absolutely nothing ritualistic about the experience. Gianna had led him to one of several small cabins that were lined up on two sides of the big arena. Once inside the cabin, Gianna undressed and lay down on the small bed that was the room's only furnishing. She didn't say a word as she lay there staring at the ceiling. Seeing Gianna naked in the moonlight streaming in through the cabin's only window did nothing to increase Alpha's desire, but he followed her example and undressed in silence. Gianna had to do some handwork to get him aroused enough to even perform. Only after she had him safely inside did she speak. "That's better. I was beginning to think you really did have the old man's sickness."

..............

Michelle was driving again as they made their way back to Midpark. Alpha looked back to make sure the four women from Trinidad were still keeping up.

"Slow down, Michelle," He told her, wondering if she was trying to lose the Rivian from Trinidad. Like that was even a possibility. Highway 40 over Berthoud Pass was the only route open between Denver and Midpark. It would be impossible to take a wrong turn.

*They still don't like this,* he thought. None of his companions agreed with what Alpha now saw as absolutely necessary. Neither Misty, Mandy, or Michelle had liked the idea of Alpha mating with someone who was not from Midpark or Montana. Then, the three of them nearly went ballistic when he told them he wanted to take four of the Trinidad women back to Midpark to mate with Midpark men. Alpha had tried to reason with them to make them understand that unless he could figure out a way to alter DNA, humanity's only hope of survival was to find the right combination of genes through ordinary sexual reproduction with a variety of partners. His efforts to convince his three companions had been futile. None of the three women knew anything about DNA. They did understand sexual reproduction, though. As far as they were concerned, Alpha just wanted to share too few men with too many women. That, and for his three companions, there was more than just a little old-fashioned romantic jealousy involved.

*How can I convince everyone that we need to put ancient emotions behind us?* Alpha was trying to figure out how to convince the council that everyone in Mid-park and Montana should start practicing reproduction like they did in Trinidad. Current reproductive practices were leading down a dead-end road, with dead being the operative word. Neither the ritualistic sex from Montana nor the old-fashioned romantic sex of James and Anna's generation would save the species. But how could he even persuade his mother and father, let alone the rest of the council and the rest of the population? *First things first,* he thought, *women can only be mated during the most fertile part of their cycle. During those few days, a woman needs to have sex with as many men as possible, and it should be different men every time, as long as the supply of men holds out. That should guarantee a woman becoming pregnant unless, of course, she isn't actually ovulating.*

Alpha thought of Gianna, who was one of the women in the Rivian behind them. He had insisted she be included in the first group of women from Trinidad because he was nearly certain that he had not made her pregnant last night. Thinking about Gianna, Alpha was confronted once again with the biggest part of the overall problem. Just because a woman becomes pregnant doesn't mean she will have a male child. Obviously, that had never happened in Alpha's lifetime. *Not yet, at least. Only me,* he thought. So, the last best hope for mankind had to be the diversification of the gene pool. That's why Alpha had insisted on the four women behind them being allowed to mate with men from Midpark. Gianna had already produced five daughters with the men from Trinidad. The odds of any other outcome with those men were pretty slim.

"Mindy, call Anna," Alpha didn't ask, he demanded. After reprogramming it, he'd left his com with Luna in Trinidad. Luna had assured him that Chelsea would be able to locate a charger for it, and he needed to be able to communicate with Trinidad to implement the plan that was coming into focus. Planned breeding of the known human population was not going to be easy to implement. It would be extremely difficult to convince some of the people of the need to change, even though everyone must know without something changing, they were doomed. The Midpark council was the place to start. That's why he had to talk to his mother. He wanted her to convene the council just as soon as possible.

# Chapter 13

T HE VOICE ON THE old CB radio was so hysterical that it was hard to tell for sure, but Jackson thought he recognized Sophia's voice. "They killed them all!" It was a shriek as much as human speech.

Jackson was on top of the hill overlooking the Abernathy dairy. He'd parked the Bolt out of sight back on the highway and made his way up the backside of the hill to the lookout post. It was the hard way up the hill but the only way to not be seen from the dairy. *Like I give a shit if the old fart knows we're watching him,* Jackson kept thinking as he packed the M4 and ammo up the steepest side of the hill.

It was Melissa's handheld CB radio that nearly scared them both to death just as he was showing her how to use the military rifle. Melissa had never been anything but an unarmed observer, but Danny wanted whoever was watching the Abernathy place to have one of the rifles from the bunker. Jackson hadn't necessarily agreed, but Danny was the leader of the newly forming militia, so here he was delivering an M4 rifle to a woman who didn't even know how to use it.

Jackson grabbed the radio and quickly turned down the volume before answering. "Sophia! Who? Who killed who?"

He tried to keep his voice low enough that it wouldn't carry down the hill but loud enough to get through.

"All of them," Sophia got out between hysterical sobs. "They killed Danny and Charlie – and the women." She was shrieking again. "Olivia – all of them – they, they just killed them all."

A thousand thoughts raced through Jackson's mind at the same time. It had to be the Narmy, but killing everybody was not their usual MO. Why? Most of the people that Sophia said had been killed seemed like perfect slave candidates. Why would the Narmy just kill them all?

Melissa, who had just heard everything, dropped the M4 to the ground and sat down beside it. She was already sobbing nearly as hysterically as Sophia. *Thank the gods she wasn't there,* Jackson thought of Charlene. Unlike Melissa and Sophia, he'd had time to form a strong emotional bond with just one person in Marysville, and thankfully, Charlene was in Beatrice.

"Logan," Jackson nearly shouted into the radio. He didn't care if the Abernathy's heard him or not. "Logan, do you copy?" he shouted again when Logan didn't come back immediately. Logan was stationed at the communications center back in the bunker.

"Jackson?" Logan's voice was soft and sounded very far away. He seemed to be whispering.

*They must be at the bunker,* thought Jackson.

"Jackson," Logan said again. "They're here, Jackson. They're outside." It was almost a question, followed by an actual question, "What should I do, Jackson? They're right outside the gate."

*Shit! They're all falling apart,* Jackson thought, hearing the shock in Logan's voice.

"Logan, listen to me. Lock it down - now. Close the blast door in the tunnel and seal up the bunker."

"But there's no one here," Logan objected. "There's just the kids and me. How will the others get back in?"

*Damn it! He's losing it.* Jackson had to make him understand.

"No!" Logan yelled into the radio, just as Jackson was about to push his own talk button. "They shot Stacey. I'll kill..." the radio went silent, and Jackson could almost picture Logan grabbing his rifle and running up the tunnel, leaving the bunker wide open.

Jackson's thoughts went immediately from the bunker to Sofia, who hadn't said a word since reporting the mass killing at Blue Rapids. "Sofia? Are you still there, Sofia?" There was no answer. "Anybody, does anyone hear me?" The radio had gone silent.

He saw it before he heard any sound, but that was to be expected from the electric armored personnel carriers that the Narmy used. There was still no answer from the radio as Jackson watched the battery-electric armored personnel carrier turn off the highway and head up the lane toward the dairy. The woman who was standing up instead of sitting in the shielded machine gun box on top of the APC barely cleared the arched *Abernathy Dairy* sign above the gate. There was a tall whip antenna behind the woman that didn't clear it at all. When it snapped back from its brush with the arch, it really was a whip, hitting the standing woman in the back. *Idiot,* Jackson thought.

Just as the Narmy vehicle started up the lane, Tom Abernathy came out of his house, followed by Ginger and Rachel. Tom was waving his arms as he ambled toward the approaching vehicle. That's when Jackson knew for sure that Tom Abernathy was one of them. He was waving to greet the invaders, to welcome them in. Judging by the way they just stood there, waiting, Jackson wasn't too sure one way or the other about Tom's wife and daughter.

Melissa continued her uncontrollable sobbing. At least, she was sobbing silently. Jackson watched through the openings in the brush that kept him shielded from the vision of those below. The APC came to a stop right in front of Tom. The side door opened, and two women got out and walked toward the old man. One of the women carried an M4 rifle like the one he'd just lugged up the hill. But the other, the one who was in the lead, seemed to be armed with nothing more than the pistol she wore on her hip. Jackson thought he might recognize that woman from his time in the Narmy, but he couldn't be sure until he heard her speak.

"Are you three the only people here?" she asked. The breeze carried her gravelly voice clearly up the hill, and then Jackson was sure. It was Helena Hunt's first lieutenant, Betty.

"Just us," the old man answered. "I'm Tom Abernathy." He stuck out his hand to shake, but Betty had a sudden cough and reached up to cover her mouth.

Tom put down his hand and took a step back to give the woman some room. She was actually bent over with the violence of the coughing fit. Just as Betty quit coughing and straightened up, the other woman, who was behind and to her right, coughed too, but it was nothing like the fit Betty had just experienced.

"You okay?" Tom asked as he took another step back.

"We're fine, just some kind of cold or something." Betty looked Tom up and down as she spoke. "You sure there's no one else?" she asked. "We were expecting a younger man."

"There are no other men." Even Jackson could hear the annoyance in Tom's voice. "I'm the one that's been talking to Commander Davis. Where is he?"

Betty ignored the question. "Too bad," was all she said as she drew her sidearm out of the holster and shot Tom Abernathy in the middle of his chest. Rachel had time to let out a shriek before the other Narmy woman mowed her and Ginger down with the M4.

"Too bad he was so fucking old," Betty told her companion before being bent over double by another coughing fit.

The woman on top of the personnel carrier was still standing straight up, being nothing more than a spectator, when the bullet tore into the right side of her ribcage and knocked her clear over the side of the vehicle. Jackson's second shot hit the woman with the M4 dead center in the middle of her chest as she started to raise her rifle. *Never aim for the head,* Jackson thought, remembering the training drills the Narmy had put him through. For once, he was glad they'd trained him so well, even if they had tried to indoctrinate him in the process. *Dead center in the middle of the torso is always your best shot.*

Betty didn't give him an opportunity to take that dead center shot. Instead of standing up, she dove to the ground, back toward the safety of the armored vehicle. The shot wasn't as easy, but Jackson hit her right between the shoulder blades as she crawled frantically toward the safety of the APC.

Other than his ears still ringing from the gunfire, the world was suddenly totally silent. Jackson looked at Melissa, who had totally stopped sobbing. She sat motionless, like a wide-eyed statue staring down at the scene of death below the hill, so totally in shock as to be almost catatonic. Jackson turned his attention back to the armored personnel carrier that sat silent in the driveway below. He fully expected that he would have to deal with one more person. *Where is she? There should be one more.* He remembered there always being four people in these small APCs, and it would definitely be a woman. Helena Hunt's people were always women.

After what seemed like an eternity but was in reality no more than a couple of minutes, the sounds of birds starting to chirp again in the brush made the world seem almost normal. Even the scene below the hill at the Abernathy Dairy would have seemed like just another day if not for the APC and the dead bodies scattered about. The cows in the barn were doing their usual bawling, and the strong smell of manure wafted up the hill on the breeze.

"Is anyone there?" the sound of Helena Hunt's voice right behind him damn near gave Jackson a heart attack before he realized it was just the CB radio laying on the ground. He turned around in time to stop Melissa, who was automatically reaching down to answer.

"Shhh," he held a finger to his lips and snatched the radio before Melissa could grab it. Carefully avoiding the talk button to avoid generating squelch, he turned the knob to shut off the radio. Just as he was turning the dial, he thought he heard the sound of someone coughing coming from the tinny speaker. The radio went silent, and the only sounds left were those of the birds and the cows.

"We have to get out of here," Jackson whispered to Melissa. He still didn't understand where the fourth woman was who should have been in the APC. "You wait here," he continued. "I'm going to work my way around to the back of the APC to make sure it's safe. You need to just stay hidden right here until I motion for you to come down the hill. Do you understand?"

Melissa shook her head, yes, but the blank look in her eyes made Jackson wonder if she understood anything. He thought about telling her to run if anything happened to him but then thought better of it. She might just start running as soon as he was out of sight. With still no sign of another living soul down below, the temptation to just walk straight down the hill was almost overwhelming. *How much time have we got?* He wondered as he made his way down around the backside of the hill. He knew it wouldn't be long before Helena, herself, showed up.

Once he had the hill between himself and whoever might be in the APC, he ran just as fast as he could with the M4 slung over his shoulder and the CB radio in his hand. It took less than five minutes to reach his destination and slink up behind the APC with the rifle in hand. The mystery of the fourth woman was solved as soon as he peeked around the back corner of the vehicle. She was sprawled out on the ground softly moaning, with one leg still hung up in the open door above. She didn't even have her rifle.

The woman was lying face down in the gravel, making low moaning sounds. Keeping his rifle pointed steadily at the moaning woman's torso, Jackson stealthily walked up to her and prodded her with the barrel. The moaning stopped, replaced by a weak hoarse whisper. "Help me," she said.

Jackson prodded her again with the rifle to make sure this wasn't just a ruse. The woman's only reaction was another soft moan, followed by another whispered plea, "help me." He reached down and rolled the woman over with one hand, keeping a firm grip on the M4 with the other.

He knew this woman, though she was barely recognizable. The fall from the APC had broken her nose and cut up the rest of her face, but it was definitely Robin. Back in Sedalia, Robin had forced him to have sex with her over and over again. For a year, he had been nothing more than a sex slave to Robin.

"Have to kill them," Robin mumbled without opening her eyes. "Kill them all. Helena...unghh."

*Did they kill Helena?* Jackson couldn't understand what the obviously delirious woman was trying to say. "Robin!" He nearly yelled as he knelt beside her. Robin's head lolled sideways in response. Jackson grabbed her by the shoulders and shook her so hard that the back of her head bounced off the gravel driveway. She was incredibly hot. An apparent fever radiated through the shirt with the wretched three-cross patch on the chest. Shaking her and yelling louder now, Jackson still didn't get any response. He slapped her hard, and blood splattered clear up onto his face, but Robin didn't move. Robin would never move again, Jackson realized as he let go of her dead body.

He pulled the dead woman out of the APC's doorway and ran around to the front to signal Melissa to come down the hill. But Melissa was already there, standing in front of the vehicle with the same blank stare on her face that Jackson was beginning to think might be a permanent feature. He didn't reprimand her for not doing what he'd said. He didn't say anything to her at all. What good would it do? Gently, he guided her to the open door of the APC and helped her climb inside.

Once again, Jackson was thankful to the Narmy, and especially to Robin. Thinking she'd converted him to their cause, Robin had taught Jackson how to operate an APC like the one in which he now found himself. He couldn't be sure, but it seemed like the exact same vehicle as the one he had learned to drive in Sedalia. Jackson didn't bother to turn the APC around. He just started backing down the lane to the highway using the view on the large driver's screen to see where he was going. It really didn't make any difference in these old APCs which direction you were traveling; the screen directly in front of the controls was the driver's only view of the world. These electric armored personnel carriers built back around 2030 didn't have any windows at all. The only person who had any view other than that provided by multiple cameras was whoever might be operating the machine gun in the open air on top.

Just as Jackson backed out onto Highway 77, a familiar voice came over the radio. "Betty - come in – Betty?" Helena Hunt was definitely not dead. There was no use going back to Marysville. What could one man and a catatonic woman do against the Narmy? Even if he did have one of their APCs. Besides, Jackson found that he was driven to do just one thing now. He had to get to Beatrice. Not just to warn Charlene, but to save her.

············

"We have to get back," Charlene told Kahina and Ember. It was pure pandemonium at the Beatrice Center. People were all yelling at once. "What should we do? Will they come here?" Zack and Marsha were trying to calm things down. Charlene heard Zack tell Marsha that he didn't think they had anything to worry about. That from what he'd heard on the radio, someone calling himself Commander Davis just wanted to take out Marysville before they could train up a militia to resist him.

"What can we do if they've already taken Blue Rapids?" Kahina asked Charlene.

"I'm not going anywhere," Ember said. "Especially not back into the hands of the Narmy."

"I don't know," Charlene answered Kahina, ignoring Ember. "But we have to try. We have to try," she said again. Her mind was racing. Maybe they could sneak in and save at least some of those she loved. Hopefully, some of them were securely locked down in the bunker. Even the Narmy couldn't get to them there. "Maybe the bunker's secure," she blurted out before Kahina could even respond.

Kahina could do nothing but follow as Charlene jumped out of her chair and literally ran to the Lordstown pickup. Charlene and Kahina weren't the only ones who seemed to be fleeing. Several Beatrice residents ran to their horses and other vehicles and took off to who knows where. At least Charlene knew where she was going. As they pulled out of the parking lot, Kahina wished they were following the people of Beatrice, who were mostly headed north, but she knew there was nothing she could say or do to keep Charlene from heading back south to Marysville.

About a third of the way back to Marysville, just south of the disintegrating old town of Wymore, there was a densely overgrown stretch of Highway 77 that had given Charlene trouble before. She had to work her way slowly through the bushes and young trees that were trying to reclaim the crumbling pavement. Backtracking along the same route where she had crashed through the smaller brush earlier took her clear off the side of the old paved section of the roadway. She had to drive through the weeds and brush down in the bar ditch to get around a substantial growth of young trees in the middle of the highway. Just at the point where she could get back up onto the roadbed before driving off into a river bottom, she could see the faded old sign she'd seen once before. The sign said, **Big Indian Creek.**

Charlene was thinking what a good thing it was that the old bridge over Big Indian Creek was still intact as she drove up the steep bank to get back on the road. She didn't make it all the way back to the road, though. The road was blocked at the top of the embankment by another vehicle coming toward her. A vehicle that looked to Charlene like a tank. If not a tank, it was certainly some other kind of military vehicle. It had some sort of gun mounted on top, and just below the gun, there were three hand-painted black crosses on the armor shielding.

"Shit!" Kahina shrieked as Charlene slammed the Endurance into reverse without even coming to a stop. All four wheels bit in hard, and the pickup shot backward too fast for Charlene to control it. She slammed into a tree at the bottom of the bar ditch and was trying to get going forward again when she saw that the tank had stopped and someone was poking their head up above the machine gun. *They're going to shoot us,* was Charlene's first thought before she recognized the man climbing out of the hatch on top. Charlene had never been so relieved in her life as she was at the sight of Jackson standing on top of the tank waving his arms. *Jackson's alive. There is still hope. Maybe the Marysville militia beat them back.* Even as she had that thought, the one that swiftly followed completely destroyed the elation she'd felt just moments before. *Then why is Jackson here?*

# Chapter 14

T HE LOOK IN JACKSON'S eyes told Charlene what she needed to know before he even spoke a word. Her family was gone, and there was nothing she could do to bring them back. Her eyes were swollen, and there was an emptiness inside that seemed to fill her entire being. As she silently rode along in what Jackson had called an APC, she thought of times and people who were now gone. No one in the APC said a word. Jackson and Kahina seemed to be just watching the scenery go by on the big screen behind the steering wheel. Melissa was still lost in a place where no one could follow, and Charlene just let the sorrow and memories wash over her in waves.

"Helena, come in." The voice on the radio startled everyone except Melissa, who showed no reaction at all. "We found her, Helena." the voice on the radio was obviously hesitant to say what she had to say next. "Betty's dead, Helena, and so is everyone else. The APC is missing."

"What do you mean missing?" Helena yelled into the radio. "Find them," she shrieked. "I…" a coughing fit apparently came over Helena while she still had the talk button pressed. "I want them dead!" she shrieked into the radio with such venom that Jackson was pretty sure one of his long-held suspicions was accurate. Helena and Betty had been more than just comrades in arms; they had also been comrades in bed.

Whoever it was that had found Betty at the dairy was silent for a few seconds before hesitantly asking, "Even if it's a man that killed them? You said you wanted the men alive."

"I know what I said," Helena yelled even louder, bringing on another coughing fit. "I don't care if the last man on earth killed Betty. I want whoever killed her found, and I want them dead." She coughed again before releasing the talk button. Then, she came back on, not yelling quite as loudly, "better yet, if you can capture whoever it was, bring them to me so I can execute them myself. I'll blow their fucking brains out right in front of the other four men we've already captured."

The woman who'd found Betty at the dairy didn't say anything for a few moments, hesitating before asking sheepishly, "where should we look? There aren't any tracks on the road?"

If it weren't such a somber time, Jackson would have had to laugh. He could almost picture the rage in Helena Hunt's face as he heard her scream into the radio, "Search everywhere, you dumb shit! How hard can it be to find a fucking APC? Start with Marysville." Then, almost as an afterthought, Helena, in a more subdued voice, added, "If you find any more women. Kill them, kill them all. If there's one thing we don't need, it's more women."

......·.....

"Jesus, you scared us near to death," was the first thing Marsha said to Charlene when they got out of the APC at the

Beatrice Center. They'd scared Ember even more than the rest. The instant she saw the three black crosses on top of the APC, she ran into the old store. Most of the people who had been there earlier were gone. Zack was still there. He'd been talking to Marsha and Ember while four of the women that apparently worked for Marsha were clearing out the parking lot. Marsha's employees had been carrying chairs back into the old Walmart store when Jackson turned the APC into the vacant lot. The four women dropped the chairs and ran to the entrance to the store to fetch their weapons. Now the four of them still had their guns, but they weren't pointing them at anyone.

"If it wasn't for that white flag you tied on the antenna, I would have had my girls start shooting," Marsha said.

"Humph, like that'd do any good," Zack laughed. "You got some kind of magic armor-piercing bullets I don't know about, Marsha?" Though he seemed to be about a hundred years old, Zack must have known a little about the more modern weapons of war.

"He's right," Jackson told Marsha and the other four women. Then he introduced himself to Zack and shook the old man's hand. "You need to get out of here," Jackson told the whole group. "Those aren't going to do you any good when the Narmy comes." He pointed at the guns in the hands of Marsha's employees.

"Zack was right then; they did hit your place?" Marsha asked Charlene, even though the grief on Charlene's face answered that question as well as words ever could.

Jackson saved Charlene from having to answer. "They did. First thing this morning, but something's changed." He looked directly at Ember, who had rejoined the group. "The Narmy isn't just taking over communities anymore. They're killing everyone. At least they have orders to kill women. I don't think they're taking female slaves anymore, just men."

If Ember's skin hadn't been so dark, it would have turned white. "Then Mya?" she didn't need to finish the question. She could see the answer in Jackson's eyes.

"But that guy on the radio, I think he called himself Commander Davis, he didn't say anything about that," Zack said. "He promised the other guy, the one from Marysville..."

"Tom Abernathy," Charlene interrupted.

"Yeah, yeah, that was it, Tom Abernathy. That Davis guy promised Tom Abernathy that he could have all the slaves he wanted."

"I think Commander Davis is no longer in charge of the Narmy," Jackson said. "I think he's dead, and I know for a fact that Tom Abernathy is. I watched them kill Tom and his wife and daughter. As crazy as Clint Davis was, I think Helena Hunt is worse. I think she's decided to just exterminate all the women she can." He looked at Zack. "And old men, too. She only wants slaves that are good breeding stock."

"But where can we go?" It was one of Marsha's women.

"Anywhere," Ember told her. "Just get as far away from New Dixie and the Narmy as you possibly can."

"Ember's right," Jackson told the group. "You need to get away, and you need to leave now. If you want to, you can follow us if that truck is charged up and ready to go." he nodded toward old Zack's pickup truck, which was the only vehicle besides the APC left in the lot.

"But where?" Marsha asked. "Where are you going?"

Jackson, who'd planned on heading straight north, was as surprised as everyone else when Charlene said, "West. We're going west."

"I need to go to the bathroom," Melissa said. It was the first words she'd spoken since witnessing the massacre at the Abernathy Dairy.

···•··•·····

*I hope they got out,* Jackson thought about the people of Beatrice. None of them were following the APC west. Both Marsha and Zack said they weren't going anywhere. They'd been born in Beatrice, and they planned to die in Beatrice. Some of the others said they would leave, but they all planned on going north. *Exactly what we should have done.* Jackson couldn't help but think.

The view on the screen was starting to change. With the coming of dawn, bits of color were slowly replacing the eerie black and white images on the driver's screen. Daylight colors were a welcome change to the infrared enhanced night view that Jackson had been staring at all night long. They had been following old Interstate 80 west through the night. It had been a slow go at first, with grasses, brush, and trees trying hard to reclaim the old road. Somewhere, just west of Grand Island, the plants suddenly just gave up. One minute they were working their way around and through tangled masses of vegetation, and the next, the pavement was covered with nothing but drifting sand and dirt. With nothing but an occasional old abandoned car or truck in the road, the going got a lot easier after Grand Island. The highway had been like that through the rest of the night. Though it didn't show up in the front view cameras, Jackson knew the first light of a new day was glowing on the eastern horizon behind them. Even with daylight, though, there wasn't much color anywhere in that great desert, nothing but various shades of grey and brown.

On the far right edge of the screen, Charlene, who was also watching the growing light, saw some trees that still had green foliage. That was a rare sight, even though she knew they were following the South Platte River. Most of the trees lining the river bottom were as bare as the desert around them, mere skeletal reminders of a greener past.

"Maybe we should camp there for the day," Charlene reached over and pointed at the patch of green on the right-hand edge of the screen. Jackson had already explained that they would have to wait out the heat of the day to conserve what juice they had left in their batteries. The energy needed for enough air conditioning to keep the interior from becoming an oven in the scorching sun would take at least half of their remaining battery power. The range indicator was already down to just over three hundred miles remaining, and Jackson didn't want to waste any of their remaining power on air conditioning.

*How far west,* Charlene thought, remembering the man in the vision telling her to "come west." The memory of her visions brought another thought to mind, *why don't I know his name? Why is it that sometimes I know people's names, and sometimes I don't?*

"How much farther?" Jackson asked, as if he'd read her mind. Charlene had already amazed him with her knowledge of the geography of what seemed to be the whole country.

"I wish I knew. I wish I knew where we're going, but all I know is west. It might be all the way to the Pacific for all I know."

"Well, I don't know much geography, but I don't think we're going to make it to the ocean." Jackson pointed at the range indicator.

"Are we there yet?" Kahina joined the conversation and laughed. "It's something kids used to say," she tried to explain. Then, "where are we?" she asked, remembering that she was the only person in the APC who was old enough to get the joke. Kahina had been asleep in one of the back seats, along with Ember and Melissa, who were now also awake. With no windows to look through, everyone watched the screen as Jackson turned to go cross-country toward that one stand of living trees.

"We just passed what used to be Ogallala," Charlene answered Kahina first. "As to how much farther, I think we can at least get out of this desert if we conserve power. It's probably just over two hundred miles to Laramie, and I bet it's high enough there to be above the desert."

"I sure hope you're right," Jackson said, "Don't know if anyone could survive for very long out here."

The words were barely out of Jackson's mouth when everyone saw the people on the screen. Actually, they saw a computer-enhanced image of two people who seemed to be trying to hide in some undergrowth at the edge of the trees. Being a military vehicle, the APC's cameras and computers were designed to specifically seek out and enhance people's infrared signal.

Jackson stopped at least two hundred yards from the edge of the trees and the people hiding there. A third person had come into view by then. It looked like someone who'd been farther back into the grove, apparently trying to stay hidden while making their way toward the other two.

Jackson started to climb up through the hatch on top, which had been open all night long for ventilation. "Wait," Charlene said. "Turn around first, so the gun isn't pointed at them."

Jackson was a little hesitant. *What if they aren't friendly?* But then he realized Charlene was probably right. The only "unfriendly" people he'd ever seen were the Narmy. Why would a few people out here in the middle of the desert, almost a thousand miles from New Dixie, be unfriendly? He tank-turned the APC a hundred and eighty degrees and started to go up through the hatch again. Charlene grabbed his pant leg and pulled him back down.

"What?" he said. Charlene pointed at the screen, which she'd switched to the rear-view cameras. One of the people who had been hiding in the brush was standing up in plain view. It was a man vigorously waving at them. As they watched, a woman stood up behind him, waving both of her arms. "Hey," the sound of the man's yell could be heard through the open hatch. Charlene let go of Jackson's leg, opened the side door, and stepped out.

The man's name was Carter, and the woman was Brianna. The third person who emerged from the trees was their oldest daughter, Yara. Charlene had never seen anyone more excited to meet other people than these three. As she and her companions listened to their story, it was easy to understand why. It had been over twenty years since Carter and Brianna had talked to, or even seen, another person. Other than the children they'd brought into the world, that is. When everyone died, they had been the only two survivors in Ogallala. As far as Carter and Brianna knew, they were the only two survivors in the entire world. `

"I was fifteen, and Brianna was twelve," Carter said. "At first, it was easy." He seemed to be searching his memory. "Just living, I mean. It was three years before we even planted anything."

"We'd probably still be eating Allpro and other canned food if Carter didn't know how to grow stuff," Brianna added. "The only thing I knew how to grow was babies," she laughed. "I was fifteen when I started growing Yara." She looked over at her sixteen-year-old daughter, who didn't seem at all embarrassed by her mother talking about "growing" her. "Carter started growing food, and I started growing babies, all at the same time."

Later on, near midday, Carter and Brianna were sharing some of their homegrown food with the five travelers from Kansas. Jackson had left the APC parked under the shade at the edge of the grove, and the group followed the couple and their teenage daughter back to their humble abode. The grove of trees was quite a bit bigger than it had first seemed. In the center of the grove, there was a large open glade. The glade was a cleared or treeless expanse that was nothing short of an oasis. The group from Marysville and Carter and Brianna's family sat in the shade, enjoying each other's company.

"I wish I could grow some boys," Brianna said, "but I don't seem to grow anything but girls." Besides Yara, Brianna had grown two other daughters who hardly spoke at all. The middle girl looked to be twelve to fourteen years old, and the younger maybe ten to twelve. For that matter Yara, herself had done no more than say hello when she was first introduced.

"How do you grow babies, Mama?" It was Chandra, the middle sister, asking the question. Yara looked slightly uncomfortable. Brianna and Carter had apparently given Yara some sex education, but not the two younger daughters.

"I want to grow a baby," Yara said. She looked directly at Jackson before adding, "but I need somebody to plant the seed."

Everyone stopped eating. Carter and Brianna both looked slightly embarrassed, and Charlene wasn't at all sure what the look on Jackson's face signified.

Carter looked at each of his unexpected guests in turn before breaking the extended silence. "You can see our dilemma." It was a statement, not a question. "When Brianna and I were the only two people who lived, I thought it was a sign from God. I thought the rapture had happened, and God had cleansed the entire earth of everyone but the two of us. I thought we'd been chosen to be the new Adam and Eve, and this was the new Garden of Eden. I thanked God every day for sparing me and for blessing me with Brianna." He took Brianna's hand. "When we set out to replenish the earth, I didn't really give much thought to how just one man and one woman were supposed to do that. I suppose I had to know it could only involve incest, but I always thought we'd have sons and daughters both. We've prayed and prayed, but God has only given us daughters. And now, here you are." He looked at Jackson before continuing, "Don't you see? You're the answer to our prayers. God sent you five to help us replenish the earth."

As Carter's gaze swung from Jackson back to Charlene and her other three companions, Charlene had the distinct impression that he had more in mind than just Jackson's seed for Yara. He was probably having thoughts of sowing some more of his own wild oats. *Maybe he's right.* The thought surprised her. The idea that perhaps this was meant to be. Charlene didn't believe in God, not Carter's, nor anyone else's. But she couldn't help but believe in fate, and fate didn't need a god. Maybe the five of them should just take up residency here in this little Garden of Eden. They could all mix and match and perhaps find the right combination to bring some male babies into the world. *But what about Alpha?* She thought, and was startled to suddenly know the name of the man in the visions. Visions that she was pretty sure didn't come from God.

"We can't stay here," Charlene said. "Someone is waiting for us out west." That statement caught everyone off guard, including her four companions. Charlene hadn't told anyone, not even Kahina, about her visions of Alpha. "I'm sorry, Carter, but you and Brianna weren't the only ones spared by God," she decided to humor him on the God thing. "There are more people like us, both where we came from and where we're going." Seeing the dejected look on Carter's face, Charlene continued, "You shouldn't feel bad about not having any sons, though. God hasn't given sons to anyone. It isn't just you and Brianna. So far, since God cleansed the earth, he has only replenished it with daughters, not sons."

"I was born after the cleansing, at least that's what I was told." Jackson's statement was so shocking that everyone was looking at him like he'd just said he was from another planet. "Of course, I don't remember. That's just what Mammi said. Mammi's who raised me. She said my mother died bringing me into the world, long after everyone else was already gone." Seeing the way everyone else was still staring at him in disbelief, he clarified, "Mammi was old, though. I don't think her mind was right. She died when I was just ten years old."

Charlene was still pondering the implications of what Jackson said when Carter spoke up. "If you won't stay, please take Yara with you." The plea from Carter was accentuated by Brianna nodding her head yes. Neither of them could know just how novel it was that Jackson may have been born after the great dying. For Carter and Brianna, just knowing there were other people still alive was itself an inexplicable miracle.

*Alpha, too. Alpha was born after V-1.* The thought shook Charlene even more than Jackson's admission. Was she truly sitting here with a man who was born after and having visions of another? The idea was so mind-boggling that Jackson's answer to Carter barely registered.

"I'm sorry, Carter, but we don't have room for Yara in the APC. It only holds five passengers."

"I'll stay," Ember said, and all heads swiveled toward her in unison, like some kind of coordinated bobble-head dolls.

# Chapter 15

J ACKSON'S EYELIDS WERE GETTING heavy. It seemed like he had been driving the APC forever. He'd caught a few hours of sleep at Ogallala yesterday afternoon, but, other than that, it was coming up on the third day since he'd had a good night's rest. *I should have taught one of them to drive this thing,* he thought, as he struggled to keep his eyes open. The terrain had seemed nearly unchanging for so long that he was beginning to feel the desert would never end. *What's that?* All of a sudden, after seeing hardly any buildings at all for hundreds of miles, a huge old warehouse appeared off to the right side of the interstate. It was the biggest building Jackson had seen since Lincoln.

"Must be Cheyenne," Charlene said, her voice startling Jackson as much as the sight of the old warehouse.

"Thought you were asleep. What's Cheyenne?"

Charlene laughed. "Well, Cheyenne was the capital of the state of Wyoming. It was named after one of the tribes of indigenous people who lived here hundreds of years ago. It was also the largest city in the state back in the before."

As Charlene continued the history lesson, more of the old city came into view on the screen. There was enough moonlight that the image on the screen was almost as good as a gray-scale daylight view. Cheyenne certainly didn't look like a city to Jackson. "Where's the city?" he asked.

Charlene had to laugh again. It felt good to laugh. It was nice to break through the spell of sorrow that she'd been in for the last few days. Even if it was just a momentary breakthrough. "I think we're looking at it. I don't think Cheyenne would have ever passed for much more than a big town back where we come from."

"Whatever it was in the before, it seems to be deserted now. I haven't seen any sign of anyone since we left Ogallala. Are you sure there's anybody left out here? Wherever here is."

"There has to be," Charlene answered. *But where?* She thought. The western part of the old United States was so vast and so sparsely populated even before; how was she supposed to know where to find Alpha in that enormous empty space?

"Well, I hope we find somebody soon," Jackson replied, "we're down to a hundred sixty-four miles of range. What are we going to do when it runs out?"

"I don't know, Jackson." She reached over and rested her hand on his leg. "But thank you for coming with me. Thank you for everything."

Jackson drove in silence for a few miles while he and Charlene both watched the light slowly changing on the driver's screen. They were both lost in their own thoughts at the dawning of another day.

"Look on the bright side," Charlene broke the silence. "We should at least make it to Laramie; it can't be more than fifty or sixty miles away."

Jackson wasn't sold yet on the idea that Laramie would be all that much different from where they'd already been. They'd been in nothing but desert for at least three hundred miles; how much difference could another fifty or sixty miles make?

Unlike the eastern edge of the great desert, the western boundary wasn't clearly delineated at all. The change was so gradual as to be hardly noticeable. The gently rolling, dune-looking hills gradually became larger, with rock formations protruding here and there into the sky. Clumps of vegetation, which had been nearly non-existent, began to appear and started getting thicker. There were even a few hardy trees growing here and there. The gauges in the APC didn't include an altimeter, but Jackson could tell they'd been steadily climbing, practically since leaving Cheyenne. The energy use indicator and changing terrain let him know they were slowly climbing out of the great desert.

The higher they climbed, the more trees there were, scattered in patches through the hills that were no longer as gentle and rolling as they had been. There were even groves of much taller trees here and there. Stretches of conifer forests with a few green trees scattered among the standing skeletons of those that had died long ago.

Everyone was awake, and everyone but Kahina was spellbound by what they were seeing. Of the group of people who now found themselves at what seemed to be the top of the world, only Kahina had ever been in the Rocky Mountains before. "You should see a real pass," she told them, seeing the expressions around her.

Charlene wasn't quite as awestruck as the rest, having seen plenty of pictures of the mountains in books, but she was impressed. With just a little over a hundred miles of range left, she was beginning to be afraid they'd have to walk to see a real mountain pass. She couldn't deny how impressive the scenery was, though, especially after the great desert they'd just crossed. The pictures in books could never do justice to the isolation one felt in that vast open space. Knowing they were no more than ten or fifteen miles from Laramie and seeing how the landscape had changed filled Charlene with hope. At least they'd made it across the great desert. *Now, if only there's water flowing in the Laramie River,* she thought. *Where there's water, there's life.* Not that they needed any drinking water. They'd filled all of their water jugs at Ogallala.

Finding Laramie as deserted-looking and devoid of life as Cheyenne was a huge disappointment, but at least the old highway was being reclaimed by growing weeds and grasses instead of blowing, drifting dirt. As they passed by houses and other buildings that had been vacant for twenty years, everyone but Charlene had their attention fixated on the driver's screen. They were all hoping against hope to see a computer-enhanced image of another human being show up somewhere.

Charlene had climbed out through the hatch in the roof and was sitting on top in the machine gunner's chair. She was tired of being cooped up in the APC, with the only view outside being whatever was on camera. It wasn't yet midmorning, and the eighty-degree air blowing through her hair felt great. The mountains on the western horizon seemed vaguely ominous as they crossed an overpass above some railroad tracks. The tracks were so overgrown that except for seeing occasional stretches of rails through breaks in the brush, one wouldn't have even known that's what they were. Charlene had expected to see a line of trees before they got to the Laramie River, so it came as a surprise when they were suddenly on a bridge crossing the small stream below.

"Yes!" she yelled in exultation. "There's water in the river."

Jackson looked over at Kahina, who was now sitting in the seat Charlene had vacated. She had a questioning look that seemed to say, "What else would be in a river?"

Charlene's joy at seeing water actually flowing in the Laramie River slowly gave way to a growing feeling of despair as the rest of the dead city of Laramie faded from view behind them. She'd so hoped there would be people, not just water, in Laramie. After crossing the great desert, they'd now found the old state of Wyoming's first and third largest cities, both devoid of life. *Where west?* She wondered. *Where are you, Alpha?*

The scenery had changed dramatically since leaving Laramie behind. Except for the mountains off in the distance, they may as well have been back in the great desert instead of the mountain west. The trees and most other vegetation had given up long ago. It was also much hotter than Charlene thought it would be. *At least there's a breeze up here,* she thought. Which was a bit of an understatement, considering that her long hair was blowing straight out to the north. She was riding on top of the APC again. They'd been taking turns getting out of the oven below. Not daring to use the air conditioning, the APC's ventilation fans blowing at full force were no match for the hundred-degree desert heat.

There was an old sign somehow still standing on the shoulder of the road, but with no more than bits of green and white paint left, what it had once said was anyone's guess. It must have had something to do with the exit ramp just behind the sign. The remains of some small town, no more than a wide spot at the edge of the highway, went by on the right. Charlene was looking back at the remains of a few buildings as they started across a bridge that was an overpass. As she glanced down at the road below, something wasn't right.

"Stop!" she yelled, as what it was that wasn't right registered. There were tracks on the road below the overpass. They were vehicle tracks through the drifted sand and dirt that covered an old two-lane blacktop road.

Jackson slammed on the brakes so hard that it nearly threw Charlene off the top of the APC. Then he joined her topside to see what the hell made her so excited. They both looked down at the vehicle tracks coming out from under the interstate on the north side. Then, nearly in unison, they both turned and looked at the same tracks going off into the distance to the south. It wasn't just a single set of tracks made by a solitary vehicle. The road below the interstate was covered with vehicle tracks. It was apparently some kind of primary travel corridor for someone. Charlene had been surprised to find people living in Ogallala. She was happy to find water in the Laramie River. She was absolutely ecstatic to see evidence of other people out here in the middle of nowhere. And not just a few people, but a lot of people. Where, though? Where did the tracks lead?

"Where do they go?" Jackson seemed to be reading her mind again.

Charlene turned back and followed the tracks on the north side as they turned left and continued to the west up the I-80 onramp. "I'm not sure, she told Jackson, but they're headed in the same direction as us on this side."

Which way to follow the tracks was a no-brainer. Charlene knew there was a whole lot of nothing for at least a hundred miles to the south. She also knew they had to be within twenty or thirty miles of Rawlins, and

Rawlins, though not much, was at least something. With their batteries nearly depleted, they really had no choice. "That way," she said, pointing off to the west. With her spirits as high as they'd ever been, she added, "Go west, young man," and laughed at the expression on Jackson's face as he crawled back down into the APC.

As the first old buildings that had once been Rawlins came into view, things didn't look too promising. There were no signs of life anywhere, and they were on one of those stretches of road where the wind had swept the crumbling pavement clean. Though they could no longer see any vehicle tracks on I-80, they continued on, stopping briefly to examine the offramp at what seemed like a major intersection. A mile or so up the road from where they stopped, they picked up the tracks again where they made an inexplicable turn. The tracks angled straight across the median through an opening that had been cut in the cable barrier and then continued across the old eastbound lanes and up what had once been an onramp. At the top of the onramp, the tracks in the dirt had once again been blown away by the Wyoming wind. They were sitting at an intersection with four different possible ways to go and not enough battery left to get more than a few miles in any direction. While Jackson was studying the screen, unable to decide, Charlene, who was still on top, was examining the old truck station that was diagonal across the intersection from where they sat.

There were several old autonomous trucks rusting away in the parking lot of the old charging station. That wasn't odd; they'd already passed plenty of old travel stations with vehicles of all sorts rotting in their parking lots. What was strange at the station across the intersection now was how the trucks were all lined up at the edge of the parking lot instead of being scattered haphazardly all over the area. Charlene shifted her gaze from the row of old trucks to the acres of solar panels that completely surrounded the west and south sides of the old travel station. Large solar arrays weren't that unusual either. Most of the travel stations built back in the thirties had large solar arrays. Still, something seemed amiss, but she couldn't put her finger on it.

"Hey Jackson," Charlene bent over and spoke down through the hatch. "Let's check out that old charge station across the way."

Jackson looked up through the hatch. "Yeah, a recharge would be great, but I'm guessing it would also be a miracle." Charlene didn't bother with a rhetorical comeback.

Jackson pulled across the intersection and into the nearly empty lot. He came to a stop just at the edge of the parking lot. Wanting to get a better look than could be seen on the driver's screen, Jackson parked in the middle of the station entrance and climbed up on top with Charlene.

The old truck lot's pavement was as deteriorated as expected and covered with dirt and sand that had blown in off the surrounding countryside. But what had attracted Jackson's attention on the driver's screen were the tracks in the sand. They were everywhere. It looked like this old charging station saw about as much traffic now as it ever had back in the before. *Who made all these tracks?* The same question was foremost in both Charlene's and Jackson's thoughts.

What neither Charlene nor Jackson had noticed before was the two other vehicles parked almost out of sight behind the old building. They were both some kind of old SUV-style cars, each parked at a charger and both plugged in.

"I don't believe it," Charlene told Jackson. Charlene wasn't the only one who couldn't believe her eyes. Kahina, who'd stayed below studying the screen, stepped out of the side door to stare in wonder. Melissa and Yara were left looking at the driver's screen and not understanding the uniqueness of what they were seeing. The front-facing cameras showed the same view that the three people on the outside could see. What the cameras didn't show was any computer-enhanced images of people. What no one saw was four women with rifles, the four women who were sneaking up on the back of the APC after emerging from behind the row of derelict trucks at the edge of the parking lot.

"Don't move," the three outside the vehicle heard from behind, just as all five of them saw four more armed women come out from behind the building in front of them.

"You two, climb down off of there. Now!" the voice commanded.

As Charlene and Jackson climbed off the APC, Kahina turned to face the woman who was issuing commands. "You're Black!" the woman who seemed to be in charge exclaimed, seeing Kahina's face. The four women who had their guns aimed directly at Kahina, Jackson, and Charlene, tentatively lowered their weapons.

"So are you," Kahina stated the obvious.

"We thought – I mean the three black crosses," the woman stammered. She walked up to Charlene, Jackson, and Kahina, who were now standing together. "We thought you must be more of them." The woman seemed to be talking to Kahina, but she also seemed unable to take her eyes off of Jackson, who obviously wasn't Black, but who just as obviously was male. "I'm Scarlett," she said to Kahina, finally pulling her eyes away from Jackson and offering her hand. It was clear that Scarlett assumed the older Black woman must be the leader of this little mixed group of travelers.

Kahina shook the offered hand and introduced her companions. Charlene didn't shake Scarlett's offered hand but instead grabbed her in a hug. Then, wiping tears from her eyes, hugged each of the other three of Scarlett's companions in turn. Her emotions were overwhelming. All the way west from Beatrice, Charlene had nurtured such high hopes of finding others while fighting the fear that they would find no one. But now, here they were. Part of her dreams had been fulfilled. Maybe there was hope of finding Alpha after all.

By the time Charlene finished hugging Scarlett and her companions, the other four women from behind the station had joined the group, who were now all getting acquainted. Melissa and Yara had crawled out of the APC and joined the group as well. Charlene didn't stop with the first four; she hugged each of the other four women in turn. And she wasn't the only one. The meeting turned into a hug-fest. Following Charlene's lead, everyone was hugging each other as introductions were made. Charlene couldn't help but notice that Jackson got an extra helping of hugs from each of the eight strangers.

"Is this all yours?" Charlene asked Scarlett as the last woman finally let go of Jackson.

"Hardly," Scarlett laughed. "If it belongs to anyone, I guess you'd say it belongs to the people of Midpark. They're the ones that put it together. We helped, of course, but they're the ones that had the crane and the know-how to make the old station functional again."

"When you say you helped," Kahina joined the conversation, "you mean the eight of you?"

"Not us personally," Scarlett answered. "At least not that I know of." She looked at the other seven, who were all shaking their heads no. She went on to explain that all eight of them were from Laurel in Montana. The people from Laurel had helped the people from Midpark turn this old truck station into a working charge station for those traveling back and forth between the two communities.

"So, you trade with the people of this place called Midpark? Are there any other communities that you trade with?" Kahina was trying to understand the relationship between Midpark and Laurel, Montana.

"Yes, we share in the rites with Midpark," Scarlett answered. "And the Midpark women share in our rites back in Laurel."

*Some kind of cult or something?* Charlene wondered. "What about the men?" she asked. "Do the men also share in the rites, or is it just the women?"

All eight of the Laurel women looked at Charlene with bewilderment. None seemed to comprehend what she was asking. Five of the eight women were really not so much women at all. They were just teenage girls. Charlene guessed that all five were younger than her. The youngest couldn't have been much older than sixteen. Even the three older women were relatively young. Scarlett appeared to be the oldest. She was probably in her late twenties.

"Is it possible?" there was hope in Scarlett's voice, like she was on the verge of some great discovery. "Can the ritual be performed without a man?"

Understanding started to dawn on Charlene, if not on the rest of her companions. "How many men and women are there in Laurel?" she asked.

Scarlett was slightly taken aback by what seemed like a change of subject, but she answered, "We have twenty-four men and nearly twelve-hundred women and girls."

"And Midpark?" Charlene asked before Scarlett had a chance to get back on the topic of a ritual without men.

"There are nineteen men and maybe eight hundred women and girls. But please - tell us, is there a way to make babies without a man?"

Charlene didn't bother to try explaining artificial insemination or in vitro fertilization, or any of the other means of reproduction that had been developed in the last century. Where would she start? Besides, no matter how it was accomplished, an egg still needed sperm, and as far as Charlene knew, there was only one place to acquire human sperm.

"I'm sorry, Scarlett," she answered. "I'm afraid I misunderstood; it does take a man to make a baby." There was a look of disappointment on Scarlett's face. "You share your men with women from Midpark, and they share their men with you, don't they?" Charlene asked, just to clarify for her own companions what she'd already figured out.

"Yes, we share in the fertility rites." Scarlett looked from Charlene to Jackson and back again before asking, "Will you share Jackson with us? Not with us," she clarified quickly, indicating the seven women who were with her. "We are on our way home from the rituals in Midpark last night." Seeing the expressions on the faces of the newcomers ranging from Melissa's blank stare to understanding and sympathy from Charlene, Scarlett added quickly, "I'm sure Colonel Montoya – I mean Angela, will allow you to participate in our rituals as well."

Jackson, who understood as well as Charlene what Scarlett was talking about, was starting to feel like nothing more than a commodity in the eyes of these people. Like he was some kind of possession being haggled over. "Do your men have a say in any of this?" he asked.

At the same time, Kahina exclaimed, "Colonel Angela Montoya? She's alive?"

# Chapter 16

T HE MEETING WAS GOING about as Alpha had expected. Not as he'd hoped, but as he had expected. Council meetings were always held at the old Middle Park High School in Granby. They were open to anyone who wanted to attend. As usual, practically no one but the council members themselves were in attendance today. The council consisted of six members: three from the Midpark community and three from the Laurel, Montana area. Besides Alpha and the six council members, there were just three other people in attendance, all young women. Alpha only recognized one of those women. He'd called Luna and invited her to attend with the idea that Trinidad should be represented in council if they were going to be represented in the gene pool. The other two women were total strangers that Angela had brought with her from Montana.

"So, let me get this straight, you are proposing that we do away with the fertility rites in order to produce more children, is that correct?" It was Lucia, Jada's counterpart from Montana. The other High Priestess Of Sex is how Alpha thought of her.

"We don't just need more children," Alpha said, pulling his attention away from Luna to focus on his interrogator. "We need more men. We need male babies."

"And you think that displeasing the Gods will make them punish us with male children?" Lucia asked. That got a chuckle from some of those present, especially Jada. The two Priestesses of the Rite, as they were officially known, both had permanent seats on the council. The other two permanent members were Alpha's mother, Anna Duran from Midpark, and ex-Colonel, Angela Montoya from Montana.

"I think the Gods have absolutely nothing to do with anything." Alpha shot back. *If they did, they'd keep you and Jada as far away from this council as possible,* he thought. "How long have you and Jada been trying to appease your gods? And how has that worked out for us?" he asked. Lucia tried to respond, but Alpa cut her off with one last question. "How many baby boys have been born from your rituals, Lucia?" Alpha practically shouted that last question.

Alpha was not a member of the council. James, his father, was this year's at large member from Midpark, and a woman named Zoe, who Alpha knew only through sex from one of the rituals, was this year's at large member from Montana.

"But Alpha, you can't deny that the Gods have granted us many children." Jada jumped into the fray. Any kind of parliamentary procedure from the old times that Alpha had read about was non-existent in these council meetings. "How many babies have been born from the rituals?" she answered his question with her own.

"And how many have not?" Anna spoke up in defense of her son. "How many times have the fertility rituals failed to produce a child at all, let alone a male child?"

"That is not our fault. We beseech the Gods, but the Gods only bestow children on the mating of two who are truly worthy." Jada spoke for both of the sex priestesses.

*It might be more believable if they were wearing their stupid costumes,* thought Alpha, before stating once again, "The gods have nothing to do with it. Reproduction is simple biology, not some mysterious miracle. Your fertility rites do no more to facilitate the joining of a sperm with an egg than random sex between any man and any woman does."

Jada and Lucia both glared at Alpha in disbelief. They were true believers in the power of their rituals, or maybe just true believers in their own power. Either way, looking at Alpha, they saw a heretic. A man who would not only strip away the power of the rituals they performed, he would strip away the immense personal power the two women had very carefully acquired over the years.

"The women of Trinidad," Alpha continued, undaunted by the withering looks from Jada and Lucia, "have no such illusions about reproduction." He looked at Luna, whom he had already introduced to the council. "Luna and her people know how precious the seed of men has become. No man's seed, not mine, nor anyone else's can be wasted on a woman who is not ready to produce a child."

James, who had yet to speak up, decided to play devil's advocate. "Is your method always successful at producing a child?" he asked Luna. Alpha knew his father, James, like his mother, thoroughly disapproved of the fertility rites. He also knew that if James didn't ask the question, one of the High Priestesses of sex would.

"No," Luna answered honestly. "Sometimes, even when it is a woman's time, conception fails. I wish I knew why." She looked down at the floor, thinking, *why has it always failed for me?*

Jada pounced at the opportunity. "So, your system doesn't work every time either. Have any of you in Trinidad ever produced a male child?" The question was purely rhetorical since everyone on the council already knew the answer, but Jada and Lucia would never go down without a fight.

Alpha came to Luna's rescue. "You know they haven't, but that doesn't mean they've been any less successful than you."

"This doesn't seem to be getting us anywhere," Angela Montoya stated the obvious with Anna and James, and even Zoe, all nodding in agreement. "I'd like to hear from Yara and Melissa," she said. "How is reproduction practiced where you came from?"

All eyes turned toward the two strangers, who were sitting together off to one side. *Where they come from?* Alpha thought. Angela had introduced the two women that she'd brought with her from Montana, but Alpha had just assumed they were women from Montana who he had never met before. He had wondered earlier why Angela, Lucia, and Zoe brought anyone else with them. Now his curiosity about the two strangers was really piqued.

"Well, we only got to Montana yesterday." It was Melissa, the middle-aged blonde woman, who answered. "But from what I've seen and heard, nothing at all like any of you. Sex has always been pretty much random where I come from. Not exactly like it was back in the before." she smiled, remembering. "In the before, as I'm sure some of you are old enough to remember, a man and a woman just sort of chose each other. People used to fall in love and then have sex. Now, a woman usually decides who she wants to have sex with, and if the man agrees, so be it." She looked pensive for a moment. "Of course, I think love does still enter into it occasionally. But basically, we don't have any rituals or systems. At least we didn't have before the Narmy came, that is."

At the mention of the Narmy, Melissa stopped talking, and a vacant stare came into her eyes, the horrors she'd seen in Marysville momentarily overcoming her once again. Just when everyone thought she wouldn't say any more, she snapped out of it. "I don't have any idea what it's like now. The only women left are probably Narmy women. Jackson said he thinks the Narmy's killing all women now and taking men for sex slaves."

"I'm a virgin," Yara spoke up before Alpha had a chance to ask Melissa who Jackson was and where she was from. Yara's statement really grabbed everyone's attention. The young woman was obviously old enough to have children. How could she still be a virgin?

"That's why I asked Lucia to bring Yara with her," Jada explained. "We believe she may be the one. We believe Yara was sent to us by the Gods to produce a son."

Alpha knew that Jada and Lucia were in constant communication with each other. How else could they coordinate the continuous flow of women back and forth between Montana and Midpark? It took a lot of planning to keep a schedule of who would participate in the fertility rites and when. So he wasn't surprised by their coordinated attempt to subvert the meeting to keep religion front and center in the discussion.

Angela cleared her throat loudly, more to get everyone's attention than anything else. "Based on all we've heard," she said, "I propose that we officially accept Trinidad as part of our community and install Luna as their representative if she agrees. I also propose that we merge our two systems of reproduction. If Luna agrees, she can work with Jada and Lucia to help schedule women for the rituals at each woman's most fertile time. Jada and Lucia can then continue to perform the rites to appease their gods."

*Their gods,* Alpha thought. He had assumed that Angela didn't believe in the rituals any more than he did, but he didn't know for sure - until now. He also could see the wisdom of what she was proposing. It wouldn't totally disrupt the current system by taking away all power from the two sex priestesses, but it would maximize the intermingling of the gene pool. *It still won't be enough,* he thought. *And Yara may be a virgin, but she is not the one.* How he was so sure that Yara would not produce a son, he couldn't say.

The counsel's vote was four to two in favor of adopting Angela's proposals, and Luna agreed to join the council and help schedule the right women at the right time for the sex ritual. *We don't need the religion,* she thought, *but if it saves us from extinction, it's worth it.*

As Luna's first official act as a council member, she asked Yara what seemed like a very simple question. "Is it your time, Yara?"

The question wasn't so simple to Yara. She'd only understood bits and pieces of the entire proceeding. Her mother, Brianna, had taught her enough about reproduction to know the mechanics of the process. And she understood that she and her two sisters had been conceived by sex between her father and her mother. Other than that, she was totally naïve. For all she knew before the meeting, sex between a man and a woman always produced a child. She looked around the room at everyone before answering, "I don't know if it's my time or not, but Charlene said I should do whatever is asked of me."

·····•·•·····

Approaching the Bioengineering Building on what had been the campus of Colorado State University in Fort Collins, Alpha was heartened to see that the area seemed free from the ravages of time and the scavenging of human survivors. As Michelle pulled the APC into the half-moon drive in front of the building, things looked even better. All of the glass that formed the southwest facade was still intact. The glass entrance doors had not even been broken. For all anyone could tell, at least from the outside, the building was just as it had been twenty years ago before the world succumbed to V-1.

Alpha walked right up to the main entrance with his armed guards, Michelle, Misty, and Mandy, in tow. It hadn't been easy for Alpha to convince the council of the need to find the genetic source of their reproduction problem. Anna, Angela, and James, who had all lived as adults in the time before V-1, were the only three who knew anything at all about genetics and genetic engineering. Jada, Lucia, and Zoe had all been young girls who may have heard of DNA but didn't really remember much about it. They had argued that the fertilization rites combined with the new knowledge that Luna brought would surely be all that was necessary to start producing male children. In the end, it was Luna's tie-breaking vote that allowed the council to sanction Alpha's efforts to bring the study of genetics back into the world. That, and Alpha had to acquiesce and agree to rejoin the sex rites. On that front, he did get one major concession, though. With Luna's help, he got Jada to agree that he would be the one to initiate Luna into the rite when it was her time.

*And what about Charlene?* Alpha thought as he walked past the empty guardhouse in front of the biomedical lab. Alpha had thought often about his visions of Charlene in the five days that had passed since the council meeting. Yara and Melissa told the council they'd traveled all the way from Nebraska with a woman named Charlene. It had to be the same woman. Alpha's first instinct on hearing that she was in Montana was to drive to Montana himself. He resisted that temptation. Somehow he was certain, just as he knew that this Charlene was the same woman from his visions, that Charlene would come to him. It was like he and Charlene were moving through some kind of cosmic dance, and each step had to be taken in the proper order. The knowing that he and Charlene would be together in due time was at a level so far below consciousness that it transcended both rationality and intuition. In some ways, the absolute knowing without having a vision to gain the knowledge was stranger than any vision Alpha ever had.

The door was locked, just as Alpha hoped it would be. He was becoming ever more convinced that the fate of humankind was in his hands and in this lab. If he could not sequence DNA to find what had gone wrong with the genetic code and then repair that code, Homo Sapiens was doomed to extinction. Other than two women, that was the only thing that consumed Alpha's thoughts. He was beginning to feel desperate. The feeling that time was running out was growing stronger every day.

"Should I break the glass or try shooting the lock?" Misty asked. Getting into locked buildings by breaking glass windows or doors was common practice for scavenging operations. Seeing that this building had not been broken into is what gave Alpha hope.

"Neither," Alpha replied. "Just wait here."

The three women didn't wait but followed along in guard formation as Alpha walked back to the APC. With a mandate to protect Alpha at any cost, the women weren't about to let him return to the APC without them. After what happened on their last trip down to the city, Alpha was no longer in their circle of trust.

The battery-powered metal cutting hole-saw with the diamond blade made quick work of opening the deadbolt lock, and Alpha recovered the hole with duct tape before even opening the door. The air inside the old building was stale but not musty. There was plenty of light coming through the south wall, which was mostly glass, for Alpha to see clearly as he walked down the hallway. There was also plenty of heat coming through those same windows. As near as Alpha could tell, the building had been left undisturbed and intact. It had also been twenty years since electricity and air-conditioned air flowed through the building.

Alpha didn't waste any more time exploring. He'd seen all that he needed to see. The lab building had been untouched, but it would do no one any good until it had power for the air conditioners, computers, lasers, spectrometers, and other equipment he would need to begin. Even after getting power, the challenges of acquiring or producing the necessary chemicals and mediums were mind-boggling. How could he, one man, accomplish all of that in time? How much time did he have? The growing feeling that he didn't have enough time was overpowering.

"Let's go," Alpha told the three guards, turning around before even reaching the end of the first hallway. The first step was to get back to Midpark to put together a crew to bring electricity back to this old building. Alpha was anxious to return to Midpark for another reason as well.

One that had nothing to do with saving humankind. Well, maybe something to do with it, but he had his doubts. Ritualistic sex was never going to save mankind, but for the first time in a long time, Alpha was looking forward to participating in the fertility rites. It was Luna's time, and Alpha could hardly wait for the ritual to begin. *She's probably already on her way.* Just that thought gave Alpha a thrill. *Maybe we'll even run into each other on the road.* He knew that possibility was extremely remote unless he called her and coordinated their travel. Deciding it best to just let the anticipation build, he climbed back into the APC. As he took his seat, he realized that he didn't feel one-hundred percent well. *Damn, hope I'm not coming down with something,* he thought as he tried to suppress a cough. Michelle, who was driving, was also coughing as she exited the half-moon drive and headed back toward Midpark.

# Chapter 17

S HARING IN THE MATING ritual with Luna was everything Alpha dreamed it would be, and then some. The same could be said for Luna. Alpha and Luna had both mated with others more times than they could remember. Neither had ever experienced the spirituality of true physical love before now. The feeling of togetherness transcended physicality itself. Lying in each other's arms, they were transported, if only for a moment, to a state of being that was beyond the confines of both time and space.

"Bless this union that it might bear fruit, that from Alpha's loins, a son will be given to Luna. So mote it be." As Jada spoke the last words of the ritual, Alpha didn't want it to end. That Jada was even there annoyed him immensely, and the words, modeled on some ancient pagan tradition, seemed offensive in a way they never had before. What he had just shared with Luna should have been private. It should not have been part of any ritual.

"I don't want you to go, Alpha," Luna whispered quietly in his ear. "I know you must. I am to mate with two more men tonight, and I know you must share with another woman." She sniffled quietly as she said it.

Alpha, hearing Luna sniffle, opened his eyes, mistakenly thinking she must be crying. Instead, her face was beaming with a radiant smile. Soaking in the emotions, he could do nothing but smile back. "Sometimes, I wish we lived in the before," he said.

"Why?" The question was in her eyes as much as on her lips. Luna didn't know much about the before. She'd read enough to know a little about the time before she was born, but she didn't have Alpha's gift for speed reading. Reading a few books and magazines was nothing like the thousands and thousands of books that Alpha had devoured in his lifetime.

"Sometimes in the before," Alpha started to say before Jada interrupted, shattering the moment. "Alpha, you must go."

For Jada, the logistics of performing the ritual as many times with as many different participants as possible every night was bad enough, without having Alpha hanging around after he had so obviously already performed his function. He'd already taken much longer to plant his seed than seemed at all necessary.

"Luna must be cleansed, and you must shower and get down to room four." Jada had a brief coughing fit before she could continue, "Carlita is already waiting for you."

*Is everybody catching some kind of summer cold, or what?* Alpha thought. His own cough had mostly gone away, but it seemed like the majority of people around him were either coughing, sniffling, sneezing, or all three. Before crawling off the bed, Alpha annoyed Jada even more by embracing Luna tightly as they shared a deep kiss. Kissing was not, and never had been, a part of the fertility ritual. Alpha enjoyed getting under Jada's skin, but he didn't enjoy it nearly as much as he enjoyed the embrace and the kiss, the feeling of complete connection that he now shared with Luna.

"Get out!" Jada shouted, which brought on another bout of coughing.

Luna had to laugh. "Go," she said softly. "We will share again, I promise."

Alpha slipped into the sacred robe that the two young attendants were holding for him. Both of the attendants wore looks of impatience and disapproval on their faces. *These two might be priestesses someday,* he thought as he stepped out of the sacred room and headed down the hall to his own changing room. Alpha knew this "Fertility Temple" had once been a simple hotel back in the before, but you would never know it by the pentacles and other sacred symbols that decorated the place now. He thought about how different the world was now than before he was born. It was hard to imagine a world with so many people. He was still thinking about those differences as he toweled off from his shower and prepared to participate in the ritual once again. He wasn't looking forward to it at all this time. This time, he would merely be performing his duty.

His second performance of the evening was scheduled with one of the lesser priestesses presiding. Jada, the high priestess, would preside over all three of Luna's ceremonies. Alpha knew intellectually, as he walked down the long hallway, thinking about Luna, that he was jealous. It was an emotion that he had never experienced before. He didn't want to have sex with another woman, and even more, he didn't want Luna to have sex with another man. Let alone two other men tonight and at least three more in Montana tomorrow night. Knowing that what he was feeling was something he'd only read about before didn't make the feelings any less real. Knowing the absolute necessity of expanding the gene pool as much as possible also did nothing to counteract his emotions. It took an extreme effort of will for him to enter the next sacred chamber that used to be nothing more than a room in a hotel. *There were probably more babies conceived in this room back then than there are now,* he thought bitterly, as he walked through the door.

·····•·•····

The following morning, Alpha didn't even want to get out of bed. He was still despondent over last night. It was strange to realize that, after all this time, what he'd felt last night with Luna was a kind of love he had never felt before. Love in the old-fashioned sense of the word that until now, he'd never understood. Having read a lot about love but never experiencing it, Alpha had assumed that love could only exist in the time before the old world ended. Or that kind of love could only be experienced by those who grew up in the before. He knew that James and Anna shared a love something like this, but he always thought his parents had been able to bring their love with them from that earlier time. *It's more than that,* he thought. *What Luna and I share is not the same. My parents share love; what do Luna and I share?*

As he lay in bed thinking that Luna was probably already on her way to Montana, he wished procreation could spring from love instead of from some ritualistic sex act. *Maybe someday it will,* he thought. *But not if we all just die out and disappear forever.*

That was the thought that finally convinced him to get out of bed. There was an incredible amount of work to do if he was going to save the human race. A good crew had been selected to help Alpha resurrect the biomedical lab. Dave

Ortiz, James, Anna, and a whole group of volunteers, would be arriving shortly. It would take Dave all day to get his crane down to Fort Collins, but the rest of the group could do a lot of the planning and scavenging of supplies they'd need in the meantime. If genetic engineering was the only way to save mankind, rebuilding and rejuvenating the old lab in Fort Collins was the only way Alpha could think of to make that happen.

·····•·•·····

One vehicle was already sitting at the charge station in Rawlins. The old Tesla was plugged in at one of the chargers. Rose, who was driving the Kia Niro to Montana, parked next to the Tesla and plugged in the Niro. Unlike Rose and the other three women with them, the scenery was all new to Luna. Before this trip, she had never been farther north than the dead city of Boulder. The country between Midpark and Rawlins was so empty that it seemed frightening. It reminded Luna of the area south of Trinidad. The charging station in Rawlins was a welcome oasis in the vast emptiness that they'd just traveled through.

Luna and the four women from Midpark were all scheduled for tonight's fertility rites in Montana. Only Luna had already been through the ritual last night in Granby. Allowing a woman the opportunity to mate with six different men was unheard of. Being allowed the opportunity to mate with more than one was an extraordinary honor. Rose and the rest of Luna's companions were all exceedingly jealous of the special privileges that had been bestowed on this stranger from Trinidad.

For her part, Luna didn't feel privileged or special at all. What she felt was empty. As empty as the land around her. It was an emptiness that she'd never felt before. It was an emptiness that couldn't be filled by mating with three men, or six men, or a hundred. *Does he feel the same,* she wondered? Luna couldn't get Alpha out of her thoughts any more than she could stop feeling how empty it was without him.

"They're awfully early," Rose said, apparently referring to whoever was driving the old Tesla. "Maybe they think if they get to Midpark early enough, they'll be able to get some on the side."

"Fat chance," Juliet laughed. "Like Jada's going to allow anyone more than one chance at a time." The laughter in the car led to coughing. *They sure seem to be coughing a lot,* Luna thought.

Realizing her mistake as soon as she said it, Juliet looked at Luna and asked the question that none of the others had dared to ask, "Why you? Why do you get all the men you want when we're lucky to even get one?"

A sad smile played across Luna's lips before she answered, "I don't want any. I don't even want to be here."

The look of incomprehension on the faces of the other four women told Luna there was zero chance that any of them had ever felt like she was feeling right now.

Slowly, the expression on Rose's face changed, the dawning of a new thought. "You like women," she said, half questioning, half stating the only reason she could think of for Luna not to want to participate in the fertility rites.

Luna burst into laughter. She couldn't help herself. "I do like women," she said, getting herself under control, "but not like that. It's just...it's just..." how could she explain to Rose what she didn't understand herself? "Oh, never mind.

I need to use the restroom." The other women had already explained to Luna that this charge station in Rawlins was equipped with a lounge where they could wait in comfort for the old Niro to charge up.

Most of the shelving inside the old station that had once held snacks and supplies for travelers had been removed, opening up a sizeable space that had been converted into a waiting lounge. The shelves had been replaced with comfortable chairs and a couple of sofas. There were even a couple of beds in opposite corners of the open space. With an electric range and microwave in one corner, along with a small well-stocked pantry and plenty of other food in the old glass-fronted cooler, a few people could easily survive in the station for quite a while if they had to.

Today, instead of the expected carload of women headed to Midpark, there were only two women in the lounge. One was sitting in one of the recliners, impatiently tapping one foot on the floor and her fingers on the arms of the chair. The other one was lying on one of the beds. She was wearing nothing but her panties, and seemed to be sweating and shivering at the same time. The visibly sick woman on the bed was quite a bit older than everyone else, maybe in her fifties or sixties. Luna's attention was immediately drawn from the sick old lady to the younger woman sitting in the chair anxiously tapping away.

The younger woman was probably about the same age as Luna, maybe a year or two older. She had long wavy black hair and a dark olive complexion. Luna felt an instant attraction to this woman she'd never felt before. Not a sexual attraction, but something that could never be explained, just felt. It was as if she already knew the other woman. Like, somehow, she'd always known her.

Charlene watched the five women get out of the old SUV and plug it in before they walked across the lot toward her. She'd been sitting in the chair much longer than she wanted to, waiting for the Tesla to charge. She needed to get Kahina to a doctor. Nothing she had tried had done any good at all, and she was absolutely sure that Kahina would die if the doctor she'd heard about in Midpark was unable to help. Melissa had died late last night after being just like Kahina was now. Angela had told Charlene there were no doctors in Montana, but there was an old man called Dr. Ming in Midpark who might be able to help. Angela told Charlene that Dr. Ming might be the oldest man alive, but if anybody could help Kahina, it would be him.

There was something about one of the women that walked into the old station. Charlene hardly looked at the other four as they came through the door but was immediately drawn to the young woman bringing up the rear. About her own age, maybe a year or two younger, a feeling, an unexplained, inexplicable feeling of familiarity, hit Charlene as she watched Luna walk into the room.

Charlene stood up. As she and Luna made eye contact, it was like some kind of ancient connection was restored. Charlene barely heard the first woman say, "Hi, I'm Rose," as she walked right past the woman's outstretched hand and embraced Luna. Rose and her companions stood dumbfounded as Charlene and Luna just held each other locked in that silent embrace.

"I'm Charlene," seemed like such an unimportant thing to say, but it was the first words that Charlene spoke to Luna.

"And I'm Luna," Luna replied, as the two women looked into each other's tear-filled eyes.

"How?" Charlene asked. "Why?" Luna said at the same time. Both women laughed. Both were filled with pure joy. Both were crying; the immense joy of just being together was overwhelming. Charlene and Luna both felt as though they were reunited after a long time apart, not like this was the first time they'd ever met.

"Do you two know each other?" Rose asked, thinking maybe this was the woman that Luna preferred to men.

Luna and Charlene both laughed while Rose and the others wondered what was so funny. Finally, Charlene turned and introduced herself to the rest of the group without even trying to offer an explanation. What would she say? How does one explain magic, or destiny, or whatever it was that just happened?

Charlene led Luna over to the bed in the far corner of the room and introduced her to Kahina. It seemed important, somehow, for Kahina to know Luna, even though, on the surface, Charlene herself didn't really know Luna at all. "We'll get you to the doctor soon," Charlene told Kahina and asked her if she needed a blanket or anything. Kahina was shivering so hard that her teeth were chattering, but she shook her head no.

The other four women had settled into the comfortable chairs and watched as Charlene and Luna walked over to the bed in the other corner of the room, about as far away as they could get from everyone else. By then, Rose and the other three fully expected to see Luna and Charlene climb into bed together. They were slightly disappointed when the two sat down on the edge of the bed and just held each other's hands while talking.

It was an epiphany, not a vision, a knowing without understanding how she knew, as Charlene looked into Luna's eyes. "You've been with Alpha," Charlene said. It wasn't a question or an accusation. It was just a statement of fact. Luna shook her head yes and didn't even wonder how Charlene knew. It didn't matter how she knew or that she knew about her mating with Alpha. It didn't even matter that Charlene had the same feelings for Alpha as she did.

"We don't have much time," Charlene continued. "I have to get Kahina to Midpark, and you have to get to Jackson."

"Who is Jackson?" Luna asked and wondered how she knew Jackson was a person, not a place.

"You'll know. He's probably on your mating schedule, but it doesn't matter either way. You'll know Jackson the same way you knew me, the same way you knew Alpha. Somehow, we're all connected."

Suddenly, Luna had her own flash of absolute knowing, and it hurt her to say, "Kahina won't make it."

"I know," Charlene said, and a wave of sorrow washed over both of them.

"Bring Jackson to Midpark," Charlene said as she stood up. "The time has come for the four of us to be together."

# PART THREE

# Chapter 18

O THER THAN THE FOUR women coughing, which seemed to be getting worse, it was a mostly quiet drive all the way to Montana. It had taken most of the day to drive from Midpark. For Luna, so much more had changed than just the passage of time. It wasn't just the change from morning to night or from one place to another. It was a completely different world when Luna stepped out of the Niro in Montana than it had been when she got in. Not just a different world; it was like entering another place in time. She could no more comprehend how that chance meeting with Charlene in Rawlins had so changed her life than she could understand the rhythms of the universe. *It just is, and always shall be.* The thought seemingly from nowhere sent a shiver up her spine.

The old hotel that had been converted into a fertility chapel was not in Park City but in what had once been the town of Laurel. Just as Granby had become the community center for all of Midpark, Laurel was now the center of the Montana community. Luna couldn't help but notice how much the fertility chapel here in Laurel resembled the one in Granby. A lot of effort had been expended, ensuring that the chapels were nearly identical. Both buildings had the same large pentagram over the entrance and the same three black crosses out front. Luna knew nothing of the ancient history of the pentagram symbols scattered liberally throughout the two old hotels, which had been converted into fertility chapels. She didn't even know the story of the three black crosses borrowed from the Modern Times Church. Luna knew only that her destiny was tied to this building in Montana and a man whom she'd yet to meet. A man named Jackson.

Rose had driven straight here from the second charging station they'd stopped at in the old town of Thermopolis. The closer they got to Montana, the more anxious the women seemed to be, the anticipation increasing with every passing mile. Luna felt that increasing anticipation as much as any of the rest, but not for the same reason. For Rose and the other three, this would be their only opportunity to mate for at least a month, probably much longer. Luna, though, had experienced that same anticipation of mating yesterday when she'd traveled from Trinidad to Midpark. Then, she was looking forward to mating with just one man, Alpha. Now, Luna found herself filled with as much anticipation as she'd ever felt before, but she wasn't looking forward to the fertility rites in general, as much as she was looking forward to a meeting. A meeting as momentous as the one she'd had with Charlene. Before meeting Charlene in Rawlins, Luna had been dreading tonight's activities. Now, unlike the others, it wasn't the sex she was anticipating. Luna may have come to Montana with Rose and the others, but it was fate that brought her here. Fate had brought her to this time and place to meet someone she'd never met before. A man who she knew was as inextricably linked to her as Charlene and Alpha.

·····•··•·····

As he undressed, showered, and donned the sacred white robe, Jackson couldn't stop thinking about how he'd come to be at this place and time. Thinking back on his life, nothing about his early childhood or even his life in Sedalia could have prepared him for the past year. When Elena and Nora were killed by the Narmy in Sedalia, he had wanted to die, too. But something always kept him going, pushing him to escape from the Narmy, driving him in a relentless search for some unknown destiny. For as long as he could remember, Jackson had felt that some special destiny awaited him. Even as a young boy, he'd felt different from others. In some ways, his entire life had been spent in search of a future that was inevitable. Just over a month ago, when he first laid eyes on Charlene, he knew his search was over. He knew in the first instant of meeting her that Charlene was the destiny he'd been seeking.

*She isn't, though.* The thought startled him. *Charlene is just a part of it.* The feelings Jackson had for Charlene were like nothing he'd ever known. He felt connected. Connected in a way that transcended time and space. It was as though they had always been together. *There are others, but where? Not where, when?* These random thoughts from nowhere had been rattling around in Jackson's head all day.

Jackson had known Montana was not the where as soon as they got out of the APC. It may not have been his destiny, but it had seemed to be Kahina's. The way she had embraced Angela Montoya, you'd have thought they were lovers instead of just two women who'd worked together in the before. *And now she's dying, just like Melissa. Maybe death is the only destiny that counts.*

The sound of the chime interrupted Jackson's thoughts. *Time for tonight's first performance.* That was how he'd come to view these nightly rituals. They weren't so much mating or sex; they were simply a performance. It seemed odd that these rituals, which were meant to bring about human life, made him feel so much less human.

·····•·····

Having participated three times last night, the ritual didn't seem quite as strange as it had that first time. Still, that first time with Alpha was so unlike anything Luna had ever experienced that she could hardly remember anything at all about the other two men. Now, she found herself thoroughly enjoying the feeling of sensual pleasure as her two attendants massaged the sacred oils into her skin. As the ritual demanded, she had her eyes closed, letting the anticipation of opening them to see Jackson for the first time build, along with the sexual tension that was about to explode.

Lucia's coughing her way through the incantation would have been a distraction for Jackson, but he was transfixed by the young woman who was receiving the two attendants' ministrations. This was Jackson's third night in a row of "sharing" in the strange fertility and mating ritual, but nothing from the previous encounters prepared him for all he was feeling now. In his rational mind, Jackson knew he'd never seen this woman before, yet he knew her. Somewhere beyond the realm of reason, where only feeling exists, Jackson knew the woman on the fertility alter more intimately than he had ever known anyone, even Charlene.

Nearly a week had passed since Jackson, Charlene, Kahina, and the others had followed Scarlett from Rawlins to Montana. For Jackson, the past week was mostly just a blur. The people and the customs were so different from those back where he'd come from that strangeness was now normal. Unlike Charlene, he had been unable to accept anything about this new normal at first. Even as Charlene took part in her first fertility rite on their second night in Montana, Jackson refused to "share" his seed. He had no desire to share with anyone but Charlene, and he was jealous and angry when she took part in that first ritual. "But you must," Charlene had told him. "It's the reason we're here. Everything, our whole lives, led to this place and time. We can no more refuse our fate than we can refuse to breathe."

Jackson had argued then. He remembered telling Charlene that he didn't believe in fate, that the only reason he was with these strange people in Montana was because she had led him here. Charlene had just smiled and told him, "You will, Jackson. When we find the others, you'll know."

And now, as the two attendants stepped back, Jackson took his place in the ritual. Luna opened her eyes, and in that instant, Jackson did know. "Jackson," she said simply, as their bodies and souls joined. "Luna," he answered, though no one had told him her name.

"What are you doing?" Lucia demanded, between coughing fits.

Luna and Jackson were oblivious. They were lying together in another world, lost in each other's eyes. Lucia's protestations were no more meaningful than the hacking coughs of the two attendants, who were standing by, wondering what to do. Nothing like this had ever happened before. The ritual was done, had been done for several minutes. Why were the participants still lying in each other's arms, saying absolutely nothing, not to them, not even to each other? They were just lying there staring at each other.

"The others are waiting." Lucia was flabbergasted. "Jackson! You must leave. Now!" The effort bent her over in a coughing fit totally unbecoming to the High Priestess. Straightening up and seeing the two still unmoving on the bed, she begged Luna, "Please, Luna, you must be bathed to prepare for the next man."

Luna finally broke her gaze away from Jackson's ice-blue eyes and turned to look at the High Priestess. "There's no need for another man," she said. "In nine months, I will bear the fruit of Jackson's seed." The words were spoken calmly, a simple statement of fact. Then Luna turned away from Lucia. "Come, Jackson, it's time for us to go."

Jackson and Luna walked right past the two attendants holding the sacred robe. Luna grabbed her clothes from the old hotel bathroom, and together they walked naked down the hall to Jackson's room. The sounds of Lucia's and the attendant's coughing echoed down the hallway behind them until Jackson closed the door to his room and turned the deadbolt lock. Luna dropped her clothes to the floor. Jackson took her by the hand and led her to the unused bed in his room. Luna knew another round of sex wasn't necessary to make her pregnant, but she could never get enough of the spiritual bond she felt with Jackson inside her. Not just physically inside her, but inside her spiritually, inside her in every way possible. They were joined together in a way that neither wanted to end, in a way that both knew was eternal. There was no beginning and never an end. Jackson and Luna had always been, and forever would be, together.

·····•·•····

Luna woke before Jackson. Her whole world had changed since she left Trinidad. *Was it only three days ago? Could so much change in such a short time?* She lay there quietly watching Jackson sleep, thinking about everything and nothing at all. It was totally quiet in the old hotel. *There is probably no one here but the two of us. I mean the three of us. Our son is already beginning to grow.* The knowledge she would have a son, the first baby boy to be born in her lifetime, should have been overwhelming, but it was simply meant to be. She pondered how much in life was fate. Looking back over her life's journey, so much of that journey had always inevitably led to this place and time, to this joining with Jackson that was always meant to be.

Jackson opened his eyes, and she was still there with him. It was too good to be true, but it had always been true. *We are one. Joined by fate. We've been joined since entering this world. We just didn't know until now.* The thought filled him with contentment. The world was as it should be. The world had always been, and always would be, as it should. He wrapped his arms around Luna and held her as close as he could.

She felt her skin against his. Felt their bodies melding together once more. She felt the union of their bodies matching the union of their souls, and for a brief moment that may have been forever, she was transported beyond the realm of time and space.

Luna was still in the bathroom getting dressed. Jackson heard the footsteps coming down the hall and someone coughing before the person banged loudly on the door. "Jackson?" it wasn't Lucia's voice, but whoever it was, they were coughing as hard as she had been last night, maybe even harder. After the coughing fit subsided, the woman pounded on the door again. "Jackson, it's Angela. Please..." Jackson pulled the door open to see a woman he didn't know start to pound the air where the door had been.

The woman outside the door looked terrible. Her skin was pale and sweaty, but she was visibly shivering between fits of coughing. Luna came out of the bathroom just as Jackson opened the door, took one look at the woman, and knew that she was suffering from the same sickness as Kahina.

"She's sick, Jackson. Angela's sick" The woman got out between coughing fits. "Everyone's sick, or, or dead. Please, Angela's asking for you."

*We brought this. I brought this.* The thought struck Jackson like a thunderbolt. He was overwhelmed by guilt as he and Luna followed the coughing woman down the hall and then down the stairs to the ground floor. *It was Robin. It was contagious. Whatever it was, we brought it here. Me and Melissa.* At some level, he'd known since Melissa and Kahina both got sick that it was the same disease that Robin died of back in Marysville, but he'd refused to accept it until now. It was too terrible. How could one live with the knowledge they were responsible for turning a terrible plague loose on innocent people? *And Luna...Luna, and Charlene both!* He looked at Luna walking beside him. She didn't seem sick at all. *And what about me? Why am I not sick?*

Luna was surprised when the woman they were following didn't go out through the fertility chapel's main entrance but instead led them through a door behind the old hotel reception desk. What had once been the management offices for the hotel had been transformed into living quarters. Neither Luna nor Jackson had any idea that this is where Colonel Angela Montoya lived. The poor woman who'd brought them here pointed to another door and said, "In there," before collapsing on the sofa.

Angela was lying on the bed and looked to be in worse shape than the woman out in the living room. She was shivering uncontrollably and had a hard time talking through her chattering teeth. "They're dead, Jackson. I think they're all dead."

"Who's dead?" he asked, fearing the worst news possible. *Had he killed Charlene? Would Luna be next?*

"All of them. The Narmy back down south...New Dixie...the radio...think they're dead...not on the radio..."

*She's delirious.* The thought was followed immediately by the memory of how the Narmy used old ham radios to communicate.

"Do you have a radio?" Jackson asked.

Angela was fading fast. It was all too apparent that she was on the verge of death. "Not on the radio," she managed to say. "Been four days now...they're not on the radio anymore."

Those were the last words Colonel Angela Montoya would ever speak. Jackson looked at the dead woman lying on the bed, trying to make sense of what she'd said. Somehow, somewhere, Angela, or someone here in Montana, must have been monitoring the Narmy's radio traffic. *What does it mean? What if it kills everybody?* The guilt that Jackson had been feeling was replaced by fear, by a terrifying realization. The disease that he'd first seen in Robin back at the Abernathy Dairy in Marysville seemed to be killing everyone who was exposed to it. *Why not me?* He looked at Luna, and fear gripped him anew. *Have I exposed her, too?"*

Luna seemed oblivious to any concerns for her health, or his for that matter. "We need to get back to Midpark," was all she said.

# Chapter 19

J AMES HADN'T THOUGHT HE would ever return to his childhood home in Castle Pines, but here he was back at the old Mendez Estate once again. The buildings seemed remarkably unchanged, considering the place had been abandoned more than twenty years ago. Unlike the house, the car barn, and other buildings, the estate's grounds were nothing at all like they had been before. James could still visualize the lush manicured greenery that used to be so inviting. The green had been gone for a long time now. Even the tumbleweeds that had completely taken over were dry and brown. James couldn't remember there being any tumbleweeds in town at all when he was young, and the ones out in the country would have still been green in the middle of June. Not like the dry brown weeds that now covered most of the estate. Tumbleweeds were piled up against fences and buildings, anyplace the wind could deposit them. A never-ending supply of the thorny weeds was tumbling and blowing on gale-force winds even as James tried to clear the front veranda of his childhood home. *Who would have ever thought the big winner from climate change would be the tumbleweed?* he thought. He pulled the last of those piled up on the front veranda away from the railing and threw them up and out into the wind. They would either be blown all the way to Kansas or deposited in the massive pile bunched up against the perimeter wall. *I don't remember the wind ever blowing this hard, either,* he thought.

Leaning hard into the wind to keep his balance as he made his way to the mechanical building out by the car barn, a strange random thought stuck in his mind. It was like an earworm of a single line from a song or poem. James knew he had never heard the line before, but there it was playing over and over in his mind, *battered by apocalyptic winds.* There was something chilling about the thought, but not the wind. It was so hot the apocalyptic wind made it feel like he was walking through a blast furnace.

"The PV panels are only putting out about seventy percent," James heard Anna tell Alpha as he got closer to the mechanical building, "but the batteries seem to be fine."

As James walked in through the open overhead door, he heard Anna cough before she added, "Not too sure about me, though. This cough seemed to just come out of nowhere."

"Maybe it's the tumbleweeds," James heard Alpha reply. "Maybe you're allergic to them."

Anna and Alpha were both studying the control panels. James had to suppress a cough of his own before asking Anna, "So, you still think we should take up residence here?" It was a continuation of the discussion they'd been having since yesterday. When they'd first discussed it before leaving Midpark, Alpha wanted to find someplace closer to the lab in Fort Collins. Anna thought it would take too much time to find and rejuvenate a suitable home away from home in Fort Collins. She argued that the old Mendez place was perfect for their needs and just over an hour away from the lab.

"I do still think we should make this our base of operations," Anna said. "Especially now that I know the electrical system is okay."

"But if the system is only at seventy percent," James asked, "is that enough?"

"More than enough. The PV panels are the only components at seventy, and the entire system was oversized by design. What really amazes me is that the batteries are in such good shape. Sure is a good thing we didn't restart the system last time we were here." Anna looked at James and smiled, remembering that first trip down from the mountains with him so long ago. "If we had, the batteries probably would have already failed, and it wouldn't be this easy to restart the system now." Anna reached over and flipped a GFCI breaker, and the electrical system sprang to life. "Kind of amazing, isn't it, how one flipped switch allowed the batteries to lie dormant for all these years."

"One flipped switch is all it takes," Alpha said. He was thinking about another kind of switch, though. "One flipped switch in the genetic sequence," he mused aloud. "Just one can mean the difference between life and death." He wanted desperately to get to work on the lab in Fort Collins, and here they were stuck at his grandfather's old estate in Castle Pines. He understood the necessity of providing living arrangements for those who would help resurrect the biomedical lab in Fort Collins, but he hated the delay. "What about water?" Alpha asked. "Electricity is one thing, but we can't live here without water."

"Dave will take care of the water; you can count on that," James said before coughing again. "Maybe I'm allergic to tumbleweeds, too," he added.

"Okay, okay. I give already," Alpha said, throwing up his hands and laughing. "We can live here and commute to Fort Collins. So, let's finish whatever we have to do to get ready and start commuting. We've wasted enough time here already."

·····•·····

Dr. Ming looked up when Lisa and a young woman he'd never seen before wheeled another woman he'd never seen through the swinging door from the reception area. He was seated at his desk looking at old records that hadn't been out of his file cabinet for a good twenty years.

Lisa introduced Charlene as Dr. Ming helped the two women get Kahina from the wheelchair to the examination table. Actually, Dr. Ming wasn't that much help. At eighty-seven years old, physical strength was no longer one of his greatest assets. Not only that, he didn't feel well himself. What had started out last night as a slight cough was getting worse as the day went on. He'd considered just going home at lunchtime, but then Jada had come to the clinic with a much worse cough than his own.

Jada was still in one of the other examination rooms. She not only had a cough but a fever as well. Dr. Ming had never approved of Jada and her so-called fertility rituals, but he, perhaps more than anyone, understood the desperate nature of the need to produce male babies. If Jada's methods could produce another Alpha, he was all for it.

Jada had walked into the clinic about an hour ago. Her arrogance was on full display as she demanded that Dr. Ming make her well before tonight's fertility rites. What really troubled Dr. Ming wasn't Jada's attitude, though; it was her symptoms. Not only was Jada's cough worse than his own, but she also had a high fever. This from a woman that he'd never known to be sick before now.

The files that Dr. Ming was studying when Charlene and Kahina arrived were his old records from back when V-1 had ravaged the world. He was troubled by the similarity between Jada's symptoms and the symptoms he'd seen in those infected with V-1. It wasn't just the cough and the fever; those could be symptoms of many things. It was more the rapid onset and the speed at which the symptoms worsened that worried Dr. Ming. Now, seeing Kahina in a coma and near death and not even needing a thermometer to feel the fever that was burning her up inside, Dr. Ming knew his worst fears were being realized. Somehow, after a twenty-year hiatus, V-1, or something eerily similar, was back.

As he performed a cursory examination of Kahina that he knew was totally unnecessary, Dr. Ming felt helpless and overwhelmed by despair. The sounds of Jada coughing from the other room were getting worse. He could feel his own cough becoming more persistent, and he knew that he would not be among the survivors this time. If there were any survivors, this time. The thought that he probably had no more than one or two days left to live was hard enough, but he was filled with profound sadness by the realization that this time, the entire human race might not survive. A few days or months, or even a few more years, didn't make that much difference to a tired old doctor, but the thought that Homo Sapiens might be on the verge of extinction was nearly unbearable. Hearing Kahina's heart beat one last time, then stop, put an exclamation point on Dr. Ming's diagnosis.

He turned to Charlene. "I'm sorry," he said as he pulled the stethoscope out of his ears. How many times had he uttered those same two words over the course of a career that spanned more than half a century? The words had never been as true as they were right now. His sorrow was nearly unbearable.

Lisa coughed, and Dr. Ming and Charlene both looked at his chosen replacement. Lisa was crying and coughing at the same time. Unlike Charlene, Lisa was old enough to remember the symptoms of V-1. Middle-aged now, she had once been a survivor herself. Like Dr. Ming, she could feel the effects of V-1 coming on, but it was different this time. Twenty years ago, V-1 had barely affected her at all. Like everyone who lived through that great dying, she had somehow been immune. She was not immune this time; she could feel it in her bones. Lisa knew that this time she would suffer the same fate as the stranger who'd just died on the examination table.

"I know there was nothing you could do," Charlene said, seemingly to both of them. "I've known since before we left Montana that Kahina would not survive. But I had to try. After everything she's done for me, I just had to try. I'm sorry for bringing her here."

Dr. Ming really looked at Charlene for the first time. She didn't seem to have any symptoms at all. As a matter of fact, she radiated good health. He felt a glimmer of hope. Maybe some would be immune once again. But would it be enough? The faint hope faded a little as he had the thought that not enough people had survived the first time. Not enough to assure the continuation of the human race. That wasn't exactly right. Lack of survivors wasn't the problem before. It was something genetic that had changed. Dr. Ming knew this, just as surely as Alpha did, but, like Alpha, he didn't know what part of the human genome had failed. He didn't know why, out of all the babies he'd delivered over the past twenty-two years, only Alpha had been born a boy.

"How long have you been with her?" Dr. Ming was back to wondering if Charlene really was immune or if she had just recently been exposed to the virus.

"Forever." Charlene actually smiled at the old doctor. "Kahina has been with me forever."

············

Alpha watched the little two-place airplane roll to a stop. Dave had dropped the crane off yesterday evening, and Liz had flown the small electric airplane down from Frisco to pick him up. Alpha and the rest of the crew had all stayed at Castle Pines last night. Yesterday, day one of the lab rejuvenation project, had been all about living arrangements for the crew. It was too far to commute from Midpark to Fort Collins every day and still have time to get any work done on the lab. So, yesterday, while Dave Ortiz was driving his crane all the way from Frisco, the rest of the Midpark crew had spent most of the day rejuvenating the old Mendez estate instead of the biomedical lab.

Alpha had never seen the old Mendez estate in Castle Pines until yesterday, but he knew of it. James and Anna had mentioned it more than a few times while he was growing up. Just as Anna had promised, the estate was almost perfect for their needs. If it only had water and was just a little closer, it would have been perfect. As it was, the commute from the estate to Fort Collins and back would use up over two hours every day. But, having everything they needed, including charging capabilities for all of their vehicles, was worth the commute.

Getting running water to the place was on today's agenda. "Did it once. I can do it again," is what Dave had said when they told him the plan. Dave's plan to get water to the Mendez estate involved using his crane, so the first thing on today's agenda was to get the crane from Fort Collins back down to Denver, where they should have taken it in the first place. The only thing Dave had accomplished with the crane yesterday was the clearing of a runway at the Northern Colorado Regional Airport. He and Liz did plan to commute daily from Midpark. That wouldn't be a problem for them. Using Liz's little Sonex plane, it would take less time than commuting from Castle Pines by car. Alpha hated the delays in getting the biomedical lab up and running, but it couldn't be helped. The crew would definitely need water wherever they decided to stay.

"How was the flight?" Alpha asked. Somewhere in all of the reading he'd done over the years, he'd come across the first question invariably asked of air travelers back when air travel was commonplace.

"Great!" Dave replied. You should try it sometime.

*Maybe I should.* Dave and Liz had tried to talk Alpha into flying many times. He wasn't really sure why he always resisted, other than the fact that it was forbidden by Anna.

"Where's Liz?" For some reason, the fact that Dave had arrived without Liz gave Alpha a sense of foreboding.

Dave started coughing and seemed to have a hard time stopping before answering. "She's under the weather. Decided to stay home and see if she can kick whatever it is." He coughed some more. "Maybe I should have stayed home, too."

"You sure you're okay?" Dave didn't sound okay at all.

"I'll be alright, let's go," he managed to get out before another coughing fit took hold.

Alpha was hesitant. He'd left the Mendez Estate before anyone else was up so he could get to the airport in Fort Collins in time to pick up Dave and Liz. At least, that's the story he had planned for his overprotective mother. In truth, he'd secretly slipped out before anyone else was up on purpose. It wasn't often that he had the chance to be out on his own without a trio of armed guardians. Besides, he wanted to let everyone get some extra rest. It seemed like everyone that spent last night at the Mendez Estate was coming down with something. Dave and Liz, too. Alpha remembered that both of them had already been coughing yesterday.

Seeing how much worse Dave's cough had gotten overnight, he wondered how sick James and Anna and the rest of the crew back at Castle Pines were. They were all coughing a lot before going to bed last night.

With a feeling of unease growing stronger, Alpha was tempted to just get back to Castle Pines as soon as he could, but Dave talked him out of it. "Take me to my crane, then you can head back. I still know the way."

Seeing how difficult it was for Dave to climb up into the cab of his crane, Alpha didn't feel like he could just leave him behind. He was gripped by indecision: indecision and a growing unknown fear. Not wanting to just leave him behind, Alpha decided to keep Dave and the crane in sight in his rearview mirror for at least a few miles. Going slow enough to keep the crane in view wasn't easy, though. Driving down a wide-open highway at a mere thirty miles an hour was just about more than Alpha could take. He was becoming more and more concerned about the health of those back at Castle Pines.

They had barely made it past Loveland when Alpha's com started ringing. It was Anna onscreen as he pulled the com out of his pocket. She didn't look at all well and had a coughing fit before asking, "Where are you?"

"You don't look good, Mom. Are you okay?"

"We're going back to Midpark," Anna managed, neither one of them answering each other's questions. "All of us..." another bout of coughing, then, "you better come, too."

Glancing up from the com to look in the rearview mirror, fear became terror as Alpha watched the crane behind him leave the interstate and nosedive into a dry creek bed.

Making a fast U-turn in the middle of the old interstate and rushing back to the crane wreck, Alpha glanced back at his com. The screen had gone black. Ignoring the fact that his mother had just hung up on him, Alpha jumped out of the Tesla he'd chosen from the Mendez car barn and scrambled down into the dry creek bed.

The crane was standing nearly vertically on its nose with the end of the boom buried deep in the sandy bottom of the old creek. It had broken loose from the trailer-full of PV panels and batteries. The trailer had stayed on the bank above.

Dave half fell and half crawled out of the cab just as Alpha ran up to help him. He was on his hands and knees in the bottom of the wash, seemingly uninjured but coughing uncontrollably. Alpha knelt beside him and placed a hand on his back, not sure what to do. Finally, the coughing stopped, and Dave turned his head to look up at Alpha. "Good thing I always wear a seat belt," he said, before another coughing fit took hold.

After several unsuccessful tries, Alpha finally got Anna to answer her com. They weren't having much of a conversation, though. Mostly, Alpha was treated to a chorus of coughing from his com's speaker, with Dave joining in from the backseat of the Tesla. He was flying down what was left of I-25 much faster than he should have been, considering the pavement's deteriorated state. Dodging potholes the size of washtubs wasn't easy at seventy or eighty miles an hour.

"Dr. Ming," he heard Anna get out between coughing fits. "Get to Dr. Ming's." The com went silent, and the coughing chorus turned into a solo. Alpha adjusted the rearview mirror to look at Dave stretched out in the back. He was not only coughing; he was sweating and shivering at the same time.

*What is it?* Alpha thought as he dodged a massive hole in the crumbling pavement. He wondered if Dr. Ming would have a cure for whatever "it" was. At the same time, he knew there was no need to drive so fast. The part of Alpha's being that knew without thinking told him there was no cure for *it.*

············

"Take the ramp to the right. The charge station is just up at the top of the hill." Giving Jackson directions while looking at nothing but the screen in front of them was hard for Luna to get used to. Not only that, being cooped up in the APC made her feel claustrophobic.

"We don't need to stop again." Jackson pointed at the indicator, which showed over six hundred miles of range left. They'd already stopped at Thermopolis when they didn't need to do so. The APC that Jackson had commandeered from the Narmy could easily make it from Montana to Midpark on a single charge.

"I need to stop," Luna said. "I don't like squatting beside the road, and besides, I need to get out of here. At least for a little while."

Jackson turned up the ramp toward Interstate 80. "You can ride on top, you know."

"Probably a good idea, but right now, what I really need is the restroom." Luna was thinking about how lucky men were in those regards as Jackson pulled the APC into the charging station at Rawlins. For his part, Jackson was thinking the same thing and wishing they didn't need to stop. He was anxious to find Charlene. Even though Luna assured him that Charlene was fine, he wanted to see it with his own eyes.

Riding on top of the APC was much better, even if it was over a hundred degrees outside. They were just passing through Walden when it dawned on Luna that she had no idea exactly where they were supposed to go. Charlene had just told her to bring Jackson to Midpark. Where in Midpark, she hadn't said. As far as Luna knew, Charlene didn't have a com, so she decided to call Alpha. Maybe Alpha would know where Charlene was. Thinking there was too much wind noise on top of the APC to make the call, Luna opened the hatch and climbed back down inside.

Alpha didn't answer. Luna wasn't sure what to do next. Alpha had never failed to answer before. She looked at the com in her hand, then tried another code. This time she punched in the numbers for Jada. Luna only had the codes for three people, and she knew that one of them, Lucia, would never again answer her com. Jada didn't answer either.

"Maybe those things quit working." Jackson didn't trust the little radios with pictures that he'd first seen used in Montana. He'd seen plenty of coms before Montana, but never one that worked.

"Maybe." Luna looked at the com Alpha had given her. "They kind of seem like magic, don't they?" *That's the trouble with magic,* she thought. *Sometimes it works, and sometimes it doesn't.*

Luna looked at the driver's screen in front of Jackson. It seemed like magic in its own right. *It's all magic. I'm sitting inside a metal object that transports me from one place to another with no effort on my part at all. I have no idea how any of it came into being or how it works. What can it be, other than magic?*

The ringing and vibration of the piece of magic she held in her hand startled both of them. Jackson glanced down at the man's face on the screen and had a strong feeling of deja vu. He knew he had never seen the man before, but it felt like he'd always known him.

"Alpha," Luna did know the man on screen. "Are you okay?" His expression told her otherwise.

"Nothing's okay," he answered. "Everybody's dead or dying."

A chill gripped Jackson as well as Luna. "Charlene?" Luna asked, the single word betraying the fear in the question.

"Charlene's fine." The picture on Luna's com shifted, and Charlene's face came into view. "Where are you?" Charlene asked.

# Chapter 20

IT WAS GETTING HARDER to keep the truck on the road. Anna slowed down some more as another violent spasm forced her eyes closed again. Her chest felt like she was coughing her lungs out, and she was so cold that her teeth were chattering. *Need to get home. Will said people are dying.* The thought was dreamlike.

"Anna, are you alright?" Will's voice seemed far away.

*Not Will. It's James.* Anna shook her head and had to swerve to miss one of the washed-out places in old highway 9. She stopped the truck. Anna knew this road so well that she could almost drive it in her sleep. Apparently, she'd been doing just that. She knew they were about halfway between Kremmling and the Blue River Ranch but couldn't remember driving here. The last thing she could remember clearly was James calling Dr. Ming while they were going through Granby. Dr. Ming didn't answer, though. That's why they didn't stop at the clinic in Kremmling.

Anna looked over at James. He looked like she felt. He was shivering and sweating at the same time. She noticed that all of the windows were down in the old truck. *That's why we're shivering. It must be cold outside.* She glanced at the thermometer on the dash and tried unsuccessfully to reconcile the one-hundred-seven degree reading with the thought that it was cold out.

She coughed and shook her head again. "Can you drive?" she asked James, who was bent over in a coughing spasm of his own.

James didn't bother to answer. He just opened the passenger door and got out. Anna opened her door and walked around the back of the truck while James walked around the front. As she climbed back into the passenger side, she noticed Mandy and Misty in the back seat. *Why are Mandy and Misty here?* It was an ethereal thought, answered by another question in Anna's mind; *Why not, it's their truck?*

The two girls in the back seat seemed to be sleeping, but they weren't girls. They were adult women. Misty was slumped against the door, and Mandy had her head on Misty's shoulder. *Better let them sleep,* Anna thought, before a moment of clarity broke through the delirium. *They're not sleeping. They're dead.* She felt a terror like nothing she'd ever known. *I'm dying, too. We're all going to die.* She remembered Will dying in Oregon so many years ago and how it had seemed like she was also going to die. *Maybe we'll get well this time, too.* She and James had both lived through the V-1 pandemic so many years ago. They survived and had a son. *Alpha! Is Alpha okay?* Her fear of dying was suddenly replaced by fear for her son. She wanted to reach for her com to call Alpha, but a coughing fit hit so hard that she blacked out.

·····••·••···

A nearly empty parking lot at Dr. Ming's clinic was not what Alpha expected to find. He parked the Tesla he was driving next to an even older model that was the only car in the lot.

He had expected to see James and Anna's truck here after his mother told him specifically that this is where they were headed. Dave, in the back seat, had stopped coughing at some point. He was now just moaning softly and seemed to be sleeping or unconscious. Alpha started to reach for his com to call Anna but decided he should get Dave inside to see Dr. Ming first.

Dave was unresponsive to Alpha shaking him and trying to wake him up. Alpha started to drag him out of the car to carry him into the clinic before remembering the wheelchair. The one that always sat next to the reception desk inside. As he walked up the ramp to get it, a young woman came out of the clinic to meet him.

Recognition was instantaneous. It was more like a dream than reality as the woman from his visions met him halfway up the ramp and threw her arms around him. They both had tears in their eyes as they kissed and held each other tight.

"Charlene, Charlene," he whispered in her ear. The lump in his throat made it hard to speak at all. Whispering her name was about all he could do as he held her tight wanting never to let go.

Without letting go, Charlene leaned her head back enough to look at the man she'd come all this way to find. "I knew you'd come here," she said. "I've been waiting. Somehow, I knew this is where you'd be."

The mixture of emotions was overwhelming. The pure joy of finally being with Charlene was at one end of the emotional spectrum, the sorrow for his friend, Dave, who seemed to be dying at the other. And the fear that both his mother and father were sick, somewhere in between.

"You're okay?" The question was redundant. Alpha could see and sense that Charlene was just as well as he was, but he was compelled to say the words.

Charlene smiled through her tears, knowing that he knew she was. "So much more than just okay," she said before kissing him again.

"Dr. Ming?" Alpha asked, allowing reality to intrude on the moment.

"Gone - Kahina, Dr. Ming, Lisa. They're all gone, Alpha. It's just us now. You and me, and Jackson and Luna."

*Who's Jackson?* Alpha wondered, then remembered why he was here. "What about my mother?" He forgot for a moment that Charlene didn't know his mother. "Anna and James," he clarified. "She told me to come here."

"No one's been here. Not since yesterday." Charlene looked puzzled. "Dr. Ming was already sick when I got here with Kahina yesterday afternoon. Kahina died before he even finished examining her. There was another sick woman here. I think her name was Jada. She died a few hours after that, and Dr. Ming and Lisa just kept getting sicker. A couple of other people tried to get in the clinic yesterday afternoon, but Dr. Ming just sent them away. Dr. Ming's com thing rang a few times today, but he died early this morning."

Dr. Ming was dead, and Dave was dying. *Where did Mom go?* There was no way James could have missed them on the road. Not unless they drove off the edge somewhere. There was any number of places between Denver and Kremmling where they could have gone off a switchback or into a canyon.

"Help me get Dave inside."

Charlene couldn't help but wonder why Alpha wanted to take Dave inside as she watched him hurry into the clinic and reappear with the wheelchair. She followed him down the ramp to the open back door of the Tesla and watched him hang his head as he looked inside and realized that Dave was already dead.

Charlene helped get Dave into the wheelchair, and Alpha rolled him up into Dr. Ming's clinic, which had become nothing but a makeshift morgue over the past twenty-four hours. Back outside, Alpha looked around at the empty streets of Kremmling. Other than a couple of dogs that had escaped someone's yard somewhere, there was no sign of life. Many of the houses and buildings in Kremmling hadn't been occupied for more than twenty years, but some had been homes for as long as Alpha had been alive. Just yesterday morning, Kremmling had been a living, growing community. Now, as Alpha looked at the old town, he saw nothing but an empty shell. A husk that had once contained a living seed, cast off now and devoid of life.

*Is everybody dead?* Alpha pulled the com out of his pocket and called Anna. *Mom isn't dead.* It was a feeling more than a thought. A sense that he would just know if his mother had died. Strange, he wasn't so sure about James; but he'd always felt more connected to his mother than his father. He wondered if that was always the case. Maybe people were just naturally connected to their mothers in a way that was different than with fathers.

There was no answer. Anna always answered Alpha's calls. *What now?* He'd no more than stuck the com back in his pocket when it started ringing. Thinking it must be Anna calling back, he quickly grabbed the com. It wasn't Anna's face looking back at him on the small screen, but it was still a relief to see who it was. It was Luna.

·····•·•····

The Tesla Charlene had driven from Montana didn't have much juice left in the batteries, so they took Alpha's car back to meet Jackson and Luna. Jackson had never been to Midpark at all, and Luna had never been west of Granby. Alpha wanted to backtrack to look for James and Anna, anyway, so they agreed to meet at Windy Gap.

The APC was sitting where they'd agreed to meet, in what had once been the parking lot and viewing area of the Windy Gap Wildlife Area. Luna and Jackson were both standing in the shade on the north side of the APC. As Alpha turned into the parking lot, Charlene noticed that some of the writing and pictures of wildlife were still visible on the weathered old descriptive panels, but the two people standing next to the APC were the only living things in sight. It was only after Charlene and Alpha got out of the Tesla and started walking toward Luna and Jackson that she heard and saw a flock of some kind of birds take flight from the creek bottom to the south. Charlene knew that tiny, gently flowing creek was all that remained of the Colorado River. Decades of drought had nearly dried it up completely.

Alpha hugged Luna as Jackson and Charlene did the same. It had only been a couple of days, but it seemed like years had passed since they'd last held each other. Like a meeting of old lovers after years apart, the two couples held on, each knowing that another love had supplanted what they'd once felt for each other. Each still feeling the bonds of some kind of love that would always be.

The couples separated, and Luna and Charlene embraced while Jackson and Alpha stood looking at each other.

"Jackson..." Alpha started to say the tired old line, I feel like I already know you, then stopped. It wasn't enough. Jackson didn't feel the need to say anything at all. What he felt couldn't be expressed in words. There was no familial resemblance between Jackson's red hair and pale blue eyes and Alpha's long jet black hair and deep brown eyes, but both men felt more like they were meeting a long-lost brother than a perfect stranger. Following the women's example, the two men gave each other a big hug.

Something dawned on Alpha as he stood there hugging Jackson. He held Jackson at arm's length and asked, "how old are you?" Not waiting for an answer, he added, "You were born after the great dying, weren't you?"

"I guess so," Jackson started to answer. He'd never known his mother who had died giving him life, but the grandmother who'd raised him had told him as much. Jackson didn't finish answering the question, though. He stopped in mid-sentence as he saw Alpha's eyes go totally blank. Alpha was still staring toward him, but Jackson had no idea what Alpha was seeing in the trancelike state that had obviously overcome him.

The fuzzy laddered spiral strands Alpha was seeing were familiar from the many photos and depictions of DNA that he'd been so diligently studying these last few weeks. There were two strands side by side. As with all of the visions he'd ever had, Alpha knew many things about what he saw that were rationally impossible to know. He knew that one of those fuzzy strands in his vision was an actual living snippet of DNA from inside one of Jackson's cells. The other was a photograph of a highly magnified strand of normal human DNA that he'd seen in a book. The two strands were different, but just how different wasn't immediately apparent.

Slowly, as if being drawn by a computer on the blank screen of Alpha's mind, a chart appeared below the super magnified images of the strands of DNA. He recognized the chart immediately as something he'd also seen in one of those books. The chart was slightly different, though, than the one he remembered. The image Alpha remembered having seen before was a charted comparison of the difference between human and chimpanzee chromosomes. It showed how chimpanzees have forty-eight chromosomes while homo sapiens have forty-six. The actual makeup of genes in the chromosomes was different in other regards, but the most crucial difference between the two species was that extra pair of chromosomes in chimp DNA.

The difference between the chart he'd seen before while studying genetics and the one he was seeing in his vision now was that this time the chart representing a chimpanzee's DNA had been replaced by a chart that represented Jackson's. There it was. The difference between normal human DNA and Jackson's DNA was as profound as the difference between humans and chimpanzees. Instead of twenty-three pairs of chromosomes, Jackson had only twenty-two. Just as with the chimp-human comparisons, there were other differences in the genetic makeup of the chromosomes as well. Jackson was a mutant. What Alpha was seeing was what he'd hoped to find using the biomedical lab in Fort Collins. In the vision, he was looking at a mutation that had to have been brought about by the virus.

Knowing how much different Jackson's DNA was from normal human DNA came as a shock, but nothing compared to the realization that it wasn't just Jackson. Alpha knew in that instant that all four of them had the same mutation. That was what they all had in common. The mutation is what connected the four of them in a way that was unlike anything before. *Are we even human?* That was the question remaining in Alpha's mind as he came back from the vision.

"What is it, Alpha?" Luna asked. All three of the others were staring at him as his eyes fluttered, and he came back to the here and now.

"It's us. It's why we're not sick while everyone else is dying. It's our DNA. Our DNA is different than everyone else's."

Of the other three, only Charlene knew much at all about DNA or genetics. Jackson and Luna may have heard the term before, but neither had spent hours consuming books like both Charlene and Alpha had done. Jackson and Luna didn't understand, but Charlene saw it immediately. "It's why we're immune. The virus can't infect us because of something genetic." She thought for just a moment before asking Alpha, "why just us four? Shouldn't there be others?"

*There should be others.* Alpha had the thought that if he had inherited his genes from James and Anna, they, too, should be immune. "I need to call my mother," he said.

# Chapter 21

SOMEWHERE IN HIS MIND, James knew that he was headed up the lane to the Blue River Ranch, but he didn't know how or why. For all he knew, he might have been on a horse or walking. Nothing but his subconscious mind was driving the truck now. Through the windshield, he saw a black and white dog come running down the lane toward them. *Grandpa Chuck should call Blackie,* he thought, though Chuck and Blackie had both been dead for many years. As he got out of the truck that had miraculously stopped in front of the big old log house, James wondered why Grandpa Chuck didn't come out to meet him. They were supposed to go find Anna today.

Anna rode up the lane to the BR on a horse that she'd borrowed from a dead man. It was a good horse, but she'd be glad to be united with her own horse, Pintada. She missed her horse almost as much as she missed her family. *No one's here.* The thought scared her. *All this way to find no one.* She'd traveled so far, hoping to find her family and Chuck alive. And James. *James has to be alive. I'll just wait for him here.* No sooner did she have the thought than James suddenly appeared. "Come on," he said, helping her get down off of her horse. Only it wasn't a horse. He was helping her get out of some kind of a machine. A sound distracted her. It was coming from back inside what Anna could now see was really just a truck. She looked back to see where the sound was coming from. "It's Raven," she told James as she reached back into the truck for the com. Anna named her com Raven before her parents even gave it to her on her fourteenth birthday. *Maybe it's Mom or Dad,* she thought before turning the com over to see someone who was neither of her parents. She took a hard look at the face on the screen, closed her eyes, then opened them again. He was still there. It was Alpha, but that couldn't be. *Alpha?* Alpha wasn't even born yet. But there he was on Raven's screen. He said something. It was a question, "Mom, where are you?"

*Silly question.* "I'm home," she said and dropped the com.

·····•·•·····

It seemed like deja vu, but James didn't know from where or when. He was riding a horse bareback, without a bridle or even a hackamore for control. The horse was taking him somewhere, his destiny totally under the control of the horse that seemed to be flying through clouds instead of running over the earth. The horse seemed to be trying to catch someone that was hidden beyond the cloudy mists. It came to him that Anna was somewhere up ahead. Not only Anna but his mother as well. The mists started changing to a glow. A light that seemed to be getting brighter. They were there, somewhere up ahead in that beautiful light. They were all there, waiting in the light. Waiting for him to catch up. Everyone he'd ever loved was somewhere in that blinding light that began to engulf him.

James didn't feel the shudder that went through his body. He didn't feel his lungs stop breathing; he didn't notice when his heart stopped beating. All that was left, all that had ever been, was that glorious light.

···•··•···

Anna was flying. Vast reaches of the earth, opening up below her. She was somewhere over plains, soaring toward mountains that were glowing in the distance as if lit from behind by the most glorious sunset she'd ever seen. Flying was effortless. It was as though she didn't have a body to move through the sky. Just an ephemeral self that had only one goal. She had to reach those mountains in the distance. The mountains were home. It was time to return home.

The glow behind the mountains grew brighter instead of diminishing like light from the setting sun. The mountains began fading from view, dissolving into the light that was growing ever brighter. It came to Anna that it wasn't the mountains that were home. The light was home. She knew she was already home as the light swallowed her, and she became the light.

···•··•···

They found Anna and James curled up together in each other's arms, with Anna's border collie watching over them. They hadn't even made it into the old log house. *At least they made it home.* The thought wasn't much comfort as Alpha knelt beside his dead parents. He'd driven back to the old ranch as fast as he could, knowing all the way that he would be too late. The same questions kept playing over and over in his mind. *Why weren't they immune? Why me?*

He looked up at the sorrow on the faces of Luna, Jackson, and Charlene. *Why us? How can we be so different from those who gave us life?* He knew the answer was still hidden somewhere in the mysterious mutations that V-1 visited on the human genome. Alpha also knew that he would never solve that mystery. It was too late. He was too late to save anyone.

"They'd want to be buried on the hill." Alpha gestured toward the hill behind the old ranch house as he stood up and wiped the tears from his eyes. "I'm not sure what to do with the others. I don't think there's room for them all in the old cemetery."

"What others?" Luna asked. None of the other three knew anything about the other people who lived here on the old Blue River Ranch. The people that Alpha knew they would find dead in both of the old houses—all those who had been Alpha's family, whether related by blood or not.

"They'll be inside the houses. There should be fifteen of them counting the girls."

The girls, some of them just children, the youngest on the BR barely two years old, were the saddest part. Other than James and Anna, that is. Luna, Jackson, and Charlene helped Alpha bury James and Anna alongside their ancestors in the Blue River Ranch cemetery up on the hill. Deciding what to do with the rest of the dead wasn't easy. They considered the possibility of a mass cremation on a giant funeral pyre, but it hadn't rained or snowed for months. Everything on the ranch was tinder dry, and it would only take one stray spark to start a wildfire.

"Guess we could dig more graves down here in the meadow," Jackson said, looking dubiously at the blisters on his hands.

The four of them were sitting around the dining table in what Alpha had always known simply as the big house. The old log home that his great-great-grandfather had built was as empty now as the place in his heart where his parents had been. Alpha looked around at the great room so familiar from his childhood. *Not the same,* he thought. *Nothing will ever be the same.* He looked down at the blisters on his own hands as he contemplated just how much nothing would ever be the same. *We may be all that's left.* He looked at the others, trying unsuccessfully to wrap his head around the thought.

"It's not just the people over there," Charlene said, referring to the old house. They'd moved the ones that died here in the big house over to the old house after burying James and Anna. There were now fifteen dead bodies over in the older ranch house. "They're all dead, everywhere. It's just us. We are the only four people left alive. Don't you see?"

Luna didn't see. "That's impossible. We can't be the only ones." She wished she'd left her com in Trinidad so she could call and prove Charlene wrong. *They're still there,* she thought. *They have to be.*

Jackson couldn't believe it either. The idea that everyone else in the whole world might be dead was beyond the realm of possibility. What he did know was that a lot of people had died. That was a fact that couldn't be denied. "I don't know how many people might still be alive, but I do know there are way too many dead people for the four of us to bury them all."

...........

Jackson pushed the last of the pile of dirt over the mass grave. Alpha had agreed that they couldn't bury everyone, but he insisted on burying those he was closest to. Yesterday, Alpha had talked the other three into loading all of the dead bodies at the BR into the horse trailer, so they could be transported down to Kremmling. He figured they could use Johnny Garcia's battery-powered backhoe to do the burying. The four of them even drove up to Frisco and collected the bodies of Liz and the other members of Dave's household. They had all been like family to Alpha.

After spending the night trying to sleep, mostly unsuccessfully, the four had driven to Kremmling early this morning with a trailer full of bodies. While Jackson taught himself how to run the backhoe well enough to dig a huge hole in the middle of what had once been a high school football field, the other three had scoured the town for signs of any other survivors. They found no one still living but added a substantial number of dead people to be buried in that one mass grave.

*What's going to happen to all of these dogs?* Charlene wondered. Pets were all that was left alive in Kremmling. Even as she asked herself the question, she knew the answer. Most would die, but some would turn wild and run in packs. Dogs would slowly devolve back into the wolves from whence they came. It would be the same with cats. It wouldn't be long before a few of the strongest would be feral creatures of the wild, while the rest would be as dead as all the people they'd just buried in that one mass grave.

"I need to go to Trinidad now," Luna said as Jackson rejoined the group.

# Chapter 22

T HE FLAMES WERE TENTATIVE at first, barely licking at the boards and logs stacked above the kindling. Slowly, the flames reached from kindling to lumber and then to the logs. By the time the flames got to the mass of bodies that were stacked on top of the pyre, the fire was a raging inferno. The fire didn't so much start burning the bodies as it completely engulfed them.

It hadn't seemed like a very good idea to Alpha when Luna insisted they cremate her loved ones. Now, watching the sparks and glowing embers carried aloft with the smoke, Alpha feared the entire compound would catch fire, not to mention the dead pinon and juniper trees surrounding this place that Luna called Trinidad. "This isn't looking good," he said to himself as much as to the other three.

Luna's home had fared no better than Kremmling, or Granby, which they'd searched on their way here. Everyone in Trinidad was dead. Her entire community was gone. "What does look good, Alpha?" she asked. "How can anything ever be good again?" Sorrow and grief didn't begin to describe what Luna was feeling. There were no words to adequately describe what any of them were feeling.

"I'm sorry." Alpha may not have had words for it any more than Luna, but he knew exactly what she felt. "I just meant the fire. The sparks might catch the whole place on fire."

Luna looked up at the smoke and sparks rising toward a clear blue sky. She imagined that the sparks in the smoke were the spirits of her people rising to some heaven, somewhere. "Let it burn," she said. "Let it all burn."

Jackson, who wasn't looking up, saw a dry pinon go up like a torch a few hundred yards to the east. Other trees started catching fire around it. "We need to get out of here!" The others heard the urgency in his voice and looked to the east. It didn't seem possible that a fire could be growing that fast. Luna still didn't want to leave, but the others half coaxed and half dragged her to Jackson's waiting APC. Jackson had insisted on using the old military vehicle because none of the other vehicles in Midpark could match its range. Now, as they sealed the hatch in the roof, another advantage of the APC was apparent; it wouldn't catch fire.

Jackson drove away from the Trinidad compound as fast as he dared, but soon the driver's screen showed a wall of flames blocking the road ahead. The wind must have shifted around to blow the sparks north of them. He stopped, not sure what to do. Switching to the rear camera, it was easy to see there was no going back. They were sitting on an island, surrounded by an ocean of fire. There was nothing to do but drive through the flames. Jackson's main concern was the APC's tires. They weren't the old-fashioned air-filled tires that could go flat, but if they had to drive too far through the fire, the rubber of the tires themselves could ignite. His other concern was visibility. Would he even be able to see the road? With no other choice, Jackson put his concerns aside and drove straight into the wall of flames.

No one in the APC said a word. Everyone stared at the driver's screen, at the mesmerizing view of a forest fire from the inside. They were totally surrounded by fire. The mostly dead and dying pinon and juniper trees weren't tall enough to form a canopy overhead, but the flames did. Thankfully, like driving through a thick fog, the road ahead came in and out of view. Going much slower than he would have liked, Jackson crept through a tunnel of fire.

The tunnel of flame ended as abruptly as it had begun. There was a collective sigh of relief inside the APC as Alpha had the thought, *So much for cremating people.* Clear of the flames, Jackson punched it. He wasn't thinking about much of anything except staying ahead of the raging inferno. *Don't slow down until we're completely out of the trees,* he thought.

..........

"We should at least go look," Jackson wanted to drive up to Montana to see if there was anyone left alive. The question of whether or not anyone besides the four of them was still alive dominated most of their discussions lately.

It had been almost a week since the disaster with the funeral pyre in Trinidad. The four of them were back at the Blue River Ranch. They had mutually agreed that the old ranch was as good a place as any to live, at least until they could find other survivors.

"If there was anyone there, they would have answered a com by now." Alpha was sure that no one was still alive up in Montana.

"What if they don't have a com? What if it's just some of the young girls who survived?" Charlene was making the same argument that she'd made before. She didn't really believe there were any survivors in Park City, but she couldn't stand the thought that there might be children there with no adults to help them survive.

"Alright, already. We can go to Montana." After listening to Charlene harp on it every night for the past week, Alpha was ready to give up. "We can go first thing in the morning, but I want to take two cars. One thing I don't want is to get stranded hundreds of miles from nowhere."

"It doesn't make any difference if we're stranded here or stranded somewhere else," Luna mumbled under her breath.

·····•·•····

The smell that greeted them in the fertility chapel at Laurel told them what they needed to know before they even entered Lucia's private chambers. The High Priestess was still on the bed where Luna and Jackson had left her, and the woman that had brought them into her chambers a week and a half ago was dead on the sofa.

*We should probably bury them,* Alpha thought. *And how many more?* They couldn't bury everyone by themselves. "Let's search some more of the community," he said. He was starting to gag from the smell and had to get back outside to fresh air.

Going through Laurel and then on down to Park City, there were dead people everywhere, but a living soul was nowhere to be found. At least not a single living human being. Most of the people who lived in Laurel and Park City had died in their homes, but a few bodies were lying about outside. The only survivors they found were pets and other animals. Alpha, Charlene, Jackson, and Luna were able to liberate some dogs and cats that were on the verge of starving after being locked inside people's homes. They also turned some stabled horses loose and opened all the pasture gates they found. They stopped looking for human survivors after entering a house in Park City and finding a large dog and a half-eaten child. It was such a gruesome scene that they just got out of the house as fast as they could, leaving that dog locked inside. That was the end of their search in Park City and Laurel.

"It can't be just us. There must be others somewhere. What about back where you came from?" Luna asked Jackson. The four of them were back outside the fertility chapel in Laurel, waiting on the APC and the Hummer to charge up.

"Maybe, but I doubt it. If Lucia or someone here was monitoring New Dixie radio traffic that suddenly stopped, it probably means they're all dead." Jackson, sitting on one of the benches in front of the old hotel, looked down at the ground in front of him before continuing. "God, Charlene, we brought it with us. It's my fault. If only I would have stayed away from Robin when I saw how sick she was."

"How could you know, Jackson? How could anyone know?" Charlene asked.

"We don't know," Alpha said, standing up and stretching his legs. "It might not have even been you. Whatever this new virus is, it might have jumped species. For all we know, dogs transmitted it to people, or birds, maybe even bats or mosquitoes. Viruses have developed in other species and then made the jump to humans over and over again. Why should now be any different?"

*What difference does it make anyway?* Charlene thought. *If we brought it with us, I'm just as guilty as Jackson, but feeling guilty isn't going to bring anybody back to life.*

"Luna's right," Charlene said, "there must be others." She didn't necessarily believe what she was saying but hoped to make Jackson feel better. "There must be others that are immune. Why would it just be the four of us?" She looked off to the east, wondering if there might actually be people who were immune back in Kansas or Nebraska or even New Dixie, for that matter. Maybe California or Canada, or somewhere else might even be possible. "Alpha, do you know of any other settlements or groups of people anywhere besides here and Midpark?" she asked.

"I don't know of any for a fact, but then again, Trinidad was only a rumor until I met Luna. When I was young, my mother talked about some people in Pocatello, Idaho that had lived through V-1. She always talked about going back there for a visit someday. Maybe that would be a good place to look." Alpha, like Charlene, was now saying what Luna and Jackson wanted to hear. It was what he wanted to believe, too, but wanting to believe and actually believing are two different things. He plowed ahead anyway. "And according to Angela, there was a woman who came to Park City on horseback a few years ago talking about a settlement northwest of here. Seems like it was supposed to be up near Missoula."

"How far are those places?" Luna asked.

*Uh-oh,* Alpha thought. *I should have kept that to myself. Unless...maybe there are others. Others who are immune.* It still seemed like wishful thinking. Besides, Alpha had no idea how far it was to Missoula or Pocatello.

"Not much over three-hundred miles to Missoula," said Charlene, consulting the atlas in her photographic memory. "Closer to four-hundred to Pocatello."

"Either one's too far for the Hummer. We wouldn't be able to get back without charging up." Alpha said.

"It's not too far for the APC, but I don't think we should take a chance on infecting any more people." Jackson wasn't necessarily buying into the theory that it might have been something besides him and Charlene that brought the disease west. "Even if something besides us is capable of spreading the virus, we know for a fact that we can spread it. If there's anyone out there that hasn't been infected, we should stay as far away as possible."

"For how long?" Luna asked. All three of the others looked at Alpha. He was the only one who seemed to know much at all about the virus that had apparently killed everyone else they knew.

Alpha thought about it before answering. "I don't know. We may not be contagious already, or we might still be able to spread it to others weeks or months from now." *Or forever,* is what he really thought.

"Then we should wait a month or two before we go traipsing off looking for other people." Charlene wouldn't admit it to the others, but she was relieved. She knew that anyone she'd ever loved was already dead. Everyone but the three people she was with right now, and what she felt toward Alpha, Luna, and Jackson was beyond description. It was transcendental, not just love. It was a state of being that had always been and always would be.

"Let's go home," Alpha said.

# Chapter 23

"WELL, DR. ALPHA, WHAT'S the prognosis?" Charlene took her feet out of the stirrups and sat up on the examination table. The four of them had moved from the BR to Kremmling a couple months back to be near the medical clinic.

Alpha laughed. They'd all taken to calling him Dr. Alpha after they took over Dr. Ming's old clinic. "You and the baby are both just fine. As a matter of fact, you are both perfect." He peeled off the examination gloves, dropped them in the trash, and bent down to give Charlene a kiss.

"Doesn't sound like a very scientific assessment to me," she said.

"Guess it's the best I can do with my limited scientific training."

Alpha and Charlene both knew there was nothing limited about Alpha's training. Over the past eight months, they'd both spent hours and hours in the old libraries in Denver, Boulder, and Fort Collins. Charlene mostly devoured fiction and thought about the way the world used to be. She also spent a lot of that time just thinking about the future. Alpha, on the other hand, consumed medical textbooks, especially books on obstetrics and pediatrics. He may not have had the experience that was once required to be a doctor, but he had already acquired more book knowledge than most medical doctors of the past acquired in a lifetime.

"Alpha, do you think there are other women somewhere – I mean besides Luna and me – having babies right now?"

"I don't know about giving birth right now. Luna isn't even due for a couple of weeks yet, and you're at least a few weeks behind her."

"You know what I mean, Alpha. I'm scared. What if there is no one else?"

It was a question that was never far from anyone's mind. A couple of months after everyone else died, the four of them had gone all the way up to Missoula in search of survivors. They found that there had once been a small group of people living in Missoula, but they were all dead. The virus had apparently arrived in Missoula at the same time or shortly after it hit southern Montana. After finding the remains of even fewer dead people in Pocatello than they did in Missoula, they'd stopped searching for survivors. After that, with Luna and Charlene both pregnant, Alpha had insisted they stay close to the clinic in Kremmling.

"I hope there are a lot of people out there somewhere who are just as nervous as we are about being new parents," Alpha said. "But right now, the only two babies I'm worried about are yours and Luna's. I'm especially concerned about Phoenix." Luna had already decided to name her unborn son Phoenix after the mythical bird that rose from its own ashes.

"Is something wrong?"

"No," Alpha was quick to dispel Charlene's concern. "Luna and her baby are both just as healthy as you and the daughter you carry. It's just that we were all so focused on producing male babies for so long. Just think about it, Phoenix will be the first boy born in Midpark in over twenty years."

"Good thing such a special baby has such a special doctor." Charlene, who had finished dressing, waddled over to give Alpha a hug. It wasn't easy with the baby belly in between them.

"Hey, our daughter is pretty special too, you know. Aren't you, little one?" Alpha bent down and planted a kiss on top of Charlene's swollen belly.

·····•·····

The headphones weren't enough to block out the sounds of the thunderstorm going on outside, and the squelch was almost unbearable. *Damn, hope it doesn't hit the antenna,* Jackson thought, as another flash of lightning lit up the room's only window. *Might as well just give up for tonight.* The lighting-caused interference coming through the headphones was too distracting to hear anything else, anyway. Suddenly, there was silence, at least from the headset, and the room went dark. "Damn it!" Jackson cursed to himself as he slipped the headset off. For Jackson, the ham radio that they'd found and brought back from Montana had become an addiction. He spent hours and hours slowly turning the dials and switches, stopping to listen whenever any kind of squelch blasted through the headphones. Jackson, more than any of the others, wanted to keep looking for other people. Since he couldn't physically search, he broadcast and listened for a reply. Jackson started every day with the same hope, hoping this would be the day that he would hear another human voice on the radio.

*Wish it would rain,* Alpha thought. The dry lightning was bound to spark fires up in the mountains. After decades of drought, down at lower elevations, there wasn't enough vegetation left to burn, but up high, there were a few places yet to be ravaged by wildfire. While Jackson was in the bedroom turned radio room, trying to communicate with the outside world, Alpha, Charlene, and Luna were engaged in a conversation of their own. The three of them were relaxing in the living room of the old stone house they'd been living in for the past six months. Chosen for its close proximity to Dr. Ming's old clinic, the house had served them well.

"Maybe I shouldn't name him Phoenix," Luna told Charlene. "Maybe I should name him Adam, and you can name your daughter Eve. The two of them can start over, just like Adam and Eve from the Bible."

"How do you know about the Bible?" It was the first question that popped into Alpha's mind, knowing that Luna hardly read at all, let alone the Bible. He, himself, had never bothered to read the whole thing. He couldn't see wasting time on myths and legends when there was so much science to study.

"Michael used to tell us stories when I was young," Luna answered. "He was the oldest man in Trinidad. I think Michael might have been the oldest man I ever knew. When I was a little girl, he was always telling us stories from the Bible. He said we needed to learn all about the Bible and follow its teachings so God wouldn't destroy what was left of the world." Luna seemed to search her memory for a moment before continuing. "Maybe he was right," she laughed. "Anyway, one of the stories I remember was the story of Adam and Eve, and how they were the very first people God created. Michael said the rest of us were all descended from those first two people."

"You didn't really believe that old man, though, did you?" Charlene asked.

"No, my mother told me it was all just stories, no more real than the story of the Phoenix rising from its own ashes. That's why I decided to name my baby Phoenix. I think the myth of the Phoenix was my mother's favorite story."

"Well, I think you should stick with Phoenix then," Alpha said. "One myth is as good as another. Besides, the story of Adam and Eve can't possibly be true. No species can regenerate from just one breeding pair. There is just not enough genetic diversity for the species to survive for long."

Luna didn't miss a beat. "Good thing there's two of us then. Breeding pairs, I mean."

Charlene laughed and then, after a moment of thought, posed a question to Alpha. "What about Lucy then, or whatever you want to call the mitochondrial Eve?" Alpha wasn't the only person in the room who was well-read. "Don't we all have just one common maternal ancestor somewhere back in the far reaches of time?"

"Ahh, mitochondrial DNA..." Alpha started to respond just as two things happened nearly simultaneously. The lights went out, and Luna let out a very audible gasp.

··········

"Can we fix it?" Jackson asked, referring to what was left of one of the large transformers at the Wolford solar power station.

Alpha had to laugh at the absurdity of the question. "There isn't going to be any fixing that," he said. The transformer wasn't just charred and blackened; the fire had been so hot that it actually melted much of the metal housing.

"Can we work around it then; the PV panels seem to be okay?" Jackson may not have known much about electrical power systems, but he knew he didn't want to be without electricity.

*Seem to be is right, but they're too old. This is all too old,* Alpha thought, as he looked at the solar farm and power station that had provided electricity to Midpark for as long as he'd been alive. "No, Jackson, there won't be any fixing this. This power station is as dead as the people that built it." He turned and headed back toward the Hummer. "Let's get back down to our family."

···········

"Do you think we're alone?" Luna asked. "I mean really alone." Baby Phoenix was nursing as she held him to her breast. Charlene was sitting across the room from mother and newborn, wondering the same thing, if not in the same terms. The two women were in the nursery of what they still called Dr. Ming's clinic.

"I hope we're not the only ones. I hope somewhere out there, another baby boy is being born right now." Charlene ran her hand over her swollen belly. "For their sake, for Phoenix and Lucy, I hope there are others out there."

Luna smiled. "So, you've decided to name her Lucy?"

Charlene laughed. "I think it was kind of decided for me last night. The storm knocked out the power, and you went into labor just as we were talking about our ancestral Lucy. How could I name her anything else? I mean, how many omens does a girl need?"

Phoenix stopped nursing, and Luna pulled the blanket up around her and her newborn son. The two women sat in silence, lost in their own thoughts for a few minutes. It was quiet in the clinic. Through the window facing west, Charlene could see that the sun was about to go down. She wished Alpha and Jackson would get back and wondered if they had been able to fix the power or not. They didn't need to get the electricity back on to supply this old clinic. Like the Blue River Ranch, it had its own self-contained power system. That wasn't the case, however, for the house in Kremmling where they'd been living these past few months.

"I hope we're not the only ones, too." Luna interrupted Charlene's thoughts. "But deep down, I think we are. I can't help it. I don't really think it, so much as I feel it. I'm afraid, Charlene, afraid that we are the only people left in the whole wide world."

*Me too,* Charlene thought, admitting to herself that she felt like the four, no six, of them were all that was left of humanity. *If we're all that's left, can we survive? Can humanity survive?* Charlene knew what geneticists and others had written about the need for genetic diversity in order for any species to survive. She thought about how small the gene pool was in their little family group and wondered if the scientists could have been wrong. If she and Luna both had multiple babies, and their babies all grew up and mated and had babies...it would still be either brothers and sisters mating with each other or with cousins. Could their progeny continue to survive without any outside genetic influence?

"We have to switch," Charlene said flatly. "After Phoenix and Lucy, I need to have Jackson's baby, and you need to have Alpha's. We need to create as much genetic diversity as possible."

"I know," Luna said. "I knew as soon as Alpha started talking about needing more breeding pairs."

Charlene thought about how mixed mating would add a little bit of diversity to their gene pool, but not enough. *What about the virus?* The thought from nowhere seemed odd. *Alpha said the virus changed our DNA. Isn't that the same thing a bigger gene pool does? Maybe the virus will create artificial genetic diversity.*

The sound of Jackson and Alpha coming through the front door broke Charlene's train of thought. She got out of the easy chair, never an easy feat now that she was in her ninth month, and met Alpha at the door of the clinic's nursery. "So, Dr. Alpha, are you an electrician as well as a doctor?" she asked, hugging him as close as she could in her current condition.

"No, I'm afraid not. Good thing this clinic has its own power, or you'd have to have this little one up at the ranch." He put his hand on her belly, hoping to feel a kick from his daughter.

Charlene looked up at him. "I think I'd like to give birth at the ranch instead of here. I think Lucy would like it, too."

# Chapter 24

"WHAT ONCE WAS, IS now once again." The frail-looking old man had a much more powerful voice than seemed possible. His deep voice boomed out through the open air, sounding like a much younger man.

"And always shall be," the old woman spoke the words as powerfully as the man who sat next to her. The old couple sat cross-legged near the top of a small grassy knoll.

*"And always shall be!"* came the chant from a crowd of people who were gathered at the foot of the hill.

There were ten more old people, six women, and four men, sitting in a line about halfway between the old couple at the top of the hill and the standing crowd below. The people at the foot of the hill were all younger than those seated higher up, but some didn't appear to be that much younger. There were probably as many as a hundred people of all ages bunched together at the bottom of that hill. The crowd seemed to be made up of nearly equal numbers of men and women, along with more children than seemed possible. The children ranged in age from infants to teens, and they were also nearly equally divided between boys and girls.

Every shade of skin and hair color imaginable was represented in this group of people, and the clothing they wore was just as varied. The elders on the hill all wore some kind of white robes. Many of those below wore nothing more than some kind of loin covering made of cloth or animal skins. Others were covered from head to toe. Some of the nearly naked people had colorful designs either tattooed or painted on their bodies.

*Like some kind of ancient indigenous tribe of hunter-gatherers,* thought Charlene. *Except for the rifles and the people wearing pants.* Many of those below the hill did indeed have what looked like modern hunting rifles, though some were armed with spears. Some, including all of the elders seated on the hill, seemed to have no weapons at all. Some had long staffs, which were probably just used to help them walk.

The surreal scene was like a bizarre dream, but Charlene recognized it for what it was. What she was seeing in her mind was a vision. It was her first vision since Alpha had told her to come west. She felt chills up and down her spine as she sat alone in the dark with her eyes closed, the vision playing in her mind like one of Kahina's old movies.

Just as one thinks about and interprets a movie while watching it, so it is with visions. *Some kind of ritual somewhere,* she thought. *But where?* The scenery was reminiscent of pictures from the African Savannah that she'd seen in books, but not quite the same. It was the lush grasses that reminded her of the African Savannah. Tall grasses that had been purposely trampled down and smoothed to make places for the elders to sit in their tiered rows, looking out over the others gathered below.

It was the red sandstone cliffs and monolith in the foreground that didn't seem right. The red cliffs and the vast tree-lined river bottom off in the distance beyond the lone rock tower didn't look like any pictures Charlene had ever seen of Africa. *It isn't Africa. Why would I have a vision of Africa, anyway?* Charlene answered her own question. *Maybe to give me hope. To let me know that there are other people still alive. Look at how many men there are and young boys.* Charlene placed her hands gently on her very swollen abdomen. *Maybe I'll have a boy.* Even as she had the thought, she remembered that she carried a daughter, not a son. The recent birth of Luna's son, Phoenix, was a miracle. Just as Alpha's birth had been a miracle. *This child I carry is his.* Charlene knew the child in her womb was Alpha's just as certainly as she knew it was a girl who would be named Lucy.

Something seemed familiar about the setting of the vision. The red sandstone cliffs seemed incredibly familiar—the red rock and the towering monolith that stood apart like some giant rock sentry. The monolith was directly behind the elders, like a god looking down on the proceedings from a lofty height. *I will bear sons. Someday, I, too, will have sons.* That thought struck Charlene at the same time as she realized she knew the setting of the vision. It was a place that, up to now, she'd only seen in photos in books. Tears of joy filled her tightly closed eyes as she looked at the people gathered in her vision and remembered searching for survivors with Alpha, Luna, and Jackson.

It was then that she knew this was a vision, not of the past or the now, but of the future. For the first time in her life, Charlene could see the future. She was watching a scene that wouldn't unfold for many decades. The towering monolith behind the elders on the hill was once named Independence Rock. It was in a place that had been called

Colorado National Park. This was a vision of how it would look nearly a hundred years from now. It was a vision of how it would be after the rains finally returned to a barren, parched desert. It would be a veritable Garden of Eden for her descendants.

That was the most joyous part of the vision. Charlene now knew she was looking at her descendants. It was a vision of those who would come from her and her three companions. Their descendants would have their own version of the biblical garden. It would be the beginning once again of the ascension of humankind. *They aren't human, though.* The strange thought was immediately followed by another. *Of course, they're human. Just as Neanderthals and Denisovans were human but not Homo Sapiens, so it is with these, our children. Our descendants are a new species of humans. We are no longer Homo Sapiens.*

Like a bolt of lightning, it struck her; *That's why the four of us could only produce children with each other and never with anyone else. That's why we survived when everyone else died. The virus changed us. Somehow, the virus changed enough of our DNA that we are no longer Homo Sapiens.*

Snippets of their future, the four of them, flashed through Charlene's mind. A future where she and Luna would not only have children fathered by both Jackson and Alpha but fathered by each other's sons. How strange to know that she would bear children fathered by Phoenix just as soon as he grew old enough to produce sperm. Or that Luna would have children by Charlene's sons who were yet to be conceived. That the daughter she carried inside her would bear Jackson's children and have others fathered by Jackson's sons from other mothers, and even those born to her own sisters and half-sisters. Mating in every possible combination all with one overriding goal, survival of the species. Survival of this new human species of which she and her three companions were the first.

In the vision, a hushed silence came over the crowd as they bowed their heads to the elders. The elders that Charlene now knew. The two oldest of those elders, seated in a place of honor on top of the hill, were Phoenix and Lucy. The ten elders seated below them were the other children who were yet to be born to her and Luna. Everyone gathered below the hill were direct descendants of those elders. All were descended from Luna and Jackson and Alpha and herself. The four of them were a new beginning in an endless time.

As the sun dropped behind the red cliffs and the giant red sandstone sentinel silently watched over the people below, somewhere on the thermals, high overhead, the chilling sound of an eagle's scream pierced the quiet evening air.

> Tomorrow arrives on wings of the past
> Riding the thermals of time
> What came before comes once more
> The fall that leads to a climb
> Yesterday and tomorrow are one
> Time an endless illusion
> Future past and the endless now
> No more than mass delusion

THANK YOU for reading the Thermals Of Time! I sincerely hope you enjoyed the reading as much as I enjoyed the writing.

If you have just a moment, it would mean the world to me if you would leave a review wherever you can. In this day and age, good reviews are the difference between a book succeeding in attracting new readers or disappearing into the waste bin of those that are seldom read by anyone.

Visit my website to sign up for my newsletter and get great deals on more great reads. Check it out:

**MarcusLynnDean.com**